D0229745

Book One

THE YOUNG MONTROSE

James Graham, the great Marquis of
Montrose, is one of the noblest figures of
history, a brilliant leader of men, a
world-acclaimed strategist, a talented
moderate in a bigoted age, a man of as great
probity as of charm and the loyalist of the
loyal – yet, a strangely modest man at heart.
And by no means a plaster saint, by any
count. If Charles the First had had even one
other servant of the stature of Montrose,
probably British History would have been
very different. But one man alone could not
alter all, when intolerance, despotism, folly
and weakness held the stage – even though
James Graham tried hard, and almost
succeeded.

In this novel Nigel Tranter takes the
fascinating, gallant, yet desperate story of
this man from the initial snub he received
from the monarch he was to devote his life to
serve, to the detriment of his own marriage,
well-being and peace of mind, through all the
reluctant involvement in national affairs,
through intrigue, violence, treachery, to
battle, more battle, and eventual
near-triumph. But expensive triumph, for
James Graham and those he loved, with all
Scotland almost in his grasp and his hated
enemy, Archibald Campbell, Marquis of
Argyll, defeated and discredited, and England
and Oliver Cromwell next on the list. But that
was to reckon without Fate . . .

Book Two

THE CAPTAIN GENERAL

THE CAPTAIN GENERAL completes the story of the Great Marquis. Nigel Tranter takes James Graham from the sorrowful aftermath of victory at Inverlochy to complete mastery of Scotland and a position to endanger Cromwell's England. Then, from betrayal and desertion, to his exile on the Continent where he met Elizabeth of Bohemia, the Winter Queen, the sister of his imprisoned master, Charles. Elizabeth was all that her brother was not, lively, vigorous – and lovely.

But Charles's execution in 1649 produced a new young King to fight for and duty took Montrose back to Scotland, on a forlorn hope. None knew it better than he. But even James Graham was not prepared for the greatest betrayal of all, when Charles the Second came to terms with the enemy behind his back and sacrificed his truest servant for expediency . . .

MONTROSE: THE YOUNG MONTROSE AND THE CAPTAIN GENERAL

Book One – The Young Montrose
Book Two – The Captain General

Nigel Tranter

CORONET BOOKS
Hodder and Stoughton

First published as two separate volumes

The Young Montrose © 1972 by Nigel Tranter
First published in Great Britain in 1972 by
Hodder and Stoughton Ltd
Coronet edition 1972

The Captain General © 1973 by Nigel Tranter
First published in Great Britain in 1973 by
Hodder and Stoughton Ltd
Coronet edition 1974

This edition 1987

British Library C.I.P.

Tranter, Nigel
Montrose : the young Montrose and the
Captain General.
I. Title   II. Tranter, Nigel. The young
Montrose   III. Tranter, Nigel. Montrose,
the Captain-General
823'.912[F]   PR6070.R34

ISBN 0 340 40763 8

Printed and bound in Great Britain for
Hodder and Stoughton Paperbacks, a
division of Hodder and Stoughton Ltd.,
Mill Road, Dunton Green, Sevenoaks,
Kent (Editorial Office: 47 Bedford
Square, London, WC1B 3DP) by
Cox & Wyman Ltd., Reading.

Book One

THE YOUNG MONTROSE

PRINCIPAL CHARACTERS
In Order of Appearance

JAMES GRAHAM, FIFTH EARL OF MONTROSE: twenty-third chief of the Grahams, aged twenty-four. *An Greumach Mor.*

JOHN GRAHAM, LORD KILPONT: son of the first Earl of Airth (or eighteenth Earl of Menteith).

KING CHARLES THE FIRST

JAMES, THIRD MARQUIS OF HAMILTON: chief of the Hamiltons, later first Duke.

WILLIAM HAMILTON, EARL OF LANARK: brother to above.

WILLIAM LAUD: Archbishop of Canterbury.

ARCHIBALD NAPIER, FIRST LORD NAPIER OF MERCHISTON: Scots statesman, brother-in-law of Montrose.

JOHN, LORD GRAHAM: eldest son of Montrose.

JAMES, LORD CARNEGIE: son of the Earl of Southesk, brother-in-law of Montrose.

DAVID CARNEGIE, FIRST EARL OF SOUTHESK: father-in-law of Montrose.

LADY MAGDALEN CARNEGIE, COUNTESS OF MONTROSE

JAMES GRAHAM: second son of Montrose.

PATRICK GRAHAM, YOUNGER OF INCHBRAKIE: known as Black Pate, friend and kinsman of Montrose.

JOHN LESLIE, SIXTH EARL OF ROTHES: Scots statesman and Covenant leader.

REV. ALEXANDER HENDERSON: Minister of Leuchars and Covenant leader.

SIR THOMAS HOPE OF CRAIGHALL: Lord Advocate.

ARCHIBALD JOHNSTON OF WARRISTON: advocate and Covenant leader, later Lord Warriston.

JOHN CAMPBELL, FIRST EARL OF LOUDOUN: Covenant leader, later Chancellor of Scotland.

REV. ANDREW CANT: Minister of Pitsligo, leading Scots divine.

REV. DAVID DICKSON: Minister of Irvine, leading Scots divine.

GEORGE GORDON, SECOND MARQUIS OF HUNTLY: chief of Clan Gordon.

JAMES GORDON, VISCOUNT ABOYNE: second son of above.

LORD LEWIS GORDON: third son of Huntly.

GEORGE, LORD GORDON: eldest son of Huntly.

ARCHIBALD CAMPBELL, EIGHTH EARL OF ARGYLL: *MacCailean Mor*, chief of Clan Campbell, later first Marquis.

ALEXANDER LESLIE: Field-Marshal, later first Earl of Leven.

ROBERT ARNOT, or BALFOUR, SECOND LORD BALFOUR OF BURLEIGH: Scots statesman and general.

QUEEN HENRIETTA MARIA: wife of King Charles.

PRINCE RUPERT OF THE RHINE: nephew of King Charles, Royalist commander.

PRINCE MAURICE OF BOHEMIA: brother of above, Royalist general.

SIR WILLIAM ROLLO: son of Laird of Duncrub, lieutenant of Montrose.

ALASTAIR MACDONALD, YOUNGER OF COLONSAY: nicknamed Colkitto, commander of Irish gallowglasses.

DAVID DRUMMOND, MASTER OF MADDERTY: heir of Lord Madderty, brother-in-law of Montrose.

JAMES OGILVY, FIRST EARL OF AIRIE: chief of Ogilvys and staunch kingsman.

SIR DAVID OGILVY: son of Airlie.

SIR THOMAS OGILVY: son of Airlie.

COLONEL NATHANIEL GORDON: soldier of fortune.

COLONEL MAGNUS O'CAHAN: Irish lieutenant of Colkitto.

WILLIAM KEITH, SEVENTH EARL MARISCHAL: chief of Keiths and Covenant commander.

JOHN MACDONALD OF MOIDART, CAPTAIN OF CLANRANALD: great Highland chief.

ALAN CAMERON OF LOCHEIL, CAPTAIN OF CLAN CAMERON: great Highland chief.

IAN LOM MACDONALD: the Bard of Keppoch.

PART ONE

I

JAMES GRAHAM STOOD, TAPPING THE TOE OF HIS HIGH-HEELED silken shoe on the waxed floor, and eyed his fellow men and women with scant approval. He was not aware that this showed rather plainly – or indeed, at all – on his handsome features; nor even that impatience was evident in his toe-tapping. For he was a young man of principle as well as of determined courtesy, and desired to offend none, except perhaps in chivalrous fashion and in a suitable cause. But these people were, in the main, deplorable to a man of any sensibility, women as well as men, unfortunately. James Graham approved of women, normally.

That there were not a few Scots amongst the posturing, painted, scented, chattering crew, was probably half the trouble. James Graham was philosophically and broad-mindedly prepared to find the English courtier more or less like this – just as he had made thoughtful allowances for the inanities and perversions of Paris, Seville, Venice, Padua, Florence, and even the Papal Court at Rome, from which he had just come; but to see Scots like John Maitland, Master of Lauderdale, with rouged cheeks and painted lips; Patrick Leslie, Lord Lindores, simpering and ogling behind upraised scented gloves; and the handsome Elizabeth Murray, though she could be no more than sixteen, not only with her gown cut so low that her breasts escaped whenever she stooped or bowed – which she did with marked regularity – but chose to find her garters in constant need of adjustment, with consequent extra stooping and disarray; all this was unedifying. The last might be all very well, indeed perhaps commendable, in private. But not in public, not in the Palace of Whitehall, surely. Here it seemed not only a betrayal of sound Presbyterian Scotland, but in the worst of taste. Not that the thronging, overdressed crowd found it so, most evidently, since all were of a similar pattern. As though determined to demonstrate that the wretched Puritans had no place here. Yet the King was a sober and religious man, much more godly than was James Graham – and Scots-born at that. That he should tolerate this sort of behaviour at his Court was scarcely believable. His flighty little French wife, of course, was otherwise, they said – and the doting Charles denied her nothing. No doubt this was Henrietta Maria's doing.

The Graham had had half an hour of this already, and wondered how much more he could, or should, stand. He was a young man not used to being kept waiting. Hamilton had said to be here at six prompt. In that half-hour he had barely spoken to a soul; just stood, apart a little, feeling out-of-place and somehow conspicuous – which last at least was no illusion, for James Graham in any company was conspicuous, of a sheer beauty of countenance which, though wholly masculine and virile, was allied to a proud grace of bearing that never failed to draw all eyes – even though fullest appreciation thereof was not necessarily the reaction of every one of his own sex.

Though he recognised many, he did not really know anyone here – nor indeed greatly desired to. Perhaps something of this attitude escaped him, despite his carefully courteous intentions. Three years on the Continent had made a stranger of him, even to the Scots present – and he had been only just of age, after all, when he left on his rather unusual Grand Tour. Nor had he ever previously visited the Court at London. It seemed that he had missed little thereby.

His foot was tap-tapping again, when a voice at his elbow turned him.

'Egad, James – it's yourself! On my soul, I scarce knew you! I heard you were home. But ...'

'Home, Johnnie . . .?' the other repeated, high brows higher. But he quickly relented, and smiled, warmly – and thereby transformed the proudly beautiful face into one of quite extraordinary attraction and charm. 'It is good to see a kent face – and an honest one! They seem scarce here! What brings you to Whitehall, Johnnie? A long way from the Carse of Forth.'

'What brings anyone to Court, James? The hope of betterment. Of justice, if you like.' The Lord Kilpont grimaced plain, boyish features. 'Not that I look like to win either, 'fore God! And yourself? What brings you, of all men?'

'Not betterment. Nor yet justice, I think,' the other returned – and his slightly scornful enunciation of the word betterment was eloquent. Then, as so often, he shook his head briefly, as though to throw off an involuntary reaction in favour of an amended and kinder one. 'I am sorry that you are not finding success, Johnnie. Or justice. For, i' faith, if all I hear is true, that you much deserve. Your father's ill-treatment was a crying scandal. Are you hoping for a reversal of the forfeiture?'

'Nothing so great. Only some small office of profit, some help with our creditors. The Customs of Airth and Alloa, perhaps. We are near penniless, James. Things have gone from bad to worse, while you have been gone. My father is a done and broken man. He will not last long, I fear. He is dunned, day in, day out. But he is too proud to ask the King's mercy, or aid. So *I* come. But to little benefit . . .'

'Poor Menteith! I did not know that it was so bad. I heard only snatches of it all, garbled. In Padua, I was then. This of Menteith is sore tidings . . .'

'Hush, man! Do not mention that name. Even to breathe the word Menteith today is next to high treason! My lord of *Airth* only, if you please!'

James Graham eyed his far-out kinsman with a perplexed frown. 'You mean this, Johnnie? Surely not! Surely Charles is not thus. A godly man, all say, and honest. Noble, indeed . . .'

'Perhaps. But weak, James – or, if not weak, with great weaknesses. Stupidities, 'fore God! The worst, that he relies on favourites who are fools or knaves. More of the first than the other, I do believe – but the end is the same! Aye, Charles Stewart looks noble enough, sounds noble – but how noble are his acts? Ask William Graham, my father!'

Lord Kilpont, a year younger than his chief, was son and heir to William, who until two years before had been eighteenth Earl of Menteith, one of the greatest nobles and proudest names in Scotland; and who, because in a rash moment, flushed with wine, had been heard to boast that his own blood was more truly royal than the King's, had been summarily forfeited, deprived of his ancient earldom with all its great revenues, and allowed to retain only his small barony of Airth, in the Carse of Stirling, with the scornfully new-minted title of Earl of Airth – this by King Charles's personal command, who, on the advice of sundry ill-wishers of Menteith's, was pleased to sense a threat to his throne and dignity in the Graham's bibulous boast, true as it was. For the Grahams were of royal descent, and closer to the main stem of the ancient Scots ruling line than was Charles Stewart himself. The new Earl of Airth, who should also have been Earl of Strathearn, a semi-royal and illustrious earldom, was a ruined man.

The imputation that the dignified and stately monarch was weak – and worse, stupid – disturbed James Graham. 'I think you mistake, my friend,' he said. 'His Grace was ill-advised in this, to be sure. I have not all the truth of it – I was a year gone when it was done, was I not? All that I may do, to put it right, I will do. But – you go too far, naming the King weak and stupid. Charles Stewart is no weakling, no fool, I swear. God forbid!'

'You have not spoken with him, I think? Even seen him?'

'No. But all declare him worshipful, wise, good.'

'I could name you some who do not!' Kilpont said grimly. But at the other's expression he wisely changed the subject. 'And you, James – what do *you* seek from His Grace?'

'Seek? I seek nothing. Only to offer him my services. As is my simple duty.'

'Your services . . . ?'

'To be sure. What else? I am Montrose.'

'Mm. *An Greumach Mor!* In Scotland that means much,' the Viscount acceded. 'But here . . . ?'

'It is in Scotland, naturally, that I would serve him. Not here.' The other's glance around him was sufficiently eloquent. 'Are you of Hamilton's mind, then, about the King?'

'Hamilton? Does that one *have* a mind? Pray, James – of a mercy, do not speak my name in the same breath with that . . . lickspittle! That empty-headed, ill-disposed, vapouring toady!'

'Save us, Johnnie – what's come to you, man? You were not always so sour! Myself, I do not greatly love Hamilton – but he is great with the King. Has his ear. And is the foremost man in Scotland today, they say.'

'In Scotland! That mincing popinjay would no more set

his dainty foot in Scotland today than in Muscovy! He is the worst of all the crew of fawning, lying, sycophants who surround the King. All you may say is that Scotland is well quit of James Hamilton and his like!' Clearly, boyish as he still looked, Kilpont was a very different man from the laughing, heedless twenty-year-old James Graham had left behind him. Then he paused in his vituperation to ask, 'What was it you meant about my lord Marquis? His mind, anent the King?'

'Merely that he warned me that the King was much offended with Scotland, these days. That I should take care how I mention his ancient kingdom to His Grace – lest it serve me but ill. Myself, I cannot believe this. Scotland, after all, is his true realm. Where he was born, where his line belongs. It is but thirty years since the Stewarts have sat on this English throne. That he should hate Scotland is unthinkable . . .'

'So Hamilton said that?' Kilpont fingered the wispy hair on his chin which he was trying to grow – with an envious glance at the neatly luxuriant moustache and trim under-lip beard of his friend and chief. 'I wonder why, egad? He has his reasons, that one, no doubt.'

'You believe it to be untrue, then? Yet you hinted, did you not, that here my name may mean but little . . .'

Montrose paused, as another man came sauntering up to them, an exquisite this, in sky-blue satin and brocade, lace, jewelled buckles, earrings and ivory-handled, shoulder-high, ribboned walking-staff.

'Save us, Basil – you too!' he exclaimed. 'Got up like a mummer at a fair, as bad as the rest! I vow, all you require now is a dancing-bear!'

'At Court, one must be a courtier, my dear James – or nothing! And I would be *something*, as you know,' the new-comer declared, laughing, and flourishing a lace-edged, scented handkerchief. A plump-featured, silky-haired, genial young man, he pointed, with the head of that ridiculous staff. 'You, now – you serve yourself but ill, dressed so. I swear it! Even the beauteous and poetic Earl of Montrose! You will but seem to rebuke others – and so smell curst Calvinist to His Majesty. See if you do not.'

James Graham looked down at his own attire, and shrugged. 'I think I am very well,' he said. 'It served well enough for half the Courts of Europe. Why not here?'

'Why not indeed?' Kilpont agreed. 'You are the most distinguished-seeming man in this Audience Chamber, for a wager!'

And that, in fact, was true. Distinguished was the apt word for this man. Without seeking to do so, he ever bore himself with a distinction, a separateness, and assurance of carriage which was something different again from the lithe natural grace and the fine features. That he should be dressed all in black, slashed with silver – even though of satin and velvet – apart from the deep white lace collar and ruffles at wrists, did further set him apart, and dramatically so, in the kaleidoscopic riot of colours in that great hall, although this was in fact his normal style for high occasions.

'Truly said,' the Englishman acceded. 'But distinction can be costly – against the undistinguished! I have said so before, James – being not troubled that way myself! But . . . I have not the privilege of this gentleman's name . . . ?'

'Ha – of course. A kinsman, John Graham, Lord Kilpont, heir to the Earl of Menteith . . .'

'A mercy, James – I told you! Not that. Never that. The name is as forbidden as that of MacGregor! Airth, if you please – to my sorrow!'

'Very well. Heir to the first Earl of Airth, though eighteenth otherwise! A sorry story. And this, Johnnie, is my good friend Basil, Viscount Fielding, who was my companion through most of the lands and cities of Europe. Heir to my lord Earl of Denbigh.'

Kilpont nodded, and Fielding made an elaborate leg, with which was associated a twirling of his staff and a flourish of the handkerchief.

'Honoured,' the latter commented. 'You Scots are so deucedly good at figures! I fear that I could never count. Eighteenth, you said? And that from the fifth Earl of Montrose . . . !'

'But eighth Lord Graham, and twenty-third chief of the name, *An Greumach Mor*,' Kilpont interpolated carefully.

'Quite – oh quite! As I say – I never could add. As well, since my father is one of the new men. The first Earl! Makes it easy for me, you see . . .'

'Enough of such nonsense,' Montrose said. 'The English can count, I think, as well as we, when it comes to most matters. Gold pieces, for instance. Acres. Houses. Servants.

16

Pay no heed to Basil's mockery, Johnnie – his tongue is the worst of him. For myself, it is the *King's* counting that concerns me. Of time! Hamilton said to be here by six o'clock. Now it is nearer seven.'

'His Majesty never appears before seven, I am told,' Fielding mentioned. 'He is a staid man, of set custom and habit. Not like his appalling and unpredictable sire. Ah – forgive me! He was a Scot also, of course! My tongue, again . . .'

'Is that truth? That the King never comes before seven o'clock? Then why did Hamilton have me here at six?' James Graham's pleasantly modulated, almost musical, voice, with the slight Highland intonation, went level, thin.

'I told you. The man's a fool,' Kilpont insisted. 'Hamilton. Or . . . perhaps he designed to keep you waiting!'

'Hamilton? The Marquis? Is he your sponsor, James?' Fielding asked. 'A strange man as I should know! My brother-in-law, no less! Married Margaret my sister – at the age of seven!'

'Sponsor, no.' That was short. 'Montrose needs no sponsor with his liege lord. I but sought his guidance, as how conveniently to approach His Grace. We are related at a distance. And his brother, Lanark, was with me at college . . .'

A sudden fanfare of trumpets from without interrupted him. The chatter in the huge gilded apartment stilled, and all eyes turned towards the top end, where great doors were flung open. Two files of Yeoman of the Guard, in scarlet and black, marched in, pikes on shoulders, to pace onward down the chamber. Right and left before them the company fell back, leaving a clear and red-lined central avenue. Behind, a gorgeously apparelled usher in heraldic tabard stalked in, and as the fanfare died away, thumped his rod on the floor.

'Silence for His most excellent Majesty Charles, by the Grace of God, King!' he cried. And everywhere men bowed low and women sank in deepest curtsy.

It was all highly impressive, dignified, suitable. Unfortunately, what followed was less so. A crowd of men came surging into the hall, some backing, sidling, even skipping, as they eddied round a small central group of three, bowing, flourishing, gesticulating, in a fatuous display of adulation. And within this capering perimeter the trio sauntered, one tall, in a peach-yellow satin, one short and tubby in rich, vaguely clerical habit, and one slender and slight in purple velvet, wearing a wide-brimmed black hat with a large curling golden ostrich-feather. Because of the hat, and the fact that its wearer was not very tall, Montrose, like most others, could not see the man's features behind his escort.

If this entrance lacked something in dignity, no less so did the waiting company's reception. Straight from their bowing and curtsying, there was a jostling rush forward, men and women pushing and elbowing each other to be foremost on either side of the lines of inward-facing Yeomen of the Guard. James Graham, astonished, found himself shouldered aside in the scramble, and although he had been waiting in a good position all this while, now was quickly edged into the background.

'Come – or we will not win near the King,' Kilpont exclaimed, starting to push, in turn.

'Never!' the other jerked. 'Think you Montrose should act so? In such rabble!'

'You heard Fielding. At Court, do as the courtiers do! See – *he* does.'

'Let him. I bide here.'

'Then the King will not see you. What you came here for.'

'So be it, then. But . . . Hamilton knows that I am here.'

The Marquis of Hamilton was the tall man in yellow at the King's right; and because of his height, he could see over the heads of most of the crowd. Already, almost as soon as he entered the room, his glance had caught that of his fellow Scot – and though he looked away at once, without any sign, Montrose knew that he had recognised him. He was a fine figure of a man, though ridiculously overdressed and prinked up with a plethora of ribbons, bows, rosettes, costume-jewellery and the like on top of his peach satin slashed with scarlet. The royal right hand rested on his puffed and pearl-seeded sleeve.

It was some little while before James Graham could catch a glimpse of the King's face, when he momentarily took off his hat to greet a genuflecting lady presented to him by one of his troupe. But at the sight, the younger man's offence and ill-humour left him, melted promptly like snow in the sun. For Charles Stewart was all and more than he had hoped to see, his features noble, splendid, stately, kingly indeed, but never proudly arrogant or distant. Sensitive, compassionate, almost sad, his great lustrous Stewart eyes looked beneath his lofty forehead and delicately arching brows. The face was long and narrow, an impression accentuated by the pointed beard, longer than was usual for the period, and the shoulder-length curling auburn hair; and the general expression was grave. But the smile, when vouchsafed, was warm and kindly. Every inch and line and movement of the man was implicit with dignity.

'Fore God, man – you said he was stupid! Weak and stupid! I think your troubles must have cost you your wits, Johnnie!'

'Perhaps.' The other shrugged. 'He looks a king, yes. But he acts . . . otherwise. You will learn!'

The King passed slowly up the avenue formed by the Guard, pausing here and there to speak to some low-bowing man or dipping woman either singled out by himself or presented by one of his posturing minions – and always, when it was a woman, he briefly removed his great feathered hat with a gesture of the most gracious courtesy. Quite soon he was past a point level with Montrose, and no sign or glance given.

'You see,' Kilpont said. 'You are not noticed. Here it is deil tak the hindmost!'

'Wait, you,' the other answered.

They had a lengthy wait, for Majesty was in no hurry, and many people were spoken to and presented. Before long, James Graham's toe began to tap-tap the floor again.

When Charles at length turned, at the far end of the room, to move slowly back, the tubby man with the slightly clerical look about his plum-coloured velvet and lace, seemed to take over from Hamilton in making the majority of presentations. And he found more to catch his eye than had the Marquis – especially amongst the women – to the Graham's ill-concealed impatience.

'That man – who is he? A churchman – but with a good conceit of himself!'

'That is William Laud, the Archbishop. The King's close confessor! An Armenian – and the most unpopular man in England! Yet Charles loves him well – even better than Hamilton, they say. He has turned the Church here upside-down. And is seeking to do the same in Scotland . . .'

'Scotland? The Archbishop of Canterbury? What has such to do with Scotland?'

'Well may you ask! But King Charles heeds him in all things. And Charles is still King of Scots.'

Slowly the courteous monarch worked his way down the long room again. And despite himself, James Graham edged a little forward. When he saw Basil Fielding briefly enjoying the royal attention, he subconsciously smoothed the lace at his throat and the ruffles at his wrists, waiting to catch Hamilton's signal the while. But the Marquis looked anywhere but at Montrose; and the King gradually passed by.

'God's curse!' the Graham swore, beneath his breath. 'This is too much!'

Kilpont eyed his chief sidelong, and decided to hold his tongue.

Biting his lip, Montrose watched his sovereign's gracious retreating back.

Fielding came pushing his way to his friend's side again. 'James! Sink me – what's this? he exclaimed. 'You are ignored. This is beyond all belief. The Earl of Montrose – spurned. On your first visit to Court. You should have pushed forward, man. As I did. As all do . . .'

'I should not,' the other snapped. 'Besides, they know that I am here. Hamilton does. He looked at me. And his brother, Lanark, mincing there. I saw him peering – and pretending not to. Yet he has brought half a dozen to the King . . .'

'It is damnable. See – people are looking. Staring. I heard many whispering your name . . .'

'Let them . . .'

'James – if you slipped round there, to near the door, behind these, you would win close enough. As they go out. There is still time . . .'

'I will do no such thing. Think you I must dodge and jouk and crawl for any man? Even Charles Stewart?'

'But . . . if he does not know that you are here?'

'Then it is Hamilton's doing. And, 'fore God, I will not crawl for Hamilton!'

In silence the trio waited. And now there was no question but that many eyes were turned in their direction. Close by, a woman tittered.

Then, as the King was about to leave the room, and trumpeters were raising their instruments for the valedictory fanfare, Hamilton stooped, and spoke in the royal ear, turning to glance back directly at Montrose.

Charles Stewart paused, turned also, grave-faced, and waited.

Everywhere a sudden hush fell on the great company. Fielding grabbed his friend's arm.

James Graham stood where he was, head high, motionless, as grave-faced as his monarch.

Moments passed thus, sudden tension in the air. Hamilton was an abruptly changed man, prominent eyes darting, nibbling at his silky moustache. Then, frowning, he flicked a gloved hand at his younger brother, the Earl of Lanark, a flick that ended in a finger pointing at Montrose. William Hamilton came hurrying, pushing his way through the throng, to where the Graham stood.

'My lord . . .' he gasped, all but panted. 'James – His Grace . . . His Majesty will see you now. Come. Come quickly – in God's name !'

The other waited a second or two longer, then bowed formally. He moved forward unhurriedly.

'Haste ye, man.' Lanark, already well ahead, turned anxiously, to mutter, 'You'll not keep the King waiting !'

The Graham said nothing to that, and increased his pace no whit.

The dandified Lanark reached the royal presence a deal before his charge. His brother looking angry, flushed, began to speak, then changed his mind. The King's expression, like his bearing, had not changed.

'Your Majesty, have I leave to present my lord Earl of Montrose?' Hamilton jerked, at last.

'Ah, yes. I know of my lord,' Charles said mildly, inclining his head. He neither smiled nor frowned. But he extended his hand.

James Graham bowed low, and reached out to take the royal hand. But he did not take it in the usual way, to raise to his lips ; instead he placed the long slender fingers between his own two palms, and bowed over it, in the traditional gesture of fealty.

'Your Grace's true and devoted servant to command,' he said, low-voiced.

The King, regaining his hand, considered the younger man from those lustrous sad eyes, but without his famed warmth. 'I did not see you come to honour my Coronation at Edinburgh, near three years ago, along with my other Scots lords,' he observed, his voice even.

'To my sorrow. I was then in Padua, Your Grace.'

'Indeed. Then I trust that Padua served you will. I bid you a good day, my lord of Montrose.' Charles inclined his head again, and turned away.

'Sire . . . !' Montrose exclaimed, and then bit back the flood of words which surged to his lips, as the King strolled off through the wide doorway, and the ring of his entourage closed round him.

The clamour of talk and exclamation rose again in the Audience Chamber behind, as the trumpets rang out.

Biting his lips, James Graham stared after the sovereign lord he had come to offer service and loyalty to, the service of a great and powerful house, great wealth, great man-power, and blood as proud as the Stewarts'. Then he flung himself round, and went stalking long-strided down the huge apartment, past the re-forming Yeomen, looking neither right nor left, caring nothing for the stares, the smirks or the tinkling laughter, making for the entrance at the far end.

He was down crossing the open palace courtyard before Kilpont caught up with him.

'Save us, James – here's your bonnet!' the other panted, clapping on his own wide hat. 'A plague on them – that was ill done! A studied insult! But, why? Why? To *you?*'

Montrose vouchsafed no answer.

'A mercy – no need for such haste, surely!' Kilpont was almost having to run to keep up with his companion's great striding. 'It was Hamilton's doing – that I swear. He has put the King against you. I was watching him. Charles is a fool, yes – but he does not lack civility. Even to me he was more civil than that – although he has not heeded my pleas. It was Hamilton . . .'

'The King it was who spurned me – not Hamilton!' the other got out, from behind clenched teeth. 'Whatever Hamilton may have said or done, it was Charles Stewart who decided. Decided to reject Montrose. Before all. I did not proffer my hand and fealty and name, to *Hamilton!*'

At the bitterness in his friend's voice, so unusual, so out-of-character, Kilpont shook his head.

'I am sorry, James – sorry. But . . . what next? Will you try again? Discover what Hamilton is at – and face him with

22

it? Challenge the arrogant lickspittle! Approach Charles again . . .'

'I will not. I ride for Scotland tomorrow, as fast as horse-flesh will carry me. Shake the dust of this place off my feet. And wish that I had sailed home direct from France! That I had never thought to visit this London, to pay my duty. It is Scotland again, for me – tomorrow.'

'Damn it, if I will not ride with you, James! On my oath, I will! I've had enough of this city of fawning spaniels and toad-eaters! And I gain no advantage for my father, here. A breath or two of our snell Scots air – that is what we both need. And leave London to its stews, its stinks and its jackals and trucklers. Especially its Scots ones!'

The other nodded. 'Aye – I long to feel the wind off the heather again, the scents of bracken and pine, hear the crackle of whins in the sun. I have been away too long, Johnnie. It is time I was home. Time . . .'

2

James Graham had never had any pronounced affection for Edinburgh, a city he had little known or had occasion to know. In friendly small Glasgow he had lived as a child, in the house of Lord Justice Clerk Elphinstone, with his own Mugdock Castle near by to the north. Of Perth he was fond, near his favourite home of Kincardine Castle, on the southern verge of Strathearn; and Stirling, to the south of this, was almost a Graham town. Montrose itself, where he had been born, though a smaller place, always pleased him. And St Andrews, where he had studied and spent his high youth gloriously, he loved as the finest little city, not only in Scotland but in all Christendom – better than Paris, Rome, Venice or Padua. But in Edinburgh, on its hills above the silver Forth, he somehow felt alien, chilled – not so much by its everlasting winds which, after all, were no colder than those of St Andrews – but by some quality in the folk, the temper of its people. He ever felt small, under the soaring tenements, the dizzy grey stone 'lands' which huddled so close on the climbing ridge between Holyroodhouse and the frowning Castle, projecting inwards over the narrow streets and wynds, so as almost to cut out the very sky – but never those winds. Yet this early May day of brittle sunlight, sting-ing showers and rain-washed colour, as he rode in beneath Arthur's Seat, past the Abbey and Palace, and up the Canon-gate and under the Netherbow Port, he almost embraced the place to him, acknowledging its magnificent setting, cherish-ing even its smells – and the blustering winds which made them more bearable than those of London and Paris – look-ing kindly on its craggy-jawed, bonneted men and shawled women, however little his benevolent glances were returned, and shook the glistening raindrops from his travelling-cloak with more cheer than he had shown for days. It was Scot-land, stern and stark and authentic, but vivid, challenging and self-sufficient as was nowhere else that he had come across in all his three years of travels – his own place, the land his love for which he had only truly discovered when far away.

He and Kilpont parted company in the Grassmarket, the latter to ride on westwards, out again by the West Port and so by Corstorphine and Linlithgow to Airth, short of Stirling, in whose small castle his sick and broken father roosted in-consolate; while Montrose, with young Graham of Morphie his esquire, Master John Lambie his secretary, his body-servant Dod Graham, and the six armed troopers who had ridden as his guard the length and breadth of Europe, turned southwards up the Candlemaker Row, climbing steeply, to issue from the city at the Bristo Port, and jingle at a trot across the Meadows, swinging westwards around the emi-nence where workmen were still busily erecting the great Geordie Heriot's Hospital, begun eight whole years ago and not finished yet. And now they were climbing on to the Burgh Muir, all whins and broom and rocky outcrops, where the burghers' thin cattle grazed, and the insolent herd-boys threw stones and lewd pleasantries at the horsemen, ready to dodge for safety amongst their shaggy charges at first sign of retaliation. Even this, today, commended itself to James Graham. Surely only in Scotland, where the independent spirit ruled all, would herd-laddies throw stones at a belted earl and his party of armed cavaliers.

Across the Burgh Muir, the ground ever rising, with the Braid and Pentland Hills soaring behind and further gladdening the travellers' hearts after too long in at countries, they passed near the turrets and steep roofs of Wrightshouse, the Napier house of a kinsman. But they did not halt, pressing on to a long ridge of yellow-blazing whins, crackling in the sun as Montrose had ached to hear so many a time. And here they saw, on the slightly downward slope beyond, a tall stone tower rising sheerly out of the orchards and formal pleasance-gardens, a strong, stout battlemented keep of five storeys and garret within the parapet, complete with wall-walk, curtain-walled courtyard and gatehouse, trim, self-contained, indomitable – and not a little arrogant – typical of the land and the people.

At sight of it Montrose reined in a little, and his fine eyes clouded. 'Merchiston,' he murmured, to himself. 'Och, Margaret!' Then he shook his head under the splendid wide-brimmed and feathered hat, and kneed his mount on.

Under the gatehouse arch of Merchiston Castle they rode clattering into the cobbled courtyard, a stout porter in leather doublet and the inevitable blue bonnet coming bustling out to take the head of Montrose's magnificent stallion.

'Hech, my lord, my lord – it's yourself'!' he cried. 'Man, Lord James, you're back! Guidsakes – here's a blessed day!'

'Aye, Wattie – I'm back. At last. To find you fatter than ever. Fat as an in-pig gilt, I vow!'

'Och, comfortable just,' the other averred complacently, handing the Earl down, 'Nae mair'n that. Yoursel', you look braw, my lord – braw. Aye, you've changed. The right cavalier now, beardie and all! She ... she wouldn'a ... och, man – my leddy ... !' He shook his greying head, and turned ruddy face away.

'Aye, Watty – as you say.' That came thinly, stiffly. Then he touched the porter's shoulder, lightly. 'Is your master at home?'

'Ooh, aye. He's up in his ain bit chamber, at the top o' the house. He's aye there, writing, writing. He has little heart for aught else, the man, these days. Awa' up wi' you.'

Leaving the others to their own devices, Montrose climbed the detached forestair, crossed the little removable timber gangway, and so entered the keep at first-floor level – a device which ensured a second line of defence should the outer curtain-wall be breached. Then on up the narrow, winding turnpike in the thickness of the walling – eight-foot thickness – lit only by arrowslits, the steps hollowed by mailed feet. At the top, the little garret watch-chamber within the dizzy parapet wall-walk, was the room with the splendid views which his brother-in-law had made his study. He knocked and entered.

The greying, lean, grave-faced man in the shabby clothing turned at his deck by one of the dormer windows, to look, peer, and then jump up, rather sombre features lit up.

'Jamie! Jamie!' he cried. 'God is good – Jamie Graham! It's yourself.' His voice little different from that of his gate-porter below, Archibald first Lord Napier of Merchiston, Privy Councillor, Treasurer Deputy of Scotland for life, former Lord Justice Clerk and still extraordinary Lord of Sessions, came forward to greet the younger man in warmest welcome.

They embraced each other with undisguised affection, for they were the greatest of friends, these two, despite the discrepancy in age. Napier, when a man of forty, had married Montrose's second sister Margaret when she was eighteen, making her an excellent husband. More than that, he had made a second father for the boy who had lost his own sire at fourteen, and had to take on the formidable business of being *An Greumach Mor,* chief of all the Grahams, and fifth Earl of Montrose while still with five years of his teens to run. Lord Napier was long past the fathering stage, as that of legal guardian – but he remained the wise and trusted friend.

'Archie! Here's joy.' James Graham held the other back, to look at him – and only just stopped himself from blurting out how he had aged in three years. He recognised, too, that he perhaps should not have used that word joy. 'It has been a long time,' he said. 'Too long, Archie.'

'Aye, too long, lad.'

The other looked away, moistening his lips. 'Margaret,' he said. 'I am sorry Dear God – I am sorry!'

Napier nodded. 'We are the poorer, Jamie. Perhaps, somewhere, some are the richer? Who knows? Your father. Mother. But . . . it is scant comfort.'

Margaret Graham had died less than a year after her

26

brother's departure for the Continent, after a dozen years of marriage, leaving three children and the still-born infant whose birth killed her. Like any husband in the circumstances, Archibald Napier could not absolve himself altogether from blame.

'She was the best of us,' Montrose said. 'The kindest, truest, most excellent. I grieve for us all – but for you above all.'

'God's will be done,' the other answered quietly.

'Was it God's will, then? You, a judge. Great in the Kirk. Tell me.' And then, at sight of the older man's perplexed and sorrowful face, he reached out impulsively to grasp his arm. 'I am sorry, Archie Forgive my ill tongue. I have learned to question much that before I accepted, these last years – perhaps too much. I did not mean to hurt you further.'

'Do not blame yourself, Jamie. But . . . questioning fate, destiny, what is ordained by the Lord God Omnipotent, serves nothing, brings no comfort but only more sorrow. This I have learned the sore way, God knows. A man must learn to accept.'

'But you yourself taught me to be a seeker. Ever a seeker, not an acceptor. Did you not?'

The other inclined his head. 'Aye. But now I seek God's *purpose* with men. And to accept His will – if I may. But – enough of this, lad. What of your other seeking? Your other sister? What of Katherine, Jamie? You still have not found her?'

Montrose shook his head. 'Not a trace. No word – nothing. As I wrote to you, I found John Colquhoun, at last. In Venice. But alone. Katherine was not there. She had gone. He said, he said that she had run off with another man! He knew not where.'

'God have mercy on her!' Napier whispered.

Montrose's prolonged Grand Tour had been rather more than just that. It had been a quest, a search, and a terrible one. Undertaken under the guise of finishing his education in the accepted fashion, to lessen the scandal of it all. And undertaken hurriedly, and against much good advice – including the Lord Napier's, which was why he had not been in his earl's place at King Charles's coronation at Edinburgh only a month or so after his hasty departure. For another brother-in-law, Sir John Colquhoun of Luss, chief of that name and husband of the Lady Lilias, eldest of the five Graham sisters, had suddenly elected to desert his wife and family, abandon his estates, sheriffdom and responsibilities, and abscond to the Continent – and, what was worse, had taken with him the Lady Katherine Graham, the unwed younger sister of twenty. To the scandal of all Scotland. Outlawed by the shocked Privy Council, excommunicated by the outraged Kirk, Colquhoun and his sister-in-law disappeared beyond the seas. And nothing would serve young James Graham but that he there and then must advance the date of his projected educational tour of the capitals of Christendom, and go in search of his erring sister.

'I did not fight John Colquhoun,' he said, slowly. 'I had promised myself that I would have his life. But, seeing and hearing him, I perceived that would profit nothing. Nor help Katherine, nor yet Lilias. The man was broken, distraught, pitiful. I scarce knew him. He was a man deserted.'

'Deserted! Colquhoun? What are you saying, Jamie? Do you know what you are saying?'

'All too well, I know. *He* had been deserted – both by my sister, and by his creature Carlippis, who had been his evil genius throughout. The poor besotted fool!'

Appalled, Napier stared at the younger man. 'You . . . you are making your sister a wanton, then? A heartless wanton . . . !'

'I know not what my sister is. I *thought* that I knew her. We were close – but a year between us. She was ever my companion, as children. And ever she was spirited. Strange, in some fashion. But, this . . . ! God's mercy – what is she?'

'You are not saying that she went off with the Italian? Or German – whatever he was. That necromancer of Colquhoun's. A mere servant! With that wretched charlatan?'

'I do not know. Except that they left John Colquhoun secretly. And at the same time. And both went none know where.'

'If it had not been yourself telling me, I'd not have believed it! Katherine! Little Katherine. But nineteen years. And you learned no more of her?'

'I sent out messengers, enquirers, from Venice, Florence, Rome. All the time I was studying at Padua, I was seeking word of her. False scents I followed, in plenty. Nothing came of any. I was told of a young Scotswoman who had appeared at the Court of King Louis, calling herself the Comtesse de Medoc. Medoc might, at a stretch, be for Mugdock, where Katherine was born. I threw up my studies at Padua, and went to Paris with Basil Fielding, Denbigh's son. But the woman was Irish, not Scots. A young widow of a true Medoc. I remained at the French Court. Still seeking. Then your letter came, telling me that it was time that I returned to Scotland. That matters were not well here, and that I should be home.'

'Aye.' Heavily Napier said it. 'And that is the truth. I am sorry, lad. Grieved that all this sore trouble should have struck you – struck us all. Grieved to have fetched you home to more trouble. Grieved for this realm of Scotland . . .'

'You said in your letter that matters were going but ill. In kirk and state.'

'Ill, yes. But – see you, here is no way to welcome you home, Jamie. You will be weary, needing refreshment. How long do you bide with me?'

'A night, two. No more, Archie. Then I must ride north to Kinnaird. I sent word to Magdalen that I was coming.'

'To be sure. I must not keep you from her – blithe as I would be to have you bide.'

'Magdalen – all is well at Kinnaird?'

'Aye. No trouble there, at least, the good Lord be praised. She will rejoice to see you. She has missed you sorely, Jamie.' The older man shot a keen, searching glance at the younger. 'It has been a long time, lad. For a woman.'

'For us all, Archie – for us all. But I do blame myself – even though I esteemed them to have little need of me, up there.'

'More than you think, James. But – come you down. You must eat and drink. You will have your folk with you. My house is yours . . .'

It was evening before, fed and rested, Montrose could again be alone with his brother-in-law. They walked together in the mellow walled garden to the south of the castle, amongst clipped box and apple-trees, with the first swallows darting about them in the clear northern light – all of which affected the homecomer not a little.

'I urged you, in my letter, to make shift to see King Charles,' Napier said. 'Did you so, Jamie?'

'I saw King Charles,' the other answered.

At the tone of voice, the older man looked sidelong at his companion.

'You scarce sound enchanted? Did something go amiss?'

'Amiss, yes. Whether my face, my name, or the style of me, I know not. But His Grace would have none of me. Scarce threw me a word. Rejected me out-of-hand, before all his Court.'

Napier had stopped. 'You . . . you cannot mean this, in truth? That the King rejected you? *You*, Montrose! One of the greatest lords in Scotland. I cannot believe it, Jamie . . .'

'It is the truth. More than rejected – spurned. Deliberately. I was there to offer him my leal support and duty, my whole strength, my all. For the word is that he may need it! But, it seems that he wants none of it. Even though my family has borne up the Scots throne for centuries. Johnnie Kilpont says that it was Hamilton's doing. That Hamilton had poisoned the King's mind against me – I know not why. I have never given offence to Hamilton, that I know of .But . . . even so, Charles could have heard me, made his own judgment. My liege lord . . .'

'This is beyond all.' Shaking his head, Napier moved on slowly along the garden path. 'His Grace needs every true man he may find, indeed. Though most of all, honest advice – dear God, how he needs that! And he will not get it from Hamilton, and his like. But – how was it? What did he say . . . ?'

Clipped of voice, stiffly – for it went sorely against a young man's pride, especially one reared as Montrose had been, to power and authority almost from infancy – he told all, as they paced beneath the trees on the drifts of fallen apple-blossom.

Napier heard him out, frowning, sighing. 'Save us – I fear, Jamie. Fear for Scotland. Fear for the King's Grace – for us all. When a man can make so many mistakes, can scarce do anything aright – how shall the realm survive? And yet, he is honest, I am convinced. Means well. And is not a fool. Indeed, I conceive him honourable, truly princely in most matters. A man apart . . .'

'As did I. And so he appears, looks, sounds. But behaves, it seems, differently!'

'He is badly advised – we all know that. He has no judgment as to whom to trust, to take into his confidence. He surrounds himself with time-servers, place-seekers, windbags. This I know only too well. He lacks his father's shrewdness. King James was as graceless a king as ever sat upon a throne – but he was shrewd. He would never have done what Charles is doing. Splitting his ancient realm in twain for the sake of a clerk's rigmarole, a prayer-book!'

'Kilpont said something of this. But he had not the rights of it, I am sure.'

'Aye – that is why I wanted you home, Jamie. I daresay young Kilpont was none so far out. This is the trouble that threatens Scotland. Dire trouble, and all for a few printed words on paper. The King, egged on by this wretched prelate Laud, this Archbishop he has made, is insisting that the Kirk changes its form of worship to the same as the Church of England! Indeed, he would have no Kirk of Scotland, but have us all worshipping God the same way, he says – his way, Laud's way. We must accept his bishops – these we have already, this while, but we scarcely bow down to them. But now he has seven of them on his Privy Council. And we are to use a new prayer-book of Laud's in our kirks, and give up the Presbyterian form of worship and church government. This, by royal command. On pain of treason!'

'But . . . but it is not possible! None can do such a thing. Not the King. Not any archbishop. Not any man on God's earth! Scotland's faith, her worship, is her own.'

'Charles says otherwise. He claims that he is head of the Church, as of the realm . . .'

'The Church of England, maybe – but not of Scotland! None but Christ Himself is head of Scotland's Kirk!'

'Aye – so we, the Kirk, have told him. But he will have none of it. He has appointed a Court of High Commission, to rule for him in matters ecclesiastical. He has appointed Archbishop Spottiswoode of St Andrews as Chancellor of Scotland, instead of the Earl of Kinnoull – the first churchman to hold the office since the Reformation of blessed memory. He has made a new diocese of Edinburgh, and declared the High Kirk of St Giles to be its Cathedral, and ordered cast down the partition-wall between the chancel and the nave. He will have none of the presbyters – we are all to be Episcopalians, bowing to his bishops whether we will or no.'

'But . . . he cannot make us, 'fore God! He cannot change a nation's religion – one man!'

'He can try. And lacks not the means, or the will to enforce it. John Livingstone, Lord Balmerino, you know. He protested, sought to rally others to protest. The King called it high treason. Had him warded and tried – aye, and condemned. To death, no less! For gainsaying the royal right to say how we should worship. But, man – there was siclike an uproar over it, that even Charles Stewart took second thoughts and issued a royal pardon. But, see you – it *was* only a pardon, not a reversal of his edicts. And, it seems, he has learned nothing by it. A new ordinance to regulate the worship of the Kirk was signed, in London, earlier this year. And this very month a Book of Canons was sent up to us, for obedience. These Canons to have the force of law. Moreover, there is this Liturgy to follow. That is Charles Stewart, by the Grace of God, King! And, stirring up this bees' bike, he yet spurns Montrose's hand and help!'

'Is he run mad, the man?'

'Well may you ask! But I think not. It is that he has a set and unyielding mind. And believes that he is right – always he is right. And has none, that he will listen to, who will tell him to his face that he is wrong! Letters we have written – but they achieve nothing. Save to put our necks at risk! I fear that we have that most dangerous of rulers, Jamie – a righteous, unbending autocrat, who believes that he, and he only, knows the mind of our God! His father before him, James the Sixth, called himself Christ's Vice-regent. The son, I swear, *believes* it!'

'And yet, he appeared a gentle man, noble. He served me less than kindly – but in himself appeared to be kindly, no autocrat, no tyrant.'

'As you say. Here in Scotland, when he came to his coronation near three years past, all men conceived him as worthy, upright. Noble, as you say. Indeed, I believe that in most things he is so – save this of religion. And here, the sorrow of it, his uprightness becomes menace, no less. In his inmost heart, Charles is brittle, unbending. It grieves me to say it, for I have served him and his father all my days. But now, it seems, none may serve him save sycophants and toadies. That, James, I will never be.'

At the heavy solemnity of his friend's voice, Montrose

shook his head. 'This all makes of my small trouble a mere nothing, Archie,' he said. 'The vexations of a halfling! I see well how the greater trouble will grow, if it is not checked. Myself, I care not greatly whether a man approaches his God through a bishop or a presbyter. Indeed, it may be that neither need come between any true worshipper and his creator, any more than need a Romish saint – only the Lord Christ's intercession being necessary. But . . . I would give my blood to defend the right of every man to choose for himself. This of the King could split the realm.'

'Well and truly said. But, indeed, what Charles is doing is not so much splitting his realm now as uniting it. Uniting it against himself. You mind how he forced through the Act of Revocation, in 1625 – to compel the lords and lairds, who had won the Old Church's lands at the Reformation, to yield them up again. For the support of his new bishops. That drove a sore wedge between King and nobles. We both lost no little by it, Jamie. Not a lord but is in fury against having to pay tithes to the Kirk and rent to the Crown. But this concerned the churchmen and ministers no whit. Nor the common folk. Indeed, they chuckled, as we know well. But now, the King is forcing his bishops and prayer-book down the throats of Kirk and people. He will have all Scotland against him, lords, Kirk and folk. Save only, it may be, the Catholics – ominous allies, on my soul! Our good and upright liege lord is sowing the seeds of hatred, Jamie. And heeds no good counsel.'

'You have told him, besought him?'

'When he was here, for his coronation, I spoke – and received but small thanks, as you may guess. Since, I have written letters. As is no more than my duty, as one of the King's ministers of state. And as result am losing the King's regard, certain offices. I have had to give up my Orkney estates, which I had of the Crown. Intriguers at Court have them now. I am no longer Deputy Treasurer . . .'

'But that was yours for life, was it not?'

'Aye, for life. But King Charles is displeased with me, and I was forced to resign the office. I was compensated with monies – but what is that, when I no longer have my master's trust? Not that I care greatly for office, or aught else, since Margaret died – but I have much experience, and ought to be able to advise the King. I am still of the Privy

Council – but no longer is the Scots Council's word heeded...'

'Dear God – the folly of it! The waste.'

'It is more than folly, waste, lad. It could spell disaster. Scotland will never thole this burden. The freedom for which our fathers fought, from Bruce's, Wallace's days, till this – it is not to be lost at the scrape of a royal pen. More especially with an English cleric's hand behind it! It must not be, *will* not be! I am the King's most leal subject, but if he insists on this, by force – which God forbid! – I, and many another like me, on whom he could have relied, will not stand idly by and see it done.' The older man's voice shook a little. 'To this end, James, to this evil end, I have brought you home.'

For long moments they looked at each other, there in the shadowy garden, sombre-eyed, silent; until, in unspoken agreement they turned and went indoors, the glowing May night gone sour on them.

3

IT WAS NOT AT MUGDOCK IN THE CAMPSIE FOOTHILLS NORTH of Glasgow, nor yet at Kincardine in the southern skirts of Strathearn, nor even at Old Montrose on the Mearns seaboard, that James Graham ended his three years' journeying; but at another's house, not his own, in the wide valley of the South Esk in Angus between the Grampians and the sea, admittedly not far from Montrose but unconnected therewith – Kinnaird Castle, seat of the Carnegies, whose lord had recently been raised to the status and dignity of first Earl of Southesk. To this great house in its spreading parkland, where the Esk coiled to join that strange landlocked tidal basin of Montrose Bay, the Graham and his little entourage rode down over the braes of Rossie Muir three evenings later – and again with very mixed feelings. It was a fair place, rich, settled, secure, and though it was not his home, he knew it as well as any house of his, and loved it well. His mind had dwelt on it long and often, and on what it contained, these past many months, even ached to see its warm brown-stone towers, cattle-dotted parks and spreading orchards, and to hear the voices that would assuredly welcome him there. But now that he in fact approached it, he knew strange doubts, qualms, almost reluctance. It had been so long. So much had changed. He was indeed a different man from the youngster who had ridden away, a man travelled, experienced, tried, mature, where he had been little more than an enthusiastic but callow stripling. All must inevitably be much altered – and not only in himself.

They had been seeing for some time the two columns of blue smoke ascending high in the early evening air, before it dawned on him that these were not woodsmen's fires but, sited on an eminence just to the west of the castle, must be twin beacons, bonfires. He had sent word of his coming, from Edinburgh; and these must have been blazing all day to welcome him back. The recognition brought something of a lump into Montrose's throat.

While still almost a mile from the great house, they saw the file of horsemen come spurring out from under the gate-house arch, to drum over the drawbridge timbers and come southwards at a canter, obviously to meet him. Keen eyes had been watching. When a banner unfolded itself, to stream in the breeze and flutter bravely at the head of the oncoming party, James Graham's own eyes misted a little. Even at that range he could see that it was of black and gold – and the only black-and-gold heraldic banner of earl's size in all broad Scotland bore the undifferenced arms of the chief of the Grahams, *An Greumach Mor*. Besides himself, only one other could, or would, ride under that ensign.

As they drew near it could be seen that of the five who rode to meet them one was no more than a child, a small figure though mounted on no pony; one was a richly dressed youngish man slightly older than Montrose himself; one was a burly man of early middle-age, who bore the banner; and the other two were grooms. Much moved, James Graham slowed his horse to a walk.

A few yards off, the man with the banner signed to the boy, who promptly pulled off his mount with some style, at the same time managing to doff his plumed hat with a

35

flourish – even though it knocked against his horse's head and ears in the process and almost fell from a small hand. Undeterred, flushing a little, the large eyes bright, the lad jerked a bow from the saddle.

'Greetings, my lord,' he said. 'I hope that I see your lordship well. And not wearied. My lady-mother sends her dev . . . devotion.' That was of a gabble, but he got it out.

'Johnnie!' Montrose said. It was not often that this adequate man made so inadequate response.

The twenty-four-year-old father and the six-year-old son sat their sidling horses and stared at each other. Inevitably they were almost strangers. The toddler of three whom the man had left behind him bore little resemblance to this fine-featured, rather delicate-looking lad with the big eyes and serious expression. Foolishly Montrose had continued to think of him as he had last seen him. And the young Lord Graham had scarcely been able to remember his sire at all – save by the portrait by Master Jamesone, which hung in his mother's chamber; and this fine gentleman hardly resembled that eager youth.

With an effort the man restrained himself from spurring forward to clasp that small, proud yet anxious figure to himself. That would never do – not when the boy had come thus formally to meet him, under that banner, playing the man, beside the Chamberlain, bringing his mother's greeting.

'I rejoice to see you, son,' he said, controlling his voice, like the rest of him. 'So tall. So well grown. And well favoured. I thank you for coming to meet me. You sit your horse fairly.'

The lad flushed with pleasure. 'He has been saddled all day awaiting you,' he said, in a rush. 'My Uncle James – my Lord Carnegie, I mean – taught me to ride. He says that I am better than you were, at six years . . .' That tailed off in something of a gasp, as realisation dawned that perhaps this might be thought scarcely tactful in the circumstances.

'Ha! That could well be,' Montrose acceded gravely. 'It is good to hear.' He turned to the other, younger, man. 'So you are Lord Carnegie now, Jamie. Of course. So much has happened. Davie's sad death. I am sorry – a tragedy. And your father's elevation. I still think of *him* as Lord Carnegie. Accept my congratulations. And my thanks for making a horseman out of my son.' That last was said courteously, but

36

just slightly formally, considering that they were brothers-in-law. These two, although brought up as near neighbours and close family friends, had never greatly loved each other. Carnegie's extra three years had made for a certain superiority and condescension, which had tended to be frustrated by the fact that he was only a second son – and of a first lord, at that – while, from the age of fourteen, the other was fifth Earl of Montrose, chief of all the Grahams, and moreover insufficiently humble for his years. The raising of his father, the Lord Carnegie, to be first Earl of Southesk, at the King's Scottish coronation in 1633, only a few months after Montrose's departure, and the death of the elder brother, David, less than six months later, had only partially evened the score.

Carnegie had been eyeing the other closely, and not failing to note all the splendid good looks, the poise, authority and maturity of the man. He recognised all too clearly, but without elation, that some further adjustment of attitudes would be necessary. His voice was curter than probably he intended.

'No thanks required. And I have taught him more than that, I hope. Lacking his father, someone must needs do so! Hm . . . welcome back to Kinnaird. It has seemed a long time.'

'Long, yes.' Eyes grey and considering locked for a moment or two with eyes brown and smouldering. Then Montrose turned to the somewhat older man with the flag, thick-set, ruddy-complexioned and plainly dressed. 'It is good to see you, Sir Robert. Kind in you to come. You at least have not changed, I swear!' That was said with a smile. 'See – I have brought back your heir to you, as you have brought me mine!'

Graham of Morphie bowed, scarcely glancing at his own son, Montrose's esquire. 'I could do no less than come, my lord James. I have looked to this day for long. You are well returned. Greatly needed. I rejoice to see you home.'

Morphie was the nearest of the Graham lairds to Kinnaird and Montrose, his property lying only some six miles to the north, at Marykirk of the Mearns. Sir Robert had been left in charge of the great Montrose estate as Chamberlain, during his chief's absence. A solid, able man, he had been one of the curators, with Archie Napier and David Carnegie, appointed by the old Earl of Montrose to look after the boy he left as heir. And he was married to the Earl of Southesk's sister.

'All tell me it is time that I returned,' Montrose said, a little grimly. 'You also, Robert. You will have your reasons?'

'Aye, my lord.' That was heavy. 'I shall not be sorry to shift a wheen burdens from my shoulders to yours! Praise to God, they look now sufficiently broad to bear them!'

'Mm.' Brows raised, the Earl shrugged. 'So be it, then. I have now to look to my own interests – thanking you who have looked to them for me.' He nodded to both men. 'Come, Johnnie – take me to your mother.'

Urging his mount forward, he was able to close with the boy, at last, and slip an arm around the slight shoulders momentarily, without any suggestion of unmanliness. Then, side by side they rode down the long slope to the marshland, to splash across the Pow Burn, and on, over the wide park-lands to Kinnaird Castle on its terrace.

A great company waited to receive them, assembled within the inner bailey, beyond the drawbridge and gate-house, of all ranks and standing, men, women and children too. The return of the Graham was an occasion indeed.

In the centre stood a big bulky man in his sixties, florid, choleric, with white hair and a bushy beard – David, new Earl of Southesk, eighth Laird of Kinnaird, first Lord Carnegie, Privy Councillor, High Sheriff of Forfar, Extra-ordinary Lord of Session and father-in-law of James Graham. He stood with arms akimbo, and looked threaten-ing; but then David Carnegie usually looked threatening. He was flanked by two young women, one bold-eyed and handsome, the other modest and plumply comely – his Coun-tess and third wife, and his daughter Magdalen. Each held a two-year-old toddler by the hand, girl and boy.

'Greeting, my lord Earl!' Montrose called dismounting, and doffing his hat with a flourish. 'I need not ask if I see *you* well. Growing younger year by year, I swear!' He bowed to the Countess of Southesk. 'My lady – you bloom! My lord looks to suit you as well as you him! Your servant.' And to the other, still younger woman, a year younger than himself, in fact, he raised an open hand. 'Magdalen, my dear.'

One countess, his own, dipped deeply, and murmured, 'My lord,' low-voiced. The other stared openly, assessingly, and whistled, barely beneath her breath, in scarcely ladylike fashion, saying nothing.

'So you are back, boy! You have taken your time, have you no'?' Southesk cried. None other than he would have thought to call Montrose boy – and even he looked just a little bit askance as he said it, perceiving that there were changes here which could not be entirely ignored. 'We looked to see you near a year back. What held you?'

'I am flattered that you so greatly missed my poor presence, my lord,' the other answered easily. 'But matters of sufficient import delayed me, I assure you.'

'Aye. Well, there's matters o' sufficient import amiss for you, here in this Scotland, man. For any man! You've come home to trouble, see you.'

'So I have heard. On all hands.' He shrugged, ruefully. 'And, I vow, you might think it all *my* doing, from the way it is laid on me! But . . . of that later.' Montrose looked round at all the assembled company, and made a comprehensive bow, flourish of his plumed hat, and friendly smile. 'My salutations to you all,' he called. 'It is good to see you again. I am glad to be back. My thanks for your reception of me. Hereafter I shall speak with you all. But meanwhile, my lady-wife demands her errant lord's attention – and merits it, you will concede! You will bear with us?'

It was superbly done, with assurance, simplicity, courtesy yet authority, such as the James Graham who had departed three years before could never have achieved. It took charge of the situation for them all, even for old Southesk, his Countess and his son. *An Greumach Mor,* Earl of Montrose, was now to be permitted to greet his wife with some measure of privacy. None found cause for complaint or discomfort.

None, that is, save perhaps for the Lady Magdalen Carnegie herself. Always a shy and retiring creature, she was apparently quite overwhelmed by this handsome, self-possessed, almost commanding presence that had come back to her after so long. Almost in a panic she bit her lip, clutching the toddler to her knees, all but shrinking back as Montrose came forward to her, eyes darting towards her father, her brother, even her small son, to anyone, for aid.

Her husband saw it, and understood, at least partially. He turned to young Johnnie, hand out, and together they moved up to the woman.

'My dear,' he said gently, 'this young man has already conveyed to me your greetings and welcome. Most worthily. How fine a son you have bred for me. I am grateful – from my heart I am. And here – here is another, on my soul! Another good Graham for Scotland!'

That saved her. 'Yes. Yes, this is Jamie, my lord.' She was constrained to stoop, and make a great fuss of picking up the little one in her arms, and so could face her husband with the child as a sort of buffer. 'Is . . . is he not a fine lad? And like you, a little. Like you . . . you were.' She gulped. 'Not now – but were. Your nose. I am sure that he has your nose. So, so long. No, no – not too long. But . . . your nose. And mouth. Yes, your mouth also. Jamie – he is strong. Stronger than Johnnie. Oh, Johnnie is stronger now. But as a bairn. When you left, Johnnie was not strong. You remember that. I . . . I . . . ' She was gabbling. And realising it only too clearly, abruptly stopped and became unutterably silent.

He nodded gravely. 'Yes, indeed. That I remember well. Which makes it all the better that you have made of Johnnie so much the man.' He patted his heir on the head, and reached out to take the younger child from her. 'So this is the second James Graham! We will have to learn to know each other, he and I. But you will teach us.' He felt down with his other hand, and raised hers to his lips. 'You have much to teach me, my dear.'

She did not answer, but something of the panic had left her. She was able to slip that kissed hand under his arm, to take her elder son by the elbow, and so face all the chattering throng, after a fashion, Magdalen, Countess of Montrose with her man and bairns. They bowed, left and right, moving towards the keep doorway.

It was long, however, before they could be alone together – nor, indeed, were either of them over-eager for that moment. It was Southesk's house, and as well as much eating and drinking to see to, he had bones to pick with young Montrose, with his son, with his brother Sir John Carnegie, who presently arrived from Ethie Castle to the south. David Carnegie was a great picker of bones – which perhaps partly accounted for his youngest daughter's chronic distrust of herself. At any rate, he kept his male company at table well into the night, long after the ladies had retired – even after his young wife, new married just before Montrose had left on his travels, reappeared on the minstrels' gallery above the Great Hall for a few moments, sought to attract her lord's attention, failed, and raising eloquent eyebrows implying complicity with the watching James Graham, departed.

When at last he managed to escape, and made his way across the courtyard, in the wan northern half-light, to the flanking-tower which his wife and children occupied, he went quietly. But light still gleamed from the window of the first-floor bed-chamber. And when he entered, seeking to keep the door from creaking, it was to find Magdalen lying awake on the great four-poster bed, staring up at the dusty canopy. She did not look at him, after the first quick glance.

'I believed that you would be asleep,' he said. 'I have been long. Your father had much to talk over. I am sorry. I have come home, it seems to a realm seething with unrest like a porridge-pot on a hob!'

'Yes,' she said.

'If you are wearied, Magdalen, would be alone, I will sleep tonight in the boys' chamber?'

'No,' she said.

'Very well.' He sat on the edge of the bed, looking down at her. It has been a long time, my dear,' he said slowly.

'Yes.'

'Your letters – I thank you for them. You are good with letters.'

'Better, better than with ... other things.'

'Do not say it. You never thought sufficiently highly of yourself. *I* think more kindly.'

'Yet ... you stayed away. For long.'

'Yes. There was so much to be done. To be seen. To be learned. And I am scarce likely ever to go back. A different world, Magdalen. A wider, richer world. Of great experiences, of treasures, of thought and learning. Of a quality of living far beyond anything we know here in Scotland. It behoves any who will have rule in this realm to learn of it all they may.'

She did not answer.

'This custom, to make the Grand Tour, is wise, lass. It broadens a man. Those who are born to lead require such broadening. Without it, those they lead can only suffer ...'

'My brother Jamie. He went likewise. On his Tour. And came home in but one year. From Padua.'

41

'Did he not come home when Davie died? As new heir. But – what of it? I am not Jamie Carnegie. Moreover, I had a task, a quest, which he had not.'

'You never found her? Katherine? No trace?'

'No trace,' he agreed, sombrely.

'I am sorry for that.' For the first time, she turned her eyes on him. 'You were close, I know. Closer to her than to any. It must hurt you sorely.'

'Yes. I did all that a man could. Searched the length and breadth of Europe. Had enquirers in every land. I wonder if, indeed, she still lives.'

'Poor Kate . . .'

'No – not poor Kate! Whatever else she is, or was, not poor! She lived ever richly, rashly, but to the full. Expended herself, never counting the cost. Foolish, often. Headstrong, yes. Unkind at times. But in herself, her life, rich. Not poor Kate.'

The woman turned her head away. 'Perhaps. And you – you are of the same stamp. As . . . as sure of yourself. And I am . . . otherwise. It is poor Magdalen, I think!' Her voice choked a little. 'You would not . . . have spent three years searching for me!'

Shaking his head unhappily, he eyed her. '*You* would never have required such search. Run away with your own sister's husband. And then abandoned him, likewise. Gone off, heedless of all, God knows where! You would not, could not. But, had Magdalen Carnegie indeed done that, I would have gone seeking for her, likewise.'

'Would you? I wonder! No – Magdalen Carnegie stays at home. A good wife. Dutiful. Waiting. Always waiting. Her husband's pleasure. A dutiful wife, mother of his bairns. Dutiful mother. Waiting – since the day we were wed. Bairns ourselves!'

'Waiting, lass? Waiting – for what? Not, I think, just for this return of mine?'

'Dear God – I do not know!' She twisted round to face him again, and a hand came out from beneath the bedclothes to grasp his lace-edged wrist, the nails digging into his flesh. 'Oh, James, James – I do not know! Sweet Christ have mercy upon me – I do not know!' she sobbed.

Frowning, the man bent to kiss that flushed brow, to stroke that thick, lustrous hair soothingly. He was not the only one whom the years had changed, it seemed. It was all true. They had been wed as little more than children. At seventeen, with his Mastership of Arts from St Andrews secured, his curators, Archie Napier, Graham of Morphie and David Carnegie, had decided that the Earl of Montrose ought to be married. What better choice than the sixteen-year-old youngest daughter of Carnegie, childhood playmate, neighbour, family friend – a sound match for both. Neither were really consulted – but, at that age, neither would have dreamed of objecting. Next to their sisters and brothers, they knew each other better than they knew anyone else, and had always been good enough friends. So all had been suitably arranged, the marriage settlement drawn up and signed, lands and dowry apportioned. Graham of Morphie had commissioned the famous George Jamesone to paint a portrait of the bridegroom. Exactly a year later, an heir was born, Johnnie – the object of the exercise. It had all been quite notably suitable, satisfactory, successful.

Magdalen, and therefore her young husband, had continued to live at Kinnaird – although he often had to be away visiting his other great estates in the south. The house of Old Montrose, three miles to the east, was old indeed – though that was not what the name,meant. It should have been Ald Montrose, from the Gaelic *alt moine ross*, the burn of the mossy point. But, more than old, it was large, rambling and neglected, indeed part derelict, for the Grahams had other and more favoured castles in south and west, and the town-house in the burgh of Montrose itself, where James Graham had been born, served them adequately as occasional base in these parts. Old Lord Carnegie would not hear of his young daughter departing for far parts, moving into the decayed barracks down the road, or setting up house amongst the burghers of Montrose town. There was plenty of room at Kinnaird where the young couple could live conveniently under the authoritative eye of father and curator. And it was so. Possibly that was a large part of the trouble.

Montrose did not withdraw his arm. With the other hand he continued to stroke her hair. 'You are overwrought, my dear,' he said. 'Tired. Upset. It has been too long a day. But you will feel better. Tomorrow. You will see. We shall talk then. I have much to tell you. Today has been too much for you.'

43

Her smothered sobs were all his answer.

'Sleep now, Magdalen lass. That is your need. I will go bed down in the boys' chamber above. I shall do very well there . . .'

'No! No – you will not!' Fiercely she cried it.

'It would serve best, I think. For tonight . . .'

'I say no.' Suddenly she threw back the bedclothes strongly, and revealed herself as lying naked, a well-made young woman, heavy-breasted but fair, her abundant white flesh warm in the mellow lamp-light. 'See – I am a dutiful wife. I told you so. Told you that I waited for you!' Her voice broke again.

He moistened his lips, and took some time to reply. 'Is this . . . what you waited for, then?' he got out. 'I think not, my dear.'

'Yes. Yes, I say.' She spread herself on the bed, in a sort of defiant invitation, but with her flushed face and tear-dewed eyes turned away from him. She spread her body in deliberate invitation - yet her abhorrence was in every inch of her flaunting yet shrinking person.

The man, who was no monk, was deeply moved. And as deeply perplexed, his body at odds with his mind and heart.

But whatever of repugnance he sensed in her, he could by no means reject that offer and demand. To do so was unthinkable. He rose, and commenced to remove his clothing. She had covered herself again by the time that he was naked and had extinguished the lamp and turned back to her.

As he moved in beside her on the warm bed, she remained still, almost breathless, but with her head turned away from him. He sought gently to caress her, to soothe the tension from her. But before long he desisted, achieving nothing and but taxing himself. He took her then, but even so seeking to waken her passion, to rouse response, until his own need overwhelmed him. She did not answer a word, a whisper, or murmur of his, throughout.

Afterwards, for long, they both lay gazing up at the shadowy canopy, wordless, listening while the curlews called wearily, endlessly, from the Montrose marshes to the east. More than once the man almost spoke, and then drew back from fruitless words.

It was she who at length broke the silence. 'You must bear with me, James,' she said slowly, carefully. 'I am no wife for such as you, I know well. But I try – God knows how I try! You are right, no doubt. Tomorrow will be better, I promise you.'

'Aye – all the tomorrows, lassie. They will be better. Now that I am home again, we shall start afresh, you and I. Who knows, the years may prove well spent, for us. Who knows, in them I may have learned more than just statecraft, the arts of rule and war, and the ways of a wider world. Give me a chance to prove it, my dear.'

'But what have I learned? Only that you have grown the further from me, James.'

'Then – help me to grow back, Magdalen,' he urged. 'Your help I need. Need, girl.'

He felt her shake her head on the pillow. But also, presently, he felt her relaxing a little, then more noticeably. In time, he slept, with an arm around her soft, still body.

It was hours later before Magdalen Carnegie closed her eyes.

4

THINGS WERE INDEED BETTER IN THE MORNING, AND ALL THE mornings – since these two were determined that they should be. They learned to live with each other again, to accept, to compromise, to withhold judgment, to help, strengthen, even comfort. The two boys were their greatest aid in this, as well as their prime inducement. With them as link they drew almost close. Marriage, even successful marriage, has been built on less than this.

That neither aimed quite so high as that was at once their safeguard and their tragedy.

The fact that Magdalen was largely free, at last, of Kinnaird and her family, undoubtedly greatly helped. Montrose had castles and estates over the length and breadth of the land; more than that, branches of his house and clan still more widely dispersed. After so long an absence, it was necessary to visit all, make innumerable decisions on the spot, put much to rights, show himself to his people. Almost everywhere he went he took his Countess and his sons, to introduce and display them, as was expected of him. Consequently they were not much at Kinnaird, or at the town-house in Montrose either, during that summer and autumn of 1636 – to the marked advantage of their union.

But if matters personal and private were thus lightened somewhat in these months, matters national and public were not. Everywhere James Graham went the talk was the same, resentment, murmurings, the stirrings of revolt. By and large, the people of Scotland, of all ranks and degrees, were angry. They were loyal enough. Indeed, it was remarkable how loyal they remained, considering that their king, James the Sixth and his son Charles, had deserted them for London, so clearly preferring everything English, and considering their old realm scarcely worth even visiting. But to the Scot, religion was highly personal and precious, not any mere formality, or separate compartment of life which could be accepted or more or less shrugged off for the sake of peace. The metaphysical implications of his faith were part and parcel of his being. New forms of worship or theology were not to be imposed on him from without, by king, parliament or hierarchy – more especially from England. For that very reason the Reformation had come later to Scotland than to almost any other nation in Christendom; but when it did come it had been more basic, comprehensive, drastic. Now their religion was not only being interfered with, but actually changed, by dictate from London, made to conform with that of England. It was not to be borne.

All this was bad enough. But there was another aspect of the situation which was worrying – especially for one placed in Montrose's position, straddling as it were the Highland Line, both in the location of his estates and the background of his blood and race. The Reformation had never really penetrated to the true Highlands effectively, certainly not to the remoter areas – except for the Campbells' Argyll. Therefore, these London edicts were of little or no interest in the Highlands. But, unfortunately, the Gordon chief, the Marquis of Huntly, not actually a Highlander himself but a strong Catholic and having great influence in all the North, was declaring himself wholly and vigorously in favour of the King in all this – and seeing that others did likewise. So that there was a serious division forming in Scotland, to the country's hurt, Highland versus Lowland, North versus the rest, Catholic versus Protestant. It was ominous and dangerous as it was grievously disappointing for all who had the unity of the realm at heart.

With the days shortening, Montrose took his little family and entourage to settle down at Kincardine Castle, on the southern verges of Strathearn. Magdalen was uneasy about this, still under her father's spell and afraid that it would cause offence. Moreover, all her life she had never lived anywhere else but at Kinnaird. But James Graham was determined on it, that they were not going back to Kinnaird, declaring that it was not suitable that the Earl of Montrose should roost always in another's house as though he had no place of his own. Kincardine was his favourite property, as it had been his father's before him.

So the old grey castle, on the rocky bluff above the wooded ravine of the Ruthven Water, was opened up and refurbished, and again young voices rang within its ancient walls, to challenge the singing of tree-top birds and the rush of falling water. The headlong Ruthven came boiling out of Glen Eagles, in the Ochils foothills of south Perthshire, to swing eastwards in its deep sylvan hanging glen above the Strathearn head-town of Auchterarder, before falling into the Earn at Aberuthven. In this winding sheltered valley, with the magnificent prospects of the Highland mountains across the wide strath, the Graham castle soared high on a rocky promontory, an eagle's nest of a hold, of lofty, mellow stone walls, crowstepped gables, steep roofs and pepper-pot turrets. Small compared with Kinnaird, or even Montrose's own Mugdock, Dundaff or Fintry, towering upwards instead of sideways, within its cramped and oddly shaped courtyard, it was a modest seat for so great a lord; but it was strong enough, and most pleasing in character as in surroundings. And it was central, not only for the various Graham lands, but for Stirling, Edinburgh, Glasgow, Perth and St Andrews, places where things were apt to happen in Scotland.

It was one golden day of belated autumn, in mid-November, with all Strathearn aglow with colour, that Montrose, returning to Kincardine with the sinking sun from hunting hinds in the Ochils, found company awaiting him. He rode over the drawbridge into the little courtyard above the dizzy drop, with Kilpont, whose home at Airth was only a score of miles to the south, and Black Pate Graham, Younger of Inchbrakie near by, who had taken over from Young Morphie as personal esquire, to find the place crowded with a dozen and more horses, their grooms and armed attendants hanging around them, indicating that it was no unimportant company.

In his hall, James Graham found Magdalen entertaining, in some evident embarrassment, two very oddly paired visitors, who in their different ways seemed to discompose her almost equally. One was burly, almost gross, of late middle years, untidy, dressed in shabby finery, a coarse-featured, red-faced, noisy man with little pig-like eyes that were very shrewd – John Leslie, sixth Earl of Rothes, and strangely enough, the most popular man in Scotland. The other was tall, thin, dark and soberly dignified, with sternly ascetic features, fine eyes and an expression of harshly restrained intensity, clad all in black.

Montrose had met Rothes only once before, when he was still a student at St Andrews; but the older man greeted him like a friend, a crony, of long standing, punching his shoulder, belabouring his back, and spluttering couthy assertions of admiration, esteem, affection. James Graham, a fastidious man, sought not to allow his distaste to show.

'Laddie, laddie – you're braw, right braw! Fair magnificent, indeed! Guidsakes – you've come on! Here's John Leslie's hand. A right swack man's come back to your bed, lassie! You'll ken the differ, I'll be bound? Hey?' Rothes almost always affected the broadest Doric.

Montrose extricated himself with difficulty from the other's salutations, at the same time seeking to come to the rescue of his flushing wife. '*I* am the more fortunate, my lord,' he said. 'The better for being home. I hope I see your lordship well?'

'You see an auld done runt, by God!' the burly man roared. 'Ask *my* wife! But, och – no' so done yet that the sight o' this weel-favoured quean doesna raise the man in me, by the powers! I was just by way o' telling hersel' the same . . .'

'Hm. No doubt, my lord. And this . . . ?' Montrose turned to the other man.

48

'Ooh, aye – this is nane other than the Reverend Henderson. Maister Alexander Henderson himsel'. Minister o' Leuchars, in my county o' Fife. A scholar, see you – and a tower o' strength in the Kirk today. He's desirous o' a bit word in your lug, James. As am I.'

'I have heard of Master Henderson – and only heard good,' Montrose said, holding out his hand. 'You honour my house, sir.'

The minister bowed stiffly, his eyes searching, but said nothing. The younger man felt that he was being weighed and assessed.

'You will not have eaten? Your horses were still steaming in my yard. No doubt my wife has bidden you bide the night with us?'

'Hech, eye. Mind you, I'd have accepted her bonnie hospitality even sharper had I heard frae her that you werena coming hame this night! But a man must sup his gruel as it's ladled out. Aye, we'll bide.'

'My lady Montrose has been entirely kind. And very patient. I am grateful,' Henderson said, and his voice was unexpectedly rich and vibrant.

Magdalen hurried from the hall.

Later, the three men sat before a log fire in the small upper chamber which Montrose had set aside as a study and lined with books, parchments and documents which he had collected and sent home during his years on the Continent – a collection which obviously much interested Alexander Henderson at least. A large flagon of wine occupied a small table beside them, and Rothes was working his way steadily through it, though the other two only sipped their liquor. The older earl's bawdy stories and outrageous and scurrilous anecdotes had been non-stop throughout the preceding meal, and still went on – his host and fellow guest bearing with them as best they might, the former with a civility in which patience was evident, the latter with a sort of steely impassivity.

Then, quite abruptly, Rothes changed his tune, and the little darting eyes he turned on Montrose were gimlet-sharp and in no way clouded with wine.

'How stand you with the man Charles Stewart?' he demanded starkly.

The younger man stroked long fingers over mouth and tiny

pointed beard, taking his time to answer that barked question. 'I am a loyal subject of His Grace,' he said, at length.

'Aye – nae doubt!' That was a snort. 'So are we all – while we value our heads! Balmerino proved the wisdom o' that! I'm no' speaking of your loyalty, James. It's your wits I'm concerned with. Archie Napier tells me that this Montrose has a head on him. And, forbye, notions beyond the ordinar'. Are you for the Kirk, man – or the bishops?'

'Must I be for one and against the other, my lord? I was never greatly concerned with forms of worship, before I left on my travels. And in the different lands of Christendom, I saw nothing which made me to believe that a man's salvation depended on the form of words he used to speak with his Maker, nor yet on the colour of a priest's clothing. Is it so different in Scotland?'

'Och, lad, dinna fence with words . . .'

'My lord Montrose,' Henderson intervened, quietly stern. 'You require freedom to worship Almighty God in your own way? Is that what you say?'

'It is, sir.'

'And are you prepared to uphold such right, for others as well as yourself?'

Carefully Montrose scrutinised the lean, strangely sensitive face leaning forwards towards his own. 'I have not, I confess, deeply considered whether I am, or not, sir,' he said. 'But I concede that, probably, I ought to be.'

'Ha – there speaks a canny chiel!' Rothes cried. 'No' that I'm blaming you, lad. The man I respect uses his head. Scotland needs men with cool heads more than men with hot tongues, in this pass.'

'Scotland needs *every* man, in this pass,' the minister amended evenly.

The Graham looked from one to the other. 'This pass . . . ?' he repeated. 'Is there a pass? Which demands our defence? Yet?'

'There is.' Rothes banged down a thick fist on the table, to make the flagon jump. 'By God, there is! I am new back frae London, man. Charles Stewart is riding for a fall. He will heed none but the man Laud and his lackey Juxon – he that's new Bishop of London in Laud's stead. These two English jumped-up clerks have our liege lord licking their prelatical feet! It makes me spew – spew, I say!'

'It is unedifying, yes. But – this pass, you speak of . . . ?'

'It is this thrice-damned prayer-book! You must have heard of it? Laud has had two Scots lickspittles, Wedderburn, Bishop o' Dunblane and Maxwell, Bishop o' Ross, to concoct the rat-rhymes and paternosters. They have finished their presumptuous blasphemies, and now Laud and Juxon have had their fell turn at it. And presented it to Charles. And he, our sovereign lord, has swallowed it all, with its mummery and its incantations and its rituals. It is being printed, and is to be imposed on Scotland forthwith. By the royal edict. On pain o' excommunication. Before Easter next.'

'Excommunication? Surely not? How can this be? Who is to be excommunicated?'

'Every parish minister, in the first place. The prayer-book itsel' isna yet printed. But the Book of Canons is, that is to go with it and enforce it. I've seen this, man – had in it my two hands. It's wicked.' All trace of the coarse, loud-mouthed buffoon had for the moment disappeared, and with it most of the broad Doric, as Rothes leant over, pointing a stubby finger at Montrose. 'These Canons are signed and sealed by the King, as head o' Christ's Church – by his way o' it. They declare that every parish minister in Scotland will have provided himsel' with at least two copies o' the prayer-book before Easter – on pain o' excommunictaion and banishment. Banishment, mind. To be used thereafter, in every kirk – on pain o' the same penalties. And any who may raise their voice against it, or fail to adhere to it, to be banished likewise.'

Montrose shook his head, wordless.

'Nor is that all, my lord,' Henderson put in. 'All presbyteries are to be put down – the courts and government of the Kirk. Even though the Scots bishops themselves accept them. Bishops alone are to govern the Kirk of Scotland.'

'It is scarcely to be believed,' the younger man said slowly.

'But it is the truth, for a' that. I tell you, Montrose, I've seen the printed and signed Canons.'

'Scotland – the realm will not accept it! Nobles and Kirk alike. The whole people . . .'

'You think not, lad? Pray God that you are right. Pray God! But, I say, it is up to us, man, who have the leadership in this land, to *see* that the realm does not! Charles will have done what the Edwards and the Henrys never could do – wiped out this ancient realm and put us under the English heel. That is the size o' it. That it should be under the heels o' damnable English prelates is the measure o' our abasement, by God!'

James Graham looked from one to the other. 'What do you wish for me?' he asked, quietly.

'Just that the Graham does not fail his ancestors, lad. At Dunbar, at Stirling Brig, at Bannockburn, at Flodden-field, at Pinkie Brae, Graham has stood – aye, and fallen if need be – for the freedom o' this sair-harried realm. Do *you* stand aside, man?'

Levelly, Alexander Henderson spoke. 'All we ask, my lord, is that you lend your name and support, when the time comes. For a stand for our liberty, our right to worship God in our own way, our determination that none shall take from us our birthright as free men.'

Montrose inclined his handsome head. 'I could do no less,' he said.

'Praise be! Aye, lad – so I believed. And so said Archie Napier. Here is right excellent augury. We came to you amongst the first, James – for where the Graham leads, lesser men will follow. And it is the lesser men, the common folk, the townsmen, that we must rally, see you. Charles himsel' has rallied the nobles against him, by his Act o' Revocation, his taking o' the tithes and teinds o' our lands to pay for his bishops. He will unite the Kirk against him by this Liturgy and doing awa' with the presbyteries. But, the common folk . . .'

'Fear not for the common folk, my good lords,' Henderson interrupted. 'King Charles has assured of them rising also, I think!'

'You say so?'

'Yes. Or the man Laud has done it for him! This of the surplices. In his Canons, you tell me, it is ordained that every minister of the Gospel discards his black Geneva gown and dons a white linen surplice. Likewise on pain of excommunication. I tell you, he could scarce have served us better! Here is something which the ordinary man and woman can see and understand. Compared with the rest, it is little or nothing I agree. But they, the common folk, will see it as popery, the trappings of idolatry. That, and these pictures which your lordship tells me are to be painted in the prayer-book, on the initial letters of each page and prayer – cherubs, angels and the like. Imagery, devices of the Devil. Aye, smile my lords – but, I tell you, who am of the people myself, that this will serve better than all your doctrine and pronouncements. Aye, or *my* sermons! This they will see as bowing down to idols! The folk will rise in their wrath.'

Rothes shrugged. 'So be they rise,' he said. 'But they must learn o' them, first.'

'They will learn, never doubt it. We – the ministers of God's Kirk – will not fail to equip ourselves with the King's white surplices, I promise you! Though we will never wear them. They will hang from every pulpit in the land, as text for our discourses. The prayer-books too, when they come. We will not use them – but every kirk will show them to the people, with their pictures and popery . . .'

'Ha – and there is more for you to display, Henderson man. Now I mind o' it. A Kalendar o' Scots saints. *Saints,* mark you. Such Kalendar to be printed with each book, by the King's personal command! Saints, and their days, for observation, veneration, worship! Show that!'

Obviously this was news to Alexander Henderson. He looked shocked, no less. 'Saints . . . !' he gasped. 'Is . . . is the man clean out of his wits?'

'You may ask! That is Charles, by the Grace o' God, King! Aye.' John Leslie reached for the flagon. 'So there you have it, James. We can rely on you? When the time comes?'

'You can rely on me not to stand dumb, my lord. Not to withhold my protest. Beyond that, I do not commit myself. I am the King's man, in all else. A loyal subject. Protest, I will support. Insurrection and revolt are another matter. I bid you both remember it.'

There was a long moment's silence.

'Pray God it comes not to that,' Henderson said, at length. 'But a man must be prepared to more than speak for his beliefs.'

'Aye, man – to be sure,' Rothes put in, rather hurriedly. 'But time enough to think o' that, when the talking fails.'

'Talking reason, must *not* fail,' Montrose declared strongly. 'The King must be shown the folly of his policy. Shown that he will rouse the whole Scottish realm against him . . .'

'Think you he hasna been told so, time and again? Balmerino told him – and near lost his head! *I* have told him – to my cost! Your good-brother Napier has told him, written letters aplenty – to no result but his own loss o' power and position. Charles ignores all – but has around him a pack o' toadies and lackeys who shout Amen to his every word. Aye, and keep the truth frae him.'

'Then he must be shown that these are false advisers. His true enemies, not his friends – Hamilton, Lanark, Traquair and their like. Time-servers. We must send the King not one letter, or two. But the voice of the whole realm must speak. Honestly, loyally, respectfullly – but firmly. A declaration. Scotland has done it before. The community of the realm of Scotland. From Arbroath. In good King Robert's time – a Declaration of Independence.' Montrose sat forward, his fine eyes alight now. 'That letter was to the Pope of Rome. Now we must needs send one to King Robert's own descendant ten generations removed. Signed by all true men whose names mean anything in Scotland. Such, the King could not ignore or dismiss. This, I say, should be done. And quickly. Before more evil befalls.'

'Mm.' Rothes rubbed his multiple chins. 'We'll hae to think on this. It might be worth the trying.'

'More than a letter or a declaration,' Henderson said. 'A covenant. A declaration is only that. Binds its signatories only to a belief, an assertion. But a covenant, binding men to action, should their demands be refused – that is something different.'

'Demands?' Montrose repeated. 'I said nothing of demands. Loyal subjects cannot *demand* from the Lord's Anointed.'

'Requests, then. A word, my lord.'

'An important word, sir. Significant. Let us be clear in our minds what we are about – that there be no misunderstanding. I will have nothing to do with demands upon the King's Grace. I will declare that I believe the King's policies are wrong – and rejoice if many others so declare with me. But I will not set myself up against my liege lord, to his hurt or constraint. Let that be understood, now and hereafter.'

'To be sure, James – to be sure,' Rothes nodded, after a barely perceptible pause. 'It shall be as you say . . .'

NEITHER KING CHARLES NOR THE LEADERS OF HIS OUTRAGED
Scots people were, in fact, so efficient and effective as they
intended. The book of the Canons was duly distributed –
printed in the end at Aberdeen – with all its dire commands
and intimations of punishments, ecclesiastical and civil,
should they be disobeyed; but the winter passed, Easter itself,
April, May, June, and still the reason and object of it all,
the prayer-book and Liturgy, did not appear. Delays in the
printing and binding were blamed; possibly the inclusion of
those ominous coloured pictures and cherubs was largely
responsible. And there were rumours of Scots sabotage, certain Privy Councillors' names being linked with the delays,
Rothes and Napier amongst them. Even sundry English
Puritans were said to have a hand in the business. The thing
became something of a joke, as time went on, hardly to be
taken seriously – despite all the dreadful warnings that resounded from practically every pulpit in Scotland. Only the
surplices appeared, shaped and sewn, it is to be feared,
mainly by busy Presbyterian fingers, to hang as dire and
inflammatory symbols in front of the said pulpits. Alexander
Henderson and his colleagues at least played their part.

And yet, even so, the forces of righteous defence were little
more competent and efficacious, or up-to-time, than was the
assault from London. Although Rothes, Loudoun, Lindsay
and others had mobilised major support throughout the
Lowlands for massive protest, and the theory of a great
declaration or petition to the King was accepted, nothing was
actually done to implement it; as the threat hung fire, so not
unnaturally did the counterblast. Many wordy forms of
protest and declamation were composed, as a sort of exercise
– Montrose and his secretary John Lambie penned two or
three themselves; but none grew into the organised and

widespread national testimony which was required – almost to the relief of the authors, those at Kincardine included.

So summer came again, and men found many things to do more immediately preoccupying than either religious or political disputation. Amongst other distractions, James Graham learned that he was to become a father once again – and rejoiced that Magdalen was greatly uplifted at the prospect.

Then, in mid-July, a letter arrived from the Earl of Rothes, to declare that the waiting and inaction was over. The prayer-book had arrived in quantity, the Scots bishops were commanded, and determined, to bring them into use forthwith, and had selected Sunday the 23rd of July for, as it were, vesting day. All the books could not be distributed round the country by then; but their spiritual lordships had decided that there would be a great service of dedication and celebration in the Cathedral of Edinburgh – in other words, the High Kirk of St Giles – before the Privy Council, the judges of Session, the Lord Provost and magistrates, and as many of the congregation as there remained room for. All persons of note in the kingdom were urged to be present – and Rothes suggested that Montrose and others like-minded could do much worse than attend. He had a town-house in Edinburgh and would be glad there to return the hospitality received at Kincardine.

So, with mixed feelings, James Graham presented himself at the lofty greystone 'land' in the Horse Wynd, off the Cowgate of Edinburgh, at Leslie's Ludging, on the Saturday evening – and was surprised to find it full to bursting. Half of the nobility of Scotland appeared to be crammed into its tiered rooms, even lining its twisting turnpike stair. Amidst much noise, argument, declamation and laughter, Montrose distinguished the Earls of Dunfermline, Home, Eglinton, Lindsay, Loudoun, Lothian, Sutherland and Wigtown; the Lords Balmerino, Stormont, Boyd, Yester and Elcho; and great lairds like Sir George Stirling of Keir, Douglas of Cavers, Fraser of Philorth, Mure of Rowallan and Home of Wedderburn. Sober-garbed and markedly out-of-place amongst this dazzling throng of cavaliers, were one or two of the Edinburgh ministers.

Many of the company were known to him, of course; some of them indeed friends from college days at St Andrews –

such as Wigtown, Lindsay, Sutherland and the former Glamis, now Earl of Kinghorne. Amongst the older men there were not a few members of His Grace's Scots Privy Council, although it was significant that none of its Lords Spiritual were present.

The talk was all about the morrow's confrontation. The Chancellor was evidently expecting trouble. He had sent orders to the Lord Provost and magistrates of Edinburgh to have the Town Guard out in force 'to ensure the peace of the King's lieges'. The Chancellor, chief minister of the Crown in Scotland, and convener of its parliament, was the Primate, Archbishop Spottiswoode of St Andrews who, three years before the old Earl of Kinnoul died, had been appointed to this key position, to the great offence of the nobility, the first cleric to be Chancellor since the Reformation. Spottiswoode himself would not be present – he would be introducing the prayer-book in his own cathedral of St Andrews; Bishop Lindsay of Edinburgh would preside – and his chief, the young Earl of Lindsay, was coming under not a little raillery for nurturing such a snake in the bosom of his clan.

Montrose was unable to get a word alone with Rothes, but could gain no impression of anything constructive being done, especially any idea of drawing up a declaration or covenant to send to the King. He put the matter to practically all he spoke with, and found no real opposition to the notion – although most seemed to feel that it would be useless, doomed to rejection by the obdurate Charles. When the Earl of Loudoun likened it to a Band, he got immediate favourable reaction. Bands, or bonds, meant something positive to these men. But Montrose demurred. A Band implied action against something. And the only target for that action, here, could be the King. That was not to be contemplated.

Montrose was glad to discover Archie Napier amongst the aristocratic throng, and in a corner confided to him that he feared that matters looked like getting out-of-hand. He was not going to be a party to civil war – and that is the way that matters were trending. There were too many hot-heads here, however gilded. Wiser councils must be brought forward, and made to prevail.

His brother-in-law shook his grey head. 'I know it, James. I pray that we can in the end win the day and see moderation prevail. Wine is talking loud here. At a council-table, could we but get to one, heads and voices would be cooler.' He frowned. 'And the King – he serves the cause of moderation nothing! He is deaf to all our pleas, and blind to his own good. He will resile not one inch from his folly.'

'But he *is* the King, still. The Lord's Anointed.'

'Aye – there's the grip of it.' Napier turned, as an imposing figure approached them. 'Ha! And here's the King's Advocate, no less! Sir Thomas – I think you will not know my good-brother, Montrose. James – the Lord Advocate, Sir Thomas Hope of Craighall.'

James Graham eyed the newcomer with interest, a big, portly, dark-visaged man, with a fleshy face and narrow-set, dark, keen eyes, scarcely prepossessing of appearance but clearly a man to be reckoned with, quite apart from being principal law officer of the Crown in Scotland. The fact that the Lord Advocate was coarse-looking, and sounded it, had thick lips, a wide mouth and a wild black and bushy beard, would only deceive the ignorant or the very unwary. Montrose knew that this was one of the most potent characters in two kingdoms – if scarcely the best-loved. Potent in more ways than one, for he had fourteen children – and what was more, two of them were already Lords of Session, to sit upon the High Court bench before which their father came to plead as King's Advocate; a fact which allowed him to plead with his head covered, an unprecedented privilege, since it would be considered derogatory for a man to take his hat off to his sons.

The younger man bowed, wordless.

'I know *of* his lordship,' Hope greeted 'Who does not? You are well returned to Scotland, I think, young man.' The Advocate splattered a little from those thick red lips as he spoke.

'You say so, sir? I appear to have returned to a seething pot of troubles, indeed.' Montrose drew back almost involuntarily, not liking what he saw – and surprised indeed to see the King's Advocate in this company, though he could hardly say so.

'Trouble, yes. But trouble is the forcing ground of change, of progress, of greatness, my lord.' Hope had a strangely light voice for a man of his appearance and reputation – and somehow managed not to sound sententious. 'Trouble is to be

58

grasped in strong hands, not jinked and jouked. Is it no',
Archie?'

'Presupposing the strong hands are available. And allied
to cool wits.'

'Spoke like an Extraordinary Lord o' Session, my old
friend! So we must needs seek strong hands, in this stir, must
we not? Aye, and cool heads. But they're scarce, Archie,
scarce.'

'You are right, Tom. That is just what we were saying,
James and I. Cool heads, a conference table. Not a stramash
of high words and flourishes.' Napier waved a hand round at
the crowded room. 'Such as we have here.'

'Cha – there may be cool heads, aye, and strong hands too,
in the land. But they maun be allied to a voice which men
will *heed*, Archie. We may conceive our ain voices clear
enough, and our heads likewise! We may even think ourselves wise, on occasion. But will Scotland heed us? Follow
us? I think not. Even you, Archie, born second Lord Napier,
these will never follow!' The Lord Advocate waved a scornful hand at the aristocratic throng. 'As for me, I am a low-
born base fellow, son of an Edinburgh burgher. What belted
earl will follow Tom Hope? Even though sometimes they'll
admit themselves fear't of me! No – the voice of Scotland
needs must be a voice high-born, younger too, of the blood
of the old leadership. Only such will our stubborn fellow
countrymen follow – and not only the nobility. The com-
monality are just as bad. I have been looking for such these
long months.'

'The Earl of Rothes has taken an active role . . .' Montrose
began.

'John Leslie!' Hope cut him short with a snort. 'Leslie –
he isna such a fool as he sounds, I grant you. But nor is he
of the stuff of leadership. Young men would never follow
the like – nor would he try to make them. And it is young
men, not old, who will decide this present matter.'

'What do you mean, sir? Saying that *young* men will
decide it? You do not mean resort to arms, surely? You, the
King's Advocate, do not advocate revolt? Rebellion? Against
the King?'

'Young man – I am the King's servant. I will do nothing,
nothing mark you, to injure His Grace. But like my lord
Napier here, I conceive him to be so ill-advised as to be in

danger of losing his Scottish kingdom. In such pass, it is my duty, as I see it, the duty of all true lieges, to save him from those who so advise him and poison his mind. From his own misguided notions forbye. And this will not be done without stark deeds. Not rebellion, pray God. But resolute, right positive action. And for that, the voices of old men will not suffice.'

Neither of his hearers spoke for a few moments. Montrose was more struck by the man's sombre words and grave tones, however light the voice, than by anything that he had yet heard since his return to Scotland. When the principal law officer of the realm, the man, next to the Chancellor, representing the King's authority, spoke so, admitted that he had been looking for strong leadership for months, to counter the royal edicts, matters had indeed come to crisis-point.

Montrose and Napier were back near-by next morning, well before the set hour of ten, to take their places in St Giles High Kirk. Nine a.m. was the usual hour, but there had been an earlier service, at eight, that Sunday the 23rd of July, in order that the common folk of the parish might have their ordinary worship and be got safely out of the way, so that there might be ample accommodation for the important people before whom the new prayer-book was to be used for the first time. Also that there might be no risk of unseemly disturbance. Normally there were no seats for the congregation – although elderly ladies and sick folk often brought their own stools with them – but there were stalls set aside for especial worshippers; and since it was inconceivable that earls and great lords should have to stand like other folk, these had today been suitably reinforced. Montrose and his brother-in-law, therefore, sat comfortably at the front of the north transept, right at the great central crossing where the massive fluted pillars supported the church's mighty lantern-tower, the south transept directly in front of them, the huge nave on their left, but the choir on their right screened off with tapestries and hangings – this because it was at present undergoing reconstruction and restoration to its former state. St Giles, before the Reformation, had been one great church, though with many side-chapels and chantries; but the Reformers had changed all that, dividing it up into three separate places of Presbyterian worship for city parishes. Now, under the new episcopal regime, it was one church again; but the choir area was not yet fully restored, in keeping with cathedral status. In front of the tapestry barrier was placed today a large Communion-table, with crucifix, candles, cloth and frontal, looking sus-piciously like an altar, rows of throne-like chairs flanking it on either side. And a little farther forward, under the cross-ing's groined vault itself, rose a carved wooden pulpit, with below it an ornate lectern or reading-desk.

The great cruciform church, undoubtedly large enough to be any bishop's cathedral, was already all but full. Half the aristocracy of Scotland, with all the notabilities of Edinburgh and Lothian, stood around. There was a mighty chatter of tongues, calling out, exchange of greetings and pleasantries, laughter, more suitable for a fairground than a church. Montrose said as much to Rothes, whom he found installed as his neighbour.

'And whose blame might that be? It's no' godly, I'll grant you. But if the bishops will make o' the kirk a place as full o' mummery and show as a playhouse, then theirs the con-sequence, say I. Eh, Archie?'

Napier looked around him distastefully, at all the colour, style and fashion. 'I'd say there's more come here today to see and be seen, than to worship God, John.'

'Aye, so. But we're no' here to worship, are we? We're here, on the King's royal command, transmitted by His Beneficence the Archbishop o' St Andrews, Chancellor o' this realm. To witness the institution o' a royal edict. Nothing more. No' to worship our Maker.'

Montrose cleared his throat. 'It may be so. But I hope nevertheless, my lord, that we get through this in decency. If we take it upon ourselves to question, and seek change, the King's commands, it must be on a plane of highest principle. And it must be seen of all to be so. If we give a lead in this, it must be with dignity. I mislike the bearing, the attitudes, I see here this morning. In a house of prayer.'

'Uh-huh. Nae doubt you're right, James. But all men – aye, and all women, for that matter – maybe havena just your fine sentiments and lofty ideals! We're no' all Jamie Graham o' Montrose!'

Directly, then, the other put it to him. 'You have not arranged any disturbance, my lord? Any demonstration, within this church, against these ordinances? I hope not. For it is no place for such. It could do our cause much harm. Set moderate men against us. You must see it?'

'Och, man – I've no' arranged anything !' Rothes declared. But there was a slight emphasis on the personal in that. 'We're here, as commanded, to hear this new prayer-book read. If folk dinna like it, and choose to make that plain, am I to blame . . . ?'

'My lord,' Montrose said urgently, 'you have taken the lead in this matter. You are one of the foremost nobles in the land. And one of the best liked, the most respected. Many will trim their sails to yours. You cannot say that what happens here is no concern of yours, no blame of yours. If folly prevails here, you must bear part of the responsibility. As indeed must I. And Archie. If you know of aught which might serve our cause ill, cause offence to moderate men – then I say it is your duty to seek halt it, before it is too late.'

'Duty, a' God's name ! *You* see fit to tell me my duty?'

'I do, my lord. Since you saw fit to come to tell me mine, at Kincardine, last November. And hence I am here.'

'And I? Suppose I conceive my duty otherwise, sir?'

'Then I suggest that you have not considered it sufficiently. Your duty cannot be to allow happen anything which might force men to abandon our cause. Men . . . such as myself !'

Rothes swallowed, his double chins quivering. Then, without another word, he rose abruptly from his pew and stalked off.

'You did that featly, stoutly, Jamie,' Napier said. 'I know no other who could, or would, have forced Rothes so. You are heeding Tom Hope's words, I think?'

'I am but looking to my own name and reputation. And yours, Archie. If Leslie wants Graham to dance, he must pipe a tune that Graham will heed ! *You* sent him to me, my friend – you should have told him so.'

His brother-in-law nodded mildly, a faint smile about his lips. 'I am glad that I sent him,' he said.

The great church was nearly full, all the stone-flagged nave being tightly packed with people. Montrose, presently, gestured towards the front of these serried ranks. 'Is that not strange?' he said. 'All this notable crowd of the quality. Yet there, in the forefront, in the best places of all, these wifies sitting there on their stools. Common folk of the town, are they not? Yet you said that such were being kept from this service? That they had their service earlier? Of set purpose.'

It was true. Whatever the official fiat about the ordinary congregation being given their normal and non-prayer-book service early this momentous day, the fact was that the first three or four rows of the close-packed ranks of the standing quality was composed of most evidently common folk, women all, sitting on little folding stools and looking entirely assured and pleased with themselves.

'You mistake, Jamie,' Napier explained. 'These are not Edinburgh wifies – not of the general run. Common folk they may be. They are maids – ladies' maids and tiring-women. It is a custom here. They come early to the kirk, with their mistresses' stools, to win a good place for their betters. Then, just before the service starts, their ladyships can come in at their ease and take over the stools – and the maids go home and make the beds or prepare the dinner! All most suitably devised, in Edinburgh fashion!' He looked beyond. 'Only today, I fear, the good ladies will be highly outraged, and denied their divine worship! For, as you see, the place has become so tight jammed that there will be no room for even the most formidable dame to win through. I think the abigails must needs serve as deputies throughout! Bishop Lindsay will be as distressed as the mistresses – what ever the Lord God thinks!'

'Save us – that is Edinburgh for you! Small wonder it gets the name it has. I . . .'

Montrose's voice was drowned by a hullabaloo from without, shouts and catcalls growing ever louder, and through it the tuck of drum. The former much prevailed over the latter – and it did not sound like cheers and applause.

'A mob,' James Graham said, frowning. 'Trouble in the streets.'

'It is the Town Guard, marching to their drums. But I fear it is not the Guard that is being shouted at!'

Inside the church the noise abated notably as attention was concentrated on what went on outside. It seemed as though the good folk of Edinburgh, even though denied their normal forenoon service, were not going to be left out entirely from the day's proceedings.

The door of the north transept was thrown open and, preceded by the city macebearer, the Provost in scarlet and ermine and the magistrates in their robes, came in, pacing rather faster than their usual procession and looking distinctly ill-at-ease, not to say out-of-breath. Two files of the Town Guard marched inside with them, and the doors were closed, shutting out the noise somewhat. As the magistrates moved to their allotted places, Rothes returned to his seat.

'Folk out there who think differently frae James Graham!' he said grimly. 'Henderson had the rights of it.'

'What do you mean?'

'I mean that these outside, the common folk, are shouting against Popery and idolatry, man. They're no' caring about the prayer-book. It's the surplices and the pictures they're crying at. Half the town's there, yelling abominations and damnation to the Papes!'

'The more fools them, then!'

'It may be. But ignore them at your peril, my lord! Yon yowling's no' *your* voice. But it's the *other* voice o' Scotland, for a' that!'

A fanfare of trumpets, from outside the south transept, stilled all conversation. The doors at that side were thrown open, while all who had seats in the church got to their feet. The noise of the crowd was much less noticeable than when the north porch door had been open, for this south entrance gave on to the enclosure of Parliament Square, a narrow area which could be barred off from the High Street. Out from Parliament Close across the way, the Lord Advocate, with Sir George Elphinstone of Blythswood, the Lord Justice Clerk, pacing slowly and with great dignity, led the procession of the King's judges, the Lords of Session.

'All this to hear a prayer-book read!' Montrose said.

'Wait you,' Rothes advised. 'There's word that Spottiswoode's here himsel', after all.'

'The Archbishop? From St Andrews? Then – he must see this as of vital importance,' Napier said. 'A trial of strength, perhaps?'

'They would bind us. Seek to commit us to acceptance of this thing, by sheer weight o' consequence.' Rothes snorted. 'They tell me that Spottiswoode came, meaning .to lead in the whole Privy Council. But most o' it has chosen to sit in the body o' the kirk, like you and me, Archie – so he'll hae to make do wi' a wheen bishops!'

64

The judiciary seated, there was another fanfare, and again the south doors were opened. First came in a delicate-looking young man, seeming almost to wilt under the brilliant splendour of a Lion Rampant tabard, carrying a baton of office.

'Save us – Balfour! Sir James Balfour of Denmiln, the Lyon!' Montrose exclaimed. 'The very trappings of royalty. Can they do this?'

'Aye, they can – it means that Spottiswoode is here as Chancellor o' Scotland, and King's representative, no' just as Archbishop and Primate,' Rothes said. 'So what is done here today has all the authority of the state behind it.'

'Scarcely that – since it lacks that of parliament,' the Graham amended. 'Here is the royal authority, yes. The great officers of state. The judiciary. The Church. But not parliament. Let us not forget it.'

A galaxy of magnificently robed prelates paced in stately fashion behind the Lord Lyon King of Arms and his heralds, vivid in rich colours, jewel-encrusted, golden croziers and crosses winking in the July morning sun. The first pair, one heavy and white-haired, the other tall, dark and stooping, wore taller, more elaborate mitres than the pairs behind, their trains borne by handsomely attired pages. To the singing of a great choir of men and boys in white surplices, who came on after, this gorgeous company entered.

'Both archbishops! Glasgow too!' Napier exclaimed. 'And four other bishops – Galloway, Dunblane, Dunkeld and Brechin. So they are not introducing the prayer-book in their own dioceses. All concentrated on Edinburgh today. Even Tom Hope did not know of this.'

'As well that parade o' play-actors came straight ower frae Parliament Close, and no' by the High Street door!' Rothes commented grimly. 'Or they'd have lost some o' their gewgaws by this! Look at them!'

Because these, like the judiciary before them, came in from the end of the south transept, the people crowded in the nave did not see them for a few moments. When they did come into sight, making for the row of chairs set on the north of the Communion-table, a great corporate sigh arose from the congregation. There was exclamation amongst it, condemnation, even a sort of unwilling admiration, but no real uproar. Clearly many were not unimpressed by the sheer magnificence of the spectacle, especially the women on the

65

stools in front. Nothing like this had been seen in St Giles for eighty years, since the Reformation of blessed memory.

Montrose's parallel sigh of relief was premature. The choir had now come into view. And where the gorgeous copes, chasubles, stoles and mitres of the prelates had got by without clamour, through their unaccustomed splendour, the simple white surplices which clothed the humble singers were as red rags to bulls. Not to the mass of this congregation, but to those representatives of the common people at the front. To a woman they rose from their stools, and cried out, pointing, hooting, skirling at the hated symbols which their ministers had been denouncing as Popery for months. Pandemonium ensued.

But the authorities were not unprepared for trouble, whatever touched it off. The choristers, after wavering momentarily, paced on, singing the louder. At a sign from the Lord Lyon King of Arms, the Town Guard present, who had been lining the walling around the crossing, stepped forward, halberds at the ready, threateningly. And from the south porch another blast of trumpets, louder than before, shook the great building.

Between them, these moves served their turn. The abigails and serving-women quietened, perceived that authority frowned on them and them alone, and that the quality behind them were looking and sounding indignant, not at the choristers but at themselves for usurping their right of protest. One or two continued to glare, one shaking a bony fist; but most resumed their seats, and none continued with the shouting.

While still the singing continued, in at the same south door came the cathedral clergy and celebrant's procession, cross-bearer, acolytes, servers and priests with the holy vessels and elements, followed by the canons, the Dean, and, bringing up the rear, the plump, rosy person of Bishop Lindsay of Edinburgh, in purple cope and mitre. He paced forward, wielding his crozier with great assurance and authority but with very wary eyes. The doors shut finally behind him.

All in turn bowing before the Communion-table and the crucifix behind to the faint murmuring of the congregation, the priests and canons took their places on the chairs facing the senior prelates. The Bishop climbed into the pulpit, and Dean Hannah moved into the reading-desk immediately below. He was a little man, with a fiery red complexion and a long nose – and could be seen to be wearing a white linen surplice under the short dalmatic and stole. He held a book in his hands gingerly, as though it might well burn his fingers.

As the singing died away, there was to be heard a steady undertone of muttering from the assembled worshippers.

The Bishop raised a beringed hand. 'By command of the King's most excellent Grace, and in the name of the Father, the Son and the Holy Ghost. Amen,' he intoned in a rich, sonorous voice.

Nobody contested that.

'The service will be that contained in the Book of Common Prayer ordained to be read in this and every other church of His Grace's realm of Scotland, by the King's command, that of His Grace's Privy Council, and of the College of Bishops.'

The company stirred restively.

The Bishop looked down on the Dean, coughed, and gestured.

Dean Hannah made some play of opening the book, finding the place with the blue satin and gold-frilled marker, and cleared his throat. 'Let us pray,' he said.

All around the Communion-table, the clerics and choristers and acolytes sank to their knees, the prelates and canons on specially provided kneelers, the rest on the floor.

The congregation thus early were faced with decision. Standing tight packed as they were it would have been difficult to kneel anyway, with more space taken up by legs than by feet. One or two may have sought to do so, at the back, for there was some slight commotion. Only those at the very front were in any position for ready kneeling – the maids, the Provost and magistrates, the judges and the great lords. Cautiously Edinburgh's civic fathers watched to see what their betters would do. One or two of the judges began to bend their knees, and then perceived that neither the Lord Advocate nor the Lord Justice Clerk were doing so, and almost imperceptibly straightened up again. All eyed the stalls of the earls, questioningly.

This problem of kneeling had not occurred to Montrose, any more than to most of his companions. He realised that innumerable eyes were on him. He bowed his head, and remained standing. Something like a moan rose from the great gathering.

'Let us *pray!*' the Dean repeated, his voice considerably higher-pitched.

From above him, the Bishop's deeper voice snapped, 'Proceed!'

'Ah. Hm. Aye. Almighty God, unto whom all hearts be open, all desires known, and from whom no secrets are hid : Cleanse the thoughts of our hearts by the inspiration of Thy Holy Spirit, that we may perfectly love Thee and worthily magnify Thy Holy Name : Through Christ our Lord,' he said hurriedly.

The assembly, standing, listened. It was a prayer that they all knew, with nothing new about it. After all, most of them had been using a liturgical service for years, John Knox's Liturgy.

Then followed the Summary of the Law. 'Our Lord Jesus Christ said : Hear O Israel, the Lord our God is one Lord...'

Only the clergy and choristers made response : 'Lord have mercy upon us, and write these Thy laws in our hearts, we beseech Thee.' But they intoned it strongly, hearteningly, and the Dean stood up a little more straight, his voice recovering.

'Lord have mercy upon us!'

'Well might ye say it!' one of the women made response, before the formal 'Christ have mercy upon us!' drowned the rest.

The congregation stirred, like a restive goaded beast.

Shocked, the Dean's voice went squeaky again. 'Lord ... Lord ... have mercy ...'

A woman's excited laughter, from the back, set off a surge of exclamation and comment.

The Dean tried to continue, raising his voice higher and higher – but with it all the noise increased. Presently Hannah gave up the attempt, and gazed about him anxiously, wringing his hands.

In the pulpit, Bishop Lindsay was speaking – but could not make himself heard. Then one of the stools was knocked over, as a woman rose to shout something – and the clatter of it produced one of those abrupt moments of silence which can follow a new and violent sound. And into it the Bishop could be heard clearly commanding, 'The collect, man! Get on with the collect for the day.'

The word 'collect' from the pulpit did indeed seem to collect and distil all the pent-up animosity and tension in the place. There was a rumbling growl from many throats, and above it all a penetrating woman's screech.

'Colic, ye say! Deil colic the wame o' ye, *I* say! Out on ye – Anti-christ!'

A great shout of laughter rose from the company, wholly and finally dissipating any residual atmosphere of worship from the assembly. But the laughter came from the assembled qual:y, not at all from the common folk with the stools in front. They were roused to rage, rather than amused – partly, possibly, by that very laughter behind them, which might seem to mock them. The maids were all on their feet now.

'Idolatry! Idolatry!' one screamed. 'It's Baal entered upon us!'

'Aye – Rome! Rome's come to Emburgh!'

'Papes! Papes! Fause-tongued thieves! Out on ye . . . !'

The Bishop rose in the pulpit, waving the golden crozier indignantly. 'Silence! Silence, in God's holy house. How dare you!' he cried. 'In the Name of God – peace!'

'I'll peace you, you crafty auld fox! You fat belly-god! Beast o' Rome!'

Stricken by such impious insults bawled in his cathedral, Bishop Lindsay gasped helplessly, at a loss for words or deeds. He turned, to gaze at the archbishops, for help, guidance. But the switching of the attack to his superior seemed to have aroused Dean Hannah to anger, where that on himself had produced only fear.

'Be quiet! Be quiet, I say!' he shouted. 'Shameless women! Daughters of Jezebel! Dare you interrupt God's servants? Defile Christ's Holy Eucharist . . . ?'

'Dare *you* read the Mass in my lug!' a short, dumpy, apple-cheeked wom in yelled back. And on an impulse, she stooped, picked up the overturned stool at her feet, and hurled it with all her strength at the Dean.

It was not a particularly good throw, for she hung on to the stool an instant too long, as female throwers are apt to do. So that it flew low, struck the lectern a glancing blow, and finished up clattering against the pulpit base. But it made a lot of noise, and had as much impact on the proceedings as though indeed it had scored a direct hit on its target.

There were a few moments of utter and appalled silence. Then tumultuous uproar broke out in the High Kirk of St Giles.

Suddenly everybody was shouting at once – and a large proportion seemed to be on the move also. The Provost bellowed for the Town Guard to clear the church. Most of the congregation surged forward – since it could not surge backwards or sideways, and motion was abruptly imperative. Prelates, judges and magistrates saw their escape route to the south porch likely to be blocked, as a result, and in their turn surged thitherwards, stumbling over kneelers, desks and church-furniture in an undignified scurry, long robes kilted high. The little Dean, who seemed to be the prime object of fury, found himself attacked by a horde of viragoes and, retiring in the face of it, defended himself as best he might, wielding the prayer-book.

Above him, islanded in his pulpit amid this turbulent sea of wrath and panic, Bishop Lindsay, hand to mouth, appealed through convulsive fingers, for aid, to the Most High, the Provost, magistrates and Town Council, the Lord Lyon King of Arms, and any and all right-thinking persons.

Montrose, shocked and dumbfounded, nevertheless recovered his wits quickly – but decided that the Dean was in greater need than his superior. He pushed his way through the milling throng to the aid of the little man, commanding order and cessation of folly forthwith, with all his notable and inborn authority. It was less effective than usual, admittedly, but he did make some impression, especially when Sir Thomas Hope and Napier materialised at his side. They got the Dean extricated, between them, and Hope led him away.

Rothes edged his way to Montrose's side. 'So much for dignity and seemliness, James!' he said. 'Have you ever seen the like?'

'I have not. Nor wish to see it again!' the younger man returned. 'It is a stain on the name of this kingdom . . .'

'Och, it's no' so bad as that, lad. If it's a stain, it will wash off! But – it changes matters. By God, it does! There will be no going back, now. No time for dainty half-measures. Mark my words – all Scotland will hear of this by the morn's morn. Of bishops and archbishops running for their smooth skins before the godly Mistress Geddes! Popery fleeing before the forces o' righteousness. And, mark you, the common folk's righteousness, no' ours! This will ring round the land – that it was the Edinburgh wifies who did it, no' John Leslie and James Graham!'

'For that I will thank God, at least!'

'You say so? I wonder.' He had to shout above the uproar. 'I say, I wonder. Think you it best that the folk should lead in Scotland? No' the nobles? Will you win your moderation that gait? Use your wits, man.'

'Mm.'

Archie Napier had come up. 'John's right,' he said, urgently. 'I have just had a word with Tom Hope. He is saying the same. That we will have to act quickly now – or the whole cause could get out-of-hand. As this morning has done. This could be like a heather-fire, burning all, bad and good alike. We must control it – if we can . . .'

6

THERE WAS INDEED MUCH TALKING, AND SOME ACTION IN Scotland thereafter. The country rang with that Sunday's doings in Edinburgh – and with the name of Jenny Geddes, stool-thrower and bishop-feller, who suddenly became something of a national heroine. Not with the gentry, of course, who could by no means countenance such abandoned behaviour. But amongst the ordinary people the die was now cast, the issue clear-cut, the anti-episcopal cause their very own.

That it must not remain so was the concern of thinking folk who sought the realm's weal. Leadership there had to be, demonstration that mob-rule would not serve. Which demonstration was not easy – for in fact this display of mob-rule *had* served, most effectively, at least for limited objectives. For after that Sunday no attempts were made to read the new prayer-book from any pulpit in Scotland, the bishops lay very low, and Archbishop Spottiswoode repaired in haste to London for fresh instructions.

So there was much debate, argument and suggestion, in castle and manor, town-house and manse; also much recrimination and dissension. Montrose's scheme for a petition of rights at last saw fulfilment – although it was not until the 18th of October that it was finally signed, sealed and sent off to the King. It was wordy, and rather uninspiredly styled *Scotland's Supplication and Complaint Against the Book of Common Prayer, the Book of Canons, and the Prelates;* not at all what James Graham had visualised. He signed it, nevertheless. None really believed that it would convince King Charles of the error of his ways.

It was not until almost a month later, when not so much as an acknowledgment had been received, that positive and effective action was taken by the born leadership of the country, after so much feeble bickering and delay. For almost every day there were scenes, crowds rioting, magistrates shut up in the Tolbooth of Edinburgh, prayer-books burned, the Lord Treasurer, the Earl of Traquair mobbed and his staff of office broken, old Bishop Sydserf almost killed. Great crowds flocked on Edinburgh from far and near, agitating against the cleric-dominated Privy Council. Sir Thomas Hope, putting at risk all his career, declared that Scotland was not so much misgoverned as not being governed at all. He suggested that the Privy Council's request for a committee of complainers was apt, permitting the calling of a Convention. He suggested that it be done forthwith, as pursuant of the Privy Council order, his own name and style being sufficient authority.

And so, on the 18th of November, 1637, a great Convention of all those entitled to attend a parliament was called in the Parliament Hall of Edinburgh. By no means all who were invited attended, many holding that to do so would brand them as having taken sides against the monarch. But sufficient did so to produce a large and representative assembly – larger than many a true parliament. Out of it all came the decision, not unanimous but carried by a large majority, that a standing commission of the Convention be set up, not just as a committee to speak before the Privy Council, but as a much more meaningful, permanent and effectve body. It would consist of representatives of the four

72

constituent sections of the Convention, the nobles, the lairds, the Kirk and the burghs, these all to meet together, but each at a separate table for their order, threat to take council for and action towards the proper regulation of the realm's affairs until parliament itself appointed otherwise. It was, in effect, a provisional government.

Montrose found himself appointed to the Table of the Nobles, but declined the convenership, when it was proposed by Rothes, who himself refused the position. It was then filled by John Campbell, Earl of Loudoun.

So, at last, the rudderless ship of state began to sail on a recognisable course, however unacceptable to some. Montrose himself by no means approved of all that was decided upon : but having spoken out against courses he objected to, he could do no less than go along with the majority decisions thereafter. It was the voice of Scotland, spoken in more democratic fashion than any there had known previously; and while he would not fail to seek to influence it, he would not controvert it.

Quickly the results were seen. Mob violence diminished, the people quietened, the Privy Council was left in no doubt as to strength of opinion throughout the country against the royal ordinances, and the ministers of the Kirk sobered somewhat in their pulpit agitation. The Lord Treasurer Traquair, a stupid man, departed for London, if not wiser, at least better informed.

Strangely, where King Charles had shown little concern over riot and fury in his nothern kingdom, he reacted sharply to these latest developments. Royal commands and edicts came flooding north. All petitioners and objectors soever were commanded to disperse on pain of treason; and not to reassemble without the Privy Council's consent. To amplify this, the Council itself was ordered to remove itself from Edinburgh and meet in Linlithgow. And as further intima-tion that the King meant business, the law courts were also commanded to leave Edinburgh. The capital was to be isolated as a plague-spot – and warning was served on the Lord Advocate and judges. Finally, Charles, with firm courage if nothing else, announced that he took complete and personal responsibility for the new prayer-book, insisted upon its immediate introduction, and gave the sternest orders to all ministers to impose it at all costs. It was to be war, at least to the paper-knife.

The Tables, meeting under the threat of treason, decided at last to take up seriously the idea of a great national covenant, no mere supplication or petition this time, but a manifesto of the people's rights, a clarion call to action, and a bond of engagement. Montrose, torn by doubts, assented.

Even such wordy warfare exacts its price on the individual – and James Graham learned something of the cost, other than to his peace of mind, when he returned home to Kincardine after that third major sitting of the Tables, at the beginning of December. He was surprised to find Magdalen, with the boys, all packed and ready to leave – despite the fact that she was nearly eight months pregnant.

'My dear,' he exclaimed, 'where are you bound?'

'Home,' she told him briefly.

'But – this is your home.'

'Is it? I think not.'

At her tone, he eyed her thoughtfully. 'Magdalen – what is to do?'

'My father is come. He will take us back to Kinnaird. For Yuletide.'

'Southesk here?'

'He is gone today to Inchaffray. To speak with the Lord Madderty. Awaiting your return. He will be back anon. We ride tomorrow.'

'But . . . I had no thought to go to Kinnaird. For Yule. Nothing has been said of this, nothing discussed.'

'You have been little here, to discuss anything.'

'I have been much thronged with work.'

'You are ever much thronged with work, James.'

'These are fateful, anxious days . . .'

'They have been long, weary days. For me.'

'I am sorry. You are drawing near your time. It must be grievous for you. But that will soon be by with. And then . . .'

'And then – what betterment? Waiting for the next!'

'My dear, you are distraught.'

'Distraught, yes. Distraught with waiting. For you! I waited all the years you were gone beyond the seas. And still I wait, idling my life away. So – I go to Kinnaird.'

'Idling, girl? With our two sons to rear? And this my house

74

to keep? Not so large as Kinnaird – but not small. Sakes – you will have less to do at Kinnaird! In another's house.'

'It is at least my home. As this crow's-nest can never be!'

'I did not know that you so misliked it here. It seems to me a bonnie house enough...'

'Then why not bide in it?' she flashed. 'If you like it so well. You are scarce ever here. I might esteem it better if I shared it with my husband!'

He bit back the hot words that sprang to his lips. 'Magdalen,' he said slowly, carefully, 'the kingdom is in grievous state. It demands the service of all its true sons. I am an earl of Scotland. One of those on whom rest the greater responsibility. Chief of a great clan. I have set my hand to the task of seeking to right some of the realm's wrongs. With others. I could do no less. Would you have me, the Graham, fail in my simple duty?'

'Have you not simple duty to more than the realm?'

'I have, yes. More than duty – love and affection, and my own concerns. But, meantime, I have no choice but to do what I was born to do.'

'Were you, the Graham, born to rebel against your king? You, one of his earls, who should be his main support?' That came out in a rush. 'My father is another of the earls of Scotland. Though a new one! He sees not his duty so!'

Montrose took a deep breath. 'Do I hear your father's voice speaking there?' he asked, at length.

'My father can say as he will. He never lacks for words! But even a woman, even Magdalen Carnegie, can think her own thoughts. I . . . oh, James, I believe you do wrongly! You are another man, since you returned from foreign lands. I feel . . . I feel that I do not know you, any more.'

At her abrupt alteration of tone and manner, the cracking of her hard-maintained front, the man reached out to grasp her arm.

'Magdalen – do not say it. I am still James Graham, your husband, father of your bairns, sharer of your bed, of *our* life. If I have changed, it is only that I have grown older, changed from a youth to a man. But – it is a man you would wish as husband, is it not? No callow youth. A man, who knows his own mind – or seeks to do so. Is that so ill?'

'If it means that you grow away from me – yes.'

'I cannot remain the bairn I was when I left you, girl.

75

But, then – nor are you the same. You are changed, like-wise . . .'

'And whose fault is that? *I* have stayed where I was, where I belonged. I have not become a renegade !'

'Renegade!' Almost he laughed. 'Dear God – James Graham renegade !' Then he frowned. 'That word, at least, is not your own. That I swear ! So, my lord of Southesk names me renegade? He, who ever makes his own laws and rules !'

'You have turned against the King.'

'I have told you, Magdalen – it is not true. I am the King's loyal subject – and will ever be so. But when the King does ill, grievously ill, to the hurt of his people and of his own name and rule, is it not my duty to seek change his course?'

'Who are you to judge the King?'

'You cannot have it this way and that. If I, as an earl of Scotland, one of the *Righ*, the princes, the lesser kings, of which Charles is the *Ard Righ*, the High King – if I must be foremost in the King's support – then I also must be one who advises the King as to right and wrong, in his rule in this land. Else I am a mere vassal; worse, a paid servant to carry out his will, right or wrong. Which, pray God, I will never be !'

'Oh, words – great, swelling words !' she cried. 'I cannot trade such words with you, James. You are ever too clever for me. But, this I say. That I believe you do ill. And . . .' she set her less than prominent jaw obstinately, 'and tomorrow we go to Kinnaird.'

'Even though I say otherwise?' he asked. 'It is not con-venient for me to go farther from Edinburgh, at this pass. I must return there for another meeting, in ten days' time.'

'The more reason that I am at Kinnaird, then. Since I am to be left alone again. As always !'

'Magdalen – I do not think that Kinnaird is the place for you. Under your father's eye and tongue. You know it – we have spoken of it, often. If you will not stay here at Kin-cardine, come to Edinburgh with me, meantime. We can take a lodging in the city. For this winter, which must be of great import . . .'

'No! What would I do in Edinburgh? Amongst all your clever plotters and intriguers? I want no part in your plot-ting. Any more than in your rabbles and riots ! I am going home – at least for a time.' Chokingly but finally, she said it, and turning, ran from him, actually ran.

He began to hurry after her, but then thought better of it. Shaking his head, he went heavy-footed in search of his sons.

Nevertheless, after an unsatisfactory night in his wife's bed, James Graham rode north for the Mearns, with his Countess, his sons and his father-in-law, having thought on it until his head spun. He was not a man to shirk the price that had to be paid – any price.

7

EDINBURGH MIGHT BE DEMOTED, IN NAME, FROM BEING capital, by the King's command; but seldom before had the old grey city above the Forth been so much the centre and heart of the country. The Privy Council – or the Lords Spiritual part of it – might meet occasionally and fearfully in Linlithgow or Stirling; but the meetings which mattered to Scotland were taking place all the time in Edinburgh; not only those of the Tables themselves, but public and private assemblies, conclaves and groups of the nobility, clergy, burgesses and ordinary folk, conferring, protesting, demonstrating. People streamed to the city from all parts – or not quite all parts, for the Highlands in the main remained disinterested, and Aberdeenshire and the North-East hostile. This latter attitude was accounted for partly by the fact that St Andrews, the former ecclesiastical metropolis and most ancient university, was the main centre of Presbyterianism – and therefore its rival, Aberdeen University, must needs support Episcopacy, to be different; and partly owing to the great influence thereabouts of the mighty Catholic house of Gordon, whose chief, the Marquis of Huntly, inevitably chose to link the Crown with the Papacy.

That winter of 1637/38, Montrose saw more of Edinburgh than he had ever done. After the birth of another son, whom they named David, in early January, he was more frequently in the city than at Kinnaird – where he found the atmosphere a little trying. The great National Covenant was in process of being drawn up; and since its sentiments and provisions were all-important, James Graham was concerned that his hand should not be absent from the wording. Also, he was beginning to regret that he had allowed the Earl of Loudoun to be appointed the convener of the Nobles' Table, with the influence this position was assuming. Loudoun, the first earl, had been Sir John Campbell of Lawers, a harsh and overbearing man, and notably anti-King. Montrose was seeking, at this stage, and on the urgings of Napier, Rothes and even Sir Thomas Hope, to restrain him from too intemperate an attitude. If the Campbell had had his way – like some of the more extreme ministers – it would have been outright armed rebellion, and the royal authority denied and dismissed.

Such was the situation when, on the 19th of February, John Stewart, Earl of Traquair, Treasurer of Scotland, arrived back in Scotland from London – but not at Edinburgh. He went to Stirling, and in the presence of the truncated Privy Council, had the Lord Lyon King of Arms read a new proclamation from the King, at the Mercat Cross, giving force of law to various aspects of Charles's policy. However, the Lyon and his heralds were ordered to come to Edinburgh and read the proclamation there on the 22nd – although discreetly.

Since one of the clauses was that all petitioners and protestors against the King's ecclesiastical policy were to be banished the city and forbidden to meet together on pain of treason, it was high time for swift decisions.

Edinburgh buzzed like a bee's-bike disturbed; but though there was strong pressure for drastic, indeed violent action, Montrose, Rothes, Napier and Henderson – guided in the background by the Lord Advocate – managed to have moderation to prevail. Meantime. The royal proclamation would be heard and its proclaimers not subjected to riot or contempt. But the Tables' own proclamation would be read thereafter, and the new National Covenant brought forward for signature in turn.

So, on Thursday the 22nd, Edinburgh was packed to bursting point, to witness this first direct confrontation, the first formal exchange of salvoes in the war of words between Monarch and people. At an hour before noon, as the bells still jangled the hour, the steady tuck of drum heralded the Town Guard, specially reinforced for the occasion, marching up the crowded High Street to the Mercat Cross outside St Giles. They had to force their way less than gently, with halberds and pikes and flat of swords, so dense was the throng; but everywhere the ministers were mixing with the people, urging restraint, a quiet reception, and the upholding of the dignity and authority of their Tables. In the main they were successful, extraordinarily so considering the intensity of the emotion aroused. There were a few scuffles, some shouts and catcalls, one or two stones thrown; but the Guard and its charges got through without major upset – these charges including the unhappy Provost and magistrates of Edinburgh, some of whom were themselves members of the Burghs' Table, Lord Lyon Balfour and his brilliantly tabarded heralds, and, impassive-featured, pacing majestically, Sir Thomas Hope of Craighall, His Grace's Advocate.

Around the platformed Mercat Cross, of course, the crowd was most dense and most illustrious. Here, standing tight-packed as herrings in a barrel, was a large part of the country's aristocracy, gentry, clergy, guildry, merchantry – and, of course, innumerable of the citizenry and country folk in for the proclamations, with screeching children, barking dogs, pedlars, hucksters, pickpockets, cutpurses, indeed all the community of the realm. It was a cold grey day, with an east wind off the sea and an occasional smirr of rain – Edinburgh in February. Every window of the tall flanking tenements and lands held its quota of womenfolk.

Through all, the Town Guard pushed. Leaving the magistrates and the Advocate at the foot of the octagonal, arched and parapeted base of the Cross, the Provost and Lord Lyon, with four heralds and two trumpeters, climbed the little winding stair to the platform, above the heads of the crowd. And there, as uncomfortably cramped as were their hearers below, the trumpeters took over from the drummers who had rat-a-tatted continuously hitherto, and blew a long and blaring fanfare.

Provost William Dick, one of the wealthiest merchants in the land, raised his hand. 'My lords, masters, citizens and burghers,' he shouted, 'as chief magistrate of this city, I require that you give ear and respectful hearing to the most honoured Lord Lyon King of Arms, who speaks by order of the King's Grace.'

One or two witticisms greeted this, for the Provost had a slight impediment in his speech which turned his Rs into Ws. But the trumpets soon cut that short.

Sir James Balfour of Denmiln and Kinnaird unrolled his parchments, and in a high clear voice, began :

'In the name of Charles, by the grace of God, King – hear me. It is hereby declared, ordained and decreed, that . . .'

He got no further. A great sigh rose from the assembled multitude, grew into a murmur, a groan that increased and began to change into an ominous growling. Shouts began to punctuate this heavy, angry sound – but they were in the main the shouts of the ministers calling for quiet, for attention, a decent respect, some of the nobility joining in. Gradually they were heeded, and an uneasy hush prevailed again.

Sir James Balfour, with an anxious frown, tried again. He got a little further, this time, managing to read the royal preamble. But when he proclaimed that the King took fullest and personal responsibility for the introduction of the new Liturgy, the murmuring began once more. Raising his voice, the Lord Lyon announced that King Charles could not possibly discuss or debate such matters within his own divine right and prerogative. Desperately, as the noise swelled, Balfour shouted the provisions that all petitioners and indeed all strangers, must disperse and leave Edinburgh forthwith, under pain not only of his royal displeasure but under all the penalties of treason. Loud, deep and steady was now the outcry from thousands of throats. Clearly no efforts of the ministers were going to have any effect now.

Montrose, whose handsome features had been growing more and more set, turned to Napier. 'They will never hear him now,' he jerked. 'We must get Balfour away. We cannot have the Lyon rabbled – the King's spokesman. Henderson, and the other ministers, swore that they could control the crowd. This is damnable . . . !'

'What did you expect?' That was Rothes, at his other side. 'The temper o' this realm will not suffer talk the likes o' that, now. Not this day.'

'We must demonstrate the authority, the moderation, of

the Tables,' the younger man insisted. 'If I could get up there . . .' He gestured towards the Cross platform. But it was closely surrounded by the thick cordon of the Town Guard, who were most obviously under orders to let no one through.

'Thank God – Balfour is getting out !' Napier exclaimed. 'See, he is folding up his papers.'

Clearly, the Lord Lyon saw the uselessness of continuing – and he was not the man to provoke any more trouble than he must. He signed to his trumpeters, and they blew a final and somewhat ragged flourish. He turned and pushed his way down the stairway.

The triumphant cheers of the crowd swelled and maintained. So soon as the trumpets sounded for the last time, there was a stir fairly close to the Cross, upstreet – nearer to Montrose's own stance, indeed. Here there was another sort of platform, semi-permanent, of timber, on which the scaffold was erected for executions. It had been brought out today, but its top kept clear. Up on to this now clambered four men, the Earl of Loudoun, Sir George Stirling of Keir, Master Alexander Henderson and Archibald Johnston of Warriston, lawyer – the conveners of the Tables. The latter was waving a large paper.

Gradually the noise subsided.

'Thank God !' James Graham murmured. 'Now – let us hope Warriston keeps his head. And tongue ! He is scarce the wisest choice . . . !'

Archibald Johnston, laird of the small property of Warriston, north of Edinburgh, looked indeed an unlikely choice to be spokesman of the combined Tables of Scotland's Convention. Young – exactly Montrose's own age of 25 – he was slight, painfully thin, stooping, pale, with long, lank black hair and burning eyes, a born fanatic if ever there was one. His was a strange character, nervously intense, utterly unconcerned with time – he was said to remain on his knees in prayer all many a night, for as long as fourteen hours at a stretch – immoderate, uncaring of the opinions of others. Yet he had a brilliant mind, a great legal knowledge, and a phenomenal grasp of detail, together with a fiery eloquence which tended to spare others no more than himself. An advocate, already he was renowned at the bar – though little liked. He had been chosen spokesman today as representing the city of Edinburgh on the Table of the Burghs, and as one of the actual compilers of the wording of the new Covenant – which Covenant indeed he was here to declare. Montrose had been almost the least certain as to the wisdom of his appointment.

Warriston raised his hand for silence – and strangely enough got it quite quickly. Despite his meagre frame he had a commanding presence of a sort, and a deep, resonant voice which carried infinitely better than either the Lyon's or the Provost's.

'My friends,' he cried, 'good folk – you have heard the voice of power and majesty. Aye, and the voice of error and shame, likewise! Even though it be in the King's name. I say to you, that yon was not in truth the voice of Charles Stewart, the King's Grace, that you heard. But the voice of the man Laud, and his minion Juxon, English apostate clerks, knaves, reprobates who . . .'

A great roar of approval drowned his words.

When he could, he went on, drawn features working. 'Not only Laud and his English jackals mislead the King. For their own shameless ends, Scots prelatical dogs do likewise. Spottiswoode, Wedderburn, Maxwell, Sydserf! Renegade Papists, idolators, chamberlains of Satan, the worse in that they are of our own nation, betraying their fellows and the blessed reformed faith, worshippers of Baal . . .'

'I feared it!' Montrose groaned. 'The man cannot contain himself. He is drunken on his own words! I told them. I told *him* . . . !' He raised his arm high. 'If I could but catch his eye. Calm him . . .'

But in the press no man's hand was going to be seen by any other. Montrose started to push his way nearer to the scaffold-platform.

'You'll no' get near him,' Rothes declared.

He was right. The younger man made but little headway. But, of all things to be there in the middle of the High Street, was an upended barrel. How and why it came to be there was a mystery. But, stumbling over it, and cursing it as so many another had done, Montrose perceived that it might serve his turn. He climbed up on to its less than stable top – while Rothes, at his back, held it, and him, steady.

'Man, James,' he chuckled, 'who'd ha' thought to see *Greumach Mor* hoisted on a barrel! Watch you – or you'll no' be at rest till you are lifted up above the rest o' us on three fathoms o' a rope!'

James Graham did not heed that sally. He was only about twenty yards from Warriston now; and, raised above his fellows thus, the other could not fail to see him – or the warning, minatory finger. The orator faltered just a little in his diatribe.

Warriston's hesitation and glance drew the attention of others to Montrose, of course. But, strangely enough, the crowd misconstrued, assuming that the great Earl of Montrose was so carried away with enthusiasm for all this eloquence that he must needs show it thus. He earned a cheer for himself, in consequence, and popular approval as the first of the high nobility to make plain his position.

His gesture, however, was not ineffectual. Warriston recollected, and thereafter applied himself to his brief. This was to summarise in digestible form the contents of the National Covenant which they had prepared, to use it as a counterblast to the royal proclamation, and to intimate that it would be set out on parchments and ready for comprehensive signature in a day or two's time.

In great, ringing tones he proclaimed the kernel of the Negative Confession against Popery, of 1581, heady, denunciatory stuff which, since it had been signed by Charles's own father, James the Sixth, made it a safe basis for this new manifesto, declaring that, as a confession of faith, they and all true Christian men did condemn the monuments of bygone idolatry.

That went down well.

The second part of the Covenant listed all the Acts of the Scots Parliament passed since the Reformation to protect and support the true faith and Presbyterian form of worship – all again signed by King James and even one or two, reluctantly, by Charles himself in his first years on the throne. These would have made but dull reciting to a crowd; but Warriston managed to summarise some of them effectively, and to emphasise that these, and only these, were in fact the law of the land, and as such must be upheld by all loyal and law-abiding subjects.

It was skilfully done, and had the effect of leaving the hearers in no doubt, not only that their course was right and lawful, but that by setting at naught and controverting the expressed provisions of parliament, the King was in fact breaking the law as well as his own coronation oaths, and betraying his father's memory equally with his realm's integrity. Even Montrose was moved to applaud.

The third and final section of the Covenant was an affirmation of loyalty.

'We, noblemen, barons, gentlemen, burgesses, ministers and commons,' he intoned slowly, distinctly, 'considering the dangers to the true religion, to the King's honour, and to the public peace, by the manifold innovations and evils contained in our late supplications, complaints and protestations, do hereby profess before God, His holy angels and the whole world, that we shall constantly adhere to and defend the aforesaid true religion, and forebear from the practice of all innovations introduced into the worship of the Lord God. Aye, and to labour by all means in our power lawfully to recover the purity and liberty of the Gospel as it was established. Also, to stand to the defence of our dread sovereign, the King's Majesty, his person and authority, as we do the laws of his kingdom. This we, the undersubscribing, promise and swear by the great name of the Lord God, that religion and righteousness may flourish in the land, to the glory of God, the honour of the King, and the peace and comfort of us all.'

Warriston paused, looked over at Montrose, and in a different and much less dramatic voice added, almost expressionlessly, 'God save the King's Grace.'

Considering the turgid nature of his material, and the fact that it was written to be read, not spoken, even the speaker must have been surprised by the enthusiasm of its reception. Men cheered, waved and capered, women skirled and clasped each other, bonnets were thrown into the air. Perhaps only the Scots, with their love of metaphysics, rhetoric and wordy debate, could have worked themselves up to such pitch over the like. With even Montrose cheering, Warriston stood back, trembling.

The Earl of Loudoun took his place, briefly, to announce that the said National Covenant would be transcribed on parchment and brought for signature to the kirkyard of the Greyfriars, here in Edinburgh, in four days' time, when this great step forward would be taken in the work of God and of the King's realm of Scotland.

*   *   *

So, the following Wednesday, the 28th, since no hall or building was large enough to contain all the people who must assemble for the occasion, the National Covenant of 1638 was subscribed and signed in the extensive graveyard of Greyfriars Church, which crowned the hill above the valley of the Cowgate to the south. The crowd was not quite so dense as that at the Cross, for guards at the gate could here keep out the mere spectators and gapers, indeed the ordinary citizens who could contribute nothing to *this* day's work, being in the main unable anyway to read or write. For all that, there were fully a thousand present, come to subscribe this dread bond and affirmation, signature of which might indeed place a noose around their necks – for none could fail to recognise that this document and declaration ran directly counter to the recent royal proclamation, with its explicit threats of treason. Whoever signed this Covenant, at least would not do so lightly. Nevertheless, not a few children had been brought to Greyfriars that day, to see the making of what could not fail to be history.

Henderson set the tone and tenor of the proceedings by mounting one of the many flat table-stones of the graveyard and calling the great company to prayer in loud and ringing voice. Head thrown back, fine eyes alight, fists clenched and often upraised to heaven, he not so much entreated and besought his Maker as assailed Him in the name of their mutual and sacred cause and duty. Harshly powerful, his words direct, unfaltering, his sincerity undeniable, he committed the Lord God to the side of liberty, justice and Presbyterianism, at length and in detail. After this, the very angels of light might not mistake.

Then John Campbell, Earl of Loudoun, mounted the gravestone, even as the Amens rang out vehemently, seeking to cut them short. He was, however, no orator, and before he was finished folk were chatting amongst themselves and tending to move around to keep warm. Frowning, the earl wound up prematurely by calling upon all present to append their names to the document – and then, at a tug from Warriston, recollected, and added that before they could honestly do so, of course, they must hear its terms, all its terms. At a slight groan from those who could hear, he commanded Archibald Johnston of Warriston to read the Covenant through.

The young advocate put things to right, despite the bad start, the chill draughts of the place, and the tendency of his hearers to stamp on the grass, rub and even blow on their hands. Once again his histrionic abilities were brought dramatically into play, and what could have been a rather dull, wordy and repetitious disquisition, despite its undoubted noble sentiments and sincerity, became a clarion call, a resounding testimony of a nation's love of freedom, a cause to die for it need be. So carried away by emotion became this strange orator, as he went on, that sometimes tears coursed unheeded down his sallow cheeks, his voice choked, and there were agonising pauses when it seemed that he could not go on. Montrose, to whom this sort of thing was totally alien and embarrassing, was astonished to perceive that, instead of putting people off, and making the occasion something of a charade, this treatment was in fact arousing the company to a high pitch of almost febrile enthusiasm. The pauses and gulping silences seemed only to enhance the tension. And cold was forgotten.

A voice murmured in the Graham's ear. 'Now you will perceive what we, in the courts, must needs contend with! There is a chiel who will have my office, if he can!'

It was Sir Thomas Hope, at Montrose's back, wrapped in a fur robe and sober black.

'How honest is he, think you? Is this play-acting? Or sincerity?'

'Oh, he is sincere enough, I think. Though, i' faith, I believe that I would prefer that he was not! A man so moved to hot feeling, as this, could endanger any cause. If allowed high place. And Warriston will not be content with lowly. But . . . he will get your Covenant signed for you, this day. Mark my words!'

Yet, despite his words, and despite the ringing, almost hysterical acclaim which greeted the end of the reading, when Loudoun, like a douche of cold water, curtly demanded signatures, the great crowded kirkyard was abruptly stricken with immobility. A silence descended. No single man stepped forward to be the first to sign this noble and applauded document. It was as though sudden realisation had dawned that this, however splendid, would most certainly be branded by the King and the Privy Council as a highly treasonable statement, and expressly contrary to the royal command.

'Does the Graham not lead in this?' came quietly at Montrose's shoulder, as none volunteered.

'Gladly,' the younger man said. 'But surely it is for Rothes to be first? Or yourself, sir? On whose advice this was drawn up.'

'Na, na – Tom Hope signing that paper could no longer remain King's Advocate, man. I will serve your cause better in that office than by writing my name yonder.'

'Perhaps. But Rothes . . . ?' Montrose looked over at that man enquiringly.

Rothes smiled, almost mockingly, but shook his head. 'After you, James,' he chuckled. 'If needs I must!'

'Very well.' Raising his voice, James Graham called strongly, 'Give me the pen, my lord.'

A great sigh arose from the company.

Taken from Warriston the large parchment was spread out flat on top of another table-stone by Archibald Henderson and Andrew Cant. Taking the quill from Loudoun, dipping it in the portable ink-horn, James Graham strode forward and, bending low, wrote the word Montrose bold and clear, just below the end of the statement, at the left-hand side.

'Praise God! And bless you, my lord,' gravely good-looking Andrew Cant said quietly, at his side. 'Scotland could ever rely on the Graham! Where you lead, a whole realm will follow.'

Doubtfully the younger man shook his head, straightening up. 'I fear, sir, that you expect too much of me.' But there was no doubt about him when Loudoun made to take the quill from his fingers. 'Wait you, my lord,' he said. He turned, and held the pen out to Rothes.

That squat man wagged his head ruefully. 'You are a hard man, James,' he complained. 'The Graham's head Charles Stewart might think twice to chop. But Johnnie Leslie's he'd have off like a thrissle's! His Grace has never loved me.' Nevertheless, he took the quill and signed, a notably crabbed, small signature for so extrovert a man, squeezed in to the left of the other, where there was scarcely room anyway – an odd choice when there was a whole sheet to choose from. Montrose looked at the older man thoughtfully.

After these two, there was no longer any holding back – save in the matter of due precedence. Since two earls had signed first, it was accepted that the other earls should come next. Cassillis, Home, Lothian, Wemyss and Loudoun set down their names in quick succession. The lords followed, Yester, Boyd, Elcho – Wemyss's son – Lindsay, Melville and Balmerino. Archie Napier did not sign, pointing out like Hope, that if he did so, he could scarcely remain a member of the Privy Council; and his membership there might yet be of more value to the cause than his signature on a paper. The long queue of the lesser barons and lairds was now forming up, in turn. This business obviously was going to take a long time.

'There is one face missing here, today, that I'd looked to see,' Sir Thomas Hope said, as they stood watching the long line of signatories. 'Where is Archibald Campbell?'

'Why should he be here? He has shown no least interest, attended no meetings.'

'There are more ways of showing interest than by attending meetings, my lord. My information is that my lord of Lorne is exceeding interested. Word of everything that is said and done is carried to him forthwith. Hot-foot, indeed. I vow that he will know by the morn's morn who first put pen to that paper.'

'Not in far-away Argyll, surely ... ?'

'He is not in Argyll. These last weeks he has been at Castle Campbell, near Dollar. Not ten miles across the Ochils from your own house of Kincardine. Do not say that you did not know it! *MacCailean Mor* and *An Greumach Mor* sitting cheek by jowl in the Ochils. Do not tell me this is news to you, my lord!'

Montrose frowned. 'I have not been staying at Kincardine. My wife is at her father's house of Kinnaird I ...' He paused. 'Archibald Campbell is not yet *MacCailean Mor*,' he said, in a different voice.

'To all intents he is. His feckless father disgraced, turned rabid Catholic in his dotage, indulging in foolish plots and banished Scotland. By decree the Lord Lorne has been given – or has acquired – all his father's powers, the management of the largest lands in this realm and complete control of

Clan Campbell. He is *MacCailean Mor* in everything but name. He is only a step from being the powerfullest man in Scotland.'

'Mm.'

'Did you expect him here today, Tom?' Napier asked.

'I conceived that he could not afford to stay away! I was wrong, it appears.'

'I do not take you, sir,' Montrose said. 'What has the Campbell to gain here? All here put their necks at risk, but stand to gain nothing. Save perhaps some peace in their souls! What is here for the Campbell?'

'What but the leadership and power in this land?' the Lord Advocate replied. 'Since it lost its kings to London, Scotland has lacked its leadership. The Campbell will lead in Scotland, if he may. And this cause and bond, this Covenant, could give him – or another – that leadership. If played aright.' And he looked directly at the younger man.

'I have said, and still I say, that *I* do not seek such position,' Montrose declared flatly, almost doggedly.

'You cannot deny your birthright, my lord. Any more than can Archibald Campbell. I think that you would not wish to see *him* ruling in Scotland?'

The other was silent.

'It is my belief that Lorne but waits his chance. To take this cause into his own two hands. Then use it to rule Scotland.' Hope paused. 'And, who knows, Scotland might do worse! For a strong hand, any strong hand, could be better than no hand at all. Or a thousand weak ones!'

James Graham chewed on that for a while, as he was meant to do. 'I do not say that I accept that,' he observed, at length, watching Douglas of Cavers, Sheriff of Teviotdale, append his signature. 'But . . . Campbell has done nothing. For this Covenant. Even though, as you say, he may be interested, watchful, he has done nothing, taken no part. Not even come to sign it. How can you think that he intends to use it?'

'He would not sign it for the same reason that I do not,' Napier said. 'He is a member of the Privy Council, likewise. Made so, though young, while you were abroad, James. He would cling to that position, meantime, I have no doubt.'

'Exactly,' Hope agreed. 'Archie Campbell is exceeding godly, for a man of his years – the more so since his father married again and turned Papist. I know no sterner Presbyterian in the land! He will, *must* approve this cause. But he is a clever man, something of a fox. And will prefer, if fingers are to be burned while lighting this fire, that it should be other fingers than his own. When he is assured of your success – then he will step in. And as Privy Councillor, Justiciar of Argyll and Chief of Clan Campbell, his step will be no light one!'

'And if we are less than successful?'

'Then he will prove to be the King's man, after all, his name unsoiled. He will have sought to save Scotland for Charles. And so gain the rule over it from a grateful monarch. So – he bides his time.'

'I think, sir, that you do not like Archibald Campbell any more than do I!' Montrose said slowly.

'Like? Liking, my lord, who or what, is nothing to the case. I am not concerned with likes and dislikes, but with facts. I conceive that it is my duty to contrive that the rule of law prevails in this realm, in the best measure possible. For that I need a strong hand at the helm – else there is chaos, as now. That I should like that hand is not necessary.'

'And you have chosen to push me towards that leadership? However lacking in strength *my* hand!'

Thinly, Hope smiled. 'The choice, my lord, is . . . limited,' he said, and turned away.

They were still signing that parchment, by the light of torches, at eight o'clock that February night.

8

THE JUNE MORNING WAS LOUD WITH THE TRILLING OF LARKS in the blue, the humming of bees in the gorse and broom, the calling of cuckoos from the thorn scrub – and the singing of James Graham, Earl of Montrose. For this man, in the right company, with stirring works to do – especially in the saddle and not cooped up indoors in long-winded talk – was a totally different character, blithe, genial, frank and relaxed, a most excellent companion. And today, the 7th of June, riding south-westwards from Edinburgh's Burgh Muir, on the Pentlands road that led eventually to Lanark, he had all these conditions in his favour. It was action of a sort, at least, after all the talking, wherein he was his own man, and in his own kind of good company – very much his own. In fact 120 mounted and armed Stirlingshire and Strathearn Grahams, under Black Pate Graham of Inchbrakie. So, broad-brimmed, plumed cavalier hat hanging at his saddle-bow, long curling chestnut hair blowing in the breeze, he sang in a rich and tuneful tenor; and Inchbrakie at his side, a swarthy, ruggedly good-looking man a year older than himself, and probably his closest friend, chimed in with a deep husky bass, here and there, when he could catch the lilts of the strange foreign airs his chief had brought home from his travels. A little way behind, in fairly tight formation, the Graham troopers laughed and chattered as they trotted, a cheerful, gallant company. Nevertheless, all except the two leaders wore jacks, or breastplates of steel, and morion-type helmets, their lance-tips glittering in the sunshine.

'The banner, James?' Black Pate mentioned, at an interval between songs. He used the Christian name when they were alone together, but was meticulous with his honorific and lordings when others could hear. 'Having brought it, should you not have it flying?'

'Time enough, Pate, when we see them, for the play-acting. That banner has been hanging in my father's hall too long, unused. Scotland has been no place for banners this century of our Lord! I fear that it will split from its staff at a blow of wind! And how would Graham look then? We must needs have a new one, if there is to be much of this.'

'I will set my wife to work on it,' the other said, tactfully not suggesting that the Lady Magdalen should have the task. 'It comes to me that we may need it.' Inchbrakie sounded as though he hoped, rather than feared it.

Consciously repressing the spirit that hoped likewise, Montrose shrugged. 'Let us pray otherwise.' He deceived nobody.

'It is barely an hour to noon,' his friend said. 'Where do you look to meet Hamilton?'

'Who knows, with that man? He passed the night at Carn-wath. Hamilton is of a sluggish temper, I think. Myself, I'd have been in Edinburgh by this. But the Marquis may like his bed of a morning. We may look for him anywhere between here and Cairns Castle. Unless we meet a messenger from the minister of Carnwath first!'

The Covenanters, as they were beginning to call them-selves, were in the happy position of finding themselves exceedingly well-informed as to what went on, at least in the Lowlands of Scotland. This because the country was divided up into innumerable parishes, and in each there was a parish church whose incumbent was, in nine cases out of ten, a whole-hearted supporter of their cause. So that nothing of importance could happen in any corner of the land without some keen-eyed divine sending the Tables in Edin-burgh word hot-foot – a great convenience. It had certainly proved so in this instance. The Marquis of Hamilton's doings had been followed and chronicled, step by step, since he crossed the Border in late May. And with particular interest.

For this was King Charles's answer. He had sent up a royal commissioner to Scotland, ostensibly to enquire on the spot into complaints and problems; but in fact, as was sufficiently well known, to gain time. When the Covenant, signed eventually all over Scotland, had been sent to him, the King's first reaction had been righteous and sorrowful wrath. Then he had sent to Scotland for certain advisers to come and inform him as to what was wrong with his Scots people. Charles was never good at choosing men, clearly no judge of character; and on this occasion, allegedly on Hamil-ton's advice, he had sent for those who would give him the kind of advice he desired – Traquair, Roxburgh, Spottis-woode and a parcel of bishops. But one summons surprised Scotland – Archibald Campbell, Lord Lorne. What made Charles so choose, and what Lorne told the King, were equally uncertain; but the Campbell came back from Lon-don, his thin lips shut like a clam. And presently a temp-orising missive followed, from the King, making certain minor concessions about the prayer-book and the law courts, but demanding the immediate withdrawal and denunciation of the Covenant itself. Also the announcement that a royal commissioner would be sent up in due course, to hear all views and deliver a proclamation to the King's local Scots subjects. It was all a much more reasonable and hopeful reaction than had been feared – were it not for the warnings of spies at Court, who declared unanimously that Charles was only playing for time, while he settled his differences with his English parliament with whom he was at loggerheads over the Ship Money issue and other questions; and a later warning that it was the Marquis of Hamilton who was on his way north, as Commissioner and that he was in fact bearing two proclamations, one of a very different tone from the other, these to be read as the circumstances indicated. Clearly Charles Stewart was still a force to be reckoned with.

His Commissioner had certainly borne out the spies' warnings, as to devious behaviour. Instead of making directly for Edinburgh, to see the people with whom he was to treat, he had swung off westwards at the Border and headed for Lanarkshire and his own territory of Hamilton. And there he had lingered for a week. But not altogether idly. The word was that he was gathering men, armed men, from his great estates. Presumably he wished to argue from strength, while in Edinburgh, in the time-honoured Scots fashion, with a fighting tail behind him.

But at Hamilton the Marquis discovered what is apt to happen to even great lords when they desert their lands and show no interest in their estates save as a source of rents. All accounts agreed that he had had the utmost difficulty in raising any sort of force. And the most reliable estimates had it that all he had managed to collect was less than a hundred exceedingly reluctant warriors. With these he apparently intended to descend upon the capital. No doubt there were plans for reinforcements to come in from elsewhere, for there were reports of musterings in other parts of the country.

It was a difficult situation for the Tables. Save for its hotheads, the last thing that the Covenanters wanted was to be the first to resort to armed force. And any attack on the King's Commissioner would be most patent treason and revolt. On the other hand, to allow an armed company of any size into the capital, especially one which could, in the King's name, demand the allegiance of the Town Guard, was a grave danger. Arrest and imprisonment for most of the principal signatories of the Covenant would be only the first almost certain result.

So Montrose, who could most swiftly whistle up a sizeable force of men, had been asked to handle the matter. Nothing could have pleased him better, in the circumstances. He sent for Black Pate.

They rode, then, jingling over the long, green Pentland hillfoots, as though with not a care in the world, scattering sheep and stirks, laughing, waving to the country folk, Montrose himself setting the tone and tenor. He had accounts to settle with James Hamilton.

They were near Malleny, and threading open thorn-scrub woodland, when keen eyes spotted, far ahead, the glint of sunlight on steel. This quickly developed into a long, strung-out file of horsemen, crossing the moorland beyond, not in any tight formation like the Grahams but straggling, scattered.

'So-o-o!' Inchbrakie commented, eyes narrowed. 'Would we could make an ambush of it! We could roll them up like babes in a plaid!'

'Would you, a leal subject, ambush His Grace's High Commissioner? Shame on you, Pate!'

Nevertheless, quarter of a mile on, where the woodland grew thicker with ash and birch mixed, Montrose reined up. 'We will wait here a-while,' he declared. 'Why ride on when we must then come back?'

'Aye.' The other grinned. 'You'll no' want the men dismounted though, I take it?'

'It is scarce worth it,' his chief agreed, glancing assessingly about him. 'See – a score of men down each side of this track. Each one length apart. Facing inwards. And lances couched. The rest drawn up in close ranks, ten abreast. Still facing west. That should serve.' Although his tone was entirely conversational and unhurried, there was somewhere at the back of it the ring of sure, almost joyous command.

With a short bark of a laugh, Inchbrakie began to marshal his men into the required hollow-square formation, closing and flanking the track, which here bent away through the woodland beyond, out of sight. The word was passed for complete quiet.

So when, after a longer wait than most anticipated, the Marquis of Hamilton and the first of his company came trotting round the corner, it was to find themselves abruptly confronted, and their way barred, by a solid phalanx of disciplined, armed and silent men, in such a position that there was no turning sideways either. There was a great pulling up and reining in of horses, with outcry and alarm – and consequent confusion behind, round the bend where the oncomers could see nothing of what went on. Chaos reigned on one side, utter and steely calm on the other.

Montrose, however, was anything but steely. He rode forward from the open front of his square, sweeping off the hat he had re-donned in a complicated flourish, his bow from the saddle profound, his smile all-embracing. A half-length behind Black Pate followed, the now unfurled Graham standard fluttering above him.

'Welcome, my lord Marquis! Welcome, in the name of the Convention of the Estates of Scotland! I am desolated that we could not express our welcome earlier. But we looked for the King's Commissioner at the Border – not coming from Lanarkshire!'

'What . . . what a God's name is this!' Hamilton exclaimed, dividing his alarmed glance equally between front and rear, and obtaining reassurance in neither direction. He was no coward – indeed he had been decorated for leading cavalry charges in the Swedish wars of Gustavus – but this sort of situation was enough to upset the most phlegmatic. 'Montrose – I say what is this?'

'What but a greeting, my lord? As *I* say. A respectful greeting for the King's Royal Commissioner – if belated. I have the honour to be sent by the Joint Tables of the Convention, to bid you welcome to Scotland, and to escort you to Edinburgh in fitting style. Er . . . God save the King.'

Like a sudden clap of thunder the 120 voices behind him rapped out a staccato 'God save the King,' and as abruptly resumed silent immobility. Hamilton jumped, rather prominent blue eyes popping.

'I . . . ah . . . devil take me! I need no escort of yours, Montrose!' The Marquis, though less exquisite than on the last occasion Montrose had seen him, was still overdressed for the road, in velvet, lace, ribbons and jewellery.

'Look on this not as mine, my lord, but as the Convention's. And now yours. At your service.'

Hamilton's own people were now crowding round the bend behind him. There was, of course, insufficient room for them, what with the trees and the stern ranks of flanking troopers. The confusion grew worse every moment. In the face of the solid, motionless, lance-couched ranks in front, the newcomers made a sorry sight.

'I require no such service,' the Marquis, recovering himself somewhat now, declared. 'And certainly not from the King's enemies.'

'The King has scarce an enemy in all Scotland,' the younger man assured him. 'I hope that it was the King's *friends* that you came to speak with, my lord?'

The other coughed.

'See, sir – here is my kinsman Inchbrakie, as loyal a subject as His Grace possesses in all his realm.'

Black Pate genuflected elaborately. 'Your servant, my lord Marquis. We have been much concerned for you.'

'I know not why, sir.'

'We heard, with joy, that your lordship was approaching the Border, eight days past,' he said, grave-faced. 'Bringing His Grace's royal proclamation to Edinburgh. Then, neither hint nor hair of you, all these days! Can you wonder at our fears for you? All Edinburgh, all Scotland, in a stir? The King's Commissioner amissing. And the King's proclamation likewise. They feared that the wild English had got you. Their Border thieves are notable rascals.' Black Pate Graham was one of the toughest characters in Perthshire. His heartfelt anxiety, mixed with reproach, for the Marquis, had to be heard to be believed.

Hamilton heard but scarcely believed. He cleared his throat. 'Not so,' he said. 'I regret any concern. But . . . private matters demanded my attention. At Hamilton. My estates. It was necessary.' Realising, perhaps, that this might sound rather like an apology – and to a mere Graham laird – he turned again on Montrose. 'You might have spared yourself your trouble, my lord. In coming to meet me,' he added thinly.

'Trouble nothing. It is all satisfaction, I assure you,' the other declared handsomely. 'After all, it is long since I had the pleasure of sight of you. It was at the Palace of Whitehall, was it not? One night two years back? When you made my poor presence known to the King's Grace!'

The Marquis looked away, frowning. 'It was unfortunate,' he said. 'The King was . . . was less than himself, that night. Of a dark humour.'

'To be sure. Distressing. I saw your lordship doing all in your power to guide him in the matter. Your great influence with His Grace is known to all. I do not forget your efforts that night!'

Hamilton, it was clear, had had enough of the subject. And of the entire encounter. 'No doubt,' he said shortly. 'And now, Montrose, if you will move your men aside, I will continue on my way to Edinburgh.'

'As you wish.' Montrose nodded to Black Pate, who raised a hand to the square of watching Graham troopers. Obedient to the signal, they moved.

It was not really a complicated manoeuvre. The two flanking lines merely turned to face forwards instead of inwards, on their previous courses, westwards; while the solid phalanx at the end of the box opened into two sections in their turn, but reined round to face the other way, eastwards. As Montrose urged Hamilton on, the former flanking files swung in quickly, determinedly, at his back – so that, save for two gentlemen attendants and one groom, the Marquis was cut off from his long and confused tail of supporters.

'Forward!' James Graham called. And, pleasantly, to Hamilton. 'On to Edinburgh, my lord.'

The tight-knit company of 120, closely surrounding the two noblemen, set off at a swift jingling trot, eastwards.

'But – s'wounds, man – how dare you! Stop! Halt, I say!' Pressed on from behind by forty horsemen, the Commissioner – or, at least, his horse – had no option but to move forward with the rest. 'What is this? Stop! I command it.'

'We must escort you to Edinburgh. As we were commanded. And as your lordship just declared. That is why we came. A guard of honour.'

'I have my own escort.'

'Our sorrow that you were forced to the trouble of providing it, sir. Now all is well. Send them home, my lord Marquis.'

'No! This is outrage! Would . . . would you lay hands on the King's Commissioner?'

'Lay hands . . . ? Save us – outrage? You jest, my lord – that is it, you jest! We provide most sure and heedful escort, never fear. An hour, little more, and you will be in Holyroodhouse. All is prepared for your comfort.'

In some agitation, Hamilton looked behind. He could not

see very well, for the forty Grahams; but it was clear enough that no attempt was being made, or likely to be made, by his leaderless and bewildered company, to rescue him. In no particular formation, they were beginning to trot along behind, uncertainly, no trouble to anyone.

'This is beyond all!' the Marquis complained. But obviously there was nothing that he could usefully do about it.

'How does His Grace?' Montrose enquired conversationally. 'We hear much of his policies but little of his royal self. He is well?'

The other, staring about him, did not vouchsafe an answer.

'It is this realm's sorrow that we do not see more of him. Much would be gained in understanding and affection, were he to visit Scotland more frequently. Tell His Grace so, my lord, when you return. This is his own true realm, as England never can be. As it is yours! It will repay closer attention, I swear.'

The Marquis's grunt was eloquent.

Montrose did not permit himself to be silenced. In the best of good-humour he chatted as they trotted on, asking questions, making points, offering advice, a man totally at ease and in control. His victim, although he did not co-operate, could not but listen and seem to consider, however stiff his back, hemmed in closely as he was.

Pate Graham presently rode up. 'Your men are straggling badly, my lord,' he reported. 'Some are a mile behind. Their part is done. Have I your authority to order that they return to Lanark? To Hamilton?'

'No!'

'There is no accommodation for them at Holyroodhouse,' Inchbrakie went on imperturbably. 'Fodder and stabling will be hard to come by, in a city already full to overflowing for your lordship's visit. And these will serve no useful purpose there.'

'My lord Marquis knows best what to do with his people, Pate,' Montrose observed judicially. 'Perhaps he will quarter them at Colinton. Or at Dalkeith. Or at Salt Preston. Since Edinburgh is so full. Costly – but his lordship is a man of great means, we know. Care no more for it.'

'As you will, my lord. Although – these towns you name

are already crowded also. Haddington, perhaps – but it is half a day's ride from Edinburgh . . .'

Hamilton, who was notoriously unwilling to spend money, save on his personal adornment, was looking ever more unhappy. He kept glancing behind him, but gaining no comfort.

'Do not concern yourself,' Montrose told him. 'A deep purse covers much. They will do very well at Haddington. Or Linlithgow, perhaps. And you could dismount them. Quarter the men in one place and the horses another. Inconvenient, but . . .'

'I am on the King's business, sir. My men will be quartered at the King's expense. Or the realm's,' the Marquis interrupted.

'Ah. How fortunate. Does the Privy Council know it? My lord of Traquair, the Treasurer, is in London, as you know. And my good-brother, Napier, of that Council, still acts Deputy Treasurer when need be. Any payment would have to be passed by him. But . . . I will have a word with him, my lord. Be assured.'

After a few silent moments the Marquis turned in his saddle and called to one of his gentlemen behind. 'Craignethan – send the men back to Hamilton,' he snapped.

'As to your own quarters in Holyroodhouse, my lord, you should be entirely comfortable,' James Graham went on pleasantly. 'My lord Rothes has seen to that. You know Rothes, of course . . . ?'

Since Rothes and Hamilton had been deadly enemies for many years, that was another conversational gambit which fell flat instead of lightening the road to Edinburgh.

In James the Fourth's grey old palace of Holyroodhouse at the foot of Edinburgh's Canongate, James Hamilton sought to play the king, in a tentative, exploratory fashion. There were some who held that his haughty and unbending manner was not just a natural arrogance but was rehearsal for the future : that in the event of Charles Stewart losing his life, or his throne, he, Hamilton, would claim it. For he was, indeed, of royal descent, being great-grandson of that Regent Arran and Duke of Chastelherault who had long been heir to the throne during the minority of Charles's father, remotely descended from James the Second. Some even went so far as to suggest that his misleading of the King in the matter of advice, was calculated, so as to cost Charles the throne of Scotland which he himself would better fill. While this last was probably nonsense, Hamilton was clearly inordinately proud of his royal blood, and found regal posturings much to his taste.

When he was ready, the King's Commissioner commanded that representatives of the Tables appear before him, to answer questions. He would have no crowd descend upon him, however, and ordered that three nobles and three ministers come as deputation. Loudoun, Rothes and Montrose were chosen, with the Reverends Henderson, Dickson and Cant. Johnston of Warriston accompanied them, but only as clerk and legal adviser.

They were received with stiff condescension and formality – reciprocated by the ministers and Loudoun, although Rothes was all mocking whimsy and Montrose imperturbably genial. They were conducted to the throne-room on the first floor, where they were kept waiting for the best part of half an hour, until Hamilton, extravagantly magnificent in the cloak and ribbon of the Garter, over pale blue satin, despite the summer warmth, stalked in, accompanied by Archbishop Spottiswoode, Bishop Lindsay, the Marquis of Douglas – married to a Hamilton – the Earl of Abercorn, another Hamilton, the Earl of Roxburgh, and the Lord Ruthven. There were no greetings. Hamilton paced to the throne, scarcely glancing at the waiting group, waved his supporters to stand on either side of him – but slightly behind – and sat down, carefully arranging his splendid starred cloak to drape around him. No word was spoken.

Loudoun cleared his throat. As Convener of the Joint Tables, he ostensibly led the delegation. 'My lord Marquis,' he jerked, 'on behalf of the Convention of the Estates of Scotland, I offer you greeting and salutation.'

'I thank you,' the other replied shortly. 'It is customary for the King's representative and Commissioner, acting in the King's place, to be addressed as Your Grace.'

'Hm.' Loudoun glanced at his colleagues doubtfully, put right off his not very certain stride.

That was how Hamilton wanted it. This was *his* audience. 'His Majesty has sent me to investigate the state of disaffection and insurrection in this his realm, and the causes of it,' he declared flatly. 'And to recommend what action is required.' He repeated the word action, a shade ominously. 'His Majesty is much distressed by all the ill conduct which prevails today in Scotland, and especially by the contumely of those who signed the treasonable and threatening Band called the Covenant. I am required to make full investigation into this matter. It is my hope that I may inform His Majesty that it is not in fact a conspiracy, but the foolish mistakes of misguided men!' The prominent pale blue Hamilton eyes surveyed them significantly. His statement had been made in an even monotone, as of a man memorising a lesson – for in fact Hamilton was little more of an orator than was Loudoun. Almost relievedly raising his voice, he added, 'You will now answer my questions.'

Loudoun grunted, but said nothing.

'My lord,' Rothes put in, 'we came to parley, to discuss, not to be inquisitioned. Did *you* came as the King's Commissioner? Or as the King's *Inquisitioner?*'

There were gasps from the throne-dais at that. Hamilton, moistening his lips, took his time to answer. 'Earl of Rothes,' he said thickly, 'if you expect response from me, address me as Grace!'

'Damned if I will!' Rothes muttered, but below his breath.

Alexander Henderson cleared his throat. 'My lords – this will serve us nothing,' he said.

Montrose took a hand. 'Marquis of Hamilton, His Grace's Commissioner,' he said cordially, 'we all rejoice to see you here as King's representative. And to congratulate you upon your appointment as Keeper of this palace of Holyroodhouse. And as such, as *both,* would pay you fullest respects. As to this matter of style and address – as you know, here in Scotland, it has always been our wont to address only the monarch in person as Grace. We seek that you will bear with us in this. In England, however, we believe that they use the term Majesty. Indeed you have used it here, yourself. Majesty presents no difficulty to our thrawn Scots tongues, as does Grace. And you, sir, in your style and magnificence, look truly majestic. I therefore, for one, have no objection to name you Majesty. If it please Your Majesty!'

If Rothes's curt intervention had aroused gasps, this amiable and mannerly contribution produced much louder ones – and not only from the dais. Everywhere men gulped, and stared. Hands rose, lace handkerchiefs fluttered. Only

Rothes looked less than shocked – indeed chuckled coarsely.

Oddly enough, most alarmed of all appeared to be the Lord High Commissioner. 'No! No!' he cried. 'Not that! A God's name, man – have a care! That is the King's alone.'

'But, Majesty – so is Grace. More so, here in Scotland . . .'

'No, sir – I will not have it. Do not say it. I command that you do not style me so. You hear?'

'As you will. You conceive Grace to be a lesser style than Majesty, then, my lord Marquis? Here, in Scotland? Would you have our kings less high, less important, than those of England?'

The other blinked. 'Not so. I said nothing such. You put words into my mouth, Montrose – ill words. I will not have it. I am the King's loyalest and humble subject.'

'As you will, my lord Marquis. As are we! So we need have no more confusion over titles and styles. And proceed amicably to our business.'

'Yes. Very well. So be it. Ah . . . hrrm . . .' It was Hamilton's turn to be put off his stride.

'We understand, my lord Commissioner,' Montrose went on quickly, smoothly, 'that His Grace intends to make certain concessions to our requests. As set forth in the petitions and the Covenant. For which we are most loyally grateful. In the matter of the prayer-book. And of the Canons. Likewise the return of the law courts to Edinburgh. Is this so? We await your lordship's announcement with interest.'

At the stir behind him, Hamilton banged on the arm of the throne, frowning. 'Not so fast! Not so fast!' he complained. 'I am here to question you – not you me! These concessions – I have said nothing of concessions. You go too fast. They are only possible. Not sure. Certain. To be granted only if I am satisfied.'

'Quite so, my lord. The concessions are conditional. But they are clear, are they not? We have heard, from sound sources, that the reading of the Liturgy in churches is to be no longer compulsory. That the Canons anent surplices, saints days and the like are relaxed. That the law courts may return from Linlithgow. These are the King's concessions?'

'Mm. They *may* be. It is possible. But only on conditions. On condition that your Covenant is given up. Abandoned. Disavowed. Only so.'

There was what amounted to a growl from the three

ministers. 'That, sir, we will in no wise do! For any concessions soever!' Alexander Henderson cried strongly.

'Never!' David Dickson agreed. 'The Covenant stands!'

'It is a treasonable document,' Hamilton asserted. 'You have risked your necks in putting your names to it. Of His Majesty's clemency he permits that you may withdraw from it. Retract. And be forgiven. It is more than you deserve, I say. But the Covenant must be withdrawn.'

'Is that your last word, my lord?' Andrew Cant asked quietly.

'It is.'

'Then we but waste our time here,' Dickson declared. 'The Lord has hardened the King's heart. This is a stiff-necked servant of a stiff-necked master! There is nothing for us here. Let us be gone, in the name of God!'

Loudoun nodded. 'On these terms it is profitless to talk. We shall bid our Commissionership a good day.'

'Wait, my friends,' Montrose intervened. 'It were as well, I think, to ascertain whose is the hard heart and the stiff neck. The master's, or the servant's? Since the master is not here.' He had not forgotten something that Hamilton had let slip, on their ride to Edinburgh – that, as a 'kindly Scotsman' himself, if they were both reasonable and firm in their attitude, they might win something of what they fought for. Hamilton had been a rather frightened man when he said that, and possibly only seeking to buy time. But it could have been a revealing remark. 'It comes to me that the King would not have authorised concessions such as these had he been so stiff-necked as now seems. A man who will make one concession will make another, be it reasonable. And to demand that a national covenant, signed by all but a whole realm, be abandoned out-of-hand, is not reasonable. We have heard that my lord Hamilton brought *two* proclamations in his pouch. Both signed by the King. His the choice which to read. Perhaps my lord has forgotten the second proclamation?'

There was a tense silence in the throne-room.

Then the Archbishop of St Andrews leant and spoke in the frowning Commissioner's ear. He spoke at some length. When he drew back, the Marquis of Douglas, at the other side, whispered likewise. Both looked anxious, urgent.

The Covenanters stood, waiting.

103

At length, Hamilton spoke stiffly. 'Very well. This once I will be merciful. Will exercise the clemency His Majesty entrusted to me. To my discretion. The Covenant is not, cannot be, acceptable to the King. But I will allow the concessions to stand, meantime. Allow that they be made known and permitted. For the present, I can do no more. I shall return to London. With this of the Covenant. To lay before His Majesty. He may command otherwise thereafter. It is probable. He may countermand the concessions. You understand? More I cannot do.'

'More we cannot ask, meantime,' Montrose acceded. 'We thank you. But knowing your lordship's great influence with the King, we will hope, with some confidence, that His Grace will be at least as careful for the feelings of his kindly Scots subjects.' Deliberately he used Hamilton's own former phrase.

To that there was no response.

Alexander Henderson spoke. 'We have brought sundry matters, propositions, outstanding questions, for consideration. To put before your lordship. The Laird of Warriston, here, has them all wrote down. Would you wish us to expand upon them now? Or to leave them with you to read and think upon?' In the circumstances he forbore from calling them 'articles of peace', as they had been referred to in committee.

'God's wounds – no! Leave them, man.' The Commissioner half-rose from his seat, in alarm at the notion of further wordy debate. 'Let them lie. We shall look at them. My lord Archbishop. And others. Leave it. Er . . . this audience is now closed. You have my permission to retire.'

If Hamilton would have preferred the deputation to move out backwards, he was disappointed, and had to be content with a selection of bows, some perfunctory.

They were hardly outside the great double doors when Rothes was slapping Montrose on the back. 'Man, James!' he hooted. 'Yon was magnificent! Threatening to call the man Majesty! You had that bladder of lard fair dumbfoonert! Fear't for his neck. We must see that Charles Stewart gets to hear o' this. That his beloved Hamilton was like to be styled His Majesty, in Holyroodhouse! It may not greatly advance *our* cause – but I swear it will no' advance James Hamilton's!'

'It served its turn,' the younger man agreed, unsmiling. 'But it was unimportant, quite. What matters is that these concessions be promulgated and made effective. They will never dare withdraw them afterwards.'

'Think you them so important?' Loudoun growled. 'When we know that Hamilton and the King but play for time? Time to muster and arm! All else is but play-acting.'

'I cannot think that you are right in this,' the Graham said. 'Even King Charles would not make war on his own people and realm.' But his voice lacked its accustomed calm assurance.

9

FOUR WEEKS LATER, WITH THE KING'S COMMISSIONER returned to London, Montrose was in the saddle again, riding north this time – to play something of the commissioner himself. Once more he had Black Pate and a force of Grahams to escort him; but this time there were many more of them, and he had the Lord Kilpont as another lieutenant. As well as these, however, he had a different kind of companion on this occasion – the triumvirate of ministers who were now the acknowledged spokesmen of Scotland's Kirk, the Reverends Henderson, Dickson and Cant. They were on their way to Aberdeen.

The Tables, and the Covenant leadership, were concerned about that grey northern city. Led by the University doctors of divinity, the ministers, and almost all Aberdeen in their wake, had taken up an anti-Covenant attitude. They were not so much for Episcopacy as against Presbyterianism, and the theories propounded by the Universities of St Andrews, Glasgow and Edinburgh. And the former Catholic Gordon influence was strong, with Hamilton known to have been in contact with the Marquis of Huntly, their chief, as to armed aid. Montrose had been made a freeman of the city at the early age of seventeen, and was fairly well known there, his Old Montrose estates being only some forty miles to the south. So now, the Graham, with copies of the Covenant in his baggage, was to convince the hard-headed townspeople, and if possible Huntly, to sign; and his clerical colleagues to show the professors the errors of their ways.

He had spent the night at Kinnaird, and now rode north-wards past the fine new castle Sir Thomes Burnet of Leys had built out of an old ruin at Muchalls, along a rocky coast-line. He had not imposed his following, even the three ministers, on Southesk and Magdalen, but installed them all in the town of Montrose, at his own charges, riding back alone to Kinnaird. Magdalen had reverted very much to being daughter rather than wife, and there was no doubt as to whom she accepted as prime authority; but she was obviously glad to see her husband, and their lovemaking that night had been more successful than for long. There had even been tears at parting. The children were all growing apace, and most evidently delighted with their handsome father, young John, eight years old, pleading to be taken with the cavalcade to Aberdeen. Their grandfather, South-esk, was less appreciative, declaring bluntly that his son-in-law was meddling in matters too great for him, and that he would be lucky if it was only his fingers that got burned. That his daughter should be wed to a man who set himself up against his king was beyond Southesk's understanding – and no declarations to the contrary affected him in the slightest. Nevertheless James, Lord Carnegie, came spurring after Montrose as he left in the morning, declaring that he wished to accompany him. His brother-in-law found this an odd request. They had never been friends; and though Carnegie's attitude towards his overbearing father was nor-mally a sulky suspicion, the fear was that here he might have been sent to spy upon Montrose. His wife, after all, was a daughter of the Earl of Roxburgh, one of Hamilton's asso-ciates and very anti-Covenant. The Graham's refusal of his company, though couched in friendly terms, was obviously not well received.

So now Montrose rode towards the crossing of Dee in much less assured and single-minded state than when he had ridden south to meet Hamilton. He rather wished that he had never called in at Kinnaird. Family relationships and public duty did not seem to harmonise.

He was far from comforted by the conversation which developed between the three ministers riding behind him, and to which Kilpont was obviously listening interestedly. It concerned King Charles, how much responsible he was personally for his policies, and what would happen if he sent an army over the Border against his Scots subjects. It was the sort of talk which greatly grieved the Graham, but of which he was hearing more and more. When David Dickson declared that, in the event of war, the King should be deposed, declared abdicate as far as his Scottish realm was concerned, and the young Prince Charles elevated in his stead, Montrose could stand it no more.

'Sir,' he exclaimed, turning in his saddle, 'in my presence such words will not be spoken! The King is the King. To whom I – and you – have vowed fealty and allegiance. Whether we agree with his policies or no. The King's person is sacred. He is the Lord's Anointed.'

'A Popish doctrine, my lord,' Dickson snapped.

'Not only Popish, sir. Christian. The Kirk assents. Agrees that the monarch is divinely appointed and sustained . . .'

'Only on condition that he maintains the true and reformed religion.

'On condition? *My* oath of fealty was certainly not so conditioned! If you, sir, and those who think like you, would ride the same road as Montrose, you will respect His Grace's royal position, and utter no talk of deposition and forced abdication. Understand it, if you please.'

'My lord – we were only speaking of what might happen in the unhappy event of war,' Henderson put in placatingly. 'I believe that it will not come to that. We are loyal subjects. The King will respect the feelings of his people, in the end.'

'But if he does not?' Dickson insisted. 'If he sends armies against us? Shall we not fight back? Shall we let them lay us low? And if we do fight, we are in arms against the King. What then, my lord?'

'We will not be in arms against the King. I will not – that I promise. We may resist religious practices imposed upon us against our consciences. But not rise in arms against the monarch.'

'It is a fine distinction, Earl of Montrose!'

'Not in *my* mind. I ask you all to remember it.'

In that spirit they came to the Dee.

Warned of their impending arrival, a great company awaited them at Bridge of Dee, the Provost and magistrates of the city and some hundreds of the townsfolk. But it was noticeable that none wore clerical black.

Provost Patrick Leslie greeted Montrose respectfully, almost effusively, declaring that the city was his, as its honoured freeman. He was affable to Kilpont and Inchbrakie also – but it was noticeable that he had little more than a glance to spare for the three ministers. He was handed a letter from his kinsman and chief, the Earl of Rothes, urging him to do all in his power, both in the city and in the country round about, to aid that noble and true-hearted cavalier the Earl of Montrose – and this he protested vehemently that he would do, in the name of God and of the Saints Nicholas, Mary and Machar, the patrons of New and Old Aberdeen respectively – a reference which drew frowns from the clerics.

On this somewhat equivocal note they crossed Bishop Elphinstone's great seven-arched bridge and into the purlieus of the granite city.

Before they reached the Town House and Tolbooth in Golden Square, where apparently a banquet awaited the visitors, Montrose was already going warily. Provost Leslie was skilfully avoiding all references to religion and politics, and behaving as though their freeman had come on a private visit.

To put matters to a test, Montrose interrupted the determined adulatory flow. 'I have a copy of the National Covenant with me, Mr Provost,' he said. 'It is my hope that you will sign it, before all. As lead to others. And urge that your magistrates do likewise. Aberdeen has been backward in this matter.'

Leslie drew a deep breath. 'My lord,' he all but croaked. 'No! Your pardon – but no. I . . . I pray to be excused. Not to sign.'

'Why, man? What ails you at it? Is it a matter of conscience?'

'Ah . . . umm . . . conscience?' The Provost bit his lip perceiving a pitfall. 'No,' he decided, after an agitated moment. 'Not conscience. But . . .'

'You are not a Catholic?'

'No, no. I am of the Kirk. All know it, well. It is not that, my lord. It is, ah, difficult.'

'Most of this realm has found it right and proper. None so difficult. Why you?'

'We, we are King's men, here.'

'And do you say that I am not, sir?'

'Sakes – no! Never that, my lord Earl – never that! But some are not. Some would have the King down. Some see this Covenant as a condemnation of King Charles. I cannot sign such a thing.'

'I tell you it is not so. Do you know better than do I, sir? Would Montrose pull down his King? If your chief, my lord Rothes, can sign, why not you?'

'My lord Rothes is . . . is far away. Others are not!'

'Ah! Do not tell me that you, a Leslie, kin to Rothes, fear a pack of college professors?'

'Hech – not them! There are others, my lord. More . . . more potent!'

'So! You mean, the Gordons?'

'Aye – the Gordons. My lord Huntly is near, where my lord Rothes is far! And can field a hundred men for every one of Leslie.'

'Mm. I will be seeing the Marquis of Huntly. But, Mr Provost, do not tell me that the great city of Aberdeen must do as the Gordon says, if it would do otherwise? You have trained bands, have you not? A Town Guard? A walled and strong city.'

Leslie said nothing. They were halted now, before the tall Tolbooth, the narrow streets crowded with watching – but not cheering – townsfolk, through which the cavalcade had had to force its way. The Provost dismounted, to aid his visitor down.

Montrose shook his head. He had been reared near enough to the Highland Line to be careful about eating the salt of any man with whom he might be at odds, and so having hands tied by the claims of hospitality.

'No, sir,' he announced. 'I regret any discourtesy. But I am here of a set purpose, my friend. At the command of the Tables of the Convention. To gain Aberdeen for the Covenant. Does the Provost of Aberdeen sign? Or does he not?'

'I cannot, my lord. Bear with me.' The other wrung his

hands. 'Perhaps hereafter. When you have spoken with my lord Marquis. Meantime – come. A banquet is prepared for you and yours. All is ready. Come, enter my lord . . .'

'My sorrow – but no. I will not sit down with those who conceive me a traitor to my King! Nor those who betray their own realm and religion, through fear.'

'But . . . but . . .' The Provost turned unhappily to stare at his fellow magistrates, all lined up to conduct their guests within.

'But nothing, sir,' Montrose said, making his voice stern. 'Here is a matter of principle. When you tell me that you will lead your citizenry in signing this paper, then I will rejoice to eat your meat. Till then, sir, I bid you a good day.'

'But your men, my lord? All your great company . . . ?'

'We shall find quarters for them in the town, never fear. At my own charges.' He turned. 'Pate – see to it. Quarters. And not only for the men. Who is for the Covenant in Aberdeen? With a large house? Your kinsman, the Earl Marischal? The Lord Forbes?'

'The Marischal is from home, I understand.' Inchbrakie's mother was grand-daughter of the fourth Earl Marischal. 'And Forbes is old, ailing, and bides at Forbes Castle. But Pitsligo is sound, and his wife my cousin, sister to the Marischal.'

'Then let us seek Pitsligo's town-house. The Provost will inform us where it lies . . .'

In the end they found admirable quarters in the great mansion of William Keith, seventh Earl Marischal, which was indeed the prior's palatial suite of the former Greyfriars Monastery which the Marischal had gained at the Reformation, the present yong earl's sister, Lady Pitsligo, gladly throwing it open for the visitors. Settled therein, the ministers set out for the University in Old Aberdeen, seeking interview with the professors and divines.

They came back later, much later, and in no joyful mood, able to boast no more success than had Montrose with the magistracy. The doctors would have nothing to do with the Covenant, although many of the students appeared to be in favour. What was worse, a meeting of the city ministers had decided against allowing the visitors the use of any of their pulpits for the next day, Sunday – one of the main objectives of the expedition, whereby they could reach the ears of the people. Whether it was love for King Charles, belief in episcopacy, or fear of the Gordon, Aberdeen was solid against the Covenant.

But the apostles thereof were by no means beaten. They hired town-criers and sent out messengers all through the city to announce a great service next day, or series of services, which would continue non-stop throughout the day from morning till night, each of the three Covenanting divines taking it in turn to preach and lead the prayers. This to be held in the large central courtyard of the Earl Marischal's lodging, wet or fine. All who professed the Reformed faith of Christ Crucified were urged at least to come and listen and pray for God's guidance.

Fortunately that Sunday dawned dry, even though a chill haar blanketed all from the North Sea. From an early hour crowds thronged the Greyfriars vicinity, and there was considerable uproar when large numbers could not gain admittance to the courtyard. Montrose's Graham troopers had to be employed in crowd-control duties. Not all, it is to be feared, were there in search of God's guidance or in Covenanting zeal; but at least the common folk of Aberdeen turned out in force; and as the day wore on, thousands heard an increasingly hoarse triumvirate of divines expound the Creator's purpose with them, men in general, and the erring city of Aberdeen in particular. There were some unmannerly interruptions; but the Grahams soon coped with these. And available Covenants soon were satisfactorily filled with signatures – even though some scoffers declared that they would be getting Hielant tinks to set their sooty marks on it next! Certainly it was not the leadership or intelligentsia of the city that were signing.

Montrose quite quickly had enough of this marathon of joint worship and persuasion, and set off on a round of visits, with his pleasantly uninhibited and hearty hostess, Lady Pitsligo, to bring a little pressure on neighbouring lairds.

By evening he was fully convinced – as the lady had told him from the beginning – that the Covenant would get nowhere in the North-East until the Cock o' the North himself, George Gordon, second Marquis of Huntly, was persuaded, if not to sign it, at least to withdraw his strong and declared opposition to it. The Gordon power was all-important. With 200 Gordon lairds within a thirty-mile radius of Huntly, their chief could count on over a thousand men rallying to his call in a couple of days, five thousand in a week. And not just bareshanked Highland caterans, but jacked and armed horsemen. Here was the shield and buckler behind which Aberdeen University defied St Andrews, Glasgow and Edinburgh.

On the Monday morning, then, Montrose rode the forty miles to Huntly, by Don, Ury and the Braes of Foudland, rounding the dominant peak of Benachie under the great skies of that rolling far-flung land. He rode practically unescorted. It would have been pointless, indeed foolish, to take any large armed party on this errand, since the Gordon could so readily outmatch it. Anyway, the ministers were probably in greater need of the protection. He took Kilpont with him, however, and half a dozen troopers.

The town of Huntly and its great castle – more properly the Castle of Strathbogie – lies secluded in the folds of the green foothills of the great mountains that form the roof of Scotland, a world unto itself. Here the Gordon chiefs maintained a strange, out-dated, semi-barbarous but princely state, undisputed lords of life and death over a vast area. Highland and Lowland.

Long before they reached Strathbogie, Montrose's little party found themselves being escorted by a large and evergrowing company of heavily armed and fierce-looking clansmen, who seemed to be concerned, not with greeting the newcomers but with demonstrating who was master hereabouts. These were dismounted Highlanders, and trotted along beside the horsemen untiring as they were speechless, a somewhat off-putting convoy. Presently they were joined by a mounted squadron of about two hundred, under a cavalier-like personage of great magnificence, who introduced himself courteously enough as Gordon of Straloch, Chamberlain to the Gordon, High and Mighty Marquis of Huntly and Lord of Strathbogie; and as politely asked the visitors' business on Gordon territory. He did not show the least surprise, however, when he was told that this was *An Greumach Mor*, Earl of Montrose, seeking word with the said Gordon.

In this fashion, then, they dipped down into the green valley of the Deveron, in now fertile and populous country beneath the high hills, and entered the narrow streets of Huntly, a place of peat-reek, smells, flies, yelling children and barking dogs. The enormous castle, with its widespread outworks, flanking-towers and soaring keep, loomed above all at the junction of Bogie and Deveron, ancient although all the upper storeys had been rebuilt in the latest architectural vogue from France not long before – elaborate stonework, mullions, string-courses, oriels, dormers and so on. Like its lord, Huntly Castle was an odd mixture.

Obviously the Gordon had known all about his visitors coming, for he was waiting at the end of his drawbridge to meet them, in full and extraordinary fig. Probably no one else in Scotland dressed quite like George Gordon, second Marquis of Huntly. A tall, finely built and handsome man of middle years, with features a shade too fine and narrow to be strong, and eyes just a little foxlike in their slant, he had a pointed beard rather longer than usual, like the King's. He was inclining somewhat to stoutness but was still a splendid figure of a man. He wore tartan trews, cut on the cross and tight-fitting, to show off long, good legs; and with them a large, jewelled, wild-cat skin sporran. Above was a tartan waistcoat of a different hue, worn under a deep-skirted, military-style riding-coat with heavy turned-back cuffs and gold buttons. If this was not enough, on a warm summer's day, a great tartain plaid of still another variety was slung and pinned down, over one shoulder, by a large sparkling brooch of Celtic design, with the ribbon of the Garter crossing it diagonally and untidily. To crown all, he wore on his curling, shoulder-length, fox-red hair an enormous beaver hat with two curling ostrich feathers in the colours of his house, blue and gold.

'Greetings to the Graham!' this dramatic personage declared, in ringing tones. 'Welcome to my poor house. Here's Gordon's hand. I knew your father, poor man. And your witch of a mother. Man, who would have thought that they would have produced the like of yourself!'

A little bemused by both his host's appearance and reception, Montrose dismounted and shook the proffered hand. He expressed his satisfaction and honour in being received in person by the great Marquis of Huntly, Cock o' the North, and introduced Kilpont, whose father would be well known to the Gordon. Apparently the former Earl of Menteith was indeed, for Huntly promptly held forth on the follies of that unfortunate, and hoped that his son had more sense – all in the best of humours however. Then, more or less as an afterthought, he selected two of the no fewer than eleven youths and children who were milling around amongst as many deer- and wolf-hounds and smaller dogs, casually identifying them as Aboyne and Lewis – the Viscount Aboyne, second son, and the Lord Lewis – though which was which was not clear.

Montrose was paying his respects to these two, and also to a somewhat slatternly but sharp-eyed dark girl who seemed to be the eldest of the brood, but Huntly's booming voice interrupted. He had turned to his hounds, and it rapidly became apparent that these were his favourite subject and study. One by one he named them, carefully, describing in detail their pedigrees, prowess and particular points, occasionally referring back for comparison and amplification – all under the admiring regard of a whole court of Gordon lairds and cadets, of varying types and degrees, and some hundreds of assorted supporters. As the recital went on and on, the visitors stirred a little. Montrose was uncertain whether this was normal procedure or a subtle form of side-tracking.

It was another of the youths, a boy smaller than either of the two who had been introduced, with a preternaturally grave expression but a bright eye, who came to the rescue. 'Father,' he said calmly, 'these lords are weary with long riding. On a hot day. Should they not receive refreshment?'

'Eh? What do you say? Dammit, boy – hold your tongue! What's the hurry? Quiet! Would you have the Graham deem you lacking in manners? See, my lords – this Luath is one of the finest bitches in all the North. She has bred some of my best hounds – but still can out-run and pull down a tall stag. Seumas is of her breeding . . .'

The brave Gordon son tugged at his impressive sire's plaid. 'My lord of Montrose has a parchment, sir,' he announced. 'I see it peeping from his saddle-roll. I swear it is the Covenant itself! Brought for you to sign. Is is not, my lord?'

'Since you ask, young man – it is! Many have signed it in Aberdeen. My lord your father's name would much grace it.'

'No doubt, Montrose – no doubt!' Huntly said testily. 'But

I mislike it, see you. I told your Colonel Munro as much, when he came here with the paper. It is not for me, all this talk of religion and faith and covenants. I prefer my hounds! A man knows where he is with them. Now – see this tall fellow, sired by younder Keiran. There is breeding for you! Look at the length of leg, the depth of chest . . .'

'Excellent, I am sure, my lord Marquis. But the Gordon has more to offer this realm than fine hounds, I swear! In Scotland many look to you for lead. Will you not give it to them, sir?'

'Not against the King's Grace.'

'Think you *I* would bring this Covenant to you if it was aimed against the King's Grace? The Graham is as loyal as the Gordon!'

'Others do not say so, my lord.'

'Then others lie, sir. Have you *read* the Covenant?'

'All those words! Why no, sir.'

'If you will do so, you will discover no single word against His Grace. That I assure you. More than that. See – here is a statement, an endorsement, on this copy, signed by myself and my colleagues of the Ministers' Table – Henderson, Dickson, Cant. I will read it to you.' Montrose picked up the parchment. 'We declare before all, that we neither had nor have any intention but of loyalty to His Majesty, as this Covenant bears.' He held it out to Huntly. 'This we wrote for some in Aberdeen who also had not read the wording. Will it not serve to content you, my lord?'

It was Huntly who suddenly thought of refreshment now. 'We must think on this. But – shame on me to have kept you thus, lacking meats, wine, sustenance. Come, my lords – my house is yours. Come.'

The young Gordon who had first suggested it, gravely led the way. The Great Hall of the castle was even more chaotic than the forecourt. All the children, ranging from perhaps eighteen down to five years, came in, the supporting lairds too, and all the hounds, to add to the house- and lap-dogs, cats, two monkeys and, of all things, a tame heron which stalked about looking disgusted, with its own tub of live frogs for provender. Housegillies and varied servants were everywhere, all on entirely familiar terms with their lord and his family – although one of the smallest girls took pleasure in pointing out to the visitors, through a cobwebbed window, to where three naked men dangled from a dule-tree on the moot-hill beside the Deveron – they had been insolent, she explained. Huntly, of course, as well as having the usual baronial powers of pit and gallows, was hereditary Justiciar of the North, and could more or less hang whom he pleased. In all this teeming and vigorous scene three more daughters of the house came to blows and hair-pulling over which should serve what to the great Montrose. Needless to say, there was no Marchioness of Huntly; the poor lady had died, probably thankfully, in giving birth to the youngest of the brood nearly five years before. She had been a Campbell.

In the perpetual confusion and noise, it took some time for Montrose to realise that the dark youth in the stained and almost ragged clothing, who had dared to interrupt his father, was in fact, despite his size, the eldest son of the house, the heir, the Lord Gordon. It was typical of this odd establishment that it was the seventeen-year-old *second* son who was Viscount Aboyne, his year-older brother bearing the lesser title. This was because Huntly himself had been created viscount before he succeeded his father as marquis, and had passed this title on to his favourite, leaving his heir the traditional Lord Gordon. It was this young man's close study of the Covenant parchment – something nobody else seemed in the least interested in – which drew the Graham to him.

'Do you find aught against the King in that, my friend?' he asked quietly, amidst all the hubbub.

'No, my lord,' this other George Gordon answered seriously. 'To me it seems sufficient loyal. And to make good sense.'

'Ha ! Then tell your father so.'

'That would serve nothing,' the youth observed simply. 'Better that you tell him, I think, that this paper seeks religious freedom for all. Liberty to worship according to a man's conscience. Even for Catholics. If so it does?' Montrose found two very level dark eyes fixed on his own. 'Can you so tell him, my lord?'

His guest fingered an arrowhead of beard. 'It is a statement of the reformed faith,' he said slowly. 'But I acknowledge that a Catholic's conscience can be as true and honest as a Protestant's. Therefore what is fair for the one should be fair for the other.'

'Aye. But that is not what I asked ! Can you tell my father

that if this paper is accepted by the King, and what it says becomes the law in Scotland, then those who would follow the old faith may do so, as their conscience guides them, without hurt or harassment? Episcopalians likewise?'

Montrose drew a deep breath, eyeing this most unlikely son of his father. 'That I cannot swear to, friend, since it has not been debated. So far, none have spoken so honestly, so bold to the point, as have you. It would require to be considered and passed by the Tables. But this I can say – that such it should be. To my mind it is no less than due. How a man worships his God is his own affair. None should constrain other, be it the King, the Kirk, or the Pope of Rome. To this I would set my hand. To this I will testify.'

'My father may require more, my lord. But I would trust Montrose,' the Lord Gordon said quietly. 'I am not of age to sign this. But would if I might.' He handed back the parchment.

James Graham gripped the slender shoulder for a moment, before turning back to the others.

When he could gain Huntly's more or less undivided attention, he put the matter to him. Would he accept the Covenant if it was declared to include religious freedom for all? Catholics, Presbyterians and Episcopalians alike? Would he sign it with a rider to that effect?

The Cock o' the North burst into a spate of indeterminate noise, a flood of words signifying nothing in particular – though eloquent enough to Montrose. This man was not going to be pinned down. Whether feckless or crafty, the Gordon would not commit himself.

One last effort Montrose made. 'My lord Marquis,' he said, 'in this matter Scotland speaks with an all but united voice. The Covenant will win. For the King will not use armed force against the majority of his Scots people. In that day, you would not wish it to be said, I think, that the Gordon, almost alone, was against it? And prevented the North-East from signing it!'

'Me? I prevent none from signing, man! That I do not do so my own self need hinder none.'

'You say so? I rejoice to hear it. Others may sign it, if they will? And you are not concerned?'

'If they will...'

'The word of a noble lord,' the other interjected quickly.

He raised his voice for all to hear. 'My lord Marquis declares that he cares not who signs the Covenant!' he cried. 'That his abstention need hinder none. The word of a generous man! For this many will thank the Gordon.'

Blinking in some surprise at his sudden popularity, Huntly shook his head vigorously, and made more of his indeterminate noises.

Now Montrose was anxious only to disengage and be off. He had as much as he was likely to get, at Strathbogie – and could lose it again all to easily. But getting away from that strange establishment was not easy, and Huntly's hospitality, once broached, was comprehensive, even embarrassing. It looked as though they were automatically expected to stay for days. It was only by insisting that it was vital for him to be back in Aberdeen by noon next day that the Graham managed to detach himself – and even so they were provided with a large Gordon escort all the way back to the very city gates.

This time it was the young Lord Gordon who led. And all the way he asked questions, sought information, views, discussed points, a young man of intelligence with a mind of his own, despite his unimpressive appearance. Montrose took to him. He would make a very different chief for Clan Gordon from his father.

10

The Covenanters presently found compensation for their non-success in the North-East, in word from London that the King was prepared to accede to their demand for the calling of a much-overdue General Assembly of the Church of Scotland – a summons which required the royal authority. This was splendid news, for whatever reason Charles was granting it. But the satisfaction in Scotland was somewhat allayed by the subsequent announcement that the

King would not attend in person but was sending the deplorable Hamilton again, as Lord High Commissioner. Nothing was said about the Covenant itself.

While there were the usual warnings that Charles was only playing for time in granting this procedural concession – although constitutionally he had no reason to withhold it – and that he was in fact preparing to outwit the Scots, Montrose at least preferred to believe that the King could be responding to reason, and behaving in honest and kingly fashion.

The great gathering was set for Glasgow, at the end of November. There had been no such General Assembly since 1619, although this was the constitutional and democratic court and ruling body of the Kirk of Scotland. Indeed, there had been only six in all, since King James removed south to London in 1603. All had been unsatisfactory, improperly constituted and conducted, each more dominated than the last by royal-appointed bishops. This one was going to be different. Much would hinge on it.

Montrose himself was duly elected as lay commissioner for Auchterarder, in which Strathearn parish stood Kincardine Castle. But when he set out for Glasgow, he rode again with Graham troopers at his back – at the Tables' request; for there were rumours that their enemies would overturn the entire proceedings by main force if no other means was open to them; and Glasgow was likely to resemble an armed camp. That 20th day of November, 1638, all Scotland seemed to be on the road to the little town between the Molendinar and the Clyde, that huddled beneath its great High Kirk, formerly St Mungo's Cathedral, wherein decision was to be taken.

In the narrow streets and lanes of Glasgow, packed as never before in its history, drama was foreshadowed. Black-clad ministers were everywhere; but that was to be expected – although the number who actually bore sword or dirk at their girdles came as a surprise to Montrose at least. It was the enormous numbers of men-at-arms and mail-clad supporters that most vehemently dominated the scene, however. They swarmed like locusts, wearing every sort of livery and colours. Every lord and laird in the land seemed to have descended upon this town of 12,000 inhabitants, each with his 'tail' of armed men. Or not quite every lord, perhaps –

for Huntly and the Gordons, for instance, was not represented; nor the Earl of Erroll's Hays, the Maxwells and Herries or other near-Catholic clans. But there were Hamiltons by the hundred, Border Kerrs of the Earl of Roxburgh, Traquair's Stewarts, Douglases of Clydesdale and Ogilvys of Airlie. It looked as though all the Glasgow decisions would not be taken inside St Mungo's Kirk.

Nevertheless, it was not so much all these that made the greatest impact on Montrose; his tight-disciplined Graham troopers under Black Pate of Inchbrakie would be a match for any of them. It was the sight of such large numbers of kilted, plaided and bare-kneed Highlanders in the streets that struck him most forcibly, and the answer to his enquiries as to their identity, the information that they were Campbells from Argyll. It was with a thoughtful mien that the commissioner from Auchterarder, after settling in at the lodging he was sharing with Archie Napier in the Drygate, went in search of fuller details.

Rothes, commissioner for Kirkcaldy in Fife, told him. 'Our cause must be prospering,' he declared, with his usual cynicism. 'The Campbell elects to bestow his support upon it! At last, openly, and for all to see. Man, is it no' great? Lorne, newly become *MacCailean Mor* and Earl o' Argyll by his fool father's death, celebrates the occasion! He discovers the Covenant is like to win in Scotland, and honours its Assembly with his presence. So now Charles Stewart can read the writing on the wall!'

'You are sure that it is *our* side that he joins? Not the government's? Hamilton's? Why bring so many men to Glasgow to join our cause?'

'With the Campbell you can never be certain-sure, I grant you. But – would yon one choose to join the King's party at this stage? Hey? Wi' the tide flowing our way? No' Archibald Campbell, I say! He wants a hand in what is decided here.'

'That could still be on the other side . . .'

Next morning, Wednesday the 21st of November, when the General Assembly, the first for nineteen years, was ceremonially opened in the nave of the vast church above the Molendinar Burn – which the Archbishop of Glasgow called his Cathedral of St Mungo and Master William

Annan its own minister called the High Kirk of Glasgow – the Earl of Argyll still provided no clear indication as to his intentions. When Montrose and Napier, having had to battle their way through unruly crowds to get in, took their seats in the body of the church as ordinary commissioners, beside Rothes and Eglinton, there was no sign of the Campbell.

There was a blare of trumpets, as the vestry door was flung open, to herald the entry of the Lord High Commissioner and his suite. All rose to their feet for the King's representative. Argyll was still not to be distinguished in the great throng. It was many years since James Graham had seen him, but he did not think that he would fail to recognise the man.

Once again Lord Lyon Balfour and his heralds led in the procession. Sundry officials came first. Then the Lords of the Privy Council – who by decision of the previous packed and unrepresentative Assemblies had been given leave to attend and vote. This, however, proved to be a very reduced attendance for many members of that august body had elected to either stay away or to sit elsewhere – as had the Lord Napier; and, more significant, not one of the thirteen Lords Spiritual, the bishops, all now members thereof, came in.

'Ha! See that!' Rothes cried out – for the din was already loud as a cattle-market. 'They too have seen the writing on the wall! No' a bishop to show his episcopal nose! Canny chiels – they ken what's good for them.'

'Thank God for that, at least,' Napier said. 'That gives us thirteen more votes. They knew they would be out-voted, and made to look small. Aye, out-talked and out-reasoned likewise. So they have chosen the better part, for once . . .'

But Montrose was not joining in the surge of exclamation which rose from all the vast company at this first hint of success for the Covenant – for the mighty church was packed, its two hundred and fifty or so commissioners only a very small proportion of the assemblage, and every aisle, side-chapel, and gallery, even the clerestory walks, crowded with far from silent spectators. He had drawn quick breath at quite another aspect of the Privy Council entrance – for second to come pacing in was the burly, bushy-bearded figure of David, Earl of Southesk.

'Look there,' he interrupted his other brother-in-law. 'Southesk has come. Come out of his retirement. When did you last see him at a Council meeting? That means he is here to take a strong line. And it will not be for us. He conceives us enemies of the King. And his son, Carnegie, will vote as his father wills, under his father's eye. The old man dominates all his family.'

Glancing sidelong at his friend, Napier nodded. 'Southesk could influence many,' he agreed. 'Especially from Angus and the Mearns. I had not thought to see him here . . .'

But Rothes was tugging at Montrose's arm on the other side, and pointing. Modestly, last of the Privy Councillors to pace in, was a slight stooping figure, limping a little, a soberly dressed, unassuming-seeming man, with a pale long face, long narrow nose and high brow beneath foxy-red, straight, thin hair. He might have been a clerk to the Council, an unfrocked minister perhaps. He kept his head lowered diffidently, the picture of a retiring nobody – but Montrose at least did not require to see the pronounced squint in the left eye, or the tight sour mouth beneath that drooping nose, to know differently.

'Archibald Campbell!' he breathed. 'By all the Powers – Argyll! Save us – it is himself! He is . . . worse! Six, seven years it is, since I saw him. And he is . . . worse!'

'Aye – *MacCailean Mor* himsel'!' Rothes said. 'The tod emerges frae his earth! How's yon to be the greatest man in Scotland?'

'Poor Scotland, then! But he is not that – yet! Praise God!'

It was strange, James Graham's ingrained loathing of this man. He was not one to hate readily; and the fact that the Campbells and Grahams were hereditary foes did not weigh heavily with him. They had only met once or twice, in their younger days, and even then they had not actually come to verbal blows, whatever their eyes said. The Campbell was only six years the elder – although he looked much more – and because of his physical defects might have been expected to be an object of sympathy and commiseration to the other's essentially considerate and kindly temperament. But the antipathy seemed to be born in him. From first sight he had abhorred and shrunk from this man. And there had been little doubt that the feeling was mutual.

'You will note,' Montrose said from between stiff lips, 'that my lord of Argyll chooses to sit, not as a commissioner for

Inveraray, but as one of the King's Privy Council, at this Assembly! Are you so sure now how he will vote?'

Even Rothes looked thoughtful.

There were ten members of the Privy Council taking their seats in a row on the dais at the chancel steps, where once the rood-screens had been, below the High Commissioner's throne but above the Moderator's chair and the Clerk's table. But at the last moment a fantastically curled, be-ribboned and painted exquisite came hurrying in alone, with tap-tapping, shoulder-high, streamered staff and lace hand-kerchief – no doubt scented – which he waved before his nose to counter the smell of less rarefied humanity. A howl of mirth went up, at the sight.

But Montrose and those beside him did not laugh as this apparition minced up, to take another of the Privy Council seats. It was the Earl of Lanark, Hamilton's brother, whose appearances in Scotland nowadays were a rarity indeed. That such as he should have come north to attend a General Assembly of the Kirk was so unlikely as to be scarcely credible; and could only mean that the opposition was in fact scraping up votes wherever it could. Presumably the King had made him a Privy Councillor specially for the occa-sion. If that was so, then they must have at least a hope of out-voting the Covenanters, or there was no point in the business. This had not been seriously considered as a possi-bility, up till now, in the Kirk's own Assembly. But the other side were experts in subversion. The very fact that Carnegie and his father were also here, and both with votes, struck a like note. Lanark, in the circumstances, was no laughing matter.

Another blast of trumpets, and Hamilton himself came stalking in, as king-like as ever, resplendent in a long velvet royal-blue cloak trimmed with ermine and held up by two pages, with a huge gemmed star of the Garter on its shoulder, and below it a riot of cloth-of-gold, satin, jewellery, bows, rosettes and contrasting slashings. Even his curled, ringleted, long hair was tied with coloured bows. He carried it off rather better than his brother, because he was taller, and well-built; but even so the absurdity shouted aloud – as did not a few of the Glasgow citizens in the spectators' galleries, church or none.

Pacing to his throne above the Privy Councillors, the

Marquis, after gazing at the scene with unease and distaste in almost equal proportions, proceeded to read his commission from the King, in a flat monotone. It proved to be in unexpectedly conciliatory terms, referring to Charles's well-beloved Scots lieges, his delight in his ancient kingdom, his support for the true Reformed religion, the concessions he had already made in that respect, and his deep interest and concern in the debates and decisions of the good fathers and brethren of his Church in Scotland, at which his trusted and entirely loved cousin, the most noble James, Marquis of Hamilton, Knight of the Garter, Lord of the Bedchamber, Master of the Horse, Chief Steward of Hampton Court, and Privy Councillor of both kingdoms, would most faithfully and ably convey his royal views and guidance. He blessed them all, and commended their deliberations to God.

Seldom was blessing pronounced in a less beatific tone of voice.

The procedure for General Assemblies was fixed and unalterable. It was deemed suitable that a proper and pious attitude should be engendered throughout, first of all, by an initial sermon. This also had the advantage of allowing all concerned time to survey the scene, size up the possibilities, and plan their campaigns – discreetly, of course, and paying at least some small attention to the preacher meantime.

The preacher, with surprising energy for one of his years, thundered and gesticulated on. Montrose got the notion that Argyll, not thirty feet away, kept staring at him personally – although with his squint, one could never tell. He stirred uncomfortably. Most of the other Privy Councillors were now asleep.

At length even the Reverend Mr John Bell ran out of strength and breath, though never of material; and thankfully Hamilton announced that the next business was the appointment of a Moderator to chair the proceedings.

Promptly David Dickson proposed their most revered and admired guide-in-God, Alexander Henderson, Minister of the Parish of Leuchars in Fife, than whom none could be more worthy and able.

Amidst ringing applause Andrew Cant seconded. Since one or the other of these two would have been the only obvious alternative nomination, there was no other name put forward. Rather reluctantly the High Commissioner declared Henderson to be the Moderator, the first for nineteen years, and asked him to come forward and take the chair. A great sigh of relief arose from the body of the church. From now on the conduct of the Assembly at least was in sure hands.

Henderson, after making a brief speech of thanks, expressing the gratitude of all for the King's gracious message, and his concessions intimated, and declaring that the Lord High Commissioner's appointment was such as to ornament the proceedings – a shaft which drew no lack of grinning appreciation – went on in changed, assured and businesslike fashion. He proposed that Archibald Johnston of Warrison, advocate, should act as Principal Clerk to the Assembly.

It was unthinkable that the Moderator's first move should be countered, and Warriston, tense in scowling embarrassment, stumbled forward to take his place at the table below the Moderator's chair. A number of lesser clerks and assessors followed him, with papers.

Henderson then welcomed all duly appointed commissioners to this great, belated and historic Assembly, emphasising that 'duly appointed' slightly. As was customary he went on, all commissions must be scrutinised, that God's work be surely and honestly done, by the due and proper representatives of Christ's Church and people. This would take some considerable time, possibly the rest of the day; and he proposed that the Assembly should adjourn until the Scrutinising Committee's work was done. Did any say otherwise?

After that sermon, none said otherwise, especially the Privy Councillors

Since the Scrutinising Committee must be wise, experienced and impartial, the Moderator then suggested that its convener should be the Reverend David Dickson, of Irvine, whose knowledge of procedure was unrivalled. Half a dozen delegates rose to second, but Henderson pointed out mildly that this was not a proposal to vote upon, but the Moderator's procedural appointment for the better forwarding of the Assembly's business. Mr Dickson should select an impartial team of assessors, and proceed with their task during the adjournment. It might well take such time as to forbid reassembly until the morrow.

There was a murmur at that, variously compounded.

Behind Henderson the Lord High Commissioner cleared his throat ominously.

Unperturbed, the Moderator went on. 'Before we adjourn, some may wish to guide the scrutineers in their task, having perhaps special knowledge of misappointments and wrongous attendances. It is suitable that His Grace's High Commissioner should so intimate first, if he is a mind to.'

Hamilton was very much of a mind to. Spluttering a little he rose to his feet, then recollecting his royal state, quickly sat down again. 'I make objection, 'he said thickly. 'Many are here who should not be. Any fool can see it! This Assembly has been packed. And sounds that it may be *more* packed!'

'I regret to hear it, my lord Marquis. This must be rectified. Perhaps your lordship will be more explicit?'

'Explicit? Man – look around you! This is an Assembly of the Church. Yet many here, I swear, represent only themselves! Or seditious parties that would endanger both the Church and the King's realm.'

'Then they must be rooted out. If you will name me names . . . ?'

'Names? What need for names, man? Look! There are more laymen here than ministers, I do believe. And many carry arms, despite my express proclamation forbidding it.'

'Arms are unsuitable in the house of the Lord,' Henderson agreed. 'But I would remind your lordship that this is a Presbyterian church, and laymen, elders, have a full say in its rule and direction. I respectfully suggest, however, that your High Commissionership is mistaken. We have the numbers of all commissioners attending. There are 142 ministers and 98 elders. The commissions of all shall be scrutinised.'

Hamilton huffed and puffed. 'I misdoubt the appointment of many here, sir. How it has been contrived.'

'Then, my lord, appoint your observers to the Scrutinising Committee, that you may be satisfied. But, I pray, give me instances, names . . . ?'

Hamilton muttered, but otherwise remained silent.

Henderson turned to look out over the company. 'If His Grace's Commissioner has no names to put before the committee, I believe that others have. As indication how there have been wrongous appointments. I call upon my lord of Montrose.'

Amidst sudden tension, Montrose rose. 'Mr Moderator,' he said slowly, 'it has been brought to my attention that there has been a mischance in the election of one of the commissioners for Brechin, in which Presbytery I am a heritor. I understand that John Erskine, Laird of Dun, was duly elected. But the Lord Carnegie now sits in his place.' He sat down.

There was a gasp and a thrill of excitement went through the gathering. Few were unaware that Carnegie was the speaker's brother-in-law.

Southesk half-rose from his seat, glaring at his son-in-law – but subsided as the Moderator's calm voice resumed.

'Is this confirmed by the Clerk?'

Warriston rose, fumbling with his papers. 'Yes, sir. I . . . I have it here. Appointment by Brechin Presbytery. John Erskine of Dun. Duly passed by the Tables, with the following note . . .'

'Tables! Passed by the Tables, 'fore God!' Hamilton roared, banging the arm of his throne. 'Hear that! Passed by the Tables. What need for further debate? Unless passed by these damned, unlawful and treasonable Tables, no man is acceptable here! A packed Assembly! Can you deny it?' He pointed directly at Montrose, not at Henderson. 'Deny it, I say!'

In the throbbing silence, Montrose perceived that Henderson was leaving it to him. He rose again. 'Is there fault in this?' he asked quietly. 'Since the King's Grace has refused to call a parliament these many years, the realm has had to be governed by some. This Privy Council, with half its members bishops, rejected by Church and people, has not done it. The Convention of Estates appointed these Tables, therefore, lacking other means. On the best legal advice! To call them unlawful and treasonable, my lord Marquis, is to betray lack of understanding. And it is right and proper that the Tables should consider who was appointed to this Assembly. No felon, malefactor, Armenian, unbeliever or Catholic may attend, by law. If the Tables did not exercise watch, who would? You, sir? Or my lords of the Privy Council?'

It is safe to say that no Lord High Commissioner had been spoken to so since the Kings of Scots had ceased to attend the Assemblies in person. Hamilton gulped and swallowed, prominent eyes popping.

'This . . . this is beyond all!' he got out.

'You asked for a denial, my lord. You have it.' Montrose sat down.

'All comments and remarks will be permitted only by and through the Chair,' Henderson rebuked them both, mildly. 'Mr Clerk, you will note this matter of the Lord Carnegie for the Scrutiny Committee.'

'I protest, sir!' That was the Earl of Southesk hotly. 'At this disgraceful attack upon my son. He is here of right. Erskine's was a rigged election. I myself had it amended.'

'The matter will be closely considered by the Scrutiny Committee, my good lord, never fear . . .'

'Fear, man? Fear! Think you Carnegie fears what any pack of clerks and preachers may decide!'

'My lord, this, I would remind you, is an Assembly of the Church, where the decisions of clerks and preachers, as you name them, has some small relevance. I urge you, and all, to remember it. Now . . .'

'And *you* remember this. Any attempt to unseat my son will cost you dear. None yet meddled with Carnegie and did not live to regret it!' It was at Montrose that the old earl glared, however.

Rothes rose. 'I move the adjournment, Mr Moderator,' he said.

There was a score of seconders.

'It seems a fitting moment,' Henderson acceded, calmly grave. 'But, perhaps, before we leave, I should wish especially to welcome to our deliberations my lord Earl of Argyll, whose renown is known to all. His presence here, and his adherence to God's cause of freedom, true religion and justice, is of the utmost value. All honest men will rejoice, I am sure.'

The applause was less vociferous than might have been. As an attempt to edge the Campbell – who had sat silent, head bent, preoccupied, throughout – into declaring himself, indeed to commit him to the Covenant cause, it was laudable but less than successful. *MacCailean Mor* raised his reddish head for a moment, in briefest acknowledgment, and then looked down again. That was as far as his commitment went, meantime.

Henderson bowed towards the High Commissioner. 'With your agreement, sir, this Assembly stands adjourned.'

On the way out, Montrose found himself treated as something of a hero – to his distaste and curt rejection. He knew well that his heroics in the cause that day would cost him dear.

Next forenoon, when the full gathering reassembled, after a long wait for the High Commissioner, it was evident that Alexander Henderson's tactics were proving only partially successful. Admittedly, there were notable gaps amongst the commissioners, indications that the Scrutiny Committee had not been slothful. But the Lord Carnegie was still in his place as commissioner for Brechin, and Erskine of Dun still in the spectators' gallery; Brechin Presbytery's changed decision seemed to have been confirmed as genuine, and Montrose's reluctant gesture gone for nothing. Moreover, sitting beside Carnegie was now his uncle Sir John Carnegie of Ethie, newly arrived in Glasgow but apparently authentic commissioner for Arbroath. He was not known as having strong views – but it was unlikely that he would vote against his brother's line.

However, when the Privy Councillors trooped in, there were seen to be significant gaps in that august body. The Earl of Southesk himself was missing; it seemed that his anger at the previous day's proceedings had necessitated bleeding by a chirurgeon, and he was confined to his bed. More actually significant perhaps, the Earls of Wigtown, Morton and Argyll were also missing. When Hamilton took his seat, his features were dark with ill-suppressed rage. Not a few hoped that he also might require the services of a chirurgeon.

Proof of a change of balance in the proceedings was fairly quickly forthcoming. The Covenant leadership put matters to the test by moving the acceptance of the Scrutiny Committee's decisions. After some undignified wrangling, in which the High Commissioner himself took large part, the motion was passed by a fairly large majority. It was notable that the two Carnegies voted against.

Encouraged, Henderson moved on to establish the constitution and power of the Assembly, a vital matter when there had been no proper precedent since 1603. This was the supreme court of the Church of Scotland, and its members had to know their authority and limitations. It was quickly asked – if a court, could they, *must* they not, try? Try not only causes, policies, matters of belief and doctrine, but men? Men who introduced error and stumbling into the Kirk?

This set the gathering by the ears – especially when all over the great church there were shouts of 'The bishops! The bishops!' The Moderator sternly called all to order – but said nothing to indicate that it might not come to a trial of the King's bishops. Montrose stirred uncomfortably, and presently rose to declare that a witch-hunt was unsuitable, and the last thing that was required in this delicate situation. For once, he gathered no applause. Henderson skilfully channelled the discussion into series of procedural issues – and gained consistent majorities for each step in a progress towards complete Assembly power, prerogative and jurisdiction. The Lord High Commissioner and the Privy Councillors remaining glared, protested, condemned, threatened – but were consistently voted down. Hamilton even had a private battle with the Moderator, claiming that he had the votes of six assessors as well as his own – which Henderson ruled against, declaring that in God's kingdom, King Charles was one man, not seven!

The day was well advanced before Montrose noticed, inconspicuous in one of the public galleries, the reddish hair and sallow features of the chief of all the Campbells, listening attentively.

'So – Argyll removes himself from the Privy Council seats, and the voting!' he murmured, to Napier. 'But stays to watch and listen. See him yonder?'

'A strange man. Henderson will rejoice. A victory for him, I think. Argyll must conceive the issue to be going our way.'

'But still does not commit himself! That such a man, so timorous, should cut so wide a swathe in Scotland! It is scarce believable.'

'Do not deceive yourself, Jamie. Argyll is not timorous. Cautious, yes, but not timorous. I know him better than do you. Trust Tom Hope's judgment of him – he is a notable judge of character. He said that he would lead in Scotland – remember it! There is a man all must watch. He is strong, despite his manner, in more than men and lands. Henderson knows it. He must have him on the Covenant side.'

At the next day's session the Earl of Argyll came down

from his discreetly modest perch, and took a seat, not with the Privy Council again but prominent amongst the nobles who were not actual commissioners – beside Morton his uncle, and Wigtown, indeed. It turned out that he was not a representative of Inveraray Presbytery, after all – although he easily could have been, since his word was law in that area. He was remaining at the Assembly as a private individual and forgoing his Privy Council vote. It was a strange decision, typical perhaps of the man – but at least it was clear indication of his disassociation with Hamilton and the King's policy. Apart from Montrose, the Covenanters were elated.

These two had to come face to face some time. It happened that evening when the Covenant leaders were invited to attend a gathering at the Earl of Loudoun's house in the Gallowgate, one of the few nobles who maintained a large town mansion in Glasgow, to discuss alarming information that the King, even while his representative was presiding over this Assembly, was making preliminary moves for the mustering of a great army; and since its assembly-place was set for Newcastle, within a short distance of the Scottish border, concern was not irrational. Argyll was one of the first persons Montrose saw, on entry to the house – he was Loudoun's kinsman and chief, of course. The Campbell saw him, likewise – but neither moved forward in greeting.

It was Henderson who presently brought them together. 'My lords,' he said, catching Montrose's arm, 'to have *MacCailen Mor* and *An Greumach Mor* in the same room, is something of an occasion, I think! You are well acquaint, I have no doubt?'

'We have met,' James Graham bowed, stiffly formal for him.

'My lord of Montrose's reputation is better known to me than his person,' the other observed. 'I am a man of retiring habit, of course.' Argyll's voice was as unexpected as the rest of him, a soft lilting Highland sibilance superimposed upon a naturally nasal rasp, allied to a slight hesitation.

'The more we value your lordship's presence with us, here,' the minister announced. 'Is it not so, my lord of Montrose?'

'Indeed, yes. It is a time for all men to declare themselves.'

'It is a time for all men to consider their position,' the Campbell amended thinly.

'There has been long for considering positions, my lord. Years. It is now time for action, I think.'

'Action against the King, sir?'

'Not against the King. Never that. Against the rule of bishops, and the suppression of parliament.'

'Will His Grace perceive the difference?'

'If he does not, his Scots Privy Councillors should inform him.'

'His Scots Privy Councillors must first assure themselves that it is so.'

'If any are still in doubt, it is because they choose to be.'

'His Grace himself has said, "No bishops, no king"!'

'Then His Grace is mistaken. So far as Scotland is concerned. For fifty years there were no bishops. Yet King James sat his throne safe enough.'

'So you are set to pull down the bishops, my lord?'

'Pull down? For myself, I care not whether there be bishops or not, in Scotland. So long as they do not attempt to rule the Kirk, change our worship, sway the King and dominate the Privy Council.'

'You would permit them to remain, lacking these powers?'

'I would, yes. If it would please the King. And those who think like him. Shorn of these powers they could do little harm.'

'There I think you err, my lord,' Henderson, who had been listening to this exchange carefully, interpolated. 'They should be rooted out quite. The Kirk has no place for them. They are a relic of Popery, and must go.'

'Which of you speaks with the voice of this Covenant?' Argyll asked. 'The Moderator? Or my lord of Montrose? When you have decided it, you may inform me.' And bowing, the Campbell limped away to alternative company.

They looked at each other. 'We are not clever enough for that one,' Henderson commented, frowning.

But next day, nevertheless, Argyll had his answer. Whether Henderson was determined to have it so, or whether this would have been the programme anyway, almost from the start of the proceedings the pressure was on the bishops, the office thereof and individual holders of it. Deliverance after deliverance was pronounced on the subject – and they were charges rather than questions for debate. In vain did the Lord High Commissioner object; the Moderator ruled his submissions as out of order. Then Hamilton revealed that the bishops had anticipated this attack, by subscribing a declinature to it beforehand, which he now insisted should be read. As no bishops had risked putting in an appearance, he called upon one of his own clan, the Reverend Dr Robert Hamilton, of Glassford parish, Lanarkshire, to read it. Again the Moderator ruled otherwise. This was not the time. Let the case against the office of bishop be heard first; then there would be opportunity for answer, defence, and this declinature.

Angrily the High Commissioner declared that he would not sit there and preside over a trial of the King's bishops. They were the highest officers of the Church, and the Church's Assembly had no right or authority to assail them.

Politely Henderson grieved to say that he believed His Grace's Commissioner was mistaken. The Assembly *had* powers to question and try bishops, if necessary to depose them. Bishops, or any other minister of the Church.

In the uproar at this statement, Hamilton could not make himself heard. When the Moderator at length gained him quiet, he shouted that it was all wind, vain mouthings, empty threats. It was disgraceful that the Moderator should make baseless statements, impossible of proof.

'Proof, my lord? If you wish proof, you shall have it.' Henderson signed to Warriston.

Then, to the wonder of all, the Clerk tapped a stack of yellowing papers on his table, to announce that these were the records of the General Assemblies of 1560 to 1590, thought to have been destroyed. It was known that the bishops and Crown authorities had indeed destroyed as much of the Presbyterian regime's records as they could. These vital Assembly proceedings had been assumed to have been amongst the first casualties. Their production, like this, was a great triumph for the Covenanters. On Henderson's promptings, Warriston read out the Act of the Dundee Assembly of 1580, duly signed by the King, abolishing the office of bishop, in the Kirk; and thereafter act after act of various others, all with the royal subscription, confirming this and wiping out all traces of the status and privileges of such prelates; likewise all subsidiary offices and titles such as deans, archdeacons, chanters and the like, all apt to be lumped under the heading of 'popish trash'. Shaken, Hamilton and the Privy Councillors sat silenced.

'This is a properly-called and lawful General Assembly of the Kirk,' the Moderator went on thereafter. 'So far as authority goes, we have absolute right to deal with bishops as we think fit. By these previous acts of Assembly the office had been shown to have had no warrant or authority in Holy Scripture, but brought in by the folly and corruption of men's inventions. Does this Assembly wish to proceed with the matter? Or to let it lie?'

The great and continuing shout left no doubt as to the wishes of the Assembly as a whole. So far as Scotland was concerned, the office of bishop was as good as abolished.

That night, Glasgow seethed like an ant-hill disturbed. The armed supporters of the various factions were involved in many clashes, and men everywhere were in a fever. The gauntlet was being thrown down, with a vengeance.

That vital decisions had crystallised overnight was immediately apparent next forenoon. So soon as the High Commissioner came in and was seated, he spoke.

'Mr Moderator – I have announcement to make. As the King's representative. The discussion of yesterday was, I rule, treasonable and not to be tolerated. If, today, there is any move towards the abolition of the office of bishop, or attempt to attack absent prelates, I shall, in the King's name, dissolve and close this Assembly as illegal.'

This bombshell shook even Alexander Henderson. When he could make himself heard, he protested. 'You cannot do this! None can dissolve an Assembly of Christ's Kirk save its own members. You have not the power.'

Hamilton banged his chair. 'I need not you, sirrah, to teach me my powers! Or my duty. I have the King's royal authority, which none can contest. This Assembly will end, if any further attack on the bishops is mounted. And meantime, I insist that the declinature of the bishops be read forthwith.'

To gain time for thought and consultation, Henderson acceded to that.

The unhappy Dr Hamilton, from Clydesdale, rose to announce that the following was signed by their lordships the Archbishops of St Andrews and Glasgow, and the Bishops of Edinburgh, Galloway, Ross and Brechin. Then, in something of a gabble, he launched into a lengthy written disquisition on the sanctity and scriptural authority of the order of bishops, with readings from the Epistles. It was clear, he said, that the King, as head of Christ's Church in these realms, alone had power over bishops, and that no Assembly, court or tribunal whatsoever, might question the royal appointments or the acts of the said bishops. The great gathering sat restive, hostile, but giving the very self-conscious reader a hearing.

All the while a succession of individuals came up to the Moderator's chair, for whispered consultation, Rothes amongst them. When he came back to his seat, he shrugged.

'Aye, then – the die is cast!' he informed. 'For better or for worse.'

'There is only one decision Henderson can make,' Montrose agreed gravely. 'I take it that he has made it?'

'God grant that it is the right one,' Napier murmured. 'Since it is like to cost us all dear!'

On the Moderator's formal enquiry, the deafening rejection of the declinature by the Assembly made counting votes superfluous.

Henderson turned to the High Commissioner. 'Sir, this court of the Church is of a sure mind. It rejects the bishops' statement, and I believe must go on to reject the bishops themselves. Furthermore, as Moderator, I declare that you have no power to keep this Assembly from discussing what it has the right to discuss and vote upon, by ample and due precedent, as quoted. You cannot lawfully dissolve it, on such grounds.'

'I can. And will. If it seeks to try the King's bishops. Does it?'

'I cannot advise that it may not. If so it desires.'

'So be it, then. You have brought it on your own rebellious heads.' Hamilton rose to his feet. 'In the name of His Majesty the King, I declare this Assembly finally and entirely dissolved. You will all disperse forthwith. The royal authority is withdrawn.' He bowed stiffly to the Privy Councillors, and turning, in deadly silence stalked to the vestry door, and out.

Glancing at each other in considerable dismay and confusion, the remaining Privy Councillors and great officers of state rose and went streaming after the Marquis.

'All will stand, while His Grace's Privy Councillors retire,' Henderson said, sternly.

Tha firm voice, measured, authoritative, pulled the shocked gathering together. Men drew deep breaths, and obeyed.

With the Lord Lyon King of Arms last to leave, this time minus any trumpet fanfares, Henderson spoke again. 'Be seated. Mr Clerk – to the next business, if you please.'

The general gasp of sheer excitement and admiration was tribute to this calm assumption that all was in order, and the situation unchanged. But not all was admiration. Dr Hamilton rose.

'Sir – Mr Moderator! This is impossible!' he cried. 'This Assembly has been dissolved. It cannot go on.'

'I rule that it can, sir. It is a duly authorised Assembly. Because His Grace's Commissioner has seen fit to withdraw, it by no means invalidates our authority. There are some hundreds of the *Kirk's* commissioners still present. You may put it to the vote, if you will.'

And so the Church of Scotland took the law into its own hands, abolished the office of bishop, and deposed collectively and individually, all who held such office. It was done formally and methodically. The holders of all bishoprics were named, declared to have accepted and exercised an office which the Kirk had officially condemned, and were therefore expelled and banned from in future holding any other ministerial office. Moreover, the present bishops' moral lapses were notorious, and were listed. Archbishop Spottiswoode, for instance, was accused of carding and dicing on the Sabbath, and tippling in taverns; the Bishop of Aberdeen of simony, the selling of benefices; the Bishop of Brechin of drunkenness, and offences against a woman and child; the Bishop of Moray of having people dancing naked in his house, and himself 'dancing prettily in his shirt'. Others variously stood accused of flagrant offences such as adultery and incest. All were deposed – and not only deposed, but excommunicated, save for the Bishop of Dunkeld who had given his Presbytery signs of repentance. Finally it was decreed that no minister of the Kirk could in future act on the Privy Council, attend parliament, or serve as judge or justice, the Church being a society independent of the State. This, of course, meant the abolition of the Church's

136

Estate of Parliament, a constitutional change of enormous significance.

So it was done. Never had there been such an Assembly. It was to go on for many days yet, passing numerous acts for the better government of the Kirk, the rectification of wrong, and the spiritual welfare of the people. But its main work was done. It would go down as the Assembly that defied the King and abolished his bishops.

It ended on its twenty-seventh session, no less, and on an unexpected note. At the very last, after the Moderator's valedictory and inspiring sermon, with only the formal prayer and parting benediction to come, who should rise from his spectator's seat, where he had sat attentively and silent throughout, but Archibald, Earl of Argyll. He spoke, at last, modestly, almost humbly, declaring that some might criticise him for his long delay in openly joining the supporters of the Covenant; which, however, was not for want of affection for so good and noble a cause, but perchance he was able to serve it better outside of it, and in the Privy Council. But when all efforts had failed with the King, his Commissioner and the said Council, he could stay no longer on the outside, but must now join with them all in the true cause of Kirk and freedom, or risk indeed being called a false knave. He therefore now assured the Assembly of his sympathy, his approval of its actions, and his convictions of its success. He exhorted all there to go back to their presbyteries and parishes and therein to do their duty and speak out valiantly for what had been decided. And to be ready to take more active steps if called upon. He urged that meantime they respect all due and lawful authority, however, lest they put themselves in the wrong. And that they pursued, in especial, peace and unity amongst themselves; for the enemy would undoubtedly seek to sow dissension and discord. With all his heart, he sought God's blessing upon them and what they had taken in hand.

It was a quite extraordinary speech, declared in the soft yet rasping voice, varying from almost servility to paternalism. And almost as extraordinary was the applause it produced – for none had failed to watch the silent, preoccupied, almost shrinking presence throughout, wondering, remembering that this was by any standards one of the most powerful figures in the land. This last-moment statement of adherence to their cause, and homologation of what at such great risk they had done, undoubtedly came as an enormous relief and encouragement to many. By those few strange words, Archibald Campbell suddenly turned himself into a hero of the Assembly, almost on a par with Alexander Henderson himself.

'And there you have it!' Rothes commented grimly. 'Hear how they cheer the man! The reward for biding his time. There's a chiel who kens when to jump, and how!'

'Tom Hope was right,' Napier agreed. 'That man will lead Scotland yet, if he may.'

'Lead? I think you misuse the word, Archie,' Montrose said levelly, his fine features strangely drawn. '*Use*, perhaps. Exploit. Manipulate. But to lead, it is necessary that a man be in the forefront, is it not? Here is no leader.'

'Perhaps I should have said master . . .'

Henderson was speaking. 'We rejoice that the Earl of Argyll thus joins, heartens and advises us,' he said. 'It is fitting climax to a great work. We have, in this Assembly, set God's house in order in this land. We have done our simple duty, spared none, nor ourselves. We have cast down the walls of Jericho; let him that rebuildeth them beware of the curse of Hiel the Bethelite. Now, my brethren and friends – go in peace. And may the blessing of God Almighty, the Father, the Son and the Holy Ghost, go with you all. Amen.'

I I

IT ALL ADDED UP TO A DECLARATION OF WAR, OF COURSE – however many in Scotland, including James Graham, refused to see it that way. Hamilton went back to his master in a fury, declaring that of the Covenant leadership none was more vainly foolish than Montrose, but that Argyll would likely prove the most dangerous man in the state, and advising the strongest measures against rebels and traitors. The assembling of forces at Newcastle, which had been rather hanging fire and more of a token threat than a reality, began to take on serious proportions when the Catholic Earl of Arundel, son of Norfolk, was appointed commanding general, the Earl of Essex lieutenant-general, and the Earl of Holland, general-of-horse, the main muster being transferred to York.

In the circumstances, while protesting their loyalty to the Crown, the Tables had either to make military preparations of their own, or to knuckle under. This last was inconceivable, even to Montrose. They asked the King for a parliament, but this was curtly refused – Charles adding that no further General Assemblies would be permitted either until the bishops were reinstated and present. So the Tables, and Scotland, set about preparing to defend themselves.

Oddly enough, the Scots, Church-dominated as they were, proved to be better at the business than was the King – who, of course, was at odds with much of his English realm, his parliament and the Puritans. At least they went about it in prompt and businesslike fashion. And they had one great advantage, apart from enthusiasm for freedom and burning convictions that they were right – they could call upon a great pool of experienced professional soldiers. For generations it had been the custom for Scots younger sons to sell their itching swords abroad as mercenaries, for they were a warlike as well as a religious people – the two seem often to go together – and found internal feuding insufficiently rewarding as a steady profesison. The Continental wars had long been a source of employment for the Scots, and many of the European monarchs would have been hard put to it to officer their armies without them. The campaigns of the great Gustavus Adolphus of Sweden, in especial, had been a notable forcing-ground for military talent. So now the Scots mercenaries were called home from all over Christendom – and not asked to come for nothing either. The Covenanters had been amassing funds for months, with a voluntary levy on all land-holders and a nation-wide appeal at parish level. Money flooded in, and the militarists flooded home.

The greatest catch in this respect was, of course, Sandy Leslie, a clansman of Rothes and younger son of Leslie of Balgonie, acknowledged to be one of the greatest soldiers of the age, outmatching Wallenstein himself, and now field-marshal of the forces of Gustavus. He was tempted to come home as commander-in-chief of the armies of the Covenant.

Meanwhile Scotland was divided up into areas of recruitment, and Montrose given the most vital and dangerous sector, as far as internal security went – Angus and the Mearns, flanking the disaffected Aberdeenshire on the south. So at last he opened up his neglected and semi-decayed house of Old Montrose as headquarters, and at least temporarily gathered his little family around him again.

It would be pleasant to recount that this was a joyful domestic interlude; but perhaps that was more than could be hoped for. Magdalen and the children came, dutifully enough at his request, the few miles from Kinnaird – even she admitting that her husband could scarcely use her father's house as base for his treasonable activities. But her disapproval of his involvement was even more pronounced than before – and after the business at Glasgow, her father and brother were scarcely on speaking terms with her husband, a distressing situation for a young woman torn by a sense of neglect, by self-doubts and divided loyalties. She would do her duty as a wife – but obviously not much more meantime. And her very evident belief that she was married to a renegade and sedition-monger was no help to strained marital relations. They both tried, and tried hard, to make their union meaningful, in more than the mere necessary production of children to heir the Graham name and tradition; but such strivings are not always a true basis for marital bliss.

Not that James Graham was able to devote a large proportion of his time to improving domestic harmony. He was, in fact, exceedingly busy whipping up and training armed men from his Angus area. In this he had the useful aid of the young Earl Marischal, at Dunnottar Castle, farther north – indeed dangerously near Aberdeen – and of the Earl of Kinghorne, head of the ancient Lyon family of Glamis. Also, of course, many of his own Graham lairds, including Black Pate and Sir Robert of Morphie. But he also had the opposition of the Ogilvys, powerful indeed in the Angus glens, whose chief, the Earl of Airlie, was a king-at-any-price man. And, of course, the Carnegies. Matters did not come to actual blows; but it was a tug-of-war business, and men recruited one day might be discovered to have changed their minds the next. And, in the absence of any obvious immediate military threat, enthusiasm was apt to be confined to the ministers, rather than the would-be warriors.

This was the situation at the beginning of March when a courier reached Old Montrose from Edinburgh and the Tables – which meant in effect the ruling triumvirate, Loudoun, Rothes and Henderson. The news was serious and circumstantial. An armed clash looked to be unavoidable and imminent. King Charles himself had come up to Newcastle, and the army now there was reliably put at 21,000-14,000 infantry under the Catholic Earl of Arundel, Norfolk's son; 2000 cavalry under the Earl of Holland; and a special seaborne force of 5000 under Hamilton himself, for which ships were assembling. This last was to sail up to link with Huntly, who was appointed Lieutenant of all the North-East, from the Esk to the Pentland Firth, and was to raise it for the King so as to take the Covenanters in the rear while the main army invaded over the Border. Moreover the Marquis of Strafford was to descend on the Clyde area, by sea from Cumberland, with an unspecified force; and the Earl of Antrim to invade Argyll and the North-West from Ireland. All assaults to be synchronised. The Scots intelligence services, at least, were proving their worth. The Earl of Montrose was herewith appointed General Officer in command of the North-East, with full powers, and the duty of dealing with Huntly – and Hamilton when he should arrive.

Somewhat shattered by this commitment, in his present circumstances, James Graham found occasion furiously to think.

Out of his cogitations, his first action was to call meetings of the known supporting lords, lairds and burgh representatives, one for the Angus area, one for the Mearns, and one for the anti-Gordon and pro-Covenant people immediately to the north of Huntly's domains, Forbeses, Frasers and Keiths, as a threat in Huntly's own rear. He chose Forfar, Stonehaven and Turriff as the meeting-places – the latter at the very north of Aberdeenshire, near the Banff border, as a secret venue – and appointed the 14th of February for the meetings. He would attend both of the southern ones personally; but for that a Turriff he sent Johnnie Kilpont and the young Earl of Kinghorne as lieutenants, to convene it

141

and convey his views and commands. Meantime he greatly accelerated his recruiting, now with promise of actually fighting, and with the definite appointment of officers and responsibilities. Grahams were sent for from other areas, far and near.

On the 13th, in the late afternoon of the very day before the meetings a messenger arrived from Keith, the Earl Marischal at Dunnottar, to say that the word had leaked out somehow, and all Aberdeen knew that the northern Covenant leadership would be assembling in Turriff the next day; not only that, but that Huntly himself, with 2000 hastily assembled Gordons, was going to descend upon the said meeting, show who was master in the North-East, and strike the first blow for King Charles against his upstart rebels.

Appalled, Montrose cursed the folly of loud-mouthed irresponsibles. But he wasted no time in recriminations. Almost before the courier was finished, he was shouting for Black Pate and his 200 Graham horse. Somebody else could attend the other meetings.

Turriff was sixty-odd miles north of Montrose, as the crow flies, almost double that by road. Moreover, Aberdeen city and all the Gordon country lay between. No level-headed man would suggest that a troop of horse could go from one to the other in less than two days' very hard riding, and without having to fight their way into the bargain. But James Graham roused, was less than level-headed. Without so much as waiting for his evening meal, he kissed his wife and baby son an abrupt farewell, saluted his older two sons, and ran out into the stableyard buckling on steel breastplate as he ran. Vaulting into the saddle, with only young Morphie there ready, he did not wait for his troop either, but yelled instructions to Pate to follow on, and clattered off straight into a canter.

Montrose rode north by west, up out of the wide vale of the South Esk, making straight for the mighty barrier of mountains that formed the fifty-mile-long north wall of Strathmore, the Grampian Line which enclosed the Highland heart of Scotland. Crossing the South Esk by Bridge of Dun, he began the long, long climb that was to take him from sea-level to over 2500 feet. By Stracathro, where Edward of England had humiliated King John Baliol, he rode, to the bridge over the North Esk at Inchbare, and so on to Edzell, the red-stone village and castle of the Lindsays within the jaws of Glen Esk. It was important for his hastily made plans that he should ascertain who was in residence and command here this night; for old Lord Edzell, of Session, was a strong King's man; whereas his son, the head-strong David Lindsay, was as keen for the Covenant, more to spite his father than anything else, perhaps. And not only did Edzell Castle command the entrance to long Glen Esk, but Lindsay towers and little strongholds were dotted all the way up, barring it and the high pass beyond, to those the Lindsays did not love. Hence this dash here unattended. Fortunately, the old judge, who spent most of the winter at Edinburgh and the law courts, was not present; and his son was not only sympathetic but bored and looking for diversion. He insisted on joining Montrose in this venture, with a small, scratch contribution of tough Lindsay horsemen. When Black Pate and the Graham troopers came beating up, there was no further delay. The combined party faced one of the most taxing equestrian assignments that the East of Scotland could produce, the Mounth passes.

Lonely Glen Esk led them north-west for some seventeen miles, through the high mountains, by a passable track, an old drove road indeed. Its strategically sited towers, however, would have sealed off access to a still stronger company than this – hence the need for Lindsay co-operation. Had the old lord been in charge at Edzell, a less dramatic and easier route, by the Cairn o' Mounth, to the east, would have been necessary – but with much more risk of trouble with the Gordons.

By nightfall they were climbing out of Glen Esk's northerly fork, Glen Mark, well above the solitary Loch Lee, and out on to the great bare hillsides. Old snow was still lying at this level, over 1500 feet, but the track was marked at quarter-mile intervals by posts – although some were down, and in the dusk, confusing as to direction. But the Lindsays, on their own ground, were little at a loss – and at least the snow gave off an eerie white glimmer which served in lieu of light.

For a full hour they climbed, slowly now, by a route few would have deemed possible for horseflesh and in winter dark – though the Graham mounts were, of course, garrons or half-garrons, the short-legged, surefooted sturdy Scots mountain-horses, of which there were none tougher. High up on the windy, bitter-cold shoulder of Mount Keen, at nearly 2600 feet, in a spectral wilderness of snow peaks sensed rather than seen, they paused to regroup. So far there were no casualties, though some were tending to lag. Montrose spoke, cheerfully, encouragingly, the biting wind catching at his breath. Ahead of them, by a long, broken and slow descent of seven miles, lay the deep valley of the Dee, at Ballater – Gordon territory.

Avoiding the Pass of Ballater, and the small Gordon castles of Knock and Abergairn, they forded the Dee at Polhillock shallows, the valley-foot seeming to be deeply dark in contrast to the open heights. Unchallenged, an hour short of midnight, they began to climb again almost at once, up Glen Gairn. Up and up, round the vast flanks of the Morven hills they struggled now, back into the snows, again almost to the 2000 feet line, their route now less known to any. Many times they lost the track, and wasted precious time beating about in that hellish, frozen desert of ice and granite outcrops. As well, of course, that the underlying peat-hags were indeed frozen, or they could not have made any progress in the darkness. It took them over two hours more to cover the ten miles from the Dee to the Don valley, near Cock Bridge, where Corgarff Castle guarded this strategic crossing. It was a hold of the Earl of Mar, not the Gordons; but the travellers gave it a wide berth nevertheless, and forded the river discreetly half a mile downstream – a dangerous preference. More mountains lay ahead of them.

Dawn found them weary, going but slowly now, straggling out, but getting into lower ground again, in the foothills of the Cabrach, with the stripling Deveron winding in the misty valleys, and the border of Banffshire near. From here Turriff was only some twenty-five miles away – but with Strathbogie and the Huntly area directly in the way. A roundabout route through the low Foudland Hills was necessary, and then a dash across the still lower and populous lands of the Ythan valley and Auchterless, going heedfully indeed, with Gordon properties and castles thick around them. They could no doubt deal with the forces which any Gordon laird could throw against them at short notice – but not without delay, and word being carried to Huntly. Many folk did see them, in their progress thereafter, of course, and stared, wondering – but the travellers interfered with none. And who would have been foolish enough to challenge such armed and determined company, however travel-worn, lacking at least like numbers?

An hour before the Covenanters' meeting was arranged to start, at noon, Montrose's scouts reporting the approach to be clear still, they rode down the green haughs of the Idoch Water and up the brae into Turriff, men all but asleep in their saddles, horses stumbling, pecking, foundered. But they had achieved what it is safe to say had never been visualised as possible, much less attempted by a horsed squadron – an eighty-mile mountain circuit of Aberdeenshire in eighteen hours non-stop.

The Covenanting lairds of the North, quite unsuspecting of any danger, were as surprised as they were delighted to see the visitor. But Montrose quickly disillusioned them, more critical and less gracious than his usual. He did not blame them for leaking the news – although somebody had done so – but he pointed out that, had proper watch been kept here, with scouts out, his own party's arrival would not have surprised them as it had done. Kilpont and Kinghorne he especially blamed, for having failed to take any steps for the defence of the gathering, however secret they believed it to be. They were not wholly defenceless, of course, for the Lord Pitsligo, Viscount Frendraught, the Master of Forbes and others had brought their usual 'tails' with them; and with lesser lairds, grooms and servants, they totalled not far off 800 men.

None having considered defensive positions, Montrose decided that the ancient parish church of St Congans, with its kirkyard, crowning a green rise to the south-east of the village, was the only place. The minister would approve. Everyone to move in there, with the horses in the manse walled-garden adjoining. Meanwhile, local Forbes scouts out, in pairs, to give warning of any enemy approach.

The newcomers thereafter lay down amongst the tombstones, and slept the sleep of the exhausted.

Montrose was awakened a couple of hours later, with the word that scouts reported the approach of a great host from the south-west, hidden in the deep valley of the Deveron – thousands, it was declared, mostly foot. Only Huntly could produce that sort of host in this country.

145

Grimly the Graham shook the sleep from heavy eyes. Even allowing for exaggeration by the scouts, it looked as though his military career was likely to be a short one; yet he was not going to start it by any ignominious flight, without striking a blow. That was not for *An Greumach Mor*. It seemed improbable that they could repel any major attack, for long – yet what other honourable course was open to them?

He placed his people to man the kirkyard walls to best advantage, using the little belfry-tower of the church for his command-post. But he did not waste his Graham troopers thus, sending them over to the manse garden, under Pate, from which they might make a suitable cavalry diversion if the occasion offered. Then they could only wait.

And so, with bagpipes playing and horns ululating, a vast and straggling host presently began to come flooding out of the dip of the Deveron valley. It gave no least impression of being an army, being more like a huge fair on the move, carefree, undisciplined, in holiday spirit. Admittedly there were groups of mounted men amongst it all, and innumerable banners, with the glint of arms everywhere; but there was no sort of military formation, nothing of wariness or tension, no hint of any unified control – or indeed *any* control. As more and more came into sight, there seemed to be many in excess of the originally estimated 2000; but somehow there was little impression of menace in the multitude. Whether or not Huntly was with it, in person, was not apparent.

As some of his colleagues exclaimed at it all, Montrose, pointing out that the Gordon presumably had expected to disrupt a meeting and arrest its members rather than fight a battle, nevertheless could not explain why such numbers should be mobilised for this; unless Huntly merely desired to make a demonstration of strength in the area.

Presently at least some sort of elementary planning was evinced, as the host began to spread itself out in a great semi-circle to south and east of the village, presumably to prevent any dash for freedom in that direction : the River Deveron would effectively cut off flight at the other side, with its only bridge almost certainly held.

At what stage the Gordons realised that their approach was to be opposed by armed and alerted force was hard to

146

say. It was not even clear just where the leadership was, for banners were wide-scattered.

A part of the great throng had come very close, almost to the foot of the kirk-brae, before seeming to realise that the frieze of figures lining the kirkyard wall above had, in fact, hagbuts levelled and pointing directly at them; and that the group up on the belfry-tower had drawn swords in their hands. The consternation, almost indignation, developing below thereupon, was quite dramatic.

But, through a kind of residual impetus and lack of any overall command to halt, the advance – if that it could be called – continued.

From the church-tower, Montrose rapped out an order. A volley of hagbut shots cracked out.

It was a distinctly ragged volley, not to say piecemeal, for the marksmen were less than expert. But its effect on the opposition was as great as though it had been fired by a crack regiment – and moreover, *at* them instead of well above their heads. All advance halted, some men fell on their faces, more turned back in haste, and confusion reigned everywhere.

'So that is the vaunted Gordon power!' the Earl of King-horne exclaimed. 'That pack of fools and cravens!'

'Do not judge too swiftly,' Montrose advised. 'They could be formidable enough, I swear, sufficiently bold, if well led. If indeed they were in fighting trim. Do not underestimate the Gordons, John. This but finds them unprepared. They would have served very well to capture your meeting – which was what they set out to do!'

Presently, when the noise abated, a voice could be heard shouting, 'Who dares to fire on Gordon? Who, I say!'

'James Graham of Montrose, Lieutenant-General of the Estates!' was thrown back. 'What rabble is this?'

There was a pause, as of sheer disbelief. Then an incredulous voice called. 'James Graham? In person? The Earl ... ?'

'In person. Bearing the authority of the Estates of this realm. Who are you?' Obviously this was not Huntly himself.

'Straloch. Gordon of Straloch. Chamberlain to Huntly. To my lord Marquis.'

Montrose sighed. He had rather liked Straloch at their previous meeting. 'Then, sir,' he answered, 'why come against me with this great host? I mislike it.'

147

There was a pause again, as the spokesman consulted his fellows. 'My lord Marquis of Huntly,' was shouted back, at length, 'is appointed the King's Lieutenant of the North. No gathering may be held lacking my lord's permission.'

'Who says so? To the Earl of Montrose, Lieutenant-General of the realm?'

That was in the nature of stalemate. All perceived it. There was another interval.

'Montrose ended it. 'Come up higher, sir,' he commanded. 'I also mislike shouting, like fishwives at a market!' And when Straloch and a group of Gordon lairds had part-climbed the hillock obediently, 'That will serve. Where is my lord of Huntly?'

'He is at the Ford of Towie, my lord. Two miles . . .'

'Why is he not here? I do not deal with intermediaries!'

'He did not know, my lord. That you were here. We believed you . . . in Angus. We did not conceive it . . .'

'Then go and fetch your master, Straloch. Tell him that I await his explanation for this display of force against an assembly under the authority of the Estates of Scotland. Go tell him, sir.'

Strangely, this arrogant assumption of authority, so contrary to Montrose's courteous habit, well served its turn. Returning to the main body, after a little delay Straloch and his group of lairds, leaving the multitude to its own devices, turned and rode away south-westwards.

It was an hour before they were back – with the Gordon host meantime settling down to wait, variously but scarcely warlikely employed, more like a fair than ever. Montrose improved the impression of disciplined strength on the higher ground by having Black Pate and his troopers move out from the manse garden, mount, and station themselves in two long lines of a hundred, on either side of the kirkyard, sitting their horses motionless and looking threatening.

A great blowing of bulls' horns heralded Huntly's arrival on the scene – what he had been doing at Ford of Towie unexplained. With his colourful entourage, and a loping pack of deer-hounds, and to the cheers of his multitude he came riding up the brae, dressed as for the hunt, but with tall eagles' feathers sprouting from his bonnet.

Montrose let him come close – although the hagbuts remained levelled and swords drawn. 'My lord Marquis,' he

148

called, 'do you come in peace or war? This great company would seem to offer me threat – me, Lieutenant-General of the Estates! I have borne with them, in your absence, with such patience as I might. I trust that you will now remove them.'

Huntly puffed, frowning. 'In this land, my lord, none speaks Gordon so. Even you! You are holding an unlawful assembly, it seems, so that . . .'

'By what laws, sir? Not the laws of Scotland!'

'*I* administer and declare the laws here, my lord of Montrose – I, Gordon! I am Justiciar of the North. And now King's Lieutenant of the North likewise. From Esk to Caithness. Perhaps you had not heard?'

'And does the King command you to interfere with the Earl of Montrose, contrary to the law of Scotland?'

'No-o-o. But meetings, assemblies of . . . of the King's enemies are forbidden.'

'You dare to name *me,* Montrose, the King's enemy, sir? He has no more loyal subject. All here are the King's loyal subjects. I urge that you remember it!'

Huntly changed his stance a little. 'This meeting? What is its purpose?'

'Its purpose is the lawful conferring together of the King's lieges. Under my authority. If you deny that authority, my lord, and that of the Convention of Estates, then *you* are an enemy of this realm, and must abide the consequences. Do you?'

The Gordon took time to consider that.

Recognising hesitation, and gauging the other's character, Montrose pressed his point. 'If you do, sir, I have many armed and trained men here, to argue that authority, as Lieutenant-General, if you so desire. If you desire a decision by arms, declare it now. Or leave us to our lawful occasions.'

While not a few deep breaths were drawn around him, at this over-bold challenge, Huntly took it seriously. He bent in his saddle, to confer with Straloch.

Encouraged, the Graham added, 'We have wasted much time over this, my lord. Hours. We grow impatient. My hagbutters. My cavalry in especial.' He waved his sword right and left. 'Do I order attack? Or is it peace?'

Huntly cleared his throat. 'I could, should, punish your insolence, Montrose – here in my Gordon country. But I am the King's Lieutenant. And I have His Grace's express command to engage in no armed warfare until . . . until my lord Hamilton comes. Or until King Charles crosses the Border. His Grace is merciful. I do not conceive you to deserve it. But I do not controvert my lord the King. These orders – I must abide by them.'

'Ha! Excellent and wise orders, my lord! Would all were so wise, used such discretion! So it is peace – until my lord Hamilton arrives?'

Stiffly the other inclined his handsome head.

'So be it. I bid you good-day, my lord Marquis. And hope that when we next meet it will be in happier circumstances.' Montrose made a gesture of sheathing his sword, and doffed his feathered hat with a flourish.

For moments the Gordon stood, biting the ends of his luxuriant moustache. Then abruptly he reined his splendid stallion around, and rode off down the brae. In some confusion his close supporters hurried after him. He drove on right through the ranks of his host, without pause, unspeaking, men drawing hastily aside for the Cock o' the North. On he went, in the direction from which he had so recently come, nor once did he look behind him.

'There goes a lamb in lion's skin!' Montrose observed, almost sadly. 'That the Gordon should have come to this! And that it fell to me to act skinner – before all his people.'

'George Gordon will never recover from this,' the Lord Pitsligo said. 'Kinder, I think, to have shot him with one of these hagbuts!'

The Graham turned away, wordless, to descend the tower stairway.

Left leaderless, uncertain, it took some time for the great host to disperse. And all the while the Graham troopers sat their mounts, still as statues – though most were half-asleep in their saddles – and the hagbutters remained leaning against the kirkyard wall, weapons levelled. The minister of Turriff came to announce that his wife had supper prepared for their lordships.

So ended the first confrontation of the Bishops' War.

James Graham was not long back at Old Montrose – having crossed all Aberdeenshire openly and unchallenged – when Field-Marshal Alexander Leslie arrived. Rothes came, briefly, to introduce him, with 1000 men, mainly foot, recruited from Fife; which, added to the nearly 3000 Montrose already had mustered in Angus, made a sizeable force, much too large to maintain in or around Old Montrose. He decided to move to Stonehaven, twenty-three miles north, in the Earl Marischal's country, where the Keiths were solidly pro-Covenant, and the impregnable castle of Dunnottar offered a secure base. Moreover, Stonehaven was only fifteen miles south of Aberdeen, and it was important to keep an eye on that city, and its harbour – where Hamilton's expeditionary force was expected to make a landing. So Old Montrose was once again shut up, Magdalen electing to take the children back to Kinnaird.

Sandy Leslie was a little, wizened, wiry man, sour and with few graces, but shrewd, decisive, with a jaw like a rattrap. He was not a man Montrose could take to; but there was no question but that he was an enormous asset to the Covenant cause, and to be accepted accordingly. The position meantime was difficult, however; for though Leslie was to be Commander-in-Chief, for some reason his appointment did not commence until May. In the interim he was to serve under Montrose in an advisory capacity. If the little veteran felt resentment at being thus presently under the command of an inexperienced amateur of less than half his own age, however highly born, he had to swallow it for the time being – though such was his jerky and ungracious manner, that it was hard to tell if he did.

At Dunnottar, with no sign of Hamilton or his fleet, a strange verbal message reached Montrose, stressed as most secret by its bearer, a Forbes laird from the Garioch. It was from Huntly himself, requesting a private meeting, as soon as possible. No reasons were given, no other suggestions made; merely the request.

The Graham pondered it awhile, while, under Leslie's keen eyes, training of the raw troops went on. Did Huntly seek an accommodation? Did he reckon the King's cause to be hopeless? Was he preparing to resile, with Hamilton's non-appearance? Or was he just seeking to lull Montrose into a false sense of security, seeking to gain time?

Other word of Huntly came from Aberdeen spies. Rumours were rife therein that the Gordons were preparing to descend upon it, with the co-operation of the magistrates and the University authorities. Certainly earthworks and other fortifications for the defence of the city were being constructed. Montrose's advisers – and now he had a-plenty – were strong that he take the town and hold it against Hamilton's arrival; but he did not wish to add to his responsibilities thus, and restrict his essential mobility. The Tables, in Edinburgh, now apparently more and more dominated by Argyll, had issued a fiat appointing Military Committees for all counties and all commands, on which the Kirk was strongly represented; and these committees had to be taken into consultation on all matters of policy. The Graham discovered that a great crowd of divines, chaplains and other long-faced gentry had descended upon his camp at Stonehaven, all claiming the authority of the Tables as advisers. Vociferously they demanded the taking of Aberdeen immediately. Whether from conviction or policy, Leslie backed them up.

Reluctantly, at the end of March, Montrose marched on the city.

There was no resistance – and no signs of the Gordons. Some of the city fathers fled by sea, as did the University professors and doctors. The citizens did not welcome the Covenanting army, nor did they provoke it. Black-robed divines descended on the erring town from near and far – like black crows on carrion, as Montrose asserted privately to Pate Graham – and did not confine themselves to monopolising the city pulpits. It was becoming most evident that many of the Kirk's ministers and supporters considered that a theocracy was now the rule in Scotland, the voice of God's ordained servants to be supreme in law and governance, and all soldiers, like other citizens, however lofty, to be subject to their guidance. Montrose, of course, saw it otherwise, and there were clashes. It was strange that Sandy Leslie should so consistently take their side – a Field-Marshall might have been expected to be the first to resent any ministerial interference in matters military. But, of course, they were in effect his paymasters.

Deciding that he did not like the atmosphere developing in Aberdeen, the Graham drew up orders for its good administration, strict but fair, appointed the Earl of Kinghorne as Lieutenant-Governor, ordered all Covenanting troops to wear a blue ribbon, as identification, imposed a fine of 10,000 merks – as advised by his Military Committee – as suitable contribution from a community which hitherto had failed to support the cause, and announced his own departure. He declared that he was going to keep an eye on Huntly and the Gordons. On the pretext that Hamilton's fleet might arrive off the harbour at any time, and coping with his reception require a skilled and experienced hand, he managed to leave the Field-Marshal behind, with his 1000 from Fife. And most of the ministers. Breathing more freely than he had done for a while, James Graham rode sixteen miles north-west, to Inverurie, a small and ancient royal burgh at the confluence of Urie and Don, and camped there.

All along, there had been stories of the Gordons mobilising their admittedly enormous war potential, in earnest. The air was thick with their reported numbers – 5000, 8000, 10,000. Oddly enough, Huntly's personal credit having suffered grievously at Turriff, the semi-legendary renown of his house had become transferred meantime to his sons. The eldest, Lord Gordon, was not much mentioned; but his next brother, the Viscount Aboyne, was said to have been so disgusted with his father's inactivity that he had run off, and sailed in a fishing-craft, south to join the King in the North of England; while the Lord Lewis, though only thirteen, was ranging round the Gordon country with a banner and a drawn sword, whipping up forces.

Inverurie, a grey-stone town amongst low green hills, with a great, green isolated mound which had supported a former royal castle – where the mighty Bruce had lain ill, before rising from his sick-bed to win a battle against the Comyns

– was an ideal spot to keep watch and ward on the vast sprawling area of rural Aberdeenshire, strategically sited not only at the junction of rivers but where the Bourtie, Benachie, Corrennie and Correen hill-masses forced road communications into a fairly tight bottleneck. If a wary eye was to be kept on the mighty Clan Gordon, this was the place to do it.

Montrose had scarcely expected, however, that his first sure word of the Gordons should be from such an authoritative level. On only his second day at Inverurie, a nondescript traveller from the north came seeking his presence – and turned out to be none other than Gordon of Straloch, Huntly's Chamberlain, though very much incognito. His master had sent him, he said, to arrange the private and secret meeting with Montrose, with a view to a possibly mutually beneficial arrangement.

Seeking to hide his astonishment, the Graham enquired further, as though this was perfectly normal procedure between rival commanders.

Huntly proposed, it seemed, that they should meet secretly, each to have only ten companions and armed only with swords, at an inconspicuous place mid-way between Strathbogie and Inverurie, each side to send forward three of their number to inspect the other, before meeting, to ensure that these conditions were scrupulously complied with.

'Does my lord of Huntly not trust my word?' Montrose interrupted warmly, at this stage. 'If I agree to the meeting, there is no need for such inspection, sir.'

'Your pardon, my lord. I said as much. But my master insisted upon it. He believes that your ministers might seek to deceive him. Not yourself, to be sure . . .'

'He wrongs them. But I will bring no ministers, I assure you . . .'

So, despite warnings of a possible trap, from Kilpont and others, two days later Montrose and Huntly did meet, at a hidden waterside hamlet under the steep slopes of Benachie. It was a strange encounter, with the Gordon strained, nervous, almost furtive, apparently wary even of his own companions – amongst whom James Graham was surprised to find the young Lord Gordon, as unimportant- and undistinguished-seeming as ever, but calmly alert and detached, in contrast to the others who presented a picture of corporate discomfort. Huntly insisted on drawing Montrose well aside, and out of ear-shot, for a start, and conducting the subsequent conversation in whispers – unlikely behaviour for the man at whose least word all the North-East was supposed to quake. The other, as a consequence, was the cooler, more off-hand.

Huntly's troubled discourse went thus. He had been deceived, shamefully deceived. Word had reached him from his son, Aboyne, now at Newcastle, that Hamilton was not in fact coming to Aberdeen at all. His force was to sail for the Forth, not the Dee. Probably he never had intended to come to the North-East. It was but a ruse to encourage the Gordons to rise. Yet now the King was criticising him for not acting more strongly. When he had His Grace's own commands to mobilise only, to await reinforcement. It was most unfair.

Montrose sympathised, distantly, agreeing that the King could be difficult, and was in most matters ill-advised. Probably it was Hamilton's fault. The man was a puffed-up bull-frog. But how did this concern himself?

An armistice, Huntly suggested, so far below his breath as to be almost inaudible. An end to this folly, in the North-East at least. An agreement – secret, of course. That there be no foolish fighting, no wasting of good lands, that Aberdeen should be left in peace, that grown men might get on with more important matters than playing soldiers.

Seeking to keep his voice level, the other agreed soberly that the situation was unsatisfactory. He would be glad to be able to call off hostilities. But what assurance had he that if he pulled back his forces, the great Gordon power would not once more resume an anti-Covenant attitude?

'You have my word,' Huntly said. 'Gordon's word!'

This was a little awkward for the man who had insisted that *his* word was sufficient guarantee for the security of this meeting. '*I* would accept your word, my lord,' he said. 'But others, I fear, might be less sure. Matters are decided, not by one man but by many, under the Estates. I am Lieutenant-General, and in the field I command. But I have the Field-Marshal Leslie to consider. And my Committee. This that you suggest is policy, not tactics. And for such I must carry a council. Such, I fear, would require more than just your word.'

Huntly tugged at his pointed beard. 'What? What would these require?'

Montrose took his time. 'I think, my lord, that nothing but your signature on the Covenant itself would satisfy them!'

Oddly enough, Huntly was clearly less shaken by this proposal than the other anticipated. He declared that he could not do such thing, of course; that he could by no means put his name to a Band against the King – but all less vehemently than might have been expected. And he listened to Montrose's disclaimers that it was nothing such, patiently enough. The other offered, as he had done once before, to endorse a copy of the document especially to cover the Gordon's loyal scruples. When Huntly questioned him on detailed wording for this, he elatedly perceived the battle won. The Gordon was going to sign.

There was a copy of the Covenant in the camp at Inverurie, he informed. If the Marquis would ride with him there – under his personal protection, of course – all could be done without delay, and the peace they both sought put in train forthwith.

After some suitable hesitation, Huntly agreed.

Unfortunately, back at Inverurie, a party of divines had arrived from Aberdeen in the interim, in their mission to the soldiery, and these reacted to Huntly and his son as they might have done to the Devil in person. There was a notable scene, with the Gordon losing his temper, and the Graham under fire from both sides. It was with difficulty that Montrose eventually got the precious signature, to a Covenant copy duly endorsed to the effect that the subscriber was binding himself in it to maintain the King's authority together with both the liberties of Church and State, Religion and Laws – an endorsement which the ministers at least were far from happy about, muttering darkly anent Papists, heretics, idolators and suchlike.

Assuring Huntly that the main step towards peace in the North-East had hereby been taken, and the King's best interests thereby advanced, just a little hurriedly Montrose saw the Gordons off, back to Strathbogie. The young lord, it was, who had the last word.

'You, my lord of Montrose, I think, are on the wrong side

in this conflict. You and the Covenant, both!' And he rode after his father.

Brows puckered, the Graham stared after them.

The Lieutenant-General's return to Aberdeen with Huntly's signature to the National Covenant, and the news that Hamilton was now likely to descend on the Forth, not the Dee, was received differently from his anticipation. The folk of the city rejoiced, of course, as did many others. But not the Covenant leadership there. The ministers, with one accord, condemned the Gordon move as a mere ruse, a snare, to trap the godly. And even if it was not, they should have no truck with the papistical horde. Huntly was nothing better than a deceitful limb of Satan, fit only for the consuming fires of Hell. And Montrose was at fault, at grievous fault, in having agreed to have any dealings with him – and, having done so, to have treated him so gently. Vipers should be stamped upon, not nurtured, by God's servants.

In vain Montrose argued before his Military Committee – which was as unmilitary a body as might be imagined. In a military situation, he declared, other matters than ethics, dogma and theology fell to be considered. Numbers of armed man-power, for instance, a hostile population, available resources, supplies, sheer tactics. Of such, as commander, *he* had to be the judge. He appealed to Alexander Leslie, but got no help from that hard-bitten individual, who declared that in his experience war was fought with wits, swords and powder, until one side was defeated – not by gentlemanly private converse between noblemen. Had he been in Montrose's place, Huntly would now be on his way to stand trial as rebel, in Edinburgh!

Coldly Montrose observed that, fortunately for the good name of the Covenant, treachery was not yet an acceptable method of gaining their ends – a statement which, it is to be feared, turned Leslie from somewhat contemptuous observance into implacable enmity. But the Graham's attitude gained little support. Kinghorne backed him, and the Earl Marischal; but most of his closer colleagues were away commanding units of the army, and the preponderance of ministers on his Committee were wholly lined up against him. They insisted that Montrose's agreement with Huntly, Covenant-signature notwithstanding, could not be ratified until the Gordon had appeared in person before them, for questioning and instruction. Moreover, declaring that Scotland was now godly and democratically governed, they demanded that the matter be put to the vote – and Montrose was overwhelmingly defeated. Announcing that he had never heard of armies and campaigns being commanded thus, the Graham all but stormed out – being persuaded to stay only by the thought that he still might exert influence if not control. When it was passed that Huntly and his son be summoned before the Committee forthwith, he announced, amid uproar, that he would personally advise the Gordons not to appear unless their safe-conduct was assured. Leslie intervened to say that the Earl of Montrose's personal safe-conduct was surely sufficient for any man. It was agreed that the Marquis and son be asked to compear, at Aberdeen, to elucidate details of the proposed armistice, on the 13th day of April.

Surprisingly, on that day, the Gordons did come, again secretly, with Straloch and his son, the Laird of Rothiemay.

That was a sorry day for James Graham, one of the bitterest in his life. Much stemmed from it; indeed nothing was ever quite the same after it. Here he tasted humiliation, of quite another sort than had been offered him at the Palace of Whitehall three years before, a shame such as had never come his way hitherto. Huntly had been enticed into a trap, baited with the Graham's given word. From the first, the Gordon chief and his heir were treated like prisoners, their interview with the Military Committee as appearance at the bar – but for sentence rather than for trial. Accusations were hurled at them, contumely, diatribes. Montrose did what he could, protested, sought to temper the blast, appealed, raged. But it was all most evidently arranged, organised, and he was consistently not only out-voted but shouted down. Time and again he was on the point of marching out. He even contemplated bringing in troops to silence these insolent preachers and orators – but recognised in time not only that this would assuredly end his influence in the cause to which he had set his hand, but that in fact almost all the troops now in Aberdeen were Leslie's Fifers, and Leslie himself was now clearly in command. All pretence of deferring to the younger man was gone. The Field-Marshall now was Commander-in-Chief indeed, and not concerned to hide it. More, Montrose gained the distinct impression that this whole affair was being staged by Leslie largely to humiliate himself.

Be that as it may, it was very much Leslie's, and the ministers' day. Huntly, conjuring up a strange dignity in the face of ranting, was harried and lambasted unmercifully, the younger George Gordon listening to all with his quiet detachment. Finally, he was told by Leslie that, having raised his forces against the realm, he was a traitor and without rights. That he had cost the realm dear, and must therefore pay a large sum in recompense. That he must bring in a number of Gordon notables as prisoners. And that he must accompany Leslie to Edinburgh the next day.

'I shall do none of these,' the Gordon answered, simply.

'I say that you shall!' the Field-Marshal declared. 'We ride tomorrow.'

'I ride, then, only as your prisoner! And I remind you that I am here under the safe-conduct of my lord of Montrose.'

'That is a matter for his lordship, not this Military Committee.'

'I protest! Most strongly I protest!' James Graham cried. 'I have listened to enough! My word stands. My lord of Huntly goes as freely as he came!'

'I care not how he goes, free or other! But he comes to Edinburgh with me, the morn. That I put to this Committee. Do you wish a vote to be taken upon it, my lord Montrose?'

The roar of approval left no doubts as to how the vote would go.

'The matter is decided. The officers will conduct the Marquis of Huntly and the Lord Gordon to their quarters. And attend on them well! My lord of Montrose – as *Lieutenant*-General, you will return to your force at Inverurie, to prosecute your campaign with all address. And with increased vigour.'

'So – you have assumed the command, sir?'

'I have assumed the chief command, yes. On the instructions of the Tables. And no' before time, I swear!'

'On the instructions of my lord of Argyll, rather than the Tables, I think.'

That remarks, injudicious perhaps, fell like a stone into a sudden pool of silence.

After a significant pause, Leslie rapped out, 'I declare this meeting adjourned,' and rose to his feet.

Before the Gordons were hustled away, the young lord caught Montrose's eye. Gravely the youngster inclined his dark head.

13

DESPITE THE NEW COMMANDER-IN-CHIEF'S ORDERS, IT WAS not long before James Graham followed Leslie south, instead of prosecuting his campaigns in the North-East with the required address. He was in a strange state of mind for that man, uncertain, perplexed, unsure of himself, and with no heart for his appointed task. He had, in fact, been struck where it hurt most – in his pride and his honour. All men know now, he felt, that Montrose's word was worthless – since a committee of divines and a fifty-eight-year-old mercenary soldier could invalidate it at their will. And all men must see him as ineffectual, Lieutenant-General in name, but harassed and thwarted by anyone wearing ministerial black. Perhaps it was the pride, more than the honour, that was the principal casualty.

But his distress was for the cause also, to which he had set his hand, at cost. Both in the long and the short term. It was going awry, falling into the wrong hands, becoming an oligarchy with menacing potential. While he was stranded up here in Aberdeenshire, far from the centre of decision. And even here matters were in reverse, with the entire Clan Gordon now raised to fury over the insult and treachery to their chief. There were uprisings and outbreaks of anarchy everywhere, even in Aberdeen city itself. Montrose found himself spending much of his time hurrying about the county putting down small conflagrations; acting the repressive policeman, in fact – a role for which he had by no means entered the cause of liberty and religious freedom.

So, leaving Aberdeen and his command temporarily to the Earls Marischal and Kinghorne, he rode south, with Black Pate and a small escort.

On the last day of April he arrived to find Edinburgh in a state of much excitement. King Charles had issued a proclamation, declaring his Scots subjects in treasonable rebellion and due to be punished by his royal self in person. He was marching north with his large force. Moreover, gallopers from Berwickshire had just brought word that a great fleet was beating slowly northwards along that coast, in the face of north-westerly winds – no doubt the Marquis of Hamilton, at last. Leslie had taken over the main Covenanting army, and was now encamped, with it, on the links at Leith, the seaport of Edinburgh, preparing to repel invasion by sea. Huntly and his son, summoned before the Tables, had been told that he must sign another and unendorsed Covenant, and make sundry other drastic concessions; and, having refused, with his heir was promptly confined prisoner in Edinburgh Castle. To some extent, it seemed, he had redeemed his Turriff-tarnished reputation, by making a resounding valedictory speech, before incarceration, which ended thus : '. . . I am in your power, and resolved not to leave the foul title of traitor upon my posterity. You may take my head from my shoulders, but not my heart from my sovereign !'

The Gordon seemed to be a hero, at last.

Repairing to Archie Napier at Merchiston Castle, Montrose learned all this, and more, and communicated his own indignation, disappointment and apprehensions for the future to his brother-in-law. The older man was sympathetic, and had like doubts and fears; but he declared that this was hardly an auspicious moment to seek remedial action and changes in policy, with armed invasion and conflict imminent. Edinburgh was in a fever of military preparedness, and all hopes pinned on their renowned and experienced Field-Marshal. He would scarcely find the Tables in a mood to listen heedfully or patiently. Especially as, more and more, they were tending to come under the sway of Archibald Campbell of Argyll.

Demanding to know how Argyll had achieved this sudden pre-eminence in a cause he had so long held aloof from, Montrose learned that the Campbell could act swiftly and decisively enough, in all conscience, when he saw fit. Given the wardenship of the West, as the Graham the North-East, with the especial task of containing the threatened invasions by Strafford in the Clyde area and Antrim's Irish on the West Highland seaboard, he had swiftly mobilised much of his great Campbell man-power, and garrisoned particularly all the landing-places on the long Kintyre peninsula, where, if Antrim was to try to link up with Strafford, he must make his short crossing from Ulster. Then, with another force of Campbells, he had descended upon the Isle of Arran in the Clyde estuary, taken the main strength, Brodick Castle, by surprise, and won the entire island without having to fight – a brilliant stroke, in more ways than one. For with Loudoun, Eglinton and other Covenant lords controlling the Ayrshire coast opposite, Arran was the key to the Clyde approaches, and Argyll could now control any invasion attempt therein; not only that, but Arran was the Marquis of Hamilton's property – he was also Earl of Arran – and the Campbells had long coveted that great island, with their lands all around. Now they had gained it, and from a man whom none would stand up for, in Scotland – a shrewd move indeed. Argyll, it appeared, would serve the Covenant and himself equally well.

Thus, Napier explained, the Campbell had made a great and swift impression, at no cost but only gain to himself – for the twin Western invasions never materialised. Vastly relieved, the Tables and the Covenanters generally welcomed him back to Edinburgh with open arms. But he was discreet, modest, on the surface, a humble, self-effacing and pious man. He did not have to beat the big drum; for the Earl of Loudoun was also a Campbell, and as Convener of the Joint Tables' Standing Council, was in a position largely to control all for his chief.

But what about Alexander Henderson? And Rothes? And others, Montrose demanded? Surely these were the true leaders of the cause, with Loudoun a mere figure-head, something of a dolt indeed!

A strategically placed dolt, now with a very shrewd and cunning brain behind him, the other pointed out. As for Henderson, he was still the true moral leader; but he had the whole uprising Kirk to manage nowadays – and a difficult and unruly horse that was to ride, puffed with its victory over the bishops. Clearly Henderson found Argyll a useful ally; more useful than Montrose, it seemed! And Rothes was less than well, a man sickening. Always he had eaten and drunk too much; and the excitements and journeyings of these days had been taxing for a man of his habits. He appeared less and less at the Tables, or in Edinburgh at all.

Depressed by all this, Montrose nevertheless decided to tackle Henderson, Sir Thomas Hope, and others, on the morrow.

On the morrow, however, the 1st of May, Hamilton's fleet, with a change of wind, sailed up the Forth, and city and port were agog. The Marquis was said to have some 5000 men aboard – much less than Leslie – but also much artillery, of which the Covenanters had little or none. The great squadron of nineteen ships made an impressive, a daunting sight, as it dropped anchor in Leith roads. The port and the army of the Covenant prepared for a one-sided bombardment, while glancing back over its shoulder towards the Border and the King's main invasion.

But no bombardment eventuated. And, oddly enough, after two days lying off Leith, the fleet up-anchored and sailed off to the other side of the Forth. There were many more harbours on that side than on the south, although all smaller than Leith; but Fife was Leslie and Lindsay country, and neither the Field-Marshal nor Rothes his chief had neglected to have these defended. Easily seen from the south shore, at most times, the invasion fleet sailed up and down the north, found no unguarded landing-places, and seemingly decided against doing anything rash. For, presently, with the easterly wind rising somewhat, the fleet split up, groups of ships seeking shelter in the lee of the undefended Forth islets – Inchkeith, Inchcolm and Inchmickery – and there remained.

Although a descent by open boats on open beaches, by night, was anticipated thereafter, and forces sent out to keep watch on a long coastline, gravely weakening the main Covenant strength, nothing such developed. Hamilton appeared to be no more successful as warrior than he was as statesman or ambassador. Perhaps it was his old mother who worried him, a dragon if ever there was one, Ann of Glencairn, Countess-Dowager and strong Presbyterian, who turned up at Leith pier, from Lanarkshire, with two drawn and loaded pistols, declaring that one was for her son Hamilton and the other for her son Lanark, if they dared to set foot on honest Scots soil.

At all events, invasion by sea remained only a threat. And King Charles's 40,000 moved but slowly, being still somewhere between Newcastle and Berwick.

Meanwhile Montrose made many calls and saw many people – although he avoided any actual confrontation with Leslie, whose authority as Commander-in-Chief might well have been turned to awkward account. This was no time for a trial of strength. He learned that not a few, especially amongst the nobility, were almost as anxious as he was about the way matters were trending in the Covenant leadership. There was much agreement that something must be done – but not at this difficult moment. Even Alexander Henderson admitted privately, guardedly, that a deal that went on was not to his liking, and would fall to be rectified. But certainly not just yet. Many in the ministry were proving over-zealous, yes. The Earl of Argyll was working himself into a position of great power, yes. But he was an able as well as an influential man, and now wholly committed to the Covenant cause. General Leslie could be harsh, difficult; but he was absolutely essential to Scotland in this pass. They must be patient, and await more convenient time for reform. Especially, he added, would patience become the Earl of Montrose! Had he not deserted his army, against the authority of the Tables who appointed him? Entered into private arrangement with Huntly, the enemy commander? Rejected the advice of his own Military Committee, with contumely? And spoken hard words publicly against the Covenant's friends and for the Covenant's enemies? Henderson was at his upright sternest, in making these charges, however quietly.

James Graham sought to be as calmly objective. He refuted the charges, explained – and added some of his own – ending by demanding Huntly's and his son's release. The other declared this to be impossible, save on the orders of the Tables who had commanded the imprisonment. And it was not practicable to summon the members thereof from their respective commands and duties, in this crisis, just to debate again on such matter. Moreover, the Tables once in session, might well take a serious view of one of their generals absenting himself from his post at such time, to come south

164

on this mission. Henderson strongly advised his lordship to return to his northern army forthwith, and make any representations by letter from there.

On that note they parted, civil but strained.

By first light next morning, Montrose was indeed on his way north again. But not wholly on account of Henderson's advice. Late the night before, a messenger came from the Earl Marischal. The Master of Forbes had been surprised and driven out of Turriff with his small garrison, by a combined force of anti-Covenant Ogilvies, Setons and Urquharts. This little victory had heartened the leaderless Gordons, who had now joined these others in force, and together they had marched on Aberdeen, gathering numbers all the way. The city had risen to welcome them – even the women were tying blue Covenant ribbons round their dogs' necks, as insult and provocation – and he and Kinghorne had had no option but to retire on Stonehaven, Dunnottar and the Keith country. He urged Montrose's return, and sought guidance, instructions.

The Earl of Marischal was aged nineteen, the Earl of Kinghorne twenty-two.

Their twenty-six year-old general cursed them, the whole Covenant leadership, the folly of men – but, above all, himself – as he raced northwards.

Even by Queen Margaret's Ferry over Forth, Glen Farg, Perth, Gowrie and Strathmore, it was 130 miles to Stonehaven. Montrose rode at his vehement hardest, but it was still two days before, with Pate and his faithful Grahams, he pounded up the steep defensive way to the gun-looped gatehouse of Dunnottar Castle, on its great thrusting rock promontory, amongst the sea-spray and the screaming, wheeling gulls. It was, however, to find the situation less bad than he had feared. The Gordons, many of them from the upland glens, had, after the fashion of hillmen, discovered the city to be a place meet for pillage rather than rescue, and Aberdeen had endured what amounted to a rape, with no single strong hand to command. As a result there had been battles between the indignant citizenry and their saviours, and more looting. Thereafter, well laden with their spoil, most of the Gordons had headed back for their glens. So the Marischal and Kinghorne had, the day previously, marched back, and retaken the town with only sporadic opposition, the Gordon, Ogilvie, Seton and Urquhart lairds and cavalry retiring before them in some confusion. The dogs of Aberdeen were now minus their blue bows again – not a few minus their lives.

The Grahams rode on into the city, tired as they were.

Montrose, deciding that Aberdeen obviously required a lesson as to where its best interests lay, imposed a much stricter regime than heretofore, a curfew, and requisitioning. Also another severe corporate fine. In war, especially civil war, the price for facing both ways – or neither – can be high.

Scouts trailing the retiring Gordon allies sent back reports that they had made, not for Strathbogie but for Gight, a strong castle of a branch of the Gordons, on the Ythan, near Fyvie, much more centrally placed. That they had settled here, rather than retired to their remoter fastnesses, seemed to indicate that this was only a reforming, a gathering of strength for further hostilities. The young Lord Lewis, the thirteen-year-old fire-eater, was said to be there.

Montrose had sent out urgent commands, on his way north, for more men to be mustered to his banner. Waiting three more days for these levies to accumulate, on the 30th of May, with a force of almost 4000, he marched north for Gight.

He found the castle a tough nut to crack, a strong place crowning a tall and rocky eminence amongst the Formartine braes, with the valley-floors around it deliberately flooded and boggy, so that the castle-crowned bluff was but the summit of a sort of island, an island only reachable by a causeway, crooked and gapped, through the marsh, and easily defended. Moreover the swamp-enclosed area was sufficiently large to offer temporary support to considerable numbers of men and horses; there were even cattle grazing there – so it would be difficult to starve out the defenders. Only by artillery could the place be fairly swiftly reduced – and Montrose had no artillery. There was little that they could do but sit down and besiege the place; but at least it would keep the enemy leadership immobilised and out of further mischief meantime. It was inglorious warfare – but anything else would inevitably have produced heavy casualties, with no certainty of success. The thought that he was facing a thirteen-year-old opponent did not help the Graham much, either.

So passed two frustrating, mosquito-haunted days and nights, as May turned to June, and the cuckoos mocked the Covenant's Lieutenant-General from every braeside. Then, almost relievedly, he received news, sent hot-foot from Edinburgh and by Henderson himself, of all people, that the young Viscount Aboyne, with Hamilton's invasion fleet, had persuaded that reluctant warrior to switch plans, leave the unrewarding Firth of Forth, and sail for Aberdeen. All the King's ships had not left, but a sizeable proportion had sailed away, allegedly with much artillery. It was the Tables' urgent commands, therefore, that a landing should be prevented if at all possible, and the city held at all costs.

So the siege of Gight was raised forthwith, and Montrose, feeling distinctly foolish, hurried the twenty-five miles back to Aberdeen. There he found no enemy force, but rumours that there had been a landing farther south – indeed in his own Montrose area. Concerned, he passed on to Stonehaven, recognising that this might be a move to cut his communications with the Covenant forces in the south. He waited at his old headquarters at Dunnottar, while probing squadrons rode off to gain firm news.

The firm news, when it materialised however, came from a different airt. No fleet, but a single small ship flying the King's flag, had made a secret landing *north* of Aberdeen, disembarking a tiny but quite illustrious company – not Hamilton admittedly, but young Aboyne, with the Earls of Tullibardine and Glencairn – the latter Hamilton's cousin – and a well-known mercenary-soldier named Colonel Gunn; also two field-pieces. Where the rest of Hamilton's fleet might be, was not clear; but the present information seemed definite and detailed enough.

Montrose was in something of a quandary. This new leadership clearly indicated a stepping up of enemy activity – especially as it was said that the King had transferred Huntly's Lieutenancy of the North to his second son, Aboyne, only seventeen years of age as he was. On the other hand, where was Hamilton himself, and the main invasion fleet? The rumours that there had been a major landing somewhere farther south, might still have some foundation – and this could have more immediate danger than the arrival of the little group farther north. No word of it came from his scouts or local informants; but it still might be a projected rather than an actual landing. Hamilton had apparently left the Forth; he must be somewhere.

So the Graham waited at Dunnottar, ready to move either way. He utilised the time further to train his forces; and was probably fortunate in having the services of one more of the mercenaries, one Major John Middleton, son of a local Mearns laird, a loud-mouthed, swaggering, uncouth soldier, but experienced and efficient at his trade.

In the event, it was from the north that the trouble developed – and more swiftly than might have been anticipated – while still there was no word of Hamilton. Aboyne made a quick link-up with his brother Lewis, and the enheartened Gordons flocked to their joint standard. They had as many as 4000 clansmen and allies at their backs in a couple of days, determined to avenge the insult to their chief. In brave style they dashed south, and once again Aberdeen fell. The young Gordons had all the traditional fighting spirit missed out of their father. Without delaying in the city, most of their host pushed on southwards for Stonehaven and a decision. Not only so, but they commandeered two Aberdeen vessels, to add to their single King's ship, and put aboard these three a collection of cannon raped from various castles in the area, heavy, rusted and antiquated pieces, as well as the two fine field-pieces brought from the South. The ships were to sail parallel with the Gordon advance, and to bombard the Covenant forces from the sea.

This bold strategy was rather spoiled by strong off-shore winds and driving rain, which kept the vessels out to sea, far out of range, and shrouded the land in dull grey curtaining. Montrose took fullest advantage of the weather – which he reckoned would be apt to unsettle and depress hastily mustered irregulars more than his better-trained and disciplined force – and moved north to take up a strong position at Megray Hill, just inland from Garron Point, two miles north of Stonehaven, where the road from Aberdeen ran through a fairly steep wooded ravine. In the circumstances, since Aboyne was so keen, he would let the Gordons take the initiative.

Whether it was the weather that indeed depressed them, a recognition that Megray was no place to fight a battle, or good advice from the veteran Colonel Gunn, the royalist army ground to a halt. There was no way round Montrose's positions, which he could not block. Artillery could have blasted him out of that ravine and its flanks – but the Gordons' artillery was at sea and nowhere in evidence. It was either a frontal assault against an entrenched foe, with most certain heavy slaughter; or retiral, with Montrose content to sit tight. It took a while to convince the Gordon fire-eaters, a wet and gloomy interval in the rain. They then turned round and retired in good order for Aberdeen again – although taking the elementary precaution of leaving a strong rearguard to continue to bottle up the mouth of the ravine until they were safely withdrawn.

Scarcely a shot had been fired.

Montrose, still concerned about his rear and Hamilton's main army, did not attempt to rush the Gordon retiral, as he might have done. He waited there in the rain, until in the early afternoon Kilpont arrived back from a three-day survey of the coast-line as far south as Arbroath, to declare that there was no single sign of Hamilton or his army. Whatever Henderson and the Tables said, it seemed that the elusive Marquis could be forgotten meantime.

Relieved, Montrose gave the order to advance on Aberdeen.

The weather cleared a little, and a pale sun was gleaming fitfully when, towards early evening, they approached the Dee, the great river which bounded the city to the south. Not unexpectedly they found the Brig o' Dee held against them, the ancient narrow bridge of seven arches, 350 feet long, endowed by the good Bishop Elphinstone, founder of the University, in the days when bishops were more to Scotland's taste. This had been an obvious point of hold-up; but what Montrose had not allowed for was the high spate in which the river was running. Presumably the rain had been even worse in the high Monadh Ruadh mountains to the west where the Dee rose. It was now a wide and raging torrent, and all ideas of fording it could be abandoned. And there was no other bridge.

Nor was it merely that the Brig o' Dee was held against them. The Gordons had stopped there, drawn up their entire army across the river, Highland foot in front, Lowland cavalry behind, flanking the bridge for half a mile on either side, with a strong party of musketeers on the bridge itself.

Montrose took counsel of his only professional. 'What think you, Middleton? Are they safe from us?'

'No force is ever safe from another, of similar strength, my lord. And we are not far off equal strength, I think. If you are sufficiently determined, you can have them.'

'By that, you mean prepared to lose sufficient men, sir?'

'War is not possible without losing men.'

'But wits and generalship may save many lives, sir. And every life a soul before God.'

'I never yet went into battle to save souls, my lord!'

'Perhaps not. But *I* do not forget it. What do you suggest, in this pass, Major?'

'To wear them down. Where they are weakest. A time-honoured maxim, my lord. And where are these like to be weakest? Not in numbers. Not in spirit, I think. Not in broadswords, or even cavalry. But – ammunition, now? For their muskets and hagbuts. I jalouse they'll have no great supplies of powder and shot. We have not, ourselves, by God – and they are like to have less. Have them to use it up, then, without us using our own.'

'Sound, yes. But how?'

'Make cavalry charges. At the bridge-head. A squadron at a time. Many charges. Always drawing off just before coming into musket range. Musketeers and hagbutters, I'll vow, will not sit close under charging horse, without firing well before they are in range.'

'Mm. That is well thought of . . .'

So the Covenant horse, of which Montrose had about 1000, were formed up in their squadrons, and sent in charging, banners waving, trumpets blowing, 200 or so at a time, to the bridge-end, time and again, always to swing away left and right, just out of musket-shot of their target. And each time the ragged rattle and crack of fire rang out. It looked, of course, as though it was the fire which consistently turned the cavalry back – though few men fell. The odd stray or spent shot at times did wound or bring down man or beast; but the losses were very small. Between charges, the enemy were given plenty of opportunity to reload and wait anxiously. In time it probably dawned on the Gordon command that they were being led grievously to waste powder and shot; but it would be an unusual commander who could prevail upon his infantry to sit tight, in an exposed position, under repeated cavalry charging, and to reserve their fire until it could be fully effective. The men, of course, never could tell whether or not this time the riders would indeed thunder down upon them, with no swinging away, and mangled death under slashing swords and horses' hooves be their lot.

Although this manoeuvre, therefore, was successful, so far as it went, and great quantities of Gordon ammunition was expended at little cost to the Covenanters, while the two main armies stood by all but inactive, the time-factor told against the one side as well as the other. The clouds had come down again, and it was going to be early dark for a June night. Admittedly the night might offer new opportunities – but that applied to both almost equally matched sides.

The Gordon command, for their part, had not been just idly watching. Much activity had been going on in the rear; and it was now seen that at least some of this was the bringing up of timber, from near and far, as fuel for great bonfires, placed all along the riverside, and even on the bridge itself. There was to be no darkness for surprise attacks. This, of course, applied equally to the Gordons, and seemed to indicate a purely defensive strategy.

Montrose, who had been bewailing his lack of artillery, decided that he might utilise the hours of darkness with profit. They were still only fourteen miles from Dunnottar; and at Dunnottar and Marischal had a number of old cannon. These were not field-pieces, but fixed and immobile features of the defence. If they could be transported here, first by boat to Covehaven, and then slung between pairs or teams of horses, they might attain a notable surprise with them, and change in the situation.

He gave the Earl Marischal himself the task, since he best knew the country and coast.

It was a wet night, which was both uncomfortable and disappointing – for it meant that the river's level would not sink, as hoped for, to permit fording at selected points.

A grey and chill daybreak, with the Gordon fires flickering low, saw four heavy cannon in position and assembled, with some ball and barrels of powder therefor – though a weary Montrose kept them well hidden meantime. Two more were on the way, but he ordered their arrival delayed unless they could be kept out of the enemy's sight. The Gordons still held to their former positions, the bridge as strongly guarded as ever – however short the defenders might be of ammunition.

James Graham, who had had plenty of time to think of it during that comfortless night, now staged a show, a play-acting, for the opposition's benefit. He sent off a small detachment to ride up the riverside, in full view, westwards. With little delay, a similar picket of horsemen moved off parallel, at the other side, to keep them under observation. They went for some three miles up, to Ardoe, where the river widened, in green levels, and there was a mid-stream island and double ford. The Dee was running as high as ever, but the party proceeded elaborately to make test of it, for depth and current. The thing was barely possible, and really out of the question for an opposed crossing – but still, leaving some of their number still prospecting there, the rest spurred back to Brig o' Dee, as though with news. Thereafter, Montrose made a great display of mounting, parading and inspecting the main mass of his cavalry, before duly despatching them off, squadron after squadron, in the direction of the ford. And, as he had hoped and prayed, almost at once the Gordon cavalry were off, likewise, to deny any crossing. Both mounted hosts disappeared westwards, up-river.

But there was a difference in the topography of the respective banks. The south side was fairly level land, and wooded; while the north was open and sloping upwards after a belt of marshy water-meadows. In consequence, the Gordons' progress was visible along the terraced roadway, whereas the Covenant horsemen were largely hidden in woodland. Moreover, beyond Banchory-Devenick's thicker forest, over a mile up, a wide bend in the river northwards pressed back the road on the far side still farther, and here was the village of Cults. The enemy commander could by no means see what was going on on the south road for well over a mile.

So, whenever all his cavalry was in this thicker woodland, Kilpont, in command, halted the main body. He sent on a small number of horsemen, with all their flags and banners, with orders to show themselves progressing westwards as much as possible. Then, with the Gordon horse well past on the other side, he turned his main body and went spurring back to Brig o' Dee.

Montrose waited long enough for Kilpont's returning host to come into sight, before ordering the cannon to be uncovered and the bombardment begun.

It was complete surprise. The densely massed Highland foot on the other side, quite unprepared for artillery-fire, and unable to hit back, fell into panic – as who would blame them? The cannon were aimed well behind the bridge – since its destruction was the last thing desired – and the defenders on the bridge itself found themselves isolated, as their main force retired precipitately and in confusion, to get out of range.

The returning Covenant cavalry was immediately switched back to charging the bridge-end, as before. And quickly, the musket-fire, fierce, almost hectic, at first, lessened. Yesterday's tactics were proving their worth. Montrose gave the order for a general advance.

It was all over in a brief half-hour. After ragged, scattered musket-fire from the bridge, the holders thereof retreated hurriedly. The cannon increased their range somewhat, and though most of their balls went wide, they made some lucky shots, especially amongst a group of Gordon lairds. The enemy command, hastily seeking to re-form and reorganise their alarmed infantry, and without cavalry support, were unable to do so before the Covenanters were surging across the bridge. Once Montrose's cavalry were over, of course, the thing was decided. One or two counter-attacks were thrown in, especially a determined one led by the new Provost of Aberdeen's own son, one Colonel Johnston; and many clansmen fought bravely. But against a thousand horse, in open country, they had no chance. Aboyne and his brother Lewis, under their father's great banner, were amongst the last to flee – but flee they did; and before there was any sign of Colonel Gunn, who had led the cavalry off, returning from the Fords of Ardoe.

When the issue at Brig o' Dee was clear. Montrose pulled out most of his horse – for a running slaughter was no part of his design, whatever Middleton vociferously advised – and sent them off westwards to deal with the unfortunate Gunn. But, in fact, no mounted battle developed, that veteran knowing at least when further fighting was useless. The royalist cavalry did not wait to make gallant gestures, but galloped off northwards for the Gordon country with all speed.

Aberdeen lay open once again, unhappy city.

There was something like mutiny, even anarchy, in the grey northern town that night. Victorious soldiery like to celebrate, especially when all the facilities lie so conveniently to hand. And when most of their officers are of the same turn of mind. For not only Major Middleton, but the Earls Marischal and Kinghorne – and, of course, all the ministers – were in favour of this wretched city being taught a lesson which would prevent it from ever again ranging itself against the Covenant. But Montrose was adamant. Without the handicap of having to defer to Leslie as overall commander, he was not hesitant about asserting his fullest authority, Military Committee or none. There was to be no sacking of the city. He had to use his own Graham troopers to impose that fiat in the narrow streets that night, and with little help from his leading colleagues – and was not entirely successful, inevitably. And next day, in a tense situation, there were hard words and threats. It was the first military victory of the Civil War – but its consequences were less than wholly happy.

Then, suddenly, unexpectedly, all was changed. Messengers arrived from the South. The war, scarcely begun, was over. Two days previously, King Charles had more or less capitulated. The Pacification of Berwick had been signed. All hostilities were to cease forthwith.

Details emerged. The King's forces, having reached Berwick-on-Tweed, and Hamilton having removed himself from the Forth, Leslie had moved his Covenant army south into Berwickshire, carefully sending word before him that they were coming in all loyalty to welcome the monarch to his Scottish realm. The host had taken up its stance at Duns Law – which could not be called a threatening position but which effectively blocked any royal advance towards Edinburgh. So the two armies glared at each other across the green levels of the Merse, neither side willing to take the first step in hostilities – the King because he was worried about reports from his inimical English parliamentarians in London, and lack of word from Hamilton and the Gordons; and the Covenanters anxious to postpone outright and treasonable attack on their lawful monarch, and concerned lest such should involve them in war with England itself. So Henderson sent secret messages and tentative terms to Berwick – and to the surprise of all, Charles accepted them. Possibly the timely arrival of Hamilton there, without having struck a blow in this peculiar war, was the last straw. A conference followed, at Birks near Berwick, and at it the King agreed that in future all ecclesiastical questions should be dealt with by free General Assemblies of the Kirk; and civil affairs should be put before duly called and regular parliaments. Charles Stewart was at his most courteous, reasonable, sadly noble. Bishops, Liturgies and the like would no more be imposed upon an unwilling people. As sovereign, he was concerned only that peace should prevail, the rule of law, and the wellbeing of his leal subjects. It was accepted that both armies should be disbanded, and all warlike behaviour cease. There were to be no reprisals, on either side, and all prisoners were to be freed.

So sanity and goodwill, belatedly, prevailed. Aberdeen in especial heaved a great and corporate sigh of relief.

Montrose was summoned south to deliver up his commission as Lieutenant-General, to attend a full meeting of the Tables to homologate all this, and in due course take part in another General Assembly and subsequent parliament. Winding up affairs in Aberdeen, he handed the place back to its Provost and magistrates, sent civil word to Aboyne and the Gordons regretting any inconvenience caused, dismissed his lieutenants, sent his army home, and said a thankful goodbye to his Military Committee – which now seemed somewhat dejected and at a loss. He took the road for Edinburgh.

It did not fail to occur to him, as he rode, that the Battle of the Brig o' Dee, the only real armed clash of the entire affair, had been fought and won after peace had been declared.

14

DESPITE ALL THEIR TRIUMPHS, THEIR CONVICTION, EVEN their talents, it was a strangely uneasy, even diffident group that waited in the Great Hall of Berwick Castle, perched high on its bluff above the town and the silver Tweed, six men who eyed each other a little askance and fidgeted rather. Yet these represented the true rulers of Scotland, their power and activities the reason for their presence here – while the man they waited to see represented weakness, failure, ineffectiveness. All were very much aware of the fact – yet achieved little confidence therefore. Bearding archbishops, high commissioners and ambassadors was one thing; facing the King in person was something quite other. That they had been *summoned* here, and had come, was indicative of their state – even though only six had come, where fourteen had been summoned, and by name; and of the six, Alexander Henderson had come without being summoned. Rothes, Loudoun, Lothian, Dunfermline and Montrose, all earls of Scotland, knew that they were in the right, held all the cards – but shuffled nevertheless.

An elegant young Gentleman of the Bedchamber, Will Murray by name, son only of a minister of Dysart in Fife but high in the King's favour, opened a door.

'His Majesty will receive you now, my lords,' he said. 'Come.'

In the end, Montrose went first, as the others all held back, it not being in his nature to insist on deferring to anyone. They were ushered into a small and simple chamber in a flanking-tower, without display or formality. Here was no chair-of-state, no heralds or trumpeters, no ranks of dignitaries – only Charles Stewart, dignity itself, sitting at a small table by the window, with an inoffensive-looking cleric in episcopal garb standing near by. Montrose bowed low, at his second sighting of his monarch, as did those behind him, the black-robed Henderson at the rear noticeably less low than the others.

The King seemed to have aged a little in those three years since the Graham had last seen him, but the process made him look only the more noble. Calm, a little sad, his great lustrous Stewart eyes so deeply full of patient understanding and care, he looked every inch a king. Bare-headed, hair falling in natural waves to his shoulders, he was dressed simply enough in the royal blue that he favoured, with deep lace collar and ruffles at slender wrists. He had been writing, a quill still in his hand.

'My lord of Montrose!' he said – and his voice was kind, almost warm. 'I rejoice to see you once more. A captain of renown now, I am told. My lord of Dunfermline. My lord of Rothes.' The smile was a little less warm. 'My lord of Loudoun . . .' He paused, fine brows raised. 'But five, six, of you? These only? Where are your friends? Whom I summoned. My good lord of Argyll? My lord of Eglinton? Of Wemyss? Of Cassillis?'

It had been agreed that Rothes, the oldest, should act spokesman; but since he said no word, Montrose made answer.

'All send their loyal devotion and greeting, Sire. But all could not leave their duties at one time. And some were at too great a distance.' In fact, Argyll had flatly refused to attend, and the Tables had forbidden others. 'But we six have full authority to speak on behalf of all, Your Grace.'

'The King's Highness prefers Majesty to Grace, my lords.' Will Murray said quietly, at their backs.

'Their attendance was a summons, my lord – not an invitation,' the King mentioned, but more in mild reproach than anger. 'I must not blame you, however, for the failings of others – you who *have* come. Forgive me, my friends. And this gentleman, whom it has not been my pleasure to have met hitherto?'

'The Reverend Master Alexander Henderson, formerly of Leuchars, now of Edinburgh's High Kirk, Sire. Moderator of the General Assembly.'

'Ah, yes. The General Assembly. I have heard of Mr Henderson. He has even honoured us with letters. I greet you, sir.'

Stiffly the minister bowed. 'Your Grace is kind,' he said. 'I came unbidden – but for good reason.'

'Majesty,' Murray jerked again.

'Your reasons, sir, I hope, for your breaking of our compact and treaty, the so-called Pacification of this Berwick? This has much grieved me, my friends.'

'*We* break the treaty!' Rothes burst out. 'Of a truth, Your Grace – Your Majesty, the boot is on the other leg! You have called the bishops to the new Assembly! After all that has been done and said! It is beyond all belief! Bishops again!' He glared at the prelate at the King's side.

'Control yourself, my lord,' that cleric said. 'Here is no way to speak in His Majesty's presence.'

'Sir – I do not require any English clerk to tell me how I should speak with my liege lord! It is my duty as an earl of the Scots realm to advise His Grace. And I do so advise him that in this of the bishops he has made grievous error. To call them to another Assembly is beyond all in folly. Against all that was decided here at Berwick. The Kirk of Scotland, in Assembly, has abolished bishops.'

'You say so, my lord of Rothes?' Charles's voice was sorrowful but restrained, reasonable. They had never been on good terms, these two. 'Did your Assembly *appoint* the bishops? No. Then how may it abolish them? But, even allowing it jurisdiction in the matter, surely the bishops had the right to appear before the Assembly that sought to depose them, to speak for themselves, to present their case? You call your Assembly the high court of the Church. It is the veriest, simplest, right of any subject of mine, in any of my realms, to appear before the court that tries him, to answer charges before judgment. You are all holders of jurisdictions, my lords. Is it not so?'

There was a pause, since none could gainsay that. Henderson, not being any sort of magistrate or judge, did his best. 'The bishops could have attended the Glasgow Assembly, Sire. None forbad them. But they chose otherwise.'

'Scarce the same thing, Mr Henderson.' That was said with a sigh, not harshly.

'To summon the bishops to attend this Edinburgh Assembly, in August, is an affront to the Kirk and people of Scotland,' Rothes went on, bluntly. 'Your Majesty must see it.'

'I see, my lord, other things. That your Tables continue to meet and to exercise authority – the authority of *my* Privy Council. Your Covenant army is not disbanded, nor your General Leslie dismissed. My Treasurer, the Earl of Traquair, is attacked and ill-used in Edinburgh streets. Others of my loyal servants likewise. These things I see, my lord – and require your explanations. And apologies. Do I have them?'

'We did not come here to make apologies, Sire,' Rothes declared grimly out of a tense silence. 'The time is past for such bairn's play.'

'Then why did you come, my lord? For I cannot believe that it was but in humble obedience to my royal summons!'

'We came to inform and advise Your Majesty. Inform that by this calling of the bishops again, you have set back the cause of peace in Scotland in marked degree. And to advise that you seek to undo some of the harm done by recalling the former bishops forthwith. Preferably to England – where they might be better thought of!'

'And if I choose to disregard such unsought advice, my lord?'

'Then Your Majesty must bear the consequences. Renewed warfare in Scotland. And the possibility that the Scots might join forces with your English Puritans – who do not love bishops any more than do we!'

That brought gasps even from Rothes' fellow Covenanters. And a hand upraised in horror from the cleric.

'How . . . how dare you speak the King so!' he cried.

'Who is this English clerk?' Rothes demanded.

Murray answered him. 'No Englishman, my lord. But Dr Balcanquhal, from my own Fife. And yours. Dean of Durham.'

'So much the worse for him!'

Charles spoke, quietly. 'Are you making a threat, my lord? To me – the King! In this of the Puritans?'

'I would name it advice, and warning, Sire.'

Charles rose from his chair. 'I cannot accept such threats from any subject of mine,' he said, head shaking. 'I find your manner and behaviour unsuitable and unsupportable, my lord. Were you not here on my royal summons, and therefore presently secure from the consequences of my displeasure, you would discover how ill-advised are your words. You have my permission to retire, sir.'

Curtly Rothes bowed, and turned away. The others, glancing at each other in doubt, began to move after him.

Not so Montrose. He had been shocked at Rothes' tone. The man was obviously not well, and all his bonhomie and shrewd canniness seemed to have disappeared with his health – like his Doric speech. His attitude in the monarch's presence was not only deplorable, but damaging to the Covenant cause. They had not come all this way deliberately to offend the King and add to their problems. Today, whatever the rights and wrongs of the conflict, Charles had become the injured party.

'Sire,' he exclaimed, 'of your royal clemency, hear me. My lord of Rothes has not spoken so by our prior agreement. He is a sick man – not himself. He and we all, are loyal subjects of Your Majesty. We did not come here to threaten nor to distress Your Highness. But to discuss with you the betterment of your Scots realm's affairs.'

'Then, my lord of Montrose, I think that you chose but an unfortunate spokesman!'

'Perhaps, Sire. But the Earl of Rothes is senior as to age. We crave your royal indulgence.'

'Very well.' The King sat down again. Rothes went out, slamming the door behind him. But the others lingered.

'We believe, Sire, that mistakes, errors, on both sides of this controversy, might have been avoided had we been able to speak face to face. Instead of through intermediaries who have proved by no means reliable. This of the bishops and the next Assembly, for instance. If Your Majesty had been advised to ask that they attend a special hearing, to answer and speak to their deposition at the previous Assembly, instead of summoning them as of their right to take part, no clash need have occurred.'

There was a stir and murmur behind him, but no outright denial of that from the others.

'You would have me submit the bishops, the lords spiritual of my Church, to your trial, my lord?'

'Such was Your Majesty's own figure, a trial and judgment. Speaking before a court. But my contention is that if we could but consult together, from time to time, much distress, misunderstanding, might be spared all. Your Highness's advice on matters Scots has, I fear, been but poor. And the first that we are apt to hear of your policies is their implementation.'

'And you conceive this to be improper, my lord? I have a Scots Privy Council to advise me.'

'Of whom the former bishops still comprise the majority, Sire!' That was Loudoun's first contribution.

'You would wish me to turn your Tables into my Privy Council, sir?'

'Not so. But your present Council has served you but ill. We urge that your interests would be better served by keeping in touch with the Tables, Sire,' Montrose suggested, moderate of voice.

'Very well. Your urgings I have heard and will consider, my lord.' There was a pause.

'And the bishops, Sire?' Henderson asked. 'Do they attend, or do they not?'

'That is for my decision, sir. But . . . they will not attend to be insulted. Nor, I think, will I.'

Quickly the Covenanters glanced at each other.

'Were you . . did Your Majesty think to attend? To attend the General Assembly in person?' Seton, Earl of Dunfermline, put their question.

'I did. That is why I am still here, at Berwick.'

'But . . . Traquair? We understood that the Earl of Traquair, the Treasurer, was now your High Commissioner?'

'My Commissioner in Scotland, yes. When I am not present. And my lord of Hamilton . . . otherwise occupied. Had I come, he would of course have stood down. But, after today, I fear, that is not possible. I can by no means attend an Assembly where the Crown is like to be insulted. As it has been today. This you must perceive.'

Montrose spoke. 'Sire – I pray that you reconsider. We knew nothing of your possible royal attendance. It would greatly rejoice and encourage your loyal Scots subjects. If . . . if . . .'

'If Your Majesty acted somewhat other than did your Lord High Commissioner at the last!' Henderson ended for him, grimly.

King Charles rose to his feet, once more. 'My lords, gentlemen – I cannot, will not, be harried and assailed thus. I think that you perhaps forget yourselves, in your pride. I counsel you to beware of that sin, that deadly sin. You, my lord of Montrose, at least I thank for your courtesy. I bid you all God-speed. You may retire. This audience is now ended.'

Bowing, they backed out – although Montrose would have waited to say more, if he might. But such royal dismissal was not to be questioned.

His colleagues eyed him not a little askance, and less than kindly, as they left the presence.

PART TWO

15

IT WAS ALMOST A YEAR LATER, AND IN VERY DIFFERENT
circumstances, before Montrose was near Berwick again. He
alone of the party of six who had so displeased King Charles
now considered the fast-flowing Tweed and wondered. His
companions now were soldiers, not great nobles and emissaries and churchmen; and although he was much more at
ease in their company, still he wondered. Indeed this wondering, doubt, questioning of self and of others, so unlike
the man's basic character, had become ever more part of
James Graham's life these many months. He seemed to be
forever being carried along on a tide, a flood, so much more
dark, swift and daunting than this Tweed, carried where he
would not, questioning the direction, fearing the outcome,
suspicious of others and himself suspect. Quite gone were
the days of enthusiasm, faith, hope. He was still a Lieutenant-
General of the Covenant forces – but more, he imagined,
that he and his Grahams and friends might be kept under
the keen and stern eye of the Commander-in-Chief, Alexander Leslie, than for any trust in himself.

For it was war again, of a sort. The Covenant army was
remustered and encamped at Duns Law once more, with
actual invasion of England imminent. And crazily, Montrose
and his 2500 personally raised men, Grahams, vassals, allies
and friends from Strathearn, Stirlingshire and the Mearns,
were to form the van, to lead the way in an exercise of which
he disapproved. To invade England – how could that be
called necessary for the freedom of worship in Scotland?
Which was his concern, all that he had joined this cause to
achieve. Even though the main object of the expedition was
not battle, but to arouse the dissident English, the Puritans
and parliamentarians, to rise and so bring pressure to bear
on the King.

This invasion, however, was only one of a long line of Montrose's disagreements with the main Covenant leadership. The Edinburgh Assembly of the Kirk had taken place last August. No bishops had dared to show their faces, despite the King's refusal to withdraw his summons to them to appear. But, under David Dickson's Moderatorship this time, the proceedings had degenerated into little more than an anti-King demonstration of snarling vehemence. Charles had held to his decision not to attend, appointing Traquair, a weak man, as his Commissioner; but he had sent a statement of his case, written by the same Dr Balcanquhal, Dean of Durham – and this was read amidst hootings, and rejected with a violence and contumely most derogatory to the monarch. And it was ordered that every citizen of Scotland *must* sign the Covenant. Montrose had objected to much, especially the arrogant declaration that episcopacy, even in England, was unlawful and to be rooted out.

Thereafter a parliament, the first in Scotland for many a year, had been held. And here the Earl of Argyll at last moved out into the open, dominating the proceedings, not so much by his strangely shrinking presence as by his influence, his cunning manipulation of the more extreme elements, his willingness now to become the focus and centre of the anti-Charles forces which were becoming ever more vociferous. That parliament of 1640, in effect, reduced the monarch, in Scotland, to a mere symbol, a name, without power. Montrose had fought against the whole trend of it, but without avail. Whispers had begun to circulate in Scotland; one, that Argyll was seeking the Scots throne for himself – he could claim descent from Bruce's sister; and the other, that Montrose had been seduced by the King from his allegiance to Covenant and Kirk.

And that was not the worst. The Tables were reconstituted by parliament a more official Committee of the Estates; and though Montrose still sat upon it he was in a permanent minority now. Argyll, oddly enough, did not let himself be nominated a member; but he had a faithful group of supporters thereon, led by Loudoun, who served him well. The Campbell had had himself appointed to Montrose's own previous duty of ensuring that the Gordons and other North-East clans did not trouble the Covenant's rear in any future activities; and very differently from the Graham he went about his task. With 5000 of his own clansmen, he proceeded in person on what was nothing more than an old-fashioned and savage clan-feuding foray against his hereditary enemies, leaving a terrible trail of ferocity, slain and tortured men, burned homes and domestic disaster, right across Scotland's North, from Argyll, through Atholl and Lochaber, to the Angus glens. The Ogilvys of Airlie were long-standing foes of the Campbells; and concerned to prevent further savagery, Montrose had persuaded the young Lord Ogilvy – his father, the Earl of Airlie, was in England with the King – to hand over Airlie Castle to local Covenanters, "in the public interest"; and had sent urgent message of the fact to the advancing Argyll. But the Campbell was not to be balked of his prey. He descended upon the Airlie country with redoubled fury of fire and sword, and burned not only Airlie Castle but the lesser and more remote castle of Forter, in which Lady Airlie had taken refuge, with unrelenting ferocity, driving the Countess into the hills, a pathetic refugee.

All this while Montrose was raising his regiments in Stirlingshire and Strathearn.

So now the Graham was prospecting the fords of Tweed, over which, in due course, he would lead the van of the Scots army into England – and doing so a prey to doubts indeed. Even the river was adding to his problems. It had been another deplorably wet season, and all the waters were running high, the mighty Tweed no exception. Royal forces still held the bridge at Berwick – although the King, of course, no longer was there. There was no other bridge. Montrose had decided on the Coldstream area, some fifteen miles from Berwick. Not that there was much choice; fords were few and far between on that wide, swift-running stream; and even hereabouts, unless the weather much improved, any crossing was going to be difficult for cavalry and impossible for foot.

Black Pate came spurring back from an investigation farther upstream, having discerned no improvement. So Coldstream it must be – where King James the Fourth had crossed, 127 years earlier, before Flodden. Might that be no ill omen.

Returning to Duns, twelve miles to the north, Montrose

found the great camp in a stir. The Earl of Argyll had arrived, from the North.

The inevitable clash was not long in coming. When Montrose repaired to the Commander-in-Chief's tent, to report his findings, it was to find the Campbell closeted with Leslie.

The older soldier pinched his bony chin, looking from one to the other. 'Here's a pleasant meeting, my lords,' he said, grinning. 'Convenient, is it no'?'

'I do not esteem it either pleasant or convenient,' the Graham answered, stiffly for him. 'My business is with yourself. I interrupt. I will return, with word of the fords, at a better moment.'

'Tush, man – not so hasty! My lord of Argyll and yourself will have much to discuss. The entire fate o' this Scotland, belike! Say on, say on!'

'My lord of Montrose will be weary with travel,' Argyll said in the softly lisping yet grating voice. 'After refreshment, no doubt, we can speak together more kindly.'

'I am not weary. And I cannot conceive of converse between us as being kindly, in this pass!'

The Campbell spread his hands, wordless.

'Come, come, my lord! *MacCailean Mor* has come all this road of set purpose to see you. Here's no way to greet him.'

'To see me? I cannot conceive why!'

'You are too modest, my lord,' Argyll said thinly. 'I have a paper, which requires your signature. Yours, and Master Henderson's. His I have obtained.'

'Ah. Then it must be important. To bring you, in person.'

'The Committee conceives it to be so. The Committee of the Estates. Requiring signature before you leave for England.'

'To what end?'

'A matter of administration. During the absence of yourselves and the army. The country will be much . . . impoverished. It is the appointment of myself, my unworthy self, as responsible for the peace of part of the country.'

'The peace? You! What part? Other than your own Argyll?'

'That part, my lord, lying north of the Rivers Forth and Clyde.'

'Dear God! Forth and Clyde? That is . . . that is more than half Scotland!'

'The stony half!' Argyll agreed dryly.

'I'll not believe it! This – this would make you, one man, master of half the land!'

'Not master – servant. My task to preserve the peace and see to good governance. At your backs, gentlemen. In the name of the Committee of the Estates. Its servant.'

'As you have just kept the peace in Angus! In Atholl. In Badenoch and Lochaber!'

'As you say, my lord. As I did, on the authority and the behalf of the said Committee.'

'Did the Committee authorise you to burn Airlie Castle? After it had surrendered to the said Committee, on my command?'

'I had full authority to take all steps as appeared to be necessary. As had you, my lord Montrose, when you were Lieutenant-General amongst that nest of vipers!' The Campbell raised his consistently down-bent, diffident gaze for a moment, to shoot a venomous glance at the younger man. Of that glance there could be no doubt – although most of the time it was hard to say just where Argyll looked, on account of his squint.

'I did not use *my* commission as excuse for rapine, torture, slaughter, war against women and bairns! I will not sign such paper, delivering thousands of my fellow countrymen into your hands, sir!'

There was a long silence. Leslie coughed, scratched a leg, and appeared to be grinning to himself.

'Your words, unbecoming in a Christian gentleman who has set his hand to the Lord's work, pain me,' Argyll said, at length, apparently considering the floor of trampled grass. 'But perhaps I should remind your lordship that this is a decision of the Committee of the Estates. Not mine. All members signed it, save Master Henderson and yourself, here with the army. Henderson has now signed. Your signature is requested. But nowhere have I heard that it is *essential*. That my commission is invalid lacking one signature. I am Lieutenant and Justiciar of the North, whatever you may say, sir. As well to recognise the fact.'

Montrose took a deep breath. Here it was again – he was faced with the damnable decision of those who committed themselves to a cause; whether to abandon it when things went wrong, or to compound, stay on, in a position where better influence might still be exercised. How many times he had put this grim choice to himself of late? To gain a little time, and aiming perhaps to shake the Campbell's hypocritical pained righteousness, he went on, slowly.

'Perhaps there is some truth in the tale that men tell, in the North? That your men, in Atholl and Angus, slew and burned to the slogan "In the name of King Campbell, not King Stewart!"'

Argyll licked his thin lips. 'I charge you, watch your tongue, Graham!' he rasped.

'My tongue is still my own. As is my signature!'

'Then take heed lest they become otherwise!'

'None will make them so, I think.'

'Be not so sure. There are powers which even the Graham must bow to.'

'To be sure. God's. And the King's.'

'And the Committee of the Estates'!'

'That Committee I lend my service to. Not my honour nor and yet my conscience.'

'Remember that, when it comes to question you!'

'Question? Me? Why should the Committee question me, my lord? One of its own members. Who has served it only well. Better, and longer, than most!'

'Served it well? Some say different. When you encourage and nurture the Committee's enemies.'

'Have I done so?'

'What of Huntly? Of Aboyne? Ogilvy? Others without number. Aye, old Southesk himself, and Carnegie likewise. All enemies of the Covenant and Christ's Kirk. Your whole campaign in the North-East has been stained with lenience to God's foes, comfort to those who oppose Him.'

'Lenience? So that is it! None will accuse *you* of that, at least!'

'God's enemies are Campbell's enemies,' the other said. In anyone else, that would have sounded as ridiculous as it was objectionable. But not in this man. He might even believe it.

Shaken a little, Montrose glanced at Leslie. That hard-bitten veteran looked as though he might be enjoying himself. He probably found them both equally absurd.

'Do you sign my commission, my lord? Or do you not?'

Argyll's voice was back to the sibilant West Highland normal.

'Let me see it.'

Scanning the paper he was handed, James Graham saw that it was a typical commission, only unusual in that it gave Archibald Campbell complete powers over.the largest if not the most populous area of Scotland. He drummed fingers on it for a moment. Then spoke. 'Have you a pen, sir?'

Leslie emitted a gleeful little croak of a laugh, and pushed over a quill and ink-horn from the clutter on his table. Argyll said nothing.

Montrose dipped the pen, and smoothed out the paper. He applied one to the other. But he wrote more than just the single word at the foot. He wrote quite a number of words, indeed. Then he signed it, in the space left for him at the top of the list, next to Loudoun's, and pushed it from him.

Argyll grabbed it, and held it close, to peer. Then he stammered something explosive, undoubtedly a Gaelic curse, rising to his feet and slamming down a clenched fist on the document.

'For the peace and good governance of that part of the realm, my lord,' Montrose observed. 'Do you believe only yourself fit to ensure it?'

'This – this is outrage!' The other was almost choking. 'Not to be tolerated . . .'

'You have what you came for. My signature.'

'These . . . these others! Time-servers. Toadies of your own!'

'Earls of Scotland, sir. With as good a right as Argyll to serve the Committee while others of us are furth the country. They are men of experience in affairs. They will but strengthen your hand!'

Leslie reached out, to claw the paper to him. He tee-heed a high-pitched, sniggering laugh. 'So – that's it! Mar! Home! Cassillis! Kinnoull! These put in to share! Share your commission. God – here's a ploy! S'wounds – here's a tod amongst the poults!' His glance at the younger man was almost admiring.

'It will not stand – it will not stand, I say!' Argyll exclaimed. 'The Committee will not have it. All the signatures made null. By this . . . this insolent addition! They will not have it. I shall see that they do not.'

'Indeed, my lord? As yet you are not a member of the

Committee. Whereas I am. It will stand – until another commission comes, requiring my signature. In England!'

The Campbell glared, just where was hard to say. But there was no doubt as to its quality.

Montrose turned back to Leslie. 'Sir – I have to report that the Tweed is still impassable. I will ford it, with the van, at Coldstream. But not for days yet. The people there tell me that the river will take three days to drop, after wet weather. And still it rains. Cavalry might cross before, but not foot.'

'Aye. As I feared. So be it . . .'

Montrose was not one to allow physical weariness to dictate his actions. Within two hours of the return to camp, he and Pate Graham were spurring northwards through the Lammermuir Hills, the rain and dusk notwithstanding.

At Edinburgh, forty miles north, they went straight to Merchiston Castle, where they got Archie Napier out of his bed, for urgent discussion. From him they learned enough to know that further riding was ahead of them. Borrowing fresh horses, and rousing some of Napier's men there and then, as messengers, they set out once more through the July night, this time almost due westwards.

Dawn found them thirty-five miles on, and half-way to Glasgow, clattering spent mounts up the steep brae to Cumbernauld Castle, in the skirts of the Kilsyth Hills. This was the house of John Fleming, Earl of Wigtown, Montrose's friend and distant kinsman. More important perhaps, here visiting was the Lord Almond, heir to the Livingstone Earl of Callander, who was another Lieutenant-General to Leslie, indeed second-in-command since Montrose himself only had charge of the van.

With more messengers sent out, the two weary horsemen retired to sleep.

When they were awakened, in the early afternoon, most of the men summoned to Cumbernauld had arrived, an illustrious company. There were the Earls of Home and Mar, whose names Montrose had inserted into 'Argyll's commission. Also Kinghorne, Seaforth, Atholl and the Marischal, plus the Lords Boyd, Erskine and Ker. The Earls of Perth and Kellie, and the Lord Drummond arrived soon thereafter. With Wigtown and Almond, they represented a good cross-section of the moderate Covenanting nobility. And the Graham believed that he could trust them all. None were members of the ruling Committee of the Estates, save himself. Others he would have called; but they were too far afield to be brought here in time. He was fortunate to have caught his two previous lieutenants, Kinghorne and the Marischal, who had been training their new regiments near Edinburgh.

When all were assembled, Montrose addressed them. 'My friends,' he said, 'some of you know why I have had the temerity to bring you here; some may not know all my mind, I think – if I know it myself. But most have come at some inconvenience – for which I crave your pardon. But I would not have asked you, nor myself come all the way from my regiments at Duns, in haste – nor prevented my lord Almond from returning this morning to the army there – had I not deemed it sufficiently important.'

There was a stir of anticipation.

'For long I have been concerned at the manner in which the Covenant cause, which we have all embraced, has become spoiled and misdirected. There are times, now, when I scarce recognise it for the noble cause to which we set our hands. You all know it. I need not labour it. But you will forgive me if I trace the beginnings of the ill to that day when the Earl of Argyll announced his adherence to the Covenant, at the Glasgow Assembly.'

There was a growl of agreement from all present.

'Argyll is no friend of mine, and therefore I must, and do, take heed against my own prejudice. But it is proven fact that the Campbell controls much of the Committee of the Estates today, encourages the fiercer Presbyterian factions for his own ends, and increasingly has his way in this realm. To its hurt, I say. He has gained altogether overmuch power, to soil a fair cause. And you all know how he has exercised that power, in the North, this last month !'

Atholl and Mar, whose lands had been overrun by the Campbell horde on its way to Angus, led the chorus of assent.

'Last night, my friends, Argyll brought to me at Duns, for my signature as member of the Committee, his new commission therefrom to have sole authority in all Scotland north of the Forth and Clyde. Argyll alone . . .'

He got no further, in the uproar of dismay and anger.

When he gained quiet, Montrose went on to describe what he had done, and the probable consequences. It was time to call a halt, he declared. 'At Argyll's instigation, the Covenant cause is fast becoming not a cause to free religion but a cause to pull down the King and raise the Campbell! King Charles has been foolish, ill-advised, obstinate; but he is still our King and liege lord. Our cause puts itself ever more in the wrong, in this. And I, for one, will not stand by and see Charles Stewart replaced by Archibald Campbell!'

'Nor I!'

'Nor I!'

'A plague on that ill-favoured fox!'

'Fox, yes. But foxes are cunning. It behoves us not to forget it. Argyll is a clever man – make no mistake. If he is to be countered, it must be by shrewd means. And unity amongst the right-minded. He will divide us if he may. We here are all loyal to the King, however mistaken he may be. He is *Ard Righ,* the High King of Scots – and we, his earls, are the lesser kings. This has always been our status in this ancient realm, from beyond history. A status that has its duties. We have the duty to advise, warn and guide the King, when he is wrong – not to pull him down. Is that agreed?'

All admitted it.

'Then I say that we should make a compact. A bond, if you like. To bind ourselves, each and all, to resist the schemings and savageries of Argyll, to uphold the true Covenant cause and freedom of worship, and to maintain the King on his throne, better advised. See you – the Campbell has his friends and bought men, who will support his every move. We must prove as united, as ready to act. Others will adhere to us, later. The Lord Napier sent his fullest support. But here we have a resounding company to begin the climbing of Argyll's wings! How say you?'

There was no dissentient voice in the loud and long acclaim.

They thereupon thrashed out a statement which would cover their intentions without specifically naming Argyll or the extreme left-wing ministers. They proclaimed their loyalty to the King, their adherence to the National Covenant, and how they had joined themselves together for the maintenance and defence of freedom. But that, by the practices of a few, their country was now suffering; so that now the undersigned bound themselves to hazard, if need be, their lives, their fortunes and estates, to see that these objectives were not controverted by any soever; and to act together in so far as might consist with the good and weal of the realm and the public interest.

All signed.

Copies were made, and subscribed; and with the ink barely dry, Montrose and Black Pate, with Almond in company now, were off again, on the long road back to Berwickshire and the army.

In the end, it was many days, weeks later, in that deplorable summer, before Leslie was able to set his force of 23,000 foot and 3000 horse in motion. The delay was not all in the high state of the Tweed, and the presence of royalist forces patrolling the far bank. The Committee had decided, sensibly, that proclamations should be sent before the army, into England, emphasising that this was no invasion, that the Scots had no quarrel with the English people nor desire to make war against them, but that it was only a means of convincing King Charles and his assembled forces in the North that they must come to terms with the dissidents on on both sides of the Border.

The river was still a formidable obstacle for men on foot. To encourage the doubtful infantry, and to set the right tone for the proceedings, Montrose himself waded in and across, alone, fully clad and armed as he was, and then back again. Where such happily uncomplicated matters were concerned he was in his cheerful element; indeed, he had been looking forward to the actual campaigning, as distinct from the politics thereof, almost more than he would have admitted. This gesture he made under the eyes of a troop of English horse which had been watching them at a discreet distance on the other shore, but prudently vanished once the real crossing began. Montrose ordered a squadron of cavalry to move into the water and there to stand, in close order, to act as a breakwater for the current and had his foot move across, arm in arm, just below them. All got safely over.

By-passing Berwick entirely, they headed southwards, un-opposed, through central Northumberland, two regiments of 1000 horse and 1500 foot. This was very much Montrose's personal force, largely drawn from his own clan and estates, the cavalry Lowland lairds and their tenants, the foot mainly hillmen from Strathearn, the Highland Line and the Lennox, some of the fastest-moving infantry in the land, lightly armed, fleet of foot. It was an ideal force for the van of a great army, the horse deployed in depth, ranging the countryside on either flank, the foot pressing straight ahead, at speed, eating up the miles, clearing the way but leaving the main force behind to consolidate.

Not that a deal of clearing or consolidation proved to be necessary. Certainly, English videttes from Berwick kept them company and under observation, but at maximum range and carefully avoiding any clash. And the local people showed not the slighest concern. Clearly the Northumbrians accepted the proclamation's terms to the effect that they were not being invaded. A less rousing Scots affray over the Border had never been mounted. It was the 20th of August.

Montrose chose a camp-site for the main army at Millfield, ten miles from Tweed, in the Till valley, and pressed on with his own force another five miles nearly to Wooler. There they spent an undisturbed night, with scouts posted over a wide perimeter.

Next day was equally uneventful. Riders from Leslie informed that the King's Berwick army of about 5000 was retiring fast down the coast towards Newcastle, definitely not concerned with giving fight at this stage. Orders were to press on to the Tyne, west of Newcastle, and there halt.

That they did, without interference, avoiding all centres of population such as Wooler and Alnwick and Morpeth. Driving fast, Montrose reached the Tyne at Newburn, some five miles upstream from Newcastle, in three more days, and there had to wait for another three while the main army came up – acting now as wary bait for Leslie's trap.

But the mouse would not nibble. The Lord Conway was the King's Major-General at Newcastle, a cautious individual with a restive and ill-assorted force which, he complained, was only fit for Bedlam and the Bridewell. Probably he was wise to hold back. Strafford was his senior officer, based at York, and he made no move to advance to his subordinate's aid, declaring that the King himself had left

London on the day the Scots crossed Tweed, to take personal command, so that, meantime, a holding action was advisable.

Montrose, at Newburn, learned off this swiftly; for the English Puritans, Presbyterians and dissenters generally, conceiving the Scots cause their own, were quick at sending information. The Graham was no less swift at passing it back to Leslie, with his own comments. The last thing they wanted was for King Charles to be personally involved. So long as he was not there, they could make use of the fiction that they were not in arms against their monarch, but against his advisers. But if he led his forces in person any attack thereon must rank as treason, and would gravely tie the Scots' hands. Montrose advised an immediate assault on Conway before the King could put in an appearance. Moreover, spies in Newcastle reported that the townspeople were mainly of dissenting mind, and also smarting from the outrages of Conway's unruly soldiery. He suggested letters be sent to the Mayor and local leaders declaring that the city would be left unharmed if co-operation with the Scots was forthcoming.

It was. Newcastle gave Conway notice to quit; and that sensible man, deciding that King Charles was the best man to direct his own strategy, commenced a retiral on York. However, Montrose now commanded both sides of the Tyne, astride the fords at Newburn; and Leslie, coming up with his cannon, was able to cut Conway's line of retreat in the most dramatic fashion by sustained artillery-fire. There was no real opposition. The English cavalry fled headlong for Durham, abandoning the foot – which turned and raced back to unwelcoming Newcastle in complete disorder, abruptly a horde of refugees instead of an army. It was all quite shameful. There were one or two local scuffles, but nothing worth calling even a skirmish. Total casualties on the royal side amounted to less than sixty; on the Scots side they did not reach a dozen. Yet this was the main part of the King's army, destroyed almost without a blow.

Charles reached York, and stayed there. He had little hope of raising another army, meantime. The Short Parliament had refused to finance this one – hence its quality; and certainly it would not finance another. The tide of Puritanism was rising. There was ever-growing disaffection in the South, with even parliamentary demands for the abolition of episcopacy. Charles was obstinate and no craven, but even he could not fail to read the signs. With the Scots beginning to settle in at Newcastle, most evidently for a long stay, he called for negotiations with his loyal Scots subjects.

The Second Bishops' War had ended even more swiftly and ingloriously than the first.

From Newcastle James Graham wrote a letter to Charles Stewart at York. It was written in sympathy and loyal duty, assuring the King that, like himself, the great majority of the Scots people were loyal, and that if His Majesty would finally dispose of the bishops' question and accept the Covenant, he would find that he had no more devoted subjects. It was a simple letter, the gesture of a warm-hearted man to one to whom he owed allegiance and who was bound to be in a sorely distressed state of mind.

It was, in effect, to change the course of history.

16

In November, still with the army of occupation in England, Montrose received a summons to attend a meeting of the Committee of the Estates, in Edinburgh. He was nothing loth, for Newcastle had its limitations as a wintering place for a Scots nobleman. Perhaps, however, he should have perceived some significance in the fact that Almond, the second-in-command, and two colonels of regiments, Kinghorne and the Marischal, travelled with him 'for consultation'.

At all events, when they reached the capital, it was to discover that Montrose was called to appear *before* the Committee, not on it – and the others with him. Not only that, but all the remaining signatories of the Cumbernauld Bond were here likewise – with the exception of Lord Boyd, who was dead, and whose demise was partly responsible for their presence here. Taken suddenly ill, on his death-bed Boyd had remembered his copy of the Bond, and had given it to a trusted servitor to burn; but the trusted servitor had served other masters. The Bond was now in the Committee's hands – and, no doubt, a facsimile in Argyll's.

This probably would not have been sufficient to give the Campbell the lever he looked for. But further unsavoury behaviour provided it. One of the King's gentlemen-of-the-bedchamber found Montrose's letter in the royal apartments, and recognised that here was merchandise for which some-one might be prepared to pay. He had no difficulty in finding a market in 1640 Scotland. Now this also was in the Committee's hands – with the Earl of Argyll's explicit instructions.

Montrose and his friends were not exactly arrested; their enemies could hardly go so far against two of the Covenant's Lieutenant-Generals, two serving colonels of regiments, and nine other peers of Scotland, seven of them earls. They could not even summon them to a trial – since all could claim to be tried by their peers; and the majority of other peers would find for them, undoubtedly. So they were requested to appear before an enquiry of the Committee – or at least the others were summoned, while Montrose was asked more politely. This was the tactic throughout, to drive a wedge between the Graham and his associates. Montrose perceived it quickly, and insisted on aligning himself with the others, accepting no special treatment.

The enquiry was as clearly intended as a warning only, to scare influential men away from forming any sort of party or alliance with Montrose, which might challenge the party of Argyll. It could not claim that the Cumbernauld Bond was in any way either unlawful or contrary to the Covenant and the realm's weal; but the implication was that it might be a secret conspiracy, with its true terms other than those written down. Montrose, as spokesman, poured scorn on that, declaring that the same might be alleged of any written agreement – including the National Covenant itself. He had signed the one as he had signed the other – the first name on both documents – for the freedom of worship and the good of the King's realm. As to the suggestion that his letter to King Charles was intelligence with the enemy, and some-how treasonable, he pointed out that such charge was laugh-able. Every liege had a right to communicate with his monarch, a *duty* if he was one of the earls of Scotland and had advice to offer. Moreover, the King was still head of this realm, not the enemy; and communication with him could not possibly be so styled. Indeed any assertion that it was, itself could better be termed treason, as an unwarrantable attack on the rights of the Crown. Let the Committee consider its own position in that respect, and that of those who sought to manipulate it, he counter-charged.

The enquiry ended abruptly, with its witnesses dismissed, and a copy of the Bond ceremoniously burned, to appease certain of the left-wing fanatic ministers. But it served at least to alarm some of the Cumbernauld signatories, to let them see that connexion with Montrose might have its dangers. Not all were proof against this sort of pressure. Argyll's name was not so much as mentioned throughout.

Montrose and his military colleagues returned to the army at Newcastle.

If Argyll and the Committee thought that by this proceeding they had warned off James Graham himself, they were far wrong. Warned he was – but in the other direction. It was clear to him now that, not only could the Campbell and he not work together for the Covenant or Scotland's wellbeing; but that the one must in the end put down the other. And since he conceived Argyll's policies, like his nature, to be against all that he himself believed in, there was no question as to what simple duty demanded of him. He owed it to his conscience, and to his country and his monarch, to see Argyll reduced from his dominant position. And not being of a secretive nature, nor seeing any advantage in secrecy anyway now that the Cumbernauld association was known to all, he went about it openly, in effect proclaiming himself focus and axis for all to rally round who hated the Campbell and all his works, as well as the rule of the zealot preachers. He even wrote to the King again, this time a long and carefully worded letter outlining a well-thought-out programme which he urged Charles seriously to consider. He advised, as vital, that the requirements of the original Covenant, regarding religion and liberties, should be granted forthwith, clearly and finally; and that thereafter His Majesty should come to Scotland in person, the realm over which his forebears had ruled for a thousand years, and which would rally to and love a monarch whom it could see and greet. Let him trust his cause no more to commissioners and' the like, men of straw, who could neither give nor gain contentment in the mighty distemper that afflicted the ancient kingdom. And let him hereafter trust, as public servants only those of known integrity and sufficiency, choosing them carefully and not on mere credit or recommendation; while avoiding absoluteness, which would only stir up further trouble.

This letter Montrose sent openly, by the hand of official couriers carrying documents to the Covenant delegation now negotiating with Charles in London.

Alexander Henderson and Johnstone of Warriston, now Procurator of the Kirk of Scotland, led this Covenant commission in London, negotiating, in the event, more with the English parliamentarians than with the monarch. This began by being a necessary fiction, for in theory the King could not treat with his rebellious subjects; but in time it was apparent that more was to be gained from parliament than from Charles. But the proceedings were delicate and long-drawn; for not only were the Scots in theory rebels, but equally they were not in theory invading England at all – yet the removing of the occupying army back to Scotland was the main item that they had to offer – at a price – with Leslie's force sitting firmly at Newcastle dominating the North of England and cutting off all coal traffic – and £50,000 of royal revenue therefrom – out of the great mining area there. London was having a cold winter, in consequence. The Long Parliament was now sitting there, and causing King Charles more anxiety than were the Scots, with Pym and the Puritans and malcontents proving their power, and the Huntingdonshire squire and grazier, Cromwell, beginning to make his mark.

The seething cauldron that was seventeenth-century politics, in England as in Scotland, was coming to the boil.

Montrose was arrested on the 11th of June 1641, by order of the Committee of the Estates. He was arrested at Merchiston Castle. He, along with much of the army, had at last returned to Scotland, most of their objectives at Newcastle satisfactorily achieved – to the tune of £300,000 paid by the English parliament, plus £850 per day 'occupation costs' for the long period in Northumberland; there can have been few more profitable and less bloody interludes in Scotland's long association with her neighbour. King Charles, at his wits' end, and now looking for Scots support rathen than enmity, in his obviously coming struggle with his English malcontents, had given in to the Covenant negotiators all along the line – had indeed promised to come to Scotland in the near future. So Leslie retained only a token portion of his army at Newcastle, as a sort of insurance, and the rest was not so much disbanded as stood down on a temporary basis. The Graham had sent his own troops back to Strathearn, Stirlingshire and the Mearns, relinquished his commission as Lieutenant-General, and was settling up sundry affairs at Archie Napier's house preparatory to heading north to Magdalen and his children at Kinnaird, when a troop of Loudoun's men came, without warning, to take him into custody. Clearly they would not have dared do this a couple of weeks before, when he still had two regiments of Grahams at his back. Napier was arrested with him; also Sir George Stirling of Keir, Napier's nephew, and the latter's brother-in-law Sir Archibald Stewart of Blackhall, who were likewise staying at Merchiston. They were escorted to the great fortress of Edinburgh Castle, on its towering rock, and there locked up in separate cells.

The charge was the vague and unspecified one of treason. Montrose, at least, had no doubts as to the real reason for it all. Argyll had been biding his time. Just as soon as the Graham was no longer part of the army, with his own protecting units and Lieutenant-Generalship, he had acted. But there must be a pretext; something more than the Cumbernauld Bond and the letter to King Charles. The arrest of Napier and the others provided the clue. It must be connected, he thought, with the business of Argyll and the alleged deposition threats to the King – although one might have imagined any treason therein to be on the other foot.

His jailers would give him no information. They were civil, and he was not maltreated, though denied his own servants; indeed he was kept incommunicado and in a small semi-subterranean room, an intolerable affront and constraint to a man of his standing and temperament. His demands to see the rest of the Committee fell on deaf ears; his letters to Rothes – now said to be mortally ill – Henderson, Eglinton and others, remained unanswered, if ever they were delivered.

So the hot summer days passed in that eagle's nest of a prison – and like a caged eagle indeed the Graham beat at his bars. Fiercely he disciplined himself to accept, to wait, to swallow his rage, forcing a proud, free spirit to steely restraint, if scarcely patience.

For six long weeks he was held there, alone, without explanation or detailed charges – and however illustrious his friends might be, none won through the barriers to visit him. Perhaps Argyll's strategy over the Cumbernauld Bond had been more effective than realised, and wise men recognised Montrose as someone too dangerous to associate with. Black Pate, Kilpont, Morphie and others of his close associates, would be seeking to move heaven and earth – that could be accepted; but what were they against the Campbell and the Committee?

Then, on the 27th of July, at last, he was taken from his cell, out of the castle, and down the Lawnmarket of Edinburgh, the sun dazzling his eyes unbearably after the long half-light of confinement. He walked between close files of an armed guard of at least one hundred, his captors taking no chances of a rescue. They brought him to Parliament House, behind St Giles. He had expected to be taken before a sitting of the Committee; but this proved to be a full session of parliament – or at least, scarcely full, for at the most cursory glance it was obvious that there were large and significant gaps in the attendance, gaps where his friends should have been. Argyll was there, however, on the notably sparsely filled earls' seats – which, of course, he could not have been at a Committee meeting.

The hush as Montrose was brought into the great chamber was absolute, the atmosphere electric. He was led to stand beside Napier, Stirling and Stewart at a central table usually reserved for clerks, as though in a dock at court. Napier looked pale and drawn, showing his years, but kept his grey head high. Sir George and his brother-in-law, much younger men, appeared nervous, unhappy and, most of all, bewildered. All showed, as no doubt did Montrose himself, the effects of their incarceration. Smiling briefly to them, Montrose bowed stiffly to Traquair, the Commissioner, and took prompt initiative.

'I wish to know, my lord High Commissioner, since this seems to be a parliament why I am not sitting in it, of right, as an earl of this realm? Why I have been held captive, without trial, for six weeks in Edinburgh Castle? And on whose authority this has been done?'

Helplessly Traquair spread his hands, in the throne. 'That is not for me to answer, my lord of Montrose. Perhaps – my lord of Argyll . . . ?'

Argyll sat still, head bent, silent, as though he had not heard.

In the Lords of Parliament benches behind that of the earls, a swarthy middle-aged man stood, John Livingstone, second Lord Balmerino, a friend of the Campbell. 'May I speak to this matter – with your permission, my lord President? The Earl of Montrose stands accused, with these others, the Lord Napier, Sir George Stirling of Keir and Sir Archibald Stewart of Blackhall, of grievous offence against the realm. For which reason he, and they, were put in ward by the Committee of these Estates, for the better weal of the same realm. And now appear before this parliament to answer questions, preparatory to trial hereafter.'

'This parliament cannot accept that statement,' Montrose answered strongly, authoritatively. 'Lord Balmerino, as a peer of this realm, knows full well that I, and the Lord Napier, have the right to trial by our peers, and by them only. That right I claim.'

A murmur ran through the assembly. Balmerino coughed. 'This is an enquiry. A questioning. Trial is not yet.'

'I will answer no questions, sir. Save to a properly constituted court of my peers. And I demand that I, and these my friends, be released forthwith.'

Amidst much stirring on the benches, Balmerino, looking flustered, glanced at the Earl of Loudoun, chairman of the Committee.

'The Committee of the Estates, which ordered your arrest, my lord, alone can order your release. It will be considered,' the Campbell rasped.

'That Committee, of which Lord Napier, Sir George Stirling and myself are all members, yet were not informed, is a committee of this parliament,' Montrose gave back. 'Therefore this parliament can and must overrule it. I request that parliament does so. Now. Orders our immediate release.'

'That request is out of order,' Balmerino said. 'Since the

Earl of Montrose is here not as a member of the parliament, but as a prisoner and witness.'

'A prisoner of whom, sir? Not of the King. Not of this parliament. Not of my peers. While parliament is not sitting, the Committee has its full powers. But when it is, the Committee is powerless in law. The greater cannot be bound by the lesser. As an earl of Scotland, prisoner or none, I am a member of this parliament. And demand a decision.'

Johnston of Warriston, that white-faced, strained and nervous young advocate, now a great man in Scotland, Clerk to the Assembly and Procurator of the Kirk, rose. 'My lord President,' he stammered. 'May I speak? This parliament cannot make any decision, save after heaving the facts. Those facts have not been laid before it. What are those facts?'

Montrose opened his mouth to challenge that, since the decision that he requested was not on the facts of any alleged offence, but on the right of a committee of parliament to overrule the parliament that appointed it. But he paused. For he, as much as any, required to know with what he was charged – otherwise he was the more hampered in his defence.

Balmerino was not slow to take up Warriston's point. 'My lord President – the facts are these. The Earl of Montrose has declared, before witnesses, that the Earl of Argyll did seek the deposition of our liege lord King Charles, on three counts – that of desertion of his ancient kingdom; of invasion thereof with English soldiers; and of vendition and bribery. My lord of Argyll entirely denies ever having said anything such. Yet one of my lord of Montrose's creatures, Stewart of Ladywell, Commissary of Dunkeld, now admits that the accusation was false, and that he aided in the forgery thereof. Nevertheless, the Earl of Montrose did cause him to send word of the said damnable forgery and traducement, which he knew to be false, to the King's Majesty in England. To His Majesty's misleading, and to the hurt of my lord of Argyll and this realm.'

There was a great uproar in the chamber now. When he could make himself heard, Balmerino asked, 'Does the Earl of Montrose deny this? We have full supporting testimony.'

'I neither deny nor confirm it, sir. I have no need. I answer no questions, save before a due court of my peers.'

After a pause, Robert, Lord Balfour of Burleigh, President

of the parliament, spoke. 'My lord of Montrose seems to have the right of this.' He was a cautious, scholarly man, occupying a curious position, one which had no precedent. The chairman of the Scots parliament was always the Chancellor. But since the Archbishop Spottiswoode was in theory still Chancellor, and the King had appointed no other, parliament had elected its own president. All knew that, hereafter, the whole proceedings might well be declared null and void, in that they were unconstitutional, without the Chancellor's presence, even though the Lord High Commissioner attended.

'My lord President – may I suggest that the Lord Balmerino puts his question to those who can claim no such right as trial before their peers?' That was Johnston of Warriston again. 'Namely the accused Sir George Stirling and Sir Archibald Stewart.'

'Ah, yes. Well said. Lord Balmerino?'

'Aye, my lord. So be it. You then, Sir George Stirling of Keir, I require you to answer before this high court of parliament, as you value your life. First – did you hear the Earl of Montrose make this slander upon the Earl of Argyll's honour?'

Agonisingly, Stirling looked at Montrose. That man nodded, smiling a little. 'Answer, George,' he said calmly. 'As you value your life! And your honour. This is no trial of mine. You can harm me nothing here.'

'Silence!' Burleigh exclaimed.

Stirling swallowed. 'I heard my lord say that he had been told it by Stewart of Ladywell,' he faltered.

'In what circumstances?'

'During the Earl of Argyll's punitive raiding on Atholl and Lochaber, last year. Ladywell, Commissary of Dunkeld, was taken into custody, along with his master, the Earl of Atholl. He heard the Earl of Argyll make the statement that King Charles should be deposed, in the Earl's own tent at Bridge of Lyon.'

'Fool! Think you that the Earl of Argyll – a wise lord who knows how to keep his tongue if anyone does! – would speak such traitorous things before any soever? Even if he thought so – as he does not. In especial before this Commissary of Atholl's?'

'I do not know, my lord. Who knows what any man will

say, on occasion? But I do know that, on that campaign, the Earl of Argyll acted so as to astonish many. Who would not have believed him capable of it. As the burning of Airlie Castle. And the harrying of the Lady Airlie!'

'Silence! Silence, I say! How dare you, sir! Answer the questions asked only – do you hear?'

'Well said, George,' Montrose remarked genially, loud enough for all to hear. 'My lord of Argyll will no doubt wish to explain that, himself!'

There was a deathly hush, as all looked expectantly at the dark-clad Campbell. But that strange man did not so much as blink an eyelid. He had a great gift for silence.

Balmerino, frowning, went on – but it was now at Sir Archibald Stewart that he looked. 'Blackhall,' he said, 'answer this, and truthfully, as you would before Almighty God. You also heard the Earl of Montrose repeat this slander? You, and others not here present?'

'I heard my lord say that he had heard Ladywell declare it as truth.'

'But Ladywell has admitted that it was untruth, a wicked forgery.'

'Of that I know nothing, my lord.'

'I think that you do. That you all, with others, contrived this with Ladywell. At the Earl of Montrose's instigation. To injure my lord of Argyll.'

'No, my lord.'

'And in concert persuaded the perfidious Ladywell to write this slander to the King, in London?'

'No. I know nothing of any letter to the King.'

'Nor I, my lord,' Stirling added.

'You lie, I say – both of you! For Ladywell has confessed to it.'

'Under torture, perhaps?' That was Archie Napier's first contribution.

'Will you inform us where the Laird of Ladywell is now, my lord?'

Balmerino glared, and glanced round for guidance. Argyll offered none. But his fellow Campbell came to his aid.

'It ill becomes the Lord Napier to make question of this matter,' Loudoun declared, rising. 'As an extra Lord of Session, former Treasurer of the realm, Privy Councillor and member of the Committee of the Estates, he was offered absolution from these charges, and his freedom. He rejected it, declaring that if any were guilty, he was guilty. Who is he to speak of torture and ill-using . . . ?'

Montrose reached over to press his friend's arm.

'My lord President – I asked a question, as I have a right to do as a Lord of Parliament,' Napier went on firmly. 'Like my lord of Montrose, if trial there is, I require it of my peers. But these friends of mine, having no such right, have at least the right to know how such testimony against them was obtained – since Stewart of Ladywell is not here present, and therefore his evidence is mere hearsay. I would remind all that I am a lord of Session, a judge, and know the law. I require to be informed – where is Stewart of Ladywell? And was the alleged retraction obtained by means of torture?'

There was complete silence in the great hall.

'Very well, my lord President. Since this parliament is not to be supplied with the evidence it requires to make any decision in this matter, I move that it proceeds to the next business.'

The Earl of Dunfermline stood. 'I second that motion,' he said.

There were not a few cries of agreement from around the hall.

The President glanced at the Lord High Commissioner, and nodded. 'Very well. I so rule. Remove the Committee's prisoners. The next business . . . ?'

Amidst some tumult, all four captives were hustled out, and marched back to their cells in the Castle.

Seventeen weary days later, on the 13th of August, Montrose was again taken to a renewed sitting of the parliament – alone, this time, his enemies at least having learned that the captives gained strength by supporting one another. Now, although still close guarded, he was treated more courteously. This was no trial, he was informed; merely an enquiry by parliament, which had taken the matter out of the Committee's hands; but which, as the Lord Napier cogently had pointed out at the last sitting, required information before it could come to any decision. Would the Earl of Montrose, therefore, answer certain relevant questions?

'No, my lord President. As a prisoner, I will not,' the Graham said, but courteously also. 'I accept the right of this parliament to ask questions. But I stand on my own right, as a prisoner, wrongfully or rightfully held, not to prejudice his trial before his peers by any reply to questions material to the issue. Free me, as you can do, with assurance of no re-arrest, and I will answer gladly.'

'But that is impossible, my lord,' Johnston jumped up to protest. 'It is to prejudge any trial, lacking the evidence. Parliament cannot release the Earl of Montrose with promise of protection, *before* it hears his defence. That is the negation of justice.'

'The negation of justice is that I, and my friends, have been held close prisoners without trial for two months, sir, on an alleged confession of one man, whom this parliament does not, or cannot, produce to substantiate it. I will answer no relevant question before my due and proper trial. But I request that Thomas Stewart of Ladywell, Commissary of Dunkeld, be produced forthwith, to inform this parliament.'

'That will not be possible,' Lord Balmerino said in a cilpped voice. 'Ladywell is dead.'

'Ha-a-a!' Montrose looked slowly round the assembly. He noted that Argyll was nowhere in evidence today. 'Dead? Convenient! Is it permitted to ask, my lord President, how this unfortunate man so fortunately met his death?'

'I understand that he was hanged, my lord of Montrose,' the President said thinly.

'Hanged! for retracting a statement?'

'For the felony and crime of leasing-making,' Johnston of Warriston amplified.

'Leasing-making! Lying! Lying in public! Dear God – if this is a hanging offence still, how many here are safe? I could myself witness to the offence of fifty! A hundred! How long since a man died under that barbarous ancient law?'

'Barbarous my lord of Montrose may call it, but it is no less the law of this land. The penalty of hanging was asked for by Sir Thomes Hope, the King's Advocate,' Johnston declared.

That gave Montrose pause. He could not be sure that Hope was his true friend; but he certainly was Archie Napier's. Even though, in his search for a strong man to rule Scotland, Hope had decided that Argyll was the answer, he would surely never sacrifice Archie Napier callously by getting rid of the witness who could save him, equally with

Montrose himself. Perhaps then, there was more to it? Perhaps Hope had conceived Ladywell to be a *hostile* witness, a danger to them, so broken by torture or other pressure as to give false evidence which could condemn them? Hope was undoubtedly the cleverest lawyer in Scotland. Whose side was he on?

Montrose looked at the President. 'My lord – if Ladywell was so notorious a liar that he was adjudged by the courts worthy to die for it, is his alleged evidence of any value to convict myself and my friends?'

'The point, I am sure, is taken,' the other nodded gravely.

'Then I request immediate release, for them and myself, sir.'

'It is less simple than this!' Balmerino cried, jumping up. 'My lord of Argyll has been most grievously injured, in his name and repute. He demands due recompense. Whether or not Stewart of Ladywell forged and invented this slander – and on whose instigation – my lord of Montrose conveyed the slander to the King. That is sufficient offence in itself. It could result in a charge of treason against my lord of Argyll.'

'Who says that I sent this information to the King? Ladywell again?'

'We have supporting evidence. A courier from the King was intercepted. One Captain Walter Stewart. Amongst others he carried a letter from King Charles to the Earl of Montrose, acknowledging receipt of a letter received by His Majesty *from* the Earl.'

'What of it? I wrote to His Grace from Newcastle, urging compliance with the terms of the Covenant, the end of the bishops, and His Grace's presence in his Scottish realm. If this is offence, then all the Committee of the Estates should be charged likewise – for that is its policy. Is it not also the policy of my lord of Argyll?'

'There was another letter. Secret. In a code of special meaning . . .'

'Saying what, my lord? And to whom addressed?'

'I say it was encoded. Clearly secret instructions . . .'

'You do not know what it contained, nor to whom it was written? My lord President – must we suffer more of this folly? Wasting the time of this parliament? And I would seek your ruling on this question. Is not interception of the

King's courier, receiving from him the King's sealed letters, and reading them thereafter – is not this treason? And lese-majestie also?'

Into the stir of excitement this aroused, the President declared that he would require time to consider that. They would take it to avisandum. Perhaps the King's Grace himself could best answer it. Perhaps those concerned would put it to him, in person? For His Grace was on his way to Scotland, and would attend the next sitting of this parliament in a few days' time. Meantime, with the situation unclear, and no further progress apparently possible on this vexed issue, with the Lord High Commissioner's permission he would adjourn this sitting . . .

Montrose was taken back to Edinburgh Castle, with a great deal to think about.

On the 14th of August, James Graham was brought face to face with Charles Stewart for the third time. And it was no more satisfactory an interview than were the other two. The four prisoners were led again to a special sitting of parliament; and it was only when they came to make their formal bows to the throne that they perceived that its occupant was now the monarch himself, and not Traquair.

Charles nodded in friendly fashion to his old servant Napier, but made no such gesture towards Montrose. He was looking at his most regal, gracious, dignified, the only man in that great assemblage wearing a hat – not his crown – and dressed in blue satin with the sash of the Garter, and over his shoulder the cloak of the Order with its large star. Just behind him Traquair stood, to whisper in his ear occasionally, and keep him right as to procedure – for the Scots parliament was very differently composed and conducted from the English model. Here the monarch or his representative personally presided, entitled to take part, although the actual conduct of the sittings, the chairmanship, was in the hands of the Chancellor; and of course, there was only the one house, peers and commons and burghs sitting together; though now, since the Glasgow General Assembly, no ministers and clerics attended save as spectators.

A debate was in progress when the prisoners were brought in; and listening, Montrose learned from it, to his astonishment, that the question at issue was whether or not the King should have the use of the Scots army still mustered under Leslie at Newcastle, against his recalcitrant English parliament, in return for sweeping reforms and concessions in Scotland. That such should be even considered, on either side, seemed almost beyond belief, but clearly this was so. When, presently, Hamilton of all men, rose from the earls' benches to commend the project, the Graham decided that he was seeing the ultimate in political cynicism, as well as in hypocrisy. Hamilton was, of course, a peer of Scotland and entitled to speak and vote; but when the man next to him rose, patting the other's padded and beribboned shoulder as he sat down, and proceeded in a sibilant Highland voice to welcome the King's royal presence in most flattering terms and then to indicate possible conditions for such a use of the Covenant army, Montrose had much ado to believe his own ears and eyes and keep from crying out. No final decision should be taken at this sitting, Argyll suggested, if his humble advice was of value to any. But the matter was infinitely worth exploring further, as the excellent and most noble Marquis of Hamilton had made clear.

While Montrose still sought to understand – and to stomach – this, the parliament moved on to discuss a motion by Loudoun that for the better governance of the realm, with the monarch apt to live furth of it, the judges and other officers of state should be appointed by the King only on the advice of parliament – powers far in advance of anything put forward even by the most left-wing English parliamentarians. Argyll rose again, briefly to commend this to the company, making it clear that it was the Committee's considered policy, and therefore his own. The King, for whom this must have been a bitter pill indeed, nevertheless sat silent, calm, unprotesting. He was apparently prepared to pay a high price for the Scots army. The motion was passed with little question.

Even then it was not the turn of the prisoners. Undoubtedly they had been brought in early just to be made to wait and so proclaim to the King and all others their captive and helpless status. More than once Montrose all but made intervention and protest, demanding his rights; but refrained, for the King's sake. If Charles was stomaching all this, he must be more than anxious to placate the present Scots leadership. For himself, Montrose, to upset this precarious balance, in the circumstances, would be unsuitable. It was part of the code that there should be no unseemly bickering in the presence of the monarch. Again, any hopes he might cherish that the King might obtain his release, could be jeopardised – and Charles had not acknowledged him at their entry as he had done Napier. He held his tongue.

Still another item of business was introduced, and by Loudoun again. All who held office in Scotland, any jurisdiction, hereditary or appointed, if they had not already done so, must sign the Covenant or forfeit such office. Was it agreed?

Since this involved every noble in the kingdom, all holding hereditary jurisdictions, barons' rights, sheriffships and the like, there was a tense hush. All looked at the King expectantly.

Charles sat his throne, impassive.

Argyll's nudge of Hamilton's arm was blatant, undisguised. The Marquis rose.

'I gladly undertake to sign the said National Covenant, my lord President,' he said. 'And therefore do second the motion.'

'And I so agree,' Traquair added, from behind the throne.

'And I,' the Earl of Roxburgh acceded.

So all was obviously arranged. Argyll, in unholy alliance with Hamilton, was as obviously in process of becoming at least uncrowned king in Scotland. Tom Hope had known what he was talking about.

Only then was broached the matter of the four patient prisoners. Loudoun declared that they appeared before parliament to answer questions, which two of their number had refused to do on previous occasions. Were the Earl of Montrose and the Lord Napier still obdurate and contumacious, even in the presence of their liege lord?

The Graham bowed deeply to the throne, but addressed the President, as parliamentary custom required. 'My lord – is this a trial? he asked. 'We are entitled to know.'

Balmerino replied, 'No, sir. Parliament still makes enquiry as to the need for a trial.'

'But not into the need for holding the King's loyal servants and subjects, let alone peers of Scotland, in close ward for eight weeks without trial or charge?' That was said as courteously as Montrose could make it.

'Silence, sir! *I* will put the questions, not you.'

'Then I, uncharged, and a member of this parliament, will reserve my answers, as do you, my lord.'

'You refuse, then, to answer the lawful questions of your realm's parliament, sitting in the monarch's presence?'

'No, sir. I but reserve my undoubted right to refuse answer to any question which I conceive might prejudice any subsequent trial before my peers. We are both sheriffs of counties, my lord – and well know the law in such matters.'

'You quibble, sir. You fence. How dare you!'

'Not so. I have, so far, refused to answer no question. If you are at a loss to know which to ask, try me. You might commence, my lord Balmerino, by asking the same that you asked before. Did I write to His Majesty of the Earl of Argyll's alleged declaration that His Majesty be deposed?'

There was an appalled silence at this bold turning of the tables on his enemies, in the very face of King Charles. Balmerino moistened his lips.

'This . . . this is an outrage!' he gasped.

'The question was asked, at the last sitting. If it was not outrage then, how is it so now? The only difference is that His Majesty is present. Who can, if he so wishes, inform this parliament that no such letter was sent by myself, or any friend of mine.'

'You dare, sir, to bring His Majesty into this?'

'*You* did that, my lord, when you intercepted His Majesty's royal courier, and took from him His Majesty's own letter to me, and read it. As you declared at the last sitting.'

That halted even Balmerino. Anyway, every eye was on the King.

Charles sat his throne as though sculptured therein, a picture of royal and dispassionate authority. But he did not speak.

When it was clear that he was not going to intervene, Balmerino whispered to Loudoun, and then straightened up. 'My lord President – it is intolerable that the Earl of Montrose should act thus, mocking this parliament and seeking to embroil the Crown in his villainies. I move that he be returned to ward forthwith. And the questions continued with the other accused.'

'Seconded,' Loudoun said.

'I move that the questions continue,' Montrose declared. 'Seconded,' Napier backed him, although not hopefully.

In the upheaval, Burleigh beat with his gavel. 'I rule that it is not in order for the Earl of Montrose and the Lord Napier, as prisoners and witnesses, to make such submission to parliament. I accept the motion. The two lords named to be removed from this sitting.'

Montrose bowed to the President, more deeply to his liege lord, and followed his guards out. The entire interlude had been merely a demonstration, he perceived, the object of which was to let the King see that he need place no confidence in himself, Montrose, or any other party, to support him. The monarch was to be isolated. Even Hamilton, Traquair and Roxburgh, his former toadies, had obviously been suborned, detached, and now danced to Argyll's tune. It was all very clear. Unfortunately, what was equally clear to the Graham, was that Charles Stewart was not going to raise hand nor voice in the matter. Argyll had calculated aright, in this also.

In the desperately slow, frustrating, lonely weeks that followed, James Graham came near to despair. Denied all contact with the outside world, a man of action, he was a prey to alternate helpless furies and deep depressions. To be utterly unable in any way to affect or influence his own fate was probably the most grievous affliction he had to bear.

Yet, despite himself, he could not but turn his mind towards the King, for aid. Charles, however circumscribed, still had powers, and could assist if he would. So he wrote letters to the Palace of Holyroodhouse – but had no way of knowing whether they ever reached their destination, however much he offered his jailers as bribes. He requested interviews with those in authority, Henderson, Loudoun, Johnston – but not with Argyll himself, never Argyll. And was vouchsafed no answer from any. He might have been already a dead man – as he would be, he knew well, if ultimately Archibald Campbell had his way – for all the notice the rest of Scotland took now of James Graham, *An Greumach Mor*, first signatory of the Covenant and Lieutenant-General. Had Magdalen and her father been right? Had he dabbled in things too great for him, and now must bear the consequences? Should he have stayed at home, tending his own wide acres, playing only the family man? He, the Graham?

It was nearly mid-October before he obtained his first gleam of hope, his first contact with other than his jailers – and also a personal blow. A new captain of the guard proved venal, and one night handed Montrose a letter from Kilpont. This began with the sad news that little David, the second youngest son, had died. He had been a weakly child from the first, and his father hardly knew him; but it was a blow, and poor Magdalen's heart would be sore. After this the letter declared the urgent loyalty of his friends, their horror at what was being done, and their constant efforts on their chief's behalf. Kilpont informed that they were ever pressing the King to act; and His Grace had assured them that he was concerned, and indeed would not leave Scotland until Montrose was freed – since he, with them, believed that the Graham's life hung on it. Charles was more sympathetic and understanding than might seem – but he was surrounded by traitors, spies and creatures of Argyll and Hamilton. These two were now inseparable. The King was desperate for an army, any army, to teach his English parliament a lesson – and only the Scots could provide one, mustered and equipped. All was subordinate to that, Leslie and his force the trump card. Edinburgh was full of Campbells and Hamiltons, in unholy alliance – it was said that Argyll had 5000 of his clan in and around the city – in name more volunteers for the King's army, but in fact . . . who knew? It seemed more like Campbell's kingdom. Much of the country, and probably most of the nobles, were now alarmed at the way things were going. But they were leaderless, and Argyll was careful to keep the Kirk behind him. But Montrose must not despair. He, Kilpont, believed the King when he said he would not leave Scotland until the Graham was freed – the only man who could stand against Argyll. The Campbell would never dare move against his life while the King was present. Kilpont ended by informing that the Earl of Rothes had died.

This very doubtfully encouraging letter was as a ray of light into the dim grey cell, nevertheless. Montrose had an objective again, not only hope but something to work for. There and then he sat down and wrote an acknowledgment to Kilpont, with sundry instructions, and another letter enclosed, to be handed, somehow or another, personally and secretly to the King. Means must be found. In it he warned Charles Stewart that there was no reason to believe that the deposition story was a forgery. He did not specifically accuse Argyll of being behind it, but he had known of it, and spoken of it – that was sure; for Ladywell was not a man who could or would have invented such a tale. Moreover there had been circumstantial rumours circulating, before his own arrest, that plans were being formulated to set up a Commonwealth embracing both kingdoms of Scotland and England, with the Crown put down and government by the parliaments only.

This letter sent, he could only wait, and hope.

He had to wait for a full month more. Then, on the night of the 17th of November, late in the evening, he was quite unceremoniously taken from his cell, conducted to the castle gatehouse by a junior officer, and told that he was free to go where he would. No explanations, no instructions, certainly no apology, was offered. *An Greumach Mor* now might have been some petty felon who had served his time in jail, casually released.

It was a wet night, and dark. In the Grassmarket below the castle, Montrose managed to hire a broken-down nag, all he could get, and made his way to Merchiston. There he found Archie Napier and the two knights, each having been freed earlier and separately, also without explanation. But from the servants at Merchiston, Napier had pieced together a strange story.

It seemed that the King was due to leave Holyroodhouse for the South first thing in the morning – hence their release at the last moment previous to the royal departure, when it would be too late for them to make any arrangements for an audience with Charles, who was, of course, kept most watchfully surrounded. But at least the monarch had not forgotten his promise.

It seemed that the royal departure was sudden and urgent. Rebellion had broken out in Ireland, and the English parliament had discovered that it required the King's authority to take the necessary steps to deal with the crisis. Charles apparently had hopes that this situation would benefit his position, proving to his malcontents in the South that they were less potent than they thought. With Leslie's Scots army to threaten them in the North, the King believed

that he might bring Pym, Hampden, Cromwell and the rest
to their senses. To this end he had hurriedly granted everything the Covenanters wanted; and had added a positive
shower of honours and appointments of office and profit,
quite fantastic to contemplate. Argyll himself had been
made Scotland's third marquis – it was said that he had
accepted only because there was an ancient West Highland
prophecy that the Argyll earldom would end with a squint-
ing, red-haired holder, and here was an ingenious way of
averting the curse, commentary indeed on the Campbell's
mind. Loudoun had been made Chancellor of Scotland.
Sandy Leslie, astonishingly, had been created Earl of Leven.
Alexander Henderson was now Dean of the Chapel Royal
and so King's personal minister in Scotland. And that strange
young man, Johnston of Warriston, although just thirty, had
actually been knighted, given a liberal pension, and made a
Lord of Session, the first of the new judges. If all this was
almost as laughable as it was shameful, the shame at least
looked like being extended and perpetuated. For there was
word from usually knowledgeable sources that the reason
behind it all, Charles's buying of the Scots army, had never
really been even remotely considered, in the first place, by
the said recipients of the largesse and titles. The information
was that, the moment the King was out of Scotland, the
new Earl of Leven was to bring his army home and disband
it. Here was Campbell diplomacy with a vengeance.

Even while Montrose all but wept for his duped and unfortunate monarch, he was told of still another and scarcely
more believable story – and one which might more closely
affect the late four prisoners. Scotland, it seemed, was ringing
– however little of it had reached the cells of Edinburgh
Castle – with a new sensation, which was being called the
Incident for want of any more credible description. A plot,
it was alleged, had been unearthed against Argyll and Hamilton, of all directions, to discredit them with the King – and
there were inspired rumours that Montrose was behind it
all. It was difficult to unravel the details and any real sense
of it, but the gist seemed to be that though Edinburgh had
been packed tight as a drum with thousands of Campbell
clansmen and Hamilton retainers, to discourage other lords
from questioning Argyll's hegemony, nevertheless the said
pair of nobles put it about that their lives were in danger,

and that they were being traduced to the King. So serious the threat, these two wronged and distressed statesmen had thereupon retired from unsafe Edinburgh to Hamilton's Kinneil Palace in West Lothian – from whence they could be back in an hour – in high dudgeon and deep sorrow. Nobody could make head nor tail of it all – save perhaps Napier, who, when he heard of Montrose's smuggled letter to the monarch with its specific information regarding the Commonwealth idea, declared that Argyll's devious mind had probably concocted the whole thing, to get him out of the King's presence until the royal departure, and to have every pulpit in the land ringing with his wrongs as a godly man endangered, hunted for his life; and to sow suspicion and mystification amongst his enemies.

At all events, whatever the rights of it, fairly obviously Charles would not be over the Border before his two marquises would be back in Edinburgh, and far from inactive. In the circumstances, it would be the most elementary precaution for the four ex-prisoners to get out of the city, and much farther away than Merchiston, before that happened, if they valued their new-found liberty. Deep in the Graham lands, Montrose declared, was the place for them, in this pass. He had never liked Edinburgh; now it stank in his nostrils.

That very November night, in thin drizzling rain, the horses were saddled and all four set out for the North with as minimal delay as disturbance.

There were times when discretion was not merely wise but the only course.

17

STRANGELY ENOUGH, THAT WINTER AND THE FOLLOWING months of 1642, James Graham came almost to give thanks to Archibald Campbell and his machinations, for so effectively cutting him adrift from all Covenant and national affairs. His name undoubtedly stank in the nostrils of the militant Covenanters and the fanatical ministers – who now, under Argyll, ruled Scotland unchallenged; but, secure within his own domains, it would have been a bold man who actually sought to lay hands on Montrose. While he had been held prisoner, Argyll had ordered the Lord Sinclair to go and harry the Mugdock estate, and pull down its castle – a piece of typical Campbell ferocity; but Mugdock was an isolated property as far as the Graham clan was concerned, only seven miles north of Glasgow. It was noticeable that there had been no attacks on Kincardine or other Strathearn lands, nor on Old Montrose, deep in traditional Graham territory.

So, for the first time in five years – indeed, for that matter, in his adult life – Montrose, unwanted by either his country or his king, could be himself and lead the normal life of a Scots nobleman, chief and landowner. And he had had enough of the alternative to appreciate it. Not that he did not frequently fret and fume with himself at Argyll's complete triumph, and his own helplessness to do anything about it – even, meantime, to avenge burned Mugdock. But the long months in Edinburgh Castle had taught him his lesson, he assured himself. He knew now when he was fortunate. After all, *he* never had had any wish to rule, to dominate. He had taken up the cause because he conceived it to be right; and if it had gone sour, and into wrong hands, he had reason to be glad that it had no further use for him. Thus James Graham in 1642.

More truly he rejoiced to become a family man – not again, for in fact he had never been one. On this score he did not have to convince himself. He went back to Kinnaird, to pick up Magdalen and the children, to take them to Kincardine Castle; and perhaps because he was so obviously defeated, perhaps because he had brought Archie Napier with him for the latter's safety, old Southesk was almost welcoming. He had been proved right – which is an excellent thing for any man; and he was able to emphasise, and to go on emphasising, the nobility of his beloved liege lord Charles, who despite all James Graham's sins against him, had vouchsafed to save the prodigal at cost to himself. Montrose, clearly, would have to listen to variations on this theme for the rest of his father-in-law's life; but at least they could live with each other again – for short periods.

As for Magdalen, she discovered that she could be sorry for her so splendid husband – and the experience was as a balm to her troubled soul. Undoubtedly she was a better mother than she was a wife; and now James Graham qualified in some measure for mothering, and she felt better able to cope with him. Perceiving something of it, however ruefully, the man also perceived that, while not really solving any problems for him, it would make life a deal easier, and certainly pleasanter for the woman he had married and whom by any standards he had grievously neglected. He suffered the mothering and sympathy, like he suffered Southesk's sermons and the periodic frustrations that boiled up within him. He was learning forbearance.

His children were his true joy. John, now twelve, was a sturdy lad, dark, keen, strong-minded, a son of whom any father might be proud – although undoubtedly he needed the said father's hand occasionally. James, with some of his mother's diffidence, was a little delicate and of less independent spirit, but a thinker, an asker of questions, interminable questions, intelligent enough for two, but not yet so much so as to be a trouble. Any fears their father might have entertained that his sons might look at him askance were quickly dissipated. Magdalen had done better by him, in this, than perhaps he deserved, bringing them up to look on their sire, not as one part of herself did – or as did their grandfather so obviously – but as gallant gentleman, cavalier, almost hero. His splendid good looks, noble bearing yet essential easy friendliness, did the rest. Unfairly, perhaps, within a day or two of his return, his sons were doting on him, and he could do no wrong.

Montrose remained no longer than he decently must, at Kinnaird. Magdalen made no objections to removing to Strathearn, and at Kincardine Castle most evidently sought to make the best of it. Almost it seemed that her recent troubles, the death of their third son, and her husband's imprisonment and fall from popularity, had bred a new strength in her, an increase in independence. And she was now preoccupied, not with living up to her husband so much as with retaining him at home and contented. So life at the little castle by the Ruthven Water was much improved on previously, for all concerned. Inchbrakie was only a few miles away; and Black Pate's wife Jean, a daughter of the Lord Drummond, was almost as much at Kincardine, with her children, as at home. Kilpont was not much farther away, on the other side; and Stirling of Keir closer still. Other friends, clansmen and supporters lived all around. Frequently Montrose asked himself why he had ever left this his own place. Archie Napier's continued presence with them helped likewise.

Not, however, that James Graham abandoned all concern for his country and its fate. He kept himself informed of what went on; and many were the discussions and arguments in Kincardine's hall, that winter and spring, on what was to be the outcome, and what ought to be done. But, more or less, by mutual consent, these were conversations, not councils, with no suggestion that any there must again involve himself.

Leaving Edinburgh, King Charles had gone back to London, to authorise the necessary steps against the rebellion in Ireland. But that done, promptly the parliamentarians had resumed their campaign against him, producing the Grand Remonstrance, a detailed indictment of his rule, and which demanded supreme powers for parliament. All his hopes of betterment were shattered – like his hopes of a Scots army. With disaster and massacre in Ireland, and the mob shouting for the blood of his Queen Henrietta Maria – whom it blamed, along with Strafford and Archbishop Laud, for most of his English policies – too late as always, Charles acted. He sacrificed Laud and Strafford, who were arrested. But to no purpose. Parliament continued to defy him; and on the 4th of January, 1642 the King took the ill-advised step of going in person to the Houses of Parliament, to arrest the men whom he considered the leaders. The gesture failed. Defeated and humiliated, Charles was forced to retire. Indeed, a week later he retired from London altogether, wiping its dust from his royal feet, and heading northwards.

But the English dissidents were not confined to the South. On the 23rd of April, Sir John Hotham shut the gates of Hull in his monarch's face. It was the final, unforgivable affront. There could be no more compromising. It was war, civil war, in England, with the King summoning all loyal subjects to arms.

Both sides wooed the Scots. The Earls of Lothian and

Lindsay were sent south, ostensibly to mediate, actually to discover which side was most likely to win, and which offered the best terms. By May, it seemed evident that the Committee of the Estates, at least, were likely to plump for the parliamentarians.

It was at this stage, reluctantly indeed, and greatly against Magdalen's urgings, that Montrose agreed to take a hand, a very modest hand, once more. The blame could be laid at Napier's door. During the long winter's evenings, he had advised his friend to put pen to paper and set down his theory of government, the art and ethics of it as he saw it, to clear his own mind and to instruct his companions. It was a change from the poetry and lyrics which the Graham had been penning, and though without enthusiasm at first, he had warmed to the task. He discovered in the process that he had indeed certain strong convictions which, set out, formulated a sort of creed. This, much acclaimed by others, presently began to nag at his conscience. Was it possible for a man of integrity to know all this, to construe it and believe in it, and yet to do nothing about it when he saw what he believed in set at naught and mocked, his country and his king at need? There was no use in telling himself that he no longer had the power to influence matters. He might not be wanted by either side – but he still could raise 1000 armed Grahams to back his word. Not that he had any intention of so doing; but he could not hide behind the screen of helplessness.

In May, Napier, who was still a member of the Privy Council, received a summons from Loudoun, now Chancellor, to attend a meeting thereof at Edinburgh, to decide on policy anent the King and his English parliament. Needless to say, he was in doubts as to whether to venture into the lion's den again. Montrose said that he should – for his voice was honoured and respected by many, and somebody must advocate the right. His friend's safety would be vouched for by the provision of a close escort of some hundreds of Graham troopers. His brother-in-law, in return, countered by advising that, in such case, Montrose himself should go to the capital with the escort – and not only he, but other like-minded nobles, to be present in Edinburgh during the period of the Council meeting, to press their views on the Councillors, in private, and to let the people see that all Scotland was not yet Argyll's.

So, towards the end of that month, a large company rode to Edinburgh – Grahams, Drummonds, Murrays and Ogilvys – not too aggressively armed, as escort for the Lord Napier, Privy Councillor, Montrose and his friends accompanying it, not exactly incognito but not parading their presence, and very much in a private capacity, their objective certainly not to provoke any clash with the Covenant leadership.

It was strange to be back in the city from which James Graham had all but fled, in darkness, six months before. He went nowhere unguarded, naturally, and so was scarcely able to test the true temper and opinion of the citizens. But he could sense the tension and unease of the place, the suspicion and fear in men's faces, the feeling that tyranny was not far away. The Kirk might be ruling here, rather than the Crown – but men's hearts were none the lighter.

Argyll was in town, attending the Council; but the two men made sure that they did not meet. They both were active, however. Montrose sought to impress on all Privy Councillors whom he might influence that so long as Charles Stewart was King of Scots they could not lawfully or morally take the side of the English parliamentarians against him. They had to accept that the King and his people were indivisible; and that monarch and parliament together ruled the state, not one or the other. His 'creed' now clear in his mind, he was the better able to convince others; though what effect he might have against Argyll's contrary influence, he could not tell, and was scarcely optimistic. For his part, the Campbell went to work in a different direction, sending out minions to rouse Fife and the Lothians to the threat of an armed bid for power on the part of the malignant Earl of Montrose and other royalists, Papists and traitors. In the event, Argyll had much the best of the exercise, the Covenanting gentry and ministers, with their retainers, flocking into Edinburgh from a wide area, intent on rescuing the Lord's faithful servants from the bloody hands of wicked men; so that to avert armed clash and bloodshed, which would serve no good purpose, the Grahams and their friends had to withdraw from the city, back to Strathearn, taking Napier with them, and leaving the Privy Council to make a carefully non-committal decision – which, in fact, had the effect of giving Argyll and the Committee all the powers they desired to make common cause with the English parliamentarians and Presbyterians.

More frustrated than ever, Montrose admitted that the non-success of this venture had been on a par with all his other recent activities, and that he was in fact beating the air. Magdalen did not fail to confirm that point of view.

The summer of 1642 stretched itself out in disquiet and tension. Another General Assembly was held, at St Andrews, now openly under Argyll's thumb – Montrose, of course, and none of his like, being summoned. Its main decision was that aid should be accorded to the English parliament if it would abolish episcopacy in England. To maintain the fiction of impartiality, it urged King Charles, in loyal duty, to see to this also. That this was shameless interference in the rights and affairs of another country, the very thing that the Covenant had stood out against for themselves, seemed to trouble few. And, almost unbelievably, the thing was accepted. The English parliament thereafter voted unanimously to abolish the episcopate, the bishops were driven from the Upper House, and the Church of England was instructed to turn itself into a Presbyterian body. For his part, King Charles did not reply to the Scots dictation.

Argyll was triumphant. He not only ruled Scotland, but was in a position largely to impose his will on England also, owing to the need of both sides for Scots aid. Oddly enough, he celebrated his ascendancy by betrothing his son, the Lord Lorne, to Hamilton's eldest daughter.

On the 22nd of August King Charles, joined by his nephews the Princes Rupert and Maurice of the Rhine, sons of his sister Elizabeth, Queen of Bohemia, set up his standard at Nottingham, the Earl of Essex moving against him, on behalf of parliament. There were a number of small, indecisive engagements, and then, on the 23rd of October, was fought the Battle of Edgehill, in Warwickshire. It was more of a drawn fight than a great victory; but the circumstances turned the result much to the advantage of the King. The parliamentarians went into retreat, and sent urgent appeals to Scotland for help.

Suddenly all was changed. It was come time for acting, not scheming, manoeuvre and diplomacy. And Archibald Campbell was less expert at this.

Late in that year of trembling balance, Alexander Henderson arrived, alone, at Kincardine Castle, for a second visit exactly six years after his first, looking tired, drawn and much more than those six years older. But still strong, stern, upright. He came, he told the younger man, at the behest of the Committee of the Estates, to seek the aid of the Earl of Montrose, and to offer him the Lieutenant-Generalship of the Scots forces about to proceed on active service.

James Graham stared at his visitor. 'Can it be true? Can you be serious, man?' he cried. 'After all that is past, you can come here to me again! In heaven's bright name – why? Why, I say?'

'For the same reason that I came before, my lord,' the other said evenly. 'Because I, and others, believe that this realm needs you, in this pass. And conceive you to love your country, despite all.'

'Despite all! Aye, well may you say it. And you? You conceive yourself, you and your like, to represent that country?'

Henderson raised dark, bushy brows. 'If not we – who? The duly elected representatives of parliament and the Assembly. If not we – who then? However unworthy.'

'And the Campbell? Your master?'

'I have only one Master, sir. But . . . my lord Marquis assents.'

'He assents!' Montrose took grip of himself, so that his knuckles gleamed white. 'Master Henderson – for you I retain some respect. Although. I mislike much of the company you keep! Argyll has taken and soiled a noble cause. And few therein have sought to counter him. I have not seen yourself prominent in this! You who brought Argyll into it.'

'As I brought you, my lord. With the Earl of Rothes.'

'As you brought me, to my cost! And now the Campbell rules Scotland, and stains its honour. And you come to me?'

'I come to you, yes.'

Helplessly the Graham shook his head. 'I cannot understand you, sir. That you should conceive it possible that I should once again put my neck into the noose. Or take up a cause which I believe to have gone far wrong.'

'The cause is not wholly wrong yet – and can be righted.

Must be righted. And I never conceived you to be so fearful for your neck, my lord!'

'The cause, the Covenant, is dead. Murdered by Archibald Campbell. You have sold your king, and mine – gained all that you wished from him, and then sold him! With such cause I will have no truck.'

'You judge too harshly. The King only gave us what we sought, and what Scotland required, because we forced him to it. Though weak, he is the most stubborn of men. Think you that he will let us keep what we have gained, our liberty to worship as we will, if we do not still press him? He is a man consumed with the knowledge that he is right, that all others are wrong. If he wins this battle with his English parliament, then we in Scotland will feel the weight of his hand. And where will our won freedom be then?'

'You call this freedom? I'd mind you, sir, that I tasted five months of it, in Edinburgh Castle!'

'That was ill done, yes. I, and others, sought to undo that wrong. But your enemies were too strong for us . . .'

'Argyll and Hamilton, you mean. Can you not say their names, man? Though indeed, Hamilton is but a jackal in the coils of a snake! He could do nothing, without the Campbell. I have no enemy in this realm that I need cast a glance at, save *MacCailean Mor*. He whom you have raised on high.'

'A national cause, my lord, cannot be over-nice in the props it uses to support it. My lord Marquis is a great noble, as are you. Entitled to take a hand in the affairs of this realm – as are you. You may not love each other, but you are nevertheless both powerful peers of Scotland whom the realm must look to in its needs. Do you blame the realm, or me, for your quality?'

'By God, sir – now you speak plain! And I will do likewise. Since Argyll is so much to your liking, appoint *him* Lieutenant-General! Yet him lead the army into England. I gladly defer the command!'

Henderson changed neither his grave expression nor his even, calm speech. 'Not so, my lord. In this, *you* can serve Scotland the better. The King has won certain victories, and the tide of war seems set in his favour meantime. The English parliament demands the aid our parliament promised them in their fight against the bishops. Such aid we must send.

But clearly such army must be most carefully led. Not to fight against the King. Not to fight at all, if it is possible. The position is delicate. It could find itself in dire straits. If the parliament cause were to go down swiftly, and the King thought to turn on it. It must therefore be led by more than a mere soldier. You understand? The Earl of Leven is a good soldier. But ...'

'To be sure, sir – I understand very well. You and your friends are concerned lest you support the wrong side, the *losing* side! You are not concerned with right and wrong, you are concerned with expediency. The Scots army is to smite its own monarch, if he is losing; but not if he is winning! That would be inexpedient. And you cannot trust old Leslie with the delicate business. Too blunt a man.'

'You judge too harshly, my lord. We – that is, the Scots parliament and the General Assembly – are committed to aid our English brethren in *their* struggle for freedom of worship and the reform of government – as we have gained for ourselves. As is only right and proper. But we are not in rebellion against the King. Our true function is to mediate, to use our army for that good purpose. Not to fight battles and shed blood. Leslie is a soldier, and nothing more. But you – you have shown yourself to have both a gift for strategy, for soldiering, and also for statecraft. Moreover, the King is disposed in your favour ...'

'And there you have it! The King is disposed in my favour. If the King's cause prospers, you may want that favour – so you turn to me. But if it fails, where would Montrose be then? Like as not Argyll's prisoner once again, with Leslie resuming fullest command! Think you I am a child, Master Henderson? Not to see it?'

'I think that you see it amiss. The position is delicate, as all must admit. It must be delicately handled, for Scotland's sake. This you cannot deny, my lord. And we conceive that *you* can handle it delicately.'

'Amiss or none, what I see is that you would have me play turncoat and trimmer, prepared to sail with the most convenient wind. That, I promise you, I will not do. Go back to our King's new marquis, better qualified than am I to so sail, and tell *him* to go south with Leslie. The Commander-in-Chief will heed *his* voice, never fear! The King chose to honour Argyll – not Montrose. Will he not be disposed further to favour him?'

'My lord Marquis conceives it is his duty to remain in Scotland . . .'

'Do you tell me so? Then, what of that other royal favourite, Hamilton? Would he not serve very well, for this delicate mission? And him so close to the Campbell.'

'My lord of Hamilton is scarce suited to it . . .'

'And, on my soul, nor am I, sir! I am a loyal subject of King Charles, one of those whom he should be able to trust. He is our liege lord, however many his mistakes. I say that he has been shamefully used by those who rule in Scotland today. I will by no means aid them in it, further.'

'So, my lord – you choose the King, in the end? Not the Covenant.'

'I chose the Covenant while still I could be loyal to the King in it. But now that Covenant is dead, trampled by self-seekers and by fanatic preachers. Aye – I choose the King!'

There was a long pause. Then Alexander Henderson sighed. 'I am sorry, my lord of Montrose. Truly sorry.' And stiffly he bowed himself out.

Slowly, heavily, Montrose climbed the narrow turnpike stair to his private chamber at the tower-head. Unlocking a drawer there, he took from it a letter, much scuffed and battered. It was headed from Nottingham, and dated the 22nd of August, the day that the King raised the royal standard there – although it had only reached Montrose recently, and by devious means, having certainly been opened, read and considered by his enemies on route, Will Murray being Will Murray. It went :

My good lord and traist Cousin,
 I send Will Murray to Scotland to inform my friends of the state of my affairs and to require both their advice and assistance. You are one whom I have found most faithful, and in whom I repose greatest trust. Therefore I address him chiefly to you. You may credit him in what he shall say, both in relation to my business and to your own; and you must be content with words until I be able to act. I will say no more but that I am your loving friend,
 CHARLES R.

*   *   *

229

He read that through again, even though he knew every word of it by heart. And then, throwing it down on the table, he slammed down his clenched fist upon it, decision taken. It was necessary. He could no longer put off, procrastinate. Magdalen was wrong, as was her father. And others. A man must do what he was born to do. Especially when he was born the Graham.

Turning, he ran down those same twisting stairs, back straighter, shoulders braced. Near the stair-foot he began shouting for Black Pate of Inchbrakie.

18

SIX WEEKS LATER, IN COLD AND WINDY FEBRUARY WEATHER, Montrose was back near his former winter quarters at Newcastle, this time not with an army but with a squadron of 120 Graham troopers, and the lordlings Ogilvy and Aboyne – the latter with him as his father's representative, to vouch for the swords of 5000 Gordons. Black Pate and Kilpont were also of the company. Montrose's numbers were carefully chosen – enough to provide a safe escort for a great noble in dangerous days, but not enough to be seen as a threat to any faction or as part of an army. And it was a company which could move fast, for they had a long way to go. They were making for Oxford and the royal Court – so close was the King to London again.

But at Newcastle Montrose heard news which changed his direction somewhat. The Queen, Henrietta Maria, had gone to France and the Continent less than a year before, to raise foreign support for her husband, taking the crown jewels and other treasure to sell, for the purchase of munitions of war. She had, it seemed, just arrived back, disembarking at Bridlington with artillery and warlike stores. Henrietta Maria was said by many to have more influence on the King's decisions even than had Archbishop Laud;

indeed it was she who had been sent to the Continent largely to get her out of England because parliament was proposing to impeach even the Queen for having undue and hostile influence on the monarch in matters of state. Montrose wanted to influence Charles Stewart in no small fashion. He decided to see Henrietta first.

The Graham company bore away slightly east of south, for Bridlington.

They found the Queen, with her artillery train assembled, on the point of setting out for York on her way to Oxford. She was a slight, pretty woman, wearing well, vivacious, hot-tempered and wilful, alleged to be much interested in good-looking young men. If so, Montrose and his young friends caught her on one of her off-days. She was, of course, scarcely at her best. A poor traveller, she had suffered much on the February seas, and was not yet recovered. Moreover her welcome back to England had been a cannon-ball, fired from one of the parliament fleet, into her own chamber in the harbour-side house; indeed the town was still under occasional fire. Enough to upset any lady. She was, it appeared, prepared to distrust most Englishmen, and all Scots. She greeted the Graham coldly, and had it not been that his 120 troopers made a valuable addition to the guard for her baggage-train, he might have got little further with her. She would by no means grant him the private interview he sought, and he had to make do with snatches of conversation as they rode, amidst the chatter of her bevy of courtiers and the fears of armed attack.

'Madam,' he urged, at an open stretch of country, as they left the village of Burton Agnes behind them, 'I pray that you hear me. In this situation, His Majesty sorely needs the help of Scotland. More, that it should be denied to his enemies. Of this none can be in doubt. But the present Scots leaders incline towards the English parliament – whatever their words. I know. So long as the King appears to be winning, they will be most careful. They intend to send an army across the Border. But not to aid His Majesty. To threaten him, rather. The moment parliament seems to get the upper hand, they will turn against the King.'

'So? Was it not ever so? The Scots are a treacherous race, my lord.'

'Not so, Madam. The Scots are amongst the loyalest folk

on this earth. But they have been betrayed, neglected, abandoned. Ever since His Majesty's father left Scotland for London, in 1603, on the death of Elizabeth, the canker has been eating in. They are a people who cherish and love their chiefs, grouped in their clans and families, a patriarchal people. They require a chief of chiefs – their King. All the system, the direction, of the Scots depends on this. But their kings have left them, to live 400 miles away, and in another land with other customs. Their loyalty, then, lacks focus, lacks its true centre. So it spends itself on the lesser chiefs, on the chieftains of clans and heads of houses. Who, lacking a master, often turn and rend each other. So we have feud, clan warfare, while he who should be ruling us, rules instead another people, differently spirited, who know him not.'

The Queen, it is to be feared, was paying little attention to this disquisition. 'I care not *why* they are treacherous, sir, so long as they are,' she told him. '*Parbleu* – what would you have? For His Majesty to give up his great English throne and return to beggarly Scotland?'

The man was patient. 'That I do not ask. Although His Majesty might do worse, I think! But in this present case, I say, he would be wiser to return to his own people, there to put his ancient house in order, first. Scotland. He cannot bend both England and Scotland to his will, at one time.'

'He came to Scotland, did he not, my lord? And was received with contumely and insult.'

'He came on a brief visit. With all the bishops trouble at his back. He chose to uphold the very men who were his enemies . . .'

'Enough, sir! Enough. *Mon Dieu* – must I listen to this, this *calomnie*, this *médisance* of my husband! It is too much!'

'Your pardon, Madam. But His Grace's situation is parlous. And demands plain speaking.'

'No. No more. Sir Peter – here come, ride by me. I have finished speaking with the lord of Montrose . . .'

Late that afternoon they were in a brush with a small force of parliamentary cavalry near Great Driffield, and the Queen had good reason to be grateful to the Graham squadron for seeing them off in gallant style. In consequence, she was rather more gracious to Montrose when they halted for the night. Loth as he was to be subjected to another

232

rejection, he did not spare her, or himself – for to this end had been his journey.

'Your Majesty will, I hope, forgive me if I offended by my plain speaking,' he said. 'It is only out of my love for the King's Grace. All along he has suffered much from ill advice as to Scotland. He wrote to me, in August, seeking my advice in this pass. It is to offer him it that I ride south now. But . . . he is surrounded by men who give him bad counsel – as, dear God, has been more than amply proved! But you, Madam, he will heed. You can greatly move him. If I could make *you* understand . . .'

'What is it that you want, my lord? What is your petition? But make it short, of a mercy! For I am tired.'

'No petition, Majesty. Only the advice he asked. Briefly this. Scotland is being mustered *against* the King. By his enemies. Argyll in especial. Hamilton aiding . . .'

'That I will not believe, sir. *Monsieur le Marquis* is the King's good friend. And mine.'

'Not a true friend, Madam – that I swear. By his acts . . .'

'Stop, sir! I will hear no more of this. If you insist on speaking evil of my friends, as also my husband!'

'Very well. I shall say no more of persons. But – Scotland *is* being mustered against the King. But the people do not hate him, despite the preachings of some divines. The people could be raised against the King's enemies, instead. I know it well. If His Majesty struck first.'

'How can he so strike? He has no army in Scotland. The Scots army is in his foes' hands. You say it yourself.'

'*I* could find him an army, quickly. Let His Majesty give me a commission to raise Scotland for him, and I will have 10,000 men in two weeks, 20,000 in six! Young Lord Aboyne, here, is empowered to promise 5000 Gordons. But give me the authority, and I will win Scotland for the King. Let him come north himself, when I have mustered his army, and all the land will fall to him. Come in strength, as a king should, not in weakness, and the Scots people will prove their loyalty.'

'You are most sure of yourself.'

'I am most sure of my countrymen, Madam.'

'Others say differently.'

'Others may not wish the King so well as do I.'

'Yet you are one of those of this Covenant, are you not? One of the most strong, sir?'

'I was. Still I believe in what I signed then. But that battle is won. And I walk no more with those who misuse the power it won.'

'In France, we have a saying how if a man changes sides once, he may do so again!'

'And in Scotland we say, Majesty, that it is only a fool who holds to a road past his destination! What I have said is true. Will you so advise the King? To his great good?'

'I will think of it, sir. I do not know. I will tell you, at York . . .'

But at York, next evening, they discovered more travellers awaiting them – Hamilton and Traquair, of all people, with quite a large entourage. It seemed that Loudoun, Henderson and Warriston, with themselves, were forming a deputation to Oxford, to urge on the King that he accept the concept of Presbyterian uniformity of worship thoughout his dominions, banning episcopacy entirely – obviously only a time-filling device while forces were raised in Scotland, since Charles would certainly never agree to it. Hearing of the Queen's coming, these two practised courtiers had waited, letting the others go ahead. No doubt they were as sensible of the lady's influence on her husband as was Montrose.

They reacted towards the Graham as might have been expected, and quickly the predictable took place. They worked upon the Queen and, old friends of hers, were not long in convincing her that Montrose was both unreliable and dangerous. They assured her that there was no cause for alarm over Scotland, that her present leaders sincerely desired only to mediate – indeed were here in England to that end – and that no threat need be looked for from Leslie's army. They suggested that the Graham mischief-maker be sent packing.

Since this advice matched Henrietta Maria's own inclinations, she took it. Montrose was told that his representations would be put before the King, but that there was no need for him to proceed farther south in person. It was not exactly a royal command not to go to Oxford, but it was a dismissal. And what point was there in going on, in defiance of the Queen? It would scarcely endear him to the monarch, who positively doted on his Frenchwoman. Moreover, Henderson,

Loudoun and the others were already ahead of him, it seemed, and would deny all that he had to say, even if he was permitted to say it.

He wrote a letter to his liege lord, then, far from optimistically, and entrusted it to Ogilvy, who, with Aboyne, elected to go on southwards. And grim-faced he turned back for Scotland, with Pate and Kilpont, a man with all the talents but whom the fates did not appear to love.

Argyll saw to it that all Scotland soon was ringing with Montrose's discomfiture. The Graham had thought to cozen and delude the King, by working on the Queen; but she had snubbed him, and sent him home – thanks largely to the Marquis of Hamilton's wise counsel. Their Majesties were happy in having true and wise servants in Scotland, to warn them against such as this trouble-maker, who would divide the country in civil war for their own ends. And as though to emphasise how right was the Marquis of Argyll, word came that on the 23rd of April King Charles had taken the almost unprecedented step of raising his good servant Hamilton to the rank and status of duke.

There was no reply to Montrose's letter to the monarch.

Everywhere, that summer, recruiting was in progress in Scotland – the more so as Charles's forces, under Rupert of the Rhine, the Earl of Newcastle and Sir Ralph Hopton, were making headway almost everywhere. John Hampden was slain, and Bristol, England's second largest port, about to fall into the King's hands. A Scots parliament was demanded – and although the King postponed a decision on this, Argyll thereupon demonstrated his complete power by calling it himself, for the 22nd of June. Lacking the royal authority, he had to call it a Convention of the Estates – but the result was the same. A General Assembly was to succeed it. The theme of both was to be the same, the unification of a parliamentary commonwealth in a Presbyterian United Kingdom, with all that this entailed.

Montrose was not invited to either Convention or Assembly, not were many other moderates and loyalists.

During those bitter months, however, James Graham was by no means idle. He accepted now that the King was unlikely to seek his services. And to muster men on his own accord, on any large scale and lacking the royal authority, would be technical treason – for in theory it was still the

King's government that ruled in Scotland, with the trappings of legality. But he also accepted that his conscience would give him no rest if he did nothing, and abandoned the royal cause – which he saw as equally his country's. He therefore sought, quietly, to form a coalition of powerful nobles, moderates, royalists, Episcopalians, even Catholics – since Huntly was so important in man-power; but he was less successful than he had hoped, lacking any commission; indeed under a cloud of royal disapproval, according to general rumour. The great lords could not be brought to agree amongst themselves, so diverse a crew. Huntly would have nothing to do with the Earl Marischal. Airlie said Kinghorne had stolen lands of his. The Lords Fraser and Forbes were at ancient and deadly feud. Crichton, Viscount Frendraught declared that nothing would make him associate with Papists. Montrose could have licked them into shape had he possessed any sort of commission; but they were mainly older men than he, and without it he was hamstrung.

Unexpectedly, in June, two events proclaimed to him that perhaps he was less ignored and ineffective than he assumed, however. He had a letter, dated the 31st of May, from the Queen, of all correspondents, declaring that she had heard a rumour that he, Montrose, was keeping ill company, was in touch with the King's enemies, the men he had warned her of, who were offering him high position, and money to pay his debts. She hoped that this was untrue, and said that arms were arriving from Denmark shortly, which might be diverted to Scotland if he was in a position to use them effectively in the King's cause; and ended by assuring him of her continuing confidence.

Utterly at a loss to understand this strange communication – or to what debts she referred – Montrose had still deferred any answer when he had an unusual visitor. Sir James Rollo, elder son of the Laird of Duncrub, was actually a brother-in-law, for he had been married to the Lady Dorothea Graham; but on her death he had wed Argyll's half-sister, the Lady Mary Campbell. He was now accepted to be in the opposite camp – although his brother, Sir William Rollo, remained faithful to Montrose. Duncrub was only a few miles from Kincardine, but Sir James's visit was rare enough to be significant. He came, confidentially, to invite the Graham to a secret meeting with Master Alexander Henderson.

'Save us – what next!' the other exclaimed. 'I saw Henderson seven months past. Has aught changed? And why secret? He came here to Kincardine before, openly enough. If he wishes to see me, why not again?'

'I do not know, James. All I was told was that this time none must know of it. And that it is important.'

'What will it serve? What that is new can we say to each other?'

But, because he still believed that Henderson was the best of the churchmen and not yet wholly Argyll's man, in mid-month he saw the Moderator and Dean of the Chapel Royal again. They met dramatically in a meadow amongst the windings of the Forth, near Stirling, Henderson's odd choice, between Highlands and Lowlands, North and South. This time, lest there be any trap, Montrose brought Napier, Ogilvy and George Stirling with him; but there was only Henderson and Rollo waiting for them.

'Why this strange meeting, Master Henderson?' he asked, without preamble. 'I gave you my sure answer last time. I chose the King, you will recollect.'

'But the King, it seems, has not chosen *you*, my lord.'

'No matter. Nothing is changed.'

'I say that much is changed, my friend. The two realms are now agreed to be done with bishops. This war in England is hateful and unnecessary. There is no need for further conflict. Only the King's obduracy. To encourage that obduracy is evil, against God's will and purpose!'

'As interpreted by Alexander Henderson and Archibald Campbell!'

'As interpreted by all lovers of peace and religion,' the other insisted patiently. 'You, my lord, do not *desire* war?'

'No.'

'Yet you prepare for war. Seek to join with other lords. In a confederation.'

'As do you.'

'*We* act in the name and on behalf of the realm.'

'But against the head of that realm. Against his express desires and commands.'

'The King acts the autocrat, beyond his due powers. And you encourage him in it. You lead him to believe that much of Scotland will fight for him, against its appointed representatives. This is to the injury of peace, to make war more likely.'

'You fight what you believe to be wrong, Master Henderson, calling it sin. You do not knuckle to the Devil, for the sake of peace. Should I?'

'I say that you should reconsider your position, my lord. If you showed a true and fitting solidarity, now, with your fellow signatories of the National Covenant, then undoubtedly the King would perceive that Scotland is not to be divided. He will be forced to heed our mediation, our mission for peace. At this Convention of the Estates that is to be, and the General Assembly to follow, a new Covenant is to be put forward. To include our English brethren. A noble document ensuring freedom of worship hereafter, and the putting down of idolatry and episcopacy in both realms. A testament of lasting peace between England and Scotland. We think to name it the Solemn League and Covenant. It is an affirmation of Christian unity and faith which will ring down the centuries to come. It would give me the greatest satisfaction, my lord, to see your name thereon. More still, if it was the first name – as it was on the other!'

'Mine! On my soul – you cannot mean it? Have you and your like not been calling me traitor, malignant, back-slider? You would have *my* name first on your new paper?'

'I would, joyfully. That is why I am here.'

'To what end?'

'To show that Scotland can unite for a worthy cause. Nothing could more powerfully convince the King that he cannot use Scotland against England. But must come to terms with both realms. For his own good.'

'For his own downfall!'

'Not so. His better state, and well-being. Only so will he regain peaceful rule over his kingdoms. You must believe me that it is so, my lord. I am as much a King's man as are you . . .'

'And as Archibald Campbell?'

'You are consumed with hate for that man. Can you not forget him . . . ?'

'I doubt if he will allow me to! For yourself, Master Henderson, I advise that you cease to blind yourself as to that same man. You I conceive to be honest. But working with him becomes you little. He is evil. And such as associate with him cannot but become corrupted, I think.'

The other said nothing for a few moments, looking across the meadows of Forth to the soaring rock of Stirling Castle.

At length he spoke. 'Supposing that you are right, my lord, should it not be your duty, as you love your country, to seek counter the works of this man you believe so harmful? By any means in your power? And will you not do this the better, more surely, within the cause than without? You chose the King. But at this moment you are rejected of King and Covenant both. You can do but little for Scotland as one man, alone. Yet Sir Thomas Hope says that you only in this realm can match the Marquis of Argyll. I accept that. Therefore I am here.'

'Ha! So that is why it is so secret? At last you are having doubts as to the Campbell?'

Henderson glanced over at Rollo, Argyll's brother-in-law. 'Have I said so? You it is who say it, my lord, not I. But – if so you believe, come back into this noble cause and make it the nobler. Take on the Lieutenant-Generalship of the army. Mediate, from that position, with the King. Sign the Solemn League and Covenant. And put Scotland and England both in your debt. You will find both parliaments not ungrateful, I warrant you. Restitution will be made for your shameful imprisonment. Your debts will be paid in full . . .'

'So-o-o! Debts, eh?' Keenly James Graham searched the other's stern face. 'This of debts interests me. I heard tell of these from . . . elsewhere. What debts, sir?'

The minister raised his bushy brows. 'Why, my lord – I have no knowledge of what they are. But the word is that you are much indebted. The costs of raising and arming your Graham soldiery, perhaps? I know not . . .'

'Nor do I, Master Henderson. In moneys, I am not a rich man. But I am not yet in debt. Even although it suits some man to say that I am! Some man who much advertises the matter. Why?'

'I am sorry if in this I offend. I but follow my instructions . . .'

'Whose instructions, sir?'

'That I am not at liberty to say.'

'I think that you are. Must be. This meeting you would

wish to keep secret. I should know what is behind it. To know how much I trust I may put in what you offer me.'

'Let it suffice to say that you may have the fullest confidence in it.'

'Does the Committee of the Estates send you to me, then?'

Henderson did not answer. Rollo it was who spoke, stepping closer.

'I say that Master Henderson speaks with the full authority of the Committee.'

'No,' the minister declared. 'I cannot so say. What I do say is that the Convention to open in a few days' time will undoubtedly confirm what I offer.'

'Which can only mean that Argyll himself sent you!'

'None sent me, my lord. I came. Believing that nothing is more earnestly to be desired, in this pass, than that you should join with your peers, and the other Estates of the realm, and by your example bring over the few, if any, who still respect merely the empty shadow of royalty. To your profit, yes. But also, I do aver, to your honour. I came, and will heartily thank God, if He but makes me the minister and mediator of so great a good.' There was no doubting the sincerity of the man. 'Will you accept, my lord?'

'No,' Montrose said quietly, simply.

Obviously Alexander Henderson was quite shattered by that reply. For long moments he could find no words.

'I am sorry,' the other went on. 'But it is not to be. I respect you, Master Henderson, and accept that you mean me well. But I believe you mistaken. Grievously so. And in the cunning hands of evil men. I will not tamper with my conscience. My debts, such as they are, I will pay myself!'

Scotland's foremost divine, in his sixtieth year, looked an old man as he stumbled away, head bowed. These two were never to see each other again.

The Convention of the Estates met at the end of the month, with the new Duke of Hamilton acting as the King's unofficial representative. It heard a declaration from Charles solemnly assuring all of his acceptance, now and in the future, of the liberties and freedoms in worship and government gained by his Scottish subjects. These assurances, however, were not accepted or believed in by the Convention, which proceeded to legislate for war. It promised the English parliamentary delegation which attended armed aid to the tune of 18,000 foot, 2000 light horse, and 1000 dragoons, on condition that their leaders signed the Solemn League and Covenant. But not without payment. £30,000 per month was the price decided upon for this support, the first monthly instalment to be paid before a man or a horse or a cannon moved across the Border. Argyll was not the man to give anything for nothing. It was astounding that the Englishmen agreed to this without a murmur – or none loud enough to affect the issue – and the whole thing was signed and sealed, the King's new duke benignly presiding. The Great Seal of Scotland could not be used on this document, since this was not a true parliament; but the Royal Signet was available, Lanark, Hamilton's brother, being its Keeper. He appended it apparently without hesitation, the King's seal to authorise the King's subjects to fight against the King.

The issue was thereafter referred to the General Assembly of the Kirk for divine blessing. More especially, the new Covenant fell to be ratified, this being very much the Kirk's business. A resounding declaration, it made it clear beyond all question that Presbyterianism was, and always had been God's own choice for the governance of His Church and creation; and that English conformity in this divine pattern was a prerequisite for any advancement in faith as in works. Moreover it showed that religious uniformity alone would produce political harmony such as all honest men desired, and peace between the King's realms. All was done in the King's name, as was right and proper.

If one man saw fit to reject all this, in his obdurate blindness, and that man happened to be the present occupant of the throne, it was unfortunate, but invalidated nothing. No man born of woman should, or could, hold up God's will and purpose. The Solemn League and Covenant was ratified – and God save the King!

Before this highly intricate and ingenious exercise in metaphysics – which probably only Scots divines could have worked out to such satisfactory conclusion – reached its happy finalisation, James Graham had seen the writing on the wall. Despite the appeals of his wife – although this time actually with the blessing of her father – he had kissed her goodbye and shaken his sons gravely by the hand. He was

on his way to join his unfortunate liege lord – and this time
he did not intend to come back until it was to place himself
at the head of a Scots army with which honest men could
link the King's name without blushing.

PART THREE

19

It was Oxford and not London, the Hall of Christ Church, not the Palace of Whitehall; but otherwise there was an uncanny similarity between this and that other occasion when Montrose had waited amongst the courtiers for King Charles – an ominous thought that did not fail to occur to him. There was the vast chamber full of the same inane, high-pitched chatter, the same exaggerated gestures and costume, the same hothouse atmosphere and strident insincerity, many of the same people. There were differences, to be sure. If anything, the women were even more extravagantly dressed, there were more contrasting colours, more ribbons and bows and jewellery, more bosoms displayed, more paint and powder, more elaborate hair-styles – for that is the way in wartime, especially well away from where the fighting takes place. The men, too, were affected; swords were not permitted in the royal presence, but military-style clothing was *de rigueur,* thigh-length riding-boots worn turned-down were all the rage, and some wore even half-armour, breastplates – though admittedly richly chased or gold-inlaid. Spurs clanked and rattled, and the general impression was one of instant readiness for the battlefield – though few indeed of the cavaliers present had ever heard a shot fired in anger. Montrose, clad again in his accustomed black-and-silver best, looked the more elegant by contrast – but most unfashionably, almost treasonably, unwarlike.

Once again only Kilpont was at his side, with most of the company eyeing him even more doubtfully than on the last occasion, a man whose name almost inevitably spelt trouble. As before, his toe was apt to tap the floor, however serene and clear his brow and assured his carriage.

The usual fanfare of trumpets preceded the throwing open of the Hall doors, and all began to dip and bow. It proved to herald the Queen alone, come from her own Court at Merton College – or, at least, without her husband, for she was by no means alone, a gallant bevy in attendance, chiefest of whom was none other than the Duke of Hamilton, gorgeous in orange and scarlet, become an inveterate traveller between Scotland and the South.

Henrietta Maria came forward into the great room at quite a pace, with little of pause and chatter, seemingly more interested in the brown-and-white spaniel in her arms than in the curtsyings and genuflections. She did however incline her ringleted head here and there – a head down to which Hamilton frequently bent to murmur. Opposite Montrose, the Duke bent lower and spoke for longer.

'Ah, yes – the Lord Montrose!' the Queen said into the hush, clearly. 'Still with us.' And she passed on, eyebrows raised.

Straigtening up, James Graham bit his lip. It was not unexpected, but none the more pleasant to endure. He had been weeks now, endeavouring to see the King, unsuccessfully, and had gained no single advantage with the Queen, or with any who might influence her. Charles had been away, first at the Siege of Gloucester – where Montrose had followed him, but failed to achieve contact – and then making a tour of royalist strongholds in the West Country. Henrietta Maria's coolness was no good augury – presumably she had forgotten what she had written earlier about the Graham retaining her confidence; but it was the King whom he had come to see, and see him he would. So he had not withdrawn from Oxford in despair. Now, with Charles only arrived back the previous night, was his opportunity. He had sent in a request for an audience, but received no reply. This was his only way to achieve an interview.

Charles was long in coming, and the Graham foot was tap-tapping again, the more so as loud laughter rang out from up around the Queen's chair-of-state at the head of the room, with Hamilton's bray predominant. It was by no means necessarily concerned with himself, but glances did tend to flicker in Montrose's direction.

Then, at last, the trumpets sounded again, and the King made his entry. This time he had only a small group in attendance, five men – and the sight of two of them lifted the Graham's heart, the young lords Aboyne and Ogilvy.

Of the other three, one, on whose arm the King's hand rested, was a dark, sardonically handsome and tall young man, with a carriage and assurance to match Montrose's own, who looked around him with a sort of grinning fierceness strange to see. Another was a paler, more stolid edition of the same, less dark and piratical. The third was a floridly good-looking man of early middle years, with twisted mouth, beaked nose and stooping wide shoulders – something of an eagle about him, but perhaps a slightly moulting eagle.

'These – who are they?' Montrose murmured, as they bent low.

'That is Rupert, with the King's hand,' Kilpont informed. 'His brother Maurice at the other side. And behind, Antrim.'

'Ah! So-o-o! The MacDonnell. Rupert, I think, I like.'

The Graham, in those moments, knew a further uplift of spirits. Here, at last, was Charles Stewart in the company of real men – not clerics, or painted popinjays or shifty, time-serving politicians, but soldiers. Rupert of the Rhine was one of the finest cavalry-leaders in Europe, despite being no more than twenty-four years. Maurice was not so brilliant, but an able and reliable commander, already experienced though younger still. And Randal MacDonnell, second Earl of Antrim, whatever else he might be, was a warrior, a noted captain of gallowglasses, descended from the Lords of the Isles though planted in Ulster; many looked on him as a Catholic monster of savagery, but he had survived in that blood-soaked land. The fact that the two Scots lordlings, developing fighters both, were included with these others round the King was itself significant.

Charles himself was looking better, less worn. Dashing about even a rebellious country appeared to agree with him. There was more vigour in his step, even in the dignified entry to this audience-chamber. His nephews, on either side of him, were no saunterers, of course.

This time, when they were opposite the Graham, Ogilvy came closer, to touch Prince Rupert's free arm. But there was no need to draw the royal attention. The King turned and paused, of his own accord.

'My lord of Montrose – welcome to my Court,' he said. 'I rejoice to see you in happier case than when last we saw one another.' And he held out his hand.

'Thanks, I am assured, to Your Majesty's gracious intervention on my behalf.' Montrose bowed low, to kiss the royal fingers. 'I am the more your most devoted servant, Sire.'

'So say many, my lord, who act otherwise! But you, I think, do mean it truly. I will speak with you later.' He nodded to Kilpont. 'My lord – I greet you.'

As Majesty passed on, Prince Rupert's glance caught and held James Graham's for a long moment.

'That was better, a deal better,' Kilpont murmured, thereafter. 'At last, perhaps, he will hear you, heed you.'

'Hear, perhaps, yes. But heed? How much influence with the King has Rupert, do you know?'

'Much, they say. More, now, even than the Queen. After all, most victories gained have been won by Rupert.'

One or two courtiers, quick to notice any change in the royal favour, now condescended to notice Montrose – and were received civilly but coolly. The King, with his wife and two nephews, at the head of the Hall, were naturally the focus of attention, accepting or summoning many to their presence. No such call came for the Graham – and he was the last man to push his way to the forefront there, as reminder. The courtiers drifted away.

When, at length, a herald announced that an acting of Will Shakespeare's play entitled *Much Ado About Nothing* would be held presently in the Hall at Merton College, at Her Majesty's gracious command, and all present were invited to attend forthwith. Montrose's patience became more obviously strained. As the company began to follow the King and Queen from Christ Church Hall and through the leaf-strewn and mist-hung gardens to near-by Merton, James Graham had to steel himself to move in their wake.

But, in an alley of dripping clipped-yew, the pair were approached by a resplendent figure, the new Earl of Dysart. This was none other than the ineffable and utterly untrustworthy Will Murray, former whipping-boy to the King, son of the minister of Dysart in Fife, and now Lord in Waiting. Charles was very free with his earldoms – or, at least, with the titles of such; for no lands went with them, and it was all a travesty of nobility to such as Montrose, for whom an earldom meant ancient lineage, great authority, vast territories and patriarchal responsibilities. This man in especial he looked upon as no more than a dangerous mountebank, and knew to be a creature of Hamilton's.

'His Majesty will see you in the Master's Room at Merton, my lord of Montrose,' he announced, almost as though he had personally arranged it. 'Ah . . . no doubt you will be able to inform His Majesty that the position in Scotland is by no means so ill against him as some ill-wishers seek to convince him? That most with any power there are loyal, and only seek the King's good.'

'What I say to the King, sir, is between myself and His Grace,' the other returned briefly.

'Undoubtedly. But there are those who, for their own purposes, seek to delude the King that the Scots are rising in arms against His Majesty. You, I am sure, know this to be untrue, and like my lord Duke of Hamilton can assure King Charles that such rising will only be against the King's enemies. If such indeed is the burden of your message, the Duke is convinced that His Majesty will be much relieved, and that you will have cause to rejoice in a successful outcome of your visit to Court.'

'Indeed? And what would constitute such success, sir, in the eyes of the Duke of Hamilton?'

'Who knows, my lord? Advancement of your personal cause and circumstances in Scotland, no doubt. The Privy Council, perhaps? The Duke is very influential. A marquisate, even, might conceivably be . . .'

'I see, sir. I shall not forget the Duke of Hamilton's interest in my concerns. Nor your own !'

'That is only fitting. And wise,' the other said, as he led the Graham past an armed guard and into a handsomely panelled chamber of Merton.

King Charles sat at a table spread with refreshments, and in the company of the five men who had attended him earlier, plus two others; one nearing middle-age, one youngish, whom Montrose recognised as Sir Edward Hyde, the Chancellor, and the Lord Digby, heir to the Earl of Bristol, and one of Charles's favourites and commanders. There was no sign of Hamilton, or of his brother and shadow, Lanark.

'Come, my lord of Montrose,' the King said, in friendly fashion. 'Let us hope that we will not long detain you from Her Majesty's entertainment. Drink a glass of wine with us. Will – conduct the Lord Kilpont to Her Majesty, and request her to proceed with the play-acting. We shall join her later.' Prince Rupert murmured in his uncle's ear. The King shrugged, and added, 'And, Will – you need not return.'

That further commended the Prince to Montrose.

'Sire, I am grateful to you for this audience,' he announced. 'I have been seeking it for weeks. I rejoice also in the company which attends you here.' He glanced particularly at Rupert. 'In what I have to say, I believe that their guidance will be invaluable.'

'Indeed, my lord? Invaluable to *my* cause, or yours?'

'Yours, Sire. And that of your Scots realm. I seek none of my own. If I did, I think I would not seek it in Oxford!'

Rupert laughed, though none other did so.

'Mm. You are frank, my lord, at least,' the King said, warily.

'I came to be frank, Sire. Only that. There has been too little of frankness to Your Majesty, in matters Scottish, I believe. I trust that I have your royal permission to be so, entirely?'

'I can scarcely say you nay. But – do you say then, that my other advisers in or on Scotland are less than frank?'

'I do. Especially the most highly placed of them, the Duke of Hamilton.'

At the general gasp, Rupert slapped his thigh, while his uncle stroked his pointed beard.

'There can be over-frankness, I think, my lord of Montrose. Especially in matters of personal opinion.'

'No doubt, Sire. But not in matters of state. As is this. I declare to you, before these many witnesses, that the Duke of Hamilton has long deceived you. To what purpose I know not, but with grievous hurt to your realm and royal cause. Others likewise. But he to your most injury.'

'I think that you forget yourself, my lord. The Duke is my friend.'

Rupert spoke, his English perfect but his voice husky, guttural. 'Sire – no man makes such charges before witnesses unless he is convinced of their truth. Or is a great fool. Does any here conceive the Earl of Montrose to be that?'

'*We* would be the fools not to hear what my lord has to say in this matter, Your Majesty,' Edward Hyde said. He looked like a shrewd cherub.

'You have never loved James Hamilton, Sir Edward. Nor

has Rupert,' the King complained. He shrugged. 'But – say on, my lord.'

'The Duke of Hamilton, Sire, I do assure you, is wholly in the pocket of the Marquis of Argyll. Than whom, I believe, you have no greater enemy. Argyll now rules Scotland, and Hamilton chooses to aid him in it. However much against your royal interests.'

'Or yours, perhaps?' Digby put in. He was a good-looking, fair-haired and blue-eyed young man, impetuous but not unintelligent, though with a petulant mouth.

Montrose nodded. 'Or mine, indeed. Or those of any loyal and honest man.'

'The Marquis of Argyll is your enemy, my lord – as all know.'

'And yours, sir, I hope! And every man's here – since he is the King's enemy. He would take the King's Scottish realm from him – has all but done so. And now seeks to aid those who would take his English one also.'

'The Duke of Hamilton assures me that the Marquis of Argyll's only intention is to mediate,' Charles said.

'Argyll's intention, Sire, is to set up a Commonwealth, in which you have no part. And in which he rules Scotland – and has much say in the rule of England.'

'This I cannot believe. This new Covenant, this Solemn League, is mistaken. But not disloyal.'

'That is not Argyll's work, but Henderson's. Henderson is honest. Argyll but uses him. And Hamilton aids him in it.'

'What proof have you of what you assert, my lord?' Digby demanded.

'Ample. Would the English parliament pay £30,000 per month for the services of a mediator? That is what they have agreed to pay for the aid of the Scots army. From the day it crosses the Border. Indeed a month's payment is already made!'

Clearly all were shaken by this revelation, staring at the speaker.

'It appears that my lord Duke has not informed you of this? Yet he was present and assenting when the compact was made.'

None spoke.

'Further to this. Your English subjects, Sire, as deputation to Scotland, were concerned that the Scots should indeed

251

fulfil their part of the bargain – which was to be 18,000 foot, 2000 light horse, and 1000 dragoons . . .'

'Christ God – over 20,000 men !' Rupert burst out.

'Yes, Your Highness – over 20,000. Large mediation! I was offered the Lieutenant-Generalship of it, under old Leslie. Indeed, it was much pressed on me. But that the English commissioners should be convinced that Argyll would fulfil what he was being paid to do, the compact was sealed with your own Royal Signet. Of which the Earl of Lanark, Hamilton's brother, is the Keeper. He sealed it in person.'

Charles Stewart gazed great-eyed past them all to the panelled wall, showing no emotion; but his long, delicate fingers beat a tattoo on the table-top.

'It gives me no pleasure to declare this shame to Your Majesty,' Montrose went on. 'But that you should know of it there is no doubt.'

'You say, my lord, that you were made offer of the Lieutenant-Generalship?' Rupert asked. 'This seems scarcely believable.'

'So thought I, Highness – until I discovered what my duties were to be! They were quite clear. If the English parliament forces were to lose, and the Scots army found itself in a difficult position deep in England, facing Your victorious Majesty, I was to be there, to mediate indeed, my known love of Your Majesty to prove that Leslie's army meant you no ill. On the other hand, if your enemies were winning, I was but *Lieutenant*-General, junior to Leslie, to do what I was ordered. I was to be, indeed, but a convenient warranty, if required, a safeguard and prudent discretion should matters go ill.' He paused for a moment. 'I think that Argyll and Hamilton overestimated my influence with Your Majesty!'

The Earl of Antrim guffawed.

Prince Maurice spoke, his voice thicker, more deliberate than his brother's. 'How many men has the Marquis of Newcastle, Sire? In Yorkshire?' he asked bluntly.

Hyde answered for him. 'No more than 6000, sir.'

'And the Lord Byron? In Lancashire?'

'He is now at Chester. With but 4000.'

Those around the King looked at each other. None appeared any longer to doubt Montrose's assertions, at least as regards the probability of a Scots invasion.

'How soon, my lord?' Rupert demanded.

'Who knows? They have been preparing, assembling, for long. I cannot think that Alexander Leslie will delay much longer.'

'Sir Alexander Leslie swore to me, when I created him Earl of Leven, that he would never again take the field against me,' Charles declared sadly.

None commented.

'Have you any suggestions, my lord of Montrose?' Hyde asked, pursing full lips.

'I have sir. What I came here to ask of the King. It were better that the Scots army, when it comes, be drawn back to Scotland than that you must needs fight it here. This I would seek to do. But, more than this – Scotland, I swear, can be saved for Your Majesty. Turned again from the evil courses of Argyll and his puppets. Most of the folk are still loyal. And the nobility much hate the rule of fanatic preachers. Give me authority to raise Scotland for the King, and I will restore Your Majesty's ancient realm to you. Or die in the attempt.'

There was a murmur of mixed admiration and doubt from his hearers. But Rupert raised his dark head abruptly, and stepping closer, thrust out his hand to the Graham, no word spoken.

The King looked troubled, nobly troubled, a man to whom decision-taking was agony. His glance at his nephew was almost reproachful.

'I esteem your courage, devotion, goodwill, my lord,' he said carefully. 'But have you sufficiently considered? You are a young man yet. Head of a notable house. But single-handed, how could you raise a whole nation? Which is already in arms against me.'

'My lord is not single-handed, Sire.' That was young Aboyne, making a first contribution. 'Clan Gordon will join with the Grahams. And where Gordon goes, will go many another.'

'As will Ogilvy,' the other lordling declared, as stoutly.

Montrose smiled at his two lieutenants, who scarcely numbered forty years between them.

Digby snorted. 'This is war, my lords – not game playing!' he declared. 'If what has been said is true, a deal more than this will be required to win Scotland from the Marquis of

Argyll and his Covenanters. I advise that Your Majesty thinks most carefully.'

'Can the King lose by it?' the Graham asked. 'I ask nothing but a commission to raise Scotland in his name. Authority. If I do not succeed, what have I cost him? A paper. And at least I will give Argyll and Leslie pause. That I promise. They will be less eager for adventures in England while I am recruiting at their backs.'

'Aye, Sire – here's a ploy!' the Scots-Irish MacDonnell, Earl of Antrim, broke in. '*I* can take a hand here, by God! I have never loved the Campbell. I will ship 10,000 gallow-glasses across the Irish Sea into Argyll, by your leave. And see how your new Marquis likes the style of them!' Antrim apparently continued to cherish the age-old Clan Donald hatred for Clan Dairmid, even transplanted in Ulster. And undoubtedly he resented the Argyll marquisate.

'We have all heard of your 10,000 Irishry!' Digby said sourly. 'But even if we were to *see* them, for a change, they would be Catholics to a man! His Majesty would needs think twice before unleashing such on his Protestant realms. Even on Scotland!'

'Insolent puppy!' Antrim snarled. 'Think you the King's subjects must all be such as you? Mother of Christ forbid it! I . . .'

'Enough, my lords – enough!' Charles said, raising his hand. 'Restrain yourselves, at least in my presence, I charge you. My lord of Montrose – I will consider this matter. Consider it well. This is Scotland. Take sure advice. I thank you for your good will. Even if I cannot thank you for your tidings.' He sighed. 'Now, my friends – let us join Her Majesty.'

'And Hamilton, Sire?' Rupert demanded. 'What of the Duke?'

'This also I must consider. Make enquiry, painful enquiry. It may not be quite so ill as my lord believes. Who knows?'

'It may be *more* ill, Uncle! Cherishing a snake to your bosom can cost you dear! I say that you should arrest him forthwith. And his precious brother. And enquire thereafter.'

'That would be too hasty, Rupert. You are ever hasty. But we shall test the matter, never fear.' Charles rose. 'Her Majesty will look for us . . .'

Charles Stewart ran true to form. He delayed decision.

Hamilton and Lanark departed again for Scotland, un-challenged. And that he should not be badgered and harried in the meantime, the King arranged it so that impatient and importunate young men should be kept occupied and out of the way while he made up his mind. The Princes Rupert and Maurice were given a variety of urgent if minor military tasks to perform, from this Oxford base – since large-scale warfare was considered to be out of the question during the particularly severe winter conditions, by both sides, with armies and garrisons more or less sitting tight up and down England. And Montrose was instructed to accompany the young princes on these sallies, as schooling and experience – and was nothing loth, finding it infinitely to be preferred to the hothouse atmosphere of over-crowded Oxford, with its excesses, its drinking and gaming and brawling, its duels and back-stabbing, its promiscuity and vice, its everlasting play-acting, dancing, music and feasting – so strange a Court for a dedicated and religiously-minded monarch, who seemed indeed so other-worldly and high-minded as scarcely to be aware of what went on around him. Montrose found in Rupert especially a fellow being almost entirely after his own heart, and they were close friends more or less from first sight – even though the prince had a ruthlessness and violence in him which found no echo in the Graham. But particularly in matters military they made a pair, audacious, swift, artful, courageous, each with his own genius to comple-ment the other's. Together during that bitter cold December and January, with small mobile forces, they dashed about the upper Thames area, relieving a castle here, and a village there, raiding in the Chilterns and Cotswolds, encouraging isolated commanders, threatening the communications of Fairfax's and Waller's armies, superintending the fortifica-tion of Towcester and other towns. Montrose found it all greatly to his taste; and had it not been for a preoccupation with the Scots situation, and a fretting that the King appeared to be incapable of positive action, it would have been one of the most satisfying periods of his life.

Then, on the 15th of January 1644, ignoring the winter conditions, Field-Marshal the Earl of Leven led the Scots army into England, and came fighting, not mediating, with the Marquis of Argyll acting colonel to his own Campbell regiment therein. Suddenly all was changed.

255

When the news reached Oxford, Charles was busy organising a parliament of his own, in opposition to that other sitting in London fifty-two miles away. His hurt was great. He actually wept. And when, presently, Montrose and Rupert got back from Towcester, Edward Hyde in person came to the former's quarters to conduct him to the King.

'I believe that His Majesty will grant your wishes now,' he said. 'He has just heard that all the North-East is falling to the Scots arms.'

'If I had been in Scotland these weeks past, instead of here, sir, Leslie might well not have marched.'

'I know it. But . . . you will be more likely to gain your ends with the King, my lord, if you refrain from mention of it!'

At Christ Church, the King had only his nephew Maurice with him when Hyde brought the Graham in. The younger men exchanged glances. Charles was looking drawn, unhappy, pouches under his fine eyes.

'You have heard the tidings from the North, my lord?' he asked wearily.

'I have, Sire, to my sorrow. If scarcely to my surprise. I grieve for your royal cause. But I believe that it is not yet too late to better it.'

'Ha – you say so? You still believe that you can win Scotland for me? Even now?'

'Even now, Sire. Although it will be the more difficult.'

'What do you need from me, to that end, my lord?'

'First of all, Your Majesty's faith and trust. If I am to imbue others with the spirit to rise and fight for you, I must convince them that Your Majesty is wholly behind me. Proof of such trust I do require.'

'You shall have it, sir. I shall appoint you my Governor and Commander-in-Chief in Scotland. Give you commission as my Captain-General and viceroy. And create you Marquis of Montrose. Will that serve to advertise my royal trust, my friend?' It was not often that Charles Stewart came out with decision at this rate.

'Hrm.' Montrose cleared his throat. 'I am deeply sensible of these high honours, appointments, Sire,' he said. 'They are altogether too much, I think. As well as undeserved. And not what I intended . . .'

'No? Then what, my lord? What more can I do for you?'

'Not for *me,* Sire. It is for the folk in Scotland that I

require this proof, not for myself. That they may accept that I have now your entire confidence. And that, hm, others have not! For me to be Marquis of Montrose would be to my much honour. But would it convince my countrymen, who have seen other marquises created? Even dukes!'

Hyde coughed, and Charles looked almost shocked. Prince Maurice's smile was probably little help.

'I regret your attitude, my lord.' That was said with royalest dignity.

'Then I crave Your Majesty's forbearance. I acknowledge that I may be too frank. But the occasion warrants plain speaking, does it not?'

The noble head inclined, but only just. 'What is it you seek, then?'

'What would convince the Scots people that Your Majesty no longer trusted those who have ill-advised you for so long. Your dismissal of Hamilton and his brother.'

'That is in train, my lord. The Duke of Hamilton and the Earl of Lanark shamefully deceived me. They have been summoned from Scotland. They will learn of my royal displeasure.'

'If they come!' Maurice murmured.

'That is a step well taken, Sire. It will please many in Scotland, and ease my path.'

'What else do you require of me?'

'Nothing, Sire – but your blessing.'

'That you have in full measure. But you have more. As Governor as well as Captain-General, you will have my *authority.* To act in my royal name. To levy and requisition as you need. To appoint to office, and demote. To bring to trial, to judge, to execute if need be. A grave responsibility for so young a man. But you will require all such powers, I think.'

'No, Sire. Humbly and with respect – no.' Montrose shook his head. 'Such powers and state I do not desire. More, I conceive it to be harmful to your cause. See you, Sire – Scotland is a proud country. And as you say, I am a young man. Offence must not be given to any who have the power to fight for you. We are a people of clans and great families, jealous each of our name and standing. I am one of the earls of Scotland, the *old* earls – that is sufficient. Your Grace alone is *Ard Righ,* the High King. None must fail to flock to your royal standard because *I* seem to set myself too high.

As many would, Sire, were I to be your viceroy. I know my own people. I will not even be Captain-General. Not at this time. Lieutenant only. Under some other. With Your Majesty's permission.'

'You are a strange man, my lord of Montrose. But it appears that you well know your own mind. And I accept that you know your strange countrymen – and mine. But . . . if you are to be only Lieutenant, who is to be Captain? Who, in Scotland, would you have me make Captain-General, master over Montrose?'

James Graham found a smile. 'None that I may think of, Sire. Since it must needs be a soldier. Rather it should be someone here, I think, in England. Close to your royal person. But someone whom the Scots will accept. Not – not an Englishman !' He paused. 'Prince Rupert you have made Master of the Horse and Duke of Cumberland. Might not Your Majesty make His Highness Prince Maurice Captain-General for Scotland?'

The King looked from one to the other, and then to Hyde. 'I cannot spare my nephew to Scotland, my lord. Not in this pass. Once the campaigning season starts, there is too much for him, for us all, to do here.'

'I did not think that you could, Sire. I will gladly send reports to my Captain-General – at Oxford !'

Maurice emitted his throaty chuckle, unoffended. 'He desires only my shadow, Sire – not my substance,' he said. 'And I shall be able to rule all the Scots at your Court here – who have until now ignored me !'

'These I intend to take back to Scotland !' Montrose countered.

Charles, who was not a man of humour, looked slightly dis-approving of this levity in his presence. But he glanced at Hyde, who nodded. 'Very well, my lord. It shall be so. Lieutenant-General you shall be, under Captain-General the Prince Maurice of Bohemia. Yet in Scotland you will have the complete command. Over all who fight for me. Including my lord of Antrim's Irish. It is agreed.'

'Mm. Sire – Lord Antrim's Irish . . . ? Is this wise? Lord Digby spoke of it, before – and I saw point to his fears. To loose a large number of Catholic Irish on Protestant Scotland might but ill serve your cause. They might make my task the harder.'

Charles frowned. None of his commanders wanted the Catholic Irish, even Lord Herbert, himself a Catholic. 'My lord – I will forgo the use of thousands of loyal troops because of unsuitable religious prejudice. We are all Christians, I would remind you! Lord Antrim's levies can best be used in Scotland. It will give you a core of experienced fighters. You cannot go to Scotland alone, single-handed, to conquer a country. You will delay your return until the Irish force is ready to join you there.'

'With respect, Your Majesty, I would prefer to find my way secretly back to Scotland, and forthwith. Once in my own place, I swear I should not be long in raising an army to fight for you – and to force Argyll and Leslie to look anxiously behind them. Without calling in the Irish . . .'

'No, my lord. That is not how it will best be done. This, from the first, must be seen to be the King's answer to rebellion. Not a further rebellion taking place behind the invading Scots army. I have spoken of it to certain of my commanders and advisers, and on this we are agreed. You must invade Scotland in *my* name – not foster a rising within Scotland on your own. The difference is important. I will send you to my lord of Newcastle, at York, and request that he supply you with a body of horse to serve as kernel of your new army. Also arms and ammunition – these are expected from Denmark any day. I will give you a commission to raise certain levies in Cumberland and Westmorland. With these, you can make entry to Scotland, in force. In the west, since the Scots army it seems controls the east. Carlisle, perhaps. When my lord of Antrim's force is ready to meet you, from Ireland. Thus you will come to Scotland as my Lieutenant-General indeed – not as a private nobleman seeking to stir up petty insurrection behind the Scots government. You understand?'

Montrose sought to keep his voice level. 'This will take valuable time, Sire. And for me to lead Englishmen and Irishmen into Scotland will not endear me to many Scots. I had rather rouse themselves to put their house in order.'

'*My* house, my lord of Montrose, I'd remind you! If you go as my representative to my Scottish realm, you will do so as *I* decide.'

The Graham bowed. 'As Your Majesty commands . . .'

IT WAS, IN FACT, FOURTEEN WEEKS LATER, ON THE 13TH OF April, that Montrose left English soil and crossed the River Esk into Scotland as royal Lieutenant. And, despite the delay, and the King's desire that he should do so at the head of an impressive force, he forded the river with only a few hundred ill-assorted men, many of them already disgruntled. The Earl of Newcastle, commander in the North of England, already short of men, with only 8000 at grips with Leslie's 21,000 on the Durham border, was in no mood, or case, to obey his monarch's command and detach precious cavalry for the Scots venture. And the royalists of Cumberland and Westmorland, seeing the way that things were going, with Leslie winning over a wide front, were much more concerned to stay at home and protect their own hearthstones from the barbarian invaders than to volunteer for a hazardous wild-goose chase into Scotland. As for Antrim's 10,000 Irish, there was still neither hint nor hair of them, although the MacDonnell had promised to deliver them in force before the end of April. Not desiring the complications that such a Catholic host might produce in the Presbyterian Lowlands, Montrose had managed to persuade the King that these should land only in Argyll and the West Highlands, where Catholicism was still the prevalent religion, there to menace the Campbells in their own country.

Montrose's company, therefore, was an almost farcical host with which to invade a warlike and already warned country – for, of course, it had all been the talk of Oxford for months, and few in Scotland had not heard that the Earl of Montrose was coming, with a ravening horde of Catholic savages from Ireland; so much so that Archibald Campbell had hurriedly withdrawn himself and his regiment from Leslie's army and sped northwards to defend his West Highland patrimony. The Graham had 1300 altogether, consisting of 800 Cumberland and Westmorland militia foot, and 500 assorted horse – very assorted, consisting of 100 ill-spared and poorly mounted troopers from Lord Newcastle, three troops of local yeomanry, and the rest gentry, Scots exiles, North Country royalist squires, and a few paid professional officers from the foreign wars. As a fighting force it was unbalanced, undisciplined, formless, and would have been laughable had it been any laughing matter. James Graham felt more like weeping. This was the last way that he would have chosen to return to his country and commence his campaign – a campaign which, even with the best of conditions and good fortune, would be a colossal gamble, all but a forlorn hope. To attempt it in these circumstances was little short of madness.

And yet, even so, the King's new Lieutenant-General could not but rejoice, in some measure, could not prevent his spirits from soaring, as he set foot once again on his native soil, with possibly the greatest venture of his life ahead of him, an endeavour which only he could make, a challenge to dwarf all others. None was better aware than he was of the difficulties and heartbreaks which must inevitably lie ahead. Yet he rode through the spring morning, amongst the blazing gorse and broom, the shouting of the larks, the long-lying snow-wreaths and the clamour of tumbling waters, with a lightness of heart – however heavy might be some of the thoughts at the back of his head.

Crossing the green plain of Gretna and the mouth of Annandale, field of battles innumerable, they worked round the wide-spreading Solway estuary and the wildfowl-haunted reaches of the Lochar Moss, to the great castle of Caerlaverock within its marshland moats. This presented no challenge, for its lord was in fact with Montrose – Robert Maxwell, head of that turbulent clan and Earl of Nithsdale. But he was a Catholic, and the Graham was loth indeed to burden his campaign with any further alleged Popish bias such as it already was being given. He got over the difficulty, meantime, by sending the Earl off into Galloway, to find and try to control a fellow-religionist, the Viscount Kenmure, who for some time had been terrorising these remote counties, all in the King's name, roaming the country with a brandy-barrel on a pole as his standard, indiscriminately pillaging, burning, raping.

Unfortunately this judicious detachment of Lord Niths-dale was promptly followed by another, neither ordered nor anticipated. Most of the Cumberland and Westmorland militia suddenly took fright, declaring that they had not enlisted for adventures in Scotland. They wanted to go home. Montrose might have taken a stern line with these, threatening them with the penalties of mutiny; but on a desperate attempt such as this, he saw no advantage in clinging to a reluctant crew. They were foot, anyway, and as a born horseman he tended to see such as more of a delaying factor to his preferred swift movement than any-thing else. He sent them home.

That he was immediately thereafter joined by a squadron of well-armed horse under the Lord Herries, was a doubtful compensation – for Herries was another Maxwell and Catholic.

A rather more welcome encouragement met them when they pressed on the few miles to Dumfries, still without opposition, in the person of Provost John Corsan and some of his magistrates and townsfolk, come out to greet them. Dumfries, where Nith joined Solway, was the first sizeable town on this west side of Scotland, and this adherence was heartening. Montrose decided that here he would take the significant step of raising the royal standard of King Charles.

So, on a cold and showery afternoon, the 14th of April 1644, in the Market Place of the trim red-stone burgh of Dumfries, trumpets shrilled and the red-and-gold Lion Rampant banner of the Kings of Scots was unfurled, to flap in the breeze, while James Graham, fifth Earl of Montrose, read out his commission as the King's Lieutenant-General – under Captain-General the Prince Maurice – with all necessary powers and authority to restore the King's rule and governance to his ancient realm. To ringing cheers he then read out a proclamation of his own composing, calling on the people of Scotland to join him for the defence of the true Portestant religion, His Majesty's just and sacred authority, the fundamental laws and privileges of Parlia-ment, and the peace and freedom of all oppressed and en-thralled subjects. God Save the King.

It was a stirring moment, long awaited. The Earls of

Kinnoull and Wigtown, supported by the Lords Herries, Aboyne, Ogilvy and Kilpont, led the cheering; but the occasion was rather spoiled by another earl of Scotland – or at least by a message which reached Montrose only a few minutes previously, to the effect that Lieutenant-General the Earl of Callander was making forced marches from Edinburgh south-westwards, to intercept him with 7000 men. This was none other than his old colleague the Lord Almond, fellow lieutenant to old Leslie and co-signatory of the Cumbernauld Bond, who had now succeeded his late brother as Earl of Callander, and moved firmly into Argyll's camp. But whatever his loyalties and politics, he was an able soldier; and the thought of him and his 7000 only three or four days' march away, was dampening to enthusiasm.

Montrose, however, gave a scratch banquet for the Provost and leading citizens of Dumfries that evening, and thereafter even danced with Mrs Corsan, the Lady Maxwell of Munches and other ladies. But however attentive he seemed, his mind was in fact filled with assessings and calculations other than such partners might have considered suitable. How fast could a host of that number, mainly foot, travel through hill country still largely snow-bound after a particularly severe winter? By what route would they come, using which passes through the Lowther Hills especially? Was there any point where a few hundred horsemen might successfully ambush such thousands? Could, in fact, such determined horsemen reach the passes in time? And if they failed, would that be the end of the King's cause in Scotland before it had even begun?

Such cogitations tended to fairly consistently depressing conclusions – which no doubt was hard on the ladies. And unfortunately James Graham perforce took the cogitations to bed with him that night – which was hard on himself. Moreover, it did not fail to occur to him that if he could think along these lines, others could do likewise. Others whom he was hopefully summoning to the royal standard. In the circumstances, with no sizeable increase in the King's force meantime, would *any* in fact, in their sane sense, rally to himself at Dumfries? It seemed improbable.

The next day and the next Montrose waited by the Nith, and learned that his fears were well founded. A few lairds, mainly Maxwells and Catholics, brought small groups and contingents. But their enemies, the Johnstons of Annandale, under the new Earl of Hartfell, though nominally royalist, kept their distance; as did the Douglasses, Murrays, Armstrongs, Elliots, Jardines and other West March clans. And Callander drew closer apace.

On the third day, James Graham accepted the bitter reality. Dumfries and Galloway are separated from the rest of Scotland by great ranges of hills and wide empty uplands. There was not another town of any size for fifty miles, no populous area where he might look for major support. And thereafter, the lowlands of Ayrshire and the uplands of Lanarkshire were both strongly Covenant, dominated by Loudoun, Cassillis, Eglinton and Hamilton. This was no country to invade from the south in small numbers. He had told the King and his advisers so; but they had known best. With under 1000 men all told, he was in no position to press on against an army seven times his size. Dumfries was not a walled town, and impossible to defend; besides, for him to be cooped up, besieged, only a mile or two into Scotland, would look pathetic, and do no service to the royal cause. There was nothing for it but to retire whence he had come – and quickly.

But one duty he had, and must attend to, first. The local volunteers must be dispersed and sent home, however much they might protest. Since obviously he could not adequately make use of them, they must at least be spared the reprisals that Callander's army would be almost certain to visit upon them.

To a man of his temperament and pride, the entire business was an agony. And, almost, he left the final withdrawal too late. Callander sent most of his horse ahead of the main body, and they came dashing down Nith only a few miles to the north of the town at the same time as Montrose was riding out to the south. It became practically a race for the Border, and Carlisle city walls. They even had to abandon some of the heavier cannon, which were severely holding them up. It was debacle, complete and shameful. Probably only because Callander's cavalry had no instructions about crossing into England and confronting the fortress of Carlisle, did the royalist force make good its escape, without loss. Its leader, set-faced, drank deep of the draught of humiliation. Only one credit was to be salvaged from the entire sorry affair. He was being taught a valuable lesson. Never again must he allow himself to be forced into commanding a military adventure which he knew to be mistaken, even by his liege lord. His duty was to serve the King – but with his mind and will, not merely with his blind obedience. James Graham was a man who did not spare himself. He blamed himself now – not for this fiasco of an invasion, but for not having refused utterly to countenance it from the beginning, when he knew it folly.

Never did a general less relish his safety as the gate of Carlisle, an English citadel, clanged shut behind him and in the face of his compatriots.

Strangely enough, this deplorable withdrawal by no means produced the storm of contumely and derision from the royalist camp which might have been expected. The English commanders cared little for the situation in Scotland; and the Earl of Newcastle in especial saw Montrose's return as admirable, heaven-sent indeed. Instead of being blamed, he found himself being treated as a wise man who had seen the better course, accepted as the sorely tried Newcastle's deputy in the North-West, and given urgent commands to raise all Cumberland and Westmorland and North Lancashire, and to assail Leslie's right flank. The impression given was almost that he had forgone pressing on into Scotland in order to return to the greater danger in England. If there was some slight balm to a young man's wounded pride in this, there was also another salutary lesson. The English, unlike the Scots, had the priceless gift of single-mindedness, of seeing matters always and entirely from their own point of view; nothing extraneous really mattered – unlike the metaphysical Scots to whom everything mattered, and too much. Here was understanding vital to any student of statecraft, any commander likely to handle troops of both nations.

Montrose, rather to his further surprise, found the Cumbrians and Westmorlanders, whom he had tended to dismiss as craven, far from it. On their own ground, fighting for something they approved of, they were both keen and valiant. Recruiting for the Scots venture had been grim; now it went with a swing. Soon the King's Lieutenant for Scotland under his new hat as royalist general in the North-West had an army of nearly 6000 under his command, mainly foot admittedly, and untrained, raw. But then, so were most of those who would be opposed to them, in civil warfare. With these he was able, not only to force Callander to keep well back on his own side of the Border, but to harry Leslie's right by making repeated brief sorties through the Pennine passes. He also formed something of a barrier diagonally across the country, to deter the parliamentary army based on Chester from moving north-east to link up with Leslie. If this was not what James Graham had left Kincardine Castle to do, at least it had the effect of salvaging his reputation as a commander – indeed enhancing it – and of giving his bevy of young Scots aristocrats, now willy-nilly officering North Country English levies, valuable experience in mobile warfare.

The strategic situation, that spring of 1644, was complex, with the centre of gravity moving distinctly into the North of England. Or at least, into Yorkshire, for the Scots were steadily pressing Newcastle southwards on that city, after being held up by the snows of a phenomenally hard winter. England was now a bewildering patchwork of loyalties, with basically, the parliament strong in London, the South and East, the King in the North and West, and the Midlands a chaos. With the Scots wholly altering the balance in the North, the Midlands and Eastern parliamentarians decided to try to join up with Leslie and take the Earl of Newcastle from the rear. To this end the two Fairfaxes moved up their central army into South Yorkshire and the Earl of Manchester commanding the Eastern Association, headed northwest. Newcastle called urgently for help.

The King ordered Rupert, building a new army at Shrewsbury and the Welsh marches, to hasten to Newcastle's aid with all speed. And he sent the hot-tempered Earl of Crawford to Montrose at Carlisle.

'You are to assail Leslie's rear,' that fiery-headed, red-bearded nobleman declared. 'Forget Scotland and Callander, meantime. Newcastle and the North must be saved at all costs.'

James Graham frowned at this chief of the Lindsays, sixteenth Earl, who had spent much of his life at the Court in England and had latterly been colonel of a regiment of royalist horse. 'Does His Majesty realise what he asks?' he demanded. 'I have here a motley crew of Westmorland squires, Cumbrian farmers and Scots gentry. Take most of them twenty miles from their homes and they mutiny! With these, the King asks me to assail the rear of an army five times as large, the best led and best trained and disciplined in three kingdoms. With another at my back, led by a man I know to be a most able soldier . . .'

'His Majesty does not ask – he commands!' Crawford said brusquely. 'But, look not so glum, man. Being cautious is no way to win battles. The King has sent me to strengthen your hand. We will tickle old Leslie's backside the way I tickled Waller's at Alton! Never fear!'

Montrose, with sad experience both of His Majesty's military commands and judgment of character, considered the dashingly picturesque but arrogant figure before him – who had lost 600 men at Alton in a grandiloquent gesture that gained precisely nothing. He could have done without the Lindsay – especially as he had not brought his regiment with him. But royal commands or none, he was the general here, not Crawford; and he was not going to make the same mistake twice. He had no faith in the royalist Northern forces, or in their leadership – indeed in any of Charles's generals other than Rupert and Maurice; nor had he any wish to involve himself seriously in the English civil war, when Scotland was tugging at him all the time. But he had to do something in the circumstances. He would interpret the King's orders in his own fashion – and endeavour, tactfully if possible, to keep the sixteenth Earl in his place.

On the 9th of May, then, leaving the unreliable and slow infantry behind to offer some sort of threat both to Callander's army over the Border and to the Lancastrian parliamentarians, with all the horse he could raise, 400 of his own and 600 Cumbrian yeomanry under Colonel Clavering, a distinctly cynical professional soldier, Montrose set out eastwards from Carlisle at speed, the fire-eating Crawford in attendance. Sparing neither men nor horses, he drove through and across the spinal heights of Cumberland and Northumberland all day, by the valleys of the Irthing and South Tyne, by Brampton, Naworth and Haltwhistle, thirty-five miles to Hexham. There, although already many of his men were complaining, he turned northwards up North Tyne, and in the long May evening half-light climbed out of the valley and over the bare empty moors, by Chollerton and Kirkheaton to the valley of the Wansbeck. Here, at Hartburn, he relented, and allowed his weary and outraged troopers a few hours' rest, not for their sake so much as that of the horses. Crawford, though eloquent on the military art for the first half of the day, had been silent now for some time; but Clavering at last was beginning to look less disillusioned. They halted in woodland, but no cooking fires were to be lit. Seven miles ahead, down this twisting vale, the main highway from Scotland to the south ran through the fortified town of Morpeth. A vital point on Leslie's lines of communication, it was held by a Scots garrison. Montrose proposed to assault it as soon after daybreak as might be.

Of a still misty early morning, divided into four squadrons under Crawford, Clavering, Aboyne and Ogilvy, they trotted on quietly down Wansbeck towards the sleeping town. Morpeth lay in the valley-floor, at a wide hairpin bend where the Colling Burn joined the Wansbeck, with gentle slopes to north, east and south, but steep banks to the west, on top of one of which perched its castle and citadel. This was, of course, the key to the place, and though not exceptionally strong in itself, nor very large, was very strongly sited. Montrose had been here during his winter with Leslie's army at Newcastle three years before, and knew the position.

At this hour of the morning the town gates would all be shut; and any attempt to storm them would inevitably arouse the castle and dissipate any advantage of surprise. Leaving his force hidden in the scrub woodland around the ruins of Newminster Abbey, Montrose went quietly forward with Clavering, to prospect.

They were able to get within 300 yards of the town gates, in cover. Neither gates nor walls looked very serious barriers, Clavering pointed out.

The other would have none of it. 'We could get ourselves into the town, yes. But what will that serve, if the castle is warned? We do not know the numbers of the garrison. And they had cannon in that citadel when last I was here. It is a Scots garrison. They might not hesitate to fire down into the town, an *English* town. Either we take that castle by surprise, or we do not take it at all, since we have no cannon. So – we await the opening of these gates. And pray that it may not be long delayed. It is market-day – for so I chose. The countryfolk will come early with their produce.'

'And if they delay?'

'Then we withdraw. Go elsewhere. The Shields, perhaps. Sunderland. Lesser prizes, but with no castles to defend them.'

Back at the main body, presently scouts watching the highway to the north reported that a party of folk were approaching, men and women, even children, with pannier-ponies. Still a mile off.

Montrose nodded in decision, and issued his orders. Crawford to take his squadron and circle the town and castle west-about by Morpeth Common, well hidden amongst its banks and braes, to as near the *south* gates of the town as possible, remaining secret. When the gates opened, to move into the lower parts of the town from that side, and to meet up with Clavering, who would be doing the same from the north. Aboyne and Ogilvy's squadrons would come with himself, and the moment the north gates were open, rush through and make a swift dash for the castle, heeding nothing else. From this side they could do so without being seen until the last moment. Was it understood?

All his commanders agreed, and Crawford led his party off south-westwards. The others mounted, and moved quietly forward to the edge of cover, to wait with what patience they could muster for the approaching countryfolk to gain their admittance, dismounted scouts out to send information.

It seemed a long wait, with every minute lessening the chances of catching the castle garrison asleep. Even with the market people at the gate, it remained unopened. More people joined these, the scouts reported. Presently, even round the river's bend, the hiding men could hear derisive shouts to the porters to waken and open up. Montrose was in a further fret now lest other early-rising locals should come down from the village of Mitford and stumble on them in this woodland – although there seemed no reason why any should leave the road to enter it. But 750 horsemen take a deal of hiding. He was at least thankful for the new May flourish and foliage.

Then, with a clanking creak they heard the gates open – no need to await the scouts' announcement. Spurring his mount, Montrose waved them on.

He was first through those gates, scattering astonished folk right and left, his squadrons thundering behind. Sleepy gatekeepers and burdened market-goers alike stared open-mouthed – and none were foolish enough to seek to halt such intruders. Down the narrow main street they clattered.

Without waiting for any marshalling and splitting of forces behind him, James Graham swung off right-handed at the Tolbooth, down a side-street, to splash dramatically across a ford of the river. Then, slithering and striking sparks from the cobblestones, he drove on through a huddle of houses, in steps and stairs, and set his mount to the steep grassy banks beyond, in the most direct route to the castle. Looking back, half-way up, he could' see young Aboyne leading his squadron across the ford in a shower of spray. The castle's gatehouse-tower entrance was at the other side, facing south, which meant a half-circuit of the curtain-walls on a steeply sloping bank. But at least there was cover here. Concerned not to show himself before the gatehouse until he had enough men with him to risk rushing it, he slowed down, in a fever of impatience.

Then, the noise of his horse's hooves and snorting breath lessening, suddenly he was aware of disturbance ahead, uproar, though the bulk of the high castle outer walling blanketed it to some extent.

Cursing, he kicked his mount onward again, rounding those walls. And as the bank levelled off southwards to a wide grassy platform, the situation was revealed. The Earl of Crawford and his squadron were milling around on the greensward, shouting challenges and hurrahing for the King, before the square gatehouse-tower with its archway – an archway in process of being blocked by the rising draw-bridge. Even as Montrose stared, angrily, the bridge clanked into the up position, and the portcullis went down with a rattle. And at the same time, a few musket shots began to crack out from the battlements.

Groaning despite himself, and caring nothing for flying ball, James Graham rode across to the sword-flourishing, martial Crawford. 'My lord – what is this?' he demanded hotly.

'Devilish ill-fortune!' Ludovic Lindsay called. 'I near had them. But a minute or two more and the place would have been mine. Marshalling my men for the assault. The Devil's own luck!'

'I am not concerned with your luck, sir!' Montrose's voice quivered. 'Why are you here?'

'The town gate, to the south, was open. We could ride in. I perceived that I could reach the castle before you – for the south gate is closer.'

Montrose held out an arm and pointing finger that shook, indicative of the effort with which he held himself in. 'Nearer, yes. But see there, my lord – visible of approach most of the way from the lower town.' He was pointing down the wide Castlegate. 'Only a guard asleep could have failed to see you approach thus. Why think you I planned to approach from the north? And commanded that you capture the lower town, making cause with Clavering?'

Gulping, he stopped. This would not do. Crawford was chief of a great family, sixteenth Earl, next to Mar the most senior of all the earls of Scotland. And an older man than he was. It was not suitable to berate him thus, to berate any commander in front of his men. Besides, musket-balls were coming thick and fast.

'I advise that you get your men down into the town swiftly, my lord,' he went on, even-voiced. 'Clavering may need your aid. And when I last was here, there were cannon in this fort . . . !'

He did not finish that, as a musket-ball screamed between them, setting their horses dancing.

Furiously the other earl reined around, and waved his squadron to retire whence it had come. Aboyne's people were advancing round the perimeter wall now. Gesturing to them to turn back, Montrose saw the first flash, and mushroom of smoke, from the keep's platform-roof, and the crash of the cannon coincided with his own urgent departure from that place.

The capture of the town itself was not difficult, with surprise, and the full thousand cavalry to devote to it. But the failure to gain the castle left Montrose in a serious quandary. Any siege of the citadel demanded cannon, of which he had none. It might be best to abandon Morpeth altogether, and concentrate on spreading alarm and confusion behind Leslie's lines by assaulting other Tyneside towns. On the other hand, Morpeth was astride the main north-south road, supply and retreat line with Scotland. Holding it would more effectively

271

embarrass the Scots army than would any other. Yet he could not just sit in it, under the threat of the castle's own artillery and garrison. If only he could lay hands on some cannon . . .

It was this line of thinking that moulded his subsequent strategy. The city of Newcastle lay only fifteen miles to the south – and there would be cannon therein. It was still in royalist hands, but being contained rather than besieged by a rearguard of Leslie's force, neutralised. If the containing force could be lured away, even for a short time . . .

James Graham did not delay. Within hours of the castle disappointment, and before the word could spread around the countryside, Crawford and Clavering were sent off south-eastwards, with their squadrons, openly, to make for North Shields, thirteen miles away. It was an unimportant place at the mouth of the Tyne estuary; but a ferry plied to South Shields across the river, with its small fort that had once been Roman. A force which could capture both North and South Shields could bottle up the Tyne, prevent supply by sea to Leslie's thousands, and bypass Newcastle's bridge as access to a wide area. No commander sitting outside Newcastle could ignore such.

Montrose waited until dusk, when a rider from Clavering arrived with news that they had taken North Shields without difficulty – likewise Seaton Delaval and Earsdon on the way – and all were now burning, to draw attention to the fact. They were making great play with the ferry-boats, and the fort at South Shields, less than a mile across the estuary, could not but assume an attempt against it. They would retire northwards during the night, but leave a fire-tending party to keep the blazes bright.

Leaving Kilpont in command at Morpeth, with Ogilvy's squadron, Montrose with Aboyne's remaining 250 horsemen, set out through the quiet May night for Newcastle.

A mile short of the city, and an hour short of midnight, scouts waited to inform them that there was a fairly large military encampment outside the northern gate but that few men appeared to be there. It looked as though the Scots containing force, at least on this north side of Tyne, had been drawn off, as planned.

Montrose had to be satisfied with that. At a brisk trot they advanced on encampment and city gates.

They encountered no trouble at the first. The guard, a

picket of Fifers, obviously assumed them to be part of their own army – as who would blame them? When Montrose called out to them in his broadest Angus Doric, the squadron was allowed to trot on without hindrance. It was a scattered camp, really a staging post for supply convoys. There might well be trouble here later, but meantime it was child's play.

Not so when they reached the high city wall and the Scots Gate, however. They reared dark, blacker than the May night, the doors solidly closed against all comers. No answer was accorded to fairly low-pitched calls and summonses, and Montrose was loth to bellow demands for entry such as would resound back in the camp and arouse immediate suspicion.

In a fever of frustration they waited, while various members of the company took turns at whispered shouting, as it were, to gain some response from within; all to no effect. It was, eventually, that lively youth James Gordon, Viscount Aboyne's suggestion that bore fruit. They tied together some of the horses' tethering-ropes, with breastplates, helmets, even swords at one end, to throw up and over the walls as improvised scaling-ladders. If sentinels there were, they could scarcely ignore such a gesture. And if the walls were indeed unguarded, then they might be able to get men up the ropes, to open the doors themselves.

This ingenious challenge was successful. The first clattering rope, after two false throws, was tossed back at the throwers even before the second was up, with some good, thick Tyneside objurgation.

'Guard, there!' Montrose called. 'Hear me. I am the Earl of Montrose, the King's Lieutenant-General. I may not shout louder, or blow trumpet, for fear of arousing the Scots camp behind. I am come to speak with the King's governor of Newcastle.'

That produced little more than a snort of disbelief.

'Quickly, man. Open the gates for us. We dare not stand waiting here.'

'D'ye think us right fools?' a hoarse voice answered. 'To let in your murdering Scots!'

'I tell you, I am the King's Lieutenant. Montrose. Fetch the guard-commander, man.'

'Ho ho! He'd thank me for that, at this time o' night! Your lord-generalship had better come back at a decent hour!'

'Fool! We cannot wait. Fetch someone, anyone in authority. With whom I may speak. In the King's name. Or when I get in, I will have you hanged, see you – also in the King's name!'

That seemed to give the spokesman pause. There was some muttered talk.

A thought occurred to James Graham. 'Guard – can you see North Shields ablaze, from up there?'

'Aye.'

'That is my doing. To draw off the Scots. You would see them ride off?'

'Aye.'

'Devil take you, fellow – have you no wits? Hanging will be too good for you. Get your officer.'

After a wait, wherein Montrose, cursing the guard's stupidity, had to admit, in fairness, that the man was only right to be suspicious, an officer did arrive above; who after some further parleying, announced that he had seen the Earl of Montrose when he had been captured by the Scots at Newburn, as one of Conway's force. If his lordship would light up his face in some fashion . . . ?

So flint and steel was struck, tinder ignited, and a letter from Montrose's pocket burned before his upturned, hatless features. The captain declared himself satisfied, and at long last the gates were opened – and closed again almost before the last of the squadron was inside.

Using all his inborn and acquired authority now to obtain swift action, Montrose spurred through the empty streets to the castle, grim, stark and strong at the riverside, where were both the governor, Sir John Marley and the wanted cannon, according to the watch-captain. Marley, who was middle-aged and portly, and mayor as well as governor, despite being put about by being found in bed with a shrilly angry wife, was only to glad to get rid of his untimely visitor by authorising the removal from the citadel of whatsoever cannon were required – since he had little ammunition for them anyway.

Montrose had less choice of artillery than he had hoped. The heavy pieces which he would have preferred would be too difficult to transport; and the light, mainly naval guns would make no real impact on Morpeth Castle walls. He took six medium cannon, but was able to collect precious few balls to go with them.

Quickly he had the weapons disjoined, and their barrels, wheels, axles and carriages tied into fishnets to be slung between four horsemen each. The few casks of powder and heavy ball likewise. Then, wasting no time in leave-taking, he wished the governor well on all counts, and hastened back to the Scots Gate, some hundred of his troopers reluctantly acting carrier.

The guard at the gate declared that there had been some stir in the Scots encampment meantime, but not any large-scale return from down the estuary, they thought; probably only curiosity as to what had become of the visitors.

Montrose formed his people up into three companies now – a fighting spearhead of 100, the transporting 100 who would inevitably be less fast-moving, and the remaining fifty as rearguard. Then he ordered the gates to be opened.

A fairly sedate trot was all the pact that his cannon-bearers could muster, with their heavy and awkward loads. At this decent rate they headed for the camp and the road.

Now there was question, opposition, it having been realised that the newcomers had gained admission to the beleaguered city; therefore they could not be what they seemed. Somebody had gathered together a fair number of men to block the way. But even in the semi-darkness they could be seen to be only a mass, a mob rather than any disciplined formation. Montrose whipped out his sword, and gave the order to his advance-guard to charge.

It was the first true charge, in anger, which many of these present had made. But led by the dashing Scots lords, they drew steel, levelled lances and spurred mounts. 'A Graham! A Graham!' Montrose cried – and some even took up that strange refrain.

They went through the mob as though it was chaff, with little or no swordery required, or indeed possible. A pistol or two cracked, men shouted, some screamed as they went down under trampling hooves, horses whinnied, and they were through.

Montrose and Aboyne tried to wheel them round, right and left, in true cavalry style, to drive back again; but of this they made a notable botch, ending up in a confused tangle, lances menacing each other. In fact, the return was not required. Seeing more cavalry coming behind, the camp orderlies, cooks and odds and ends of an army perceived no point in further interference in what seemed to be no business of theirs. Prudently they drew aside, and the transporters and rearguard trotted through, swords out but unchallenged.

After that it was merely a matter of following the winding road through the night northwards, keeping the rearguard well behind and watching keenly for pursuit. Also seeing that all took turns at the miserable duty of carrying artillery. They reached Morpeth exactly twenty-four hours after their first arrival.

Crawford and Clavering were already back from North Shields.

That afternoon, rested and refreshed, Montrose tried out the reassembled cannon. He had them dragged to the top of the Ha' Hill, the best vantage point, and from there fired a few trial shots. Unfortunately no trained nor born artillerymen showed themselves amongst his force, and their trial-and-error education in the science was grievously wasteful of the small store of ammunition. Moreover, the castle's own cannon promptly fired back, and with rather better aim and much greater prodigality. He set his men to dig trenches for shelter – but even so there were casualties, largely due to splinters from trees and rocks. As an artillery duel it was scarcely a success; but, with one good hit they did demolish a turret of the gatehouse-tower – proof that, given time and ball, they could batter their way into the place.

Accepting that patience was the quality required now, Montrose gave orders that every smith in and around Morpeth was to be set to the manufacture of cannon-balls of the required calibre. Lead and iron must be gleaned from near and far. Gunpowder was less difficult, for most mansions and manors had stocks for small-arms and sporting use.

All this took a lot of time, and Montrose used the waiting period to good effect. The fact that the Scots force left to contain Newcastle was making no move to attack him, despite the provocation, seemed to indicate its poor quality and leadership. He was emboldened, therefore, to initiate a hit-and-run cavalry campaign from this base at Morpeth, both to north and south-east. His flying columns took Amble, Rothbury and Alnwick in quick succession, from small Scots garrisons. Clavering, after burning North Shields, had declared that he believed South Shields could be taken, without too much difficulty, from across the river. This Montrose now gave him permission to attempt. Quickly the place fell – and for the meantime at least, Montrose held the mouth of the Tyne. He could not retain it for long, of course, with only cavalry; but his objective was to create maximum confusion behind Leslie's lines, not to occupy territory.

Clavering and Crawford went on to assault Sunderland.

Then, at last, Leslie reacted. Eight hundred first-class cavalry were detached from the main Scots army before York, and sent north hot-foot, to be followed by a larger body of infantry. This was success – even though it gave the besiegers of Sunderland a fright when the Scots horse was reported at the other side of the town, and they had to beat a hasty retreat, via the Shields South and North, sinking the ferry-boats behind them. That evening the Graham recognised that his time at Morpeth was probably short. He did not intend himself to be besieged.

He had now assembled a sizeable supply of cannon-balls and powder. Deciding that little was to be gained by waiting for daylight, with the target the size it was and the marksmanship erratic anyway, to say the least, he had the guns dragged up to a point of vantage on the Ha' Hill, there and then, and bombardment opened, darkness or none.

He made an awesome night of the 28th of May, with the town shaken by the thunder of explosions, the lurid flashes of the charges, the fires started in castle and town, the billowing acrid smoke-clouds. The garrison fired back, of course, but less vigorously than heretofore; perhaps they themselves were running short of ammunition. The besiegers suffered a few casualties, but not many – for the defenders' aim was poor in the darkness, with nothing so large as a castle to fire at. The town itself suffered more. It was difficult to assess just what impact their own cannon made.

Some time during that hideous night, after the castle guns had been silent for a notable period, Montrose called a halt. In the relative quiet he went forward with a trumpeter, to near the battered gatehouse-tower. After a fanfare which even to his own ears sounded crazy in all that smoke, he shouted, coughing a little.

'Guard, ho! Guard, I say. Bring the governor of this

castle. I, James Earl of Montrose, would speak with the governor.'

Almost immediately the reply came, quite clearly. 'You would, would you, James Graham – a plague on you!' In these nightmarish conditions the casually conversational tones taxed credibility. 'My compliments, James – frae Sandy Somerville o' Drum. Here's no way to spend a night, man!'

'Dear God – is it yourself, Sandy!' Montrose cried. 'Sandy Somerville, by all that is wonderful! Are you . . . are you well?' Even the speaker all but choked at that ridiculous question. The Master of Somerville, heir to the ninth Lord thereof, was an old friend from St Andrews University days.

'Never better, James – never better. Save for an empty belly. You caught us with the larder empty. What can I do for you?'

'You can come out of that Englishman's house and let me shake you by the hand, Sandy. And be done with this folly.'

'Ooh, aye. We'd have to think about that, James. Shaking an excommunicate by the hand, man, may no' be allowed! It's an ill thought.'

'Eh? What did you say . . . ?'

'Don't tell me . . . don't say nobody has told you, James? That you are excommunicate? Utterly damned! Hech, aye – bell, book but nae candle!'

Into the pause which succeeded that announcement, the Master of Somerville shouted again, 'Have they not told you?'

Even then it took James Graham moments to answer, 'No.'

'Och, well – never heed. You're no' the only one,' the other called. 'What terms will you offer me, James?'

Montrose pulled himself together. 'This shouting. We could talk the better face to face. Come out, man, under safe conduct, and we'll discuss it.'

'I'll send a depute, James. Mysèlf, I'll bide, and have a bit look round this auld rickle o' stanes you've been battering. To see if we can hold out a mite longer! Till auld crooked Sandy Leslie sends a wheen stout lads to our aid, may be.'

'I have still much ball and powder, Sandy. Must I batter on?'

'We'll see. I'll send you Jock MacCulloch to discuss the matter . . .'

So presently Captain MacCulloch, a Galloway mercenary, came out under a flag of truce, and after a certain amount of formal parleying, informed Montrose privately that the Master of Somerville was indeed anxious to yield, if he could so honourably, for they had had no food for three days, and all their powder was exhausted. But he did not wish to seem to do so precipitately. Let them wait until daylight ...

Soon after a misty sunrise, on the 29th, Montrose formally slammed another couple of cannon-balls at the drunken-looking gatehouse-tower; and thereafter, almost at once, the white flag was run up from Morpeth Castle keep and all was over. Presently the governor and garrison of some hundreds – more than anticipated – marched out to tuck of drum, and James Graham shook hands with his friend and offered a short speech of congratulation to all concerned. Somerville and his officers retained their swords, his men laid down their arms, and thereafter all marched down to the town, where Montrose had been having a large meal prepared, out of his own pocket paying for oxen, poultry, ale and bread in abundance. In courteous style he entertained the Master, the enemy officers and his own, to dinner in the Tolbooth, while the men feasted cheerfully in the streets.

It was a rousing and pleasant occasion – and it would have been more so had Montrose himself been in a happier frame of mind. But this news of his excommunication weighed heavily upon him. It had come as a great shock, such a thing never having occurred to him as possible. Though not intensely religious, and less than patient with fanatical divines, he always had been a God-fearing man, and for years had carried everywhere with him a pocket-Bible, well-worn and much annotated with his own hand-writing. His Presbyterianism was no mere outward form. That the Kirk of Scotland should officially declare him excommunicate, expelled from salvation, was scarcely believable, and bore sorely on him. It had been done, according to Somerville, when he had invaded Dumfriesshire at the head of 'a foreign host.'

His banquet guests, however, had other tidings, by no means all of it more cheerful. Sir John Gordon of Haddo, impatient at his chief Huntly's failure to rise again on the King's behalf, had led a raid on Aberdeen, kidnapped the Provost, and ridden off triumphantly. This had made a great impact, but had split Clan Gordon – for though Huntly had tentatively emerged from Strathbogie to occupy Aberdeen thereafter, his eldest son, the Lord Gordon, had declared this to be folly and had actually elected to join the Covenant side – the fruits presumably of Montrose's own influence on that serious young man. Argyll had sent a force north to deal with this – and Huntly, much alarmed again, had handed over the city and its keys to his son, and decamped northwards at speed, not stopping it was said until he reached the Pentland Firth at Strathnaver. The young Lord Gordon was now, to all intents, chief of the clan, and co-operating with Argyll – a serious situation and strange end-product of James Graham's association with him. His brother, Aboyne, all but exploded at the news. Argyll had executed Gordon of Haddo, out of hand, for treason – and, sadly, also hanged the Provost of Dumfries who had been rash enough to welcome Montrose.

Coping with these indigestible tidings, Montrose was a little heartened to learn that Hamilton and Lanark, at least and at last, had met their deserts. They had been summoned south to Oxford from Scotland, by royal command, had come, and had been arrested and tried before a commission of enquiry. Found guilty of deliberately misleading the King and aiding the King's enemies, they were condemned to imprisonment – despite strong pressure from a powerful party, led by the Queen, on their behalf. On the way to ward in Cornwall, somehow Lanark had made good his escape and was now with the Covenant army. The Duke, it seemed, was held secure at Pendennis Castle.

It was perhaps typical of King Charles's Court and methods that news of this should reach his Lieutenant-General only from the enemy.

Montrose, sending Somerville and his people back to Scotland, was faced with the question whether to get out of Morpeth and back to Carlisle while the going was good, having created a sufficient diversion behind Leslie's lines; or to stay where he was, further to fortify the town, and seek to hold it in the face of the larger force Leslie must inevitably send north from York when he heard the news. It was tidings from York, indeed, which eventually decided the issue – but not from Leslie. A letter arrived from there – but by a messenger of Prince Rupert's. That dashing commander had hastened north to the Earl of Newcastle's aid, had reached York and pushed Leslie back somewhat. But he was now threatened by the Fairfaxes' northern army, and Manchester's Eastern Association, as well as by the Scots – and with only 15,000 men was much outnumbered. He ordered Montrose to leave whatever he was doing, and march south to join him immediately. As a sort of postscript the Prince added that His Majesty had, on the 6th of May, signed a warrant creating his well-beloved James Graham, Marquis of Montrose, in recognition of services rendered.

Heavy at heart, and filled with foreboding, the new marquis – who had no particular desire to exchange his proud and ancient style as an earl of Scotland – wound up his affairs in Morpeth, and set out with his very reluctant force, first westwards into the Northumbrian hills and then southwards, by devious ways, to avoid Leslie's army. It beat in his mind that he, the King's Lieutenant for Scotland, was proceeding deeper and deeper into England, to involve himself ever more inextricably in the affairs of another country when his own was crying aloud for his return. Although, he had to admit, that cry was so far of his own will and imagining.

On the 3rd of July, at the Durham-York border near Middleton in Teesdale, a group of fleeing North Lancashire troopers gave Montrose the dire tidings. There had been a great battle, the day before, on the Marston Moor west of York. Prince Rupert and the royal army had been completely defeated, with great slaughter. All was lost. It was every man for himself. No, they did not know how fared the Prince, or where he was – nor greatly cared, it seemed. But some of the royalist officers, it was said, were seeking to rally at Richmond. Much good it might do them . . .

Montrose, distressed, was again placed in a dilemma. Every impulse tugged at him to turn back. His thousand far-from-eager warriors could not effectively alter the situation, and were most likely merely to run their heads into a noose. And behind him, Scotland pulled. Yet, his orders had been to join Rupert. And to seem to desert the Prince now, in his hour of need, was unthinkable. Yet he might be dead, a prisoner, or fleeing far.

Contrary to the advice of most of his colleagues, he

decided to go on, warily, at least as far as Richmond, another twenty miles.

They found Richmond an armed camp, in a touchy state of alarm but Rupert himself in command. Weary, slightly wounded and harassed, he was by no means despondent, and greeted Montrose warmly. Indeed their arrival seemed to give him an accession of vigour and hope. The Graham found that, once again, his own reputation had outgrown his deeds. His taking of Morpeth and cannon-ball raid on Newcastle was being looked on as a great victory, and the belief here was that all the North of England was in his sure hands.

Rupert had nearly 6000 of the royal troops collected at Richmond – which meant, of course, that 10,000 at least were lost, 4000 said to be dead. More might come in, and he had sent far and wide for new levies. But he dare not wait here much longer. That devil-damned Cromwell was coming – indeed had allegedly sworn to take him, Rupert, and hang him!

Montrose had heard of Oliver Cromwell, a Huntingdon-shire squire who had been making a name for himself in the English parliament as a stern opponent of the King. But now, it appeared, he had changed to a military role, and the defeat at Marston Moor seemed to be largely of his making. He had raised and trained and disciplined a body of heavy cavalry, almost as fanatical religious zealots as the Scots divines, and used them with diabolical, almost unbelievable skill. Rupert had been caught between Leslie's veterans and Cromwell's horse. Newcastle's army had collapsed on his flank, and the day had been lost. But it had been this Cromwell's tactics that had turned the scale late in the day. And he was now heading west, by Skipton and the Ribble, to Wensleydale no doubt, to approach this Richmond from the rear, while Leslie circled the Cleveland Hills to make a frontal attack.

That evening, in the inn in which the Prince had taken up his quarters, his surviving commanders urged on him differing courses – to head west and then south, in front of Cromwell, for Oxford and the King; to retire north-east, to Marley and Newcastle; to do what would be least expected, disperse the foot and make a dash back to York with the cavalry and surprise the Fairfaxes denuded of Cromwell and

Leslie. Montrose urged his own old and favoured theme. Use Scotland. Move up over the Border with this 7000. Callander would not hold them. That land was basically loyal to its King, in a way England was not – a Scots-born king. Rouse it by a show of strength. Lacking Leslie's army, Argyll would be lost. He was no soldier. Then, strong, turn back to England.

When even Rupert shook almost pitying head at this totally unacceptable suggestion, the Graham changed his plea. Give him just 1000 crack cavalry, to replace his hotch-potch of a force. Give him these, and he would cut his way through south Scotland like a sickle through corn, to his own territories, and there raise Scotland for the King. He asked no other help than that – he, the King's Lieutenant for Scotland.

But again Rupert shook his dark head. He needed every man he could raise – and crack cavalry were more precious than fine gold. He needed five times his present numbers. He could afford to detach not one. They would ride north, yes – but not to Scotland. To Carlisle, where they would be protected by hills and sea. The North-West had scarcely been touched by war. There they would re-form and renew their strength. To turn again in a month or so – and teach the King's rebels who was master in England.

James Graham sighed.

But next morning he was more cheerful. At least they were moving northwards, not south.

21

IT WAS SIX WEEKS LATER BEFORE JAMES GRAHAM HAD finally had enough of England, the English, even of Rupert of the Rhine, six weary weeks on the very verge of Scotland, yet all the time with their backs to it, considering only the South. Earlier he had sent Ogilvy and his connection by marriage, lame Sir William Rollo, secretly into Scotland disguised as pedlars, and after three weeks they had returned, their news not such as to ease Montrose's mind in any way. The proposed Irish landing had at last taken place, months late, but in a half-cocked fashion and anyway up on the Ardnamurchan coast of Argyll; and not 10,000 men, not Antrim himself – only 1600 commanded by a Scots Mac-Donald chieftain, Alastair, son of MacDonald of Colonsay, commonly known as Colkitto and a kinsman of Antrim's. This character was said to be busy ravaging the Argyll seaboard with fire and sword, from Mingary Castle on Loch Sunart; but so far none of the clans had risen to aid him in what looked like merely a typical incident in the unending MacDonald-Campbell feud. And elsewhere in Scotland the royalists were completely inactive, having lost all hope under Argyll's savagely repressive regime. Even the most moderate nobles were kneeling to the Campbell. The two emissaries' report amounted to this – that if the King's Lieutenant-General for Scotland was ever going to achieve anything in that unhappy land, it had better be soon.

But any such move had now no sort of priority with the King or the royalist command in England. Rupert was sympathetic, but wholly concerned with his all too serious problems in the South. Not only were not troops available to lend for a Scots adventure, but the new Marquis's own services were required for more immediate campaigning. All were to move towards Oxford, with the new levies.

So Montrose came to a decision, a dramatic one. He duly set out for the South, with the rest. But a short distance from Carlisle, leaving his own party and personal baggage under Ogilvy and Aboyne, he dropped to the rear, ostensibly for a word with William Rollo who had been deliberately delayed. With Rollo, and a Colonel Sibbald, a tough mercenary from the Swedish wars who had fought under him in the Bishops' War in Aberdeen and whom he had had his eye on for some time as a useful man, he trotted along at the very end of the long column for a little, dropping ever farther behind, a led horse with them. Then, in close timbered country in the Eden valley, all three quietly slipped away into the empty woodland, and turned their horses' heads northwards again.

In an hour's hard riding they were back on the Scots

border, but now in lonely country. Here they halted, and from their saddle-rolls drew out very different attire from their normal fine cavalier costume. Rollo and Sibbald produced and donned uniforms taken from captured Scots officers of Leslie's force, while Montrose himself dressed in the garb of a groom, tucking up his splendid curling hair under a rusty morion helmet. Thus, riding with the led horse decently behind his betters, Lieutenant-General the Marquis of Montrose forded Esk and rode back into his native land.

It was a curious and hazardous interlude – for inevitably they had to ride through parts of Callander's army which was holding all the passes of the South-West. They chose unfrequented and awkward routes, by Sark and Kirtle Waters, Wauchope and Ewes; but even so could not avoid Callander's pickets. Rollo and Sibbald claimed to be wounded Scots officers returning from Yorkshire, and got away with it – although some rather odd glances were cast in the direction of their groom, who made only a poor job of looking like a menial, whatever his clothing. Disaster, indeed, came close on one occasion, when one of a party of Scots troopers, ignoring the officers, sidled his mount close to Montrose after some staring. He spoke low-voiced.

'The Earl o' Montrose, by a' that's holy! Here's a ploy!'

'You mistake, friend,' James Graham said stiffly. Then remembered his Angus Doric, 'Och, wheesht – dinna be daft, man!'

'Nae mistake,' the other asserted. 'D'you think I wouldna ken the Earl? Marquis noo, they say. I've seen you wi' my Lord Newcastle one time, at Durham. But . . . gang your way. And God go wi' you!' And, grinning, the man reined round, and away.

Montrose, catching his companions' glances, let out a sigh of relief. Presumably the fellow had been a deserter from Newcastle's army; or had been captured and changed his coat, but still retained some loyalties.

They rode on, for Eweswater and the North.

A devious journey they made of it, seeking to avoid all centres of population, especially where there were churches – for Montrose conceived the ministers to be his greatest hazard, keen-eyed divines who might have seen him at General Assemblies and the like. Obviously his disguise was less than effective. James Graham could hardly be expected to recognise that his whole bearing, carriage and the essential cleanness that always characterised his person, shouted aloud that he was no groom.

Putting up at lonely alehouses and remote hill farms, they were accepted as Leslie's and therefore Argyll's men, and feared accordingly. Clearly all Scotland now feared Argyll, who appeared to be exercising more arbitrary power and harsh authority than ever had any of her true monarchs. Although he used no style or title as yet, other than Marquis, Privy Councillor, Justiciar of the West and chief of his clan, professing to be merely the lowly servant of Christ's Kirk, the squint-eyed King Campbell nevertheless now held the fullest authority, and ordered matters as he would, and with a heavy hand. He was hated, yes – but cared not a snap of the fingers for it. His rule was not concerned with love, affection, even admiration. Effective power he wanted – and effective power he had.

The furtive travellers avoided Edinburgh like the plague, skirting well to the west much as Montrose would have liked to see and talk with Archie Napier at Merchiston. Stirling also fell to be by-passed, for the Graham was well known there. They crossed Forth by the little-used Fords of Frew, by dark, as many a hunted Graham had done before them – and thereafter slipped through unfrequented territory which he and Rollo knew like the back of their hands. *An Greumach Mor* was scarcely ready yet for his own country-side to know of his return.

On the fourth day – or, rather, night – of journeying, avoiding Perth by crossing Earn and Almond to the west they rode in the early dew-drenched August morning up through the birchwoods of little Strathordie, past the lonely little kirk of St Bride's, to the remote fortalice of Tullybelton on its shelf of the great Highland hills, looking southwards across the wide middle vale of Tay. To a great barking of deerhounds and shouting from tower-windows, they made their presence known, declaring true identity openly at last.

Black Pate Graham himself, bellowing incoherent delight and greeting, came hurtling down the turnpike stairway, to slide back the great drawbar with a crash, unbolt the iron yett and fling open the heavy oaken door, to throw himself bodily upon his chief and friend, still only in his shirt. Never before had James Graham seen that man sobbing. His growing and boisterous family had rather outgrown his ageing father's castle of Inchbrakie in Strathearn, and for two years they had been roosting here in more remote Tullybelton – a place with its advantages for a man unsure of his popularity with the powers-that-be.

'Man, Jamie! Jamie!' Pate cried. 'Yourself! It's yourself! At last – God be praised, at last! Och, James – you're back? Look at you, man – look at you! Come chapping at my door like, like any tinker! Christ God! I heard tell you were the King's General. And a marquis, no less. But . . .'

'Empty names, Pate, meaning little. Yet! But we'll make them mean something, you and I! Save us – it's good to see you. Good to be back in my own place. It has been too long . . .'

'Too long indeed. For us all. For Scotland. The Campbell, God's everlasting curse upon him, has all at his feet. But, now, you are back . . .'

'Back. With two men!'

'And one of them lame!' Rollo mentioned, from behind.

'Guidsakes! You . . . you're alone, man? No tail? No army? You've come back empty-handed?'

'Alone, yes. But not quite empty-handed, old friend. I have in my pouch the King's commission. To raise all Scotland for His Grace. With all and every power and authority that Charles Stewart can give me. All the authority I needed before, and did not have – if not the power. The power we must forge, Pate. Forge, until it is tempered steel, to free this land from shameful tyranny. No – I am not quite empty-handed now, lad.'

'But no men . . . !'

'Scotland is full of men. Full of men who hate Argyll, I have learned. And I am still the Graham. And you are Black Pate of Inchbrakie, as good a recruiter-captain as any in the land. You will raise the men for me. Starting with our own good Grahams. How long till I present Scotland to King Charles, Pate? Purged and free? How long?'

'God knows!'

'Give me a year,' James Graham said slowly, quietly. 'Give me but one year . . .'

There was a moment's silence, there before the door of Tullybelton House.

As its laird beckoned them within, Montrose's voice

changed. 'Now – your news, Pate? My wife? What of Magdalen? And the bairns? Have you heard? You will have watched out for them. What of my sons . . . ?'

Much as he would have liked to ride to Kinnaird, less than fifty miles as the crow flew, or even to Kincardine, nearer still, Montrose forbore to do so. Within a day or two, already somehow the rumour had got around that the Graham was back in Scotland. Perhaps that trooper near Langholm had talked; perhaps some other had recognised him, without immediately declaring it. At any rate, like wildfire the word spread – no bad thing, from one point of view, paving the way for his recruiters. But it did mean that certain places would be watched, for sure, Kinnaird where were the fugitive's family in especial. It might well be fatal for his chances, and no kindness to his dear ones, to approach there. Letters he risked – but not a visit. The same even applied to Tullybelton itself, for Pate Graham was well known as his close friend and lieutenant, and his house a likely refuge and venue. So, after that first day, Montrose kept away from its close vicinity, hiding in the spreading woodland and secret deans and valleys of central Perthshire.

But this was no idle skulking. James Graham was like a spider at the centre of its secret and ever-shifting web, now, sending out emissaries, messengers, scouts, to lairds and lords and chieftains, receiving reports, replies, secret visits. It was a risky business, for even some of his own Grahams, despairing of their chief's and the King's cause, had compounded with circumstances and were now, for their very necks' sake, toeing the Covenant line. The dangers of betrayal were serious. For the answers and accounts that reached Tullybelton told a sorry story. Clearly the morale of the country was low, seldom had been lower. None saw salvation from Argyll and the Kirk Militant as likely, even possible. The King seemed to be no longer concerned with Scotland, the ministers had taken over the entire parish system and purged it of anti-Covenant and moderate elements, and no sane man saw any future in revolt, with the entire nobility now truckling to the Campbell. Montrose's name might mean much still; but what could one man do?

After days of consistent temporising, foot-dragging and sheer refusal on the part of those to whom he looked for support, even James Graham grew depressed. A few rallied to his call, or to Black Pate's bullying mainly young Graham lairdlings and Drummond relatives of Pate's wife Jean; but, with their men, these did not make up so much as a squadron of horse. There were many more promises – but clearly these were unlikely to be fulfilled until it was evident that defeat was not inevitable.

A demonstration was needed, indubitably, some small victory which might serve as a beacon of hope for the many doubters. But how to achieve anything significant with so few? And not jeopardise all by courting early disaster?

It was at this juncture that, as Montrose declared to Pate, his prayers were answered – and in strange shape. It came in the form of a weary Irishman, a messenger on foot, hungry, tattered and demoralised, who arrived at Tullybelton, having been directed there from Inchbrakie, seeking help, food, if possible a horse, to aid him on his way to Carlisle. He carried a letter from his master, Alistair Colkitto MacDonald to the Marquis of Montrose, and he had been told that Inchbrakie would help him on his way.

Ever suspecting treachery, a trap, without informing the man that Montrose was within a mile of him, Pate fed him, promised a horse, and gave him a bed. Then, managing to extract the unaddressed letter from the Irishman's clothing, he took it to his friend in the birchwoods of Strathordie.

Under its blank outer cover, the missive was indeed addressed to Montrose, the King's General at Carlisle. And it was a cry for help, from Colkitto. It seemed that, after landing on the Ardnamurchan peninsula in early July, with 1600 gallowglasses and exiled Islesmen from Ulster, he had, as instructed by his kinsman the Earl of Antrim, harried the Campbell lands of North Argyll and called upon the Highland clans to rise for their King. This they had notably failed to do and the Campbells had rallied mightily against the invaders. He had had to fall back on his base at Mingary in Sunart. There he found his ships had been destroyed in an Argyll raid. Desperate, unable to get away by sea, he had decided to march right across Scotland to the only clan he believed he could rely on to rise – the Gordons. By Loch Eil and Lochaber he had trailed his ragged crew, reaching the fringe of Huntly's country at Badenoch. There he had discovered that the Gordons' revolt had fizzled out, and Huntly had fled to the North. Partly hoping to join him there, and partly in the hope that the Mackenzies under Seaforth, hereditary foes of the Campbells, would aid him, Colkitto had marched northwards. But he had found neither Mackenzie help, nor Huntly's elusive person. He marched south again, issuing on his own initiative a summons in the name of the Marquis of Huntly, for the loyal clans of the North-East to rise. Some 500 men, mainly outlying Gordons, did join him; but the Covenant clans of Grant and Fraser prevented him from reaching the true Gordon country. Argyll himself was now hot-foot on his tracks, and he had mutiny amongst the new Badenoch men, who did not like the Irish. Hungry, weary, short of everything needed for even a small Gaelic army, he did not know where to turn. Could and would the Lord Marquis of Montrose help him? Otherwise he feared complete disaster faced him. The letter was four days old, written from the Badenoch-Atholl border at Dalnaspidal.

'Dear God – hear this!' Montrose cried. 'To think that we knew nothing of it! This MacDonald stravaiging the Highlands in the King's name!'

'Achieving nothing,' Pate commented. 'Indeed, worse. Irishmen, barbarians, offending better men!'

'Tcha, Pate – use your wits! The Irish are Catholics, yes. But none so ill. And he says there are Islesmen, too. Properly led such are good fighters. Here is an army of 2000 men, but fifty miles across the hills! An army awaiting me, it's General!'

'An army, James? A rabble of starving, bog-trotting savages . . .'

'Armed men. Savages – who knows? But at least they will rise and fight for *something!* Which is more than most Scots will do this year of grace!' Montrose thumped fist on tartan-clad knee – for he was now dressed as a Highlander, in trews, doublet and plaid, to be less kenspeckle in this country. 'I'm for Atholl, Pate.'

'You could pay over-dear for that sort of army, James.' That was Sir William Rollo, looking grave. 'Scotland will never accept the Catholic Irish.'

'That is to be seen. Scotland will not accept *me*, in this pass. I think Scotland must be taught what things come first! I will see this messenger. Now.'

So the unfortunate courier was roused from his well-earned rest, given a Highland garron and sent off again forthwith northwards, with a letter for Colkitto. The Marquis of Montrose requested Alastair MacDonald, Younger of Colonsay, to meet him at Blair in Athol, in two days' time, for their mutual pleasure and conference.

At midday on the 18th of August, then, Montrose, alone save for Pate Graham, came by devious ways to Atholl, midway between Badenoch and Strathordie, that great mountain tract in the north of Perthshire, to find the Blair district in the wide vale of the Garry in a turmoil. Colkitto and the Irish, it seemed, had misinterpreted the message. Instead of coming quietly to a secret meeting here, the MacDonald had marched south with his whole ragged force, had taken forcible possession of Blair Castle, with the young Earl of Atholl – still a minor – within it, and had run up his banner at the tower-top. Promptly the Atholl Stewarts and Murrays, with their neighbouring Robertsons of Struan, had gathered to rescue the young earl, and take vengeance, and were still gathering. Battle appeared to be imminent.

'I told you!' Pate declared. 'Savages! And fools, forby. What good are such as these?'

'Wait, you,' his friend advised.

Quite openly. Montrose led the way, though anonymously through the ranks of the angry clansmen and towards the opposing crowd that surrounded the castle on its green terrace some 400 yards away, an alarming proceeding.

'Pray God they don't shoot us down like dogs!' Pate muttered.

'They will not do that. We present no threat to them. Keep your head up, man.'

Some distance off still, a rich and powerful voice hailed them. 'Who comes so bold, in the name of God?'

Montrose raised a hand in acknowledgment, but did not answer, and kept on walking. Perforce Pate did likewise.

'Stand you!' the great voice bellowed. 'You heard me – Alastair? Who walks so swack to his death?'

Even then the other took his time to answer. 'James Graham,' he called, at length. 'And I do not shout. At my friends. Or my foes.'

'Graham, d'you say? Graham? Stand you, then, Graham

– or you'll never shout again, I promise you! What Graham thinks he may outface Alastair?'

Pate could not restrain himself longer. 'Montrose, you fool!' he cried. 'Who did you come here to meet? The Marquis. The King's General.'

'Blessed Mary Mother o' God!' That was almost a howl. 'Montrose? Himself? By all the saints – if you lie . . . !' A giant of a man burst out from the ragged throng that faced them. Dressed in red-and-green short kilt and plaid, with ox-hide long sleeveless waistcoat, shoulder-belted broadsword at side and bristling with pistols and dirks, he was nearer seven feet than six and broad in proportion, with a shock of curling red hair and savage down-turning moustaches at strange variance with the almost boyish freckled face. A man of Montrose's own age, in his early thirties, he had hot blue eyes. He came forward, great-strided and grim-visaged.

But James Graham, for better or for worse, seldom managed to look other than he was, however dressed or circumstanced. The calm assurance was not to be mistaken. The big man, as he came close, slowed his stride and then halted, chewing his lip under those wicked drooping moustaches.

'Saviour Christ born of Mary,' he muttered. And then bowed, deeply. 'My lord Marquis – your servant. Alastair.'

'Not mine, Alastair – not mine. The King's only. We are both the King's servants. And here is another – Patrick Graham, Younger of Inchbrakie, my kinsman and friend.'

Those two sized each other up, stiff as suspicious dogs.

'I looked . . . I looked for you otherwise, my lord. I looked for the Captain-General. With an army . . .'

'And found only James Graham and his cousin! I fear that we are a grievous disappointment, Alastair. I am not even *Captain*-General. Prince Maurice is that. Only Lieutenant.'

The other swept that aside with a mighty arm, the shirt-sleeve of which was torn and far from clean. 'What are styles and titles?' he asked.

'What indeed? Do I call you Alastair MacDonald, Colkitto, Dunaverty . . . or my Major-General?'

The giant drew a quick breath. 'Major-General . . . ? Did I . . . hear aright?'

'To be sure. Mere style and title – but yours!' Montrose smiled wryly. 'I may have no army, no power – but I have all the authority that King Charles can give me. I am his royal voice and hand, in Scotland – God help me! So I make Alastair MacDonald of Dunaverty, son to Coll of the Left Hand, his Major-General and my second-in-command.'

For a long moment the other stared, perceiving what was here involved, the ramifications of that statement – or some of them. Then he inclined his red head, and held out a huge hand, large as a ham. '*Your* servant, my lord,' he said. 'At your commands.' He turned, and gestured sardonically. 'Your army!'

Montrose considered the fierce and motley throng of shaggy and unwashed Irish kerns and Highland caterans, armed to the teeth with steel but with hardly a musket, pistol, jack or helmet amongst them, and nodded gravely.

'Excellent,' he said, and there was no mockery in his voice. 'With these we shall do great things, you and I, Major-General. Now, bring to me your host, the Earl of Atholl, whose aid I seek. And make your officers known to me . . .'

The easy and quite unassuming assertion of command was accepted by the fiery Colkitto without a murmur. As was the later move, when with the boy Earl and Pate, Montrose walked back across the no-man's-land to the watchful, waiting ranks of Atholl and Robertson clansmen, to declare to them his identity and authority, and to announce that he had come, in the name of King Charles, to take charge of and discipline Colkitto's Irish and Islesmen host and to raise the Highlands for His Grace. With the Earl's, and Robertson of Struan's permission, he would request all to disperse to their homes forthwith, assured that there would be no further trouble; and thereafter, as many as loved their King and Scotland's cause and freedom, to rally to the royal standard, here in Atholl, next day. Let the Fiery Cross be sent out. Not for the first time the Highlands would teach the Lowlands their duty!

So, for the second time, and on a day of hazy August sunshine, with the heather glowing richly purple on all the Atholl braes, the Marquis of Montrose unfurled the banner of King Charles in Scotland. It was a very different occasion to that at Dumfries nearly five months before. Instead of a town square on the very southern edge of the land, the ceremony took place in the wide green hazel-rimmed haughland where the foaming Tilt met the peat-brown Garry under the soaring mountains of the very heart and centre of Scotland. Instead of decent, hodden-clad burghers and mounted Border and Solway lairds and their levies, infinitely more fierce-looking Highlanders and Irishmen surrounded him, however softly musical their voices, most shooting suspicious if not downright hostile glances at each other, a sea of colourful if ragged tartans, flashing steel and brawny bare limbs. A big crowd was present, but it made a very small army. Colkitto had proved to have remaining only some 1100 men of his own, after his West Highland campaigning – if so it could be called – to which he had added another 500 or so from Badenoch, mainly outlying Gordons. He had no cavalry at all, nor ever had. A large number of Athollmen, Stewarts, Murrays and Robertsons, turned up for the occasion – but how many would remain as part of the fighting host remained to be seen. Summonses were sent out now, urgently, far and wide, for all who had promised aid, all who ought to have promised, to rally to the standard here in Atholl; but it would take time for any appreciable number to assemble from a distance. Montrose had only the boy Earl of Atholl, Donald Robertson, Tutor of Struan, Sir William Rollo, Colonel Sibbald, and a number of local lairds, with Colkitto and Black Pate, at his side.

'My friends,' James Graham said, in the Gaelic – since few there knew English – when horn-blowers had gained him silence, 'today we set our hands to a great and goodly venture. This land is most grievously oppressed by men, not all evil but most shamefully mistaken, and eaten up with the arrogance of spiritual pride. These men have risen against the King's Grace, to whom all owe allegiance and love – as do we. Tyranny reigns, imposed above all by Archibald Campbell of Argyll, *MacCailean Mor...*'

A great roar of execration interrupted him, at mention of that name.

He held up his hand. 'The Campbell rides high. But not so high that he cannot be pulled down. To that end have I come. Come with the King's command to save Scotland from such evil and disloyal men. And with his royal commission to do all that is necessary to that end, naming me Lieutenant-General and Governor in Scotland, with all powers as

Viceroy. In that name and authority, therefore, I, James Graham, call upon all loyal men soever to arms, to fight under my command, until Scotland is cleaned of the Campbell, of his minions, and of fanatic men who set themselves up as the very voice of Almighty God . . . !'

Again the bellow of approval. Deliberately, that was all he was going to say anent religion, with a host before him three-parts Catholic, and his own Covenanting background known to all.

'In the King's royal name, then, I unfurl the King's royal standard, the ancient emblem of this realm and kingdom, for which I am prepared to die. How many of you, my friends, do say as much?' And he tugged loose the cord which tied the great red-and-gold flag, and the Lion Rampant of Scotland streamed free in the breeze. He had carried that flag, rolled in his horse-blanket, since Dumfries.

Everywhere hands, swords, dirks were thrust up, bonnets soared into the air, and the uproar rose and maintained, echoing from the surrounding hills, in fierce, hoarse and continuing acclaim and assertion. Even the Irishmen joined in, affected by this heady draught.

When he could make himself heard, Montrose added, 'Your word I will test! And you, mine. Today we are not many. In a month, we shall be a great host. In our proud and sacred cause may we ask Almighty God to go with us, to strengthen our hearts and our arms, and to give us the victory. Amen. God save the King !'

Out of his own pocket thereafter, James Graham bought great quantities of beef and ale, whisky and victual, from the Earl of Atholl's steward, and fires were lit all over the grassy haughland to roast the meat, providing a rough-and-ready feast, with as much to eat as even the most starveling bog-trotter could desire. This while the necessary business of enrolment and forming into companies and commands proceeded. Montrose went round making himself known, speaking with the men, encouraging, questioning.

That late evening, with much good cheer in the camp, merriment, singing, story-telling, dancing – and some superficial fighting – all the well-fed relaxation of a Gaelic host, Montrose slipped away. Major-General Alastair MacDonald was roaring drunk and challenging all comers, three at a time, to wrestling bouts; so Black Pate was left in effective command. Borrowing a Highland garron from Atholl, James Graham gave himeslf twenty-four hours' leave of absence while they awaited the results of their widespread summonses, and rode off quietly, unescorted, south-eastwards.

He went down Garry, and into the mouth of the shadow-filled Pass of Killiecrankie. All night he rode, at a steady mile-devouring trot, bearing ever more into the east, by heather-tracks and drove roads, by mere footpaths and no paths at all, leaving the Garry near where Tummel joined it, to climb to Moulin, and up and up beyond, over the quiet, empty darkling mountains, by the Pass of Dalnacarn into Glen Brerachan, and so to the head of Strathardle. He knew the road well, having travelled it many times as a young man – but never by night. Down the long, long strath he went, barked at by the occasional dog but otherwise unchallenged. At its foot, where Ardle met the Blackwater of Glenshee, he forded that river to Strone, to start his climbing again, this time by the high Muir of Drimmie, eerie, strange, where the Stone Circles of the ancient people reared themselves out of the night like upraised fingers warning of the brevity and unimportance of all men's lives and activities.

In six hours of great riding he was looking down on Strathmore, or its grey vacancy, from the very lip of the Highland Line above Alyth, only level lands below him now, after over thirty miles of the mountains. It was two o'clock of a still August morning. This was Ogilvy country, where he cold feel reasonably secure; but he still went secretly, seeking to disturb none. In two more hours he had crossed the wide strath slantwise, almost due eastwards, by Glamis and Aberlemno, avoiding Forfar and Brechin, and could smell the sea in his nostrils as he rode down through the marshlands to the wide landlocked bay of Montrose. At the reedy head of it, on a little hillock amongst the cattle-strewn saltmarsh meadows, his tough garron going slowly, wearily, now, he halted at a low-browed, reed-thatched cot-house amongst the misty tidelands, where dwelt old Sim Mather, once his father's chief falconer, who had taught him that sport twenty years before. He had no need to rouse him – the old man's dogs had already done that – and his greeting, on identification, was heartfelt and heart-warming.

'Sim,' he said, after some account of his circumstances,

'you will serve me kindly by crossing the saltmarsh to Kinnaird. Does my lady still occupy the south-east flanking tower? Aye. With my sons, my children? Do you know?'

'Aye, lord. I saw the young lord but two days back.'

'Good. Go there then, Sim, secretly but swiftly. Tell my lady that I am here. Bid her, if she will, come to me, for a spell. As secretly. For an hour or two. With the boys. The baby, the girl, will be too young.' Eight months before Magdalen had given birth to a daughter, as yet unseen by the father. 'Bring them to me. Do not disturb the castle, or my lord of Southesk. There is a postern-gate. You will know it well . . . ?'

'Aye, lord. I will have them here within the hour.'

'Yes. She is well?'

'Well, and bonny. And the young lords fine lads. You will be proud o' them . . .'

Sim Mather was as good as his word. Montrose had dropped asleep on the settle by the smoored peat fire when, with the first hint of dawn beginning to whiten the coiling mist wraiths that rose from the saltings, the shack door burst open and his two eldest sons flung themselves in and upon him in a breathless flurry of exclamation.

'Save us – who are these!' their father cried. 'Robbers! Hielant caterans! Grown and ill-favoured men, for certain! Do not tell me you are Grahams of some kidney?' It was over a year since he had seen them.

They shouted with laughter, two tousle-headed, long-legged, good-looking youngsters, all knees and elbows, one fourteen, the other eleven years, bursting with excited questions and competing declarations.

The man's glance lifted from them. Magdalen stood in the low doorway, biting her lip, her youngest son Robert at her knee and a plaid-wrapped bundle in her arms, peering in.

The anxiety, uncertainty, implicit in her stance, her whole person, went to his heart. Life had been less than generous to Magdalen Carnegie – and he was no husband for her, no husband for any woman. He rose, and went to her, hands out.

She could find no words, only gazed at him from great eyes, holding out the baby a little way, as something which might have been part offering, part barrier and reproach.

297

Gently but firmly he took them both in his tartan-clad arms.

'My dear, my very dear,' he said, kissing her.

He felt her trembling. At first she did not, could not speak. But there was no doubting her emotion.

'So long, lass,' he said. 'So very long. Even since I returned. To Scotland. I could not, dare not, come to you. Even now, I come like a hunted beast. What a husband I have made for you, Magdalen!'

She nodded, and shook her head, in one.

'And this is Jean! Little Jean. We have a daughter.' He took the baby from her, easing the plain back from the tiny wide-eyed face. 'A poppet. Like you, my dear – comely.' He kissed the child's brow. 'Jean Graham – deserving of a better father.'

The transference of attention to the infant seemed to loose Magdalen's tongue 'Oh, James – at last! How I have feared for you! Thank God you are back. Safe. All these weary months. Years. Waiting, hoping, praying.'

'Aye, lass. I know it. I can only beg that you forgive me. It seems to be my fate to fail you. But – at least I am in Scotland again. Not so far away. I can see you more often, God willing. This small one – to think that I have never seen our daughter till now. She looks well, well. As well as she is bonny. And these.' He turned to his eager sons. 'My dear, you have done well. So very well. I thank you.'

She shook her head. 'They need their father.'

'The *King* needs our father,' John said stoutly. 'All Scotland needs our father.' That 'our' was distinctly emphasised.

'He is the greatest man in all the realm,' young James declared. 'Tell us how you beat the English. At Newcastle. And at that other place. More . . . Morepath.'

'I did not beat the English, lad. I did not even *fight* the English. Only the King's enemies. And many of those are Scots, to their shame.'

'When can we come with you, my lord? *I*, at the least. To fight for the King,' John demanded. 'I am fourteen now. And can use a sword very well. As well as Tam Keith. And he is sixteen . . .'

'Hush, John!' his mother said. 'Do not talk so. I have told you . . .'

'But I am the Lord Graham, Mother! I must serve the King, too. I am old enough now. Tam Keith says . . .'

'You are a child still. Enough of such foolish chatter.'

'Lewis Gordon was fighting for the King when he was thirteen . . .' James declared – and then looked shocked as he realised that at that time his father had been on the opposite side.

'We will not talk about fighting now, for the King or other,' Montrose said gently. 'Time enough for that. Now let us talk of kinder things. For I have not long. I must leave here before most men are abroad. To get me into the hills of Glen Clova, just as quickly as may be, and so over the mountains to Glen Shee and Atholl again. I am too well known hereabouts to remain unrecognised for long. We have an hour, little more.'

'Oh, James – so little?'

'I am sorry, my dear. But I may not be away from my men – folly to call it an army yet – for longer. And I dare not risk capture, or the cause is lost. Kinnaird is bound to be watched. Argyll is no fool. There may be spies even in your own house.'

'If I found one, I would run him through! I swear I would!' John announced.

'You see! How they grow, without their father's hand. They see themselves as a hero's sons . . .'

'We are! We are!' the boys chorused. 'He *is* a hero. Everybody says so. Next to Prince Rupert he is the King's best general.'

'At the least, let me be a hero to my sons!' the man said, ruefully humorous. 'Now – enough, I said. And that is as good as a royal command. Let us talk of homelier things. Magdalen – how is it with your father?'

She smiled, despite herself. 'My father! Even he now reckons you hero. Since you chose the King's side! He but encourages these foolish children.'

'And you do not, my dear?'

'Oh, James – I cannot *afford* a hero for husband! Can you not see it? Understand? I want only an ordinary man. At home. A husband by my side, after all these years. I care nothing for heroes and battles and causes. Even for the King's Grace, I think! I want only my own, my husband and the father of my children. Is that too much to ask?'

Wordless himself now, he shook his head.

'But . . . I have but an hour with you, then? One hour!'

'I fear so, lass. Unless you would have me in one of Argyll's dungeons. He has a price on my head. Then, you would never see me again!'

'Oh, God!' she said, chokingly. 'Is that what we have come to?'

'I fear it is. But I *had* to see you. See you all. The Campbell does not scruple to fight women. Remember what he did to Airlie's wife.'

'*I* will see to Mother,' John assured. 'She will be quite safe.'

'Spoken like the Earl of Kincardine!' his father approved.

'Earl . . . who?'

'Earl of Kincardine. You are an earl now, Johnnie. Did you not know? Since the King made me a marquis. Earl of Kincardine. And you, Jamie, the Lord James Graham. How like you that, my lords? And your mother the Marchioness of Montrose.'

'Me! I am as little a marchioness as I was a countess! What do I care for such . . .'

'Quite so. Yet it does put you one step above, say, your stepmother! I conceive that might be to your satisfaction, on occasion! No? And two steps above your brother's wife! All folly – but if I guess aright, not wholly without advantage!'

Magdalen paused to consider that, while the boys yelled their new titles at each other excitedly. Sim Mather had discreetly made himself scarce.

Setting down the baby on the old man's pallet-bed of reed straw, Montrose took his wife in his arms again. He was no monk, and his need for a woman frequently was fierce – but he had never yet allowed himself to surrender to it. To that extent, at least, he had been a better husband than some. Now, with Magdalen's plumply rounded body under his hands, the urge to possess her, after so long, was all but overwhelming. But he could not possibly send his sons out of the shack; and they were still too young to recognise his need. Magdalen herself was tense within his embrace – although that might well have been her own frustration and necessity. With almost an unspoken curse, he put her away a little, and turned to pace the earthen floor.

'Can I come with you? With your army?' In a rush, she blurted it out. 'I could do it. Other women have done it.'

He stared at her, scarcely believing that he heard aright. 'Magdalen, lass . . . !'

'At least I would be with you. I could be a camp-follower – if soldier you must! I am none so delicate – only timorous! Take me with you, James.'

'My love – it is not possible. I thank you, with all my heart I thank you for saying it, offering it . . .'

'I am not offering. I am asking, praying.'

'No, lass. You do not know what you ask. It is not possible. What I go to do is too harsh, too hazardous, for anything such. You do not understand. How could you? I have no army – only some two thousand beggarly kerns and caterans. With that I must needs try to win Scotland. And I will do so, God willing. But for months, a year, it will be not warfare but skirmishing, banditry, ranging the land. No place for you, or any woman. Living in the heather, with never a roof or a bed. Moving all the time . . .' He went to take her hands again. 'No, Magdalen – it cannot be. But my heart goes out to you for saying it. Bless you!'

Her shoulders slumped. 'Am I never to have you, then? Never? Is it always to be . . . thus?'

'No. I swear it will not be. Give me this year, lass. I shall see you from time to time. But – give me a year to win the King his kingdom back. And then, on my oath and honour, I will come home to you.'

'If they do not kill you first,' she said flatly.

'That is in God's hands. But, never fear, I am none so easy killed. Now – tell me of yourself. Of your days, your life. How you spend your time. Of little Jean's birth. Of Ald Montrose. The lands, the folk – there is so much to hear. And so little time . . .'

They had their hour, and a little more, before the man could drag himself away.

'The parting,' he declared, then, in a strained voice. 'The parting again is damnable. Too high a price to pay. For us all. But this time it will not be for so long.' He put his arm around Magdalen's shoulders, and pointed to his sons. 'My Graham lords – look well after your lady-mother, I charge you. And these little ones. Grieve her nothing. It is the Lieutenant-General's command! This is *your* part. To hold my rear secure, in good order, while I advance. Else I cannot do so with a single mind. It is all part of the battle. And you, my dear, you hold so much that is precious to me beyond all telling, in these two hands. Do not fear that I will not come back to claim it. And soon. God keep you all.'

He left them there in that lowly hut, tears blurring their image, one lonely man to go and conquer Scotland. And he did not, dared not, look back.

The morning was further advanced than he had intended. He had to get into the empty hills as swiftly and as unobtrusively as possible, unable to return to Atholl by the shortest route, as he had come – and his garrison was tired. He rode west by north, by the Muir of Dun and the Muir of Pert, and by little Stracathro to the Catherthun hills, and so over into the quiet hidden valley of the West Water; and although he saw and was seen by a henwife or two, herds with their cattle, and some men with their sickles cutting the scanty oats, even raised his hand to them as a decent traveller should – while keeping his too-handsome head bent or averted – none challenged him. None of the quality, of course, were abroad at such hour.

Once the great rolling heather hills received him into their abiding quiet, the man relaxed somewhat. The chances of interception, of significant encounter, or any encounter, were now minimal. But instead of fifty miles to ride, he now had nearer seventy, and by rougher ways.

He elected to make one encounter. At the lonely Lindsay bonnet-lairdship of Craigendowie, where the rivers forked, instead of avoiding the house he turned in there, and exchanged his tired garron for another, plus a tankard of milk and some oatcakes, leaving a golden guinea as acknowledgment. He did not name his name, nor was it asked. And thereafter he had Scotland to himself.

At least he had time, and opportunity, to think, as he crossed the wide watersheds of Glen Clova, Glen Prosen, Glen Isla and Glen Shee, to Glen Tilt, in Atholl.

It was dusk again when James Graham rode down Tilt to the camp at Blair, heavy-eyed, drooping in the saddle, having covered a total of over 110 miles of mountain and moor in twenty-fours hours. The place was in an identical stir and clamour of singing, dancing and general uproar as when he had left it, almost as though it had never paused. But one change there was, to lift the droop from Montrose's shoulders. John, Lord Kilpont had arrived from Stirlingshire with

300 men – and these were trained in archery, an old-fashioned but especial interest of Kilpont's. They were mainly Menteith Grahams and their adherence, with the support of his friends, was an incalculable fillip.

Before he allowed himself to sleep that night, Montrose penned a formal letter to Archibald Campbell, Marquis of Argyll. As the King's Lieutenant he informed Argyll that he was in a state of armed and treasonable rebellion against the monarch, and that unless he withdrew immediately from this activity, and made full and suitable restitution and submission to His Grace, he would be proceeded against with all vigour forthwith by the King's forces, to his considerable and swift injury. An immediate submission was required. The letter-writer, tired as he was, smiled grimly to himself as he added his signature to this crazy if old-fashioned chivalric challenge.

22

THEY MARCHED AT DAWN ON FRIDAY THE 20TH OF AUGUST, 1644 – and from the very first, Montrose was at pains to show all concerned what manner of commander he was and what he expected of the troops under his command. He himself marched on foot, targe on arm, pike over shoulder, broadsword at side. He sang the lilting, fast-stepping Gaelic marching-songs with them, and laughed and joked with all. But he led at a fierce pace, and continued to do so, ignoring all roads and even tracks unless they took them directly or substantially in the direction he aimed to go. This was to be the fastest-moving force in Scotland, necessarily.

For that, of course, it was in fact ideally composed, cavalry or none. Lean and agile Highlanders and Irish kerns, lightly armed, carrying no more kit than their plaids, brogans of rawhide on feet hardened to roughest going, they were mobile light infantry par excellence, as far as swift movement was concerned – and could go where even garrons could not. Living off the country, with no bases to tie them, no communications to guard, a pouch of oatmeal each man's rations, they had no baggage-trains to hamper them, no cannon. Such as had firearms had in the main flintlock pistols and light sporting muskets, not the more ponderous military matchlocks which required V-topped supports and rolls of slow-burning fuse to fire. If the lack of ammunition for these was appalling – it was reckoned that the Irish contingent did not muster more than one ball apiece – at least it meant that they travelled the lighter.

There were some 2700, now, in all, 800 Athollmen and other North Perthshire clansmen having joined. They forded the Garry near Glackmore, waving goodbye to the young Earl of Atholl and his folk, and moving up-river to Invervack, climbed then straight up the long, long braeface, three miles and 1000 feet of ascent, to the heather ridge of Tulach which separated the valley of the Garry from that of Tummel, the men sweating out the effects of much beef and liquor of the last days. Over the lofty summit they spilled down to Loch Tummel-side at Tressait, without pause, nearly 3000 men brushing through the knee-high, dusty, scented heather of a golden August morning. At the loch-shore, Montrose swung right-handed, westwards, not left, as might have been expected.

His spies and scouts had informed him that the Lord Elcho, son to the Earl of Wemyss, was commanding the Covenant army being raised to deal with Colkitto's Irish, in co-operation with Argyll's Campbells. He was based on Perth, near his own castle of Elcho, and was estimated to have 7000 infantry and 700 horse, mainly from Fife and Angus. Whether he knew of Montrose's assumption of Alastair's command was uncertain; but at least he would not expect an immediate advance and attack by this beggarly host on his vastly larger and properly equipped army. The Graham, aiming at this stage for a gesture, a demonstration to arouse confidence, rather than any conventional battle, intended at least to surprise his former colleague – for Elcho had served with him in the Second Bishops' War.

Rounding the head of Loch Tummel, they crossed the river between it and Loch Rannoch to the west, and commenced to climb again, up and up under the mighty cone of shapely Schiehallion by the Braes of Foss. To the lofty, lonely small loch of Kinardochy they mounted, and so southwards beyond, down the green Strath of Appin, with the great valley of Tay beginning to yawn before them. By early evening they were down amongst the levels of Dull, where the ancient Celtic Church had once dispensed its urbane and genial faith. They had covered twenty-one miles – whereas the man Cromwell had recently declared that the utmost that even the best and most lightly armed infantry could achieve in any day was thirteen, and that not in mountainous country.

They were on the verge of Campbell lands here, filched from the MacGregors, and Montrose sought no conclusions with such, or any distractions at this stage. They turned eastwards down Tay – and soon found themselves in some trouble from Menzies clansmen, who sniped and skirmished – their chief, Sir Alexander Menzies, having Campbell connexions. Black Pate and a party were despatched to deal with these, and a few were slain, some roofs and corn-stacks burned – the first blood to be shed in this new campaign. Castle Menzies itself, above the haughs of Tay, was too strong to assail without cannon, so they attempted nothing. But, since he would assuredly have messengers off to Perth, to warn Elcho of this new danger, with the darkening, to keep such couriers delayed for at least a few hours, Montrose settled his men for a much-needed rest in a wide circle around the castle, lighting cooking-fires to roast Menzies beef and poultry. Neither welcome nor recognition came from the chief. When darkness fell the fires were fed anew, to keep them blazing for some time – although their lighters thereafter stole away quietly into the scrub woodland to cross Tay secretly by the ford west of Aberfeldy. With luck it might be long before Sir Alexander discovered that those fires were untended, morning even.

With even Alastair silent now, Montrose led his weary host up the steeply climbing drove road that lifted southwards out of the vale by the strung-out Falls of Moness, towards the next pass in that vast system of serried mountain-range and valley. But they were all now too tired for much more of this, and in a wide hollow by the shadowy Loch na Craige they threw themselves down in their plaids, to sleep in the heather. It was nearly midnight.

Even so, four hours only Montrose allowed them before they were on the move again – and men learned anew what sort of general the King had sent them. Down Glen Cochill and across the head of Strathbraan they hastened as the light grew on the mist-capped hills, by Amulree and another, lower, pass, and so down into the dramatic gut of the Sma' Glen and the rushing Almond. Nearing more settled lands now, Pate Graham was sent ahead with an advance-guard – and there was some excitement when he sent back word that a fairly large body of men was awaiting them at Buchanty, near the southern jaws of the defile, a strategic spot which the Romans themselves had recognised and fortified. However, a second courier came to say that the party was friendly; and on approach it proved to be 200 more mixed Menteith Grahams and Drummonds, under the Master of Madderty and Sir John Drummond, younger son of the Earl of Perth, on their devious way north to join Montrose at Atholl, in answer to his summons. All were much heartened by even this modest accession of strength – Montrose the more so in that he was desperately short of officers, and here he gained three of some experience. The Master of Madderty, son of the Drummond Lord thereof, was another of his own brothers-in-law, having married Jean, the youngest of the five Graham sisters, an impetuous young man but with the makings of leadership in him. Sir John Drummond, a kinsman, was actually brother to Black Pate's wife. And Major James Stewart of Ardvorlich, whose mother was also a Drummond, though strange, indeed known as the Mad Major, was a brilliant fighter. Almost forty of this party were mounted – the beginnings of a cavalry arm.

Thus reinforced in numbers and morale, they crossed the last of the intervening ranges, a comparatively small one, into Strathearn, with the Lowlands before them, by Fowlis Wester. This was all Drummond and Graham country, so that they could now go openly, and even gather up the odd extra adherent as they went. Montrose still marched on foot, dressed as a Highlander. They camped for the night just east of Fowlis, having covered exactly another twenty-one miles. For an infantry force to have marched almost forty-five miles in two days was next to unheard of.

During the night not much sleep was achieved by Montrose or his officers. Recruiters were out all around, seeking

especially horses and ammunition; also food and money -
partly Montrose's and Black Pate's rents, with Inchbrakie
only two miles off. Scouts came in with reports – one being
that Sir John's elder brother, the Lord Drummond, had gone
to join Elcho at Perth, as had the Lord Murray of Gask,
son to the Earl of Tullibardine, another of Montrose's
former colleagues and kinsman of some of the Murrays in
their own force. This was part of the heartbreak of civil war,
with families shamefully divided. Elcho was also reported
to have gained the support of a very experienced professional
soldier of the Swedish wars, Sir James Scott of Rossie – a
serious matter.

They were marching again by dawn, heading eastwards
towards Methven. It was Montrose's aim to achieve a surprise by cutting off Perth from the south and east, and so
confining Elcho's force in the city, unready, with only the
mainly hostile north to retire on – for the Graham had many
friends in Perth, and might expect considerable sympathy
from the townsfolk. But, unfortunately, before they reached
Methven, six miles down the strath, scouts brought word
that Elcho, after early-morning devotions – it was Sunday,
the 1st of September – had left Perth and was marching
westwards by the Burgh Muir to meet them. Clearly, the
Menzies chief had got his message through, by swift horsemen presumably, in time to reveal the secret advance.

It was a sore blow. The situation was wholly changed.
Despite all their Homeric marching, Montrose's plan was
now unworkable. He could not possibly work round to south
of Perth now – Elcho's 700 cavalry could intercept any such
attempt. They must either fight a battle, or turn back.

It made a dire choice. Outnumbered three to one, out-
armed and out-classed, lacking cannon – Elcho was reported
to have nine five-pounders – and cavalry, any head-on confrontation looked suicidal. Yet, to retreat now, at the first
threat of action, could be nothing less than disastrous for the
morale of his force, for his credit as the King's general, and
for all royalist hopes in Scotland. Nothing could be worse
than that.

In this cleft-stick, it was a strange chance which decided
James Graham. Almost as an afterthought, the courier who
had brought the news mentioned to Sir John Drummond
that the city was ringing with the dread word that the

ministers attendant on Elcho had decided, after due prayer and deliberation, that the slogan for the encounter should be 'Jesus, and no quarter!' Shocked, Drummond came to tell Montrose.

The Graham was utterly appalled, scarcely able to believe that any men calling themselves Christian, quite apart from being ministers of the gospel, could so blaspheme and traduce the name of their Saviour, who was Love personified. But when he had questioned the messenger, and satisfied himself that it was true, Montrose was a changed man.

'In the name of Almighty God,' he declared, voice trembling, 'I do swear before all that if He will give me strength, aid, this day, I will burn that infamous cry from the lips of damnable, ranting bigots who besmirch His Son's holy name! God help me, I will!'

His friends stared at him. Never had any of them seen the equable, calm and assured James Graham, the compassionate, the courteous, like this. None spoke as, white-faced, he turned away.

'Continue the advance!' he commanded, harshly.

When David, Master of Madderty, presently sought to ask tactics of his brother-in-law, Montrose cut him off short in a fashion hitherto unknown. Men repeated those awful four words to each other, throughout the host, and considered all that they implied, looking askance at the stiffly slender, tartan-clad back of their leader, as they marched, doubtfully now, on to Methven.

But though Montrose was more furiously angry than ever he had been in all his life, he was not wholly beside himself with rage and sick disgust. One part of his mind continued to work coolly, clearly. He saw in his mind's eye all the layout of the land between himself and Perth, knew it well, sought its advantages and problems. Much of it indeed belonged to Lord Madderty, and many a time he had hunted and hawked over Methven Moss and Tippermuir. The other side would know it equally well, of course, since what did not belong to Madderty was owned by Murray of Gask – Ruthven land given to the Murrays of Tullibardine by the late King James after the Gowrie Conspiracy of ill fame. But, if clash there was to be, the land itself must be made to fight for its king.

Since Elcho was coming by the Perth Burgh Muir, he was

obviously going to occupy the long, low ridge of Lamberkine, which lay to the south of this shallow side-vale of Strathearn, in which lay Madderty, Gask, Methven and eventually Perth itself. His own force was approaching along the northern flanks, also rising ground. Between lay the two-mile-wide soggy bottom-land of the sluggish Cowgask Burn, Methven Moss first and then the open levels of Tippermuir to the east. Neither force was to be expected to leave its secure higher ground to cross that low open waste; yet the advantage lay all with Elcho, for he could send his cavalry east-about, round by the lower Almond valley, to come in behind the royalist force – a manoeuvre Montrose himself could by no means attempt, first because he had no cavalry to do it, and secondly because the Almond fords would inevitably be guarded by the enemy. Any such move on the western side would be under observation all the way.

Catching up with Black Pate's scouting party on the Methven slope, Montrose could see the enemy already drawn up in position on the gentle north-facing Lamberkine braes opposite, less than two miles away, arms and armour glinting in the forenoon sun, banners flapping, all looking highly effective and frighteningly potent. Elcho clearly had his cavalry fairly equally divided between left and right wings, with his great mass of 7000 foot in the centre, a row of nine five-pounder cannon grouped ominously in front of them. That cavalry alone, sent in at once in two complementary thrusts, could so roll up and disorganise the royalist infantry as to leave them more or less helpless prey for the Covenanting foot – if they did not sweep them away entirely, without the foot's aid. To discourage any such early move, and to give time for his own dispositions – as well as to establish his constitutional position in proper fashion – Montrose sent forward the Master of Madderty under a flag of truce to inform the Lord Elcho that he was facing, in arms, the Marquis of Montrose, the King's Lieutenant-General and Viceroy, and that he was therefore in a posture of rebellion which could amount to treason. He conceived him, and his colleagues, to be essentially loyal subjects of King Charles, however; and therefore, looking on them as former comrades, for the good of all and to avoid shedding the blood of Scots fellow subjects, he required the Lord Elcho to disperse his forces forthwith, and come to make his due allegiance to the

King's Grace. Moreover, on the Sabbath Day, any such warlike posture was singularly unsuitable. If time was required to reconsider their duty to their undoubted liege lord, let them withdraw to Perth meantime and make submission on the morrow.

So soon as young Madderty rode off, his brother-in-law set about positioning his ragged host. Disaster could most easily and swiftly come by outflanking; therefore his main preoccupation at this stage was so to extend his line and make use of the terrain that this was impossible, or nearly so. His sheer lack of numbers told against him in this, forcing him to thin out his front in almost crazy fashion, so that, in the main, his men were ranked no more than three deep. On the other hand, his knowledge of the ground, plus the eye of a born tactician, enabled him to base the horns of his great semicircular front on marshland, the swampy Cowgask Burn where it emerged from Methven Moss, on the west, and the Tippermallo Myre on the east. It was a ridiculously long front for less than 3000 men; but it would be hard to outflank, at close range. Colkitto he put in command of his Irish, Islesmen and West Highlanders, in the centre; Kilpont, with the Graham bowmen, he placed on the left, overlooking the Tippermallo Myre; while he himself took the right wing, with the Athollmen and more local volunteers.

While these dispositions were hastily taking place, the Master of Madderty reached the enemy lines. Montrose could not actually see what then took place, but there arose a great shouting and hooting, and white flag and envoy both abruptly disappeared. Then, three horsemen came galloping from the Covenant centre, to rein up some two hundred yards away, across the Cowgask Burn and its reedy bed, there to shout that the Lord Elcho and the Military Committee held no truck with traitors and excommunicates of Christ's Kirk; that they had chosen the Lord's Day to do the Lord's work; and that the insolent envoy had been arrested, was being sent bound to Perth, and would be hanged just as soon as the Lord Elcho had leisure to arrange the matter. No quarter would be granted to traitors, in the name of Jesus Christ and His Holy Kirk.

The bold trio wheeled their mounts, and raced back whence they had come.

Even before they were back, to a great and fierce chanting of 'Jesus, and no quarter! Jesus, and no quarter!' from the thousands of infantry, led by black-robed divines, the enemy cavalry charged, the Lord Drummond's banner at their head. It was the left-wing squadron, and no doubt was intended partly as a feint, to force the royalist centre into a premature break-up of formation, for it was aimed to right of centre. Not for nothing, however, had Montrose placed Alastair MacDonald and the most experienced fighters in the middle. Although only in three ranks, they stood their ground stoutly as the cavalry bore thundering down on them, the front rank kneeling, to fire their single musket-shot from that position, the second crouching, and the third standing – only these last were mainly without muskets and had only stones to throw, which their leaders had had them collect.

They waited until the charging horsemen were almost upon them, so that even stones would have maximum effect. But well before the clash, and just as soon as Montrose had assured himself that the other squadron of enemy cavalry were not immediately being thrown in in support, on the right, he had a trumpet – borrowed from Atholl – blown high and clear as signal to Kilpont, half a mile away. That man promptly swung his bowmen down into the Tipper-mallo Myre, and from that wet and difficult stance faced west to pour a shower of arrows into the flanks of the advancing cavalry just as they reached Colkitto's front – at extreme range but galling. At the same time, Montrose led his own people down into the Cowgask bog, from which, however uncomfortably, they also could discharge their muskets against the left flank of the enemy horse.

The Lord Drummond, therefore, found himself under fire from three sides – in a box, in fact. He could have smashed his way, no doubt, through Colkitto's centre, though at severe loss almost certainly; but then would as certainly have found the royalist horns closing in behind him, between him and his army, so that he would either have been out of the battle for good or have to cut his way back through the enemy. As probably most cavalry commanders would have done in the circumstances, he chose to swing away to the side, his feint not having worked. To swing to his right would have brought him closer to those hundreds of archers, already sorely harassing his flank. He swung left-handed, westwards, for Montrose and the Athollmen, and out of the range of the arrows.

Casting aside their useless muskets, the Atholl Stewarts and Robertsons drew swords and dirks, while those with pikes formed up into hasty hedgehogs, many of them up to their knees in mud and water. Drummond was no fool – and, after all, he knew this place as well as did Montrose, with his father's castle not a dozen miles away. He saw those fore-shortened legs, and knew that his horses would inevitably get much more seriously bogged down than men on foot, and that this mire was a trap for him. He yelled and gestured for what remained of his squadron to swing still farther round, and keep on swinging, so as to ride back to the main army.

But it is not so easy to control a cavalry charge gone wrong, with a third of its men down, riderless horses career-ing everywhere, men shouting and screaming. His Fife yeo-manry were far from highly trained, and yelling Highland-men darting out, bent low to avoid swinging cavalry swords from above, but dirks out to rip open horses' bellies, are apt to distract even the most stolid. The entire turning manoeuvre became little short of a shambles, which quickly developed into complete and disorganised flight.

Out of perhaps 350 horsemen, only some 120 were down. But the remainder, in fact, now offered Montrose a sudden and unexpected opportunity. They were fleeing back singly and in groups, anyhow, across the levels of Tippermuir, widespread, scattered. Taking an enormous risk, the Graham shouted to his trumpeter to sound the General Advance; and, in a fever of urgency, himself raced forward, broadsword on high, to lead his Athollmen out of their bog after the fleeing horse. Those 200-odd cavalrymen were wholly mask-ing their own cannon.

Alastair saw the situation and its possibilities, and swiftly flung his own three regiments forward at the run. It all meant abandoning their good positions, but he obeyed his com-mander's summons. Kilpont, farther away and less well placed to co-operate, lagged somewhat.

Yelling their clan slogans, the 2000 Highlanders and Irish-men charged, steel brandished, behind the fleeing cavalry, with half a mile to cover. And seeing them coming, a savage tide, and their own cannon unable to fire without shooting down their own folk, the prudent artillerymen did the sensible thing, and fled likewise.

Down – or rather up – on Elcho's waiting centre, then, pounded and flooded a host of men and horses, in flight and charge, in panic and pursuit, in chaos and yelling confusion. But the panic came first – and panic is perhaps the most infectious disease known to man. The thought that nine loaded cannon were now lost to them and could well be turned point-blank upon themselves, no doubt contributed. Despite the screaming, furious ministers urging death to the Philistines, and too full of the wrath of God to be frightened, the foot from Angus, Dundee and Fife wavered, appalled, gave ground involuntarily in anticipation, and then turned and bolted in a vast human flood.

It was not all fright and shame, of course. Elcho sought to rally those around him, and succeeded in forming at least an island in the rout. Sir James Scott, the mercenary veteran on the right wing, did not flee, but wheeled the second squadron of cavalry round to come up behind the advancing royalists – since he could not assail front or flanks without riding down his own folk; but now Kilpont was coming up fast on that flank, with his bowmen, and they paused to wing hundreds of vicious arrows at the circling horsemen at short range, to devastating effect. It was enough. Seeing all else disintegrating, all so suddenly lost, and no doubt worried also about those captured cannon, the cavalry, after a single ragged charge, rode off in the general direction of Perth.

Elcho and his lieutenants, recognising reality all too clearly, retired while still they could, and hurriedly.

Montrose himself was quite dumbfounded at the speed and scale of his unexpected success. But despite his continuing anger over the shameful 'Jesus, and no quarter' sacrilege, he by no means lost his head in triumphant glee. He perceived very well that this was not a true victory, but something of an accident, a fortunate chance for him and a mere superficial defeat for his enemies. Excellent for morale and prestige though it would be, he had not really vanquished the Covenanting army, only dispersed it in panic. At the end of the day it would recover itself, and be still twice as large and many times as powerful as his own – and that much wiser. In *his* circumstances, he needed much more than that.

Panting then, at a lull in the flailing, stumbling swordery, he gasped to Black Pate who never left his side, 'On ! On !

Smite! Tell Alastair. Pursue. To the . . . very gates . . . of Perth! No let-up. Tell all – on !'

'Aye. God, aye! Trumpeter? Sound Advance again . . . ?'

The other nodded, and plunged on.

And so took place, along the Lamberkine ridge, over it on to the Aberdalgie side, and on across the east-facing slopes of the Burgh Muir and the braes of Friarton and Craigie, what was nothing less than a running and interminable slaughter. And deliberately, torturing himself, the man who had ordained it, and who hated bloodshed, steeled his heart to it all, and pressed on and on towards the outskirts of Perth. This army, this impious army that chose to pervert the very name of the Saviour in its arrogant savagery, must be destroyed. Destroyed, not just scattered. The cavalry could get clear, and did; but the foot, the staggering, stumbling, frantic foot was their prey. Some stood and fought, of course, some few grouped together and cut their way to safety, some managed to outrun their pursuers; but the great majority not only just ran, but threw away arms and armour to run the faster – and were in consequence cut down by the hundred. Included in the shambles were not a few citizens of Perth who had elected to spend their Sabbath watching the sport of the Host of the Lord destroying the Midianites hip and thigh. When Montrose discovered this and perceived what they were, he sought to command that all such should be spared. Also any of the ministers fleeing. But to control Irish and Highland fighting-men in the heat of victory, and over a wide area, was wellnigh impossible. Many non-combatants fell with the rest, undoubtedly.

It was a long, bloody and vastly exhausting business for all concerned – save the cavalry – despite the brevity of the actual battle, a four-mile carnage over a great expanse of moorland, rough pasture, and latterly quite steep scrub-covered braesides down around Pitheavlis and Craigie. Weary, hoarse, mud- and blood-spattered, but unhurt, Montrose at length found himself at the very southern walls of the city – indeed exactly at the place which he had originally hoped to reach by surprise. Under-officered as his host was, he sought at last to hold on, to draw up and take a firm grip of his fevered, excited horde, his trumpeter blowing and blowing, big Alastair's bull-like voice bellowing, hunting-horns winding. Long before there was any real semblance of order, and with running fights still going on over a wide area, a deputation of magistrates and leading citizens of Perth came hurrying out under a positive forest of white flags, evidently believing that the trumpeting represented a summons to surrender, shouting aloud for mercy, forbearance, peace, declaring complete submission. Their Provost was amissing, none knew where; but the city was the Lord Marquis's, and all therein. If he would but spare it, and them . . .

A little dazed by the suddenness of it all, as well as by sheer physical fatigue, Montrose drew strongly upon his reserves of wits, discernment, even courtesy, and switched from playing the guerilla leader to playing the King's representative and responsible governor. He accepted the city's surrender, the third greatest in the land, declared that he had no quarrel with its leaders, promised order and good treatment for all, so long as his needs were supplied, his orders obeyed and his men well treated and catered for; but demanded that all arms and ammunition, and all horses, should be brought and handed over to his officers before nightfall. All fugitives who had taken part in the late treasonable fighting must render themselves to him as prisoners; and if they did so without delay and further resistance, there would be mercy and no more slaughter. Let the magistrates and bailies take fullest charge of their city; he would require a good accounting. But he hoped that there would be no need to make examples. God save the King!

And so, that night of the 1st of September, the man who had started the day as little more than an outlawed fugitive with a price on his head – £1600 sterling – and only the stars for a roof, ended it as master of the third largest city in Scotland, and complete victor over the country's second-line army. Admittedly this was a poor affair compared with Leslie's great professional force in England; but it had represented the largest assembly of armed men mobilised north of the Border, and had been well equipped. To all this equipment, arms, ammunition, commissariat, tentage and some horses, as well as the nine cannon, Montrose fell heir – as well as whatever Perth could supply to him. By the most abrupt change of fortune, he who could lay hands on little or nothing, now had a superabundance at his disposal; and for the moment, undisputed sway over a large area. It was exactly fourteen days since the victor had crossed the Border disguised as a groom.

Before he slept that night, between sheets for the first time for long, in the house of one Mistress Donaldson, he was concerned to send out invitations to all the ministers of Perth to dine with him next day. The diplomat and statesman was in control again. Not that this precluded him from sending a messenger hot-foot to Kinnaird Castle.

23

THREE DAYS LATER, THE ARMY OF KING CHARLES WAS ON the move again – they were daring to call it that, now, though perhaps still a little ambitiously. Certainly it looked, and was, a very different host from that which had fought the Battle of Tippermuir. It was no larger – for though some Perthshire lairds had rediscovered their courage and duty to the King, and some numbers of Elcho's men had elected to change sides, nevertheless most of the Athollmen, not to mention the Highlanders recruited by Colkitto earlier in Badenoch and Lochaber, were no longer present. This was not desertion, but the normal pattern of Highland military service. These clansmen were nobody's servants, crofters, cattle-herds, drovers, fishermen, hunters, supporting a chief but not employed by him or by any man. They would gladly wield their swords in his cause, unpaid; but when the battle was over, they went home, to get on with the business of living and keeping their families alive. Moreover, this was harvest-time in the Highlands, and their cattle stock, the basis of the whole Highland economy, could not survive the long winter without the oats now waiting to be gathered in from a thousand glens. They would fight for the Lord Marquis another time, and for this King Charles perhaps, to a lesser extent – but meantime they were going home, with the booty of their victory.

Montrose knew all this too well to seek to dissuade them. And he saw that they went adequately rewarded.

So there were large changes in personnel. And those who remained *looked* different – the Irish, the Islesmen, the Grahams, Kilpont's bowmen and some Gordons. They were no longer ragged and ill-equipped. Now all who wanted them had breastplates, helmets, good Lowland clothing and boots, and were armed comprehensively with firearms, and ample ammunition therefor – for, after all, they had captured over 5000 stands of arms. Most of the Gaelic warriors would by no means wear Lowland gear, so Montrose had demanded a vast amount of cloth, tartan where possible, from the Perth merchants, to renew kilts, plaids and jerkins. Apart from that, the horses, and a £50 levy – to give Alastair, who had not a penny-piece left in his war-chest – James Graham had imposed no further penalty upon the city, and had kept his troops from any excesses, with a stern hand. It was important, since he could by no means remain there to hold the place, that Perth should thereafter look fairly kindly on him and on the royal cause.

For he had to move. Static warfare was not for him and his – and Perth no place to be besieged in even if it had been. Already there were reports that the Estates were mobilising feverishly in Edinburgh, Glasgow and Dundee; and they said that Callander, with Leslie's reserve army on the Border, had been called home. More immediately threatening, Argyll himself was known to be hastening eastwards from his own Highland territories with a large force of Campbells and their allies, and demanding reinforcements from all sides in the name of the Privy Council and Estates. And there was said to be a sizeable Covenant force in the North-East, based on Aberdeen – although who was its general was not clear, the young Lord Graham adhering but presumably not in command.

Above all things, the royalist force must not be trapped between three converging armies – or two, for that matter. Montrose decided to move north by east, partly because the opposition in that direction was the least specific, and with the Gordon element in it liable perhaps to change allegiance again; and partly because he wanted to recruit men in Angus and the Mearns, Graham and Ogilvy territory. Even the Carnegies might now be persuaded to join forces with him, on the King's behalf. But few would risk it, he believed, if the city of Dundee remained hostile, so close at hand. Therefore he would make for Dundee first of all, where he had hopes that the ruling party might be dislodged without too much difficulty – the Graham lairdships of Claverhouse, Claypotts, Fintry, Strathdichty and Mains circling the place on north and east.

So, on Wednesday the 4th of September, they marched away from Perth, crossing the Tay and up its eastern bank, making for the wide mouth of Strathmore in the first instance, and the Ogilvy country. They made quite a gallant show, for they had cavalry now, to the number of 200 – Grahams, Drummonds and 100 Hays under George, Lord Dupplin, the old Earl of Kinnoull's heir, the only new recruit of any note. Most of the officers were mounted – although Alastair MacDonald scornfully refused a horse, preferring to march with his men. As indeed Montrose would have done, had he not had occasion to ride escort. For this day, trotting at his side, were his Marchioness and his eldest two sons, the Earl of Kincardine and the Lord James Graham.

On the Sunday night, after victory, Montrose's messenger to Kinnaird, as well as informing Magdalen of success, had also invited her to join him for a day or two at Perth, with John and Jamie. None would hinder or assail the Graham's family, within a fair radius of Perth, in the meantime – so it would be safe enough. They had come the next day, to a joyful reunion – even though Magdalen did not fail to declare her continued fears for the future, and her loathing of all warfare, victorious or otherwise. The boys, of course, were in a seventh heaven of delight, sons of a manifest hero now, for all to acknowledge. Two nights and a day they had had together – and at least the nights had been their own.

Now they rode, and marched, up the wide pastoral vale of fair Strathmore, between the Sidlaws and the Tay, through the pleasant settled land of North Gowrie and the Stormont. At the junction of Isla and Tay, they swung eastwards for Coupar-Angus, the slow cannon already left far behind. And near where the Romans had once made their great camp, at Lintrose, Montrose halted likewise, and sent out probing parties southwards through the Sidlaw passes of Balshando and Glack of Newtyle, to discover the state of affairs at

Dundee, and to make contact with the Grahams of that area, while he waited for the slow cannon to catch up. Meanwhile, he sent to the Earl of Airlie, at Cortachy Castle, and to the Earl of Kinghorne at Glamis, for reinforcements, mounted if possible.

He gained little joy at Coupar-Angus – save for what he obtained from his wife and sons. Airlie was loyal King's man enough, and answered the call personally, bringing his sons Sir Thomas and Sir David Ogilvy with him – but only forty-five men. This was a grievous disappointment, even though they were all horsed, from one of the most powerful lords in the East of Scotland. Montrose had looked for many times that number. And Kinghorne sent only his regrets. He did not actually declare that he was not so agile at changing sides as was James Graham – but he indicated that he still adhered to the Covenant which he had signed, and did not feel that he could rise against it in arms, with a clear conscience. Nor was he in the best of health . . .

Only a comparatively few other recruits joined them at Coupar-Angus.

Old Airlie brought sad news as well as few men. His eldest son, Montrose's faithful lieutenant, the Lord Ogilvy, with most of the rest of the Scots whom James Graham had left so dramatically and secretly south of Carlisle, had fallen into an ambush on the way to the King at Oxford, at Ribble Bridge, and were now the English parliamentarians' prisoners. Aboyne had apparently escaped, for he it was had sent the word from Carlisle; but many others were taken. Airlie may not actually have blamed Montrose for desertion of his son; but undoubtedly it still rankled that he had failed to save the Ogilvy castles of Airlie and Forter, and the Countess herself, from Argyll's savagery, when he was still Covenant Lieutenant-General in these parts. Probably this accounted for the merely token force of Ogilvys he brought with him.

On the second night at Coupar, while still they awaited firm news of Dundee, Montrose was aroused in the tent he was sharing with Magdalen by the agitated captain of the guard. Not attack, no. But trouble. Great shameful trouble. Murder . . . !

Hastily seeking to quieten and reassure his alarmed wife, James Graham ran, half-naked, through the drizzling night and the slumbering camp, to another tent, where three men lay dead, horribly contorted in a sea of blood – his friend, John, Lord Kilpont, and two sentries, all stabbed with savage, multiple wounds. By the light of a flickering lamp, he starred, appalled.

'John! Johnnie!' he choked. 'God in heaven – what is this? Dead? Dead? All dead . . . ?'

'Dead, my lord. When I got to him. The sentries gave the alarm. Then these two slain likewise. Another wounded . . .'

'But . . . why? Who? How came this . . . ?'

'Ardvorlich, my lord. Major Stewart of Ardvorlich. He did it. Him they call the Mad Major.'

'But . . . but Kilpont was Ardvorlich's friend. His closest friend, in this host. Some mistake, here . . .'

'No, my lord Marquis – none. They were together in this tent all the night. Playing at the cards. See.' He pointed to the overturned ammunition-box, the scattered cards and the fallen wine-flagon and tankards. 'The wounded sentry is one of my lord Kilpont's bowmen. He heard shouting, and came running. He saw his lordship on the grass, and the Major stabbing at him, stabbing and stabbing with his dirk. He ran for aid. Fetched these two others, and went back. Ardvorlich was a man crazed. He knifed them all. He shouted "Mac-Gregor!" at them. MacGregor – though they were none of MacGregor. Then he bolted. I heard noise at the horse-lines. He is gone. And . . . these are dead. All dead.'

'Sweet Jesu – MacGregor! That old story! Of a mercy – so sore a sin, so ancient a sin!'

'But there were no MacGregors in it, my lord . . .'

Montrose did not explain what he meant to the captain of the guard, but knelt down beside his friend, head bowed, to take the limp hand and try to pray. Pray also for the souls of the two innocent sentries, who had all unwittingly paid the price of a thirty-year-old enormity. He knew the story well. All who dwelt in Strathearn knew it. How Ardvorlich on the south shore of Loch Earn had been a Drummond property, and how the son of Stewart of Glenbuckie in Balquhidder had wed the daughter of Drummond-Earnoch, Keeper of the royal forest of Glen Artney, and had been given this Ardvorlich as her tocher. Dying, Drummond had been succeeded by his son, as Keeper, and one day a marauding band of MacGregors, poaching the forest, and who had a grudge against the father, chanced upon the son in Glen Artney, and slew him there and then. Satan-inspired, they cut off the dead man's head, and took it across the hills and down to Ardvorlich House. Stewart was from home, but his lady only temporarily out-of-doors. When she came back, it was to find the MacGregors sitting round her kitchen-table, feeding themselves and her brother's severed head bread and cheese. In screaming horror she had run away, away and away, up into the empty hills, a crazed and preg-nant woman alone, wandering, out of her mind. And there, by a lonely lochan, still known as the Loch of the Woman, her child had been born – James Stewart. He had survived, and indeed had grown up strong, handsome but with a strange look to his eye, renowned for strength, temper and courage, utter disregard for danger, waging ruthless and un-relenting war on all MacGregors. Whenever he saw one, he killed him if he could, as he would a fly; and all such learned to keep their distance from Loch Earnside. Half a Drum-mond, he had joined Montrose with that party, and had been given a company of the Athollmen. None had fought more bravely or fiercely, or wrought more havoc, at Tipper-muir, than the Mad Major. And now – this.

Montrose took the business hard – harder than many deemed was necessary. Kilpont had been his especial friend and loyalest lieutenant. Save for Black Pate, there was none closer to him. And had it not been that he had brought his wife to share his tent with him, this would never have happened – for Kilpont and Pate and he had always been together hitherto, and only Magdalen's coming had caused his friends to tent elsewhere. Had his lust, his need for his wife's woman's body and softness, been the cause of his friend's death? The thought of it would not leave his grieving mind.

James Stewart did not return. Where he had gone, none knew.

Next morning, Pate Graham, as ever master of scouts, brought the waited news from Dundee. Any assault on the city was out of the question, he advised. To it had gravitated all the Covenant zealots and friends of Argyll from a wide area. Heavy cannon had been gathered in, from Broughty Castle and elsewhere. Three shiploads of arms and ammuni-tion had just arrived from Leith. The place was like an armed camp, and no amount of Graham lairdships round about would avail against it.

Montrose was in no mind to disagree with his friend's counsel. Siegery was foreign to his temperament anyway; and though the cannon he had captured from Elcho would be useful on a battlefield, they were far too light for use against a walled town. It was not by sitting down and seeking to starve out cities that he would conquer Scotland.

They would move north for Aberdeenshire and the Gordon country. Angus would never rise wholeheartedly for the King with Dundee secure on the other side.

So, in a strangely remote, self-critical, almost harsh mood for that man, the King's Lieutenant turned his face to the North-East. Magdalen, troubled, had never known him like this, he who was usually so courteously sure of himself, so unfailingly master of the situation. His sons took it all in their stride, of course.

It was no more than an easy two days' march to Kinnaird and Old Montrose, achieved without opposition – but also without any influx of support from the Angus gentry, worth mentioning. One battle obviously did not constitute any sure foundation for success. Approaching Kinnaird, where Magdalen and the boys were to be dropped, his elder son John made shift to speak with his father, apart from the others.

'My lord Marquis,' he declared stiffly, jerkily, in most formal style. 'Request permission to speak with the King's Lieutenant-General.'

Brows raised, his father eyed him. 'To be sure, Johnnie. But – you have never sought such permission before! Is aught amiss?'

'No, sir.' The boy coughed, but went woodenly on. 'I have never so spoken you before, my lord. As . . . as the Lord Graham. I would rather not be named the Earl of Kincardine, if it please you. I need not be, need I? The Lord Graham is . . . better.'

Surprised, Montrose looked at him with a new interest. 'Indeed, you are probably right . . . my lord! There have been Lords Graham for centuries. Yes, I think you have the rights of it, lad. The Lord Graham you shall remain.'

'Yes, sir. The Lord Graham means more. Always meant a deal, in Scotland. It must do, yet. Permission, my lord

Marquis, for the Lord Graham to remain with His Grace's army.' That came out in a breathless rush.

'Mm. So that's it! Laddie – you are only fourteen.'

'The Lord Lewis Gordon was only *thirteen* when he raised the Gordons! I will be fifteen soon. And I am the Lord Graham! I have learned all that they can teach me at Kinnaird, see you . . .'

'You say so? But – your mother needs her eldest son to look after her, Johnnie. Jamie is only eleven and Robert four – too young.'

'Mother, and my lord of Southesk, my grandfather, say that I must go to St Andrews. To the University. So that I will not be with my mother. And I could not study at the University when you were fighting for the King in Scotland. I *could* not! Father – take me!'

Montrose stroked his tiny beard. 'You think of war as glory, adventure, lad. It is not so, believe me. In especial, civil war. It is blood and bestiality and cruelty. Aye, and treachery too. Do not see it as a thing fine, splendid . . .'

'*You* are not cruel. Nor treacherous. You are noble – all say so. And you make war, for the King. I am the Lord Graham, sir. I have . . . I have been too long at Kinnaird, my lord. With women. With old men. And I do not want to go to St Andrews. If they send me there, I swear that I shall run away! To fight for the King. As a common soldier.' The boy was flushed now, stammering, but determined.

'So! You would threaten, Johnnie?'

'No. No – never that. But – I cannot stay at Kinnaird. Do you not understand? I . . . I *hate* the Carnegies, I think! They think only of lands and properties and marriages. My grandfather is already seeking a wife for me! I heard him telling Mother so . . .'

'He is, is he! We must see about that, must we not?' Unwittingly, the boy had struck the right note, now. 'Hm. Your mother would not thank me for taking you, Johnnie.'

'My mother knows my intention, sir. I have told her, often.'

James Graham pondered. Magdalen had said nothing of this to him. Nor of any going to University. And certainly not of possible marriage contracts or betrothal. Was the boy indeed being smothered at Kinnaird? By Carnegies? He was right, in that, indeed; the Carnegies were concerned with the Carnegies, to be sure! But this boy was the heir to Graham.

Young he was, but conceivably he might have the rights of it.

'I will think of it, Johnnie,' he said.

One night at Kinnaird, with the army camped at Old Montrose near by – one night of his father-in-law and his brothers-in-law and their women, decided James Graham. The Carnegies and the Grahams just did not look at life from the same standpoint. Which might be right, the dear God knew. They might even both be right. But their all too evident difference of outlook must not be allowed to damage and distress his spirited sons, at a significant and impressionable age. Magdalen had been too long at Kinnaird. If Kincardine was too far away, and too vulnerable in present conditions, at least she should keep her own house again, and his, here at Old Montrose. This he would insist upon. With separate schooling for James, Robert and little Jean, free of the crowd of Carnegie children. And Johnnie, the Lord Graham, would come with him, at least meantime.

Surprisingly enough Magdalen did not take nearly so much objection to this programme as her husband anticipated. Perhaps she had been getting a little tired of being under the thumbs of her father, brothers and step-mother, not being mistress of her own house; perhaps she had been reconciled for some time to losing the spirited Johnnie; perhaps Tippermuir, and her husband's suddenly increased stature, had even affected herself, however little she was likely to admit it. At any rate, her opposition was half-hearted and brief. Montrose promised that he would look after Johnnie like a hen with one chick, and see that he was kept out of danger, as far as in him lay. And when the campaigning was over, he should certainly go to St Andrews University.

On that note they allowed the matter to rest, and permitted the more personal concerns of their last night together to possess them.

In the morning, the Ensign Lord Graham rode proudly northwards, as aide-de-camp to the King's Lieutenant-General, while the Lord James swallowed the tears which would have branded him as unfit to do likewise. Biting her lip, the Marchioness of Montrose watched them go.

Two days later, on the 11th of September, they had crossed the Mounth and were descending the empty uplands to the Dee valley near Banchory, with all Aberdeenshire and the Gordon lands before them, when at the same time riders approached the long-strung-out host from front and rear. The first was a hard-riding, gallant group, Nathaniel Gordon of the Ardlogie sept, with thirty mounted men; and the second was none other than the Master of Madderty, who had escaped from his captors and come hastening after his friends. Both brought news, and both Montrose was glad to see – even though their tidings furrowed his brow.

Nathaniel Gordon's adherence, even with only thirty men, was at least an augury for the future. Montrose had been looking for large-scale Gordon support for days. This was the very modest first of it. Nathaniel of Ardlogie was hardly influential, however notorious. He was in fact a wild character, even spoiling for a fight and seldom out of trouble; but if kept under control – such as Huntly had never found possible – he was a daring and seasoned fighter. It was not so much his presence as the news he brought that was important. It appeared that the Covenant army of the North-East was near by, on the outskirts of Aberdeen itself, only some fifteen miles away. It was under the command of the Lord Balfour of Burleigh, and he had as lieutenants the Lords Fraser and Frendraught – old Covenant colleagues of Montrose at Turiff – and the younger Lord Gordon with his brother, the still younger Lord Lewis. According to Nathaniel, the young chief was unhappy about the entire situation, his father having sent orders from the far North that he was not to involve the clan in fighting on either side; in consequence he was looked on with suspicion by practically everyone, especially Burleigh, Fraser and the other leaders.

The Covenant force was some 3000 infantry and over 600 horse – much of the latter Gordon.

This was significant news. Balfour of Burleigh was the man who had acted President of the parliament which had sought to try Montrose, in King Charles's presence, a creature of Argyll's. The Graham had no high opinion of him as a soldier or anything else. Fraser and Frendraught had not proved themselves masters of the military art at Turiff or thereafter – and they were at permanent feud with the Gordons. Any army, with such leadership, was unlikely to be at its best – especially with the man who controlled most of the cavalry already harbouring doubts and resentment.

The Master of Madderty's tidings clinched the matter. He brought word that Argyll himself, with 2500 foot and over 1500 cavalry, plus a number of large cannon, was only three or four days' march behind, at the western end of Strathmore and thought to be going to advance up Glen Shee from Blairgowrie and into Deeside from the west. He added that Stewart of Ardvorlich had fled to join Argyll, and now was being fêted as a hero for his slaying of one of Montrose's principal lieutenants. Indeed, Argyll was offering £12,000 Scots to anyone who would do the same for Montrose, payment to be made on production of the Graham's head at the Mercat Cross of Edinburgh.

Montrose, forcing himself to swallow meantime his anger and revulsion at this second part of the report, concentrated on the more important item – Argyll's 1500 cavalry and large cannon. Here was menace indeed. He must not allow these to get within striking distance of his own force, or all would be lost. Nor, if he could help it, must he allow Argyll's army to join up with Balfour of Burleigh's, or to sandwich his own between them. Aberdeen city, unlike Dundee, had been on the side of the King, and anti-Covenant, formerly. Argyll would change all that.

So James Graham altered his plans there and then. Instead of going recruiting in the Gordon lands of Central Aberdeenshire, he would seek to strike an immediate blow at Burleigh, the weakest link in the chain threatening to encircle him – even though it seemed to be considerably stronger than his own force. Aberdeen must be shown, at all costs, that the King's cause was far from lost. After a word with Alastair, he ordered a change of direction in the march, to the east.

They crossed the Dee, near Durris, where there was a mid-stream island which permitted fording. There was no sign of opposition. They camped for the night at Crathes, to whose hospitable castle Sir Thomas Burnett of Leys made Montrose welcome. He was that rare character for Scotland, a quiet inoffensive man, who took no sides; and although he was a good Protestant and Presbyterian, he acknowledged his duty to his monarch. He had no armed men, but he offered the King's Lieutenant a sum of money – which Montrose courteously refused. He said that Aberdeen, fifteen miles away, was in a great stir, having heard that Argyll was coming, and was tending to believe that the Covenant must win.

By sunrise they were on their way down Deeside, on the north bank. Montrose, held back by the infantry and slow-moving cannon, sent his few cavalry ahead now, with orders not only to scout and clear the way, but to secure the vital Bridge of Dee. He had vivid memories of its military significance heretofore. Riders presently came back to declare that they were not meeting with resistance, but that their arrival was expected. Not that they could have hoped for surprise, with such slow-moving force. Balfour of Burleigh had moved out from the city and taken up a strong defensive situation on the slopes of a gentle hill, between the How Burn and the Craibstone, just two miles south-west of the centre of Aberdeen, the Covenant forces flanking a climbing lane, with houses and walled gardens and orchards on either side. These were being held by parties of forward troops, so that the entire position resembled a quite extensive and elaborate strong-point. Balfour was known to have some heavy cannon from the citadel, and had high ground on which to site them. This could be no easy contest. He had made no move to hold the Bridge of Dee, however, which had fallen without trouble.

Montrose's instinct was to start his attack with the least possible delay, giving Balfour no time to lay plans and perhaps call up reinforcements from the city. The man was no firebrand, deliberate, stolid, the sort to be put off by his stride by sudden, swift, unexpected moves. Also, there was Argyll pressing up behind from the south-west. But James Graham, despite the black mood which had gripped him since the terrible revelation of his enemies' attitude in the 'Jesus and no quarter' slogan, deepened by the murder of

Kilpont and the murderer's welcome from the other side, would not abandon his principles. Aberdeen must be given the opportunity to declare for the monarch. He was in Scotland not merely as the King's General but as Viceroy. His first duty was to win over his fellow citizens to their due allegiance rather than to make war on them. Therefore he disappointed Alastair MacDonald, Black Pate and other impatient warriors – including the Lord Graham, aide-de-camp – by ordering camp to be set up on the other side of the shallow valley, in view of the enemy but just out of cannon range, between the Lower Justice Mills and the Ferry Hill Mills. It was late in the day, anyway, with thirteen miles covered since Crathes.

Now that hostilities were imminent, he rather wished that he did not have Johnnie with him, hero-worshipping, itching for splendid action.

In the morning, he sent Sir William Rollo, under a white flag and with an Irish drummer-boy of Colkitto's to beat a rat-tatting way for him, through the enemy lines and into the city, to proclaim the King's greetings to his royal burgh of Aberdeen, to require its due allegiance and support for the King's forces, and to expel any obdurate enemies of His Grace and minions of the rebellious Marquis of Argyll. If, however, the magistrates and townsfolk refused loyally so to do, Rollo was to inform them to send out of the city to a place of safety all old and infirm, all women and children – for the Marquis of Montrose, the King's Lieutenant, would surely put such rebellious and disloyal town to the sack, and those who remained could expect no quarter, as the Covenant leaders were proclaiming no quarter to the royal forces. He hoped that this would have the desired effect of avoiding bloodshed and preventing the citizens from aiding Balfour.

While they awaited the return of this embassage, Montrose deployed his force. As at Tippermuir, he gave the centre to Colkitto's Irish and Islesmen. The right wing, of Perthshire men, he placed under a veteran of the foreign wars, Colonel James Hay, with Rollo to aid him if he returned empty-handed. And the left, taking a chance, he allotted to Nathaniel Gordon who, coming from the country, knew the area like the palm of his hand, having conducted nefarious private ploys of his own hereabouts. The few cavalry he split into two groups, stiffened with Kilpont's bowmen and some lightly armed Highlanders, who could race with the horses, clutching a stirrup, an employment only for the boldest and most agile, but which could yield notable dividends.

Montrose was returning from making these dispositions, almost at noon, when he heard uproar in the main camp, the Irish in particular yelling in anger. Rollo was back – but alone. The magistrates and leaders of Aberdeen had received him warily, coolly, and returned an equivocal answer to the Lieutenant-General's summons, committing themselves to nothing and most evidently playing for time. They sought elucidation of the Lord Marquis's terms, particularly his threats of no quarter. They gave the drummer-boy a silver piece and sent Rollo away. And as they had come back, fire had been opened upon them, flag of truce or none, and the boy had been killed.

The news touched off a highly unusual outburst of sheer fury in Montrose. He was not a man of violent passions, and though he could be roused, was able to keep his temper under stern control. But now he was suddenly and excessively enraged. Or, perhaps, it was no so sudden, in fact, and the anger had been boiling up in him for days – at the savage hatred of his opponents, the price on his head, the shocking slaying of his friend, the reluctance of those who should be aiding him to rise in support of their King. Also, there is no doubt that the fact of the drummer-boy being of a like age and size to Johnnie affected him strongly. He burst out in a storm of cursing – and when an outraged and red-faced Colkitto came demanding vengeance for the lad and declaring that he could not promise to control his Irish if any order was given to spare Aberdeen, as Perth had been spared, the Graham grimly assured him that no such order would be forthcoming. If they won this battle, Aberdeen should pay the price. He sent Alastair back to his post, and commanded the trumpets to sound for action.

Although very much the weaker force, it was the royalists who now set the pace. Colkitto was ordered to move individual parties forward, to clear the houses and gardens flanking the lane, which must inevitably be the main axis of advance – fairly certain that Balfour would not train his cannon on this area where his own people were hiding. Also, because of the slope of hill, it would be difficult to depress

329

the gun-barrels sufficiently; this must be a central point in Montrose's strategy.

The clearing of the orchards and houses was achieved without too much difficulty, although it took time, place by place. Prisoners sent back informed that the Gordon cavalry on the enemy left was under the command of young Lord Lewis, his elder brother having apparently returned to Strathbogie in disgust with the ministers who dominated the Covenant host. Fraser and Frendraught were on the same left wing, with the infantry; while the right was commanded by Sir William Forbes of Craigievar, a man of some stature. The main body, in the centre, was under Balfour of Burleigh himself, with the cannon.

Presently, there was a counter-attack on the enemy left. A sudden wild charge down the hill by Gordon cavalry led by Lord Lewis took everybody by surprise, since it was unsupported by any other, infantry or artillery, and was not in great force. More surprising still, this attack was not pressed home against Hay's and Rollo's Perth men, the Gordons dashing only to within range, discharging their pistols, and then wheeling round in fine style and galloping back. When this odd performance was followed by a tentative advance of left-wing infantry which sent forward relays of ranks, each to fire muskets and then hastily retire out of range again, Montrose recognised that it could only mean one thing – a distraction. The enemy centre was strongly dug-in, and therefore unlikely to move out at this stage; so it must be on the right. Hastily he sent word to Nathaniel Gordon to be ready for surprises, and also to Rollo to be prepared to switch to their aid.

It was only just in time. Down a sunken and hidden lane between the Upper and Lower Justice Mills, well to the west, some 400 Covenant foot and 100 horse suddenly erupted upon the royalist left flank. Nathaniel Gordon, who had been raring to make some spectacular advance in typical dashing fashion was hardly in a posture or frame of mind for dogged and effective defence. Recognising the danger, Montrose sent in half of his cavalry in support, and called Rollo's foot to make swift transfer behind the centre lines.

It was then that Sir William Forbes charged, with the main body of Covenant horse on the now cavalry-denuded royalist centre, a full-scale and determined attack and no mere demonstration like Lewis Gordon's. It was as well that Colkitto's men were veterans, the survivors of long and bloody campaigning; other infantry might well have panicked. But they had experienced cavalry charges before this. They stood their ground, waiting to fire their muskets until the horsemen were almost upon them – and then shooting at the mounts rather than the riders. Hastily darting aside, to open ranks and let the horsemen through, dodging swinging sabres, they closed in again behind, and turned to attack the cavalry's rear. It took strong nerves – but whatever else these kerns and Islesmen lacked, they had these. Forbes's horse, disorganised, suffering heavy casualties, and now detached from their own forces, were then faced with a furious charge by the other half of Montrose's scanty cavalry, under Madderty, Black Pate and Dupplin. They broke and scattered.

Rollo had succeeded in rescuing Nathaniel Gordon, so that now the advantage on both wings lay with the royalists. No artillery had so far fired, on either side; nor had Montrose so much as drawn sword, but sat his horse on a vantage-point, young Johnnie at his side, where he could oversee all and direct, a general's stance, however frustrating for an excited youth – and for that matter for his father likewise, who always itched to take the active role. Now he ordered a general advance, with Nathaniel Gordon to make a swift encircling move to the west. The trumpets shrilled.

Strangely, the two centres never really came in contact. Those trumpets, in fact, sounded the real end of the Battle of Aberdeen, without a cannon-ball fired – for Balfour and his main body, seeing what had happened to their flanks and alarmed at the obvious flanking move on the west, did not wait for some specific defeat. Led by their mounted leaders, they fled – though the ministers with them, shaking fists upraised to heaven, called down the wrath of God on weak-kneed back-sliders and craven sons of Belial, some still screaming that 'Jesus and no quarter' cry. These were the last to go – and the Irish made short work of such as left it too late, cloth or none.

So now there was another running fight, like that after Tippermuir – only the distance to run was much shorter and soon the fighting was taking place in the streets of Aberdeen. This time, of a set and harsh purpose, Montrose made no attempt to call off the dogs of war. It is doubtful indeed whether he could have done so effectively, if he would. The Irish had Colkitto's promise that on this occasion they should have their way. Aberdeen required, and had asked for, a lesson. It should have it. James Graham deliberately turned his back on the city which had opposed him four times, and returned to his camp with his disappointed son. Major-General Alastair MacDonald should show Aberdeen who was King in Scotland.

The night Montrose paced the dusty floor of the mill granary he had taken over as headquarters, in no mood for sleep, handsome features set, fine eyes bleak, with none of the victor's triumph, no sense of duty well done. For once, none of his lieutenants dared seek his company, even Pate Graham keeping his distance. He went through the hell of his own deliberate choice, steeling himself to do no more than this dire pacing, when every inch of him, every nerve, screamed to him to go, go back to Aberdeen and halt what he knew must be taking place therein, the terror and horror of a great city sacked. He won that savage fight with himself and his better, or weaker, nature – but at a price, a terrible price. He would never be quite the same man again, and knew it. But . . . he was the King's Lieutenant, no private individual. And Scotland, as well as Aberdeen itself, required, demanded a demonstration of unmistakable vehemence and proportions. An infinity of lives might well be spared, years of warfare saved, by this stern decision. Somewhere, sometime, someone must take it. It had to be he, and it had to be here.

The recurrent thought that Archibald Campbell would have taken it without a second thought, and slept sound thereafter, was no least help to him.

Hollow-eyed and still awake, he watched the new day dawn. He did not wait to see his son John, felt that he could by no means face him. Thus early he rode into the city.

Bodies still littered the route of the fleeing Covenant army – in the main naked bodies for, it seemed, the Irish were particular about this, stripping their victims before finally despatching them so that good clothing might not be spoiled. In the city streets it was the same – although here not a few of the bodies wore tartan and lay about drunk rather than dead. Smoke billowed from burning buildings, blood was splashed on walls and cobbles, furnishings lay smashed everywhere, warehouses spilled their contents. Sickened, Montrose rode to the Town House and Tolbooth, where he unceremoniously roused his snoring Major-General out of drunken slumber on the Council-table with an unclothed lady, and ordered him to get his men rounded up and out of the city as quickly as might be, without further licence. They, and Aberdeen, had had their night. At Colkitto's incoherent protests, he rounded on him with a harsh vehemence hitherto unknown, eyes blazing. Muttering, the giant MacDonald stumbled off, dragging his bewildered bedfellow with him.

All morning James Graham sat in the Town House receiving complainants, petitioners, protestations, of individuals and deputations, magistrates, ministers, merchants, prominent citizens. Stony-faced he heard their woes, their pleas, their charges. From these assertions there could scarcely be a citizen who had escaped death, injury, rape, pillage or outrage. Considering that Colkitto's total force was now less than 1200, and that the population was nearly ten times that, this seemed less than probable. He demanded details, numbers, specific instances. He did not get them – only allegations that men, women and children had been slaughtered indiscriminately by the hundred, and things done which it was not lawful even to mention. That it was heathen Papists who had committed these enormities was the prime complaint, especially of the ministers; a woman raped by a good Protestant seemed to be another matter. Montrose dismissed them all, refused to see more, sent out a fact-finding team under Black Pate, and himself rode out of town northwards, unaccompanied, to be alone with his thoughts.

If it was peace of mind that he sought, he did not find it so easily. Nor was it so easy to impose the discipline and order he had commanded – even for Colkitto to round up his Irishry and Highlanders. Many of them had gone to ground, with women and drink, all over the city, making up for long months of privation, danger, hardships. Covenant soldiers too had likewise gone to ground and were equally beyond discipline. From the ordinary Aberdonians' point of view, there was probably not much to choose from between them.

That night was only a little better than the last.

Pate Graham's team reported to Montrose, back at his

headquarters, such facts as they had been able to uncover. The city had had a bad time of it, undoubtedly, and many were dead, there had been much looting and a deal of rape and assault likewise. But there had been no wholesale slaughter of the citizenry, nor yet of women and children, as some alleged. So far as they could ascertain, out of a total of about 200 dead within the city, only nine women were included, these apparenly slain in drunken brawls. Most of the others were Covenant soldiers who had got as far as the streets, and to whom Colkitto's men had given no quarter admittedly. A few houses had been fired, undoubtedly much gear stolen and warehouses rifled. Also a number of women were missing – but some of such who had been run to earth proved to have gone with the newcomers voluntarily and quite happily. All in all, Newcastle had suffered much worse from Leslie's army, and even Cromwell's Puritans made greater havoc in conquered towns.

Nevertheless, James Graham was sick at heart. God willing, never again would he allow himself to be manoeuvred into a position where such a decision and responsibility was demanded of him.

Meantime, he was determined to get away from Aberdeen at the earliest possible moment. Argyll was drawing near – and if he sent any large proportion of his 1500 cavalry on in advance, they could be here in a day or so. In the present drunken and demoralised state of his force, this could spell disaster. They would move out tomorrow, for the north.

But the morrow saw Colkitto still 300 men short of total, and angrily refusing to move without them. They were the backbone of the royalist army, and both men knew it. Montrose could only fret, and send out search-parties and wait.

It was next day before the blear-eyed, jaundiced, grumbling, overladen, over-dressed horde straggled out of Aberdeen northwards, up the Don valley, everyone out-of-temper. Despite Montrose's objections and offence a long tail of women now accompanied them. Colkitto informed him that they were part of the price he had to pay for his veterans – and he could have the choice of any one of them any night! Argyll was reported to be only twenty miles away, coming down the Dee – but from all accounts going very warily, and certainly not rushing his cavalry ahead of him. Presumably he had heard of Balfour's defeat, and was more impressed by it than was the victor. Indeed Montrose had to remind himself more than once that he *had* just won his second major victory. He had no least feelings of triumph – quite the reverse.

They made slow progress, slower than ever, for now they had the heavy cannon captured from Balfour, as well as the lighter Tippermuir pieces, to hold them back. And, of course, the women and the lengthy, untidy train of booty. It was a humiliation and a disgrace for James Graham to trail this sorry spectacle through the Aberdeenshire countryside; but he was not in a position to take strong action with the Irish and Islesmen. He needed them too much. Also, he was feeling less than well. Not only his mental state was depressed. He had seldom felt less lively.

But at Kintore, where they camped that first night, amidst an uproar of drunkenness, skirling women, and general indiscipline, he wrote a despatch to King Charles, at Oxford, in determinedly cheerful note, announcing victory and sending all encouragement – so much more than in his present frame of mind he felt. Duty has many facets. Right away, in the September dusk, Sir William Rollo was sent off with it, on the long road south, before Argyll could block the way.

In one way, in his present angry mood, a trial of strength with Archibald Campbell, a once-and-for-all set-to, would have appealed to Montrose, even lacking his accustomed energy. But the other's 1500 horse precluded anything of the sort. Until he himself could build up a powerful cavalry wing, or arrange it so that any clash took place on terrain where the advantage lay with the foot, he dare not come to conclusions with Argyll, galling as it was to seem to flee before him.

They were in Gordon country now, however, and would be for days. At Kildrummy, two days later, farther up Donside, he sent off Nathaniel Gordon to Strathbogie, with a message to his young chief, urging that he join him and give command to his clan to do likewise. The Gordon lairds could produce horsemen by the hundred, the thousand almost, basis of the cavalry force he so greatly needed. He would have gone himself so important was the requirement; but Colkitto was still resentful over the Aberdeen business and his men must on no account be allowed to get more out-of-hand

335

than they were already, in this Gordon country, or all hopes
of co-operation could be forgotten. He sent his son with
Nathaniel however, as of equal rank to the Lord Graham –
his first duty in the King's cause.

Aberdeenshire is a vast county, and progress was painfully
slow. On the 20th, they heard that Argyll had entered Aberdeen city the day before – his first act to levy heavy contributions on the already outraged citizens. But so far there
was no sign of pursuit. It looked as though the Campbell
was little more anxious to come to blows, meantime, than
was his foe.

Nevertheless, always concerned about the enemy's great
preponderance in cavalry, which could so rapidly catch up
with his cumbered and crawling host, Montrose pressed on
farther into the west, following Don up into the mountains
of its birth, by Glenbuchat and Inverernan, Forbes country
with no friendliness shown to the visitors. And when
Nathaniel Gordon and young Johnnie caught up with them
again, he pressed on farther and faster. For they brought
word that he was not going to get his much-needed cavalry
from the Gordons. The Lord Gordon had listened to them
courteously enough, and admitted that he was at a loss to
where his allegiance lay. But his father, Huntly, had sent
categorical commands from his hide-out in Caithness, that
there were to be no Gordon levies lent to Montrose, King's
commission or none. Was not he himself King's Lieutenant
of the North? If King Charles was so foolish as to trust the
wrong man, and to choose such as Montrose to represent
him, instead of his old and tried friends, so much the worse
for His Grace. George Gordon had an excellent memory,
however lacking he might be in leadership. And he was still
chief.

If the Gordons would not rise for the King, none of the
lesser North-East clans were likely to do so, the low-country
clans, from whom Montrose might have looked for cavalry.
The Highlands were different – but they did not produce
horse-soldiers. He might be the winner of two battles – but
he was no nearer winning Scotland for Charles Stewart than
when he had crossed the Border. Or so he told himself.

Dispirited and now feeling physically sick – no doubt the
result of too continuous strain and fatigue – he decided that
it was the Highland fastnesses, now, for him and his dis-

tempered horde. Scouts informed that Argyll was slowly following him up through Central Aberdeenshire. In the mountains, those cannon which so grievously delayed them, would be no more than a useless impediment; so reluctantly he buried them, with all the heavy ball and powder, in a riverside haugh near Corgarff. Then, lightened at least, though now encumbered with large herds of hill-cattle which he was buying from scowling Forbes farmers, and which were going to be a deal more valuable than artillery where they were going, he turned away from Don at last, to climb up into the heather, into the outliers of the mighty Cairngorm mountains, by remote Tomintoul and the lonely desolations of Stratha'an. He did not think that Argyll would follow them there.

25

JOHN GRAHAM SAT ON A LOG OF PINE BESIDE HIS FATHER'S couch of horse-blankets, biting his lips, great-eyed. This was nothing like the going to war, to fight for the King, that he had visualised. He was worried, frightened, and rather disappointed. Nothing was as he had imagined. He would have admitted to none, not even to himself, that he was even a little disappointed in his hero-father, who had won a battle, true enough – although he himself had been allowed no part in it – but had been leading a retreat ever since. And now he was ill, tossing and muttering on this bed in the forest, while his lieutenants quarrelled and bickered amongst themselves, and that great bull of a man. Alastair MacDonald, strutted, shouted at everybody, and got drunk. Not that he blamed his father for being ill; but surely they should not be in this ridiculous Rothiemurchus Forest, hiding like beaten fugitives – the King's army, led by the King's Lieutenant-General! And a heathenish Papish Irishman, or Highlander or whatever he was, ordering about good Scots lairds, even earls like Airlie. John Graham rather wished that he was at home with Jamie.

His father was mumbling again. The boy leant forward to listen. It was very hard to make out what he said – and what words were distinguishable did not seem to make sense, anyway. It was very frightening. Could his fine father, the great Montrose, the King's and Scotland's hope, be going to die? Pate said no, that it was just a fever, that he would be right again soon, with rest and quiet. But Pate was not a physician. They had no physician with the army – except one of the Papist Irish who called himself a doctor, but whom nobody would allow near his father, naturally. Pate, indeed, was allowing practically nobody into this tent, he or one of his men standing guard like a watchdog at the door, by day, and sleeping across it by night. Pate was good. So was Lord Airlie. And his sons. He didn't like Dupplin very much – he should now call him Earl of Kinnoull he supposed, since his old father had evidently just died. And the Master of Madderty, whom he *did* like, was away on a deer-hunting expedition. It was daft, surely, that so many of the King's soldiers should spend their time hunting deer in this out-landish forest, when all Scotland was waiting to be won for the King. Though, at least, the forest was a good place for deer.

They had been here for three days.

Suddenly Montrose sat up, peering straight ahead of him out of strangely vacant eyes, a trembling hand out, finger pointing. A flood of words spilled from his lips, disjointed, harsh, utterly unlike his normal calmly assured, almost musical speech. Campbell and Henderson and Rothes and other names, the boy could make out; but though his father seemed to be asking questions, he had not the least idea how to answer him. It seemed terribly important, too. He did not know whether Pate was still outside the tent. He called for him, urgently.

Only a sentry looked inside, a Graham admittedly, but only one of the bowmen. 'Get Inchbrakie,' John cried. 'My father – my lord wants something. Quickly – get Major Pate.'

But Montrose had fallen back again, and was staring at the tent roof, lips moving but without words. But when presently Black Pate came running in, and the boy began to explain, a weak voice from the couch interrupted.

'What's to do?' it asked, flatly, a little querulously, but quite sanely. 'Pate? Johnnie? What's to do?'

Surprised, they both turned to stare. These were the first lucid words for three nights and two days.

'Glory be, man – you are yourself again!' Inchbrakie exclaimed. 'Thank God!'

'Father! You are well? Can you see me now? Hear me? You have not known me. All these days.'

'Days? Days, you say?'

'Yes, many days. You have lain there . . .'

'This is the third day, Jamie,' Pate amended. 'We . . . we feared for you.'

'I have been . . . on a journey, I think. A strange journey.' That was said slowly. 'Far. Where all was very different.' His eyes travelled round the tent, seeing eyes now. 'I doubt . . . if I am very glad . . . to be back.'

'*I* am glad – and that's God's truth!' his friend declared. 'You were strange, yes – sick, Jamie. Sick. Knowing nothing. And this camp has been in a stour while you lay. They are all crazy-mad, I swear. That Alastair . . .'

Montrose was not listening. 'This Scotland,' he said, his voice ruminative. 'I saw it all. As in a picture. A fair realm. All this goodly land. But doomed. Fated. Betrayed by a fatal disease. You hear? Doomed.'

They stared.

'Betrayed. By disunity. And treachery. This Scotland. Every man a law unto himself. So that he will unite truly with none. Each esteeming his own freedom above all else. Above the realm's freedom. To think. To speak. To act. As each will. And so distrusting all other. It is our curse . . .'

'Aye. Maybe.' A little askance Inchbrakie eyed him, unsure whether or not he still might be wandering in his mind. 'But, Jamie – there's closer trouble than that. Here, in the camp. High words. My lords Airlie and Kinnoull cannot get on with your Alastair. Nor he with them. Or any, save his own barbarians. There's been near to bloodshed. Here is no army, any more . . .'

'I say this Scotland is torn apart,' the other went on, in the same quiet, withdrawn voice. 'Torn by ravening wolves, while the shepherds tear each the other. I saw an army. An army of dead men. All dead. Weeping for this Scotland. The King led it . . .'

'The King? Dead!' John cried. 'Never that! It was but an ill dream. Father, you but dreamed...'

Montrose turned his head to look thoughtfully at the boy. 'I saw other in that army,' he said. Then he turned away again. He did not say that he had seen himself and his son, both, behind the King.

Pate fidgeted uneasily. He did not like such talk. Montrose's mother, the Lady Margaret Ruthven, was reputed to have had 'the sight', even to have dabbled in witchcraft. The Ruthvens were that way inclined. Abruptly he changed the subject.

'You will be hungry, Jamie? No food has passed your lips these three days. Nor drink. I will bring you something . . .'

There was a commotion at the tent-door. Stooping, the huge person of Alastair MacDonald came striding in. He was a little unsteady on his feet – but that was nothing unusual.

'So you *have* come to your wits, my lord Marquis!' he said. 'The whisper is round the camp. Not before time, 'fore God! I was near away, your warrant or none.'

Not very interestedly, Montrose eyed his Major-General. He inclined his head, but did not speak.

'Mary-Mother – are you yourself, man? In your right senses?' the big man demanded, raising his voice.

'I can hear you very well, Alastair.' That was quiet.

'You can? Then hear this, my lord. I have had enough of lurking and idling. As have my men, whatever! It is time that we were off, by God! About our own affairs. It is October now. Soon the snows will block the passes. No time for campaigning in these mountains. I am for off, my lord Marquis.'

The other moistened his lips, but said nothing.

'We serve no good end here.' Colkitto's great voice was rising again. 'My men are fighters, see you – not dodgers and sitters! This idling and scuttling mislikes them. They are less than the men they should be. We must be off.'

'Where, Alastair? Whither?'

'To the West. To the Western Sea. Where we came from. To winter there. Where there are no snows. I go to my castle of Mingary, in Ardnamurchan. My lord Antrim was to send me supply ships. More men. Provisioning. Arms. From Ulster. They may be there now. We go winter on that western seaboard.'

'But not as . . . scuttlers? Idlers?' That was mild, gentle almost.

'God's wounds – no! All the Campbell lands lie south of Ardnamurchan. We shall not spend our winter idly!'

'Scotland will not be won for King Charles from Ardnamurchan, Alastair, I think.'

'Is it being won here? Thus?'

'If I can coax Argyll into these mountains, where his cavalry are little use to him, much may be won.'

'He was leaving Castle Gight, on the Ythan, last word to come in, my lord Marquis,' Pate interpolated. 'Turning westwards towards the Spey. Still following. But slowly.'

'A cat to your mouse!' the MacDonald snorted, scornfully. 'You will not win Scotland so, either! I am for the West.'

'Even if I am not, Major-General?'

The giant frowned. 'Aye,' he said. 'You are a sick man, my lord. I, and mine, cannot dance attendance on a sick man, who prefers to skulk than to fight. Through a Highland winter. My sorrow – but that is the truth of it. I am for Ardnamurchan.'

'You have not forgiven me for Aberdeen, I think? That I called in your dogs of war.'

Colkitto said nothing.

'I cannot hold you, Alastair,' Montrose said, with a sigh. 'You will do as you must. Who am I to *command* you to stay. But . . . I ask you.'

The other shook his red head. 'There is much to be done in the West. Nothing to be done here. I go. Tomorrow. Come with me, my lord – if you will.'

'No, sir.' Sir James Graham's voice was weak now, only a whisper – but lacking nothing in decision. 'If I go . . . to the West . . . Argyll will follow me. Where he is stronger than ever. And Lowland Scotland . . . will lose what heart . . . it has. I bide.'

Shrugging, the big man turned, and stalked out.

'Hielant barbarian!' Pate growled. 'Papist scum! I told you they were not to be trusted. Any of them. Treacherous dogs!'

Sinking back, staring at the tent-roof again, Montrose shook his head. 'Not treacherous,' he murmured. 'They fight a different war. That is all.'

So, next morning, weak and leaning against the gnarled trunk of an ancient pine, but on his feet again, the King's Lieutenant-General watched two-thirds of his force march away from the tree-clad shores of Loch-an-Eilean in Rothiemurchus – with bickering and vituperation between the Gaelic and the Lowland contingents right to the end. At least they took their pathetic trail of women with them – the cause of much of the strife. Montrose himself had carefully refrained from acrimony; but he could not hide his sadness at the occasion, nor his awareness of the blow this was to the King's cause. He had asked God, the King, his friends, even Magdalen, for a year, one year to win Scotland – and he had been given five weeks. In this time he had won two battles, taken two cities, covered a deal of Scotland, countenanced a great evil, besmirched his name – and lost his army. Only O'Cahan and a party of 120, out foraging, were left him of Colkitto's force. With the last bagpipe notes of the Gaelic host fading away amongst the pines, James Graham, refusing all company, even his son's, but accepting a stick Johnnie found for him as support, moved shakily down to the water's edge and along the loch-shore. His mind was still bemused, woolly, far from incisive; but he had to think clearly.

Gazing out across the lapping waters to the little castle on its island, built by that shameful royal brigand, Alexander Stewart, Earl of Buchan and Wolf of Badenoch, two centuries before, he sought to concentrate his thoughts. His strange illness had affected him as strangely, causing him to see things from a different standpoint. That it was a more philosophical perhaps fatalistic standpoint, he was aware. For too long he had been fretting, anxious, harassed by great matters and small, of national import or merely personal. And alone – always and essentially alone in it all. Now, it seemed that somehow his body and mind together had called a halt, taken their own steps to relieve the strain he had long been under. He was still weak, of course, and this might be partly responsible; but the fact was that in his mind he now felt strangely at peace, unconcerned with what had so worried and frustrated him hitherto – or perhaps resigned might better describe it. The pressure, somehow, was relaxed. By some means or other, in those past three days and nights of wanderings in far places, he had reached and emerged from a crisis. And now, on the other side of it, he was, he knew, a slightly different man. He believed that he would never be quite the same again.

Which was all very well – but obviously such relaxation, such resigned attitude, held drastic dangers for a commander of men. In his new frame of mind, was he no longer fit to be the King's Lieutenant-General? Even of so small a host as was left to him? It might be so. But he certainly could not be relieved of his command for a considerable time to come; and he owed it to his men, and to Charles Stewart, to be at least as good a general as he had been hitherto, if not better. No change in his outlook, or state of mind, however attained, altered his simple duty.

Eyes lifting to the great heather mountains behind the loch, above the dark green sea of the pine forest, already turning to the ochres and sepias that spoke of coming winter, James Graham considered what he could and must, do for Scotland and King Charles, with 500 men. First of all, he must try to keep alight the flame of hope which he might have lit in loyal hearts, hope that the cause was far from lost – this above all. So it meant gestures again, devices, continuing tokens, constant activity to make men talk and wonder, even to chuckle. To do that, he had to continue to keep Argyll involved, winter or no winter. He could not now hope to engage the Campbell in battle; but he could trail him endlessly across Scotland, harass and weary him, make a fool of him for all the land to see, show the King's flag here, there and everywhere, to set tongues wagging. Pin-pricks perhaps – but if these were persistent enough they could have cumulative effect far beyond their actual worth. The Campbell had shown himself to be a slow and cautious campaigner in the field. He must be baited, outstretched, mocked. So would his name, and the menace of it, sink in Scotland. It was the only way . . .

His mind made up, Montrose returned to the camp.

The following day, therefore, with the early morning frost making diadems of all the myriad spiders' webs that decked the juniper-bushes of the great forest, weak still but determined, James Graham hoisted himself into the saddle and led the way out of Rothiemurchus, southwards. Argyll, scouts said, was three days' march behind, down Spey.

*　　　*　　　*

As a programme of attrition it was not unsuccessful. But attrition is a double-edged weapon, and not without effect on both sides. Fighting men do not take kindly to continual retreat and coat-trailing – especially when they see no end to it. And when they have lands, farms, crofts, with wives and bairns at home, all calling them. Alastair and his Irish were not the only ones affected.

Seeking to keep no more than three days ahead of Argyll, Montrose led his reduced company up Spey and into Glen Truim, with the mighty mountains ever closing in and the forests dropping behind. And on, over the dreich high Pass of Drumochter, the very throat of the Highlands, and so into Atholl again. Thus far he had no real trouble; but Atholl was home to not a few of his following, and almost inevitably he lost men there. Nor could he find it in his heart to blame them, and did not call it desertion; with the Campbell coming behind, a man had every reason to prefer to be in his own place, with his family, to protect what he could from the avenger. Nevertheless, he did not risk proceeding much farther south, where he might lose more, the Drummonds, the Hays, even his own Grahams. At Dunkeld he swung off eastwards, by Butterstone and Clunie and Blairgowrie, for Strathmore once again, always having to slow their pace, not too greatly to outdistance Argyll. It was weary work, with a dozen miles a day a maximum progress, and a wet autumn turning into an early winter. At Coupar-Angus, where they had camped five weeks before and Kilpont had died, the Earl of Kinnoull and his Hays took their departure, despite pleas. The King's army now numbered barely 300.

They were close to Ogilvy country again, and Montrose feared the worst. But instead of deserting him, the old Earl of Airlie and his two sons found an extra fifty men, and mounted men at that, and continued with him – warming the Graham's heart as nothing else had done for long. It was a pity that there were not more like the Ogilvys.

It was galling to be so near Old Montrose, Magdalen and the children, and not be able to visit them; but to do so would only have endangered them when Argyll came up. He sent word to his wife to go to Kinnaird meantime, where her father's name and standing would presumably protect them from any Campbell reprisals. And he urged Johnnie to return there also, now that he had sampled soldiering and discovered it less than glorious, and his father to have feet of clay. But the boy clung to him, seeing his sire now as deserted by so many. All but in tears, he pleaded to be allowed to stay. Montrose could not find it in his heart to insist.

Instead of swinging eastwards towards the sea, then, they climbed due northwards over the Mounth again, by the same route of narrow valleys and steep hillsides over which once he had led a hard-riding troop to Turriff – in what seemed almost another life. They went still more slowly now, naturally – but not nearly so slowly as would Argyll if he chose to follow through and over these wild hills where the larger and more heavily equipped the force the greater the difficulties. He believed in fact that the Campbell would not attempt it. For himself, he wanted a day or two's grace, at Strathbogie. The young Lord Gordon there still could produce what he himself needed above all – cavalry. The thought was seldom out of his mind, the hordes of Gordon horse which could be raised from the vast Aberdeenshire lowlands, literally in their thousands. The waste of it all. They could transform his, and the King's, cause almost overnight. Denied them through an old man's stubborn pique and a young man's doubts. It was worth any effort, any sacrifice, to win such prize. Even if he had to go down on his bended knees to Huntly . . . !

By Dee and Don, then, they came at last to Strathbogie, on the 21st of October, with the first snows whitening the mountaintops to the west. The Gordons they passed looked at them askance, doubtful. At the castle, George Gordon, solemn and old-seeming for his twenty-four years, at the head of a swarm of brothers and sisters, received Montrose and his party civilly but warily. They were welcome, he said. His father's house was theirs. But only as guests; not as combatants, it must be understood. And where was Argyll?

Old Airlie cursed Argyll, and by implication the Lord Gordon, and advised that young man to let the Devil look after his own. The King's Grace expected better than that of Gordon. But Montrose was more careful. He conceded that they were only come as friendly visitors, and were grateful indeed for any hospitality Gordon might furnish them, after weeks in the heather. Argyll was far behind, and was not likely to try conclusions with Gordon in Gordon country.

Huntly, it seemed, was still discreetly absent in the far North. And the impetuous Lord Lewis, now nineteen, remained with the Covenant forces of the North-East, somewhere in Buchan. Aboyne, of course, was still in England, fighting for the King. The remainder of the brood were here, and although six years older than on Montrose's first visit, were as noisy, untidy and unruly as ever.

Later, after a chaotic meal, protracted, with a piper strutting up and down the hall, blowing lustily the while, children shouting, dogs barking, and the general chaos which seemed endemic to this establishment even when its master was not present, when he could get George Gordon alone and in quiet, James Graham put the matter to him straightforwardly.

'Once, you told me that you were the King's man,' he said. 'And now the King's cause suffers hurt for lack of horsed men. You can supply such horsed men. By the thousand. And do not.'

'Not I, my lord Marquis. My father.'

'Your father is as good as abdicate. He has left his clan in your hands. Yours must be the decision, now.'

'No! Who am I to go against my father's expressed wishes, in this? To put hundreds, thousands, of men's lives at risk? For a doubtful cause.'

'Your liege lord's cause, my friend.'

'Once, my lord, you said to *me* that our liege lord, having chosen bad counsellors, fell to be shown the error of his ways. That God's cause was higher than the King's.'

'Aye. You do well to remind me. I said it, and meant it. And still hold to it. But, under Archibald Campbell and the fanatic preachers, God's cause has been perverted, shamefully betrayed. The King is still the Lord's Annointed. He gave in to all the Covenant's fair and legitimate demands. And to more. His cause is now God's cause.'

'Many in Scotland think otherwise,' the younger man said.

'No doubt. But when has Gordon – or Graham – acted on the thoughts of others? Think for yourself, my friend.'

'Think you I have not thought a-plenty!' the other cried, his unnatural calm cracking. 'It is not as *I* think – but as my father thinks. He it is who commands, not I.'

'He has left you in the rule of the clan. Himself prefers to bide afar off.'

'No. My father is still chief of Gordon. Wherever he is. I only act for him. And he has said that no Gordon shall be lent to the Marquis of Montrose, my lord. That is his express command.'

'But – he is the King's man. Ever has been. He boasts of it. He does not love me, no – and perhaps with reason. But he loves Charles Stewart. Will he sacrifice the King for his hate of *me?*'

'He holds that you are not the King's friend, or ever have been.'

'I am the King's Lieutenant-General. Hold his royal commission.'

'He also holds the King's commission. As Lieutenant of the North.'

'Then should he not be fighting for the King? Using his Gordon host in the royal cause? See you – it need not be used *under* myself. I care not who commands the Gordons – so long as they fight for the King. *You* lead them, my friend. I will give you commission as a major-general. An independent command. Be your own master. Do not serve under me. But co-operate with me, for the King's sake.'

Nibbling his lip, George Gordon shook his head unhappily. 'It is not possible, my lord. I would it were. I would fight with you, serve under you. Gladly. But I will not go deliberately counter to my father's wishes. Would you have *your* son do so?'

It was Montrose's turn to hesitate. 'No-o-o,' he admitted, at length. 'I would not. But, nor would I divorce myself from my responsibilities, and leave my son to face them. With his hands tied. That I would not.'

The other said nothing.

'See you,' James Graham went on again, urgently, 'the King's cause requires your cavalry more than anything. I ask you, in God's good name muster your men. If you will not serve with me, or independent of me – at least have them muster. Argyll will not know what you intend. Will go warily. Give him pause – and me time. Though you do not strike a single blow, will you do this, my friend? Not for me – for Charles Stewart?'

'I . . . I do not know. I shall have to think on it. My father would not have it so – that I *do* know . . .'

'Think, then. Remembering what the King's Grace will

347

expect of Gordon, in his hour of need. Seek the advice of your lairds, if you will. Straloch, your father's chamberlain. Consult your conscience, above all. I will wait . . .'

Montrose waited at Strathbogie for three days, not in the castle but in camp with his men. In that time a few Gordon lairds came to him, offering support – but not the Lord Gordon. They were all small men, and welcomed gladly, with Nathaniel Gordon active in persuading them, some kinsmen of his own. But their offerings did not increase his strength by 200 all told, and less than a quarter of that horsed. The large lairds, with the mounted followings, awaited their lord's commands.

Then, on the 24th of October, the Graham could wait no longer. Word was brought that Argyll was nearer than he had anticipated, less than two days' march away. Worse, this unaccustomed speed was accounted for by the fact that he had been reinforced by no less than fourteen troops of regular cavalry under Montrose's own old lieutenant, the Earl Marischal, who remained loyal to the Covenant, and had been sent north by Leslie, with the Committee of Estates adding the Earl of Lothian as second-in-command in case the Marischal should fail in his duty. The royalist irritation, obviously, was to be disposed of, and quickly. And William Keith, the Marischal, had always been a hot-tempered, hasty young man.

Montrose, ordering an immediate move, went for a last appeal to George Gordon. But there was no moving that unhappy but dutiful son. His father's will must prevail in this matter. He would not muster Clan Gordon. The best he could do, he declared in evident distress, and apparently at Straloch's suggestion, was to offer a single troop of say 100 cavalry, not as any sort of contribution but purely to escort the royalists off Gordon territory. If it served to make the Lord Marquis's force look slightly the stronger, from a distance as it were, that was as might be. But it would return at the limits of Gordon land, and would on no account draw sword on their behalf.

Montrose looked at the young man, his handsome features set. 'Very well,' he said, carefully. 'If that is the best that Gordon can do, in this pass, I accept it. As King Charles's Viceroy. I thank you.'

George Gordon turned and strode to a window, to stare

348

out. 'I am sorry . . .' he said over his shoulder, his voice choking.

So the King's army left Strathbogie, some 800 strong, with less than 250 of it horsed, and 150 of that number under orders not to fight.

26

WITH THE WORD THAT ARGYLL – OR RATHER, THE MARISCHAL, who in this context was the greater menace – was coming up Donside, circling the Correen Hills, by Alford and Lumsden, Montrose headed eastwards for the upper Ythan and Gight rather than into the wild hills, westwards. On two accounts. In increasingly wintry conditions it grew ever more difficult to feed and forage his host in empty mountains; and there were still vast Gordon lands far to the east, in Formartine and Buchan, remote from Strathbogie, where Huntly's writ might run less strongly, according to Nathaniel Gordon.

They camped that first night in the bare uplands west of Rothienorman, above the Ythan, the Gordon cavalry keeping very much to itself and looked on with suspicion by the rest. The maintaining of adequate scouting parties had been a big problem for long now, owing to lack of the necessary horsed men; but with Argyll's slow if steady pursuit this had been of no great moment, a small cavalry rearguard serving the main purpose, with a few pairs of riders well ahead and to the flanks. At Strathbogie, Montrose had relied on Gordon's own in-built system of intelligence – and that now proved to have been an error of judgment. Next morning, they had barely left camp when couriers arrived, from Strathbogie admittedly, but grievously delayed, almost too late. The Covenant cavalry under the Earl Marischal, it seemed, had moved on fast, far ahead of Argyll's main army, and was now only a short distance behind.

Nathaniel Gordon looked grave when he heard that the

349

couriers thought the large cavalry force had passed the night in the Culsalmond area – and it took a deal to sober that optimist. If this was true, they could be on them in an hour or two, he declared, knowing the country. Montrose, who was a comparative stranger to these uplands, demanded at once where was the nearest defensive site. It was bare open country of green grassy slopes hereabouts, ideal for cavalry. No use in telling the infantry to disperse and make a bolt for it; they could be ridden down and hunted like hares by hounds. They must fight, whatever the odds. Was there any position which they could reach in time, where they could make a stand? Any Gordon castle, for instance? For such were apt to be set in strong natural sites.

None worth calling strong, the other lamented, amidst a volley of curses. The nearest castle was Towie, a Barclay place and a fine house – but not strong. Fyvie was better five miles to the south. But it was a Seton hold, the Earl of Dunfermline's, allied to Gordon. It stood amongst the Ythan marshes. But the Earl did not live there. And his sympathies were doubtful . . .

'Marshes, you say? Fyvie, amongst marshes? How far?'

'Four miles. Five. In the Ythan valley, north-by-east. The castle stands on a spine of higher land in the flooded valley. A sour place . . .'

'Then Fyvie it is! With all speed. Pass the word. Hasten!'

The infantry almost at a run, they turned in their new direction. And as they went, Gordon of Lethangie, in command of the cavalry escort, drew up to Montrose's side.

'We leave you now, my lord,' he cried. 'My orders are that we be concerned in no fighting.'

'But . . . dear God, man! We have not even *seen* the enemy! At least bide with us to Fyvie. Draw no sword, if you must not – but *be* there. Five-score cavalry, in a prominent place, could save a day, without moving a foot!'

'No, sir – my orders were clear. To leave you at first hint of conflict. And – you intend to fight.'

'I intend to fight!' the Graham agreed, grimly. 'Go, then – and God pity Gordon!'

Nathaniel thereof swore himself hoarse.

One hundred and fifty men short, they reached Fyvie without interception, and found it much as described. The Ythan here sprawled in its fairly narrow valley amidst bogland, water-meadows and scrub, with a long narrow loch to the east. There were islands in the waterlogged vale. Two were linked by a low ridge of higher, drier ground. On that to the south clustered the village – a strange place of turf-roofed huts and wooden cabins, whose folk must have webbed-feet, according to Colonel Sibbald. And on the higher end of the ridge, to the north, soared the tall and handsome brown-stone castle, with drum-towered gate-house and three other great towers, turreted, gabled and splendid, although with an air of desertion. It had been the seat of the ancient Thanes of Formartyne, though much of the present building had been erected within the last century by the great first Earl of Dunfermline, Chancellor of Scotland, grandfather of the present rather feeble lord. Montrose eyed it all assessingly.

'We shall give a good account of ourselves there,' he said, to Johnnie at his side. 'Charles Seton was my friend once. We shall assume his hospitality in his absence!'

'Will . . . will it be bad?' the boy asked. 'We cannot win, can we?'

'No, I fear we cannot win, lad. But it may be that we can keep *them* from winning. With God's help. Which may serve.'

'We cannot all get into that castle. What of those left out . . . ?'

'None of us will be in the castle, Johnnie. It would be but a trap. We will hold this wooded ridge, between the river and that marshy loch. Backs to the loch, which cannot be crossed. Castle on our right flank, village on our left .River and bog before us. Afoot, where cavalry cannot reach us.'

John, Lord Graham, swallowed, and tried not to look dismayed.

Black Pate was away with some of the precious cavalry now, scouting, watching the enemy, reporting back. The Marischal, following the line of their former advance, had eben taken by surprise at the turn towards Fyvie, and had overshot towards the east, on the way to Gight. He had now turned back – but it allowed them a little longer. He was in major strength, in three groups of some 500 each – dragoons, trained heavy cavalry. Argyll, with his thousands of foot, was still miles behind, to the south, but coming up as fast as he might.

That message, reporting 1500 horse, was like a blow at James Graham's heart. But he allowed no hint of his distress to show. His fifty or so remaining cavalry he spread along the summit of the spine, where they were very evident, and, interspersed with scattered thorn trees, might seem rather more than they were. In theory they were commanded by the Earl of Airlie, but in fact by Nathaniel Gordon, who would lead in any desperate action. The foot would be divided into three companies of less than 200 each, to man the west slope of the ridge, amongst the trees and stone dykes – but later. Meantime all must be massed to hold the south approach to the ridge, from the village – for this was the only approach for cavalry, the Ythan and its belt of haugh- land and water-meadow being too soft for horses. Montrose would have held the village itself, if he could; but his num- bers were too small. There was a drystone dyke across the spine about 300 yards north of the houses, with a gateway for the road to the castle. That must be their holding line, with open ground before it. All men with muskets to man that wall.

Hardly were these dispositions completed when Pate Graham and his dozen horsemen came back at the gallop, hotly pursued by a troop of Covenant cavalry, so close had been his shadowing. They clattered through the village, now discreetly deserted by its inhabitants, and into the elongated box which was the royalist position – and a volley of precious ball from O'Cahan's veterans brought down a few of their pursuers, and warned off the rest.

Pate actually had a prisoner with him, a sergeant of Lothian's dragoons captured from a picket they had sur- prised. He informed that the Earl Marischal was in personal command just behind, with his brother George Keith lead- ing one cavalry group of 500, and the Earl of Lothian the other. Argyll was thought to be some four hours' march away still with more cavalry and some 4000 foot, the latter in two sections, one much farther forward than the other which accompanied the baggage and artillery.

They had not long to wait. In gallant if alarming style, the Covenant horsed host appeared over the skyline of the Cairn Hill shoulder to the south, rank upon rank, in good order, banners flying, a daunting sight.

Soon trumpets were blowing, as the Marischal perceived

the situation, and drew up his squadrons in a great extended line, scores deep. In contrast, the three-score royalist horse, however carefully placed, looked little short of pathetic.

'Thirty times our number!' Pate Graham growled. 'Damned traitors!'

'Not that,' Montrose demurred. 'Misguided, shall we say? Fellow subjects misguided. William Keith was ever head-strong. But no traitor.'

However headstrong, the Keith was not precipitate now. The problems, from a cavalry attacker's point of view, were all too apparent – debarred from making any assault on three sides, and the fourth narrow, and partially blocked by the village, which might well be held. He could not know that Montrose's men were desperately short of powder and shot.

After quite prolonged deliberation, the enemy moved on towards the village. Halting his front ranks just out of musket range, the Marischal dismounted a troop of about one hundred, and sent them creeping forward, skulking behind dykes and hedges and barns, to test the village defences.

When it was established that the houses were not held, the cavalry moved on, but warily, clearly fearing a trap, Montrose's reputation as a tactician inhibiting all.

Beyond the village, the spine of higher ground was barely 200 yards wide. There was open, cultivated space, with some orchard, before the first barring drystone dyke with the gateway to the castle in the centre. Every foot of that dyke was manned, with every musket the royalists possessed. But such was the lack of ammunition that there was not enough for two complete salvoes.

When the Covenant leaders were almost within range, Montrose rose from his hiding-place, ordering a single shot to be fired in the air. 'Will Keith,' he called into the sudden hush. 'You ride under the banner of your King's enemies. It is my hope that you come to place yourself under my command, as His Grace's Lieutenant-General, as is your duty. If so, your past offences will be overlooked. Also those of your company, so be that you serve the King loyally hereafter. That on my word. If not, you will suffer my wrath, and the King's forthwith.'

There was a pause, and some laughter from the ranks opposite. Then the Earl Marischal spoke. 'James Graham –

my lord Marquis – I do not wish you harm. My orders are to convey you before the Committee of the Estates. At Edinburgh. I have no lack of men to serve that duty. Many times your numbers. And my lord of Argyll approaches, with a great army. Yield you then, I pray you.'

'I repeat, my lord Marischal – make your loyal duty to myself, as royal representative. Or I open fire on rebels. Quickly, my friend.'

'I tell you, it will not serve, Jamie . . .'

Montrose cut him short, nodding to two marksmen with muskets aimed over the dyke, glowing matches at the ready. They fired, and gravel and dirt spurted into the air a yard or two in front of the Earl's horse.

The beast reared in fright – and not alone in that. Being cavalry, this mounted host had no muskets – which could not be fired from the saddle, requiring supports – but only flintlock pistols, with less than half a musket's range. In considerable confusion the front ranks reined round on the crowded pack behind. Quite a few pistols were fired, but to no effect. A distinctly unseemly retiral was made to the houses.

'They must attack now,' James Graham called along his lines. 'Hold your fire until you are certain of a hit. But before they gain pistol-range. Every ball must tell. The horse cannot jump this dyke.'

The inevitable charge came quickly. Two troops came spurring forward, yelling, with a third trotting more slowly behind. Knowing that their mounts could not leap that wall, they came bunched, five or six abreast, making for the gateway, some 200 very brave men, hoping by sheer weight and momentum to break through. It was like a clutch at the heart for the Graham to give the order to fire – for this would be sheer massacre, and these were his fellow countrymen. But what option had he?

It was the pistols that fired first, and uselessly, morale-aiders only. Then the slaughter, as the royalist muskets brought down their targets in flailing, screaming ruin. The dragoons had no least chance. The first ranks crashed like ninepins – and the others tripped and stumbled into and over them. The rest sought to spread right and left, inevitably, even though there was no possibility of passing the wall in front. These merely died at closer range and more dispersed.

In only a few seconds, a troop and a half of dragoons were down, without inflicting a single casualty on the defence. The survivors swung away and round, desperately, and ploughed back into the supporting third troop. With good sense, these turned also and streamed back to the village.

'Mary Mother – I'm hoping they will not try that again !' Colonel O'Cahan cried. 'We have used up most of our shot in one stroke.'

'I think not. They will attempt the waterside now,' Montrose said. 'They have no other choice. A score of your best marksmen, Colonel. As near the river as they may venture. Take shot from others. The Master of Madderty's bowmen behind them. Spread along the slope. In cover. You will find good targets, I think.' He sent a trumpeter out into the shambles in front, under a white flag, to announce that the Earl Marischal could recover his wounded, unassailed.

There was a quite lengthy interval thereafter. Then the anticipated infiltration along the riverside haughland commenced. A troop of horse began to pick their way through the reeds and willows there – and quickly were in trouble. In a dry summer it might just have been passable for cavalry horses, but after a wet autumn it was a quagmire. Only by most careful testing and probing could the riders make slow and individual progress. And as they came within range, marksmen with bow and musket picked them off one by one, at leisure. It was a quite hopeless endeavour – so long as arrows and shot held out.

The enemy did not fail to recognise the fact. The attempt was soon called off.

'What will they do now?' John Graham asked.

'They could dismount their men and send them in on foot,' the Earl of Airlie said. 'Men could cross that soft ground where horses cannot.'

'They could. But I do not think they will,' Montrose reasoned. 'They cannot know that we are short of powder and ball. They have only pistols, until they get close enough for lance and sword. They could be shot down while out of range as was the cavalry charge. They will not take kindly to fighting on foot, see you, being regular cavalry. And why should they – when they have us bottled up here, and have only to wait for Argyll's infantry to come up? I say they will wait.'

'And if they do? What will we do then? When my lord of Argyll comes?' his son demanded, voice less than steady.

'We will counter the Campbell as best we may – and pray for God's aid. But meanwhile we shall not waste such time as we are granted. There is much to do, trenches to dig . . .'

James Graham's assessment of the situation was accurate. No further attacks developed. Stalemate had been achieved, meantime.

While the trench-digging and barricade-building proceeded, Montrose repaired to the castle of Fyvie. Its keeper was an elderly kinsman of Dunfermline's, who wanted no worse trouble than he found himself in already. When it was announced that the castle was being taken over in the King's name, he offered no opposition. The Graham did not set about further fortifying the place, however, contenting himself with requisitioning all foodstuffs and forage, and setting up a rough manufactory in the old kitchen for moulding musket-balls, stripping the roofs of lead for the purpose. Fortunately, there was no lack of it. A squad of men were soon working hard.

It was late afternoon before Argyll arrived – and for every minute of that delay Montrose gave thanks. Again they watched the endless files of men come over the shoulder of Cairn Hill, this time with only the officers mounted, in the main. Keenly James Graham watched that vast, slow-moving column, so much less gallant than the Marischal's had been, but more menacing in these circumstances, and assessed its numbers at some 2000. Which meant that this was only about half the Covenant infantry force. Presumably Argyll had left his slower-moving units and baggage behind, hastening on with these. Two or four thousand would not greatly affect the issue, however, as far as the 650 royalists were concerned. What was highly important was that there seemed to be no artillery present. Again the Graham praised his Maker.

The thought of his particular, personal enemy so close at hand had an almost physical effect on the man, incompatible with his God-inclined thanks. He knew a churning within him, almost a nausea. It was sheer hate, he knew, deplore it as he might. He had to control himself sternly.

Archibald Campbell was seldom the man to rush matters.

But with only two hours of daylight left, any attack to be made that day had to be launched quickly. Within thirty minutes of the infantry's arrival, an assault was mounted. As Montrose expected, it was ostensibly on two fronts, the main advance along the riverside, with a diversion straight up from the village. This meant that the royalist force had to be spread out grievously, most of it facing west along the wooded spine, with no massed concentration at the dyke, as before. O'Cahan's men were left to defend that front on their own. They were all now reasonably well supplied with ball, and these were the veterans of the force. But it would inevitably be touch-and-go.

About four companies of foot, something under 1000 men, made the main riverside move, creeping along the reedy bank just out of effective range, parallel to the royalist positions, ploutering and floundering in the marsh and mire but managing to make progress where the horsemen had failed. It took them some time, and there was nothing Montrose might do to stop them. Presently, at a trumpet signal, they halted, and turned to face eastwards forming a quarter-mile front. Then, at another blare, a great hullabaloo developed on the short village front, with musketry and shouting and milling of cavalry. Under cover of this feint attack, the riverside assault commenced.

This was the real test, as all the defenders well knew. Once the enemy infantry won out of the soft ground, it would be hard to halt them – and no doubt Argyll would be throwing in more men than these. They would be well equipped with muskets. To face them, sheltered by the scrub woodland and dykes, plus the trenches, Montrose divided his force left, right and centre. He left O'Cahan and his six-score veterans to hold the short village front, facing south. Along the west-facing river front he put Sibbald, with the remnant of the Athollmen on the left, the Master of Madderty and his bowmen on the right, while he himself took the centre. The cavalry still waited, prominent on the ridge.

At first, the advantage lay with the defence, who had cover, a firm base, and for the time being sufficient ball. In the musketry exchange they undoubtedly were a lot more effective than the enemy, who suffered many casualties, out in the open. But numbers told, and the attackers came on undeterred. And as they advanced, in short rushes rather than concerted charge, more men picked their way along the waterside behind them to take their places. When these were in a position to give covering fire, the first waves made better progress. And once these won their way up onto the firm ground, with broom bushes and the like to hide them, their advance was inexorable.

Thirty yards or so before the thicket woodland, Montrose had had his men dig the first and principal trench, a very rough ditch and rampart amongst tree-roots and stones, with the soil piled into a parapet riverwards. This now proved to be an enormous asset, against which the enemy flung wave after wave of men, between musket volleys, without success, losing large numbers. But the royalists were now running short of powder and although Madderty's bowmen on the right supported them wonderfully, with a vicious hail of shafts in flank, when the powder ran out the trench had to be abandoned, since it then became a death-trap for men fighting only with sword and dirk.

With the first of the attackers actually penetrating the skirts of woodland, and the second wave leaving the waterside more or less unmolested, Montrose recognised that drastic action was necessary if all was not to be lost. He ordered O'Cahan and his Irish and Islesmen to leave their position by the south wall, where they had stood more or less inactive, with no real attack developing from the village, to mount one of their terrifying Gaelic charges, with cold steel, from the left flank. They were to be replaced at the dyke by some of Sibbald's Athollmen. And Black Pate was sent racing, to make a minor cavalry gesture on the right flank, with a dozen or so horse, in the hope that it would be assumed that considerably more would in fact be committed. He sent young Johnnie to Airlie and Nathaniel Gordon sternly forbidding them and their fifty mounted men to move from the ridge meantime.

O'Cahan's charge was magnificent. One hundred and twenty strong, his company leapt in sword-slashing, yelling fury, shouting their Celtic slogans, bounding slantwise across the scrub-dotted slope above the river, sweeping the advancing Covenant infantry aside like chaff. Montrose had given Pate his trumpeter, and now, with much blowing and to-do, horse-men dashed into action on the right, supported by a lesser but noisy charge of about fifty of Madderty's Drummonds. As the advancing enemy faltered, Montrose ordered a general advance, ridiculous in fact as this might be.

It turned the tide – of this attack, at least. The already wavering ranks broke and ran, pursued back into soft ground by the shouting if far less numerous defenders. As ever when a front breaks and bolts back through a supporting force, chaos ensued.

Montrose did not rush forward with his centre. As commander, he knew what he would do were he in Argyll's or the Marischal's position. A flank attack at this moment, from the village, could change all. Only some seventy Athollmen held the dyke – although the enemy could not know that. He hurried to take charge of them.

He was too late. He had been prepared for a fairly massive infantry assault, under heavy covering musket-fire, on the narrow front; but not for another full-scale cavalry attack over the killing-ground already littered with most of two troops of dead dragoons and their mounts. But this is what emerged from the cluster of houses, tight-packed, rank upon rank of horse, pennons fluttering, trumpets blowing, cheering, a daunting sight for seventy men behind a dyke.

Montrose, while still running, began to shout, saying to hold their fire almost until pistol-range. But the Athollmen were not trained veterans like O'Cahan's kerns, however stalwart. Before their commander's words were able to have any real effect, they had begun to shoot, wildly, haphazardly, at long range. They emptied a few saddles and brought down a few horses – but made no major impact.

Urgently Montrose turned and waved to his impatient horsemen sitting up there on the ridge. Nathaniel Gordon's raised hand and ringing cry answered him, as he dug in his spurs.

Gathering a few men round him to guard the vital gateway through the wall, Montrose shouted to the remainder of the Athollmen to retire a little way, back to the shelter of the tree-trunks, so as to keep out of pistol-range. Shoot from there.

Then came confrontation as the cavalry swept up to the very dyke. They tended to bunch towards the gate, naturally – and it was the leaders who reached it first. Montrose, using a hastily grabbed musket now, saw the pale face of William Kerr, Earl of Lothian, one-time colleague and shot his horse from under him. He saw also George Keith, the Earl Marischal's brother, go down with a ball smashing his forehead in bloody horror. Other leaders were crushed against the shut gate itself by the weight of horseflesh behind. The gate's timbers splintered and crashed. But there was no pouring through. The fallen men and horses piled up, to form their own limb-lashing barrier. Some behind did manage to clamber over – and were promptly shot. The gateway held.

All along the wall horsemen were rearing up, ranging back and forth unable to leap it, cursing, firing their pistols, being crushed against the stones by the press coming on. But it was only a drystone dyke, and already men dismounted, deliberately or otherwise, were pulling, clawing, at the stones. By keeping below the level of the wallhead, raising their arms to it, these could not be shot – even though they might be trampled down by their own colleagues. It was only a question of time, brief time, before there would be gaps for a breakthrough.

Then, with ringing cries, the royalist horse thundered down on the rear flank of the Covenant cavalry. Fifty upon 500 is poor odds; but a downward slope, impetus, an attack to the rear, plus sheer desperation, make potent allies. They created major havoc. Montrose caught just a glimpse of his son John charging down just behind Nathaniel Gordon and Sir Thomas Ogilvy – and cursed himself for failing to command the boy otherwise.

Now there was complete confusion on both fronts, men fighting everywhere at close quarters, with little that even the best leadership could do to regulate affairs. Another squadron of Covenant dragoons thrown in at this juncture could have changed the entire scene – but strangely enough was not forthcoming. What did happen was that Magnus O'Cahan and his wild men came storming back, warned by the trumpeting with which the enemy horse had heralded their charge. Just as portions of the wall fell his Gaels with their dripping swords hurled themselves upon the first through the gaps, crouching, to slit the horses' bellies with their dirks, blocking the entries again, even clambering over to launch themselves from the walltop, crazed with the bloodlust.

It was just too much for the now leaderless dragoons. They broke right and left, and streamed off, pursued by the yelling Irish and Islesmen. Both Covenant attacks had failed.

Montrose shouted for his trumpeter to sound the recall.

He was stooping over the fallen George Keith when Johnnie rode up, flushed, eyes alight, sword in slender hand – but, his father was thankful to see, unblooded sword. He gabbled excited words, and Montrose forbore criticism. Then the boy looked down at Keith, and his flush faded. He put his hand to his mouth.

'What now?' Airlie demanded. 'Will they attack again? They have the men ...'

'I think not,' the Graham answered. 'The sun has set. It is near dusk already. Dark within the hour. They could not mount another attack in time. No, they will wait until morning, I believe. And by morning, God willing, we shall not be here!'

'Ha ... !'

'Colonel Sibbald – the trumpeter, under a white flag. To the Earl Marischal – not to Argyll. I will not have dealings with the Campbell. Tell the Marischal that he may remove his wounded. Tell him also, with my regrets, that his brother is dead. Pate – see you to the wounded – all wounded. And put those screaming horses out of their pain ...'

'Permission, my lord Marquis, for my men to collect powder from the dead enemy,' Colonel O'Cahan came to enquire, panting. 'We have scarce a snuffboxful left between us.'

'To be sure, my friend. I think you can do so unassailed, now. And – Colonel, you and yours played a hero's part this day. I shall see that the King hears of it. And recommend that His Grace bestows the accolade of knighthood upon a most valiant soldier.'

The dark Irishman smiled, and bowed. 'A man does what comes naturally, in such pass,' he said lightly. 'But – my thanks. Did I hear your lordship say that we are to be out of this? With the dark?'

'You did. Six hundred cannot fight six thousand for overlong. And when Argyll's artillery comes up, we are lost. On this island in the marsh. We shall slip away under cover of night, secretly. The old man in the castle, Seton, says that there is a way through the bog. To the north-east. A causeway of a sort, between the loch-head and the Tifty Burn. Just passable for horses, in single-file. He will lead us. I trust him – for he desires only to be quit of us. We shall leave camp-fires burning here, where they may be seen. And steal out when the men have rested and eaten, horses led. Now – go gather your powder ...'

Four hours later, after replenishing the fires, the royalist army snaked away in utter silence from Fyvie, its castle and its ridge – and found none to interfere with this quiet going, although all the slopes to south and west blazed with the lights of the Covenant host.

The clash at Fyvie would not rank in any annals as a great battle, nor yet a victory; but as a military exploit it was one of the most extraordinary of the troubled century.

27

IN THE GREAT HALL OF THE LARGE AND ANCIENT CASTLE OF Balvenie, in Banffshire's Glen Fiddich, a lofty thirty miles west of Fyvie, Montrose was reluctantly holding a council of war. At least, that is what he called it, though in fact it was nothing of the sort – for he himself knew what he intended to do. It was, rather, an adding-up of accounts, an opportunity for heart-baring – though scarcely his own – and a test, a test of loyalties, of staying-power, of determination. And James Graham had put off making it, almost afraid to do so, until that morning's courier from the South had forced his hand. His was a sensitive nature not difficult to make afraid – however little his fears were allowed to show or to dictate his actions.

In the flickering light of two great log-fires beneath the pointed vaulted ceiling, which but emphasised the grey, wet gloom of the mid-November afternoon, he looked round at the faces of his officers and companions – so pitifully few of them round that long table which could have seated five times their number. He was even glad of his young son's presence there, to help swell the company – to such ebb had they sunk. Besides Johnnie, Pate of Inchbrakie was there, and Graham of Gorthie; the Earl of Airlie and his sons Sir Thomas and Sir David Ogilvy; Colonel Magnus O'Cahan and the Master of Madderty. That was all, all above the rank of captain, in the King's army of Scotland. These, and their host, Sir Robert Innes of Innermarkie and Balvenie, with his son – looking doubtful, as well they might.

Montrose cleared his throat. Thin, worn, he still carried his head high, and his courtesy was consistent. 'So, my friends – there you have it,' he declared, into the argument which had developed. 'Argyll is content to fight, for this winter season at least, with other weapons than sword and musket. Weapons more to his own taste, I think! But sharp, see you – sharp.'

'The man is a dastard!' old Airlie growled. 'We all know that. But that sound men should heed his lying, deceitful words, play his foul game – this is the crowning shame. Betrayal – it is nothing less! The man Sibbald I could believe it of – a mercenary, his sword for sale to the highest bidder. But gentlemen, like Hay and Drummond and Nat Gordon! To buy their skins at the price of their honour! Treachery...'

'No, no – not that, my lord. I will not have it so black!' Montrose protested, if a little wearily. 'Do not judge our friends so hard. They have served the King, and myself, so very well. Be not so sore on them because they have not quite so great hearts as your own. These were against a winter campaign, from the start...'

'As was I. And am still,' the Master of Madderty interjected.

'I know it, John. And you shall have your say. But do not let us call those who have elected to leave us traitors. Because they have had a sufficiency. The Campbell's blandishments are potent. His promises of pardons, lands, gold, to all who will desert my banner – these speak loud to weary men who have already given so much for the King's cause. I do not find it in my heart to blame them, merely because I·myself am beyond the range of the Campbell's generosity!'

'But Nat Gordon...!'

'The Gordon has not defected, my lord. Only seemed to do so. Of a purpose. I may reveal it now, within these wall, I think. Nat has gone as my envoy, to the Lord Gordon. Seeming to accept Argyll's offer of indemnity, like the rest, but in fact still in my service. To remain at Strathbogie and seek to play upon his young lord on our behalf. Never forget as I do not, that north of Tay only Gordon can provide the King with the cavalry we require. The numbers necessary. Nat, a Gordon himself, believes that he can work on George Gordon, in his father's absence, to alter his stand. And on Straloch, the chamberlain, his own near kinsman, who has great weight with the young lord. Better that he should be so employed in these winter days than traipsing the Highland hills with us, and no cavalry to command – for that is his worth.'

The Earl shrugged. 'As you will, James. But these others – Drummond, Hay, even Sibbald. If these are not traitors they are cravens at least.'

'Even that I will not allow, my lord. All have shown themselves brave men. Steel, mark you, is not all of the same strength and spring. Some swords will snap before others, if bent too far. As we, my friends, all have been bent those past months. I but thank God for you that remain to me. And pray that I keep you by me, even so, until better days. Colonel Sibbald I grieve over. He fought with me at Morpeth, and rode with Rollo and myself from Carlisle, secretly into Scotland. A good soldier. But . . .'

'But tested, and found wanting!' Sir Thomas Ogilvy put in, shortly.

'Perhaps the testing was too stern? Who am I to judge? Even you, Sir Thomas? Or your brother? Or your noble father, here. I shall not judge *you* if even you are tested too hard.'

'What do you mean, my lord Marquis?' the quiet Sir David asked.

'I mean, my friends, that I have ill news for you. The same courier who brought me news of Argyll's seducing of our friends, brought me other news also. I have scarce known how to tell you. Your brother – and your elder son, my lord – who is my friend and comrade-in-arms, the Lord Ogilvy, we all know was captured in England on his way to Oxford soon after I left Carlisle. Now he has been bought – *bought*, mark you – for gold! For £1000 sterling. By the Campbell. To be *his* prisoner. So hot is his fire. Brought to Edinburgh. Confined in the Thieves' Hole of the Tolbooth, like the foulest felon!' The Graham's voice quivered. 'That any man

364

calling himself Christian, and fighting in the name of religion, should so act ... !'

Sir Thomas had half-raised himself from his seat. But at a gesture from his father he sat again, tense-featured.

'Nothing is beyond the Campbell,' the older man said, carefully. 'I have learned that lesson, ere this. And he hates my house. But . . . Ogilvy will fight him from a pit in Edinburgh's Tolbooth as Ogilvy does from these Highland hills! My Jamie will give *MacCailean Mor* no satisfaction, there or anywhere.'

'It will not be all black hatred, my lord. He will seek to use your son to bring *you* to his heel.'

'Then he is a fool as well as a dastard and a rogue!' Airlie growled. 'Jamie will not yield him a word, much less a whimper. And nor will I!'

Montrose spread his hands. 'What can I say, in face of such steadfast constancy? Save to salute the house of Ogilvy. The King's Grace is fortunate in *some* of his friends, at least!'

'My lord Marquis,' Sir David said, 'we but take yourself as model.'

'Aye, and do not tell us that the Campbell reserves all his spleen for Ogilvy,' the Earl added. 'Since he hates you still more than he does me.'

The other nodded, his handsome face composed, his voice almost expressionless. 'You are right, my lord. Archibald Campbell has not forgotten Graham. I learn that he has ordered the imprisonment of most of my kin and friends. Innumerable of the house of Graham, in the South. My good-brother, the Lord Napier, and his son. Aye, and their womenfolk. Stirling of Keir, and his. John Fleming. And many more. My castle of Mugdock is sacked and despoiled, and much of my other lands harried. Southesk, my good-sire, is to ensure that there is no traffic between my wife and children and myself – on pain of excommunication! And has so agreed. Here is how King Campbell makes war – in the name of the Lord Jesus Christ and no quarter!' With an obvious effort, James Graham controlled the voice which had risen and harshened. 'Forgive me, gentlemen. All this is scarce to the point. Save to sharpen our resolve. What *is* to the point is that I have sure information that Argyll is not now following us, but has turned back. Is making his way down Strathmore for the South ...'

'*Dia!* We gave him his bellyful at Fyvie, then?' O'Cahan cried.

'I think rather that he, at least, has no stomach for a winter campaign in the mountains.'

'In that, on my soul, he shows good sense!' John, Master of Madderty averred.

'You think so? I do not, John. It is a backward step. He has a great army – but has won no battle. He will garner no credit with this – and a general must have credit, as I know to my cost! Covenant Scotland and the Committee of the Estates will only accept his retiral, and a winter's inaction, if *I* do no more. If we are equally inactive. And I do not intend to be!'

'Ha! What means that, my lord?' Graham of Gorthie demanded.

'I mean that we should surely use what we have. However small. Now only 500 men, yes – and no cavalry. But 500 toughened, fast-moving, light of foot, unburdened by gear. Five hundred who can climb mountains, cross bogs, swim rivers, live off the land. You, Colonel O'Cahan – tell us what such a force may achieve, even in winter mountains. You, who have led the like.'

'Anything, my lord Marquis – anything, by the Powers! So be it that *you* lead it!'

'Thank you, my friend. Would that I could be worthy of your so great trust. But at least we can achieve much, where others could not. Or *would* not. And so will not think to look for us. I propose to march through the great hills, up Spey, into Badenoch again. It is Huntly's country, but less under his hand than this. We may gain men there. And from Badenoch slip down through the passes to Atholl, once more. The back door to the country where most of us come from. Drawing men from there into our ranks. And then, gentlemen – strike west!'

'West . . . ? To Colkitto?'

'Partly. But mainly, my friends, to Argyll itself. Inveraray. The Campbell's homeland. Teach *MacCailean Mor* what it means to take up arms against his liege lord. On his own secure doorstep. Without cavalry we cannot fight a Lowland campaign. But we can attempt a Highland one. And the Campbell homeland deserves a taste of war, perhaps . . .'

He knew, of course, that he would have them, with that

366

programme. He could not go on, for the noise, the stamping of booted feet, the banging on the table, the cries of acclaim. Even old Sir Robert Innes, their host, who was scarcely concerned though a loyal King's man, applauded with the rest.

Only Madderty doubted. He declared that they would never get volunteers such as they needed, for a winter's campaign, especially horse, which was the prior requirement. Now that the pressure from Argyll had relaxed, he believed more than ever that they should take a much-needed rest, to regain their strength; and spend the winter months secretly visiting their friends and possible supporters, seeking enlistments rather than actually campaigning.

Montrose acknowledged that there was some sense in this. But he held that there were dangers too. Lose impetus and it might be exceedingly difficult to restart hostilities. Better to keep going – especially when the other side was flagging. Moreover, word of the King's cause in England was not good, and Charles badly required encouraging news from Scotland. It was their duty to give him it, if they could.

He had his way, of course. They would move up Spey, for Badenoch, next day.

It was ten days later that a courier reached them in the Dalwhinnie area, some way north of the grim Pass of Drumochter which linked Badenoch and Atholl, in their camp by the rushing Truim amongst the snow-covered mountains. He was an Atholl Stewart, brother of one of the men with Montrose – and his news was startling. Argyll himself, with a large part of his foot, was less than thirty miles away. He had billeted his men at Dunkeld, on the very verge of Atholl, but was himself now at Blair Castle, pressing the young Earl of Atholl to change his allegiance. He seemed to be settling in for the winter in that area, and was attempting to seduce the loyalties of the lairds round about, with a mixture of threats, promises and money. All his cavalry were dismissed to winter quarters in Perth, Fife and the south.

It was dusk when the Stewart arrived, but despite this, and the windy dark, within an hour the camp was struck, and all were ready to move. Before they set off, James Graham spoke to the assembled company, by the flickering light of the last camp-fires.

367

'My good friends and companions,' he said, 'we face an unexpected challenge and opportunity. Your enemy, and mine, the Marquis of Argyll, is all but within striking distance of us here. Unsuspecting. At Dunkeld, his troops settled for the winter, his cavalry gone south. I had not believed that he would remain so far north, on the verge of these Highlands. He is seeking to lay Atholl under his evil sway. The homes of many of you. Are you with me in surprising the Campbells?'

The throaty roar greeting that left no doubts as to the reaction.

'I need not tell you what it would mean to the King's cause, to all Scotland, if we could capture Argyll ... ! Wait, you! Wait, you! I have boasted of you, my friends, that you can cover more miles of this land in fewer hours than any other men living. Now, prove it! You know the shortest way to Blair, where the Campbell has come to threaten the young Earl. Thirty miles by the roads men follow. But less through the mountains, I am told. How long until you are chapping at Blair Castle door?'

'By daybreak tomorrow!' somebody yelled, and there was a gleeful shout of approval.

'See to it, then. And I with you ...'

So, leaving Lord Airlie to bring on at a more modest pace the older men, those slightly wounded, and such as might hold them back, some 350 of them set out on as major a physical test as could have been devised for an armed force, even mountaineers. It was not a march, more of an endless loping trot, by drove roads, cattle-tracks, deer-tracks and no tracks at all, contouring dark hillsides, ploutering through bogs and peat-hags, crossing high passes, threading woodland, wading rivers. There was half a moon, fitfully shining through scudding clouds, and for late November the weather was reasonably kind. But conditions for travel were appalling nevertheless, and could only have been endured by such men as these, hardened hillmen and veterans, toughened by hard campaigning and challenged to their utmost, travelling light, untrammelled, bearing only shoulder-slung swords, pistols and dirks.

They avoided the long, long bend of the main drove road threading the Pass of Drumochter by heading almost due eastwards, climbing high to start with, up the deep scar of a corrie, or hanging valley, and so over the snowy ridge of Carn na Caim and down over wicked country to lonely Loch an Duin beyond. Here they could turn south down the Edendon River, mile upon mile of it, the watershed behind them. The snows of the upper reaches at least meant that the bogs were frozen hard. But it was a killing journey.

At last the Edendon brought them down into the main central valley of Atholl, at Dalnacardoch where they joined the drove road again, having saved almost six miles. At least they had had no lack of guides, for many of the Athollmen knew even this empty wilderness. They had covered some thirteen savage miles, and taken almost seven hours to do it. Already Montrose was desperately weary, not yet fully himself after his sickness of six weeks earlier. Stewart of Dalnacardoch, roused at two hours past midnight, provided cold venison, raw oatmeal and whisky. All had a little. His son was with the party.

There was still a dozen miles to go to Blair, and before they were half-way down the wide Strath of Garry, it was sheer spirit that was keeping James Graham going, a determination at all costs not to fail the others – and not to betray legs of clay, as well as feet thereof, to young Johnnie who was still going strongly.

With the moon setting behind the black mountains of Craiganour to the north-west, they reached Blair-in-Atholl thirteen hours and twenty-five miles after leaving Glen Truim, a feat possibly unrivalled in Scots military history for any large body of men on foot. There and then, silently, avoiding the township which was the home of not a few of them, they surrounded the great castle, and began to close in.

They were fairly near before the alarm was raised. Montrose had his trumpeter sound the summons and make his presence and identity known. But known only to the Countess, the Earl's mother – not to Archibald Campbell. To the grievous disappointment of all, they learned that Argyll had moved back to Dunkeld the previous afternoon, taking young Atholl with him. Their Homeric efforts had been in vain.

Dunkeld was another twenty miles to the south. And Argyll's main force was there – although in cantonments, unprepared for fighting. Montrose decided to press on. But not yet, hardly yet. Flesh and blood, his own in especial, was capable only of so much. They must have rest, food, refreshment. A few hours ...

It was mid-forenoon before they set out once more, their fine enthusiasm not quite recaptured, though still they went fast, Montrose refusing the offer of a horse. They were almost at the junction of Tummel and Tay, with Killie-crankie and Moulin behind them, when a small party coming in the other direction halted them. It was the young Earl of Atholl returning home.

He was only a little older than Johnnie, and in a great state of excitement. All was well, he cried, to Montrose. All was well. Argyll was fled.

Astonished, unbelieving, the Graham questioned him. It seemed that, while they had slept at Blair, somebody had slipped away, on a fast horse, to warn the Campbell at Dunkeld. And whenever that man had heard that Montrose was so near with an armed force, he had flown into a dire panic, declaring that he was betrayed, that all was lost, that his encamped troops were in no state for fight. And without more ado he had taken horse for Perth and the South, leaving the Earl of Lothian to do as he thought best. He had not so much as taken leave of Atholl.

'But ... but this is madness!' the Graham objected. 'There are less than 400 of us. He must have thousands at Dunkeld. Has the man taken leave of his wits?'

'The messenger did not say but 400, my lord Marquis. He but said Montrose was coming with a Highland host. That was sufficient for *MacCailean Mor!* He believed you on his heels – and fled.'

'Dear God – and this is the man who holds Scotland in thrall! This he who sets himself up against his King, the hope of the Lord's elect!'

'What to do, now? Argyll was escaped; and however unprepared, the camp at Dunkeld was now warned. There could be no surprise. Atholl estimated between 3000 and 4000 men there – and even if their general was a craven, these would not be all the same. More than ten times their own number.

Reluctantly they turned back. Bold grasping of an opportunity was one thing; foolhardiness quite another.

Back at Blair they waited for Airlie to turn up; and then

stayed longer, welcome, to give the Athollmen a chance to see their own people, and to seek to rally more to the royal standard. Argyll's extraordinary behaviour aided them in this. – although it was recognised that when Montrose was gone, the Campbell and his threat would re-emerge. Over another 100 volunteers were added to their strength.

They were still at Blair, safe behind the closely guarded Pass of Killiecrankie, when ten days later there were surprising developments on two fronts. Word came from Dunkeld that the entire military scene was changing. Argyll had gone straight to Edinburgh, where he had had but a cool reception from the erstwhile loot-licking Committee of the Estates, who now criticised his generalship. In high dudgeon the Campbell had there and then resigned his commission as commander-in-chief of the home forces and shaken the dust of Edinburgh from his feet – while still, of course, reserving the right to make all important political decisions. He had retired to Inveraray and his own territories. What is more, he had commanded all his Campbell levies, which made up the main bulk of his present infantry, to return home to Argyll forthwith, likewise. If the Covenant leadership did not appreciate his services as a general, they could see how they got on without him, and his.

Evidently in some considerable confusion the Committee had been unable to persuade either of the Major-Generals, the Earl Marischal or the Earl of Lothian, to take on the thankless task of commander-in-chief. Neither would the Earl of Callander, commander of the Borders area, consider it. In desperation they had turned to old Leslie, in England, and he had sent them an almost unknown individual, one of his own major-generals, by name William Baillie of Letham, a veteran of the Gustavus Adolphus wars.

Montrose, although intrigued by the news, was less delighted than were some of his lieutenants – for he knew Baillie, and had few doubts that a professional soldier as commander-in-chief would prove a more potent opponent than most high-born amateurs. But the resignation of Argyll was heartening and significant – even though it was only as general that he was stepping down. He would remain the political master of Scotland. The tidings therefore, although an unexpected present encouragement, could also mean more effective military measures against them hereafter.

The second development was more consistently heartening, and as unanticipated. The day following the first, all at
Blair were excited to hear the distant sound of bagpipes –
intrigued rather than alarmed. Coming from the north, no
attackers would so advertise their approach. All were agog
to see what this could mean. When a large host appeared in
sight, marching down the strath, there was some misgiving.
But when the proud black-and-white Galley of the Isles
standard could be distinguished flying at the head, and
beside it the Red Hand banner of Ulster, there could be no
doubts. Colkitto was back.

Montrose went out to meet the prodigal, forgiving all,
thankful of heart. But as he and his neared the front ranks
of the host, even the mighty figure of Alastair MacDonald
failed to monopolise the attention. For, flanking the blond
giant, was such a galaxy of eagles-feathered Highland chieftains as the Graham had never before seen at one time, fierce-
looking, barbarous-seeming men, dressed in tartans, both
kilts and trews, calf-hide jerkins, antiquated armour and
helmets, with Celtic jewellery, bristling with symbolic arms,
pride emanating from them in an almost visible aura.

'Major-General Alastair – I rejoice to see you,' Montrose
cried. 'With all my heart, I do. And . . . in such bonny
company!'

'Ha, my lord Marquis – I see that you are on your feet
again, by the Mass! I heard that you might have work for
me, once more! And for mine.'

'Always I had that, my friend.'

'Aye. Well, see you – I have brought some kin of mine.
You will not fail to know their names, I think.' He turned
ceremoniously towards his right. 'It is my honour to present
Sir James of Sleat; Aeneas of Glengarry; John of Moidart,
Captain of Clanranald; Alastair MacRanald of Keppoch;
MacIan of Glencoe; MacIan of Ardnamurchan.' He paused
there, for effect – as well he might.

No comparable play-acting was required of Montrose. A
sensitive man, he was in fact concerned that tears of emotion should not well up into his eyes. For this resounding
catalogue represented the greatest clan in Scotland, greater
even than Gordon or Campbell – the Clan Donald Federation. Here were the chiefs, or their near representatives, of
the age-old dynasty which had been undisputed rulers of

the North-West and the Hebrides for half a millennium. He held out his hand, stirred as he was not forgetting to do so in due order of precedence, the same in which they had been presented.

'Gentlemen – you gladden my eyes and my heart,' he cried. 'I salute the Sons of Somerled !'

That pleased these proud Islesmen, it was clear – although none actually smiled as Montrose grasped each hand.

Colkitto was not finished. 'And here, to present to *An Greumach Mor*, is Clan Gillean. Sir Lachan Maclean of Duart; Hector Maclaine of Lochbuie; Ewan Maclean of Ardgour; Lachlan Maclean of Coll.'

'I greet the great Clan Gillean.'

'Here is Alan of Locheil, Captain of Clan Cameron; Mac-Master Cameron of Letterfinlay; MacSorley Cameron of Glen Nevis.'

'I rejoice to meet the MacGillonie, the Camerons of Lochaber.'

'Moreover, Seumas my friend, here is Duncan Stewart of Appin; Alan Stewart of Ardsheil; Ian Stewart of Invernahyle; and Dugald Stewart of Achnacone.'

'The Royal Race ! My salutations . . .'

And so it went on. With meticulous care, Colkitto presented group after group of chiefs and chieftains and captains, all in their due order, rank and precedence. And as heedfully, Montrose acknowledged them, thankful not only for their presence there but that he could remember sufficient of the Gaelic polity and tradition to greet each properly and aptly. For these men were prouder of their ancestry and lineage than any grandees of Spain, the proudest probably in all Christendom, and easier to offend by any failure in address or order. Yet they were some of the finest irregular fighters ever born – and for that the Graham's heart was full. Even though apparently they had brought with them no more than some 500 clansmen, mere token 'tails'. But engage and involve these chiefs, and they could provide their thousands.

That Colkitto was highly pleased with himself over producing this impressive support for the King's wilting cause, went without saying. That they were all probably more deeply imbued with hatred of the Campbell than with loyalty to King Charles was beside the point. Colkitto had been operating for the past month or two on the northern fringes of Argyll, raiding into Campbell country – a proceeding which commended itself to all other western chieftains. However much they might disagree with each other, their antipathy to *MacCailean Mor* was sufficient to produce a kind of unity when opportunity arose to smite the Campbell with some degree of success. Colkitto had promised them such smiting, and consequent rich pickings, in this laudable pursuit.

If the adherence of these Highland chiefs provided its own problems, at least it cleared Montrose's mind as to what must be his next move – something which had been concerning him not a little. Now there could be no question. He had to continue to concentrate on Archibald Campbell. And since the Campbell had retired to his own fastnesses, there they must follow him. Mid-Argyll was a vast natural fortress, of course; and no major assault on its central citadel area had been attempted for centuries – not since the Bruce's campaign against John of Lord in 1308, when the hero-king had won his brilliant victory at the Pass of Brander. Modest hit-and-run raids such as Colkitto had been engaged on, mere pinpricks, were always possible, on the perimeter; but full-scale invasion was something other. There was probably not a commander in Scotland who would even consider it. But, on the other hand, neither Archibald Campbell nor anyone else was likely to expect it, therefore. It had taken the immortal Bruce to do it before. He, James Graham, might humbly try his hand – with God's help. Only so could he make best and enthusiastic use of his imposing new supporters. And the King's cause meantime could as well be served in Argyll as elsewhere.

So it was decided. They would leave Atholl and turn their faces to the west, marching by Breadalbane and Mamlorn. And, God willing, they would teach Archibald Campbell who was king, even in Argyll.

Quickly thereafter Montrose learned how difficult a team he now had to handle. For Breadalbane was itself now largely Campbell territory, stolen from the MacGregors, MacNabs and lesser clans, by the Glenorchy branch of the Campbells. And Colkitto and his friends were for letting the Campbells of Lawers, Balloch, Lochtay-side, Finlarig, Glen Dochart and Strathfillan learn something of what it meant to have the

same name as *MacCailean Mor,* as it were en route. James
Graham's insistence that this should not be was not well
received. Indeed it looked almost as though the authority of
the King's Lieutenant was going to be flouted before even it
was acknowledged – for these men he now spoke to were
little kings in their own way. He declared earnestly that
surprise was the very basis of anything they might achieve
against Argyll. Forfeit that, and they might as well remain in
Atholl. They must avoid all such populous Campbell areas
like the plague, meantime, lest word be sent to Inveraray.
Their turn might come, afterwards . . .

That the Graham had his way, in the end, was thanks
wholly to patient persuasion and nothing to command.

28

GOD, IT SEEMED, ON THIS OCCASION, WAS WITH MONTROSE –
or so decided the Highland chiefs. As well He might be, of
course, since it was the heretical, Covenanting and thrice-
damned Campbell who was equally His enemy as well as
theirs. For that month, from mid-December 1644 to mid-
January 1645, the wind blew lightly but steadily from the
east, cold but dry, frost and clear skies, sun by day, bitter,
splintering starlight by night, such consistent cold as had
not been experienced for long – but dry cold. For moving an
army across the very Highland roof of Scotland, nothing
could have been better. No snow fell – and what was already
there was solid as iron. Rushing rivers were frozen over, and
crossable. Bogs became level, if slippery, highways. The
passes were not drifted up. All the natural hazards of winter
travel in the mountains were modified – for men who could
cope with the cold. This, admittedly, was terrible – but there
was fuel in plenty, for Breadalbane and Mamlorn were well
wooded with the old Caledonian pine-forest. And cattle were

available in large numbers, huddling conveniently on the low ground, not scattered over the ironbound hills – and being Campbell cattle, and therefore free, tasted the sweeter. Whatever the chiefs thought of present Montrose tactics and strategy, they recognised his luck. And acknowledged his energy, and the sustained speed of their going.

They made excellent time indeed, in this epic move – for nobody had thought to transport an army, now numbering some 3000, across the highest and broadest barrier of Highland Scotland, in deepest winter, in memory of man. Even the Bruce had done his Argyll campaigning more seasonably. Leaving Atholl on the 11th of December, they marched south first, to Tay, and then west up Strathtay by Aberfeldy – taking the opportunity to pay a call at Castle Menzies, at Weem, and take into custody Sir Alexander Menzies, who had betrayed Montrose before Tippermuir. His strong links with the Campbells might well make him a useful hostage. Then on down both sides of Loch Tay – carefully avoiding any assault on the Campbell castles there however, much as the chiefs grumbled. In long Glen Dochart they were joined by quite a large contingent of MacGregors and MacNabs, welcome recruits, whose hatred of their dispossessors, the Clan Campbell, was deep and personal indeed. And these saved a bloody encounter at the narrows between Loch Dochart and great Ben More, where a hastily assembled party of Glenorchy men might have held them up indefinitely; and Montrose was shown how to avoid the pass by a secret route on a high terrace to the north. Then up Strathfillan to Tyndrum, where they had a most unexpected adherent – none other than Patrick Campbell of Edinample, brother to Robert of Glenorchy himself, who had quarrelled with his brother and Argyll both, a shifty character but who also might be useful. The long pass of Glen Lochy, under Ben Lui, then opened before them, stark white, bleak savage – but unguarded by man. Through its grim miles they passed unopposed, until the wide lowlands of Loch Awe spread spectacularly before them, a stirring, heart-lifting sight after the close constriction of the mountains. It was the Campbell homeland and very fair.

They had thus reached the borders of the central Argyll citadel in five gruelling days, eighty miles across the high hunched back of the land. And without a single conflict worth so calling. It seemed highly unlikely that any warning could have gone ahead of them, to Inveraray.

Kilchurn Castle, the large and strong main seat of the Glenorchy Campbells, stood in an almost unassailable marshy site at an inlet of the great loch ahead of them. To take that would be difficult and time-consuming, without artillery. But it had to be neutralised somehow – and especially prevented, from sending a warning boat up the twenty-three-mile length of the great loch, from which word could be got over the hill to Inveraray on Loch Fyne. Fortunately, Campbell of Edinample, who had been reared here, knew how the lochward approaches to the castle could be blocked by means of a boom across the narrows of the inlet – part of the place's defences against attack by water. The boom was permanently there and only a constricted channel had to be blocked, and no boat could get past. A small party was given this task, and the guarding of the boom thereafter. Montrose was loth to thus use the services of a traitor – but dealing with Archibald Campbell made such scruples too costly.

Farther west still, the mighty jaws of the famous Pass of Brander yawned, barring off all central and coastal Lorne. This was where Bruce had won his great victory, improbable as it seemed. Bruce had not been aiming at Inveraray, however, but at Dunstaffnage, John MacDougall of Lorn's fortress. It was on the MacDougall's consequent fall that the Campbells arose. So Montrose did not require to seek passage of that fearsome gorge between the steep sides of towering Cruachan and the deep black waters of Awe. But it had to be sealed off, nevertheless, lest any enemy assault developed through it, to outflank them. So he sent a detachment of 200 MacGregors and MacNabs, the former once owners of this territory, to stop it – and 200 could hold up 10,000 there, one way as the other.

These dispositions taken, the Graham faced south along the loch-shore.

Loch Awe-side was rich, fertile, long-settled and sheltered territory, highly populous. The loch lay in a north-easterly and south-westerly direction, averaging just under a mile in width. On the eastern side, the access to Loch Fyne area was by a small pass some six miles onward and so down Glen Aray to Inveraray itself, nine miles. But that was the way any attack would be expected to come, and almost certainly it would be kept well guarded. A much less convenient approach was to the north, across high boggy trackless moors to the headwaters of the Shira River, and so down its long waterlogged glen to Fyne. In normal conditions this would be almost impassable for any large body of men, however agile. But with the country frozen solid, it almost certainly could be done. Colkitto, with 500 of the toughest men, would attempt it. But there was still another way over into Loch Fyne-side, almost equally awkward. This entailed proceeding two-thirds of the way up Loch Aweside, to a place called Durran, from which a steep and difficult bridle-path struck off up over the intervening range, eventually to descend into Fyne-side some seven miles below Inveraray, also traversing undrained and evil uplands. This would be Montrose's own route, with the main body.

But there was still another factor to be taken into account. The *west* side of Loch Awe was also fertile, if somewhat less populous, and would have to be taken care of likewise if warning was not to be sent to Inveraray by boat up the loch and then over the hill. Moreover away beyond the head of Awe, the coastal lands of Kilmichael and Kilmartin were densely populated, and could raise thousands of men, who could come up Lord Fyne from its foot, if warned or summoned. The fact was that this whole area, aroused, could produce 10,000 men in a couple of days, and fierce fighters, defending their homes. This must be avoided at all costs. So the veteran John of Moidart, Captain of Clanranald, the most experienced in war of the Highland chiefs, would take another 500, and attend to the west side of Awe, making sure that there was no burning, to send smoke columns of warning high into the still air; and thereafter proceed over into the coastal plain to the south, to block any reinforcement of the central Inveraray citadel from thence.

So the three divisions parted company, with Montrose himself still commanding the best part of 2000 men. Before him, along the eastern lochside, he sent a swift advance party of 300, under Magnus O'Cahan, with instructions to do no fighting but only to seal off any routes and tracks over the hills south-westwards, so that no warnings should go ahead of them; and especially to hold the point, at this Durran, where the main body would branch off, seventeen miles

ahead. No Campbells were to climb up on to those intervening hilltops, to light warning beacons or smoke-signals.

It was midday as they moved off, with a bare five hours
of daylight left to them, and vast mileages to cover. Despite
the temptations of fat Campbell houses, farms and townships,
for Highlandmen with old scores to settle and booty to be
won, Montrose was adamant that there should be no harrying and time-wasting. And certainly no burnings. All that
could wait. They had richer targets ahead. Fortunately, and
advisedly, he had got rid of most of the high-born Highland
firebrands, with Colkitto, who might have felt it incumbent
upon them to demonstrate that they took orders from no
Lowland lord, even though he called himself *An Greumach
Mor*.

They made good time up Loch Awe-side then, despite the
grumbling, with the Campbell population prudently keeping
out of the way, cowering behind their doors and walls, fleeing discreetly into woods and ravines, as well they might, and
putting up no useless resistance at this stage. It was a green
and pleasant land, and ripe for spoiling, all agreed. But they
would be back. There was no snow down here, almost at
sea-level; but the frost remained hard as ever.

Montrose's eyes tended to look across the loch almost as
much as forward. Two things he feared from there – smoke
from undisciplined burnings, and boats setting off up-loch
to bear grim tidings. But neither materialised. John of
Moidart knew his task, and was authoritative enough to have
his men well in hand.

The early dusk found them half-way up the long loch; but
there was to be no halting this night. On they pressed, and
presently a thin sliver of moon rose above the south-westerly
hills slightly to light their way, and to glisten chilly on the
sparkling frost. Montrose sent word that the older and less
able could go slow if they would. Stop if they must. But the
main force must keep going through the night. None would
hear of hanging back, however, with old Airlie and young
Johnnie as examples – both insistent that they were good for
another ten miles at least. Montrose worried a little about
these two. His son was looking thin, these days – as indeed
were they all – but with dark rings to his blue eyes, and a
cough which, though not deep, seldom left him. He certainly
never complained, and seemed to have ample energy, never

379

flagging. But a father's anxiety was not to be quenched entirely. As for the old Earl, for whom the Graham had acquired a great regard, even affection, he was clearly being taxed to the utmost. He frequently fell asleep at the briefest halt, and collapsed of an evening into a kind of stupor.

At about 8 p.m., three hours after dark, they came up with O'Cahan, and a picket, at Durran, near the loch-shore. He had been awaiting them for hours, of course – but not altogether idly. He had sent most of his men over the bridle-path, to hold the high ground. Some were ahead, farther up the lochside. And others were just back, in a purloined boat, from a visit across the loch to see how John of Moidart was getting on. Their report was encouraging. Clanranald was almost level with this point, and going strong. He would be rounding the head of the loch by midnight. No boats nor messengers had eluded him, at least during daylight.

To take a host of almost 2000, in darkness over a 1200-foot ascent, by a narrow drove road in a rockbound land was a nightmare-proceeding almost beyond contemplation. The ascent, their guide told them – one Black Angus of the Glencoe MacIans – was over two miles long. Then there was three miles of lochan-pocked peat plateau to cover, and the descent of another two miles to Loch Fyne. Only the hard-frozen state of the land made it at all possible. But if one man could do it, Montrose declared, so could 2000. Given time.

It took them, in fact, over six grievous desperate hours, the stumbling across the terribly broken if iron-hard peat-hags of the high plateau quite the direst part of it. But by two-thirty in the morning, most of the now mile-long strag-gling column was down at salt-water, on the shores of the longest sea-loch in Scotland, at Inverleacann, seven miles south of Inveraray. At last, Montrose called a halt. Three hours for rest, he said. He had told Colkitto that he would look for him at the other side of Inveraray, at sunrise.

By 6 a.m. they were on the move again, half-asleep on their feet, cold beef, raw oatmeal and as raw whisky in their stomachs. Fyne-side was less densely populated hereabouts than was Aweside, but even so the passing of such a host could not go unnoticed, even in the darkness, with dogs to give tongue at every farmstead. Occasionally there were cries of men. Whether any raced ahead to warn Inveraray there was no means of knowing. Boats might well be launched on the dark loch to carry the news. That could not be helped.

Dawn of another cold, clear day found them at Dalchenna Point three miles south of their objective. They were on time – and so far they had not had even to draw sword.

Then, presently, ahead of them, distant, faint but clear, they heard the sound of bagpipes on the north-easterly air, many bagpipes, shrilling, ebbing and flowing.

Even as his heart lifted to the sound, Montrose frowned. That could only be Colkitto and the Clan Donald chieftains. None other would blow martial music before sunrise on a winter morning on Loch Fyne-side. The MacDonalds were *ahead* of time, then, not hiding their presence, and presumably not waiting.

It scarcely required the Graham to urge his weary host to greater speed. All perceived the situation. Practically at the run now they surged on northwards.

Rounding an intervening headland of the loch they saw their goal at last, capital of the Campbell's kingdom, a town of whitewashed houses and church spires, with the massive tall castle rising behind and above all. The blue smoke of morning fires was rising from hundreds of chimneys there. Down at the double jetties, fleets of boats lay moored. *MacCailean Mor's* great banner flapped lazily from the castle's topmost tower in the light breeze.

But even as they stared, two developments became evident. Black smoke, thick and billowing, began to rise amongst the blue, and across the still waters of the loch shouts and screams and the clash of steel came clearly though the shrilling of the pipes. And out from the cluster of shipping suddenly shot a large many-oared craft, with a covered canopy at the stern, to set a course down-loch at impressive speed, alone.

'Himself!' Black Angus, the guide, at Montrose's side, cried, pointing. 'The Campbell, whatever! The forsworn, devil-damned craven himself!'

'You mean ... ? You mean ... ?'

'Aye – by Christ God, I swear it! That is *MacCailean Mor's* own galley. None other like it, see you. He flees, the dastard – he flees, leaving all.'

Montrose shook his head, wordless. There was neither glee nor scorn in his mind, any more than satisfaction. Rather a sort of pang and anxiety. Would he ever succeed against this man, he wondered? For to fight a man adequately, one had to understand him. And he did not. He just did not know how Archibald Campbell's mind worked. And that, he was well aware, was highly dangerous.

They raced on to the town.

There was little to be done there – save to restrain the MacDonalds' savage ire. Half of the houses seemed already to be ablaze. Colkitto had pressed on, to the castle – whether or not he had guessed the significance of that fleeing galley.

There was only a token defence at the castle. By the time that Montrose reached its walls *MacCailean Mor's* banner was being hauled down, and the chagrined MacDonald chieftains were stamping about, cursing, at the discovery that their quarry was gone. The Graham had the greatest of difficulty in preventing them from putting all within to the sword there and then, and burning the building over them, in sheer frustration – after certain of the treasures had been extracted, of course. It was a fine house, and full of valuables. Argyll's wife and two sons were not there, being evidently domiciled meantime at Roseneath Castle in Cowal, far to the south, on the Clyde estuary – where, retainers informed, the Marquis was now proceeding.

So Inveraray, the vaunted Campbell citadel, fell almost without a blow struck. It was a wonder, an anti-climax of the first order, almost an affront, somehow. Men could hardly credit it, especially the proud chiefs, who went about as though somehow cheated, tricked, offended. Archibald Campbell's credit would never recover from this – at least in the Highlands. But that was scant consolation. Malice was not to be sated.

Montrose sought, with indifferent success, that at least it should not be sated, by proxy, on Inveraray town and district. Some harrying and spoiling there had to be, of course – it was the terms on which Highland armies fought; but wholesale slaughter, sack and destruction the King's representative forbade in the King's name. Not that his commands received strictest obedience. But at least no more of the town was set alight, and the proposal to hang every able-bodied man on a large extension of *MacCailean Mor's* already commodious gallows – where so many MacDonald clansmen had dangled – was negatived.

A large proportion of the population, in the event, escaped in the fleet of boats, leaving the town to the victors.

That night, in Archibald Campbell's hall, Montrose sat in Archibald Campbell's chair at the head of Archibald Campbell's table, while his colleagues and lieutenants ate and drank the Campbell's provision and made merry. MacDonald pipers paced up and down the great stone-vaulted chamber, blowing their hardest; captains and chieftains, many of them already much drink-taken, shouted and sang, banged their flagons and stamped their feet; Campbell serving-wenches skirled and squealed as they ran the gauntlet of lecherous hands; deer-hounds snarled and squabbled over bones and scraps. James Graham was no spoil-sport and enjoyed the relaxation of convivial company with any man. But he was tired, and not being addicted to the bottle, was stone-cold sober – which is a handicap in such circumstances. None better, he recognised that his hard-pushed supporters and allies deserved their recreation and amusement. Young Johnnie had fallen asleep over the table, at his side, and near by, Airlie snored. But if Montrose knew anything of Highland festivity, the noise and excitement would increase rather than lessen, soon the dancing would commence, the trials of strength, the outdoing of one's neighbour in song and story and muscle, and steel might well flash. These clan chiefs were only temporarily in alliance, with each other equally with himself; most of them were at timeless feud and rivalry. By the time such stage was reached, the King's Lieutenant intended to be safely if less than peaceably elsewhere.

It behoved him to say what he had to say soon, therefore, while men might still take it in – since it was important, and the morrow might present no opportunity. He banged on the table with his goblet, he rose to his feet and clapped his hands, Black Pate bellowed for silence – all to no least effect other than to wake up Johnnie Graham, but not the Earl of Airlie.

At length, taking up a great silver tankard half-full of wine, and engraved with the Campbell arms, Montrose suddenly hurled it crashing down the centre of the long table, with fullest force, after the manner of a curling-stone, whereon it smashed aside dishes, goblets and broken meats, spilling its contents and that of others, splashing diners,

383

shouters and sleepers alike, in a spectacular if limited ruin.

This, at least, attracted attention. Men jerked back, startled, and stared. Voices died away – even though the pipes and the hounds still gave tongue.

Montrose smiled at them all, gently, genially, and raised his hand to the pipers – who raggedly choked and wailed to a temporary close.

'My lords, chiefs, friends,' he said, 'a few moments of your time, I pray. I shall not detain you for long. But some matters require your attention, and I crave your patient hearing. Firstly, I would thank you, thank you all, from my heart. These last days, you have done what has seldom, if ever, been done before. What few might have believed possible to be done. You have nursed and coaxed an army across Highland Scotland in mid-winter in five days, most of it in hostile territory. You have made traverse of trackless mountains in darkness. I will not thank you for beating the Campbell in fight, since he did not stay for that . . .'

The roar of derision, abuse and contumely drowned his voice. He waited.

'So much for thanks,' he went on, when he could. 'Now for a word of warning. We celebrate here in Campbell's house – but celebrate what? One man's craven spirit? We have won no victory, gained no battle – save over rock and heather. One Campbell, and he *MacCailean Mor*, has fled before us. But there are others, my friends. You have not, for generations, hated – aye, and dreaded – the Campbells because of one man or one house. There are, I am told, over 150 Campbell lairds who can field over 100 men, some of them up to five times that number. And we are in the midst of their land . . .'

Again interruption, this time growlings and cursings.

'In two days, or three, my friends, 10,000 men could be surrounding this town. We have but a quarter of that, with John of Moidart still at the coast. Nor do the Campbells lack for leaders. Think of these – Campbells of Glenorchy, Auchenbreck, Dunstaffnage, Cawdor, Lochnell, Barbreck, Ardkinglas, Saddell – aye, and a host of others. Men of stature and power.' He paused, and looked down the table at Patrick Campbell of Edinample, who sat beside Sir Alexander Menzies, both not a little uneasy. 'How say you, Edinample? Are there not stark enough Campbell chieftains by the score to lead Clan Diarmid? Even though *MacCailean Mor* plays craven?'

'Plenty, my lord Marquis,' the Campbell agreed. 'And do not forget my lord Earl of Irvine, my lord of Argyll's half-brother. He is banished to Ulster by his brother. But could be back within the week, to Kintyre. Would that he were *MacCailean Mor,* instead of Archibald. Then, I swear, you would not be sitting in this hall tonight!'

That statement was received with mixed feelings by the company, and there were more than unkind glances directed at the speaker — with whom many of the chiefs had been loth to sit down in the first place, and only pursuaded by Montrose's firm notions of courtesy. All, James Graham included, were apt to forget Argyll's half-brother, James Campbell, Earl of Irvine, cordially detested by Archibald and living almost in exile on Campbell lands in Ireland. He was a man of some vigour and ability, it was said. If he came back to lead Clan Campbell in the field, there might be a different story to tell.

'You make your point, Edinample,' Montrose acknowledged. 'It behoves us, therefore, to watch how we go. To recognise that we are not victors in a conquered land — not yet. Let us not behave as such. We cannot *occupy* all this great Campbell land — such would take ten times our number, and more. And be unprofitable, besides. So we must seek to subdue it piecemeal, by careful campaigning. Our task has only begun ...'

There were less than respectful comments, protests, assertions as to what real men could and would do to this Campbell kingdom, claims that no Sassenach would teach true Highlandmen how to deal with Clan Diarmid. Even Colkitto demonstrated a defiant attitude. How much it all was strong liquor talking was not to be known.

The Graham allowed them their say. Then resumed, conversationally, easily, but assuredly. 'You fight under the King's banner. And under my generalship. So long as you do, my good friends, you will heed my commands. Your good advice and offices I will seek on all occasions, as to tactics. But as to policy, my decisions prevail. All understand that, I am sure?'

There was an ominous silence.

'Good,' he went on, smiling slightly. 'We have done great

things together, gentlemen. And shall do greater. But in order, and of a set policy. And that policy necessarily forbids widespread pillage and rapine of this country. For nothing is more sure to arouse and unite against us this whole clan and people. Bring them in fury about our ears. This you will understand, I am sure.' He raised a hand as the snarling began. 'Hear me. I say that you shall have your booty and spoil, in full measure. Campbell beasts and gear and goods you shall not lack. But it shall be done decently and in order. On the authority of the King's Lieutenant. I will have no burning and slaying and raping, no lawless harrying of this land. I will not have the King's name soiled, nor the King's cause jeopardised by such, and the wrath which it would stir up. Is it understood?'

Only a few men nodded or said aye to that – and none of them Highlanders, Islesmen or Irish, save only for Magnus O'Cahan.

Montrose looked around at a preponderantly hostile company. He smiled still. 'I do not know how best *you* impose your will and command, gentlemen, on your men. For myself, I intend to hang any in my own command guilty of disobedience to this. It is my belief that your own authority will be no less effectively upheld. I have not heard that any of you are backward in maintaining your supremacy.' He paused, to let that sink in. Then he nodded, and shrugged. 'I end, my friends, as I began – with my thanks and my esteem. And my apology that I should so interrupt your well-earned diversion. The night, and this house, is yours. I bid you enjoy it. Myself, I say a goodnight to you all.'

He bowed and touching young Johnnie on the shoulder, turned and made for the door. The clamour rose behind them.

Up in a small tower bedroom with his son – he could not stomach Argyll's own great bedchamber; Colkitto could have that – James Graham lay listening to the noise from below and riot from the town, long after Johnnie slept. It appeared to be his lot to seem responsible for the sack of towns, hate it as he did. But, dependent on the unpaid armies of fierce lords and chiefs, what could he do? Aberdeen had stained his name. He prayed that Inveraray would not further tarnish it. But he feared that the Campbell capital would not forget its Yuletide of 1644 for many a year.

29

THE SLEET-LADEN WIND SCREAMED AND SOBBED THROUGH
the pine-wood where 1500 men lay or crouched, wrapped in
their plaids, asleep. When the wind abated for a moment,
the noise of the waves on the near-by loch-shore filled the
night, in its place. It was the 29th of January, 1645, a month
after that celebratory feasting at Inveraray – and dramatic
was the change in the circumstances of the royalist army.

Montrose himself was not asleep, nor most of his remaining leaders – for this was only half the company that had
taken Inveraray, the rest having gone home with their booty
after the age-old fashion of Highland armies. He paced the
wet pine-needle floor now, head bent, brows knitted, a man
in the throes. Around him his officers watched and waited,
huddled shoulders hunched against the storm. None ventured to interrupt the Lieutenant-General now, none were
over-ready with advice. It was past midnight, and all save
the sentries had been asleep for hours.

Montrose halted his pacing in front of an elderly man who
sat, eating cold meat ravenously, on a fallen pine trunk.

'You say that Argyll has 3000 *Campbells*,' he put to him
'Before we left Inveraray we had word, from the South, that
the Estates had sent sixteen companies of infantry, Lowland
militia, under General Baillie, to *MacCailean Mor*. Are
these with him now also? At this Inverlochy? Are they
included in the 3000.'

'I know not, lord,' the older man said, his mouth full. He
was soaked, dead-weary, but tough, lean, despite his grey
hairs, a notable man if an odd choice as courier to send
over the winter mountains, Ian Lom MacDonald, the Bard
of Keppoch. 'Myself I have not seen them. Keppoch sent
me, just, with the word. He said 3000 Campbells.'

'But . . . a mercy, man – it makes a mighty difference! If

it is 3000 Campbells *and* sixteen companies of trained militia, see you, it makes a force twice as strong. How may I decide what I should do lacking this knowledge?'

'Your pardon, lord. I am but a messenger from my chief.' That was said with quiet dignity and reproof.

Quickly Montrose relented. 'Aye – forgive me, friend. I must seem both graceless and ungrateful. *Your* pardon, it should be. You have come far and fast, in evil weather, to bring me this news, and I thank you from my heart. *And* MacDonald of Keppoch. But – my problem is heavy, my choice hard. To press forward, as before? Or to turn back?'

'It is not for such as my own self to advise you, lord. But . . . you might save much of Lochaber, and Keppoch too, from the Campbell's wrath.'

'Aye – there is that also. You do well to remind me.' He did not rebuke the man that his chief, Keppoch, was no longer with the army, but had dropped off at his own country, with his men. 'See you – I am between two fires. Seaforth lies ahead, with 5000, at Inverness. Not more than thirty miles away. And now Argyll, you say, is on my tail, at similar distance, at Inverlochy. If I have to fight, I'd liefer fight the strongest first, while I am fresh. If Argyll has but 3000 of his own Campbells, he is less strong than Seaforth. And in hostile country, where Seaforth is not. But if he is joined by those sixteen companies . . . !'

Pate Graham spoke. 'Strike Seaforth, and you still have Argyll to deal with. Defeat Argyll, and Seaforth and his Mackenzies will melt back into their Kintail.'

'True. Or likely so. It depends on what Huntly said to him. But, if Baillie is now with Argyll we are up against an experienced general. I know him.' He turned back to Ian Lom, the poet. 'You heard no word of this General Baillie, from Keppoch? Or other leaders of Argyll's force?'

'None. Save only that Sir Donald Campbell of Auchinbreck leads, under *MacCailean Mor*. Who fell off a horse to hurt his knee, they do say.'

'More like running away!' O'Cahan commented briefly.

'Auchinbreck? He that was soldiering in Ireland? A hard man, they say. But a trained soldier. If he has Baillie also . . . !'

'Then there will be no doubt which army will be the stronger. To deal with first,' Airlie put in. 'I say, Seaforth

388

can wait. Even if he has Huntly in his pocket. And is reinforced by that fool Balfour of Burleigh, from Moray and Speyside.'

This was what had brought Montrose hurrying northeastwards from Inveraray five days before, in vile weather – the information that George Mackenzie, second Earl of Seaforth, had raised his great northern clan for the Covenant at last, and marched on Inverness with the declared object of linking with Balfour's force skulking north of Aberdeenshire. Worse, it was rumoured that he had come to terms with the disgruntled Huntly, who was still in the far North somewhere, and that it was his intention to enroll much of the Clan Gordon against Montrose. The Graham could not sit at Inveraray, whatever the weather, with such a threat building up behind him. He had decided to dash north and deal with Seaforth, before the slow-moving Argyll could organise the retaking of his kingdom, from Roseneath. But it seemed that Argyll, for once, spurred on by humiliation, had moved fast; and instead of merely setting things to right in his own territories, had pushed swiftly on to bring fire and sword into Lochaber of the Camerons and MacDonalds of Keppoch, at Montrose's back.

'Very well,' he said, sighing. 'We turn back. Seaforth can wait. Let us pray that he does not convince the young Lord Gordon, whatever success he has had with his father. For the Gordon cavalry could cost us all Scotland. We turn back, and at once, gentlemen. This hour we march, storm or none. See you to it . . .'

And so, thereafter, with even Ian Lom MacDonald saying that it was impossible, Montrose led his force southwards, by the selfsame route that the MacDonald had just come. The normal route, down the Great Glen from this Kilchumin where they were encamped, by the side of the River Oich, Loch Oich, and the long Loch Lochy, to where Spean joined the Lochy, was difficult enough, in winter. Did they not know it, who had just come that way? But thereon the Campbells would have their scouts out, their advance parties probing. To avoid them Ian Lom had come from Keppoch, in Glen Spean, by difficult and hidden ways to the east of the accepted route, by Glen Roy and Glen Turret, crossing the watershed of Teanga and so down into Glen Buck and the Calder Burn. Then avoiding Aberchalder and the gap into the Great Glen again, he had climbed steeply over another small watershed, high above the Oich's valley, and so down the Cullachy glen to Glen Tarff, the Tarff leading him down to Kilchumin here at the head of Loch Ness. He all but wept at Montrose's declaration that so he would lead them back to Spean and the Lochy. The passes were blocked with man-high drifts, he said; the rocks were glazed with wet ice; the burns were in raging spate; the wind was a yelling demon, on the high ground . . .

The Graham patted his shoulder, and smiled. 'You are an older man than most here, my friend. You, guiding us, will cross it again – and take us with you. We will find no Campbells thereon, I vow! To give word of us. We have done the like before, see you. We will not be put to shame by your grey hairs!'

Nevertheless, as they soon discovered, they had *not* done the like before. There was little comparison, in fact, between the traverse of the hard-frozen heights, on the way to Inveraray, and this storm-lashed hell of soft snow, roaring rivers and steep rock-bound mountains. They could not hasten, with every mile a challenge to muscle, wind and will, a trial, a torment and an achievement. By the direct route they had some thirty miles to cover to Inverlochy, where Lochy joined Loch Linnhe, and where Argyll seemed to have made his base meantime. By Ian Lom's route it was nearer forty. And averaged a thousand feet higher.

No words are adequate to describe that march. None who made it would ever forget a mile of it. Almost at the start they lost three men, swept away in fording the icy thundering waters of the Tarff. Then the fierce rock-climbing ascent of the steep hanging valley of Cullachy, with its half-frozen waterfalls and deep drifts, only two miles up to the watershed but two miles of sheer agony, rising almost a thousand feet, with the south-west, snow-laden gale battering in their faces. Across the bare peat-pitted high ground of Meall a' Chulumain and Druim Laragan they staggered no more than four miles from their starting-point and over four hours later, stumbling over hidden hags and rocks, deafened by the wind, breathless with the cold, weary already.

From the heights they slipped and slithered down a desperately steep burnside into Glen Buck, the valley of the Calder. It was wooded down there, and more sheltered; but the snow lay deeper and the river was in high spate. Daylight found them there. Montrose had been determined that they should get over that intervening high ground before dawn, however stormy a dawn; for though a thousand feet above the Great Glen, they had been little more than a mile from it, parallel, and would have been visible, crossing the open heights, to keen eyes below on the other side of the Oich valley. That danger was now past; and according to Ian Lom there would be no more similar hazards of discovery until they came to Keppoch and had to cross Glen Spean.

The climb out of the head of Glen Buck and over the high tableland of Teanga southwards to Glen Turret was the highest of all the route, reaching 2250 feet, an unrelenting inferno of screaming blizzard, of sleet now rather than snow, for over four miles. It took them almost six hours, men jerking forward with stiff, small steps, numb, almost blind, falling, tripping. Most of this army was bare-legged, in short kilts, with only worn rawhide brogans on their feet. Muscular Highlanders took it in turn to carry the old Earl of Airlie on their backs – to his own almost sobbing protests but the Lieutenant-General's commands. Montrose himself went much of the way his arm linked in his son's. It was mid-afternoon before they were staggering down short Glen Turret.

The wide, major but coiling Glen Roy now lay ahead of them, ten miles of it, in comparative shelter, its extraordinary terraces forming natural roads contouring both sides of it, good as even the Romans could have made – beaches of some forgotten loch, the learned said. Along these they could make better time, even though the soft snow thereon was a hold-up. Half-way down that long glen they rested for some hours, huddled in wet plaids, eating cold meat and raw oatmeal, lighting no fires. Although this was Keppoch country, Montrose was taking no chances. Keppoch itself was only five miles ahead, where Roy reached Spean, and a warm welcome would greet them from MacDonald, Ian Lom assured. But the Graham would have none of it. One tale-bearing traitor, one Covenant-inspired zealot, in the Spean valley, was all that would be necessary to bring to nothing all that they were suffering, he pointed out. One man hurrying down Spean to Lochy, to the Campbells, and all was lost. They would cross Spean by night, avoiding Keppoch, however wrathful its laird might be afterwards. He was willing to pay almost any price for the benefit of surprise.

That they did, then, that evening, leaving the wide mouth of Glen Roy well to the west of Keppoch, in driving rain and darkness, and fording the raging Spean at its wide shallows a mile and more downstream, at Coire Choille, using a human-chain device to help numbed legs and feet support their owners in the ice-cold waters. They turned up the Cour Burn thereafter, in fairly thick woodland – and almost at once ran into trouble, stumbling upon a foraging party of Campbells already camped for the night in the shelter of the trees. Black Pate and his advance-guard made short work of these, leaving none to flee with the news. It was an inglorious brief interlude, the Campbells being cut down as they rose from their plaids, given away by the glow of their dying fires; but it had a most enheartening effect upon the half-starved, half-frozen royalists – first blood in this contest.

On up the Cour and Loin Burns they trudged, and into the ancient pine forest of Lianachain, under the frowning outliers of the mighty Ben Nevis itself – even though they saw none of it.

Dawn found them still in the forest, with the rain ceased and the wind dropping. They were actually crossing another watershed, but a low one this time, no more than 500 feet high, and tree-covered, though the pines were stunted and wide-scattered. It was much less killing going for exhausted men – but still desperately slow. By midday they were dropping down into Glen Lundy – and the Lundy River ran for only four or five miles before emptying itself into the wide Great Glen again, into the River Lochy, only a mile or so above salt-water at the head of the great sea-loch of Linnhe. Inverlochy lay at the junction.

Two hours later they halted, a mile from the mouth of Glen Lundy, still in open woodland. They had accomplished the impossible. Not even the mighty deeds of the old Celtic sagas and legends could outdo the achievements of the last forty hours. Montrose, dizzy with fatigue himself, sought to praise, say his thanks – and could not.

Nevertheless, an hour later, as a murky sunset, the first such for days, was staining the waters of Linnhe and Loch Eil, its westward arm, the Graham and a small advance party under Black Pate, as always, reached the last of the trees in the very mouth of Glen Lundy and gazed out over the suddenly far-flung scene. Remaining carefully within the shelter of the pines, they stared. Directly ahead, wide and level, lay An Moine, the Moss, the flood-plain of the Lochy at the head of the sea-loch. And in strong position amongst its reedy flats, the massive walls of Inverlochy Castle rose on a grassy mound, a great quadrangular stronghold of lofty curtain-walls and rounded flanking-towers, antique in appearance. Semi-ruinous now, it had been the seat of the great House of Comyn, Lords of Lochaber, home of he whom Bruce had slain before the altar at Dumfries. The Gordons had gained it, eventually – indeed it still belonged to Huntly; but they did not use it, and the place was now mouldering away. But strong still.

It was not the castle, however, which held the Graham's interest and concern – even though, if Ian Lom was right, his arch-enemy might well be even now within those crumbling walls. It was the great camp which lay to north and east of it, amongst the scrub alder and hazel, where scores of evening cooking-fires gleamed and sent up blue columns into the sunset sky. He heaved a mighty sigh of relief. The Campbell host had not moved on. Their own desperate journey had not been in vain.

Montrose transferred his gaze to the land itself, its lay-out, features and scope. It was a terrain, from a military point of view, not so very unlike that of Fyvie, though on a much greater scale. There was the castle on its spine of firm ground, and a lot of wet and low-lying land around, with the impassable barriers of the sea-lochs to south and west. A strong defensive position – but this time it was not he who would be defending it. Nor had he any desire to attack such a position. His task was to bring the enemy to battle – but in a position where he himself would have the maximum advantage.

He did not dare peer for very long, in case there were keen eyes watching from that camp, or patrols circled it. Besides, the light was failing. One matter was clear. Whatever strategic surprise he might attain, *tactical* surprise was impossible – at least in actual attack. For, in front of him there was no cover or screening whatsoever. Glen Lundy opened widely on to the flat cattle-pastures. The moment

393

any large force appeared farther forward than these last trees, they would be seen. And they had a mile of these levels to advance over before contact – unless the enemy indeed advanced towards *them*.

Thoughtfully Montrose turned back, leaving Pate Graham, with a picket, to watch there. A night attack might get over the problem of the approach – but bring other and larger problems. He was handling wild and undisciplined troops, however bold – too bold. Without being able to *see* how the battle went, he would be quite unable to control them or the fighting. Night fighting might serve well enough for taking a difficult position; but for actually defeating an enemy army so that it would not reassemble and fight again later, it was of little use. Men could escape in large numbers in the darkness. The attackers would follow, and disperse themselves hopelessly. They might gain the central position, and seeming victory – but with most of the foe undamaged. For his present purposes Argyll had to be defeated in the field, and be seen to be defeated – otherwise their fine and hard-won surprise would be wasted. And it could not be repeated.

He had made up his mind by the time that he got back to his men, wet, cold and hungry, round the first bend of the valley. He conveyed his regrets to all, but they must put out those fires, and no more must be lit. They were less than two miles from the Campbell host, their presence unsuspected so far. It must remain that way. It would be an uncomfortable night – but surely nothing to the discomforts of the past two nights. At least they need not flog their bodies into movement. Tomorrow night, God aiding them, it would be different . . .

Presently Black Pate sent a runner to announce that two mounted patrols had left the Campbell encampment, obviously to make a circuit of the neighbourhood to see that all was well. One was heading in this direction. He requested instructions.

Montrose, half-asleep already, had to think fast. If such a patrol came up this glen any distance, it could not fail to discover them. And, mounted, some would certainly escape back to tell the tale. At all costs that must be prevented. He called for Cameron of Locheil, who was still with him – and who might be expected by the Campbells to be in the vicinity

394

anyway, with his home not five miles away – telling him to take a score of his men and hurry forward to the glen-mouth. Let the enemy discover them. Have a small clash with them, even. Then hurry away southwards, into the Nevis foothills. Draw them away. That should arouse no suspicions of a large force being near at hand. Marauding Camerons, keeping an eye on the Campbell host, were only to be expected.

Locheil gone, all waited tensely. An hour later another runner from Pate Graham came to tell them that there had indeed been a tulzie at the Lundy ford, some small swordery, and then the Camerons had fled off, into the hills, the Campbell horse after them in full cry. None had so far come back.

The encampment relaxed again.

It was near midnight when Locheil got back, grumbling at a frustrating and shameful task. He could have ambushed the wretched Campbells more than once, and ensured that none got back to Inverlochy to tell their story. But that had been forbidden, and he had had to play the feckless poltroon, leading them on into the nightbound hills. He had left them well up the slopes of Sgurr Finnisgaig. They might conceive the Camerons fools and cowards – but they would not conceive an army to be hiding near by.

Satisfied, Montrose thanked him, and resumed his attitude of crouched and shivering slumber. Not that he thought to sleep; too much was on his mind.

Some snatches of uneasy oblivion he did achieve that grim night; but long before dawn he was fully and finally awake, and had said his daily prayer. It was his wont to read a portion in his battered little pocket Bible, which he had always carried everywhere with him, at the start of each new day; but with no fires to give him light he could not do so this dark morning. He repeated a favourite psalm to himself, committed himself and the cause of the Lord's Anointed into God's hands – with especial care sought for his son John – and went to rouse the camp.

Well before daylight all were massed at the wide mouth of Glen Lundy, in a chill drizzle of rain. They watched the fires brighten in the great camp a mile away, as it came alive to another day. Not a man of his host would not have preferred to put all to the test there and then, with no more waiting, to advance under cover of darkness and fall on the unsuspecting foe. But it was not to be. That camp area was no suitable battle-ground; and there were ditches and drainage-channels in the mossy pastures between. Montrose had other plans.

When it was light enough to see what they were doing, and the exact lie of the land, Montrose quietly moved his people forward and some way to the south, extending them into a long line along the skirts of the foothills – which were in reality the first swellings of the mightiest mountain in the land. But he did not move them too far, either forward or southwards – and he kept almost one-third of his numbers back, to hide them behind a long grassy, whin-covered bank, too low to be called a ridge but sufficient to screen them from the west and north. The line he formed with the rest was nearly half a mile long and slightly crescent-shaped, with Colkitto and his Ulstermen on the right, O'Cahan, the Macleans and Islesmen on the left, and, recessed somewhat, in the centre such Highland chiefs as remained, with John of Moidart, Captain of Clanranald in command, with Glengarry. The hidden reserve behind was under another Ulster veteran, Colonel MacDonald, known for some reason as O'Neill, with Locheil and Stewart of Appin. Who was nominally in command of these clansmen was vitally important, since most of them would fight under none save their own chiefs. It made dispositions difficult for a general. The crescent-shaped front faced the Argyll camp and the old castle, at almost a mile's distance. But midway between, rising out of the flood-plain, was a sort of whaleback of firmer ground, not very high admittedly, but solid and fairly wide, with even some rock outcropping, and scattered whins. The previous evening, Pate Graham had pointed it out to his chief as the place for them. Montrose had merely shaken his head. He had perceived another use for it. That was, he prayed, for the Campbells.

At what stage the silent waiting host became apparent to the Campbells in the camp was not evident to the watchers a mile off. Certainly no sudden outcry arose, no obvious alarm. The waiting period had been partly filled, for the Catholic portion of the royalist army – which was the major part of it – by their priests stepping forward and making the sign of the cross with their arms while the men knelt bare-kneed in the wet grass and prayed aloud. There was no snow lying at this sea-level, and the drizzle had ceased; but the chill was daunting, especially for men with empty stomachs, stiff with wet lying. It was Candlemas Day, the 2nd of February. Let them pray.

But chilled waiting, and even prayer, was scarcely the best aid for morale in fiery Celtic troops; and presently, with indications that a wintry, watery sun was rising behind the vast rearing bulk of Ben Nevis, Montrose decided to seek to expedite matters somewhat. He had two trumpeters, his own and Colkitto's, for use in blowing certain basic calls during battle, advance, charge, pause, retire and so on. Now he unfolded the great and handsome Royal Standard – which he had carried these many grim miles wrapped within a plaid around either his own shoulders or his son's – and ordering the trumpeters to sound the Royal Salute, he had the silken banner hoisted high on a lance in the morning breeze, while the mountainsides echoed and re-echoed with the stirring, challenging bugle-notes. A great yell went up from the ranks of the Celtic host – and they would have surged forward there and then had not the leaders sternly held them back.

At last, visible reaction came from the Inverlochy camp. It was not to be credited that they had not been observed hitherto; therefore the enemy must have been making some hurried decisions and dispositions, even though nothing was visible from this distance. But now horns sounded from the Campbell positions and the movement of men became evident and purposeful. Then a flash drew all eyes and a single resounding explosion shook the surrounding hills. A column of water and mud spurted up from the flats half-way between the two hosts. An involuntary indrawn sigh spoke eloquently from the royalist ranks. Argyll could also make a gesture. He had artillery at Inverlochy, even though it was as yet well out of range.

Montrose frowned, but not too blackly. He had hoped that they would not have to face cannon-fire; but he had not excluded the possibility. They would only be field-pieces, here, pray God – in which case they could not have an effective range of over half a mile. He hoped what he had planned might nullify any such, in some measure at least.

Then, to the astonishment of all, Argyll staged another gesture. Three horsemen suddenly emerged from the castle gateway, and went cantering down the quarter-mile track

397

to the loch-shore, plain to be seen. There a number of small fishing-cobles were drawn up on the beach. Two of the horsemen dismounted, clambered into one of these, and were rowed out to a larger craft which lay moored offshore in deeper water. The third turned and trotted back to the castle with the horses.

None who had witnessed what had happened at Inveraray that other early morning five weeks before was in any doubts as to what this meant. That was a similar vessel, probably the selfsame galley in which *MacCailean Mor* had fled that day. Here he was at the same ploy, removing himself to safety before any possible danger could arise for himself.

A howl of execration, contempt and sheer fury arose from the royalist ranks – and was promptly answered by another shattering discharge, and a second cannon-ball – which did not reach even so far as the first. Somebody in the camp, no doubt Sir Donald Campbell of Auchenbreck, was more aggressively inclined than was the chief of all the Campbells. Although aggression could be demonstrated on more than the physical plane.

The galley was up-anchoring and its double banks of oars beginning to impel it out into mid-loch.

'The man is at least consistent!' Montrose declared to Airlie. 'I fear that he will survive us all!'

'For so ill-favoured a creature he rates his own hide high!' Airlie's son, Sir Thomas Ogilvy, snorted. 'Has he no sense of shame? In front of all his people!'

'His sense of his own consequence outdoes all,' Sir David the brother, said. 'After a fashion, there is a sort of pride in it, He cares not what others think of him, knowing himself to be all-important, irreplaceable. Few men, I vow, are made of such stuff!'

Montrose nodded. 'You are right, David. I have come to believe it is not all craven cowardice. The man is unassailable in his self-righteousness – and therefore dangerous. Harder to deal with than a dozen paladins!'

'Aye. And what paladins has he left behind to fight for him there?' Airlie wondered. 'I think we shall soon know. See – he hauls to in the loch. Out of harm's way. To watch. Auchenbreck, his own cousin, has the name of a hard and savage man.'

'But proud,' the Graham added. 'I have heard that he is

398

notably proud. I pray that he is, indeed. For so I hope to draw him. He has twice our numbers – and will see but part of us. I cannot believe that he will relish his master's careful departure. He will be smarting under it – as any true soldier would. His cannon cannot reach us, here. I believe, I hope, I pray, that he will come out to teach us our lesson, advance to show us that the Campbells are not all poltroons. Get within cannon-shot of us. And to do that, he must do so, directly to yonder tongue of firmer land between us. Or else make a great circuit round to the north. Which would take time, and allow us opportunity to retire and take up new and stronger positions on the hillside. I think that he will come directly at us. Where we want him!'

Very quickly thereafter it became evident that Montrose's thinking had been accurate. To tuck of drum, disciplined companies of foot began to issue from the camp almost straight for them, long columns of musketeers and pikemen, marching four abreast, with banners. The Graham sighed a little at the sight – for this answered his questions to Ian Lom. The sixteen companies of Lowland militia regulars *had* reached Argyll – for only such would advance thus. The odds, therefore, were lengthened considerably.

It was trying to stand idly by and watch the enemy power build up, so much greater than their own, march forth and take up advantageous positions before them, without lifting a hand to interfere. It went against every instinct in the Highland fighting man. But Montrose's orders were emphatic. This battle was to be fought his way, or not at all. Outnumbered three to one at least, no amount of wild heroism was going to serve for victory – although plenty of that would be required also. Only carefully thought-out strategy could win the day for them – with God's help – which was why James Graham had hardly closed his eyes that cold night.

The seemingly unending companies of militia filed steadily forward across the soft and marshy pastures, no doubt congratulating themselves on not being attacked while they were doing so, leaping the ditches and runnels, until they reached the long whaleback of good ground, where they split into two, one half marching on to the extreme right, the other left, eastwards. Clearly they were to form the wings of Auchenbreck's array. The rise was about one-third of a mile long, and averaging some 300 yards in width. Montrose reckoned that 1000 and more of the militia were taking up their stance thereon.

Now the mass of the Campbell irregulars were surging out from the encampment area, not in any orderly ranks. There was no counting these, and however undisciplined, they were known to be fearless fighters. For long they streamed out and across the levels, making it clear that there must be much more of the camp beyond the castle, in the dead ground behind. It seemed as though the whaleback rise could never possibly hold them all.

When at last this great host was all out, came a group of mounted men, not cavalry but Campbell lairds, in the Lowland garb which most of them affected. There were some thirty to forty of these, sitting proudly, some with banners. At sight of them, a long snarling arose from the MacDonald ranks. These were the hated ones, rather than the ordinary Campbell clansmen, these were the oppressors of the Highland West, the rich and able men with the Lowland law in their pockets, the ear of government, the proclivity for being always on the winning side – and the heavily laden gallows-trees. Behind them staggered long columns of men straining and tugging on ropes, drawing two brass cannon, which made heavy going on the soft wet ground. With them came files of shaggy garrons, laden with panniers no doubt containing powder and shot. Finally emerged the reserve and rearguard, more militia and a mixed crowd of clansmen, with some mounted officers.

'It is a great host,' James Graham said. 'Far more than we are. Can we hope to hold them? Those cannon – they bring them near to us. Will they not shoot us down, and we can do nothing? They will be in range, will they not? On that bank?'

'Range, yes,' his father admitted. 'Just. But . . . wait you. More than range is needed. They require a clear field of fire. Do you see them getting it?'

The boy bit his lip. He considered himself to be a veteran soldier now – even though a less robust one than he tried to appear, with an unmanly cough like a bairn and a tendency to shakes and shivers, fight against them as he would. He had, however, no experience of artillery.

Soon his father's meaning, and planning, became evident, to him as to others. The cannon, even when dragged to the highest point of the whaleback, were still too low set to fire over the heads of the massed men thereon, so slight was the rise. And so tight-packed were the enemy that clearing any sort of avenue down which to shoot would be a difficult matter. The great numbers of the foe were here working to their own disadvantage.

Not that Montrose intended to allow them any time for a reappraisal of the situation. As the field-pieces reached the firm ground, and the long teams of haulers pushed in amongst the crowded ranks of clansmen, causing maximum upset, the Graham raised his arm towards Magnus O'Cahan waiting and watching eagerly on the left flank. And with a deafening yell, long continued, his force of Islesmen and Macleans flung themselves forward, at last, in headlong charge, broadswords out.

This tip of the royalist crescent was the nearest of all to the enemy, only about 400 yards separating them from the Lowland militia. These musketeers and pikemen had been in England fighting the Cavaliers, and had never seen or faced a Highlanders' charge – quite the most terrifying and unnerving ordeal in the military experience. Casting aside their plaids, stripped to the waist, dirks in left hand, broadswords in right, yelling their fierce slogans and bounding like deer over the soft ground, 300 of them bearing down on any static body of men, however disciplined, was a fearsome sight to contemplate. Not too much to be blamed, undoubtedly, the officer in command of the enemy right wing was over-early in giving his order to fire – and his men all too eager to respond. At far too extreme a range the matchlocks blazed, and the ball went whistling across the levels amidst impressive clouds of smoke and with a mighty banging. But only one or two men fell as a consequence. And it was highly doubtful whether there would be time to reload the unwieldy muzzle-loaders, as the officers bawled orders to do.

Trumpets rang out again, and horns blew, and the entire royalist front moved forward, not in any charge at this stage, but steadily, sufficiently to further upset worried militiamen.

Montrose halted his centre still outside musket range. But the right wing, under Colkitto, surged into a charge, pipers playing his Ulstermen on, wild Irish screeches rising to a crescendo.

It was more Lowland militiamen who faced them, for the Campbell clansmen mass formed the centre. Colkitto had farther to go than O'Cahan – but his charge was just as fearsome.

Montrose was now dividing his attention principally between O'Cahan and those cannon. There was a great stir and confusion in the middle of the Campbell position and towards the rear, where no doubt the pieces were being manhandled into position and turned to face the enemy, and the ponies with the ball and powder were being pushed through the press. Little could actually be seen because of the dense ranks of clansmen in front. But, by the same token, the cannoneers could not see their targets, and there was just not enough elevation to fire over the heads of their folk. So crowded, indeed, was the whaleback that there was just no room for the cannon and garrons.

On the left, O'Cahan's men reached the rising ground, and went leaping up in full cry, naked steel flashing in the new-rising sun. And without waiting for the impact, the militiamen turned and fled, without getting in a second volley. The ground immediately behind them there was much waterlogged, so they streamed off half-right, back towards the castle area, 500 of them, throwing into some confusion the rear ranks of the Campbells and utterly demoralising their colleagues of the reserve who were still advancing across the levels. O'Cahan's Islesmen, seeming to race after them with unabated enthusiasm, suddenly followed their leader in swinging round behind the main enemy front, between it and the faltering rearguard. Ignoring the massed Campbells altogether, they dashed on towards the rear of the left-wing militiamen facing Colkitto, caring nothing that for much of the way they were splashing through pools and runnels of icy water.

These Lowlanders stood their ground rather better than did their colleagues, but not for long. They had seen what had happened on their right, and they quickly became aware of the extraordinary threat in their rear. The gigantic Colkitto, leading the screaming Irish, was large-enough anxiety, especially as many of the latter had pistols as well as swords and pikes. There was a ragged exchange of fire, with little effect on either side, and the militia front began to waver and cave in.

Montrose drew his own sword, pointed to John of Moidart, and his trumpeter blew the general advance. With a mighty earth-shaking roar the royalist main body of Mac-Donalds broke into a run, like hounds unleashed. And from behind the little ridge at their backs, the reserve emerged, shouting likewise, to take their place.

It was probably the sight of that unexpected reinforcement, even though there were no more than 250 of them, that broke the militiamen of the left. Throwing down their fired muskets, they bolted. O'Cahan was on their left and Colkitto at their backs, so they ran half-right also, north-westwards into the bog.

The Campbell mass stood solid, isolated, on its whaleback, deprived abruptly of flanking cover, and with rear threatened.

Montrose did not actually lead his centre's advance. It would not do to seem to supersede the Captain of Clan-ranald. He contented himself with remaining in the racing front line – and with keeping an eye on young Johnnie. In the main, his own major part was played. He had brought the two sides to grips, as advantageously as he could. It was now up to others.

Or, almost. Just before the front clashed, he ordered the trumpeter, who stayed almost as close to one shoulder as Black Pate did to the other, to sound a special and repeated call. This was for O'Cahan and Colkitto's men to break off from whatever they were doing, and to concentrate on making a ring of steel round the Campbell position.

And so the real battle commenced. The Campbells still outnumbered their attackers two to one. But they were cramped and crowded in a vast huddle of 3000 men, with no room not only for manoeuvre but for free work with sword and pike. Moreover, only those on the perimeter were in touch with their foes, and the rest, half their strength, could effect nothing. This whaleback was in fact a death-trap, its illusion of firm ground little more than a constricting menace.

The Campbells fought bravely, or rather died bravely; but it could not be said that they fought well – since they could not. Surrounded, restricted, hampered, frustrated, they fell where they stood and were replaced by their fellows, from behind, almost with relief. Soon the MacDonalds, in their element at last, were standing on top of banks of slain, thus gaining desired additional height and reach. And the great circle, or rather ellipse, shrank.

Montrose had fallen heir to some of the garrons which had carried the ammunition, and mounting himself on one's broad back was able to survey the battle from something of a vantage-point. There was little that he could do to affect the issue of the ding-dong struggle. But he was able to summon forward the reserve when the doubtful enemy rearguard looked like reassembling and joining in the fight. And he sent Sir David Ogilvy and a company of Athollmen to silence marksmen in the castle, musketeers who had taken refuge there and were sniping long-distance at any who came within range. For the rest, he circled the fearful conflict, with Johnnie and Airlie, not knowing whether to cheer or to weep. Massed slaughter and bloodshed at close quarters was not to his taste, general or none.

The eventual outcome was not long in doubt, barring unforeseen developments. The Campbells might break out, but they would never gain the mastery now. From the start they had been out-manoeuvred, their advantage in numbers nullified. Their leadership might be brave enough, and conventionally effective, but it had lost the initiative and allowed itself to be trapped in the centre of an ever-narrowing circle. At this rate, it was achieving nothing – even though it might be the last to die.

Colkitto, however, had ideas about that last. Collecting a team of mighty sworders about him, he spearheaded a wedge of smiters in a drive into the Campbell centre, himself out-doing all in the fury of his onslaught, his enormous reach, untiring energy and bellowing bull-like roaring enough to clear a way through the dense pack so long as his back was protected. He was, of course, a superlative captain of gallowglasses, however odd a major-general. Steadily he hacked and hewed a passage through, towards the enemy leadership, still sitting their mounts in the midst.

Montrose, Johnnie at his side, watched fascinated. He saw the giant reach the central group, apparently unharmed. He saw Sir Donald Campbell of Auchenbreck, from horseback raise a pistol and fire at Colkitto. He heard that man's great shout of laughter even amidst all the unholy din so that presumably the shot had missed its mark or done scant damage. And then he saw a huge bare arm and sword-hand come up to sweep the small, neat and grizzled Campbell right out of his saddle, the dirk in the other hand struck fiercely but expertly, once only, and Auchenbreck disappeared in the press while Colkitto strode on.

Whether it was the fall of their principal leader, or the fact that the whole enemy position was now practically cut in two, the Campbells' dogged defence thereafter began to falter and disintegrate. They still fought vigorously, but they were of a sudden concerned with cutting their way through and out, rather than with maintaining a front. It was every man for himself.

Soon the whole battle had broken up into innumerable struggling groups and running men. In every direction the enemy fled – if they could. And after them raced the yelling MacDonalds, Macleans, Camerons and Stewarts, doing at last what they had sought to do all their lives – hunting down defeated Campbells.

At this stage, with all obviously over save individual killing, Montrose would have called off the fighting. He ordered his trumpeters to sound the retiral – and to go on sounding it. He might as well have shouted commands to a pack of wolves. None save the Athollmen, Drummonds and Grahams heeded. The rest were about their own business. The Battle of Inverlochy might be over, well before noon-day, for better or worse; the killing was not.

Montrose did his best. He divided his officers amongst parties of the troops who would obey them, and ordered them to protect the Lowland militia who had laid down their arms back in the camp area. He sent out tough men such as Black Pate and O'Cahan to try to halt, or at least limit, the running slaughter. He himself led a company to capture the castle – but the snipers here fled without further opposition. From the ramparts thereafter he gazed out over the scene of his triumph, set-faced – and saw Argyll's antiquated galley starting to speed seawards with all the power of its double-banked oars, even as scores of his clansmen desperately hurled themselves into Loch Linnhe to swim out towards it and safety from their hunters.

James Graham, a patriot, groaned for Scotland.

*   *   *

That evening, feasting on Campbell provision once more, in the Great Hall of Inverlochy Castle, part-derelict but a palace compared with their quarters of recent nights, Montrose called together such of his officers as were available – many of the Highlanders had just never returned from their Campbell-slaying – and such as were sufficiently sober, and sought to gain a full picture of the situation, its implications, and how fullest advantage might be taken.

The details of the battle, now marshalled before him, were extraordinary, scarcely credible. Although they had sustained many wounded – and one of these, unhappily, had died just an hour before, Sir Thomas Ogilvy, youngest son of Airlie – only three others were dead on the royalist side. Whereas the Campbell slain already counted amounted to over 1500. A large proportion of these, undoubtedly, had been hunted down and despatched as fugitives, and the bodies of many others would no doubt never be found. On the ridge of the whaleback itself, over forty Campbell barons and lairds had died, in addition to Auchenbreck. More than half of the total Campbell army had been wiped out, therefore, a proportion unknown in any battle since Flodden. The Lowland militia had suffered comparatively lightly, the majority of them now prisoners, strictly guarded for their own protection. Not that the Highlanders seemed to have any interest in them – except as a source of booty and matchlocks, despising them as beneath their notice.

Arms, munitions and supplies captured were more than enough to re-equip the entire royalist army – if such a thing there was, any more. This was the question that was worrying Montrose, even as his companions congratulated him, and themselves, on the scale of their victory.

The Master of Madderty summed up the attitude of most of the Lowland officers. 'You have not won only a battle, James – you have here won a campaign, possibly even a war, a nation indeed! For you have broken the power of the Campbells now – that is certain. Argyll will never again put a Campbell army in the field. And Argyll *is* the Covenant, his name and his power its strength. This day we have demolished that name and strength.'

'The Covenant has more than Argyll, John. He is uncrowned king, yes. But do not forget that it has the best-trained professional army in the two kingdoms. Even the man Cromwell has said as much. Sandy Leslie's army. It is in England – but it could be brought home, and quickly, if need be . . .'

'Mercenaries, in the main. At least, its officers, from Leslie downwards. Hired men. Think you they would not quickly perceive who will pay them best to fight for? When *you* sit master in Edinburgh !'

'He is right,' Graham of Gorthie agreed. 'Leslie and his like will not support the losing side, ever. Show yourself master in Scotland, and the army will not come back to challenge that master.'

'Perhaps, friend. But before I am master, or make the King master, in Scotland, I have three other armies to defeat. Four, it may be. Seaforth's at Inverness. Burleigh's in Moray. It may be that they are now one. Callander's in the Borders. And Baillie at Perth – though we know not the size of the force he has there. Or may gather. And he is a notable general.'

'But another mercenary, a paid soldier. As for Seaforth, he is a waverer. It has taken him years to make up his mind to this. Argyll has been at him since '39. He will melt away, with the Campbell prop and spur removed. And Burleigh is a fool. Callander is otherwise, but his is only the reserve army. And I do not believe that he would fight *you*, if he may avoid it. He used to be your own man, signed your Cumbernauld paper.'

'Aye – and he refused the chief command, after Argyll,' Madderty added. 'He will act cannily, will Callander. I say, strike from here swiftly at Baillie, at Perth. Another fast march. He can have no large numbers there yet. Then make straight for Edinburgh, dismiss the Committee of Estates, and call a parliament in the King's name. I swear you would have Scotland in your two hands in a week !'

'Aye ! Aye !'

'To be sure. That is the way of it !'

'Strike while the iron glows red . . . !'

It was heady talk, and men rose to it.

James Graham raised his hand. 'My friends – I think you forget one matter, of some import. You would not do so if you were Highlandmen. Donald here, who is one, will tell you, I think.'

Donald Farquharson of Braemar, a quiet modest man,

beloved of all, who had joined Montrose soon after Tippermuir, sighed. 'You must needs wait, I fear,' he said. 'Until,
let us say, the spring. The clans will now return to their own
lands.'

The others stared at him.

'It is true,' Ian Lom MacDonald assured. He was already
turning over in his mind the mighty fast stanzas of an epic
to describe this day's doings for all time to come. 'It is the
way, the custom. You will not hold them now.'

'You see?' Montrose asked. 'You have forgot that it was a
Highland army which won this fight for us. As only a Highland army could have done. And Highland armies, when
they have won a battle, thereafter retire homewards with
their booty. Such are the terms of their fighting. Always.
Even now we are already missing one-third of our numbers,
who have not come back from chasing the Campbells. We
shall not see them again, I think. All Argyll, Lorne and
Cowal lie open to their raiding. Think you any will march
with me to Perth and Edinburgh?'

There was a shocked silence, and then some growling.
Again the Graham raised his hand.

'*I* do not blame them,' he declared. 'Most of them joined
us only to fight the Campbells. All along I have known that.
They have fought, and won. And never was there such
booty, so much Campbell treasure. I fear that when we leave
Inverlochy, it will be with Colkitto's Irish and Islesmen, the
Athollmen and those from Strathearn and Strathmore. Little
more than a thousand, all told. Shall I march on the Lowlands with a thousand men?'

None answered him, nor had to.

'It is hard,' he went on. 'In a day or two, when Scotland
learns of this day's work, the land will lie all but open for us.
Almost for the taking, I believe. Only, I shall not have the
wherewithal to take it. I would march on Edinburgh
tomorrow, blithely. But I may not.'

'God's curse on them all! What then will you do?'
Madderty demanded.

'I think, march north again. Noth south. Send Seaforth
back to his northern glens, if we can. Then go talk again with
Gordon. Aye, my friends – well may you grimace! But
young Gordon, and only Gordon, has the answer to our
problem. Perhaps Inverlochy will convince him that his

King's cause is not lost, is worth his support, whatever his father says. Who knows – even Huntly might think again . . .'

At the heavy silence and downcast looks of his friends, James Graham changed his tone of voice, his whole demeanour. Throwing up his head, he smiled. 'Come gentlemen – not so sober! We should be rejoicing, not glooming. I crave your pardon for drawing so long a face. We have won a great victory – and thanks to those same Hielantmen! We have struck a blow for King Charles today such as has not been struck yet in all this long war. I go write the good news to him now. It will, I swear, cheer His Grace mightily. Here at Inverlochy, they do say, stood an ancient capital of our Pictish kings, from whom our liege lord descends. It is an excellent omen. The King's cause triumphs, at least in Scotland, and the King's chiefest enemy flees, discredited before all. This is a day for cheer, not gloom. All who made it possible, I thank from the bottom of my heart . . .'

But when he turned away, that brilliant smile was gone.

30

THE GREAT GORDON CASTLE OF BOG OF GIGHT WAS SET amongst the spreading and desolate sea-marshes and tide-lands of Speymouth, its tall gaunt tower a scowling plaything for the winds that howled and swept across these level wastes, with the boom of the great seas on the long sand-bar three miles distant like the muted roll of artillery in some endless battle, and the sad scream of seabirds and marsh-fowl serving for the cries of the dying. James Graham, only too well aware of that background of ominous sound, as he was the more immediately obsessed with the grievous sound of his son's difficult breathing, knew a great fear, almost despair. Not a man to be oppressed by conditions or atmosphere or omens, however strong his emotions and vivid his imagination, he nevertheless knew a hatred for Bog of Gight and wished that he might never have come here. Wished more than that, God knew . . .

There was wicked pride speaking in that, wearily he told himself there by the bedside, in the high tower room round which the sea-winds sobbed. He hated Bog of Gight partly because he had once before come to it on a begging mission, seeking aid of Gordon, and had been rebuffed. And now, victor as he was acclaimed, had come again, on the same sorry mission, a beggar, a suppliant — and dreading further rebuff. He had heard that the Lord Gordon, that young man whom once he had felt he could love, was here, at the second greatest of the Gordon castles, the seat from which Huntly took his odd but time-honoured title of Gudeman of the Bog. It was a humiliating posture for any man of spirit, he told himself, the more so for the King's Lieutenant and winner of so many battles — to be soliciting, beseeching a young man barely out of his teens. But the basic situation had not changed, victories or none. To conquer the Lowlands for King Charles, he required cavalry, much cavalry. And Gordon was the only major source of cavalry north of Tay. Now, with Inverlochy behind him, and Scotland ringing with his deeds and wondering what the great Montrose would do next, he was back cap-in-hand at Bog of Gight — to find the Lord Gordon departed for Strathbogie only two days before.

They had marched northwards from Inverlochy and Lochaber in consistently bad weather, driving rain and biting winds. And Seaforth, hearing that they were coming, and what they had done to Argyll, had turned and marched away from Inverness, north-westwards into the remote hills and fastnesses of his own Kintail and Gairloch. Balfour of Burleigh's force was said to be hiding in Banff and Moray, and they had turned south by east seeking him. They had taken the towns which he had so lately occupied, Nairn and Forres and Elgin — but found none to fight. And there, to the surprise of all, they had been joined by the Laird of Grant, with 300 men, fifty of them horsed, the first cavalry Montrose had had for long. This was an encouraging first-fruit of Inverlochy's victory, and a good augury, for James Grant of Freuchie was a notoriously careful character, and had joined the Covenanters as early as 1638 and never wavered in his canny support – indeed was one of the Committee appointed to try all 'malignants' in the North. Moreover, he was married to Huntly's favourite niece. A proud head of a proud line, his grandfather had refused James the Sixth's suggestion that he should make him Lord Strathspey, by demanding who then would be Laird o' Grant? Meantime he had been left in command at Elgin, capital of Moray.

It had been with no lightened heart, however, that Montrose halted at Bog of Gight, and sent only messengers on after the Lord Gordon, to Strathbogie. He stopped because Johnnie could go no farther. The boy had been ailing all the way from Lochaber – that terrible hill-march from Kilchumin to Inverlochy having been just too much for him, after earlier privations. And ever since, he had been shrinking and fading before his father's eyes. Desperately anxious, James Graham had watched him, sought to shield him and protect him in all those winter rains; would indeed have left him behind in some warm house had he dared trust his son to a stranger, in a potentially hostile land. He had even thought of sending him, in Black Pate's care, back to his mother at Old Montrose; but the fever-stricken, dark-eyed boy had pleaded, with tears, not to be parted from his beloved father and hero. Now he lay in this tower-room, in warm bedding and with a great log-fire blazing cheerfully; but still he shivered and was racked with coughing, cold sweat on his young white brow. James Graham was almost beside himself. In the next chamber the Earl of Airlie lay in bed, in not much better shape. Campaigning with Montrose was not for such as these. The old man, hit by the death of his youngest son, and sorely concerned at lack of all news of his eldest, the Lord Ogilvy, imprisoned by Argyll at Edinburgh when last heard of, had travelled latterly in a litter slung between two Highland garrons.

It was the second day of March, in the afternoon. Montrose was roused from sad introspection at his son's bedside, and the boy in uneasy dozing, by the sound of horns blowing at a little distance, ululant above the sobbing wind. Rising, he moved to the window, to gaze out. It was to see a large body of horsemen approaching from the south, down the riverside from Fochabers village. And since no alarm had been given by his pickets, they must be at least ostensibly friendly. Peering, for the window glass was thick and dirty, he saw a banner blow sideways in the wind. It was blue, with three golden charges, two and one. In that country, such could be no other than the three golden boars' heads of Gordon. And the banner bore no difference, tressure, or other mark of cadency.

'Gordon, Johnnie – Gordon !' the man cried. 'And horsed ! Scores, hundreds. Do you hear? Gordon cavalry !'

The boy's eyes opened, over-large, glittering, filled with weak tears. No words came, but he licked his lips and nodded, with a caricature of a smile, as his father hurried to the door and went racing down the winding turnpike stairway.

Two hundred Gordon cavalry indeed came riding to Bog of Gight, Colonel Nathaniel Gordon at their head, all gallant cavalier in great feathered hat, gleaming half-armour and thigh-boots. Two others rode beside him – the slight dark figure of the Lord Gordon himself, and his young brother, the Lord Lewis. Montrose, those emotions of his at their tricks, found his throat all but choked as he watched them ride up in jingling proud array. He held out his two hands, wordless.

'My lord Marquis !' Nat Gordon sang out cheerfully. 'I greet you. I acclaim you ! And . . . I bring you friends.' And he swept off his hat in a flourish that was both salute and waved introduction of the company.

George Gordon was more quiet, just as he was more quietly dressed, a serious, almost diffident young man, but with a still, grave strength of his own.

'My lord – your servant,' he said. 'Come belatedly, to your side.'

'For that I thank the good God. Welcome, my friend. Welcome to our liege lord's cause.'

' 'Tis to *your* cause, rather, that I am come. Of His Grace's I am less sure.'

'My cause *is* His Grace's, my lord. Only that, be assured.'

'Yet Charles Stewart has not brought me here, sir – only James Graham. You persuaded me to the Covenant. Then the Covenant locked me and my father in cells in Edinburgh. When they freed us, it was on condition that we provided men to fight for the Covenant. *I* would not have agreed. But . . . it was done. I am scarce nimble at changing my coat, my lord Marquis. And my father is hot against you still . . .'

'Yet you are here, friend.'

'Yes. It has taken me much time and thought. But I have come, at length. Against my father's express commands. Because I believe in James Graham. That only.'

'Mm.' Montrose eyed him thoughtfully, and sighed. 'You put a heavy load of responsibility on my shoulders, sir. I shall dread that you find me unworthy. But – so be it. The King's cause and mine are one. I welcome you from my heart – and not only for the men you bring. We shall talk of this hereafter.' He turned to the younger brother with the impatient frown. 'And you, Lord Lewis. Your spirit all Scotland knows. Now, it will serve a worthy cause. I will have work for it, never fear.'

That headstrong, hot-eyed youth, still in his teens but a thorn in the Graham's flesh ere this, shrugged. 'So long as we have an end to talk – talk, and creeping caution and care!' he jerked, his scorn of his sober brother, and of Montrose himself probably, undisguised. If he was the antithesis of George Gordon, he was strangely like his father – strangely, in that Huntly's fox was replaced by Lewis Gordon's wolf, young but unmistakable. James Graham knew well that he would have to watch this new recruit.

'Care I cannot swear to spare you, young man. Nor a modicum of talk. But creeping caution, I think, you may avoid in my service! Nathaniel, my good friend – I rejoice to see you. We have missed you, indeed . . .'

'*My* grief, to have missed Inverlochy!' that bold man cried. 'But – I have been busy.' He glanced behind to where the Gordon ranks sat their mounts. 'Training these. And others. My lord of Gordon has more to come.'

'A token, only,' George Gordon nodded. 'Give me a week or so . . .'

The Gordons had scarcely been ushered into and installed in their own house of Gight when a second arrival kept James Graham from his son's bedside. These were no additions to his strength, however, even though they were two of his own servants from Old Montrose. They brought a letter from Magdalen his wife, and had been roaming the North-East for days seeking him, having just come from Elgin. He took the letter up to Johnnie's room – which was also his own.

'My lord,' it commenced – and he sighed at that cool beginning, not Jamie, or James or even my dear lord.

I send you greeting, in the hope that you are in health, and that our son John is well. I have heard tell of a great battle in the West, and that Thomas Ogilvy is slain. He was my good friend. Once, as a foolish child, I thought that we might wed. God rest his soul. I hope and pray that you do keep Johnnie from all danger.

My lord James, I must tell you that I cannot go on further as I have done so long. I am less than well, in body as in heart. You have chosen to be neither husband nor father to me or mine. No doubt but that the fault is mine, for I am not of your quality, nor have the heart to partner such as you.

These are evil times and all the land in a stir of trouble. Of which you, my lord, are not guiltless. There is much bitterness here, and threats are made against us. My lord of Argyll has imprisoned your good-brother the Lord Napier, but his son the Master is escaped they say. Also Sir George Stirling of Keir and others of your friends. There is talk of execution. My father fears for the safety of myself and my children, as indeed do I, or I am no heroine and desire but to live in peace. I have therefore left your house and gone to live at Kinnaird with my father and brother. You will not relish this, my lord. I know of your ill-will to my father Southesk. But you do provoke hatred and enmity in others, yet omit to protect your own wife and children. My father is come to some agreement with the Committee of Estates, I thank God. And my lord of Argyll. With him I should be safe. But there is talk of them taking Jamie, as hostage. For your better behaviour and submission. And even little Robert they may take from me. It is my hope and prayer to God that this may not be. But no thanks to you, my lord.

It is my belief that all these threats and reprisals against me and mine who am all innocent of injury to any cause, would be lessened were my Johnnie to be returned to my keeping. So says my father. It is wicked and a sin that one so young and tender should be turned into a man of blood. He is not yet fifteen years. I cannot sleep of a night thinking of him, in war and danger and bloodshed, amongst

*savage men. So, my lord, if you have any heart for me,
and for him, any regard for a mother's feelings and a
father's duty, do you send him again to me at Kinnaird,
where he shall be safe. I am assured that this will commend itself to the Committee and to my lord of Argyll.
You have no right, to be sure, to engage a child in this
your rebellion. James, if you too would come back, with
Johnnie, and forswear further rebellion and war, it would
greatly commend you to your*

sorrowing but dutiful and faithful wife
MAGDALEN CARNEGIE

*The lords Crawford, Maxwell and Reay, of the King's
faction are all captured, and Master George Wishart,
once your secretary. They say they are to be executed.
Also the Lord Ogilvy. Because of your rebellion. Your
excommunication is renewed by the General Assembly.
And the Committee of Estates, have proclaimed you infamous traitor, and forfeited of life, lands and goods.
What have you done, James – what have you done . . .*

The writing tailed away in a tear-blotted scrawl.

For long, unseeing, James Graham stared at the letter,
knowing a terrible hurt, pain and sorrow, almost despair.
When he raised his eyes, it was to his son, lying in a snoring,
restless semi-coma, thin, wasted, broken. Was Magdalen
right, then? Was this the end and price of his victories?
This, and the fate of those friends of his lying awaiting the
ave? Was it all the most shameful, appalling mistake? *His*
mistake, his arrogant faith in his mission and the King's
cause? Was he shockingly at fault, in prideful wrong?

Yet, that pitiful letter, from a wronged and distracted
woman whom he had vowed before God to love and cherish,
the mother of his children – was not right, surely. Nothing
of it was right, true, just? Nothing of true judgment? Those
were the words, in fact, of David Carnegie, of old Southesk,
a man concerned only for his lands, his properties, his position. And behind these were the words of Archibald Campbell's dictation – of that there could be no doubt. Magdalen
would scarcely know it, bue he could read it in every line.

Yet . . . if he had any regard for a mother's feelings and
a father's duty . . . ?

415

How long he sat there, lower in spirit than he had ever been in all his days, there was no knowing. The noises of an over-full house and a great armed camp came thinly into that high tower-room, and did not touch him. Only the difficult shallow breathing of his son, and the grief of that letter. Head in his hands, he groaned.

The clatter of many more hooves below, and the shouted greetings of men did presently penetrate his tormented consciousness – but this time did not take him to the window. Later a while, Black Pate came to the door, to knock and enter quietly, concern and compassion on every line of his dark, strong features. He looked from man to bed, and drew a deep breath.

'Jamie . . . my lord,' he said. 'Will you go down? Seaforth is come. My lord Earl of Seaforth.'

The other raised his haggard head to look at him, but dully, and did not speak.

'Seaforth, Jamie – the Earl. The Mackenzie himself. He is here. Asking for you. Seeking the King's peace.'

Montrose rose. 'Johnnie is . . . worse,' he said.

'I will bide with him. Go you down,' his friend said, gently.

Obediently, almost like a child, the King's Captain-General went to the door, and out.

Book Two

THE CAPTAIN GENERAL

PRINCIPAL CHARACTERS
In Order of Appearance

JAMES GRAHAM, 5th EARL and 1st MARQUIS OF MONTROSE: twenty-third chief of the Grahams, Viceroy and Captain-General of Scotland.

PATRICK GRAHAM, YOUNGER OF INCHBRAKIE: known as Black Pate, friend and kinsman of Montrose.

GEORGE MACKENZIE OF KINTAIL, 2nd EARL OF SEAFORTH: Chief of Clan Kenneth, doubtful royalist.

JAMES OGILVY, 1st EARL OF AIRLIE: Chief of the Ogilvys, staunch royalist.

GEORGE, LORD GORDON: eldest son of Marquis of Huntly.

ALISTAIR MACDONALD, YOUNGER OF COLONSAY: nicknamed Colkitto, Major-General to Montrose.

SIR JOHN HURRY OF PITFICHIE: Covenant Major-General.

DAVID CARNEGIE, 1st EARL OF SOUTHESK: father-in-law of Montrose.

MAGDALEN CARNEGIE, MARCHIONESS OF MONTROSE.

WILLIAM BAILLIE OF LETHAM: Covenant General.

COLONEL MAGNUS O'CAHAN: Irish commander of gallow-glasses.

LORD LEWIS GORDON: third son of Huntly.

SIR DAVID OGILVY: second son of Airlie.

COLONEL NATHANIEL GORDON: soldier of fortune.

JAMES GORDON, VISCOUNT ABOYNE: second son of Huntly.

ARCHIBALD, MASTER OF NAPIER: Montrose's nephew.

JOHN MACDONALD OF MOIDART, CAPTAIN OF CLANRANALD: great Highland chief.

ALEXANDER OGILVY OF INVERQUHARITY: young lieutenant.

PROVOST JAMES BELL: chief magistrate of Glasgow.

ARCHIBALD, 1st LORD NAPIER OF MERCHISTON: statesman, brother-in-law of Montrose.

JAMES, LORD OGILVY: eldest son of Airlie.

REVEREND DR. GEORGE WISHART: Montrose's chaplain and secretary.

WILLIAM, 1st MARQUIS OF DOUGLAS: Chief of that great house.

LUDOVICK LINDSAY, 16th EARL OF CRAWFORD: royalist Major-General.

GEORGE GORDON, 2nd MARQUIS OF HUNTLY: Chief of Clan Gordon.

KING CHRISTIAN IV OF DENMARK: warrior, and uncle of Charles I.

QUEEN ELIZABETH OF BOHEMIA: daughter of James VI and I, sister of Charles; known as The Winter Queen, and Queen of Hearts.

PRINCESS SOPHIA: daughter of Elizabeth.

PRINCESS LOUISE: daughter of Elizabeth.

PRINCESS ELIZA: daughter of Elizabeth.

ARCHDUKE LEOPOLD: brother of Emperor Ferdinand III, Governor of the Spanish Netherlands.

JOHN ASHBURNHAM: Gentleman-in-Waiting to Queen Henrietta Maria.

HARRY, LORD JERMYN: Master of the Household to Queen Henrietta Maria.

QUEEN HENRIETTA MARIA: wife of Charles I, and Princess of France.

JEAN FRANCOIS DE RETZ: Archbishop-Coadjutor of Paris.

EMPEROR FERDINAND III.

WILLIAM HAY, 3rd EARL OF KINNOUL: royalist officer.

SIR EDWARD HYDE: Chancellor of the Exchequer, adviser to Charles II.

KING CHARLES II: aged eighteen.

JOHN KENNEDY, 6th EARL OF CASSILLIS: Covenant representative.

JOHN MAITLAND, 2nd EARL OF LAUDERDALE: Scots statesman.

JAMES CRICHTON, VISCOUNT FRENDRAUGHT: royalist officer.

SIR EDWARD SINCLAIR: Orkney laird.

MAJOR ALEAXANDER SINCLAIR OF BRIMS: royalist officer.

NEIL MACLEOD OF ASSYNT: Highland laird.

MAJOR-GENERAL HOLBOURN: Covenant officer.

GENERAL DAVID LESLIE: Covenant commander-in-chief, later Lord Newark.

SIR JAMES STEWART OF COLTNESS: Provost of Edinburgh.

ARCHIBALD JOHNSTON, LORD WARRISTON: Covenant lawyer and judge.

JOHN CAMPBELL, 1st EARL OF LOUDOUN: Chancellor of Scotland.

ROBERT GORDON: an Edinburgh boy.

PART ONE

CHAPTER ONE

The thin slanting sunlight of a March forenoon was sore on eyes that had not closed all night, and James Graham frowned. Some ridiculous corner of the man's mind was even grateful that he could so frown and narrow his eyes unashamedly; it might not be perceived that the King's Lieutenant-General and representative in Scotland was in fact fighting to keep the tears from spilling from those narrowed eyes, the firm lips from quivering under the luxuriant moustache and above the trim little pointed under-lip beard. Bare head high, frowning straight into that level dazzlement, and seeing nothing at all, he sought not to hear either, hear the dread words of the Gordon minister of this remote northern parish of Bellie where mighty Spey spreads itself over wide marshlands before reaching the sea; those words, of dust unto dust and ashes to ashes, that signified the end of the earthly journey of one who had barely started along it. Somewhere in the same numbed mind, the man was trying to pray, seeking to assure himself that this was indeed but the beginning, the start of an infinitely fuller and finer and more rewarding journey, for Johnnie Graham, a journey on which, one day, his father would join him again and they would continue together towards a goal of unimagined fulfilment. For himself, that day could not come sufficiently soon.

James Graham was not aware of it, but there were many eyes, other than his own, damp and strained and narrowed, that March morning of 1645, hundreds, it might be thousands, the eyes of harder, fiercer men than he, tough Irish kerns, proud Islesmen, bare-shanked West Highland clansmen, veteran Athollmen, Grahams and Drummonds from Strathearn, Ogilvys from Strathmore. If the serried ranks of Gordon cavalry were dry-eyed enough, it had to be remembered that they had but newly joined the royalist army, and had neither known Johnnie Graham nor yet come to love the father whose slender and so upright figure in the black, rusty half-armour, thigh-length, mud-stained riding-boots and tartan plaid, stood alone beside the open grave – and all but broke other men's hearts. John, Lord Graham, titular Earl of Kincardine, aged fourteen, had served with his sire, and these others, all through the most savagely taxing winter campaign of Scottish military history, and choked to death in his own blood, in his father's arms, the day before, worn out by his privations. Now he lay there in the new-dug earth, beside the little parish kirk, wrapped in the same Royal Standard which had flown over the stupendous victory at Inverlochy a month before, and which he and his father had taken it in turns to carry, wrapped round their persons, in snow and rain and mist, across flooded rivers and ice-bound passes, through screaming storms and freezing nights in the heather. Now they would lie together, the thin, great-eyed boy and the King's banner both, on the curlew-haunted flats of Speymouth; and father and army would march away and leave them there, to win Scotland back for its feckless, high-souled monarch, without his flag.

As the minister's harshly vibrant voice died away, the darkly swarthy hatchet-faced man who stood a little way behind the Marquis, and was his aide, kinsman and closest friend, Black Pate, Colonel Patrick Graham, Younger of Inchbrakie, raised a hand to the trumpeter near by, who lifted his instrument and blew a simple high reveille, clear, sweet, a little tremulous, its last pure note long-maintained, almost insupportable.

In the quivering silence that followed, Montrose took a single hesitant step forward to the very lip of the grave, his upright carriage drooping suddenly. He stared down into it, lips moving. So he stood for long moments, while, ranked outside and around the little riverside kirkyard, 3,000 men waited motionless, hushed. Then, turning his back on his son, the man straightened up, squared his shoulders and swung round to face the vast array, sun behind him also now. Head high, he raised his hand.

'Pate – have the March sounded. We have work to do,' he called, clear for all to hear. 'Advance in column.'

Even as the trumpet rang out again, this time in the stirring, cheerful bugle-notes that commanded forward in order of march, Montrose paced briskly between the table-stones to the group of officers who stood near the long, low thatched-roofed church of St. Ninian, a motley group, some in the extravagant magnificence of Lowland cavaliers, some in the tartans and calfskins of Highland chieftains, some in sober broadcloth, some in dented and dulled breastplates and ragged nondescript captured clothing – the veterans, these.

'My friends,' he said, and sought to keep his too expressive voice even, businesslike. 'Time we were amove. To your stations of march, if you please. My lord of Gordon – you will ride with me. The Master of Madderty and Sir David Ogilvy command the rearguard.' He held out his hand. 'My lord of Seaforth – I bid you a good day and God-speed. May you find your lady fully recovered, at Brahan Castle.' That was James Graham, Marquis of Montrose, *An Greumach Mor*, gentleman, to the man who less than a month before had led an army against him.

George Mackenzie of Kintail, chief of the name and 2nd Earl of Seaforth, blinked little pale eyes, and bowed low. 'My lord Marquis – you may rely on me to hold the North secure for you . . .'

'For His Grace, King Charles,' the Graham amended, but courteously – even though, at his back, somebody muttered 'Treacherous Hielant tod!' sufficiently loud to be heard by all.

Seaforth elected not to hear it. He was not in a position to do anything about it, having come in from the North with only one or two of his chieftains two days before, to submit himself to the King's Lieutenant – but leaving his army of Mackenzies, Macleods, MacRaes and Rosses safely behind, unblooded, in his own glens. Inverlochy had convinced him that he was temporarily on the wrong side. But an equivalent defeat would as swiftly detach him again.

Montrose turned to the old Earl of Airlie, who was sitting on a tombstone, wrapped in a borrowed ragged plaid. 'My good lord,' he said, in a very different tone, 'we part, for a space. You have been beyond all men faithful, splendid. It is my pride to have served and striven at your side. You will regain your strength at Strathbogie. There to act my recruiter, to send me more Gordon horse. And when you are fully well, to come to me again.'

The Ogilvy chief shook his grey head. 'It grieves me sore, James. To leave you thus. With so much still to win. But, God pity me, I but hold you back. I am a done auld carle, and by with it. But – come the good summer days and I'll be with you again, lad. And . . . and meantime, you have my sons.'

The other spread his hands. Sir David Ogilvy had already taken leave of his father to go with Madderty to command the rearguard. Sir Thomas lay dead in Inverlochy Moss. And the eldest, the Lord Ogilvy, lay rotting in Edinburgh Tolbooth's darkest pit, there long months, bought from Cromwell for gold by Argyll, to humiliate and use as weapon against his father. The old earl had indeed served his King to the full, and broken his own health in winter campaigning in the process.

'I will lift Jamie out of Argyll's pit for you, my friend, never fear,' the Graham assured. 'And I will look to Davie's safety – if I may. God knows you have paid sufficient price. My thanks – and we shall meet again, with the King's cause triumphant . . .'

So they went their ways, Seaforth north, Airlie west to the Gordon hills, and Montrose and his ragged army east by south, with a kingdom to conquer.

*   *   *

Through South Moray, Banff and the uplands of Buchan they went, in predominantly hostile country. This was the land where the Committee of Estate's General, the Lord Balfour of Burleigh, had been lurking for many months, hiding his Covenanting army out of harm's way. They had been safe, if inactive, supported by the majority of the local lords and lairds. Now it fell to the King's Lieutenant to teach these Northern gentry that it did not pay to forsake their allegiance to their monarch and maintain His Grace's enemies. Montrose was in stern mood, as well he might be, and forced himself to unrelenting severity in spelling out this lesson, burning many a laird's-house and tower and granary, levying fines, requisitioning food, horses, gear, in a wide swathe south-eastwards. None put up more than token resistance. He was, however, equally stern with his own people, that there should be no bloodshed, rapine, savagery. He was a mild, almost gentle man for a great captain, but only deceptively so where principle was concerned. He had hanged men in the past for such conduct, and assured that he would do so again, be they heroes or none. His army was a wild one, mixed, of Irish kerns, Islesmen, Highland clansmen, Gordons, Angus lairds, few loving the other; under a less sure hand they would undoubtedly have run riot. But in coming to love this handsome, courteous, warm-eyed man, tested and tested again in the fiercest fire, who never asked his men to do anything that he would not, or could not do himself – they accepted this firm hand surprisingly well, with even the ungovernable giant major-general, Alastair MacDonald, Younger of Colonsay, showing a sort of reluctant respect. The Gordon cavalry was new, and less biddable; but they obeyed their young chief; and the Lord

16

Gordon, now that he had at last made up his mind where his allegiance lay, was attentive to James Graham's word.

They reached Turriff on the 9th of March, without any major clash of arms, with no word of Burleigh, or where he might now be hiding himself. It was six years since Montrose had last been at Turriff, when as Covenant lieutenant-general himself he had thrown down the gauntlet before Huntly and his Gordons. It would have been a bold prophet who would have forecast the changes and realignments which had taken place since then, and that King Charles's throne should now be tottering in England and Scotland both.

At Turriff further proof of Inverlochy's profound effects was demonstrated in the arrival of a deputation from the city of Aberdeen, no less, seeking the Marquis of Montrose and pleading that he would not again descend upon their much-fought-over town. Burleigh was not in Aberdeen, they declared, and all Covenant forces had been sent away. The citizens were at heart still loyal to King Charles, and all they wanted was to be left in peace.

James Graham was only moderately responsive. Although an honorary burgess of the city, Aberdeen had latterly shown him little but ill-will. They had cherished his and the King's enemies, had welcomed Argyll and accepted a Covenant garrison for long months. Why should they expect clemency from the King's Lieutenant?

The Irish, they quavered – the Irish . . . ! Like so many Lowland Scots, the Aberdonians conceived Colkitto's Catholic Irish – and the West Highlanders and Islesman likewise – to be little better than barbarian savages and fiends of hell. Their descent upon the city after the Battle of the Bridge of Dee, six months before, was being called the Sack of Aberdeen, and ever becoming, in retrospect a greater nightmare.

Montrose yielded so far as to assure that he would not let Colkitto's men nearer than Kinellar, nine miles from the city. He himself, however, must and would take over Aberdeen, in the name of King Charles. He required that the Provost and magistrates had the keys of the city ready to hand over, with all cannon, weapons and ammunition, and the citizenry orderly and well-behaved for his entrance in, say, four days' time. With this the emissaries had to be content. The Graham sent them away hoping that they did not really recognise how tiny and ill-equipped was his force, and that the train-bands and burghers

17

of Aberdeen could overwhelm them by sheer numbers – if they plucked up the courage for the attempt.

Three days later, at the little grey town of Kintore on the lower Don, Montrose encamped, and ordered forward an advance party of Gordon cavalry, some eighty strong, to show the King's standard and make due arrangements for the entry of the royal representative on the morrow. He would have sent them under their own chief, the Lord Gordon; but that young man was not a little self-conscious about his change of sides – for the last time that he had been in Aberdeen it was as leading a cavalry brigade *against* Montrose; moreover, he was very well known in the town. So he asked to be excused. Instead, Colonel Nathaniel Gordon was sent. But Nat was something of a wild character, and liable to do rash things. So the reliable and level-headed Donald Farquharson of Braemar, whom all men respected, and was also a familiar figure in Aberdeen, was chosen to accompany him.

That evening, in the Manse of Kintore, with most of his officers happy to seek what amenities and facilities even a little town had to offer those starved of such modest delights for long, James Graham found himself alone with George Gordon for almost the first time since their reunion. Armies on the march offer little opportunity for private converse. His back to the minister's well-doing log fire, he considered the younger man thoughtfully.

'You are less than happy, I think, my friend, over your change of allegiance? You still are anxious about your father?' he asked. 'That he will be much angered. It distresses you?'

'My father? No – I have won past that. I have known for long that my esteemed sire is blessed with but poor judgment. For himself, or his family, that might be of little consequence. But as wielder of the Gordon power, it is of great account. I *had* to take decision of myself – since he has washed his hands of all leadership. No – it is not my father's frowns that trouble me now.'

'What then, George?'

The other leaned forward, slight, dark, still-featured, but with deep-set glowing eyes. 'You will not understand, my lord. But ... I fear to hear men call me turncoat!'

'Turncoat! And you think *I* will not understand? I, whom so many have called that same. Have I not grieved over it?' Montrose shook his head. 'Too well I know your trouble, friend. But a man is no man, a poor creature indeed, who cannot change his mind. When issues change, when he gains new light, when he learns better. The man who truly uses the wits God gave him, *must* change his mind. Frequently. All men err. If they never may change, they are of God's creatures the most pitiable.'

'Aye – but to lead men, on one side, in a great cause. And then so soon, to lead them on the other! I see the fingers pointed at me, too clearly. You did, yes. But you are Montrose. Of the stuff of greatness. I – I am but one of Huntly's brood, who has now changed sides twice . . .'

'And both times on my account! At my pleading.' Montrose nodded. 'I know it, lad. And recognise my responsibility in this, as in so much else. *I* changed – but I did not change lightly. Nor lightly besought others to do so. Mine was the first signature on the National Covenant. I helped set up the Tables and the Committee of Estates. I was the Covenant's lieutenant-general. And believed that I did well, in the sight of God and of honest men. And then, when we had won what we sought, the freedom to worship as we believed right, the reform of government in Scotland – when I learned that many of those with me were not content, that they fought indeed for other ends, to pull down the King's Grace and set themselves up to rule in his stead . . . this I could by no means stomach. To seek to dethrone the Lord's Anointed! Charles Stewart made errors amany, and had to be shown it. As one of the earls of Scotland it was no less than my duty to show him the error. But I am the King's loyal subject, always was and always will be. When the ministers turned against the King, in their overbearing spiritual arrogance, I could no longer walk with them. And when they allowed Archibald Campbell of Argyll to use their cause, and mine, for his own evil ends, and make himself master of this kingdom in place of his liege lord – then I had to draw my sword against them, and him. And to urge others to do likewise. As their simple duty. You, George, have done so. If this is to be turncoat, would God there were more of the breed!'

'You speak truth,' the Gordon admitted. 'All this I know. Have told myself many times. But . . . I have not your strength. I am weak, foolish. Too concerned with how men think of me . . .'

'*I* would not think that! Of George, Lord Gordon? With a mind of his own. When I remember the long months when my chiefest thought was how to change that mind of yours! On King Charles's behalf . . .'

'And I in a misery of remorse, indecision, hating myself! You have won a sorry lieutenant, my lord Marquis.'

'I have won the man I wanted most to win,' the other declared simply. 'And not merely on account of the Gordon cavalry.'

Almost hungrily the younger man stared at him. 'If I could believe that ... !' he said.

'It is plain truth, man. Since the day we first met, at Strathbogie, I have known that one day we would be brought together. It was fated.' James Graham smiled faintly, ruefully. 'Although I near cursed you thereafter. For you it was who made *me* first to doubt. Really doubt. Doubt my Covenant cause. You who asked if religious freedom meant freedom for all – or only for the King's Protestant subjects. Forced me to admit that a Catholic is equally entitled to a conscience. And then, later, at Inverurie, not five miles from this place, told me that you had decided that I was on the wrong side in this conflict. I, and the Covenant both. Do you remember? George Gordon's well-considered opinion!'

'And you were!'

'And I was.'

They considered each other, these two, so dissimilar, the assured, nobly-handsome man of thirty-three, looking older, thin, worn with fierce campaigning and personal sorrow, yet with an air almost of gaiety in the high purpose he emanated; and the twenty-seven year old, looking so much younger, diffident, slight, lacking poise but with a great sincerity.

Slowly, wordlessly, the Gordon nodded, rather as though a binding agreement had been contracted.

'You ride at my side into Aberdeen tomorrow, then?' the other asked.

'Yes.'

'Praise be for Gordon!'

George Gordon drew a long breath. 'Before you say thanks for Gordon, I would warn you. To my sorrow, I fear that you cannot altogether trust my brother. Lewis. He has his virtues. He will make a better captain of horse than ever will I. But ... he has much of our father in him. Although more fierce. He is not wholly your man, I think. As I am. Do not rely on him too heavily, my lord.'

'You say so? I have never esteemed the Lord Lewis to be of *your* calibre, friend. Headstrong – but spirited. He would never betray us?'

'Not betray, I think. But he might fail you. In a pinch.'

'In a pinch, I might fail myself! But – would he let *you* down, and the Gordons likewise?'

'He might see it otherwise. His mind works differently from mine. And he might carry some of the Gordons with him. He has done, before.'

'You think that your father might work on him?'

'I do not know. It is a sorry business when a man cannot trust father or brothers.'

'We live in sorry days, with house divided against house. Civil war is of all evils the most grievous, I believe.' Montrose quelled a sigh. 'But you trust Aboyne, at least.' The Viscount Aboyne, second of Huntly's sons, had been fighting for the King for years, since his late teens, and was even now beleaguered in Carlisle, besieged by General David Leslie.

'Aboyne always gangs his ain gait. So long as *you* go that gait...'

The calm acceptance in the younger man's estimation of his family's failings was somehow moving. Huntly had eleven children, and had let them grow up wild, professing more interest in his dogs. Lady Huntly, with the last of them, had gone to her reward.

Montrose, whose own family life held its problems, changed the subject to that of logistics for the morrow's entry into the third city of the kingdom. With man-power so low, all would have to be most carefully stage-managed.

In the event, it was not stage-management that was called for, but something sterner. In the early morning Nat Gordon came back to Kintore at the gallop – but with only some thirty of his eighty troopers. And minus Donald Farquharson.

The roused royalist camp heard with mixed sorrow and fury what had transpired. The advance-guard had been well enough received by the city fathers, and suitably entertained, arrangements for the next day being agreed upon with every appearance of amity. But while this proceeded, couriers had been sent hurriedly southwards into the Mearns – whether with official knowledge or no was not clear. The Earl of Balcarres, Master of Horse to the new Covenant commander-in-chief General Baillie, was in the Mearns, protecting the flanks of Baillie's army, which was based on Perth. And with Balcarres was Sir John Hurry, or Urrie, of Pitfichie, an Aberdeenshire laird turned professional soldier, impartial as to his loyalties and methods, but effective and swift in their execution. Hurry, with a couple of squadrons of cavalry, had made a dash northwards from Conveth, reached Aberdeen that same evening, and fallen upon the unsuspecting Gordons – or such as were not bedded down with the ladies of the town. No quarter had been given. Donald Farquharson had been cut down where he stood, along with most of the advance party. Where Nat Gordon had been during this interlude was not specified – but he had managed to gather together what remained of his company and escape from the city, northwards, even as Hurry and his dragoons dashed away southwards again.

Montrose's heart sank within him at the news. Aberdeen seemed fated to destroy his good reputation and character. The major stain on his name hitherto had been its so-called sack, when after the treacherous killing of his Irish drummer-boy, under a white flag mission, he had allowed his angry troops to teach the city a lesson. He had never ceased, since, to regret that relaxation of discipline – even though probably he could not have prevented it in any case. The trouble was, he was not really a soldier at all, however successful at times he appeared at the business; he was a partisan, an enthusiast, a strategist and tactician, a would-be righter of wrongs, God forgive him – and he could not bring himself to accept the inevitable concomitants and horrors of war.

George Gordon took the blow hard, conceiving the blame as in some measure his own, since he had brought these men out but had failed to accompany them into the city. But he did not rant and rave like his brother Lewis, who immediately demanded that he should be given the rest of the horse to descend upon Aberdeen and demonstrate the price to be paid for assailing Gordon. Refusal of this demand was not well received.

Montrose laid down his programme in more assured and certain terms than he felt. He would enter Aberdeen as planned, swords sheathed. He would take steps to discover who was responsible for sending for Hurry, and deal with them. He would recover the bodies of the slain, and give them due and proper burial, with military honours. He would ensure that the city paid their dependants an ample sufficiency. And he would impose a collective fine for the King's cause, on account of Aberdeen's harbouring of the King's enemies. But there would be no reprisals, no looting, no savagery. This was no conquered city, but one yielding to the King's peace.

The growls of dissent were undisguised and general amongst his officers. Here was no way to deal with rebels and traitors. The blood of slain men demanded better than this, he was told. The King's cause must be vindicated.

'It is the King's cause that I am concerned with,' James Graham asserted, though reasonably. 'Aberdeen is a large city. We cannot garrison it, or hold it. When we pass on southwards, as we must, on the King's behalf, I would have behind us a city thinking well of us rather than hating us. To ride through its streets, shooting and slaying and burning might draw some of the hurt out of *you*. But it would serve King Charles nothing, for these are his subjects, as are we. Until I have five times so many men as I have today, I will not make Aberdeen more my enemy than it is now.'

Only a few agreed with him. It was ironic that one of those who could have been relied on to support him in this was Donald Farquarson of Braemar. George Gordon's support was dutiful rather than whole-hearted.

'I could use this evil circumstance to clear me of my promise to keep the Irish at a distance,' Montrose went on. 'But I shall not. No good would come of it, and much ill might. But you, Alastair, and you, Magnus, and some of your officers, should come with me, I think. You the citizenry will not fail to recognise – and so perhaps also recognise what they are escaping!'

His gigantic major-general snorted. 'A God's name – I'd have Aberdeen praying on its stiff knees that it would never see me or mine again! They would recognise me, to be sure!'

'No doubt, my friend – if afterwards you survived, with a great and hostile city at your rear, and the rest of Scotland to conquer!'

'I'd take my chance on that, whatever!' Colkitto shrugged bull-like shoulders. 'Soldiering, I'd sooner be feared than loved!'

A murmur of approval ran through the company.

'But more than soldiering is required of the King's Lieutenant, Alastair, I'd mind you of it. All of you . . .'

And so, that March afternoon, only a token force of about five hundred marched by Bucksburn and the Forest of Stocket, into Aberdeen, watchful, wary, grim, but with swords in their scabbards and at least a superficial aspect of peace. They were met at the city gates by the Provost and his anxious-looking magistrates and chief burgesses – but with no ministers, it was to be noted – with the keys, and urgent protestations that they had had nothing to do with General Hurry's attack, had no knowledge that he was coming, and greatly deplored the bloodshed and slaying. They prayed that the Lord Marquis would not hold the city in any way responsible . . .

'You may not have been responsible, gentlemen, but you did nothing, I think, to halt this shameful killing in your streets. Nor to detain Hurry thereafter,' the Graham replied, at his sternest. 'You have train-bands, guildry, thousands of able-bodied citizens. Yet you interfered nothing. You cannot escape responsibility, sirs. Keep your keys. I prefer to hold this town, in the King's name, by my own strength than by your leave.' And, as the municipal eyes were busy counting the numbers of men he had behind him, added, 'Major-General MacDonald's Irish and Highland Brigades are rather nearer than the nine miles I spoke of to you. But they will remain outwith the city, as promised, unless there is occasion to call them in.'

'One blast on my horn, and they will be here, by the Mass!' Colkitto roared, coming in on his cue. 'And Donald Farquharson shall be avenged!'

Hastily, fervently, the city fathers assured that that would not be necessary, that Aberdeen was the King's loyalest town in Scotland, or England either, that all was at the disposal of the Lord Marquis and his officers, every soul and stick and stone.

'Very well. I will hold you to that. I accept this city in King Charles's name, and require its due adherence to His Grace's rightful cause. So long as this is forthcoming, the citizens may go about their lawful occasions in peace. Now – I want discovered to me the identity of those who sent for Hurry. And I want the bodies of my friends slain . . .'

There was little or no trouble thereafter, on either side. They buried Hurry's victims at the great church of St. Nicholas next day, with an impressive and dignified service unflawed by incident – although there were one or two tense moments in the kirkyard. It was almost unbearably poignant for James Graham, who read the Lesson, so soon after that other funeral at the little kirk of Bellie; he realised that every such that he attended hereafter would amount to a re-burial of his own son. He had to remind himself that it was the souls of Donald Farquharson and forty or fifty Gordon troopers that he was praying for, not Johnnie Graham's.

Any sad preoccupation with Johnnie's present situation was

rudely shattered that evening, when a rider arrived hot-foot from Kinnaird and the Marchioness of Montrose. John Hurry had not halted again at Conveth on his southward flight, it seemed, but had gone on to Kinnaird, on his way apparently to Dundee. And from there he had forcibly taken Jamie, the new Lord Graham and Earl of Kincardine, despite his mother's, and the Earl of Southesk's entreaties, declaring him necessary hostage for his father's better behaviour, and moreover in need of proper upbringing and schooling. The boy was now aged twelve.

Montrose had been learning, for long now, how to control his passions, hurts and angers, learning the hard way. But this latest blow taxed all his resources of will-power and enforced calm. No doubt Hurry, a plain soldier, was acting under orders from Argyll, for he would be unlikely to make war on women and children. And no violence was beyond the godly Archibald Campbell. What would they do with the boy? Where would they take him? Would Hurry and the military keep him? Or hand him over to the Campbell and the Estates? What would *he* do, to aid Jamie? Could he do anything at all...?

As well as the news itself, another thought came to prey on the man's mind. The courier brought only the grim news from Kinnaird, no letter, no message from Magdalen. Questioned, the man declared that her ladyship had given him no other instructions to carry than the bare tidings. Her husband found the implications ominous. He had written to her, at length, over the death of Johnnie, detailing, commiserating, seeking to comfort, as best he could. She would have received this letter days ago, and had ample time to reply. She had not done so. And now this. He feared, he greatly feared, for Magdalen's state of mind.

Private fears, however, were no more permissible for commanders to show than were hot anger and reprisals. Two days later they marched out of the city, for Stonehaven and Angus. Old Montrose, his own house, and Kinnaird Castle where Magdalen had returned to stay with her father, lay but two score of miles to the south.

CHAPTER TWO

William Keith, 7th Earl Marischal, next to Gordon was the most powerful man in the North-East. He was a cheerful, unsubtle individual, younger than Montrose a little, undistinguished as to features and apt to have a wide grin for most occasions. He had been James Graham's lieutenant once, and they were good enough friends; but he had not changed sides when Montrose did. Not particularly able as a soldier he nevertheless could muster large numbers of men, a considerable proportion of them cavalry – and for this reason had been Argyll's Master of Horse for a while. But Montrose's prowess at the Battle of Fyvie had damped his ardour, and his brother's death there, plus many of his trooper's, had made him less active in the Covenant support. But he had not succumbed to appeals to join the King's cause. And so Stonehaven burned.

Stonehaven, fifteen miles south of Aberdeen, was the Marischal's town, and head burgh of the Mearns, a pleasant place in a sheltered bay between headlands, with offshore the great rock which gave the place its name. Its houses were close huddled together and mainly thatched, and it was this that Montrose burned, and of a set purpose. There was no killing allowed, no raping and a minimum of looting – two of his men hanging at the Mercat Cross helped to ensure that; and the fired reed thatch could be readily replaced and no great harm done. But it all made a most impressive smoke, guaranteed to be seen at Dunnottar, the Earl Marischal's mighty fortress-castle on its sea-girt rock two miles to the south. Will Keith was safe in his eyrie, even from cannon – it was said, in the company of the Reverend Andrew Cant, third in the Covenant hierarchy of ministers, who had slipped out of Aberdeen hereto at Montrose's arrival. But the sight of the billowing smoke, and that of other and lesser properties of his along that seaboard, might convince the earl that he was in fact on the wrong side in this business – where letters from James Graham had gone unheeded.

No evident response had been evoked when operations had

to be called off. Scouts brought alarming news. Hurry, whether or no he had gone to Dundee as the Kinnaird courier reported, was back at Conveth, not much more than a dozen miles away – but now with 600 cavalry. As Montrose's horse were reduced to 150-odd, the situation was perilous in the extreme – especially with great black smoke-clouds rising 500 feet in the spring air to shout aloud their whereabouts. Something had to be done, and quickly, for 2,000 infantry, however bold and experienced, could not prevail against 600 cavalry save in a strongly defensive position. And Stonehaven was far from that – a trap, rather, in its deep hollow, cut off by the sea.

Typically, Montrose decided on advance towards the enemy, as the tactic least to be expected. But he did not do it directly. Conveth was on the rising ground at the south side of the wide, level Howe of the Mearns, with much bare and open country in between. He ordered his march due westwards, by Fetteresso and the high ground of the Braes of Glenbervie, the foothills of the Grampians, which here came fairly close to the sea; and once amongst them, turned south by Glen Farquhar and Strathfinella, closed, hidden ways, to emerge at length at the southern end of the Cairn o' Mount pass, at the mouth of the Howe indeed, but from the north-west, not the north-east where Hurry's scouts might have looked for them. Conveth lay across the levels no more than five miles away, as the crow flies. They camped in the wooded foothills just north of Fettercairn, which they reached in the dusk.

Montrose was up with the dawn next morning, to make his way, with Black Pate, to make survey of the spreading levels of the Howe of the Mearns from the high viewpoint of the old ruined royal castle of Kincardine, a mile or so to the north-east. Presently he sent Pate back for George Gordon, while he himself quartered every acre of the land spread before him with his calculating retard. He knew it well, had hunted over it, hawked and fished, not ten miles north of his old home.

He put it to George Gordon – would he be so kind as to take his Gordon horse and act decoy? In due course, let them ride openly forward from hereabouts, as though unaware of Hurry's presence at Conveth – which could be seen smoking blue against the green of Garvock Hill, in the new-risen sunlight. There was nowhere between where a body of cavalry could remain hidden. Hurry's look-outs would be bound to see them. If they were to ride, openly, unhurriedly, towards the House of Halkerton, there, two-thirds of the way across the Howe, then turn west-wards along that slight ridge. They could see it from here. The chances were that Hurry would not resist the chance to make a sally out to deal with them, 600 against 150.

'Decoy, you said?'

'Yes. You would get plenty of warning, see you – for Hurry will have as little cover to approach you, as you to hide from him. You would pretend not to observe him, at first. Let him get within half a mile, perhaps. Then turn and spur back in seeming panic, north by west, as though direct for this Kincardine. Not the way you had come – but direct. It is important. You are not to know it, but there is the deep and mud-lined Ducal Water in the way, a wide and evil stank draining the marshlands of Halkerton. You do not know of it, see you – but Hurry could not fail to. And to know that horse cannot cross it. Hawking, I have often cursed it. Now it must serve us. He will conceive you trapped by it.'

'And I am *not* trapped?' the other wondered, without enthusiasm.

'Think you I do not value you, and your cavalry, too highly for that, man? You will turn due westwards along it, as in alarm, and dash with all speed, seeking a crossing. There is none for miles He will believe he has you. See – you can trace the line of the Ducal from here – alders and willows. You will gallop along its southern lip. And just over that lip, I will have every musketeer and archer I possess, in a long line, hidden in the dip of the stank. Lining the bank, all my infantry. We shall let Hurry pursue you. He will seek to cut you off, but must himself follow that river-bank, strung out. And so we shall have him!'

Pate Graham slapped his thigh. 'Glory be!' he exclaimed simply.

'Mmm. But supposing Hurry thinks better of it? Senses a trap? Does not follow ...?'

'Then no harm done. But why should he? I will keep my infantry hidden. I promise you. From now on. No fires, no movement. Hurry will see only your cavalry, on a reconnais-sance. When you flee north by west, you will seem to heading for this gap in the hills behind us, the entry to the Cairn o' Mount pass, whence you have come. A natural retiral. What would *you* do, Pate? In Hurry's place?'

'If I knew that I was dealing with James Graham of Montrose, I'd turn and ride for Dundee as though Auld Nick was at my tail!' that dark man declared, grinning. 'Otherwise, I'd chase Gordon, to be sure. The more so if I knew about that Ducal stank.'

'Hurry has been in this Conveth area for ten days at least. He cannot fail to know of it. He is a professional cavalry captain. Knowledge of the ground around him will be ever in his mind. He will know. And will not fail to know, likewise, that Gordon's 150 is all the cavalry that I have.'

'My men will not relish fleeing from Hurry,' the Lord Gordon pointed out. 'After he slew their comrades at Aberdeen.'

'Their chance will come. Once the trap is sprung. Tell them so, George . . .'

And so, that sunny first day of April, the royalist infantry spent an uncomfortable forenoon bent double much of the time, Colkitto leading in stupendous if breathless swearing, as they crawled down burn-channels, ditches and marshy hollows of the wide flats south-east of Kincardine, dodging, scuttling, creeping, in most undignified and unsuitable fashion for veteran warriors. It was not until nearly noon, when almost all were in position, that Gordon rode openly out at the head of his squadron.

From a carefully chosen spot midway along the line, Montrose scanned the wide prospect, dividing his attention between the Gordon's progress, plainly visible, and the distant Conveth. Assuming Hurry was there, he knew what he would do were he in his place.

And presently, keen eyes could discern Hurry doing exactly that. What looked like a dark cloud shadow moved out from the scattered housing below Garvock Hill and its woodland – but since the morning was bright, it could be only a tight-knit body of horse, a large body. Gordon would not see it yet, for the shadow was keeping to the east of the Halkerton woodland which would screen it from the north.

Owing to the watchers' angle of vision, however lowly, they could see exactly when the two sides came into mutual view. Suddenly the smaller Gordon group changed direction – and speed. Now they were coming directly northwards, across the marshy flats, at the gallop, spraying up mud and water, towards the hidden burn-channel and the line of waiting men. Gone was any neat formation, as the horsemen spread out to find their driest and swiftest way across the wet lands. From his low-set position, Montrose now could not see beyond them, to what

Hurry might be doing. But obviously the Gordons were fleeing in a major and sustained fashion, so that the enemy could be taken to be not far behind. All along the line the infantry readied themselves, tense now.

From the Halkerton woodland to their stretch of the Ducal Water was a good mile; but at the speed of the flight, it took only two or three minutes for the Gordons to cover the distance. As they approached the waterside area they tended to do so at an angle, as it were cutting the corner. And now behind them, could be seen the masses of Hurry's dragoons, spread wide across the levels, between quarter and half a mile away, a daunting sight even though they were being deliberately coaxed hither.

'Gordon is going to strike us midways,' Black Pate objected. 'Coming in where he will, he'll waste half our men. Those to the left will not be able to engage.'

'A hard thing for Gordon to judge. With those devils at his tail! But, no matter, We have enough . . .'

Presently the Gordon horse were thundering up the burnside track not a stone's throw from the crouching infantry, divots and stones from urgent hooves coming raining over on the watchers. The Gordons were strung out now, and the drumming of hooves, the snort and pant of the horses' breath, the creak of saddlery and the clank of steel beat a tattoo of excitement that set men's fingers itching at triggers and bowstrings.

But they had to be patient yet awhile. With the Gordons all streamed past, it was not long until the first of the Covenant troopers came pounding up, Major-General Hurry well to the fore, lashing his foaming beast with the flat of his drawn sword, a gallant figure dressed as cavalier rather than Covenanter. His men were all armoured in steel jacks and peaked-and-necked helmets, riding notably heavier mounts than the Gordon garrons, low-country beasts from Fife and Lothian. Montrose had given the strictest orders – no shooting until he gave the signal, on pain of dire penalty.

'Pray George Gordon remembers his instructions,' he murmured to the Master of Madderty, who was cursing steadily, monotonously, beneath his breath. 'If he goes too far . . .!'

But the Gordons did not overshoot their mark, which was a slight rise half a mile to the north-west, where Montrose, even from his lowly position, could see them. Here, as though realising that there was no crossing of the Ducal Water, they all abruptly turned to swing away at right angles south by west again, leaving the burn-side for the open levels. And, seeing it, James Graham gave them a few moments, and then raised a horse-pistol and fired a deliberate shot at the nearest of Hurry's horse, in front of him.

Immediately pandemonium erupted along that line of the burn. Every musket and pistol in the royalist army blazed out – at least, save for those too far to the east to have any targets. Every bowstring twanged. And even the poorest marksman could scarcely miss – for the enemy rode within fifty yards of them in the main, totally unaware of their presence.

More complete surprise could not have been achieved. Horses went down like ninepins in lashing ruin – for they made a surer mark than did the riders – and many that escaped the shooting tripped and crashed over the fallen, men being hurled in all directions. A fair proportion survived that first assault, of course, and most of these turned to face the unexpected attackers. But even so they were at a hopeless disadvantage. For the mud-splattered infantry were protected by the steepish bank which dropped to the water, a bank no horseman could cope with. Some who attempted to ride down the shooters, as they reloaded, slithered and fell in screaming, flailing disaster down into the stream. More drew over and swerved along the bank waving swords or firing pistols – but to little effect. None dismounted to come to grips. These were professional cavalrymen, and never considered fighting on foot.

At this stage the Gordon horse wheeled round and came dashing back, decoys no longer, swords drawn.

Hurry, up at the front, and so far unharmed, was no fool. Recognising a quite impossible situation, he shouted to his trumpeter to sound the retiral. He and those about him clearly preferred to take their chances with the Gordon cavalry than to run the gauntlet again of that grim river-bank, and swung off to the south-east, back towards Halkerton, forthwith. But others took retiral literally and merely reined round to spur back whence they had come – and these largely fell victims to Montrose's men before they perceived their error and pulled out desperately, anyway, eastwards, The Gordons got most of them.

It was all over in ten minutes – not a battle, nothing like a battle, since there was no fighting, as such, but only killing, with no royalist casualties at all save one Gordon whose horse pecked at a ditch and threw him, and one Irishman who toppled to fall into the burn and was fished out half-drowned. But it was a victory, undoubtedly, cheaply won. There were many more horses killed than men, but even so they captured eighty good mounts. The nearly 200 prisoners were something of an embarrassment; but thirty of them offered to change sides and serve with Montrose – indeed some had already done so – and the rest were sent under guard to Aberdeen. But the morale victory was much more important than the actual, Hurry made to look a fool, his Aberdeen raid avenged, and yet another infantry triumph over cavalry chalked up for all Scotland to consider, to enhance the legend of Montrose.

Always meticulous about such matters, James Graham held a burial service for the enemy dead, using the prisoners as gravediggers. And in the evening, when his scouts brought word that Hurry and his remaining dragoons had evacuated Conveth and were heading south fast, Montrose handed over command temporarily to Major-General Alastair, and taking no companion, despite protests, rode off southwards himself, public duty yielding at last to private.

*   *   *

It was only ten miles from Fettercairn to Kinnaird, in its great parks at the head of the vast landlocked bay of Montrose, and he came to the castle before dark. Even so the drawbridge was up and the gates locked against troubled times, and the caller had to wait some time at the moat-side before the porter obtained instructions to let him in.

David Carnegie, 1st Earl of Southesk, received his son-in-law in the Great Hall, an irascible, florid, heavy man, with a shock of white hair, white beard and choleric eye. He had his brother John with him, from nearby Ethie Castle, created Lord Lour in 1639 and since Montrose had last seen him, a less strong character but perhaps with a nimbler brain. No women were present.

'I hear that you have been showing that knave Hurry his business!' Southesk greeted, without preamble. 'Not before time. If you had done it a mite sooner, we'd all have reason to be the better pleased, by God!'

James Graham did not specifically answer that. His father-in-law had never loved him, even though he had been one of his guardians – which was why he had been married off to Magdalen Carnegie at the age of seventeen.

'I have come as soon as I might, sir,' he said, bowing. 'I hope I see you well? And you, my lord? May I offer my belated congratulations on your advancement?'

John Carnegie began to reply, but his brother interrupted brusquely. 'He came here, to Kinnaird, with hundreds of his bullyrooks. Hurry. To Kinnaird. Insulting me in my own house – me, Southesk! Declaring that he came in the name of the Estates. The Estates in which *I* sit! To browbeat my daughter. And remove my grandson. For *your* faults, sirrah! On your account. I hope that you are proud of yourself!'

'I have no reason to be proud, sir. But nor have I reason to reproach myself in this, I think. I conceive it to be Argyll's doing. Only *he* makes war on women and bairns. And Argyll is now a friend of yours, I am told?'

The other spluttered. 'Friend – no! We work together, on occasion. That is all. For the realm's weal. No more.'

'The King's greatest enemy, sir. An ill man to work with, I would think.'

'Not so. Be not so insolent, man. I'd mind you to whom you speak. Old enough to be your father . . .'

'And the King's former friend!'

'The King's friend still, damn you! If he had but taken my advice! Can I help it if Charles Stewart acts the fool? I am his loyalest subject. Nor is Argyll his enemy. He but cherishes the realm, until His Grace comes to his senses.'

'Cherishes, you say? Dear God, sir – do we speak the same language, you and I? Argyll cherishing Scotland, with sword and dagger and hangman's rope! Ask you Archie Napier how Argyll cherishes Scotland – your old colleague and fellow Lord of Session. Or ask Airlie. Or George Stirling of Keir. These will tell you, from Edinburgh's dungeons!'

'Cha! Men who rise against the lawful authority must be prepared to pay the price.'

'Perhaps these believed the *King* to be the lawful authority in this realm! As did once yourself, my lord. In whose name are you Earl of Southesk? Or Lord of Session Extraordinary?'

'Do not lecture *me*, on my duty, young man! His Grace rules Scotland through a lawful parliament of the Estates . . .'

'Of which Argyll is but one member! As indeed am I! Not even President, Convener or Chairman. Not Chancellor – he leaves that to his minion Loudoun. Yet do you deny that King Campbell rules in Scotland today? Who did Hurry obey? You,

33

or Argyll? From whom does Sandy Leslie take his orders? Or this General Baillie? Or Callendar, Balcarres and the rest?' The younger man paused, drawing deep breath. 'But I did not come, sir, to reproach or suffer reproach. We choose our own paths, as we see best. Have you any word of my son? Of Jamie?'

'Only that he has been sent to Edinburgh. To the care of the Estates.'

'The care of Argyll! Where is he kept? How treated? Is he well ...?'

'I know not. He was well enough when Hurry took him. How can I tell? You should look to your own bairns, James Graham ...' Even David Carnegie paused there, no doubt recollecting the other bairn, whom James Graham had looked to, and taken with him on his campaigns. He coughed.

Hurriedly his brother intervened. 'I go to Edinburgh in two days, my lord Marquis,' Lour said. 'On affairs. I shall make it my business to discover how Jamie does. And to aid him if I may. I have promised Magdalen ...'

'Aye, Magdalen,' Montrose echoed 'I thank you, sir. I shall be your debtor. Magdalen? She ... she is ... well?'

Her father produced something between a sniff and a snort. Her uncle spread his hands. Neither spoke.

'I will go to her. With your permission.' And not waiting therefore, Montrose bowed briefly and left them.

The Grahams, in their early married life, had been allotted a flanking-tower of the great courtyard castle, and thither the man hurried now, his heart leaden. This house of Kinnaird had always depressed him, its influence on his marriage not to his taste. Well he knew that his wife had always looked on it as home, rather than on any house he had provided for her. Not her fault, but there it was.

He climbed the twisting turnpike stair to her little sitting-room on the first floor; but only a dying fire was there. He climbed higher – and would have gone still farther to the third floor, but stayed himself. Up there would be his two remaining children. Robert aged five and Jean three. In their beds, no doubt. That he had to steel himself to knock at the other, second-floor door, was the measure of his failure as a husband.

There was no response, and quietly he opened the door. The room was unlighted, and beyond the great canopied bed a woman sat, staring out of the north-facing window at the last of the day's dying on the distant Grampians. Hunched, she sat, silent – and did not turn as he came in.

'Magdalen! My dear!' he said, his voice tight, choking.

'Yes,' she answered, flatly. She did not so much as glance behind her.

He moved over to her, but almost hesitantly for that assured and positive man. 'Lassie,' he murmured, 'it is I – James.'

'Yes,' she repeated, after a moment, and with no more emphasis.

He looked down at her hunched shoulders and drooping head, and knew a great pity. She had always been a plump, big-made girl, comely enough, however shy and retiring. Now she was almost fat, flabby, slumped there, a picture of dispirited dejection, of letting go. Was this his doing? She was younger than he was, only thirty-one.

'Magdalen, girl – I am sorry. Desperately sorry.' He put hand to her shoulder – and felt her shrink away. 'You are sore hurt. And I – I am much to blame.'

'Aye, you are to blame,' she agreed, but lifelessly, an acceptance rather than an accusation, challenge.

'My sorrow – what can I say? I am desolated, as you are. It is hard, grievously hard. But . . . Jamie will be well enough, never fear. They will not harm him. We will get him back. He is but hostage . . .'

'And Johnnie? Shall we get him back? My Johnnie. Whom you stole from me. And killed.'

Shocked, the man gripped her. 'Magdalen! How can you say such a thing!'

'You took him. In your pride and folly. A child. And where is he now? My fine Johnnie. Where is he now?' She turned, for the first time, to look up at him. 'Tell me, James Graham – where is my Johnnie now?'

Now that he saw her full face, he was shaken by the change in her, the puffiness of flesh, the sag at the corners of her mouth, the lack-lustre eyes and the heavy droop of eyelids. This was not just sorrow and pain. Here was sickness of the mind.

'Johnnie is, I think, better off than are we, my dear,' he said, slowly. 'His troubles are by with. We still have ours to thole. Johnnie was tested, tested hard. And proved a man, whatever his years. He will fare none so ill on the next stage of his journey – of that I am sure. What do we have to take to the hereafter with us? Only the character we have fought to forge on earth.

This must be our charter and warrant in the next world – only that, and God's infinite mercy. So – I do not fear for our Johnnie. We shall see him again, one day – and know him well blessed, I think.'

'Words!' the woman declared. 'Fine words, meaning nothing. Johnnie is dead – *dead*, do you hear? Because you took him to the wars, a child.'

He sighed. 'Dead, yes. But I believe that there are worse states than to be dead. More especially for those who have lived well. Struggled. Striven. And died well. As did Johnnie. He . . . he was fine. Courageous. Cheerful. To the end. A son to be proud of. He died in my arms . . .'

She put her hands over her ears. 'Stop! Stop, I say. I do not want to hear. Enough! Enough that he is dead. And gone. You may keep your fine swelling words, James. You always had them, in plenty. I have less faith in them.'

'You do not wish to hear how it was? With him? What I could not tell you in my letter . . . ?'

'No.'

'There could be comfort in it.'

'There is no comfort for me. Comfort! I am done with comfort. Save it for those who know no better.' She turned away again.

'Magdalen – this will not do. You torture yourself. You *need* comfort. As do I, God knows! We are husband and wife. We should cherish each other . . .'

'*You* say that! When are you with me, to cherish me and mine? You cherish only James_Graham. And need nothing from me. Nor ever have.'

If that had been said vehemently, harshly, with any spurt of feeling, it might have been less hard to bear, in that it could have engendered retort, perhaps indignation. But it was said levelly, hopelessly, and the man knew only sorrow, pain, guilt.

'I have come, now, at least. I would have come sooner, if I could,' he said, on a sigh. 'But Hurry lay between. He is gone now – but only to Dundee, I think. I must follow him, before he raises that city against us; against the King. I must be back with my little army by dawn. We have not long together, lass. Do not let us squander it, in this fashion.'

'Together?' she asked, simply.

He swallowed 'It was for that I came.'

'If it is the bed that you want, I cannot say you nay, my lord.' That was a whisper.

Biting his lip, he shook his head. 'No. Not so. I came only in love. Seeking to give, and receive, comfort, affection, help.'

'Then you came too late, James. Too late, by years. I am your wedded wife, and you may do with me as you will. But you are too late for these things – love, affection, comfort. They are dead, James. Like . . . like Johnnie; I am sorry.'

'No! I will not accept that, Magdalen. I cannot. But . . .' He touched her shoulder again, lightly, and changed the subject. 'I would see the children, my dear. Let us go upstairs to see young Robert. And Jean. They will have grown much . . .'

'Go, yes,' she said.

'And you. Surely you also . . . ?'

His wife shook his head.

Sighing, he turned and left her.

They had had five children. David, the third, had died in infancy. Robert and Jean were asleep in cots in the room directly above their mother's. Their father did not disturb them, although he longed to take them in his arms, especially the cherubic, pink-faced little girl. He scarcely knew them, having been but little at home these last five years and more – confirmation of Magdalen's indictment. Was he grievously at fault? Had he done altogether wrongly in choosing to concern himself with the affairs of the realm and the King, instead of those of his own family, his wife and children? He need not have done so. Nobody forced him to it. But . . . he was one of the earls of Scotland – he never thought of himself by this new-fangled title of marquis – one of the lesser kings, whose traditional duty was to advise, guide and support the monarch – *Ard Righ*, the Great King. Others admittedly had not taken this duty so seriously. But he was not one of the new men. He was *An Greumach Mor*, head of the house and line of Graham, which had been a sure support of the Crown since Celtic days. The land where he stood, although it was Carnegie's now, had been given to his ancestor Sir David the Graham by the Bruce himself, 320 years before. And that David was far down the long line. Should *he* have shrugged that heritage away? How could he have done – the Graham – and continued to respect himself? Yet – what sort of a father had he been to these sleeping innocents? What sort of a husband to that unhappy woman downstairs? Was it all selfishness of a sort, crass pride? Had he indeed taken the wrong turning, years ago? And now bairns were paying for it? What was duty? Where did it lie? To a man's country, heritage and liege lord? Or to wife and bairns?

Stooping over those cots, suddenly he was aware that Magdalen was standing just outside the door, looking in. He turned to her – and at once, like a shadow, she was gone.

He took a step or two after her, and then halted. What use? But at least she had come so far ..

He stayed there with the children for some time, perhaps half an hour, just sitting, watching, even after the last of the light was quite gone. He would not do better in this house. And it might give time for Magdalen to think, to reconsider.

At length, he reached out lightly to stroke those small heads and whisper something incoherent. In present circumstances, he had little assurance that he would ever see them again.

Downstairs, he was disappointed. Though the lamps were unlit. Magdalen still sat at the window, as before, silent, withdrawn. She had nothing to say to him, no comment to make. Clearly she now inhabited some sad, grey world of her own – and, try as he would, he could by no means penetrate to it. Presently he gave up the attempt, and stooped to kiss the heavy coils of her hair.

'Goodbye, my dear,' he said. 'God keep you until I come again. God have mercy upon us both. For we need it. Perhaps, when next I come, things will be better, kinder, for us. I pray that it is so. You must try to forgive me, Magdalen – for all our sakes. I have failed you grievously. But I must follow the road I have taken. There can be no turning back for me, now. Thousands depend on me – God pity me! But ... we will have decision soon. And then – we will do better. Do not despair, lass. Time will heal much – and we are young enough yet. Try to pray for me.'

She made no response. But nor did she round on him.

He left her then, and made his way back to the main keep, to take leave of her father. The old man sat still at the head of the dais-table in the hall, a great wine-flagon before him, his brother sprawled over the board and snoring.

'Well, man – you have seen what you have done to my daughter,' Southesk growled. 'Are you satisfied?'

'I am sore at heart,' the younger man told him. 'How long has she been thus?'

'Too long. Months. Do you wonder?'

'It was before ... before Johnnie died?'

38

'Long before. That worsened it. She has pined for you too long, man. Now all is gone sour in her.' The old man took a great draught from the flagon, and then banged it down on the table. 'God's curse on it!' he cried. 'My lassie!'

'I should have taken her with me,' his son-in-law said, slowly.

'Eh . . . ? Taken her ? To the wars ?'

'Yes. She asked it, once. After Tippermuir. At Perth. Pleaded with me. When I took Johnnie. He pleading also. She said she would be a camp-follower. I said that it was impossible, not to be considered . . .'

'I should say not! What folly! *My* daughter, trailing at the heels of an army, like any Irish drab . . . !'

'*That* was not my concern. It was the hardship, the danger, the rough living. But . . . it might have saved her from . . . this.'

'Nonsense, man. If you think that, you are an even greater fool than I took you for!'

'There are fools and fools!' his son-in-law observed, sombrely.

In that spirit he left Kinnaird.

CHAPTER THREE

With Hurry gone and no Covenant forces remaining in the neighbourhood, the countryside hastened to make at least its provisional peace with Montrose. Deputations arrived at Fettercairn from Brechin, Forfar and Montrose itself, announcing these towns' welcome to the King's Lieutenant. But James Graham, what with one thing and another, was not in forthcoming mood. He sent Colkitto to Brechin, which had shown active hostility, and Madderty to Forfar, permitting them to requisition, with a little plunder – but not to harry or ravage, making clear distinction. For old times' sake, he himself went to Montrose, where he had spent much of his boyhood. It was the best port north of Forth until Aberdeen, and its merchants prosperous, its warehouses well-stocked. There was much his ragged army required which Montrose town could supply – but here he would pay for his purchases, on the principle that it is a dirty bird which fouls its own nest. And he had hopes that he might raise a troop of cavalry from the local lairds.

At Montrose, however, messages from his advance scouts informed him that General Baillie, spurred on by Hurry's discomfiture, had at last moved out of his comfortable quarters in Perth and was heading north against the royalists, evidently directly, via Strathmore. James Graham knew Baillie, another professional, who, like Leslie had trained under the great Gustavus Adolphus, and had much respect for his abilities as a soldier. Especially as he now was reinforced by 3,000 of Leslie's seasoned infantry sent up from England and withdrawn from Ireland, as a result of the Invergarry affair, in addition to his own local forces and Balcarres's horse. But Montrose was not going to forfeit his valuable image as a bold and victorious general by avoiding the superior enemy. He sent out hurried couriers to his scattered units, and headed south to meet William Baillie.

Next afternoon the two armies met near Coupar Angus – or almost met. For the winding but major River Isla lay between them, and it was in fairly high spate with the melting snows from the mountains. There was no bridge across it all the way from where it emerged from the hills of Glen Isla to its confluence with Tay, nearly twenty miles, only fords. The best of these, for any large body of men, was just north of Coupar, at Couttie – part of the reason for the town's existence indeed. Baillie having arrived first, had taken possession of this ford. But he had not brought his army across.

Halting on a low rolling ridge of the Strathmore plain called the Hill of Bendochy – hill being an exaggeration – Montrose had the Covenant army in full view before him, four times the size of his own, gay with flags and banners, a fitful sunlight glinting on steel, a stirring sight.

Drawing up his own force extended along the ridge – so that it might appear as large as possible, and that there might well be more behind – Montrose sent mounted gallopers dashing hither and thither with great urgency on mainly mythical errands, to give the impression of great activity and marshalling, he himself scanning the terrain intently the while. It was highly significant, of course, that Baillie had not crossed the Isla when he had opportunity. It showed, as well as caution, probable doubts as to the royalist strength – a state of affairs to be fostered and exploited, if possible. It would be strange, of course, if Hurry had not given an exaggerated report of the force which had so humiliated him.

But how to exploit the situation, in the face of that impassable river, taxed even Montrose's fertile imagination. No flanking or encircling move was feasible, no feint or gesture was of any validity that did not involve crossing the water; and that could be attempted only at the guarded ford. Admittedly the same applied to Baillie – but he had clearly *chosen* to remain where he was. It looked like tactical stalemate.

James Graham made up his mind, and quite quickly. It was vital that he retained the initiative, or seemed to. He hoisted a white flag alongside the new royal standard he had had made, and ordered his trumpeter to blow a fanfare. Then, with a few of his officers, he rode down to the river-side. Swiftly Covenant officers appeared on the other bank, cantering over the green haughland.

After another trumpet flourish, Montrose spoke. 'The King's Lieutenant and Viceroy, James, Marquis of Montrose, requests the courtesy of speech with Lieutenant-General William Baillie of Letham,' he called.

'To what end? Are you surrendering?' somebody called back.

'I would speak as one gentleman with another. That is all. Kindly convey my request to your general.'

The horsemen spurred off.

Montrose sat his mount, patiently waiting.

Presently a little stout cherub of a man, mounted on a horse much too big for him, came unhurriedly down, surrounded by aides, lordlings and black-robed ministers. James Graham recognised many faces amongst them, including the sardonically handsome Hurry, the Earl of Balcarres, Master of Horse and the young Earl of Lauderdale.

'You desired speech with me, my lord?' Baillie shouted across, in a surprisingly deep and strong voice to emerge from so small a man.

'I do, sir. I greet you kindly. And since you come into my country with a large host, I wish to ask whether you come to submit yourself, and it, to the King's peace, as is your duty? Or whether you remain in shameful rebellion to that peace, as creature of my lord Argyll?'

'I come as commander of the forces of the Estates of Scotland, my lord marquis. With warrant for your arrest and trial on a charge of high treason.'

'Ah! And whose signature is on that warrant, sir, I pray you? A Campbell's, I swear!'

'Hmmm. It is my lord Earl of Loudoun's, Chancellor of this realm.'

'Aye – a Campbell's, as I thought. And how can he be Chancellor, when the realm's lord and master, King Charles, no longer recognises him?'

'Did you call me here to barter words, my lord?'

'No, sir. I did not. Since you come in declared enmity, I crave your co-operation that we may come to a fair decision, on the matter which divides us, like gentlemen. That is why I sought your presence. At present we cannot do so because of this river. Either, will you stand your force back while we cross over unassailed, so that we meet in fair fight? Or shall I do so, that *you* may cross unhindered? The choice is yours, sir.'

There was a brief pause, and then Baillie answered, more roughly than hitherto. 'There is no choice in it, man. For I will do neither. I will fight my battles at my own pleasure and convenience – not yours!'

42

'You hesitate to put the matter to the test in fair fight, then? Perhaps you are wise, sir.'

'Enough of this!' The other jerked his horse's head round. 'Good day to you. But – I will have you in Edinburgh Tolbooth before long, never fear!'

'But not today, General? You prefer to leave it till an occasion when you feel that you might win?'

Without another word, Baillie and his suite rode off.

'Are you disappointed, my lord?' Colonel O'Cahan asked.

'I am not, Magnus. Relieved, rather. Since we are in no state to fight four times our numbers, and without advantage of surprise or site, I am well content.'

'You expected it thus, b'God?'

'Indeed, yes. Given a man of cautious temper, like Baillie, he was all but bound so to choose. Now *we* can choose our course, and declare aloud that Baillie refused to fight.'

'If the King had even one more general like yourself, James,' the Lord Gordon declared, 'he would sit secure on his throne.'

Back at the main force, Montrose gave orders to remain drawn up, there on the rise, but for the infantry to seem to make camp. And to endeavour to give the impression that there were many more of them behind the ridge. The Covenant army likewise remained where it was. And all that afternoon and evening they watched each other at a mile's distance.

As night came down and cooking-fires were lit, Montrose gradually withdrew his regiments and squadrons behind the rise. But he left a small working-party of Gordon cavalry to keep these fires lit and replenished all night, with whatever they could find to burn, and only to follow after the rest at dawn. And he left an advanced picket, with its own fire, down not far from the ford at Couttie, to discourage any night ventures. Thereafter, he commanded fast, silent marching – and when James Graham said fast marching, he meant fast indeed.

They went north-eastwards now, as steadily so as the land would allow with tributaries of the Isla to cross and marshland to circumnavigate, difficult in the darkness. But these were all Airlie lands, and Sir David Ogilvy, with some of his men, made excellent guides. It was nine or ten miles before they could cross Isla, at Inverqueich Mill ford; but this they avoided, Montrose giving Baillie credit for having pickets as far out as this, to prevent his flank being turned. In another four miles, however, they were well into the Grampian foothills, and mounted scouts

43

reported that the ford at Kilry was not held. Cheered but wary still, they pressed forward into the deep den where, below rapids, was a shingly stretch passable for determined men.

If many of the company now expected their general to swing back, southward to bear down on the Covenant left, they were surprised. For Montrose led his force on almost due westwards, against the grain of the land, over rather than through the billowing skirts of the hills, taxing, trying work. But at least here they were safe from observation, with only cattle lumbering off into the night affrighted, and they could march openly and less silently. They went behind the Hill of Alyth, avoiding the Ramsay castle of Banff, and on across the high desolation of weird Drimmie Muir with the eerie stone-circles looming up like giants in the darkness. The deep valley of the swift-running Ericht then fell to be crossed. which they managed at Strone of Cally, to start climbing again, but now swinging directly south-wards over Cochrage Muir to the long remote valley of the Lornty Water, amongst more ancient burial-cairns and the constant reminders of long-dead races. Finally, having circled all the populous area of Rattray and Blairgowrie, they came down to the east-west Stormonth road at Drumellie Loch, an hour short of dawn. Even then there was only a brief rest, with Montrose not satisfied, for security reasons. There were still eight miles to Dunkeld, in the throat of Atholl, but now easy going, with a drove-road all the way. What was another eight miles to his heroes?

He had his way, and three hours later the royalist army limped into the haughs of Tay across from Birnam Wood, just short of Dunkeld, weary and spent – but having transformed the entire strategic position. Now Baillie was left islanded in Strathmore, friendly Atholl and the Central Highlands were at Montrose's back, and the great Tay valley open in front, the way to the south, unguarded. Perth was theirs for the taking, Strathearn and Strathallan, Graham and Drummond country, beyond. Argyll, in Edinburgh, would feel the cold draught from the north, with nothing but miles between him and his enemy.

But James Graham, in his strategic brilliance, had forgotten something – the great weakness of any Celtic army,. the pull of home ties and families. Even before he wakened, around noon that day, men were slipping away. After the Ulstermen and Isles-men, the bulk of his infantry were Athollmen – and now, after long absence, they were within smelling distance of their own hearths and peat-reek. It was not desertion, for they would come back in due course. But meantime, the call was too strong for them. The Stewarts, Murrays and Robertsons faded away. The Drummonds likewise, heading southwards, even some Grahams. Up Strathbraan, down the Sma' Glen, and they were into Strathearn. The exodus from Dunkeld began. Montrose, in his heart, could not blame them, disappointed as he was.

Waiting, fretting, at Dunkeld, while he sent out officers all around to try to raise more men from lairds and lords who *should* be friendly, Montrose learned that Baillie also had wasted no time, that he was now hurrying southwards diagonally across Angus, for Fife, undoubtedly to defend the Forth crossings. It was going to be too late for any descent on the capital.

Then further trouble developed at Dunkeld. The Lord Lewis Gordon declared, out of the blue, that he for one had not come all this way just to skulk and hide and twiddle his thumbs, awaiting the pleasure of a wheen Hielant barbarians. He could do better than this for King Charles back in Aberdeenshire. Unless Montrose led them on to Perth and Stirling, at least, he personally was going back home – and he did not doubt but that he would take not a few of the Gordon horse home with him.

After an angry scene, his brother managed to persuade him to stay his hand. But things said could not be unsaid, and there was bad blood now between the brothers and amongst the Gordon ranks. The fact was, Gordon as a power had always acted for itself, never made a satisfactory *part* of any force under the controls of others.

Not only the Gordons were demanding action. It was another weakness of the Celtic host that it did not find waiting easy. None bolder, braver, more gallant when the clash came, the Gaelic warrior had little gift for patient restraint and inaction. Colkitto did not join the Lord Lewis in threats; but he urged action, any action. Otherwise his Islesmen would be the next to head for home.

Since keeping his force in being was, after all, the first priority, and since the south was now barred and Perth warned, Montrose decided to make a strike at Dundee. It was twenty-five miles back to the east, and would never anticipate an attack; but it was a major city, and in royalist hands would support a claim that all the North was the King's. In a war which was being waged for the soul of a nation, that sort of claim could be important.

That night of the 3rd of April, he sent off his baggage, sick and less able men, to march by easy stages for Brechin, towards the north-east end of Strathmore, whilst with some 600 infantry and such horse as remained he himself slipped out of Dunkeld as suddenly and discreetly as he had come. At the last moment Lewis Gordon decided that Dundee was an insufficient target for Gordon. It was the flimsiest of excuse – but the break had to come. Montrose did not seek to hold him, or those who felt like him, despite the Lord Gordon's protests, but requested that they escort the baggage-train as far as Brechin, on their way home. It was a grievously reduced host, then, which set out for the coast and Dundee.

Since his men had wanted action, they got it now. They had twenty-five miles to cover, and it was necessary that any descent on Dundee should be a surprise. This time they followed Tay directly down through the lower Stormonth to Meikleour, by level lands, comparatively easy going, to cross the Isla at the same spot near Coupar Angus formerly held by Baillie and now deserted. Then they slipped through the green range of the Sidlaws by the easy Tullybaccart pass, just as the grey dawn was breaking; and in an hour or so saw the walled town of Dundee before them, between the towering law and the dazzlement of the sun's rising over the Tay estuary. Scouts sent word that the gates of the city were being opened for the new day. The necessary surprise would be achieved.

But it could only be a limited surprise, sufficient to ensure that there could be no reinforcement of the town's small permanent garrison. For there was no way of hiding the little army's final two miles of approach. Inevitably the gates would be shut again, and the walls beginning to be manned.

Montrose had two small cannon, which he had borrowed from the Earl of Atholl's castle at Dunkeld. These he had dismantled and slung in panniers on garrons, with a limited supply of ball. Dundee's garrison would have many and much larger cannon – but they would be distributed at various points round the perimeter of the walls, and it would take time to assemble them at any given point of assault. Therefore time, now, was of the essence – despite the weariness of men who had marched twenty-five miles. Also the point of attack was vital. The town walls were substantial and high, and Montrose had no illusions about his chances of taking them. But he had a precious item of information, obtained when he lay at Fettercairn, that there had been a collapse of the wall, where a burn flowed beneath, near the north-east corner, and his scouts confirmed that this point was still under repair. He planned his tactics accordingly.

His main force marched forward, swiftly and openly, towards the main west gate, where the road from Perth entered. But secretly he sent a small party, with those cannon, by devious hidden ways, with bales of hay on the horses' backs to hide their burdens, the men looking as like ordinary countrymen as they might, arms not in evidence. These, under Magnus O'Cahan, were to get into position near the broken portion of the walling, set up the cannon, but to remain quiescent meantime.

As expected, they found the West Port shut and barred against them – and Montrose could imagine the panic and frenzied activity within the city. And, he hoped, the hasty dragging of heavy defensive cannon to this threatened western area. There was an eminence here, just within the walls, ideally situated for artillery defence, called the Corbie Hill. Montrose knew it well, and knew that any commander would use it. To give time for a concentration of the city's artillery here, he sent a trumpeter and a Gordon laird, under a flag of truce, as emissary to the Provost and magistrates, requesting the city gates to be opened to him in the King's name, and assuring that no harm would befall Dundee if all was done peaceably and without delay.

'What hope have you of submission?' George Gordon asked.

'None,' he was told. 'The city is much too strong to consider it, I think. They can see that we are but a small force – we cannot hide it. If I know them, they will parley with our messenger, delay, while they get their cannon assembled and into position on yonder Corbie Hill. These will be scattered round the town. Then we shall have our answer – in the shape of powder-and-ball. Watch you that hill-top.'

'You will let them get so far? Into position on the hill?'

'We cannot stop them. But we are out of range, here. They will do us no harm. We wait, with what patience we can summon...'

Sure enough, after the best part of an hour, waiting, they could discern much activity on the top of Corbie Hill. It was only a gentle eminence, and the city walls were too high to allow the watchers to see all but a small hummock on it. But men's heads and shoulders could be observed, and presently the upper parts of straining horses – undoubtedly dragging cannon up the slope. Montrose was satisfied. But their envoys did not return.

Another trumpeter was sent forward, to the foot of the walls, to announce to the gate-keepers that the King's Lieutenant's patience had run out. Unless the authorities threw open the gates to him in ten minutes, he would take it that they were in rebellion against His Grace, denying his Lieutenant entry. He would take the city by force.

At the same time, he sent another runner racing round to the north, to the party opposite the broken portion of walling. Open fire five minutes after receiving the message, he directed.

No reply came from Dundee's leaders. Nor did the Gordon and the trumpeter return. Everyone waited, tensely now.

Then the crash of cannon sounded from the north. Immediately, all was transformed. As yells and shooting rose from the walls and within, the royalist ranks swung around in disciplined units, and went off at the double northwards, following the perimeter. There was some delay before the city's cannon on Corbie Hill thundered raggedly – but their ball did no damage to the running regiments.

Another two shots boomed from the pieces at the north-west angle. Magnus O'Cahan had much experience as a cannoneer.

By the time that Montrose got round to the point of bombardment, there was little need for further preparation. The collapsed wall had by no means been fully rebuilt, and at point-blank range the cannon had battered a sizeable gap in it already. There was no sign of defenders, as yet – certainly no artillery reply in this sector.

Montrose's trumpeter sounded the advance, breathlessly, and the Irish infantry poured through.

There was no real opposition, at this stage. The guns on Corbie Hill were masked from here, useless. Citizens wisely stayed indoors, and such few armed men as were about faded rapidly away. One troop did come rushing down a narrow side-street, from the south, saw that they were too late to prevent entry, also much outnumbered, and turned to bolt back whence they had come.

Montrose and Colkitto kept their men very closely under control – for nothing is so dangerous as for a comparatively small force to take a town and to become dispersed therein. They led them back in roughly the direction they had come, only inside the walls, a swift-racing silent band of 600, the cavalry left outside. It would have been a brave train-band commander who attempted to stem that Celtic flood.

Montrose, in front, took them directly to Corbie Hill, approaching it from the north-west side now. When it came into view, there was again great activity on the crest, a dragging round of cannon, a milling of horsemen and shouting of orders. When the hill-top cannoneers suddenly saw the Irish regiments breasting the hill at the run, in grim, panting silence, they were scarcely to be blamed that they bolted also, to a man. There was no fighting, no resistance. The cannon, and horses harnessed to them, were left as they stood.

'O'Cahan!' James Graham shouted, and pointed eastwards, into the city centre. 'These pieces to face there. Down Overgate and Nethergate, to Market Gate. Do not fire until I give word.'

The situation was now almost laughably reversed. Corbie Hill commanded all the centre of the town, the principal streets, the Tolbooth and Town House, the high tower of St. Mary's Church, all spread conveniently below. Their own cannon now held Dundee at their mercy.

When O'Cahan's men had the pieces turned and trained – they were already loaded and primed – Montrose said, 'Two shots, Magnus, if you please. Where they will do least hurt. The graveyard perhaps, if you can. The Howff, there. Two only.'

The first two cannon-balls produced no recognisable reaction. Montrose was loth to order a bombardment of the city. He waited, his men impatient now. Presently he sent another four shots down into the Market Gate. Thereafter, fairly quickly, a white flag was hoisted from the top of St. Mary's tower. The magistrates could see, as well as anyone else, that the heart of their city could be pounded to pieces by the artillery.

It was a practically bloodless victory.

But all was not over yet. As the victors marched down the Nethergate, there was sniping at them from side-streets and wynds. Angered, the Irish infantry turned hunters, and Montrose now had to use all his powers of command and persuasion to prevent savage reprisals. He did not want a sack of Dundee on his conscience, to add to that of Aberdeen. But at least this behaviour gave him excuse to allow a certain amount of pillage, taking of food, forage, clothing, footwear and other gear, which the ragged army so desperately required, without payment. James Graham's personal fortune which, for so long had borne most of the cost of the King's campaign, was by now in shaky condition indeed.

When he had accepted the surrender of the city, and warned

what would happen if guerrilla resistance continued, he went back to the Corbie Hill, partly to maintain the threat of those cannon – for 600 men in a city of thousands were vulnerable indeed – and partly because it was the best look-out point within the walls.

It was as well that he did. Two galloping horsemen caught his eye almost at once, heading from the district of Invergowrie, for the West Port. Their haste and urgency was eloquent, as of men chased. Raising his gaze, he scanned the area to the west, behind, screwing up his eyes in the slanting late afternoon sun. And there, a dark shadow was spilling out from the wide dip which was the valley of the Gowrie Burn. It could only be men in large numbers, an army . . .

His trumpeter was blaring the Recall, with three blasts for urgency, within seconds, and messengers were racing off.

Montrose waited there only long enough for his galloping Gordon scouts to reach him, their horses lathered in spume. Baillie had turned back from Fife, they panted. He had ferried his men across Tay, farther up, Hurry's cavalry first. Now they, the cavalry, were not two miles behind.

'How many ?'

'God knows ! A great force. All Balcarres's horse, by the looks o' it . . .'

James Graham was shouting orders before the words were out. The cannon to be slewed round again, to face and fire westwards. The West Port to be manned by musketeers. It would not take Hurry long to find the gap in the walls, to the north – but the delay might be just sufficient. He would send cavalry to pick up the cannoneers and musketeers, as soon as he might. Start the gunfire right away, without ball – it would serve to warn their own people that there was trouble, and might make Hurry cautious, slow him down.

Jumping on a horse, he dashed down to the Market Gate.

Gathering together 600 men in a city, especially when they have been given a licence to pillage, and where there are women available by the score, is no swift and simple task. The trumpeting and resumed cannonade helped; but even so it was an infuriatingly slow and involved process. When a different note in the cannon-fire indicated that it was now ball being fired, in earnest, Montrose sent Nathaniel Gordon and a troop of horse back, to evacuate the cannoneers by pillion. He decided that he had no option but to cut his losses. He had no illusions as to what a large force of cavalry could do to a smaller scattered infantry force shut up inside a town. Almost a hundred men short, he commanded immediate and speedy retiral by the Seagate and East Port, himself waiting for Nat Gordon. It was ignominious, heart-breaking. Little or nothing of their pillage could be taken with them. But it was necessary if the force was to be preserved as a weapon of war.

They were only just in time. Had Hurry known the full circumstances, of the Athollmen's absence, Lewis Gordon's defection, and the fact that there could be no real attempt to hold the town against him, undoubtedly he would have pressed on faster, rushed the gates, and thereafter foregone the checking of side-streets and lanes. As it was, Montrose, with his cavalry as rearguard, were clattering down the Seagate to the East Port as Hurry moved heedfully down the Nethergate.

It was the measure of Hurry's respect for Montrose as a tactician that, with the evening descending and the light beginning to fade, out in the open country with room to manoeuvre, skirmish and ambush, he did not attempt any brash riding down of the retiring royalists. He followed on, but with care, scouts and pickets testing every yard of the way. Only that, a beneficial result of the Ducal Water affair, saved the Irish infantry – for the cavalry of course *could* have made good their escape – as they hastened along the Angus coast, eastwards.

Sundry delaying tactics Montrose did attempt. He lit the whins behind them near Broughty Castle which, with the evening breeze, made a swift-running moorland blaze calculated to alarm and puzzle following cavalry. At the ford of the Dichty Water, short of Monifeith, he left two more fires, like beacons, with the same purpose. And he sent a picket of swift horsemen, under Nat Gordon to ride round and back, in the darkness, to fire a fusillade of pistol- and musket-shots *behind* Hurry's ever more preoccupied force.

The cumulative effect was satisfactory in so far as it prevented the Covenant cavalry from finally catching up with the hard-pressed Irish and Islesmen regiments. And about midnight, having crossed the wide sandy wastes of Barry, at West Haven just beyond Carnoustie, Montrose swung his desperately weary marchers abruptly north-westwards, away from the coast, at right angles to their line of retreat hitherto, to slip up the shadowy and hidden winding den of the Monikie Burn, passing close to the Kirkton of Panbride, and on beyond. The cavalry he ordered to continue on their former course meantime, to disguise if possible the sudden change of route of the foot, and draw Hurry after them. They could rejoin them later, in the Guthrie area, on their joint way to Brechin, where they would rendezvous with the baggage-train, and all detachments and stragglers.

The ruse worked. Scouts came to report that the large force of Covenant horse had not so much as paused at the Monikie ford, but splashed, across and on heedfully, towards Arbroath.

They were climbing up from the coastal plain now, by cattle pastures and thin-dotted moorland. In the Carmylie vicinity, at Guynd, Montrose reckoned that he could allow his panting, weary men a rest. Many of them, tough as they were, were in a bad way, liquor too hastily consumed at Dundee having its effect. Hurry would never find them again tonight. Two hours they could have, he declared. Then on to Guthrie and Brechin.

But before they made a move, the scouts that Black Pate Graham never failed to have out, front, flanks and rear, brought reports of a new threat. Another large force was in front of them, heading fast through the night north-easterly up Strathmore's southern flank, diagonally across their own line of march. It could only be Baillie, seeking to cut them off from their safe refuge in the Angus glens and the mountains beyond. Someone must have talked, told him of the Brechin rendezvous. It looked as though they had underestimated their enemy. Baillie must have been closer behind Hurry than they had thought, and proving that he could move fast when he put his mind to it.

Montrose was in no position to challenge Baillie any more than Hurry. He could only take avoiding action. He sent fast horsemen off to warn the people at Brechin to disperse northwards and make for Strathfinella and the entrace to the Cairn o' Mount pass. Others to try to find the Gordon cavalry at all costs, in the region between Arbroath and Brechin, watching out for Hurry meantime, and order them to flee at their fastest up the Howe of the Mearns to Glenbervie, and there turn south and west again, through the Glen of Drumtochty, to reach Strathfinella from the north – this to avoid the risk of bringing Hurry in pursuit, down on the infantry again. They would all meet at the mouth of the pass. God willing.

The main body resumed its northwards march cautiously, swinging somewhat to the west now, across the scrub birch, pines, whins and marshes of Montreathmont Moor, hoping to strike the levels of Strathmore well behind their foes.

At Markhouse, with still two hours to dawn, they reached the wide plain, scouts assuring that the way was clear and that Baillie's rearguard was fully three miles ahead. Thankfully, Montrose led his desperately tired men across the ford of the South Esk and out into the levels, Brechin seven miles on their right, Forfar the same distance to the left. Nothing was likely to hold them up now, except sheer fatigue.

The sun was up long before they reached Strathfinella, in the throat of the mountains; but this was Ogilvy and Lindsay country, where they were relatively safe. They found both the Gordons and the Brechin party already there, awaiting them, having had no contact with the enemy. All moved on a mile or so up into the steeply climbing gut of the Cairn o' Mount pass. They were out of Baillie's or Hurry's clutches now; none could trap them in such a place, none would venture to follow them, mountain-warfare veterans, into these lonely barren heights. They might go hungry, but they would not die.

Montrose had saved his pathetic remnant of an army from disaster. But he was not proud of himself. He had acted against his better judgment, taken grave risks for insufficient purpose, taken for granted enemy dispositions which he should have more closely checked, and not given Baillie and Hurry credit for being the professionals they were. He could blame none but himself. He was the commander, and the responsibility was his.

James Graham was not to know that, with the military historians of the future, this retiral from Dundee was to rank with his greatest victories, outshining some of them indeed, as a feat of arms. Not for him to evaluate the worth of a general who could take a walled and warned city almost without a drop of blood shed; halt what amounted to a sacking of that city in a matter of minutes; collect, marshal and extricate an army of half-starved, part-drunken and notoriously independent Irish and Gaelic irregular infantry from a major cavalry assault; and thereafter, already weary with great marching, get them over thirty desperate miles in the darkness, avoiding one army in pursuit and another intent on heading them off. Such a man was, by any standards, no ordinary commander.

They rested all that day and the next night – and their scouts sent no word of enemy approach. The day following they marched northwards, unhurriedly now, into the mighty mountain spine of Scotland.

CHAPTER FOUR

The valley of the Feugh made as good a place as any to halt, to lick their wounds, to consider the future. It lay at the northern end of the long Cairn o' Mount pass, a hidden side-glen of the great valley of Dee, populous enough with Gordons and Farquharsons to provide food and forage for this modest army, yet sufficiently remote and inaccessible to be secure. Amongst the green mountains, with their pine-forested lower slopes, dark Lochnagar itself dominating the scene to the west, Montrose settled for a space, to rest his troops and rack his wits.

Here in the Forest of Birse three days later a courier found them, disguised as a packman, after a month on the road seeking Montrose. Despite his lowly and undistinguished appearance, this was a very special visitor, an Irish Colonel Small, from King Charles himself no less at Oxford, the first link James Graham had had with his liege lord for many a long month. The colonel carried brief despatches, but longer and fuller message by word of mouth – even Charles Stewart was learning discretion, it seemed. The verbal royal commands would be backed by written authority as soon as it was practicable.

Small's tidings were to this effect. His Majesty had received Montrose's letter, after Inverlochy, and was highly delighted and encouraged by that great victory. His well-beloved and trusted friend was now Captain-General in Scotland, endowed with every power to act in the King's name in all matters, supreme – royal warrants to follow. The King intended to act on Montrose's advice, and come to Scotland in person, just so soon as it could be arranged. It was his royal intention that he should advance over the border from Cumberland and that Montrose should strike southwards, and they would trap the King's rebels between two fires. Meantime, recognising his friend's great need for cavalry, His Majesty would send north a body of horse, to be entirely under Montrose's command.

James Graham reacted to these tidings in entirely positive fashion. The fact was that, for once, Charles had given him what he needed. Not the Captain-Generalship, which he had once refused and which, as a mere title, was unimportant. But the feeling that he was not, after all, alone, forgotten, a man chasing cloud-shadows; that his so strenuous efforts were not just a beating of the air but part of a great and noble purpose. Desperately, indeed, he was requiring such assurance.

He was sufficiently moved, therefore, almost elated, to shake hands with the colonel a second time. 'My friend – I cannot sufficiently thank you for risking your life to bring me these tidings,' he said. 'And His Grace for sending them. It is long since I had any news of his cause and progress. I am like a man in a dark room, to whom you have brought a gleam of light. To let me see my way ahead, again. To know that I am not forgotten is, in itself, as good as a regiment of cavalry!'

'Sakes – you are not forgotten, my lord!' Small assured, grinning. He was a cheerful, devil-may-care Ulsterman, stocky, blunt-featured and with a slight cast in one eye, dirty, unshaven and clad in ragged clothes that stank. 'Forgotten is the last state of the Marquis of Montrose, b'God! Though some might wish that you were! For the King builds you up before all, no less. As a shining exemplar, see you. The only one of his generals who can win battles! Your name is seldom off the royal lips these days. And not all loving the sound o' it!'

'Mm.' James Graham looked perturbed. 'That is unfortunate. I do not merit such acclaim, besides. I have won some few encounters, yes – but am almost as far from winning Scotland for the King as ever I was, I fear.'

'You say so? I will not tell His majesty that, by the Powers – however much it might please some close to him!'

'Close? How close?'

'Of the closest, sir.'

'You mean – the Queen?'

The other glanced about him, at the Lord Gordon, Sir David Ogilvy, Pate Graham and other officers who listened interestedly. 'I did not say that, my lord Marquis,' he observed, after a moment.

'No, sir – you did not. All witness it. But . . . I have my enemies at that Court, I know well. To my sorrow. Two close to His Grace will support me, however, I believe. His nephews, the Prince Rupert and Maurice.'

'No doubt, sir. But Rupert is not in the highest favour, these days, see you. And his brother with him. The King is led to believe him too rash. They are scarce in the royal confidence . . .'

'But – these are his own kin. His sister's sons. And, moreover, his best commanders . . .'

'No doubt. But *Her* Majesty no longer finds them altogether to her taste, my lord.'

'I see. It is that way?' Montrose took a turn across the greensward before the cot-house which presently was his head-quarters. 'Tell me, Colonel – how goes the cause in England?'

'Ill,' the other said, baldly.

'So! How ill, man?'

'Ill enough to cause His Majesty consider coming to Scotland!'

Montrose's colleagues exchanged grim glances. But, though he himself stared thoughtfully at the speaker, the Graham was not surprised. Deep within him, he had guessed as much, recognised that the war *could* not be prospering in England, or the reactions of the hard-headed realists of the Estates of Parliament would have been very different from what it was. And even though it was desperation that was to bring Charles to Scotland, that might be none so ill a contingency.

'You mean, it will be flight rather than policy which brings him here?'

'You could say so, yes. The man Cromwell has the King's high-born generals trussed like fowls for market! There is not one of the noble lords who can face him. If *you* were to come south, now, sir . . .'

'No – I am well content that it should be His Grace who comes north. Whatever the reason. This I have long urged upon him. The Stewarts, I believe, made their greatest mistake when they forsook their own Scotland for England. They represented a thousand years of rule in Scotland. But what in England? The English have no *Ard Righ*, nor ever had. Their kings were always conquerors – and if they could not conquer, they fell. The idea of kingship, as of government and religion, is quite different in the two realms. And James Stewart threw his Scots heritage away – for what? A poorer, lesser, uncertain thing. And, to be sure, vaults of English gold!'

'That was forty years ago, my lord.'

'True. But the situation remains. Charles, I fear, has lost England, at least for the present. But there is no reason why he should lose Scotland, his ancient inheritance, also. He should have come back, long ere this. Come back, to bide. Let England take its own course, meantime. Let them choose King Crom-

56

well, if they will. Charles is still, and will always be, King of Scots.'

'Yet the Scots seem to love the King little more than the English do. Or the Irish! Was it not here that revolt started? With your Covenant?'

'You mistake, my friend. That was not revolt. Protest, yes. A plea for reform. But with no thought of putting the King from his throne. Putting down some of the King's ill-advisers, yes – but never the King. Scotland lacking a King of Scots is inconceivable. It is the oldest kingdom in Christendom, old when there was no England, only warring German tribes. Charles should return home, prepared to make concessions, call a true parliament – and summon Argyll before it. If he stayed away, the Campbell would be forfeited, outlawed. If he came, he would be voted down – nothing surer. He is the best-hated man in the kingdom. King Charles, if he relied on honest men, not on Hamilton, Lanark, Lauderdale and the like, could put down King Campbell.'

'And Leslie? Baillie? Callendar? The armies of the Estates?'

'These are paid soldiers. Mercenaries. Not Callendar, but the others, the important ones. Able, but venial. They serve who pays highest, who seem to win.'

'That, then, is your advice for His Majesty, my lord? To abandon England and come to Scotland. So soon as may be. With his armies...?'

'With his English armies – no! The King must not bring English troops against his Scottish subjects. Or very few, and officered by Scots. We are a prickly race, sir, the thistle not our emblem for nothing! But there are many Scots serving in England with His Grace. A corps of these, coming over the West March with the King, would draw much support in Dumfries-shire and Galloway. To threaten the Earl of Callendar from the south. I would move down from the north, and we would have them between two fires. Callendar is no rash hero. He would temporise, and then slip away, if he might, I do believe. Leslie would be forced to come home from Yorkshire. Before he could do so, we would be secure in Edinburgh, calling a parliament. Leslie would wait at the border, to see how the cat jumped. And his men, so near home, would not all wait with him! I know! Scotland would be the King's within a month.'

'A fair dream, my lord Marquis. But a dream, nevertheless, I fear.'

'I do not content myself with dreaming, Colonel,' Montrose said briefly – and his friends smiled.

The Irishman made hasty amendment. 'I meant nothing such, on my soul!' he assured. 'All the world knows your lordship's prowess as a general. None esteems it more than I do. I meant only that such a campaign would be more easily planned than carried out. So much might go awry . . .'

'No doubt. But that could apply to both sides. The King would start with advantage, because he *is* the King. And takes the initiative.'

'And because *you* are Montrose!' Colkitto, who had just come up, declared from behind

'That is as may be. But at least I have the most seasoned and renowned infantry in Europe, to strike terror into more humdrum forces!'

'Very well, my lord. That message I will carry to His Majesty. Whether he will heed it is another matter! For few at Court will agree that England should be abandoned . . .'

'That is for His Grace's ear alone, man – of a mercy! Do not stress it, even so. Just the seed to be sown. What is important is to hasten the King's coming to Scotland. How soon was he minding to ?'

'That I cannot tell. You know His Majesty! Time is of small account to him . . .'

'But it is of large account to his cause! To me, and mine, it is vital. You must impress it upon him, sir. It is now April. All must be done by August, or it will be too late. With harvest, the clansmen go home. Request His Grace to come in June, if he can. And I will come to meet him.'

It was left so, and that night Colonel Small took his departure southwards.

Now, spurred on with new drive and purpose, Montrose was all energy again. He had to build up his army once more, and swiftly. He sent George Gordon back to Strathbogie to recruit more cavalry and counter any ill influences of his brother Lewis. Colkitto was despatched westwards to the MacDonald country of the Hebridean seaboard, to seek to involve Clanranald, Glengarry and Keppoch once more, with others of the Western clans. Black Pate and the Master of Madderty went south, by Glen Shee and Kirkmichael to Atholl, Strathtay and Strathearn, seeking Stewarts, Robertsons, Murrays, Drummonds, Hays and Grahams. Other emissaries went elsewhere. They were all to rendezvous at Skene, some fifteen miles down the Dee, by the end of the month or thereabouts.

James Graham was not the man to sit idly waiting while others were busy. Moreover, his Celtic troops were not the sort who improved with inactivity. When, two days after his messengers had left, his scouts brought intelligence that Baillie had retired to his former quarters at Perth, while Hurry, with 1,200 foot and an unspecified number of horse was pushing northwards for Aberdeenshire, he decided on an interim ploy of his own. He asked for volunteers, and when practically every man raised hand, selected the 500 fittest. He had only a small number of horse left, so he took fifty of these, warning all concerned that they were in for an exercise in swift movement. Let any who had second thoughts say so now, and stay comfortably at Feughside. Needless to say not a man resiled, however many may have wondered what they were letting themselves in for.

Leaving Magnus O'Cahan, despite pleas to be taken along, in command of the residue, they set out up the Feugh, through the Forest of Birse and over the skirts of the great hills to Loch Muick. Then southwards by the high passes of the Capel Mounth, at well over 2,000 feet, to the head of Glen Clova. By nightfall, after a tremendous day, they were in wild Glen Doll, Montrose pointing out that this was a mere flexing of muscles. They must do better hereafter.

Next day they crossed the shoulder of mighty Mayar, at a height of nearer 3,000 than 2,000 feet, to the head of Isla, and down that fair glen to Airlie's burned castle of Forter, where Argyll had played the savage five years before. Then, through a short side-glen below Mount Blair they reached Glen Shee, which when crossed brought them down past the lonely Spalding castle of Ashintully into Strathardle, at Kirkmichael. They were, of course, travelling wholly against the grain of the land, crossing the vast ridge-and-valley system all the way, desperately difficult going that only notably fit, active and determined men could maintain for long. Montrose treated it as an exercise and a challenge, to himself as much as to the rest. Any force which could swiftly and unexpectedly move about Highland Scotland like this would possess an enormous advantage and set at naught all the accepted strategies.

The third day they crossed from Strathardle, by remote Loch Broom, to Tulliemet and the Tay above Dunkeld, safely into Atholl again. But they did not pause there, save to eat mightily of the young Earl of Atholl's provision. They had word of Black Pate nearby, recruiting, but did not seek him out meantime. *They* were not really recruiting. They struck off up Strath Braan, to Amulree, and then down the Sma' Glen. That night they lay at the head of lower Glen Almond, and Lowland Scotland stretched before them, Perth itself no more than fifteen miles away, and to the *east*. They had covered nearly eighty miles of mountain territory in three days' mighty marching, and were where no one in the land could have expected them to be. James Graham was bone-weary, but satisfied – meantime. With such an army he could tie his enemies in knots.

In the morning they marched, openly and leisurely, down to the town of Crieff, near the head of Strathearn, to proclaim the King there and summon all loyal subjects to his service. Montrose reckoned two hours, at the most, for General Baillie to learn of it at Perth.

William Baillie was not a rash or impetuous man, but even he, after his first surprise had worn off, could not resist the challenge of this impudent handful at Crieff. He waited until nightfall, and then moved out in force, westwards up the Earn. Montrose's skilfully placed Drummond scouts, knowing every yard of this their own country, swiftly brought him word. Between 5,000 and 6,000 men were on the march. But Balcarres's horse, such as were not with Hurry in the north, were in Fife, and could not be involved for at least three days.

Well content, the Graham marched his rested men out of Crieff and over the Earn, to the south. Then turned westwards again, along the river-side, the three miles or so to where the fairly wide strath narrowed suddenly with the steep, intrusive wooded hills of Torlum and Lennoch. Here, beyond Strowan, he turned his force around, and settled to wait.

In due course, with the early sun behind him, Baillie found them there, blocking his path. Obviously it was a strong position, a narrow, thickly-wooded pass, and even with ten times the opposition's number, the Covenant general was not going to risk an assault. Which was entirely as Montrose had anticipated.

So now he commenced his drag-wing progress. Leaving a screen of men to guard the narrows, he quite openly withdrew his main force westwards, to take up another defensive position about three miles on, beyond Dalginross, where the Romans had done the like before him. There was no lack of such sites in the upper Earn valley, with the mountains shouldering close. Settled there, he called back his rearguard.

Soon Baillie was before this position also.

It was no more of a practical proposition to attack here than had been the other. Soon Montrose made another strategic withdrawal. In the process even David Ogilvy observed that this was an undignified proceeding and singularly lacking in profit, in his view. What was the object?

'The object, my good friend, is that of any commander in the field – to defeat the enemy. With our small numbers, and lacking cavalry, we cannot now defeat Baillie by force of arms. But we can, I believe, bring low his name and credit, which means much in this sort of warfare. He has come out against us with ten times our numbers. Now, he must either follow us thus, until we choose to fight – which will be on ground of *my* choosing. Or he must give up, stop following, turn back. He has no other choice. In which case, we blazon it to all Scotland. For the second time, the Covenant commander-in-chief has refused battle with a vastly smaller army. He cannot win, today, see you.'

'This was your intention . . . ?'

'If I could coax him to it, yes. Another four miles, and we are at the foot of Loch Earn. We must take one side of the water, or the other. So must he – if he comes at all. We shall take the south shore, the longer by a little, with more headlands to circle. It is my hope that Baillie will choose to take the north shore, to hurry along at all speed, so as to turn the head of the loch before us – try to bring us to battle on the open flats there, where his numbers would tell.'

'Your hope . . . ?'

'We would turn up the glen of Arvorlich. Where the mad major is laird,' Nathaniel Gordon intervened. 'Climb the hill over into Glen Artney. And so mock them.'

'You are wrong, Nat. We would turn *back*. Back whence we have come. Down Strathearn again, and fast. Twice so fast as Baillie can move. Nor halt at Crieff.'

'You mean . . . ?'

'Aye. Perth lies undefended. We could take it this night. All Baillie's stores, ammunition, cannon, will be there. It is the key to Fife and the South, down to Stirling. To my own Graham lands. If Baillie lost Perth, his credit would scarce recover.'

'Dear God in heaven . . . !'

But, tremendous as was this conception, for a few hundred

men, it was not to be. Baillie, whether he saw the trap, or merely tired of this fruitless stop-and-go procedure, called a halt. At St. Fillans, at the foot of Loch Earn, where Montrose took the southern shore, he neither followed nor took the northern but remained where he was. Probably he did not guess at the sheer bold extravagance of Montrose's design on Perth; but he would recognise that the royalist commander was seeking to lure him farther into the mountains for some purpose which could scarcely be to his advantage. Wary, as ever, he halted while he still had options open to him, room for at least some manoeuvre, and a clear line of retiral to his base.

When, half-way down the seven mile long loch, this became clear to Montrose, he was disappointed but in no way cast down. He still held the initiative, still could go where he would, and could declare that he had won a moral victory over the Estates commander who was abandoning the fight. It was as much as he had set out to achieve, in this exercise.

They passed Arvorlich where his former officer, Major James Stewart, was laird, Stewart who had murdered Montrose's kinsman, lieutenant and friend, the Lord Kilpont, in a fit of mad anger – but Stewart was from home, indeed acting turncoat with Balcarres's cavalry in Fife, and the Graham did not wage war against women and bairns. They marched on to St. Blane's Chapel at the head of the loch, and then turned south for Balquhidder, to camp in an excellent defensive position in the jaws of that valley.

It would be interesting to see what Baillie would do.

But in due course scouts reported that the Covenant army had in fact turned back, and was in steady retiral down Strathearn, pride swallowed in the interest of good sense. The royalists were on their own again.

From Balquhidder they crossed the passes above Glen Gyle and down to Loch Katrine-side. The Gregarach, Children of the Mist, were out-of-love with the Crown – Charles's father, King James, having persecuted them sorely and even denied them their name. But they had as little love for the Covenant, judging the Campbells as worse than the Devil. Donald of Glengyle supplied food and forage for Montrose's gold, and even contributed a token force of fifty clansmen – pointing out that this was as good as any 200 ordinary mortals. More interesting he disclosed that there was a little group of royalist refugees hiding, by his good offices, at Portanellan, along the lochshore, where there was an island nearby to offer sanctuary if necessary. Some were wounded, including their leader – who would not give his name but had a lordly way with him, though young.

Intrigued, Montrose went on ahead of his people, with only two companions to avoid alarming the fugitives, to investigate.

They were spied from afar, and could perceive men scattering off into the birchwoods and junipers from the lonely reed-thatched house of Portanellan. A little group of four, however, got into a boat and pulled a few yards from the shore, to await the arrival of the visitors in safety.

Coming down to the pebbly strand, Montrose doffed his Highland bonnet, and raised his hand. 'Friends,' he called, 'have no fear. I am James Graham of Montrose, your King's Lieutenant. Glengyle told me of you . . .'

There was a great shout, out in the boat, and a hasty and far from co-ordinated splashing of oars to bring the craft back to the beach. Out into the shallows jumped one of the young men, arm in a grubby sling, to come running in a splatter of water.

'My lord! My lord James!' he cried. 'God's mercy – it's yourself! Here's joy. It is I, James Gordon. Aboyne . . .'

'Aboyne! You – of all men! My dear lad – I believed you beleagured in Carlisle . . . ?'

It was the Viscount Aboyne, second son of Huntly, next brother to the Lord Gordon. Montrose had left him, a year before, when he had made his secret and unauthorised dash back to Scotland from Cumberland, and Aboyne, with the Lord Ogilvy and other Scots of Montrose's English army had remained in the King's service in the south. Ogilvy had been captured by Leslie's Covenanting force and sold for gold to Argyll, at Edinburgh; but Aboyne had been with the remnant driven back on Carlisle, where they had been besieged and shut up for long months.

'I escaped,' the younger man cried, a slight, sharp-featured redhead, hot-eyed like his brother Lewis but with less wolflike an expression. 'I contrived to bolt. One night. A sally, with a score of troopers. From the Scots Gate postern. I wearied for home. Had enough of Carlisle, by God! And the English, too! One night, we slipped out. Unknown to any. We cut our way through Callender's lines. Lost two. My horse shot under me. My shoulder put out.' He patted his slung arm. 'Came north by Annandale and Douglasdale. At the ford of Frew, near to Stirling, we fell in with these . . .'

63

Montrose had raised his glance to the other two young men who were disembarking more conventionally. 'Archie!' he exclaimed. 'Young Archie! I did not know you – my own sister's son! Dear God – *you* I thought deep in Edinburgh's Tolbooth!'

'Aye, Uncle, and so I was. But Sandy here and I got out; Sandy Alexander you will know, son to the late Earl of Stirling? We bribed a gaoler to let us in with the women – strumpets, slit-purses, thieves – and there changed clothing with two of them. Lord – you should have seen us! And so won out, offering our favours to drunken guards! Only *we* did the poking, not them – with dirks! We were on our way north, to join you . . .'

'And your father? My good lord?'

'He rots there still. With Ogilvy, Stirling of Keir, your chaplain Wishart. And many another. Argyll's prisoners. Held below ground. In worse case than the cut-throats and pickpockets . . .'

'Aye!' That was almost a groan. 'The price of being friend to James Graham!'

'The privilege, sir!' his nephew declared, proudly. He was a delicately good-looking youth, just twenty, Archibald, Master of Napier, son of the late Lady Margaret Graham and of Montrose's friend and former curator, the first Lord Napier of Merchiston. His companion, even younger, was Alexander, a son of the poet 1st Earl of Stirling, from Menstrie Castle.

Montrose was greatly enheartened by this encounter. Apart from his pleasure in the company of friends long-parted, he had a great sense of kinship, of community. Moreover, he badly needed lieutenants, officers on whom he could rely. He did not know much about young Alexander, although his father certainly had been a man of great initiative, inventor of the new-fangled degree of baronet of Nova Scotia. But his nephew Archie was sound, steady and less delicate than he looked. As for Aboyne, despite his youth he was a proved leader of light cavalry, with a flair for hit-and-run tactics. He had not the sober worth of his brother George – but he had far more dash and vigour, yet without Lewis Gordon's moody fickleness. They were a strange family, admittedly, their father Huntly little short of an oddity and their mother, of course, a Campbell.

That night Montrose moved to Cardross, amongst the extensive marshlands of the Flanders Moss in the wide vale of the upper Forth, in an effort to coax Baillie southwards and to alarm the Convenant leadership – for here he was only a dozen miles from Stirling, less than fifty from Edinburgh itself, and moreover with the barrier of the Forth turned. They dared not press on, of course, with so small a force and without cavalry; but the threat was there, and the lower Forth crossings which Balcarres was so heedfully guarding, were outflanked. But at Cardross, in Graham country now, a courier from the north found them, from George Gordon. Hurry was pressing him hard, and devastating the lower Gordon lands on Deeside and Donside. If Montrose wanted to raise a Gordon cavalry force, he had better come quickly.

Once more strategy had to yield to immediate necessity. They left the wildfowl-haunted marshes of Forth that same night, on one of Montrose's major cross-country marathons. But at least they were reinforced in numbers – although the newcomers were liable to hold them up in their prodigious marching.

It took them three strenuous days and nights to win slantwise back across Scotland to Aberdeenshire. At the Skene rendezvous they found Black Pate and the Master of Madderty just arrived. with Atholl and Strathearn recruits. But Colkitto was not yet back from the Highland West; and George Gordon was still in Strathbogie, for it seemed that Hurry had now moved on north-eastwards to threaten the Gordon lands from the territories of their hereditary foes on Speyside and the Deveron, the Crichtons, Forbses, Frasers and Inneses.

James Graham decided to wait for Colkitto. Hurry was alleged to have 4,000 foot now, and over 400 horse–a major army, for the foot included the regular line regiments of Loudoun's, Lawers's, Buchanan's and Lothian's – although the last seemed to have been in some sort of mutiny, details unclear. Hurry was playing a waiting game too, it appeared, for recruits were flocking in from Moray and Nairn, mainly from hatred of the Gordons – this was the price Montrose must pay for the essential cavalry. And worse, that turncoat, the Mackenzie Earl of Seaforth, had changed sides once more, only two months after parting from Montrose at the graveside at Bellie, and was now marching from the far North-West, with the Earl of Sutherland and a large force of clansmen. Hurry would wait for that.

Fretting, Montrose marked time.

As usual, his light-foot host was short of supplies and ammunition, a chronic state for an army which refused to lumber itself with a baggage-train and commissariat. Yet Aberdeen was close and comparatively undefended. Montrose refused to saddle himself with the responsibility of the city which could only hold him up and fritter away his energies. But the Viscount Aboyne came to plead and urge that he give him such cavalry as there were – these were mainly Gordons anyway – and let him make a swift raid on the town, while they waited. He promised that he would bring back all the supplies they required.

James Graham knew him well enough to recognise that this was a necessary Gordon gesture, the signal to Scotland that Aboyne was back on his native heath, and the Gordon power no longer in wavering hands. There were only some eighty horse, all told – but skilfully led, eighty determined Gordons descending on Aberdeen might achieve much, given surprise. Besides, it was the sort of thing Montrose himself would have liked to have done. He gave permission.

Aboyne's raid, essayed in broad daylight, was astonishingly successful. He suffered no single casualty and even included ships in the harbour in the assault. His eighty came back not only richer than they went, but more numerous, with an extra score of laden horses and a dozen volunteers to ride them. Also with twenty kegs of gunpowder, from one of the ships, and food enough to solve their problems meantime. With May upon them, forage was now no difficulty.

When, two days later, Major-General Alastair turned up from the west, he proved to have been worth waiting for, bringing 1,100 MacDonalds, Camerons and Macleans, under the Captain of Clanranald – who had led them at Inverlochy. This made the royalist army just over 2,000 strong, with some of the best infantry in the world. Once they had their Gordon cavalry . . .

There was no waiting now. With all speed they marched north for Strathbogie.

Montrose found George Gordon in something of a stew. His brother Lewis had got home before him and had sent out emissaries to all the main Gordon lairds urging them not to get involved with Montrose, saying that he spoke in his father's name. Since all knew that this indeed was Huntly's attitude, wherever he was hiding himself, they were all more prepared to listen. And when Hurry's troops were menacing Gordon lands, it was reasonable for able-bodied men to stay near their homes and guard their hearthstones. When the Lord Gordon arrived, then, recruiting, he met with a distinctly cool reception, by and large, and now had less than 250 men assembled. His delight at finding his brother James with Montrose was in fact as much relief as fraternal affection, and he thankfully handed over

66

responsibility for things military to Aboyne, his junior by a year but who had always taken the lead in that young family – a situation which was oddly reflected in their titles, for James was the Viscount Aboyne whereas the elder George was merely the Lord Gordon. This was explained by the fact that James was Huntly's favourite; he could not make him his heir, but he himself had been created Viscount Aboyne before he succeeded his father as 2nd Marquis of Huntly, and he had passed on his personal title to his second son. Aboyne lacked the depth of character of his elder brother, but he was a born leader.

Leaving him at Strathbogie to get on with the business of countering Lewis and his father's influence, and enlisting somehow or other the essential cavalry, Montrose pressed on northwards with George and his 250 horse. Despite the disparity in numbers, he was anxious to bring Hurry to battle before the large Seaforth and Sutherland reinforcements could reach him.

But Hurry was not going to be rushed. He retired before the advancing royalists, backing away from the Spey through the laigh lands of Moray, towards Nairn. The faster he fell back, the sooner he would link up with the oncoming North-West Highland contingent. Baillie was now said to be in Atholl, burning his way northwards also, punishing that mountain province for its continuing support of Montrose. No doubt he intended to join up with Hurry, perhaps at Inverness.

Montrose was in something of a quandary. He was anxious to keep Hurry isolated, but, with only half his numbers, was in no position to force attack, in any but very favourable conditions. And he would have preferred to wait for Aboyne and maximum cavalry support. He followed Hurry on, by Avon and Spey, not pushing, with scouts out far and wide. Hurry and Baillie had to be defeated before he could strike south again to meet King Charles. But he himself must not be defeated, at this stage, or the King's cause was lost. He must play this very heedfully.

It was hardly James Graham's normal procedure. And he had a spirited team to hold in. Oddly enough, and to his own surprise, when decision at last came, it was not he who made it.

CHAPTER FIVE

The village of Auldearn lay in the Moray plain not much more than two miles east of Nairn town, a poor place and small. When the royalist army reached it, on the wet, chill evening of the 8th of May, Hurry was declared by scouts to be no more than an equal distance the other side of Nairn, and still retiring. Montrose called a halt here, for it was in a fair defensive position, on a low U-shaped ridge, with much marshy land around. They had been as near to Hurry as this before – but James Graham always took due precautions. He found the village deserted, no doubt horror tales of the barbarous Irish having preceded them; but though it was a wet and miserable night, he had his troops camp in the open, and himself with them. There were not enough roofs to shelter a quarter of his people; also, once men got settled in houses they were less readily turned out swiftly in an emergency.

Montrose had information that the Earls of Seaforth and Sutherland had indeed at last reached Hurry, but not with their full strength, having merely come on ahead on horseback, their trudging main body still in the vicinity of Inverness. Strangely enough, almost the same position applied with himself, for though Aboyne had now come on, it was only with some fifty more horse, the larger body he had assembled, almost 300, still being equipped and given elementary training by Nat Gordon at Strathbogie. They would come on in a few days. Montrose decided, however, that if at all possible he must bring the enemy to a stand the next day, before the main Highland host reached them. A swift circuit west-about, by Geddes and Cawdor, fording the River Nairn at Kilravock, to trap them between that river, the lochy swampland of Flemington and the sea, perhaps? An early start, while it was yet dark . . .

As well that they did make that early start. For they were just moving out of Auldearn, at dawn, when racing scouts arrived to announce that Hurry was almost upon them. He had apparently changed to the attack, slipped round behind Nairn in the darkness, with his whole force, and was heading this way. Undoubtedly he knew that the Marquis was at Auldearn . . .

68

Taken by surprise, for once, James Graham reacted swiftly and without panic. He had little time, and little choice of manoeuvre. But at least their present position was a good defensive one, and might be utilised to advantage.

Much depended on Hurry's intentions. If he was planning an immediate dawn attack, though it gave little time for dispositions, it meant that the fighting would be on ground that Montrose knew, an immense advantage. It must be his objective, then, to *make* Hurry fight here, if he did not already intend to.

With this in view, Montrose divided his force into four groups. Five hundred of the Irish and Islesmen infantry he sent forward, under Colkitto, to hide in scrubland at the northward approaches of the village. The slight ridge on which it was built ended here in a knoll called Castle Hill. A sluggish burn found its way round this from the south-west, and because the ridge was shaped like a wide U, the burn had spread itself as bog in the central basin. The road from the north, therefore, shouldered the Castle Hill and kept to the higher ground, and on down the village street; and to the east of it the ground sloped down through scrub-birch and whins to more marshland, the saltmarsh of the sea nearby.

The cavalry, about 370 strong, under Aboyne, were sent to the extreme south-west horn of the ridge, to wait there on the crest, in view, as a threat – though the soft ground before them was far from ideal for cavalry. But then, the same would apply to the enemy. Magnus O'Cahan was given the best of the musketeers and bowmen, some 300 all told, with most of the powder and shot, to man the yards, back-gardens, pig-sties and cattle-sheds of the village itself. Most of the houses, stretched along the ridge, had long riggs of cultivable strips reaching down to the bogland on the west, with dry-stone dykes to keep the beasts out; and at the foot were the sties and byres, where the animals could be herded on to the common land. These, in the hands of skilful marksmen, could serve as so many strong points. The main body, about half the total infantry, Montrose himself took, to hide, as it were hull-down, behind the ridge to the south and east.

Hurry did not keep them waiting long. A mounted picket appeared on the skyline of the shoulder of Castle Hill, and there halted, scanning the scene. The rain had stopped, but it was a grey chill morning. Presently they were joined by a small group of mounted men. Hurry and his officers, almost certainly, gazing across the half-mile and more of the village, the bogs and the U-shaped ridge.

'Pray that he does not move 200 yards to his left, from that road,' Montrose almost whispered. 'Or he might glimpse Colkitto's men in the scrub. However low they lie.' He shrugged. 'But – why should he ?'

Hurry had learned not to be rash in dealing with James Graham. He sent his mounted picket forward, to canter along the deserted village street. This was of no danger, so long as they did not proceed much farther along than the last of the houses, where Montrose's own main body would come into view. To counter any threat of this, Aboyne sent a small detachment spurring to intercept – a perfectly natural-seeming gesture. The picket did not wait for them, but turned and hurried back. O'Cahan's musketeers and bowmen lay low.

Satisfied, Hurry waved on his hidden columns.

It was a nerve-racking business for the watchers to contemplate, inactive, as the seemingly endless files of men, the four regiments first, disciplined, confident, then the local Moray and Nairn volunteers, hundred upon hundred, then the spreading, teeming multitudes of the northern clans.

'His cavalry ? Where is his cavalry ?' Pate Graham growled. 'He is not sending them forward.'

Montrose was frowning. 'Either he keeps them in reserve. Or he has sent them off west-about. To win behind us. Cut off our retiral. Perhaps both.'

'He has 500 horse, they say. This could hit us sorely,' Gordon exclaimed.

'Could. But not necessarily. It could be a blessing. Pate – you scouted the area last evening. How far west does this bogland reach ?'

'Two miles, perhaps. Or three. Broken, sour land. It has been a loch, in part, once. I think . . .'

'And as wide ? Bad ground for cavalry, then. A long circuit. This might serve us none so ill. So be it that the battle is short! Much of his cavalry out of action the whole . . .' Montrose paused, and pointed. 'Ha – see. We spoke too soon.'

Mounted men were now appearing to the west of the marching infantry columns.

'Thank God they are on the right !' Gordon said. 'On the left they would mask Colkitto.'

'Wait, you,' Montrose murmured.

'It is Colkitto who will not wait – if I know him . . .!'

'I told him to. Till most of the host was well past. Into the village.'

'That is not all Hurry's cavalry,' Pate declared. 'Here is but a squadron. A plague on it – are the rest behind, in reserve? Or riding west, circling the bogs?'

'Pray the latter . . .' Montrose began, when he was interrupted. A great shout arose, and maintained, over there on the right front, as Alastair and his Irish, tired of waiting indeed, leapt up from their cover amongst the scrub and flung themselves, forward in a wild charge, to cross the 300 yards of rising ground between them and the enemy's flank.

'Too soon!' Montrose groaned. 'Half Hurry's infantry is not yet into sight. And if his main cavalry is still behind there . . .' He left the rest unsaid.

'It may be that he can see more than we can . . .'

'Shall we advance now?' David Ogilvy demanded.

'No!' That was a bark. 'Colkitto has struck too soon. But he will not force my hand! All depends on the next minutes. Wait.'

Colkitto, if he had failed to contain his impatience, at least had not forgotten some of his general's commands. He had the proud Royal Standard fluttering above him as he flung himself onwards at the head of his warriors – calculated, of course, to give the impression that here was the King's Lieutenant himself, and the main host. Whether Hurry in fact so interpreted it, there was no knowing; but if he did, it could have a major influence on the proceedings.

The sudden Irish eruption on the scene was as dramatic in its effects as in its appearance. The Covenant force was marching in column, naturally, and though not wholly confining itself to the muddy roadway was nevertheless strung out along and alongside it in very extended order. Abruptly assailed on its left flank, it was easy enough for its columns to turn and face eastwards. But then they represented a very thin and elongated front, and one very difficult for any unified control. Colkitto had let the four regular regiments past before he struck, so that these now represented the enemy's nearly half-mile-long right wing, with Buchanan's regiment just right of centre. The local volunteers of Moray and Nairn and Speyside formed the actual centre and immediate left – and it was at these that the Irish and Islesmen hurled themselves directly, no doubt considering them to be the weakest link in the chain. The mass of Mackenzies, Sutherlands and northern clans were still streaming over into sight from the north, in no sort of formation. And the cavalry, or such squadron as had shown itself, was islanded on the west, behind all.

There was a great confusion, officers bellowing commands, trumpets blowing, slogans being shouted, and the blood-curdling, ululating roar of a Celtic host in a life-and-death charge.

'God in Heaven, hear them!' Pate cried. 'Four hundred against five thousand! Look at them! What folly – but glorious folly!'

'And we stand here watching, idle!' young Napier exclaimed.

'Where, now, is Sir John Hurry?' Montrose asked, voice calm, steady, almost conversational – even though he had to steel himself to keep it so. 'I see no banner. And his position is of some importance in this.'

The sound of the clash, as the charge struck home on the Moraymen, was like the clanging of hammer on anvil, a metallic crash ringing through and above the rest of the din, a frightening noise indeed for men whose own flesh shrank momentarily from the impact, in sympathy.

But there was no real fighting, at this stage. No fairly narrow cordon of men, however brave and experienced, could have withstood that first furious onslaught – and some of the Moraymen had not waited to try. In seconds only, the yelling Irish had surged right through, sweeping away the entire middle section of the enemy column, like chaff. Hurry's army, in those brief moments, was cut in two.

'Pray the good Lord he remembers!' Montrose all but croaked, forgetting his own nonchalant pose. 'Remembers his orders. To turn left. *Left!* Or he is lost . . .'

But Major-General Alastair MacDonald, Younger of Colonsay, was a most able commander of his kind, if impetuous and no strategist. He was not so busy wielding his great sword like a windmill as to be unaware of the squadron of enemy cavalry standing waiting on the ridge to his right. Now that he was through the infantry line, those horsemen could plunge down upon him if he continued to pursue the broken remnants he had smashed; or equally, if he swung right to roll up the enemy's left wing. Whether he recollected his leader's prior instructions or no – and he was no slavish obeyer of orders – he could see his dire danger staring him in the face. Urgently he waved and yelled his screaming cohorts round to the left, southwards into a dip of the ridge.

'Holy Mother of God be praised!' George Gordon, whose Reformed state was only politic, breathed. 'Now, shall we move?'

'No. Not yet. Let them be.'

Colkitto was now facing the four regular regiments detached from Leslie's Yorkshire army and sent north to aid Baillie on Argyll's instructions. They represented a vastly greater challenge than did the Moray levies, and between them added up to almost 1,800 disciplined men, well-equipped and officered. But they were meantime at a disadvantage, caught unprepared in no defensive posture, and now their flank turned. Given a few minutes, they undoubtedly would have marshalled themselves into a state in which they could have cut Colkitto and his people into ribbons. But those minutes were denied them. Moreover, there was no coherent command – for it appeared that wherever Hurry was, he was not with them. He was a cavalryman always, of course, a master of horse not of foot, and was unlikely to march with the line regiments.

The Irish charge, although it had lost some of its impetus, was by no means spent; and now, in renewed fury if less than any coherent line, flung itself upon the hastily turned columns of Buchanan's regiment, while the shattered ranks of Moray and Nairn were left to stream away north and westwards in flight, masking their own cavalry for the time being. The Buchanans did not break, but began what was intended to be an orderly retiral up towards the village, where the houses would offer the cover they needed for regrouping and a stand. The other regiments' lieutenant-colonels were of the same mind, obviously, and a general falling back on the line of the village ensued, standard tactics indeed for such a situation.

It was then that Colkitto seemed to remember Montrose's orders. The sort of commander who always led from three or four paces in front of all others, he abruptly left off the direct attack, and swung his swordsmen on to follow him, racing along the east flank of the enemy regiments, southwards, parallel with the road. Shots began to crack out now, as the Covenant musketeers had time to bring their weapons into action. Men fell. But racing men, crossing a front, do not make good targets, and there was no major hold up.

'Bless him!' James Graham whispered. 'I wager O'Cahan is blessing him likewise! Alastair remembered him, at last!'

Colkitto was concerned now not merely to get parallel with the

73

enemy, but to get beyond him, as it were to head him off, like a sheepdog might do with a flock. That he was able to achieve this in any degree was thanks to various factors; the waiting and obvious Gordon horse in the distance, for one – the columns would not want to be driven towards that. Also, their natural tendency would be to move back northwards, to rejoin the rest of their army. Moreover, without uniform command, they were scarcely in a position to take sudden and unified aggressive action. They drifted to a halt, and remained more or less stationary, uncertain, content with musket-fire meantime.

'Can he do it?' Gordon demanded. 'Force four times as many back. On the village? Now there is no surprise?'

'I will go aid him.' Clanranald had moved up to where Montrose and his aides lay peering over the grassy crest of the ridge, amongst the whins. He was anxious for his fellow-MacDonald. 'We will roll up the Sassenach between us. As we did at Inverlochy.'

'Bide you, friend, if you please,' Montrose told him. 'No doubt you *would* roll them up. But those four regiments do not represent half Hurry's infantry. And he has still 400 cavalry somewhere. Since I can see no sign of him, I guess that he is commanding this himself, a cavalryman always. He is saving them for something.'

'But, Alastair . . .! By the Mass, Alastair could be cut to pieces there, whatever!'

'Alastair knows what he is doing. He will not be trapped. He has miles of marsh behind him. But, see you – those Lowland regiments with their mercenary officers – they will not wish to stand there in the open, facing an Irish charge, when there are houses behind to give them cover. It is against all their training. Those village houses will be drawing them as water does a thirsty man! For a wager, in a little, they will retire on the houses – safety. Which is what we want . . .'

'O'Cahan is there? He lies low, I say!'

'On my orders. O'Cahan is perhaps the best infantry officer I have. He is not in the houses, but down in the pig-sties and byres at the garden-ends. He will do nothing to warn the enemy away from those houses. But once they are in, he will keep them engaged. And Hurry's best weapon will be bottled up, wasted . . .

Sure enough, as Colkitto's 500 began to get into a position to charge again, the regiments began a steady and orderly withdrawal, by platoons, towards the long single-sided street of

74

houses – although it was hardly a retiral, since they were, in fact, advancing in relation, to their main army. But they moved back from the Irish threat meantime. And Colkitto, for once, restrained his fierce companies, so that they edged forward instead of charging. It was probably one of the hardest things that he had ever had to do, for the platoons which covered the withdrawal of the others were now using their muskets to better effect, and on good slow-moving targets. Montrose gnawed his lip as he watched his Irish fall. But he did not give the sign his agitated and impatient officers waited for.

It was O'Cahan who came to his fellow-countrymen's aid, then – but did it heedfully, so as not to invalidate his orders. He sent a number of his musketeers and bowmen out from their hiding amongst the pig-sties, to race to the north end of the village gardens and riggs, and from there to open fire on the rear of the retiring regiments. At the sight and sound of it, Colkitto's men let out one of their terrifying yells, as though to commence their charge indeed. It was sufficient. The Covenant infantry decided to forget orderly and planned withdrawal meantime, and turning, made a run for the shelter of the houses.

Presumably somewhere Hurry was watching, and deemed this the moment to throw in his counter-attack. Or it may have been that he was only now ready with it, for all the action hitherto had taken place swiftly, in much less time than it takes to tell. At any rate, over the Castle Hill's northern shoulder came the hordes of irregular infantry, in their thousands, shouting, to bear down upon Colkitto's right. The squadron of cavalry on the ridge began to move down on the flank.

Hastily the Irish reformed to face this new threat. But Alastair was not the man to await any attack in a passive posture. Leaving a screen of some scores to preoccupy the regiments in the village, he turned and plunged forward with the rest of his people, towards the oncoming, shouting host, their own fierce war-cry ringing high above all. At the same time, all O'Cahan's musketeers from the line of the village gardens, opened up on the backs of the houses, further to surprise and perplex the infantrymen milling there.

'That Colkitto is a hero!' Archie Napier declared. 'Look at him! Numbers mean nothing to him. One in a thousand!'

His uncle nodded. 'Ten thousand, rather. I told him that, if this day should be ours, the victory would be his. We see him earning it.' He had been scanning the entire scene keenly, as he spoke. He turned abruptly to the Lord Gordon. 'Off with you now, George. To your brother. My compliments. And my thanks for his patience. So long. He may charge now. Destroy that squadron. And assail the foot's flank. But . . . to watch for Hurry's main cavalry. Away, now – and God be with you.'

'We go now ?' Clanranald asked, urgent.

'A little longer, friend. Until I am sure that Hurry's main force is engaged. We are dealing with a veteran fighter, see you.'

Again the clash of headlong collision. But this time the odds were hopelessly against Colkitto, and he must be forced back and overwhelmed. The cavalry squadron had not yet been able to engage, with a stretch of soft bog to cross. But it was only a question of time.

The blaring of Aboyne's trumpeter sounding the charge whinnied high, and like a coiled spring released the horsed ranks plunged forward and downhill at last, slogans of 'Strathbogie!' and 'A Gordon! A Gordon!' bursting from nearly 400 pairs of lungs. They had marsh to get over, likewise, but would skirt the worst of it.

'Now we should learn what Hurry has in reserve!' Montrose said.

The enemy squadron did not fail to perceive its danger, and pulled away hastily in its descent upon Colkitto's hard-pressed flank.

O'Cahan's musketeers were keeping up a constant fusillade against the village and the close-huddled regiments therein.

Even Pate Graham, loyalest of the loyal, was uneasy now at his chief's inaction, with all the detachments of the army engaged – save only for the main body. The Irish foot and the Islesmen were in extreme danger. If the regular regiments should sally out from their cover, it would be the end of Colkitto.

James Graham was no steely calm imperturbable, however straight he sought to keep his face. His knuckles gleamed a tell-tale white now, as he watched and waited. Then, with a great exhalation of breath, he pointed.

'There! There, at last, is Hurry! His standard. Cavalry only. Aye – and no great numbers, by the Powers! Thank God! He must have sent his main horse to the west. To encircle us. As I hope. There is no more than another squadron there. Praise be!'

On the ridge of Castle Hill, behind the forces locked in battle, had appeared a new fringe of horsemen, with three banners fluttering above them, one of them very large. But it was no large force – one hundred perhaps. And no further masses of foot had moved up, to support them.

At last, Montrose was satisfied. 'To your commands, gentlemen,' he cried. 'Clanranald – you will lead the van. With Glengarry. No trumpet-calls. No shouting, until we are in plain view. Forward, my friends – in the King's name!'

That they achieved complete and demoralising surprise was obvious. With over a thousand fresh men, mainly MacDonald swordsmen at that, hurled into the fray unexpectedly, the enemy quailed and faltered. Even though they still greatly outnumbered their attackers. They were badly split up, and, by a masterly piece of psychologically inspired manoeuvring, their best units, the four southern regiments, were cooped up in the village, secure but almost useless. Long before Clanranald and his kilted, half-naked van reached them, Hurry's main infantry were hurriedly breaking off their assault upon Colkitto and streaming back whence they had come.

And now the Gordons had their revenge for all the humiliations they had had to suffer of late. Ignoring the two squadrons of Covenant horse altogether, they thundered up the slope from the waterlogged ground in the central basin of the great U, to fling themselves upon the retiring enemy infantry, in sabre-slashing fury. Almost immediately retiral became a rout, every man for himself. The first Covenant cavalry squadron, instead of turning to attack the Gordon's flank, turned the other way altogether, and actually rode down many of their own fleeing foot, either by mistake or blind panic. Hurry, on the ridge, saw all disintegrating before his eyes, and though he himself rode forward, to rescue what he could, his reserve cavalry turned and disappeared sensibly northwards.

Montrose and most of his main body had not so much as blooded their swords. But it was not time yet for cheering. The regular regiments which O'Cahan had been keeping preoccupied were still unbeaten, in their cottages and out-houses and gardens. If they chose to sit tight there, as in a strong point, the royalists were unlikely to be able to dislodge them lacking artillery, and short of powder and ball as they were. And to sit down around them, in a sort of siege, would be to give Hurry time to halt and reassemble his fleeing irregulars, and possibly return to the attack. Moreover there was the main Covenant cavalry force still to consider – for the two squadrons they had seen could represent little more than a third of it. Presumably it was somewhere

77

to the west, circling the marshlands. But it could be highly dangerous still.

Montrose sent Black Pate and a horsed picket to go look for it; and word for the Lord Gordon and half his Gordon horse to keep up the pursuit of the fleeing enemy, to prevent any rallying. Aboyne and the remainder to round up stragglers near at hand, and hold themselves in readiness to deal with a sudden enemy cavalry attack.

When opportunity offered, he strode forward to grip the panting and slightly wounded Colkitto by the hand, wordlessly, and led him along to consult Magnus O'Cahan, amongst the pig-sties.

'Here's the hero of Auldearn, Magnus!' he declared. 'Alastair has done his part. Now, I require *your* aid. How are we to dislodge these coneys from their warren?'

'A charge – and a plague on their muskets!' the irrepressible Colkitto jerked. 'Then cold steel. House to house.'

'No, Alastair. Not that. So we lose many, many men. Enough of your fine fellows have fallen this day. The main battle is won. I will not sacrifice more brave men than I must. Rather would I march away and leave these . . .'

'If the weather had been dry we might have burned them out, my lord. Or smoked,' O'Cahan suggested. 'Flaming arrows to the thatches. But I fear they would not catch, so wet it has been.'

'Whins pulled, and set alight? And a charge through the smoke? Shrouding their musket-fire. There's a notion . . .'

Montrose was interrupted by a great rattle of musketry from the north end of the village – which was strange, for though the entire perimeter was now surrounded, there was no particular target there for the enemy marksmen. Then, as this died away, out from the same northern extremity of the houses sallied a company of men, orderly, close-knit, but running hard.

'Sainted Mary! A bolt . . .!' Alastair cried. 'They flee, the fools!'

'They were safe there,' O'Cahan muttered. 'If they all come out . . .!' He left the rest unsaid, and ran off to his command again.

Whoever was responsible for the decision, it seemed that the Covenant regulars had elected to leave their security and make a dash to regain the retreating and defeated army – possibly with the object of rallying it. Whatever the reason, it was folly as

78

unexpected as it was desperate – and doomed to failure. For heavily accoutred Lowland foot to pit themselves to outrun light-footed and half-naked Highland and Irish sworders was hopeless beyond all telling. Although the companies emerged in planned order, in a leap-frogging procession, intermittently running and halting to cover the escape of their fellows, such disciplined tactics could not be kept up in the circumstances, and over broken ground, with no central control. Not with Colkitto, Clanranald, Glengarry and O'Cahan leading their veterans against them. Even so, had they accepted the fact, and bunched together in schiltrom formation, hedgehogs, squares, they might have saved much from the wreck, even against Aboyne's horse. But no such refinement developed, and the flight quickly deteriorated into a prolonged shambles, just an endless killing, one-sided, terrible, shameful. Indubitably the Lowland foot fought gallantly enough; but leadership was almost non-existent and they fell by the score, the hundred, almost the thousand, without profit.

When Montrose could stand it no longer, he called off his dogs of war – but with difficulty. The enemy, imbued with the spirit of that Covenant hymn of hate, 'Jesus and No Quarter!', seemed to prefer to die rather than surrender – perhaps Argyll's tales that the Catholic Irish tortured, even flayed and ate their prisoners, conditioned them. At any rate, prisoners were few, and the killing took a deal of stopping. Loudoun's, Lothian's, Lawers's and Buchanan's regiments came to a bloody and complete end there at Auldearn's ridge and bogs, in the name of God and Archibald Campbell. That two of the regiments were Campbell-officered, Loudoun's and Lawers's, made the MacDonalds especially difficult to draw off. Sir Mungo Campbell of Lawers himself was one of the last to die, on a heap of his own dead. No fewer than nine kinsmen of Douglas of Cavers fell, in the Lothian ranks.

With Black Pate's scouts returning to report that a fairly large body of enemy cavalry had been spotted, but had suddenly turned back, inland in the Kinsteary area, it could be accepted that all was over. Hurry was not only outmanoeuvred and beaten, but destroyed as a force, Seaforth taught a lesson. And Baillie was isolated, and in the Highlands, where he was at a disadvantage.

Baillie was a better general than Hurry, and would have to be tackled with care.

Montrose, assured that Hurry and the remnants of his force were in full flight for Inverness and beyond, turned back for Elgin, to rest his troops, treat his wounded, bury his dead, and consider how to trap William Baillie.

CHAPTER SIX

It was a curious reversal of roles. James Graham sat in the castle hall, and waited for David Carnegie, suppliant. It could be only as suppliant that old Southesk came all this way to see his son-in-law, eighty miles from Kinnaird by the shortest route, over the Cairn o' Mount, by Deeside and up Don, to Corgarff, at the very head of Strathdon, amongst the high mountains. Admittedly Corgarff was a small and stark castle, nothing like great Kinnaird, and not even Montrose's own to sit in, but forcibly taken from the hostile Forbeses; but at least he sat in authority here, and his father-in-law must be well aware of it. Not that Southesk was liable to be obsequious, or even mildly respectful, under any circumstances. But he must want something strongly to have travelled all this way.

Nevertheless the younger man rose courteously to his feet, as Pate Graham knocked and came in, to announce impressively, 'My lord Earl of Southesk craves audience with the King's Captain-General, the Most Honourable the Lord Marquis of Montrose.'

'Damn you, man – I crave nothing!' the older man snorted, stamping into the small bleak stone-walled hall, reeking with peat smoke. 'I am here to see my good-son, James Graham – that is all.'

'Then greetings, sir,' Montrose said. 'You are the more welcome in that visits from you are . . . unusual. I see you well – or you could scarce be here. I hope that you bring me fair tidings from Kinnaird?'

'Are there any fair tidings in all Scotland, these ill days?' the other demanded. 'Or England either! The world's awry, and an honest man knows not which way to turn, on my soul!'

'Ha! Can it be that you are unsure of your course, my lord? You – Southesk? That, surely, is for lesser men!'

Balefully the earl glared, tugging at his bristling white beard. '*My* course is not in doubt, man. It is others' courses that gar me grue.'

'Mine, I take it, sir?'

'Aye, yours. Man – do you care naught for the hurt you cause others? Those akin to you, and who have done no harm to any? Have you no heart?'

'I esteem myself to have a heart, my lord. Indeed, it causes me a deal of trouble! But – what are you at? My family? Is there trouble there? Or since *you* have come all this way seeking me, is the trouble yours?'

'Hm. There is a guard put on my house, sir! Day and night. Quartered on me. A company of wretched soldiery. At my cost! On your account . . .'

'Mine?'

'Aye, yours. Since Auldearn. My house is in ward, by God! Mine! Your son Robin in custody . . .!'

'Little Robert? But six years? I'll not believe it!'

'It is true. In Magdalen's custody. So she is in ward also. My daughter, in my own house! She may not leave it. A prisoner. Because of you, sir.'

'But why? How will this serve Argyll?'

'I know not. But I will not be treated so. I am Sheriff of Angus. A Lord of Session . . .'

'Argyll is your friend, is he not? Your colleague . . .?'

'No longer, 'fore God! This is too much. Has the man lost his wits? He'll no treat David Carnegie so!'

His son-in-law smiled faintly. 'And Magdalen? How is she? How does she take it?'

Southesk snorted. 'She . . . she isna caring. No' in her right mind. You have seen her. She seldom speaks. But she is sore about Jamie – that I can tell you . . .'

'Jamie? What of Jamie?'

'He's been put in close ward. In Edinburgh. In the damned Tolbooth, they say. With the others.'

'The Tolbooth! A twelve year old! God – no! A mere lad . . .'

'But your *heir*.'

'Was holding him not enough? They are monsters.'

'Just angry men. You shouldna fight battles against them, if you canna look after your own wife and bairns! Aye, and your friends, too. You've young Napier with you now, I hear? Cocking a snook as a soldier, eh? Well – tell him his new bit wife's flung into the Tolbooth too! His sister, forby. It was as a wench that he made his escape, they say. So they've filled his bit cell wi' wenches! Besides his father . . .'

Montrose turned to pace the stone-flagged hall, his features set. He found no words to express his hurt, resentment, shame.

'You'll no' lie down under it, I'm thinking?' the other observed, in a different tone of voice.

James Graham looked at his father-in-law sharply. 'Is not that what you wanted me to do?'

'If you hadna started this folly, aye. But, now, the situation is ... changed a mite.'

'You mean, I have defeated Hurry. And Baillie is intent on avoiding battle, these eight weeks since Auldearn.'

'Aye, well. Maybe.'

'What is it that you want, sir? You have not come all this way, to Donside, just to give me ill tidings. Out with it, of a mercy!'

Southesk came to tap him on the shoulder. 'Come you to Kinnaird, James,' he said. 'With your army. Rid me o' these insolent knaves. Then I'll ride with you to Dundee. I warrant that they'll no' hold out against you in *my* company. With Dundee and Aberdeen, you'll have the whole North-East. Come you to Kinnaird, I say.'

It took Montrose some moments to grasp the message, to realise what the older man was proclaiming. It was a complete *volte-face*. Battles won did produce results, after all. Southesk was changing sides. Or, at least, was proposing to commit himself. Presumably, therefore, he now conceived the King's cause as likely to prevail.

'You surprise me, sir,' he said. 'You wish to be identified with *my* campaign?'

'His Grace's campaign, is it not?'

'To be sure. But the King has now made me Captain-General, with fullest vice-regal powers in Scotland.'

'Aye. But he will soon be here, himself, to take command. Will he not?'

Montrose drew a quick breath. 'You ... you know of that?'

'Aye.'

'Dear God – how? How could you have heard it? Who told you? This was the strictest secret ...!'

'All the Council knows it. A courier was captured. On his way from you to the King. Small, by name. Irish. Calling himself a colonel. They hanged him, anyway ...'

'Damnation! Small captured. And *hanged*? God rest his soul. And ... and he talked? He had little in writing ...'

The other shrugged. 'Men can be made to talk.'

'Yes. With the shame on the makers, rather than the talker!'

So that was it! Why Southesk had turned. And come all this way. Montrose's own victories and the King's coming, together. Charles must not be displeased with the man whom he had built up, made lord, then earl and judge.

'When do you look to see the King?'

'Did not Small tell you? Or the Council?'

'Only that it was to be soon. How soon?'

His son-in-law did not answer. He was thinking hard. If Small had never reached the King, Charles would not have received his own message. Urging haste. And he was notoriously dilatory, never doing today which might be put off till the morrow. There would be no June or July rendzevous, then. He must get off another messenger, forthwith.

'Does Charles seek to bring an army with him?' Southesk went on.

The younger man was wary. He did not altogether trust such sudden conversions. 'That remains to be seen,' he said.

'He'd be wiser not to, man,' the other declared. 'Leslie's been ordered from York. To Westmorland and Cumberland. To cut off any descent on Scotland, on the West. That's the way he was to come, was it not? And the other Leslie, David, is still besieging Carlisle. Charles will not have an easy road home. If he tries to bring an army. No' that he's got that much of an army left, since Naseby, by all accounts.'

'Naseby? What is this?'

'You havena' heard? Guidsakes, man – has none told you? There was a mighty defeat of the King's host, at this Naseby. In Northamptonshire, it is. By the man Cromwell. In mid-month. They had near double the numbers, mind – Cromwell and Fairfax. Rupert's horse broken quite, the foot annihilated. The King's greatest disaster. Small wonder he comes to Scotland...'

'Defeat in England! Rupert beaten again, by Cromwell! My sorrow – these are ill tidings to bring me. But . . . but it will serve to bring the King the sooner, yes. To let him see that his first duty was to be King of Scots. The ancient kingdom of his race. The lesson I have been trying to teach him, for long. Let Cromwell and Fairfax and their friends have England – which never has owed the Stewarts true allegiance. Scotland, their true heritage, the most ancient kingdom in Christendom, may correct but will never do without its king.'

84

'Aye, well. Hrrm. You will come to Kinnaird, then? And on to Dundee?'

'I will send a company, to dispossess your invaders at Kinnaird. If so you wish. But I will not seek to take Dundee. Now is no time to risk being shut up in a city. I have not the men to spare, to hold it . . .'

'But it could be yours – or the King's – for the taking. I am Sheriff there . . .'

'Then *you* take it, my lord. In the King's name. His Grace would take that kindly, I am sure! And hold it, if you may. For myself, I play a game of mouse-and-cat with Baillie. Have been doing these past weeks. Dundee would be as good as a trap for me. I need space, country, wide lands to cover. My task is to destroy Baillie – if I can. Not to hold cities.'

'And the King? What of Charles?'

'I shall send him warning. Of the Leslies. Tell him better that he comes all but alone. With only Scots for company. And secretly. So long as he is back in his own Scotland, it will serve. Give me six months, with His Grace in the country – four – and he will sit his fathers' throne secure.'

'I hope so . . .'

'Now – tell me of Magdalen. And the children. Is she more herself? Less low in spirits? And are the bairns well? These soldiers – they do not harry them . . . ?'

*   *   *

Southesk's visit to his son-in-law was brief, for the very next morning riders came from the Lord Gordon, at Strathbogie, thirty-five miles farther north, calling for aid and action. Both the Gordon brothers were at home, meantime. Montrose had sent Aboyne on sick-leave after Auldearn – for his damaged shoulder was not improving as it should, with all this campaigning. And Aboyne had sent urgently for George, when a new and specific command had reached Strathbogie from their absent father. Huntly straitly ordered all Gordons, all tenants and all who owed him any sort of allegiance, immediately to retire from any service with the Marquis of Montrose, on pain of his direst displeasure. The Lord Lewis would take strict note of any defaulters, and they would pay dearly when their lord returned. This fiat had been too much for Aboyne to counter on his own. He required his elder brother's authority, for once.

Now the Lord Gordon sent word of new trouble. General

Baillie, whom Montrose had been trailing back and forth across the North-East, trying to manoeuvre him into a position where his superior strength could be successfully negatived, had apparently tired of the process, and had changed tactics to harrying the Gordon lands. He was now in fact besieging the great Bog o' Gight Castle near the mouth of Spey – the same where Johnnie Graham had died. This was of little strategic importance; therefore Baillie must be doing it merely to trouble the Gordons, and possibly to coax Montrose to come to the rescue. And he was successful in this, if so, for George Gordon declared that nothing was reinforcing his father's commands like this blatant assault on the second-greatest Gordon stronghold. He could do little or nothing with his father's clansmen so long as this harrying and siege continued.

Montrose, as ever desperate for cavalry, had no option but to head north without delay. He did so, however, with his eyes wide open.

Sending his father-in-law, grumbling and more or less empty-handed, back to Kinnaird, with only a small detachment under young Napier to eject his intruders, a move was made from Corgarff.

Montrose was by no means anxious to thrust himself upon Baillie, at this stage, and well aware that Bog o' Gight might be something of a trap. Apart from the Gordons, he was suffering other detachments from his strength. Clanranald and his Moidart MacDonalds had returned to their western glens and islands – although Glengarry and his Knoydart MacDonnells remained – and Colkitto had gone with his friend to try to raise an alternative force. So the royalist army was for the moment short of both infantry and cavalry – the price which had to be paid for a purely volunteer force, unpaid save for what booty it might collect. Montrose's own fortune was by now entirely dissipated, and all his properties confiscated. Although he had total powers to requisition and tax, in theory, for policy's sake he seldom used them. This was why it had had to be cat-and-mouse with Baillie for so long – until they might fight on *his* terms.

He marched north to threaten Baillie, then – but marched warily. At Strathbogie he picked up, thankfully, the Lords Gordon and Aboyne with 250 welcome horse, and pressed on for the Spey. But not too fast. The last thing that he wanted was a pitched battle with Baillie outside Bog o' Gight. Indeed he positively dragged his feet as they neared the Speyside area. Once across Spey, he could turn Baillie's flank, get round behind him. This would have suited him very well, had he had a larger force. As it was, he must just try to coax the enemy away from the level Moray plain. And a threatened crossing of Spey, *behind* Baillie, might just do it.

His reasoning proved accurate. Baillie, well served by his scouts, came up to contest the Spey crossing. He did more, he advanced to the line of the Banffshire Isla, at Keith, which gave him a double advantage, Isla before him, Spey behind. Even a Montrose could not readily outflank him here.

And so, once again, the Graham and Baillie faced each other across a river valley, with neither able to cross it save at dire loss – especially in the case of the royalists, for Baillie had artillery drawn up on the heights. Not that Montrose had any intention of crossing. Once again he took the initiative, and went through the charade of trumpeting, parleying and challenging the other to a set battle one side of the river or the other. And with the same result. Baillie was a down-to-earth mercenary soldier, no romantic warrior. He sent word that he would fight at his own time and place; and when he did it would be the end of James Graham of Montrose and all his traitorous rebels. He reinforced this reply with a salvo from his cannon – which fell short, of course, but had its own eloquence.

Montrose waited for one inactive day. Then, in full view of the enemy, staged a dramatic interlude. He arranged an elaborate altercation between himself and the Gordons, which ended in the entire cavalry force mounting and riding away north-east-wards, pursued by the shouts of the rest. Whether Baillie interpreted this as a serious difference of opinion or not, he at least would be apt to assume that the Gordons were making for the Bog o' Gight area, to discover what had happened to their important stronghold.

Soon afterwards, minus cavalry, the royalist army packed up and headed southwards, whence it had come, in some obvious confusion.

By late evening rearward scouts brought forward the information Montrose hoped for. The ruse had worked. Baillie was following on.

The problem now was to keep the enemy cavalry at a distance, while enticing Baillie on. And this for about thirty difficult miles, two days retreating, until the Gordons could circle east-about to rejoin them unobserved. But by dint of his previous well-tried tactics of setting fire to whins and hillsides by night, and making sham ambushes, traps and obstacle-courses by day, Montrose managed it. The fact that he skirted Strathbogie again undoubtedly helped, proximity to the Gordon heartland having an inhibiting effect on the enemy, naturally enough. On the evening of the 1st of July, Montrose crossed Don at the ford near the village of Forbes, above Alford – to find the Gordon horse drawn up under cover of woodland below the Gallows Hill, at the far side, near where the Leochal Water came in. He heaved a long sigh of relief. He was where he wanted to be, he had his cavalry back – and Baillie was only a few hours march behind.

'Now we stop trailing our wing,' he declared. 'Tomorrow, we will force Baillie to fight on ground of *our* choosing, God willing!'

* * *

James Graham, in his innumerable journeyings back and forth about the North-East, had often noted the excellence of the Ford of Forbes as a sheer copy-book battleground – at least, for *his* purposes. The long and level Howe of Alford was a flood-plain, with the Don meandering through extensive meadows for miles. This was not unusual; the same applied at the Isla, the Deveron and dozens of other rivers of the undrained land. What was unusual was that the ford at Forbes was so wide; indeed there were really three fords, over almost a mile's extent. Moreover, there was no high ground to overlook them, until the Gallows Hill of Forbes was reached, on the south, a low, wide eminence, wooded round its base, a full mile back from the river. This meant that an opposed crossing of the Don here was almost impossible, especially with a lesser host opposing a greater. Baillie need have no fears about being able to cross here.

What was not so clear, without careful investigation, was the course and behaviour of the Leochel Burn which joined Don from the south-west just above the fords – whose deposited silt and stones, indeed, helped to form the ford's shallows. The Leochel seemed an open and placid enough stream for the first half-mile, all that might be seen from the other side of Don, broad but shallow. But thereafter it changed its character dramatically, cutting its way through rocky and steep ravines, with rapids and cauldrons, a formidible barrier. Thus it curved round the western slopes of the Gallows Hill. But half a mile farther it once again changed character, to open out in widest sprawl and spread, flooding the hollow basin at the back of the hill, and turning it into a swamp. Accordingly, though not apparent from the Don, there was only one practical way round Gallows Hill for an army, east-about – and this was much complicated by bog. The road itself steered a clear course, well to the east.

Montrose, that morning, made no attempt to hide his presence, not wishing Baillie to suspect any sort of trap. He drew up his foot on the upper and bare part of Gallows Hill, visible to all. But the rejoined cavalry he kept hidden, partly in the woodland below. Also behind the hill he kept a reinforcement he had met with on the way south, Farquharsons, Ogilvys, Hays, Baillie would see only the units he had been following all the way from Keith.

In mid-forenoon the enemy appeared, and duly made his crossing. Baillie sent his horse, some 450 of them, splashing over first, then the serried columns of foot, followed by the oxen-drawn artillery which had so held him up, with the lengthy baggage-train last. He took his time, and Montrose did not interfere. They watched each other warily.

When all were safely over, Baillie, cautious man, divided his cavalry into two, and sent half round the east base of Gallows Hill and half round the west. As would be expected of him, to avoid being outflanked and cut off on the hill-top, Montrose retired openly to a new position on the north-east face of the hill. But he did not move his hidden cavalry.

Baillie advanced his main body of infantry to the foot of the hill.

Montrose waited. Soon the east-going enemy horse would come into view of his infantry behind the hill – and vice versa. This might not upset them over-much – though they would surely send back to inform Baillie. This reserve was under the young Master of Napier, who had rejoined his uncle after expelling the Covenant guard from Kinnaird. The royalist right-wing cavalry and foot were under the command of the Lord and Nathaniel Gordon respectively, the centre infantry under Angus MacDonnell of Glengarry, the left-wing foot under O'Cahan and horse under Aboyne. All knew Montrose's plan of action.

From his point of view it was all more like an elaborate game of chess than a battle, whatever was felt by the participants in general. Every move was predicted – even though some were not exactly as timed. The Lord Gordon, for instance, left his cover too soon, and charged the enemy left-wing infantry before he should, tempting target as they made – with the result that Baillie's right-wing cavalry, riding back from the Leochel-narrows impasse, as was to be expected, were hastily switched to the other flank, and created considerable havoc – admittedly also amongst their own foot – as a cavalry battle ensued, the wretched infantry expendable amongst the lashing hooves.

Baillie, on the word that the west-about route was impossible, since he could scarcely retire across Don again with all his artillery and baggage, had either to press on east-about, or to stay where he was. But his present position was cramped and limited as to possible manoeuvre, no ground for a battle. He sought to push on.

Aboyne now charged on the left, to give this move impetus; and the Highland centre, under Glengarry, went bounding downhill in yelling fury. Bugles from Baillie recalled his left-wing cavalry in haste. This should have been Lord Gordon's task to intercept – but he was fully engaged already. Nat Gordon did his best with the right-wing foot, throwing in his men in a do-or-die effort, not to stem the new cavalry threat, since that was impossible, but, once they clashed with his young chief's hard-pressed squadron, to dash in amongst the enemy horses, dirks drawn, hamstringing the poor brutes and slitting their bellies. It was an expensive way of fighting, but effective.

O'Cahan came in then, as Baillie rallied his strung-out centre, and Aboyne was able to leave his wing altogether, on Mont-rose's urgent command and dash through the woodland to the aid of his brother.

It was a curious situation. On the royalist side, all went with almost clockwork precision, save for George Gordon's costly lapse. On Baillie's side, however, it was an utter confusion from start to finish, with no pattern followed or indeed possible. Even so, the enemy losses, at the start, were not great, and Baillie still had many more men in the field than had his opponent. But then young Napier came on the scene, with the reserve, afraid that his uncle had forgotten him. Loud-voiced, clamant they appeared from the back parts of the Gallows Hill, in no sort of order, a very mixed bag of raw recruits, uncertain of their target but full of fervour. They won the day, without striking a blow for as it seemed, by mutual consent, the Covenant horse broke at sight and sound of them, and turned to dash for the Ford of Forbes again, led by a group of mounted officers, notably not by Baillie himself. The infantry was unable so to escape, though much of it tried. Amidst indescribable chaos, Baillie himself was presently forced to ride off – escaping only by moments and inches, indeed, as George Gordon himself slashed his way through the press to try to grab him by the sword-belt. The Battle of Alford was over.

There was less killing thereafter than at Auldearn and Inverlochy, with Colkitto and his Irish absent, and Montrose better able to control his victorious troops. Not that he was not otherwise preoccupied. For George Gordon lay dead on the bloody field, amongst many of his clansmen. At the last moment, as he sought to capture Baillie, he had been struck down from behind by a Covenant pistol-ball.

James Graham stood over his friend, tears streaming down his cheeks unchecked. He was even more distressed than was Aboyne. The Lord Gordon was not a great soldier, or even a very notable figure on the national scene. But he was the man closest to Montrose in spirit, with whom he could talk and discuss, partner of so many evening camp-fire debates, sensitive, intelligent, conscientious, responsible. Baillie's defeat had been dear bought, as far as James Graham personally was concerned, with the heir of Gordon's fall.

The Gordon horse had, in fact, borne the brunt of the fighting, sandwiched between two assaults. Only amongst them were casualties high, or indeed more than nominal, on the royalist side. Baillie's infantry losses were large, and a great many butchered horses lay around; but basically his cavalry and officer-corps had made good their escape. The artillery and baggage, of course, remained with the visitors.

The pursuit was maintained for the rest of a long summer's day – a pursuit intensified by the extraordinary information, obtained from a captured officer, that the Marquis of Argyll himself had been with Baillie, and was now presumably fleeing northward somewhere. His presence with the army was said to be accounted for by Baillie's pleas to be allowed to resign his command, repeated more than once during the last weeks. The Campbell had not only refused this, but had come up himself in order to ensure that the reluctant general did his duty. According to Glengarry he had almost managed to dirk a richly dressed character whose description corresponded.

Hurry and Baillie both were now defeated.

The Lord Lindsay of the Byres had a small army based on Angus, local levies almost entirely – but they could be discounted. The Earl of Callender's force remained in the Border area; but it had proved itself a singularly inactive and non-aggressive body, to date. The two Leslies were still in England, although only just. Montrose might hope that the road south lay open to him, at long last.

He marched the very next day, going to Aberdeen, to inter his friend, with fullest military honours, in the great granite cathedral of St. Machar. That city did not oppose him. No city in all Scotland was likely to oppose James Graham's entry that early July of 1645.

He made but a sombre victor, nevertheless. Quite apart from the loss of George Gordon, Montrose did not forget that he had a son, and sundry good friends, to free from Edinburgh's Tolbooth. And there were reports that the plague was raging in the capital.

CHAPTER SEVEN

Some weeks before, the Earl of Southesk had urged his son-in-law to come to Kinnaird. But when he came, his reception was less than enthusiastic. Perhaps David Carnegie had some small excuse for his lukewarmness; it had never been his intention that Montrose should bring 5,000 others with him – and the vast preponderance of them Irish and Highlandmen, in the Carnegie's opinion little better than animals. Kinnaird was a handsome and civilised house, one of the first seats in all Scotland no less, and not to be defiled by such cattle.

James Graham gave him no option, however. Kinnaird was near their line of march, only three miles east of Brechin, his troops were hungry and he had spent his last penny in providing meagrely enough for them; moreover it was important at this stage that the Lowlands should not be antagonised by any whole-sale requisitioning and looting. Whereas his father-in-law was one of the richest men in the land – and, so far, his ostensible support of King Charles had cost him little. Moreover, Montrose wanted to see his wife; and it might well do Magdalen no harm to meet some of the men with whose names Scotland was ringing.

For his wife's sake mainly, then, he put on quite a show. Marching his army, unit by unit, into the great park of the castle, trumpets blaring, pipes playing, banners flying, clan slogans shouted, cavalry jingling at the trot. Never, in fact, had he had such a large force at his command since his Covenant days, for Colkitto had rejoined him at Fordoun, at the foot of the Cairn o' Mount pass the day before, and had been more successful in his recruiting in the West than hitherto. Aboyne was absent again at Strathbogie, where he had retired after his brother's funeral; but any day he was expected back, with more of the precious cavalry. Hence this breathing-space.

With his thousands marshalled in the great park, Montrose led his officers over Kinnaird's drawbridge and into the courtyard of the castle. Southesk stood there, glowering, with his youngish Countess – a second wife – his son, the Lord Carnegie, and his brother the Lord Lour. Magdalen and the two children were not present, but two small faces could be seen at an upper window of their flanking-tower, and James Graham thought that he could just distinguish the outline of a figure behind.

'Greetings, my lord,' he called out. 'You invited us to Kinnaird, a month back. We rejoice now to avail ourselves of your hospitality – in the King's good cause.'

'Man – you've brought *thousands*!' the other spluttered. 'And ... and the half o' them Hielantmen, 'fore God!'

'All His Grace's loyal subjects, sir – stout fighters for His Grace's rights.'

'But ... but ...'

'It is our hope that you will add to our numbers, at Kinnaird, my lord. With a fine troop of Carnegie horse, in especial. A captaincy for your son, my good-brother, at least.'

That closed the old man's mouth almost with a snap. He stared, appalled.

'I have the honour, my lord, to present to you some of my officers, men whose names I pronounce humbly but with pride. First, my Major-General, Alastair MacDonald of Dunaverty, Younger of Colonsay, whom men call Colkitto. The bravest of the brave!'

'Umph!' Southesk said. Highlanders and Irishmen were almost equally to be deplored, in his view. A Highlander who led Irishry was quite beyond the pale.

'We have all heard of General Colkitto,' his Countess said, admiring the blond giant's sheer rampant masculinity. 'Welcome to Kinnaird, sir.'

'*Your* welcome I would savour to the full, lady!' Alastair answered, grinning – with a distinct emphasis on that first word.

'And here is John MacDonald of Moidart, Captain of Clanranald. And Angus MacDonnell of Glengarry. Two of the most illustrious names in all Scotland.'

'Ooh, aye. No doubt.'

'Lachlan Maclean of Duart's fame must be known to you. Likewise Murdoch Maclaine of Lochbuie and Ewan Maclean of Treshnish.'

'Mm. Aye, well ...'

'Here is MacDonald of Keppoch and MacIan of Glencoe.' It was highly important to get all these Gaelic chiefs and dignitaries in their right and due order, a subject Montrose had early set himself to master. Nothing was easier than to give dire offence by a single misplacement.

'Cameron Younger of Locheil, Macpherson of Invereshie MacGregor of Glengyle . . .'

'Aye, man – aye,' Southesk interrupted testily. 'But where are the Scots ?' Like most Lowland noblemen he did not concede that Highlanders – the Erse as they named them, lumping them with the Irish – were Scots at all.

Montrose frowned. 'All are Scots, my lord. None less so than yourself.'

'Davie means your *Lowland* lords, James,' the normally silent Lord Lour intervened.

'You see here the Master of Madderty, the Master of Napier, Sir David Ogilvy son to the Earl of Airlie . . .'

'Lords he said, man – *lords*!' Southesk insisted. 'No' younglings and landless whippersnappers! Where are your solid Scots lords ?'

His son-in-law's determinedly pleasant and patient voice took on a sharp note. 'Most, I fear, are like yourself, my lord – less eager to prove their loyalty to His Grace than are their Highland brothers! A matter I shall not fail to bring to His Grace's notice.'

There was a sudden hush at that. The thing was so unlike James Graham. Even David Carnegie was struck silent at the implied threat.

It was the Countess who set things to rights. 'You are all welcome to Kinnaird, gentlemen, Highland and Lowland alike,' she declared. 'And Irish also,' she added, after just a momentary hesitation. 'But in especial, General Alastair – who is the size of man I find to my taste!'

'Lady, I improve on closer acquaintance, whatever!' Colkitto assured genially.

'As half the women in Ulster and the Highland West will vouch!' Magnus O'Cahan observed conversationally from the background.

There was a great shout of laughter, and the day was saved. In that spirit the reception broke up.

As soon as he might, James Graham went to his little family's own tower across the courtyard, only too concerned with the fact that Magdalen had not come to welcome him – and presumably had kept the children from so doing, for surely it would have been an exciting occasion in their constricted lives. But when he saw his wife, any hurt or resentment was driven from his mind. He was shocked at the sight of her, at the sheer physical deterioration. It was not so very long since since last he had seen her – three months, no more. Then she had been direly mentally depressed and heavy, lethargic in body. Now she seemed to have shrunk, her flesh dwindled on her bones. She had always been a big, well-made woman. For the first time her husband saw her looking gaunt. She gazed at him, her eyes haunted, her mouth drooping, and with no smile of greeting, no word indeed.

'Magdalen, lass – are you ill?' he cried, going to her. 'My sorrow, this is no way to find you.' He took her in his arms.

She was totally inert, passive, in his embrace. Last time she had resisted him. There was nothing of that now. Limp, unresponsive, in his arms, she might have been an inanimate thing.

Cradling her, he groaned.

He looked up, to see Robert and Jean watching them from the open doorway. He raised a hand to them, and they came forward, shyly.

'Did you see them all?' he asked. 'All the King's soldiers?'

'We saw you. And Colkitto. And Cousin Archie Napier,' Robin said. 'Colkitto is very big.'

'I saw the Hielandmen,' Jean told him. 'Why do they wear feathers in their hats?'

'That is to show that they are chiefs. Chiefs of clans. When they have three feathers. Chieftains of septs, branches, only have two. Lairds of name, but one. They are eagles' feathers . . .'

'Could *you* wear them?'

'I suppose that I could. Your grandfather Graham had a feathered bonnet, I mind – though I never saw him wear it. *An Greumach Mor.*'

'How many feathers? Three?'

'Three, yes.'

'My lord is chief of all the Grahams, silly!' her brother told her. 'And he is the King's general, too. Greater than Colkitto. Though . . . though not so big. He is the most important man in all Scotland. Perhaps he could wear *four* feathers?'

'Three would be enough. And I fear that I am not the most important man in Scotland, by any means. But . . . in this room, now!' He looked down at his wife. 'I am the important man, here. Have . . . have you no word for me, my dear?'

With an obvious effort, as though bringing her mind back from afar, she nodded. 'You are well?' she said, each word separately enunciated.

'Well, yes. I have been blessed with great good health. Would God I could say the same for you. Have you been sick, Magdalen, lass?'

'No,' she decided, after a moment or two.

'But you are so thin. And . . . and not yourself.'

'Who would wish that I should be . . . myself?' she asked, bleakly.

'Eh? I, for one, girl. Mercy on us – that's not way to talk! Your children . . .'

She said nothing.

He looked at the children, unhappily. How much of all this affected them?

'The bairns look well,' he said. 'Growing fast. A credit to their mother. They suffered no hurt when the soldiers were here?'

'No.'

'Cousin Archie Napier sent them packing!' Robin declared. 'They ran away. To Dundee. They did not even fight. I like Cousin Archie. Can I go see him, Mamma?'

'I am going to take you down, to meet my officers, my friends,' his father assured. 'Your mother too.'

'No,' she said dully.

'But yes, my heart. You will find them excellent company. You must see them. In your father's house. It will be my pleasure to present them, my good companions, to the Marchioness of Montrose. Some of the most renowned and kenspeckle names in the land.'

She shook her head.

'But, Magdalen – why? It would do you good. Take you out of yourself.'

She looked up at him, pain in those lack-lustre eyes. 'Please – no!' she whispered.

'What's wrong with you, girl? What's wrong?' he exclaimed.

'I do not know,' she answered, slowly, head drooping again, as though this brief display of decision had been too much for her. 'But . . . I must be . . . alone.'

'This is . . . this is . . .' He shook his own head, eyeing the watching, interested children. 'We shall speak of this again, Magdalen. When we are alone.' Sighing, he went and took a child's hand in each of his. 'We shall go down and see them,' he said. 'Meet Colkitto. And Clanranald. And Glengarry. And Duart. And my friend Magnus O'Cahan, the best Irishman that

97

lives. Cousin Archie, too. And all the others. The bravest men in all this land. Shall we ? And perhaps Mamma will come later, if she feels better . . .'

*   *   *

That night, quite frankly if shamefully, James Graham put off the moment when he must leave the great and cheerful company gathered round his father-in-law's hall table, and betake himself to his wife's bedchamber. He had his excuse, for his lieutenants were discussing an ambitious scheme of Nathaniel Gordon's to take a flying column to the far north of Scotland. To Strathnaver, on the very Pentland Firth, where his chief, the Marquis of Huntly was hiding himself, and to bring him south, whether he would or no, to Montrose's presence, and ultimately, the King's. Until Huntly could be persuaded to change his petty and offended attitude, the vast potential of the Clan Gordon strength could never be fully harnessed. Once they had Huntly in their hands, they could change his tune, for he was a weak and basically simple man, however proud; and honours, appointments, titles, would be apt to seduce him. Montrose's own reaction to this notion was less than enthusiastic, for severely practical reasons, in that it would demand a quite large detachment of cavalry to achieve, in any reasonable time – the very thing they could not spare. In their cups, his friends were fairly consistently and vociferously in favour, the 200-odd grievous miles conveniently shortened by wine. James Graham, sober, listened patiently. He would prick their alcoholic bubbles on the morrow.

At length, with snores – his father-in-law's the loudest – tending to overbear laughter and argument both, further delay could not be supported. Excusing himself to such of his companions as were still in a state to be concerned, the King's representative went leaden-footed towards his connubial couch.

James Graham was a wholly masculine man, however gentle of manner, and as appreciative of the other sex as any of his lusty company. His need for women was often very strong, and his denial of that need through the long campaigns no light matter. But he was a sensitive man also, and not one to find any satisfaction in forcing himself upon any woman, wife or other.

He found Magdalen's room unlit by lamp, but the northern July night was only a dove-grey. He could see his wife lying in the great four-poster, canopied bed, but whether asleep or no he could not tell. In that moment he hoped that she was.

His voice, therefore, was very low, as he spoke from the doorway. 'Are you waking, Magdalen?' he whispered.

'Yes,' she answered, after a moment.

'It is late. I am sorry. There was much discussion below.'

'Yes.'

'If you are tired, wearied, I will leave you. Sleep in the bairns' room. Tonight.'

She did not answer.

'I would not wish to disturb. When you are less than well . . . '

'No.'

He did not know what that meant. Whether she meant that he would not disturb her; or whether she agreed that she was not well, and wished him gone. 'Shall I go, then, lass?'

'I am your wife,' she said, flatly.

'Yes. But . . .' He paused. The last thing he wanted was to seem to reject her. 'If it does not . . . disturb you? Thus late?'

When she made no reply to that, he came inside and closed the door. As he took off his clothes, she did not speak, although he told her of the good impression that the children had made on his friends and colleagues, and what they had said.

When he climbed in beside her, she did not move, neither welcoming nor repulsing him. The bed was large, and he kept his distance at first, to give her time. But at length he put out an arm, to encircle her. There was no disguising the shrinking from his touch. She was naked, nevertheless. He felt her bones near the surface as never before.

He kept his arm about her, hoping for the tension to relax. But she remained stiff, silent, her breath short, shallow. Her mind apparently accepted that she should do her duty, but her body did not.

He did not press her. Instead he talked to her, gently, soothingly, speaking of many things, of their childhood and youth, when they had been good companions, of their kinsfolk and friends. Did she remember this, recollect that? Sometimes she murmured briefly, sometimes she made some monosyllabic reply; but that was as far as it went.

Slowly, almost imperceptibly, he moved his hand lower down her person. Immediately she stiffened further, drew away slightly.

Sighing, he continued to talk softly, but now with increasing intervals between remarks, for he was tired, whether she was or not. And presently he slept, although he did not intend it, still with his arm around her.

Magdalen Carnegie did not sleep – or not until just before daybreak. She lay staring up at the heraldic plaster ceiling, wide-eyed, and occasionally a great slow tear welled up and rolled unheeded down her cheek. She did not move throughout, lest she disturb the deep-breathing man at her side. She was lost, lost in a grey and endless wilderness, alone. And she would never win out. Until, until – and if – she saw her Johnnie again, beyond the grave. None understood . . .

*   *   *

In the morning Montrose received information that the plague had struck Edinburgh with great severity. And Stirling likewise. And that the Committee of the Estates had transferred itself, and the parliament it had called, for later in the month, to Perth – though it was no true parliament, since it had not the royal authority, but could be only a convention. Orders had gone out for a further 10,000 men to muster in arms, at Perth, and Baillie summoned to take command of them, his renewed resignation not accepted. Argyll was not beaten yet, it seemed.

Montrose recognised that this recrudescence should be stamped upon, if possible, before it grew into a serious threat. He ordered a move right away – to his father-in-law's unconcealed satisfaction. James Graham's leave-taking of his wife was harrowing for him. He knew now that she had gone far beyond his grasp, beyond any hope of return, and his heart bled for her. Previous partings had been disappointing, upsetting, resentful – but at least he had been able to ride away hurt, angry, or determined to do better, emotionally roused. Now there was nothing so positive. Only the grim knowledge that she was, in spirit, little better than a corpse. And that, undoubtedly, it was in the main his neglect of her that was responsible, wherever the fault lay. Other contributory factors there were, almost certainly; but that with him lay the principle blame he could not question. It was a sorry thought to ride away with, from Kinnaird.

They made their way by the so well-known route down Strathmore, to cross the Isla near Coupar Angus and on up Tayside to their old base at Dunkeld, in the mouth of Atholl. Here, on the 24th of July, Montrose sent out his spies for detailed information – and learned that Baillie had indeed a new army, not of 10,000 but of over 5,000 foot and about 800 horse, at Perth, guarding the convention of parliament which was to open that very day. More reinforcements were said to be on their way, from Ayrshire, under the Earl of Cassillis, from Clydesdale under Hamilton's ineffable brother the Earl of Lanark, and from Fife where Balcarres was raising more cavalry. Argyll himself was at Perth, with the rest of the Covenant leadership.

When Aboyne arrived at last from Strathbogie with another 300 horse, to add to the 100 already at Dunkeld, there was no more waiting. The royalist force moved southwards, openly, by way of the Almond valley, for the Perth vicinity.

Within sight of the city walls, near their old battlefield of Tippermuir, they halted, challenging Baillie to come out and fight. But he would not.

Montrose tried a few feints and provocative gestures, circling, parading, sending forward bold forays right to the walls. But retaliatory action was not forthcoming. Any other commander but Baillie, Montrose believed he might have coaxed.

At a council of war amongst the Methven woodlands it was Colkitto, not usually a strategist, who propounded the stratagem. 'Be damned to Baillie for a fat slug!' he declared. 'Forget him. Think on his master – Argyll. The Campbell. He is the man to push, whatever.'

'Argyll got a fright at Alford, I swear, Alastair. He was never nearer capture. He will be learning Baillie's caution – or we would have had action before now.'

'Aye – but Argyll is in different case, see you, from Baillie. He has a weakness that Baillie does not have. Property! He is a great man for possessions, is Campbell. So we may move him, I think.'

'How so ?'

'Castle Campbell is not far away. His house in the Ochils. Let us go spoil it. As he has spoiled *your* houses of Kincardine and Mugdock. And Keir, your kinsman's house. Burn Castle Campbell, I say. And Argyll will send Baillie out to fight!'

There was a shout of acclaim from the others round the fire. Montrose stroked his little beard thoughtfully.

'Aye – and if we get between Perth and the Forth,' Sir David Ogilvy pointed out, 'they cannot fail to see it as a threat. To cut them off from all the southlands. They must move . . .'

'Yet I would not myself wish to be trapped against the Forth,' Montrose mentioned. 'That could cut two ways, my friend. Nevertheless . . .' He drummed his fingers on his tree-trunk. 'It might serve.'

'Where would we fight, then ?' Colkitto asked.

'That I would have to consider. Not in the Ochils, certainly. We must be able to disperse back into the Highland hills should we be overborne.'

'You have never lost a battle yet, man!'

'But always I have been prepared to lose, Alastair. A way of retiral left open. That one defeat might not mean complete disaster. A general's duty is to survive defeat as well as to gain victory.'

An unexpected addition to their strength, the next morning, was the Earl of Airlie arriving with eighty more mounted Ogilvys, a most welcome accession, the old man claiming that he was now wholly recovered and fit for the wars. When he heard of the proposed descent upon Castle Campbell, he was gleeful indeed, declaring that he claimed first torch to the blaze. He had not forgotten Argyll's savage burning of his own castle of Forter, in Glen Isla, and the turning out of his pregnant countess into the wild hills.

So they marched. This was Montrose's own country, of Kincardine of Strathearn, and he knew every inch of it. They were not followed, their move apparently not perceived. By mid-forenoon they were at Kinross, on the shores of wide Loch Leven; and by mid-afternoon were climbing above the levels of the Forth plain, at Dollar. Castle Campbell crouched on a terrace, in a cleft of the Ochils, directly above them.

It was a strong place, in site as in building, with high square keep and towering curtain-walls rising from the naked rock of a pointed spine between two deep ravines. It might have held out for some time, for Montrose lacked artillery, as usual. But its keeper yielded at the first summons, and there was no fighting.

The spoiling of the castle went with a will, and Airlie thereafter duly applied the first flame. Great was the conflagration, for the place was most richly stocked. The smoke of its burning rose high above the green Ochil summits, for a sign that could be seen from Forth to Clyde, from the Lammermuirs to the Highland Line; its blaze a beacon which kept burning all night, while men feasted around it and in the little town below. Castle Campbell on its proud terrace blazed its message to all southern Scotland indeed. The King's Captain-General had left the North at last. Here was the token of things to come.

Wearying of the business early in the August evening, Montrose himself left it to others, and rode down to Alloa, on the shore of Forth, where the Earl of Mar, young Archie Napier's new father-in-law, had his great house.

And the following night, at dinner in Alloa Tower, James Graham received the word he awaited. Baillie was on the move. He was marching hurriedly along the north flanks of the Ochils, westwards – undoubtedly to cut off his enemy from his northern and Highland bases. Moreover, Black Pate's scouts, far ahead, reported the Earl of Lanark, with 500 horse and 1,000 foot from the Hamilton lands, had reached Glasgow and was moving up the Lower Kelvin Valley. Only thirty miles separated the two enemy forces.

It was time to be up and doing. Moreover, his Highlanders and Irish were getting out of hand in Alloa town . . .

CHAPTER EIGHT

The Campsie Fells lie south of the upper Forth valley, isolated, and could represent a strategic trap. And the hanging valley of the upper Kelvin a swamp, a waterlogged quagmire, where men must flounder and plouter and horse must sink and sprawl, is immediately to the south of the Campsies. Yet James Graham chose this to be the site of the battle which could decide the fate of Scotland. For a quagmire might be as valuable as squadrons of cavalry to him. And it was the great Flanders Moss which isolated the Campsies from the security of the Highland hill-skirts of Menteith and Strathearn – and Donald MacGregor of Glengyle knew the secret ways through that mighty morass, and could lead them safely if the worst came to the worst. Those hidden causeways, part under a foot of water, some said belonging to Roman times, had been Clan Alpine's bread and butter for generations, the route by which they brought back their stolen Lowland cattle to their Highland fastnesses.

How to bring Baillie to action where he wanted him? The enemy was following on fast enough, with Argyll and the entire Covenant leadership with him – no doubt to his grave embarrassment. Baillie had rounded the Ochils west-about, and come down Allan Water, by Dunblane, to Stirling, avoiding the plague-stricken town itself, as Montrose had done; but had delayed long enough to burn the Alexander castle of Menstrie, and re-burn Airth – no doubt Argyll's fury showing itself. Now, on the evening of the 14th of August, he was only some four or five miles away, at Hollinbush near the head of Kelvin, with 6,000 foot and 800 horse. And no more than ten miles to the west, on the other side, was Lanark and his force. They would join up on the morrow – or else seek to trap the royalists in a joint attack, front and rear. Montrose's army stood in a strong position on the ridge above the little town of Kilsyth, his back to the Campsies. It would be difficult to trap him there.

The situation was not to James Graham's taste and requirements, nevertheless. He was far *too* strongly placed. Baillie would never attack him here. Which meant that the two enemy forces would link up. And that would give Baillie at least 1,200 horse. The 7,000 foot did not worry Montrose unduly; but such number of cavalry was a serious matter.

That warm August evening, then, Montrose rode out unattended, along the Kilsyth ridge. He climbed the Campsie foothills. At last, almost two miles east of their camp he found not exactly what he was looking for, but what he believed might serve, a sizeable depression in the hills, over half a mile long and somewhat aslant as to floor. A burn came in at the head of it in a quite deep ravine, forming almost a waterfall as it came down the sudden drop. At its lower end the depression, or great hollow, opened out to a levelish apron, over which the burn spread itself wetly, before the long and gentle descent to the waterlogged Kelvin valley below, where the road from Stirling rimmed the Dullator Bog. But the central part of the hollow, because of its slight slant, was relatively dry, well-drained, the burn disciplined by gravity. The floor of it was perhaps 400 yards wide, and the slope down into it from the west, as Montrose had ridden, comparatively easy, smoothish grassland dotted with whins. The other, east, flank however, was steep and rocky, especially towards the foot, no cliff or scarp, but a difficult braeside.

For long, as the light and colour faded from the hills, the man stared, his mind busy. Then abruptly he wheeled his surefooted Highland garron around, and trotted back to the camp.

'Sound the Rally,' he cried, to his trumpeter. 'Fires out. Assemble in companies and squadrons. We move.'

'Move?' Colkitto exclaimed, flagon in hand. 'March – now? To attack? A night attack? You will never take the cautious Baillie by surprise, man. In all those Kelvin bogs. His camp will be like a moated fortress, my God!'

'Not to attack, Alastair. To *be* attacked. If God so wills. And before Lanark and his cavalry join up.'

'You'll not force that one's hand, whatever.'

'He has the misfortune to have advisers with him! The entire Covenant leadership. They will not fail to advise him as to his duty, never fear. *I* know. I have suffered under their militant guidance. They will not let Baillie resign his command. But they will not let him command it in his own way, I swear. So – we move.'

In two hours, little more, the entire royalist army had exchanged a fine strong position for a wretched one, security for obvious hazard. Baiting traps was all very well – but the trap had to have jaws. This place was a death-trap.

James Graham smiled. '*There* are my jaws,' he said, and gestured to all the ranks of Irish and Highland infantry, settling down in their plaids for the night.

Aboyne, very much casualty-conscious since his brother's death, looked around him uneasily. 'This is no place for horse,' he said.

'Precisely, James. It is their horse that I fear. Suppose – suppose, I say, that Baillie has sent an order to my lord of Lanark that *his* horse should hasten forward, leaving the slow foot? That would give Baillie 1,200 or 1,300 cavalry. Three times our numbers. Would you accept those odds? In cavalry?'

'Holy Mother! Twelve hundred . . .! You think it possible?'

'It is what *I* would do, in his place.'

While men slept around him, James Graham settled down by a single tiny and aromatic fire of bog-pine, to read, peering, the little pocket-Bible which was his constant companion and mentor. Scouts came and went throughout the night – and none found their general asleep.

By dawn the entire camp was roused and standing to arms, eating the handfuls of raw oatmeal as they stood, washed down with burn water. If God willed, they might do better hereafter. Pate Graham informed that the enemy scouts knew where they were. Baillie, only two and a half miles east of this position, was preparing to move. As yet there was no sign of Lanark's horse, from the west.

Montrose disposed of his forces with simplicity but particular care. The Gordon cavalry he set on the right, under Nat Gordon, near the slow drop to the Kelvin valley, with the spreading water-apron and emerald-green mosses of the burn before them, and the comparatively easy western hillside behind. It was going to be a frustrating day for the Gordons, whatever happened. On the left he placed Colkitto and his veterans, 2,000 of them, crowded below the very throat of the ravine with its waterfall, allotting him Ogilvy's eighty horse as a sort of reserve. In the centre he placed the main body of the Highland infantry, 3,000 strong, under that puissant triumvirate of chiefs, Clanranald, Glengarry and Duart. All were inevitably close-packed, with little or no room to manoeuvre. Even Black Pate looked doubtful when he came hurrying in, from the eastern slopes, to announce that the enemy were on their way. It would not be long now.

Young Alexander, his lieutenant, who had shown an aptitude for scouting, still reported no hastening Clydesdale cavalry, from the west. In reserve, beside himself, Montrose kept Aboyne and a small squadron of horse, for eventualities; also a company of Gordon foot.

There was one final disposition to make, small but important. On the higher ground, up on the lip of the ravine, above the cataract, was a group of roofless, deserted cottages, the huts of a cattle-herder's shieling. Young Ewan Maclean of Treshnish was sent up there, with a token company, to hold it – and to be seen to be holding it. That done, there was nothing for it but to wait.

From his point of vantage, Maclean of Treshnish presently signalled. The enemy, in force, was in sight.

Aboyne was still unhappy, impatient. 'Suppose your stratagem does not serve ?' he objected. 'Baillie is no fool. He may not fight as you would wish. What then ?'

'Then there is no harm done. If we look as though we might be trapped down here, we can retire up this easy brae behind. So long as Lanark's horse does not arrive. Alexander will give us warning of that.'

'But will not Baillie seek to outflank us ? Round, on this high ground to the north. Keeping high ?'

'Pray you that he does, James!'

It was not long before the first ranks of the enemy began to appear over the high skyline to the east, the morning sun behind them. It was going to be another hot day, sultry, windless. Mounted outriders came first, then whole squadrons of cavalry, seemingly endless; and finally the vast cohorts of the foot, steel glinting, banners flying, regiment upon regiment.

The front ranks halted, in full view of the royalist army in the hollow, the rest pressing on. And still they came, over the swelling hill-ridge, their numbers greater than those of any previous Covenant host.

'Now we shall see!' Archie Napier said. That was almost a whisper.

Less than half a mile apart, but with 250 feet of difference in their altitudes, the two forces eyed each other.

'If he has cannon, he could smash us into bloody ruin, here,' the Master of Madderty declared.

'He cannot bring his cannon up over these rough hills. One of the reasons for my choice of battle-ground.'

A group of mounted men moved forward from the enemy front, to the very edge of the sharp drop. There they halted, peering down.

'Baillie. Argyll. Hurry. Lindsay. Balcarres. Elcho. Burleigh.' Montrose enunciated the names clearly, his fine eyes narrowed into the sun's slanting glare. 'I cannot see them, distinguish them – but they will all be there. The ministers, too. Dickson. Law. Guthrie. Traill. The men who have torn a nation apart, in the name of religion. Who have caused the deaths of thousands, in their damnable pride. So near . . .!'

The party up there reined their horses this way and that along the lip of the drop, and then gathered again in a knot. Voices, of course, could not be heard; but there could be little doubt as to what they were saying. There was no way down for cavalry, here. The brae was steep and grassy for two-thirds of the distance, then steeper and stony, at a long out-cropping escarpment. No horsed force could negotiate that descent without grievous casualties.

'What would you do if you were William Baillie, Archie?' Montrose asked his nephew.

Young Napier looked around him, nibbling his lip. 'If he sends his horse left, to the south, they must drop down into the wet ground at the tail of this valley. Or into the Kelvin bogs. He will not do that. If he sends them round to the right, they have to cross that ravine. That done, they could win on to this smooth slope behind us, and charge us down.'

'They will see young Treshnish and his lads at the cottages, on the edge of the ravine. They must assume the ravine held.'

'*I* would leave my horse out of it,' Madderty put in. 'Divide my infantry. Send the main body down this steep hill-side, straight at us. Foot could negotiate it, though horse could not. Send the rest right-about, to clear that ravine. Make a way for the cavalry to cross it. Then we are at their mercy.'

'No doubt. But Baillie well knows that we are strongest in our Highland and Irish foot, weakest in our cavalry. *He* is strong in cavalry. He will wish to use it, not merely keep it in reserve. And his foot would suffer terribly from our musketeers and bowmen as they descended. Heavy-armed infantry could not run down that hill. They would lose their footing.'

'He will do nothing, then. He is a cautious man,' Napier said. 'He will wait for *your* move.'

'He has half of the Estates advising him, up there. And the

fire-eaters of the Kirk, wanting blood! I do not see them allowing him to sit and wait.'

'What, then?'

'This smooth slope behind us must surely tempt them all. If they could but gain it, they have us. Pate – you say that they have four regiments of regular foot again? As at Auldearn. More of Leslie's army which Argyll has demanded.'

'Aye – Home's, Cassillis's, Glencairn's and Argyll's own. You can see them – their breastplates shining.'

'They will never send *them* down this brae, I swear! And Baillie knows passing well that my Highlanders and Irish like the bogs! Bogtrotters, do they not call them? He will not risk a major assault on his left, then. He will send a probe right. That is why I have put Colkitto at the foot of the ravine. If the probe is held, and cut up, he may send in more, to their aid. We may force him to fight there, around the ravine, where his horse is useless to him, where we have every advantage . . .'

It took a long time for Baillie to make up his mind. Perhaps he was arguing with his masters. The sun rose steadily in a pale sky. It was going to be unbearably hot, limp-making. Sweating already, himself, James Graham removed his shoulder-slung sword-belt, threw off his doublet and unbuttoned his shirt.

'Off with these cloying clothes!' he cried. 'Up there they roast in their iron pots! Let the sun fight for us! As well as the hills. *We* shall at least fight in comfort – if they intend to give us battle, at all! Pass the word down . . .'

Nothing could have pleased his men more, the Highlanders in especial. It was their custom, anyway, to cast aside their clothing in the heat of battle – and, oddly enough, a naked man, with naked steel, hurling himself upon one, is a deal more alarming than a man fully clad, or even armoured. So now they gladly threw aside kilts and plaids, and either tied the tails of their saffron shirts between their legs, or discarded shirts altogether. Laughter, hooting, challenge rang out, coarse jesting. Better for morale, this, than just idle, silent waiting.

As though it had been a signal, the enemy suddenly were spurred into activity. Bugle-calls resounded up there on the hill, shouts, commands. The Covenant cavalry reined round, and began to trot off, right-handed, squadron after squadron. Then the foot turned, likewise, and led by the extreme right, commenced to march in the same direction. The entire enemy army was gradually setting itself in motion.

Montrose stared, scarcely crediting what he saw. This was no probe. This was Baillie turning his entire line of battle at right angles and marching across his enemy's front. He could only be making for the ravine, or to go above it, higher still, intending to turn the royalist flank in the biggest way.

Furiously James Graham had to consider anew, scrap all his tentative plans. Never had he anticipated this, that the enemy should take so enormous a risk, so utterly unlike Baillie. However secure he believed himself to be up there, by turning into column thus, he put his army out of effective concerted action for some considerable time.

Suddenly Montrose was presented with an astonishing opportunity – if he could take it in time. He had the men to do it. But could he get his orders to them in time . . . ?

That problem solved itself. For Colkitto and Clanranald, veteran commanders and used to operating on their own, perceived the situation as swiftly as did their general. Nor were they of the sort who considered orders sacrosanct. Leaving perhaps one-third of his men, under Magnus O'Cahan, to cope with that ravine itself, Colkitto pointed his sword straight up the eastern hill-side and waved his men on, leaping forward himself, longer-strided than any. Clanranald, in the centre, was beginning to do the same even before Montrose's shouted commands were relayed to him.

And so thousands of Highland and Irish warriors launched themselves, racing and bounding, half-naked, up the steep brae-side, swords and dirks in hand, jumping, scrambling over the stones at the bottom and flinging on up the grass slope above. Only such hillmen, toughened in gruelling campaigns, could have done it, without bursting hearts and lungs.

The elongated enemy column did not at first perceive and realise its danger, for owing to the steepness of the slope and the curvature of the hill they could not see what was happening immediately below. No doubt, however, like their betters, they assumed that the ascent was unclimbable, at least for an armed force. By the time that they became aware of the true situation, it was too late to engage in any major reforming movement. They could only turn and meet the eventual charge in column, a thin end slender line indeed.

That Colkitto's and Clanranald's men had any energy and breath left to charge, after surmounting the brae, was a wonder, and a tribute to their fitness as well as enthusiasm. But charge they did, furiously if raggedly, and along a wide front, hurling themselves upon the long, extended column in waves. The first wave suffered fairly heavily from musket-fire, but thereafter it was all steel and muscle. Minutes after Baillie's trumpets had sounded the march, his army was cut, not into two but into many parts.

It was not defeat, of course, merely disruption. But since it did away, for the time being at least, of the possibility of unified command, it laid the foundations of defeat, thus early.

Perceiving that a diversion at this stage would be valuable, Treshnish opened up with musket-fire, at extreme range, from the cottages, upon the Covenant cavalry at the head of the column, thus preoccupying Balcarres. A detachment was sent to deal with him. He had only 100 men there – but the enemy could not know that. To help in this issue, Montrose sent orders to Magnus O'Cahan to advance with all speed up the eastern side of the waterfall, in the ravine itself – and to make as much noise about the business as he could. And, recognising that here was a quite extraordinary chance to strike a crippling blow, he despatched Maclean of Duart with the entire infantry reserve, up the main steep eastern slope, to join Colkitto and Clanranald on the high ground.

Aboyne, with the small cavalry reserve, was agitatedly pleading for work to do; and no doubt, on the far right, Nat Gordon and the main horsed force were equally upset. But there was no role that they could usefully fill at this stage. The same applied to Airlie's eighty Ogilvys. From the first it had been Montrose's determination that this should be no cavalry battle. He sent Aboyne up the smooth hill-side at the back, to work along to the north, towards the western lip of the ravine, as possible counter-cavalry threat – although this was really only a gesture, for the deep wooded ravine would be fatal for horse, on either side.

Baillie was not inactive in all this, of course. Cut off from most of his own foot, he still could control his cavalry. It did not take him long to perceive that much might yet be saved, and the royalist command and cavalry, at least, be defeated. He sent word to Balcarres to leave the wretched ravine area and spur on due northwards at maximum speed, up and up the long hill-side, to where the burn's channel shallowed amongst the heather and it could be crossed with ease – the best part of a mile, by the look of it. Then back down the west side and on to the smooth slope behind Montrose. A charge, in overwhelming strength, down there, and it would be the end of James Graham and the Gordon horse both.

When Montrose saw the enemy cavalry swinging away and uphill again, he swung on young Napier.

'Archie – up the ravine, after O'Cahan! Tell him to get most of his force back across the ravine. Somehow. Have them spread out as a line across the hillside. Using all the cover they can – peat-hags, burns, anything. He will know. To try to hold Balcarres's horse, when they cross higher and come down. I will get horse up to support him. Quickly, now! You understand?' He turned to Madderty. 'You, John – to my lord of Airlie, with his Ogilvys. Up this hill behind to, Aboyne. Then on up the main hillside to the north, to support O'Cahan's foot. Nat Gordon not to move meantime. You have it?'

He gazed backwards and up. Young Alexander still waited, high on a ridge to the west, giving no signal of Lanark's army. He must stay there.

Tempted as he was to leave his central stance and hurry up the steep brae in front, to see how the infantry were faring up there beyond the curve of the hill-side, James Graham sternly controlled himself. His place must remain here, where he could be seen by all, calm, assured, under the Royal Standard of Scotland, the King's Captain-General in total command of the situation. He sent one of the few aides he had left, young Alexander Ogilvy of Inverquarity, with his compliments, to Major-General Alastair, to enquire how he did? He and Black Pate were left almost alone.

'This is damnable!' that stalwart muttered. 'Standing here idle. *Watching!* Like . . . like auld wives at a marriage! Is this a battle, God's mercy?'

'If God's mercy does not forsake us, you are watching the end of the Covenant, Pate! It is a strange battle, yes. We can see little or no fighting, from here – but we see that our ally is strong! The hills – it is the hills, Pate. The hills of Scotland are fighting for us.'

'And these?' The other pointed upwards to where they could see the great mass of the Covenant cavalry streaming uphill, in no sort of order and scattered over a wide area.

'Those are Fife and Ayrshire and Lothian farm-folk, in the main. Riding low-country horses over steep heather and peat and scree. See how they flag and scatter. What state will they be in, or their beasts, when they can get across that burn-channel and come down upon our flank ? The hills, I say, fight this battle for üs.'

Nevertheless, the two Grahams put in a grim and trying half-hour there, in the lap of the hills, watching, waiting and unable to affect the issue for the time being. They saw the leaders of the enemy cavalry reach sufficiently high on the main spinal ridge for the burn-channel to offer little obstacle – but, even so, the emerald-green ground there was obviously very wet and progress was slow. They saw O'Cahan's line of Highlanders and Irish pouring out of the ravine, much lower, and spreading across the hill-face to form some sort of line, uneven, patchy, broken, as they utilised the natural barriers that the ground had to offer – peat-hags, hollows in the knee-high heather, outcropping rocks, burns, aprons of surface water. They saw Aboyne and Airlie spurring up to reinforce O'Cahan – but not making good time of it in the atrocious going up there. They saw Balcarres's men marshalling themselves, and then their descent upon the royalist front, a move that was so far from a charge as to be almost laughable, horsemen having to pick their way with heedful care. Soon muskets were taking their heavy toll of easy targets, men and horses both. In high old heather, which O'Cahan had deliberately chosen, horses were at a major disadvantage, as against bare-shanked Highlanders, unable to see where they were placing their hooves, turning hocks on loose stones, sinking into peat-broth, slipping on outcropping rock. Clearly it was a bloody business, up on the high hill, for both sides; but the enemy did not appear to be gaining any appreciable headway on that wicked ground.

Then young Inverquharity came leaping and slithering down the western steep to them again, scarlet faced, panting.

'Colkitto has . . . them beat!' he gasped. 'The foot. On the run. Everywhere. Dead men, dying men . . . all over the hill. Clanranald killing, killing . . .'

'Gently, lad – gently,' Montrose said. 'Take your time.'

'Yes. Yes, my lord. But . . . but, the blood! I saw a headless man . . . running . . .!'

'Aye. Your first battlefield is no bonny sight. But – your message, man. What says my Major-General ?'

'To tell you, my lord, that all is near over. With the enemy. The foot. He broke them up. It was easy, he said. He was singing! Colkitto singing. He is . . . terrible! Blood all over his body. Not his own, I swear! Shouting. Laughing . . .'

'Yes, yes – I know him. But what of the four regular regiments? These I must know of. Are they still fighting?'

'They retreated. Lochbuie told me. To a line of dykes. Drystane dykes. Up the hill. As redoubt. But the Macleans leapt the dykes, Lochbuie said. And the MacDonalds. Pushed the dykes over on the enemy. Cared naught for the musket-fire. Crawled on their bellies up to the dykes, where muskets could not fire over at them. Then leapt over. They are gone, too. Home's, Cassillis's and the other regiments. Broken, fleeing, being cut down . . .'

'Glory be!' Black Pate cried. 'Then the day is ours?'

'Not quite,' his chief said. 'I thank you, Inverquharity. Now – get you back up there to the Major-General. As quickly as you came down! My congratulations to him. And request that, leaving half his men to finish off the enemy foot and make sure they do not rally, he takes the rest and gets him as quickly as he may across that ravine. To yonder battle on the great hill. You have that? Off with you, then. And you, Pate. My compliments to Nat Gordon. He has been very patient. Have them up there now, also. To Aboyne's aid, and Airlie's. The whole cavalry force. To fight it out, at last.'

But it was not to be. When Balcarres and his horsemen saw Colkitto's legions coming streaming towards them, and fresh squadrons of the Gordon horse spurring eagerly upwards, they could discern no advantage, or future, in their situation. Without any direct orders to break off battle, in fact a general disengagement began. And, in the circumstances, that soon developed into every man for himself. Uphill, downhill, over towards the ravine, northwards and westwards for the empty hills, riders broke away and fled, singly, in pairs and groups. And were pursued by bounding, hallooing Irish and Highlanders, more like wolves than men.

The Covenant leadership had not waited thus long. From an eminence well back on the eastern slopes, they had watched their hopes collapse. And well before Balcarres's horse broke, with two companies of Clanranald's half-naked MacDonalds heading purposefully in their direction, they were off, hurrying back towards Stirling, whence they had come, Argyll to the fore, Baillie amongst the last. A reinforcing body of Fife horse, come late to the battle, turned and fled with them.

The Battle of Kilsyth was over. Only the killing remained.

That killing was perhaps the most wholesale yet. Because of

the wide-scattered nature of the battle, and the subsequent flight in so many directions at once, it took longer than usual for Montrose to establish any measure of overall control. Moreover there had been a heartless and gratuitous slaughter of royalist camp-followers at Methven Wood, after the move to Castle Campbell, and revenge was much in men's minds. Much of the cavalry undoubtedly made good their escape; but the infantry in the main ran downhill, into the Dullator Bog of the Kelvin valley – overlooking the fact that their bare-shanked and lightly armed enemies were considerably more at home in bogs than were they. They died there in their hundreds, before James Graham might stop it. But not the men who gave the orders, of course; only those who obeyed them, the others being safely away in good time. That was the prime sorrow of it.

For a commander, Montrose disliked the aftermath of victory almost as much as of defeat. He felt less at one with his colleagues and subordinates then than at any other time. Disillusionment, reaction, disgust, even remorse, surged over him, instead of any sort of triumph. His lieutenants, in consequence, tended to win scant acclaim, at this stage.

When old Airlie, who had led his Ogilvy horse up that hillside like any youngling, came to him down at the Kelvin road, the congratulations tended to be one-sided.

'Magnificent, James!' he cried. 'Total victory. As great as Inverlochy.'

'Great is not the word *I* would use, I think.'

'Eh? Och, man – great is Argyll's defeat, you'll no' deny?'

'Perhaps. But that does not make it a great victory. Only a great slaughter. God forgive us!'

'You do not win battles without bloodshed, lad. War is not just a game of chance, of skills, with no real cost. You play it passing well, to be sure. But the reckoning is aye in men's lives.'

'I know it. But unnecessary slaughter is vile. Unworthy of our cause.'

'But not our enemies' cause, it seems! You must fight as you are fought.'

'That I cannot accept. Or we are worse than the brute creation. Besides, that way breeds hatred, continuing strife. I have a kingdom to save for His Grace. Not a desert of hatred and death. These were the King's subjects, equally with ourselves.'

'The King's rebels, in treasonable uprising, man. A difference there is. Remember our two sons in Edinburgh's Tolbooth!'

'Think you I ever forget it ? Nor the other two who lie in their graves, mine and yours both.'

'Aye. I am sorry. Forgive me, James. You have paid your price for the victory of Charles Stewart. I think that you have Scotland, now, to present to him. I hope that he is sufficient grateful.'

'You go too fast, my friend. Scotland is not ours yet, to give to the King – grateful or no.'

'I believe it may be, James. At last.'

'Wait, you,' James Graham said.

CHAPTER NINE

As the sweltering August days passed, and the reports came in, it grew to seem almost as though the Earl of Airlie had been right. Although his triumphant legions pursued the fleeing Covenant forces far past Stirling, to Fife and Lothian, and southwards and westwards towards Clydesdale and Carrick, Montrose remained at Kilsyth for a couple of days, gathering intelligence as to the national picture, to decide on his next move. He had sent a flying column, under Aboyne, to deal with Lanark and his army, to the west – only to find that hero had already fled and his people evaporated. And, that Lanark was not alone in his readings of the situation, quickly grew more apparent as the messages came in.

Baillie, it seemed, had made for Stirling town, despite the plague, and had gone to ground in the impregnable fortress-castle on its rock, along with Balcarres, Burleigh and others of the military leaders. Argyll had been much more prudent, not drawing rein until he reached South Queensferry, on the Forth, where he had actually taken ship for England no less, via Berwick-on-Tweed. The Campbell had a preference for escaping by boat. The Earls of Loudoun and Lothian were also on their way to England, on horseback – no doubt to join one or other of the Leslies, Sandy at Newcastle, David at Carlisle. The West Country earls, such as Glencairn and Cassillis, were reputed to be on their way to Ireland. The ministers, without the resources of the nobility, were dispersing to their parishes over the length and breadth of the land – possibly to their parishioners' benefit.

It seemed that no major figure remained, of the Committee of the Estates, to lead the fight against Montrose.

James Graham himself was scarcely able to credit it, however confidently jubilant were his friends. He kept enquiring of this lord or that. What of the Earl Marischal? What of Seaforth? What of Lindsay? What of Balmerino? What of the Duke, Hamilton himself? And that fanatic Johnston of Warriston, now a Lord of Session no less? Above all, what of James Livingstone, Earl of Callander, and his Border army? All these could not have dissolved into the mists ...

'Callander would not be such a fool as to assail you now,' Pate Graham of Inchbraikie averred. 'Having avoided any encounter all this while, will he hazard all now that you are master of the land?'

'It is his duty, no less. With an army in the field, unblooded. And it is folly to call me master of the land, Pate, because for the moment no host harries us.'

They were sitting alone on the hillside above Kilsyth, with the great camp outspread below them and the afternoon turning towards evening, though heat still shimmered on all the landscape and drained it of colour.

Pate eyed his friend and chief keenly. 'What has come over you, Jamie? These last days, weeks almost, you have not been yourself. Moody. You are not sick? As you were at Rothiemurchus, that time? Or is it ... is it Magdalen? Or young James, in Edinburgh Tolbooth? That will soon be over, at least.' Almost the first thing that Montrose had done, once he heard that the Covenant forces were not reassembling against him, had been to send Archie Napier and a hard-riding squadron under Nat Gordon, to Edinburgh, to open that Tolbooth, praying the while that neither the plague nor any dread emissary from Argyll got there beforehand.

'I am well enough, Pate. Would God I could say the same for Magdalen. She is sore afflicted. I do not know what to make of her, where to turn. I have failed her grievously. But ... I cannot blame myself for all her ill. God has laid His hand heavily on us, in this. As for Jamie, again I do blame myself. I should not have left him there, at Kinnaird, to be made hostage. Knowing the Campbell! Magdalen blames me for this, too, I know. Yet I could not take him with me on campaign. After Johnnie ...' He shook his handsome head. 'Is there a curse on me, Pate? To bring hurt on those I love? Is it my fate to beat the air, to make great swelling gestures – and to achieve nothing save the sorrow of those close to me?'

'Achieve nothing, Man! You are losing your wits indeed, if you say that! What have you *not* achieved? One man! I mind you saying, that day at Tulliebelton, when you came to my house in guise of a groom, with William Rollo – you said, God give you one year, but one year, with the King's authority, and you would hand Charles Stewart back his Scots kingdom. That was August last. I mind not the day of it, but it was late in the month. So you have scarce had your twelve months, This is August likewise, but only the 17th. In those months you have raised armies out of nothing. Out-fought every host sent against you. Made every other general look a fool. Made the King's cause to mean something, and given Scotland hope again. And you say that you have achieved nothing, but to beat the air!'

'You are kind, Pate – but biased not a little. Winning battles without holding territory is of doubtful value – even though a necessary step. I have yet to be convinced that even this last one will solve that problem for us.'

'I say that you are too gloomy, James, by far. Their leaders are fled. What more do you ask for?'

As though in answer to that question, they perceived a small mounted party riding uphill from the camp towards them, led, they recognised, by young Alexander. There were two splendidly dressed individuals and two grooms, all in marked contrast to the campaigners' stained and tattered clothing. One of the new-comers was elderly and distinctly stout, the other of early middle years, sallow, sober.

'Visitors, my lord Marquis,' Alexander called. 'From the city of Glasgow, no less. Have I your lordship's permission to present them?'

'Glasgow, you say?' Montrose got to his feet. 'This interests me.'

'Sir Robert Douglas of Blackerston, Lord of the Manor of Gorbals and Bridgend, my lord. And Master Archibald Fleming, Commissary. Representing the Corporation of the city of Glasgow. Humbly crave audience of Your Excellency.' Gleefully, young Alexander was piling it on, rather, as they dismounted.

'I am happy to receive representatives of Glasgow,' Montrose said, 'I have happy memories of the city. I had some of my schooling there. My house of Mugdock is – or was – nearby. And my grandfather was your Provost for a while I think.'

Sir Robert Douglas, the younger of the two representatives, coughed. 'Mugdock,' he said. 'I . . . we . . . regret it. Most un-happy. That we could by no means save it.'

'Unhappy, yes.'

'Did you try?' That was a bark, from Inchbrakie.

Douglas looked uncomfortable. 'My lord Marquis of Argyll gave strictest orders . . .'

'To be sure,' Montrose nodded. 'I understand very well. Now – how can I serve you, gentlemen?'

'It is our wish to serve *you*, my lord Marquis,' the Commissary declared. 'We have the honour to seek your protection, and to offer you the hospitality of our town. In the name of the Provost, magistrates, the Dean of Guild and the Deacon-Convener of Trades.'

'Ha-a-a!' The two Grahams' glances met.

'We offer our complete support, my lord,' Douglas added.

'That I shall require, yes. In the name of the King's Grace. As I do of every other city and town. But . . . I could have done with Glasgow's sooner, see you! Before Kilsyth, rather than after! When, for instance, the Earl of Lanark marched his rebel army through your streets.'

'We are not postured for war, my lord. We are a peaceable city. Traders, merchants, craftsmen, scholars, not fighting-men . . .'

'You have city walls, strong gates, a Town Guard, train-bands, have you not ?'

The emissaries were silent.

James Graham relaxed the stern expression which he had assumed – and which indeed did not come easily to him. He was in fact greatly encouraged by this development. Perhaps it was an augury, proof that Pate and the others were right, that Scotland was at last prepared to throw over the zealots and fanatics and bigots, to acclaim the defeat of Argyll and the Covenant leaders, and to rally to the King's cause. Glasgow was a smaller city than Edinburgh or Dundee, but it was important too, the key to the South-West, its university a source of great influence, its churchmen powerful. Moreover it was very wealthy, its merchant and craft guilds the most prosperous and organised in the land.

'Belated support is better than none,' he said. 'I accept it. But for King Charles, not myself. I will inform His Grace.'

That produced no outburst of loyal enthusiasm. 'Yes, my lord,' the Commissary acceded.

'You will come to Glasgow ? Enter the city ?' Douglas asked.

'Mm. Probably. But first I shall require a token of your support. My army, after long months of campaigning, is in need of much. I shall require from your city guilds clothing, shoes, bonnets and the like. Also money.'

There was a heavy silence.

'You do not sound eager, gentlemen.'

'We must speak with our colleagues on this . . .'

'A whole army, my lord! It . . . it would be costly. Very costly.'

'Not so costly as the blood which that army has shed, sirs. Remember it, if you please. Cost is a relative matter. Moreover, I have the fullest authority – and ability – to take what I require.'

Hastily the emissaries changed their tune. The stores and supplies would be forthcoming, they were sure.

'Very well. Inform your Provost and colleagues to that effect.'

'When will you come, my lord ? To Glasgow ?'

'In a day or so. When you confirm this matter of supplies. That is, if you have not the plague, there ? I will not put my army at risk by the pest.'

'No plague, no. It has not come to Glasgow, God be praised. The city will rejoice to honour you.'

'Will it, sir ? I wonder! And why ?'

'Because your lordship won a victory almost on its doorstep!' Alexander declared. 'And for no other reason. Another twenty miles, and they would have looked the other way!'

'Not so, sir. Not so, I say!' Douglas protested. 'That is not true, I swear it . . .'

'You will have opportunity to prove your loyalty, never fear, gentlemen. Tell your Provost so,' Montrose said, smiling pleasantly again. 'I shall inform him of the time of my arrival. A very good day to you, friends . . .'

*   *   *

So, on the 19th of August, the Captain-General and his victorious host approached the city, crossing the Molendinar Burn to the Drygait Port. Ahead, beyond the gates and walls, the Townhead area rose in a huddle of roofs and spires and towers to the vast mass of the Cathedral dominating all, with the parapets and battlements of the Archbishop's Palace and Castle near by. There was more green to be seen than in most cities, for Glasgow was a place of trees and gardens at this north-eastern end, with the cathedral-manses' orchards, and the College Garden bowered in foliage. The army metaphorically licked hungry lips at the sight – or part of the army, at any rate. For the inevitable process had already begun. The clansmen were going home, large numbers already gone. Battle won, the defeated spoiled – and there were major spoils after Kilsyth, with the entire Covenant leadership's baggage captured, to say nothing of Baillie's commissariat. Even Aboyne was anxious to be away, back to his Gordon lands, with the responsibility for the clan now his, no one knowing what Lord Lewis might be up to. Airlie himself was talking about returning to his Angus glens, where the harvest was over-ready. When the economy depended almost entirely upon cattle, as it did practically everywhere north of the Highland Line, the getting in of the oats for winter feed was a vital matter. And the hot weather had brought on the grain early.

What was left of the royalist army, then, marched to the strains of such pipers as remained to them, until the bells of Glasgow's cathedral and churches rang out a jangled welcome to compete, a new experience for them.

'It almost sounds as though they were glad to see us!' the Master of Madderty declared.

Colkitto hooted. 'They will be as glad to see us as they would the Devil!' he said. 'They'd ring the bells for *him*, whatever – if no saints were in sight to come to their aid!'

An official party was waiting to greet them just outside the Drygait Port, on the beaten dusty fairground. Here, under a silken canopy upheld on poles by halberdiers, stood Provost James Bell and his magistrates and bailies, with the Dean of Guild, the Deacon-Convener of Trades, the university dignitaries and one or two ministers, all colourful and prosperous-seeming in their robes and chains-of-office. By comparison, Montrose's army looked a shabby, ragged horde, lean, unkempt, unwashed. James Graham himself, although always he kept his person neat and as clean as might be, his bearing assured, easily commanding, was still in the stained and patched tartan doublet and trews, scuffed and battered riding-boots and shoulder-slung sword-belt he had worn while campaigning. Until his men were reclothed, he would remain thus.

The Provost was a small, ferret-like man, red-haired, with no presence but keen-eyed, shrewd, a wealthy bonnet-maker.

'My name is Bell, Lord o' Montrose – Jamie Bell. I'm the Provost,' he announced, in a sing-song West Country voice. 'And these here are the bailies.' He pronounced it bylies. 'And the Dean o' Guild. I was Dean mysel' three years back.' He sounded prouder of having been Dean than Provost. 'And this is Deacon-Convener Ninian Gilhazie – och, the trades just, ye ken. And . . . and others. You're welcome to Glasgow, you and yours.'

'I thank you, Mr. Provost, Gentlemen. I rejoice at the goodwill of this great city. I accept your submission in the King's name – whose humble servant I am.'

'Eh . . .? Submission . . .?' the Provost said. 'Whae said

anything about submission ?' He glanced quickly at his companions. 'It's no' a submission lord – it's a welcome.'

'You did not offer us a welcome *before* we won Kilsyth battle, Mr. Provost. Though we were but a dozen miles off, and could have done with Glasgow's kindly aid. And you permitted my lord of Lanark and his rebel force to pass through your streets. Before that battle. Therefore I do assume that it was that battle which constrained you. To change your attitude. Correct me, pray, if I am wrong ? And when battle, armed force, constrains men to change their policy, I deem it submission, sir.'

'But . . . but we never fought against you, lord . . .'

'You are a man of God. I am sure, Provost ? To represent this city whose motto I well know is that it flourishes by the preaching of the Word. Then I answer you from the Word. Thus. "When saw we thee an hungered, or athirst, or a strange, or naked, or sick, or in prison, and did not minister unto thee ? Then shall he answer them, saying, Verily I say unto you, inasmuch as ye did it not to one of the least of these, ye did it not to me." How say you, then ? I have been fighting for King Charles's cause in Scotland for a whole year – and I have not received a man, a groat, or even a word of support, from the great and wealthy city of Glasgow. How say you, sirs, to Holy Writ ?'

Provost Bell did not say anything. Nor did his companions, even the ministers. Undoubtedly they were unused to having Scripture quoted at them save from the pulpit.

'Is it submission, then ? Or no ?' Montrose glanced behind him, at his serried thousands. 'I would prefer not to have to *make* it so, gentlemen.'

'No! No, lord – no' that! Och, use what word you will. Submission, aye. So long . . . so long as you dinna let *them* loose in the toon! The Irishry and the Hielantmen. Anything, lord – anything but that.' The little red-lashed eyes kept looking in the direction of the gigantic Colkitto.

'Very well, Mr. Provost. Glasgow submits to the King's Captain-General, and kindly welcomes him and the King's army. Is that correct ?'

'If you'll no' let them loose . . .'

'Sir – I command an army, not a rabble. If I accept your submission, then your town comes under my protection. All shall be done lawfully and in order.'

'Aye, well . . .'

'Good. Then there is the matter of the supplies, sir. Which I stipulated. Shoes, clothing, bonnets and the like. And money. This is part of your welcome? A practical part – and very necessary.'

'My lord Marquis,' Commissary Fleming spoke up, from the rear. 'It is not possible to gather large quantities of these goods at short notice. You will understand, at this time of year . . . With the best will in the world, my lord. We, ah, we suggest an alternative.'

'Indeed, sir? I am not used to be offered alternatives to my legitimate requirements.'

'No, my lord. But . . . but it is difficult, see you. We suggest that you, your soldiers should be given £500 – sterling, not Scots – £500 distributed amongst them. To *buy* such things as are necessary.'

'You'll agree that's generous, lord?' the Provost added.

'Should I, sir? I shall require much more of this city than that, I assure you! But – this is for my men? In their hands? In lieu of shoes, gear and the like? Is that it?'

'Well . . . aye.' The Provost sounded doubtful, glancing around.

Hastily Sir Robert Douglas put in, from a flanking position. 'My lord Marquis – it shall all be as you say. We are in your hands, and are glad to be. We are all assured of your gracious goodwill towards our city. And your protection. We hope that you will now enter it, and test our loyalty. A banquet is prepared, feasting for all your men. Entertainment. Without stint. We must not keep you standing here, outside the walls . . .'

His points made, Montrose acceded, and moved forward in restrainedly friendly fashion to greet the bailies and guild representatives. Then he summoned the pipers once more, and after a preliminary flourish by his trumpeters, they fell in behind the musicians, one and all, and proceeded to march through the towered gateway, and into the narrow Drygait, Montrose at the front with the city deputation – and having much ado to limit his stride to their notably non-military and various gaits.

No crowds lined the narrow streets to greet them, although people were at windows and congregated in groups at close-mouths. Booths were shuttered up, stalls folded away, packmen and hucksters conspicuous by their absence. Even the poultry and pigs which normally cluttered up the wynds and alleyways had been hidden away by their prudent owners. But some attempts had been made, presumably at official level, to strike a more welcoming note, for leafy branches and bunches of fern and bracken were tied on wells, pumps, louping-on stones, braziers and the like; and now and again the head of the procession was halted for a moment or two for children dressed as angels or cherubs to present to the King's representative flowers and stammered recitals. Montrose rewarded each with a smile, a pat and one of the few coins he had managed to preserve – and was thankful for the scent of the flowers at least, for the smell of the city, in that hot airless August noonday, was appalling.

With the College in its gardens on their left, and the Archbishop's Castle on their right, unoccupied this long while and looking dejected, at the junction of the Drygait and Rotten Row, they swung northwards up the Stable Green, climbing the hill past all the cathedral manses in their orchards to the Vicar's Alley, to where the Kirk Port gave access to the mighty Cathedral of St. Mungo, Glasgow's pride – although it was now divided, in good Presbyterian fashion, into the High Kirk, the Outer Kirk, and, in the semi-subterranean crypt, the Barony Kirk. The majestic bulk of it brought back memories to Montrose, for here had been held the vital and dramatic General Assembly of 1638, the turning-point in his public life, wherein his hand was finally set to the plough. The cathedral graveyard, together with the grassy expanse of the Green outside, was the only open space large enough in the city to contain the thousands of men. On the Green oxen were already being roasted on open fires, many of them, barrels were being broached, and vast quantities of loaves laid out, using the table-stones and recumbent slabs of the graveyard as convenient dressers and benches – with the cooks and scullions furiously warding off the hordes of stray dogs which the savoury smells had brought from near and far. The swarms of flies were equally attentive. The many children, no doubt warned about the dreadful, possibly cannibalistic habits of the Irish and Highlanders, fled as the procession came up.

Here there were more speeches, by Baillie Colin Campbell – an unfortunate name, in the circumstances, which drew forth uninhibited groans from such MacDonalds and Macleans as still remained with the force – by Dean of Guild Henry Glen, and by Master Henry Gibson, the Town Clerk. All could orate better than did the Provost, but even so were listened to only by those in the immediate vicinity, and not all of those. Then the Principal of the university, the Reverend Dr. John Strang, had his say – the Chancellor, being the Duke of Hamilton, was wisely absent –

but by this time nobody wanted to listen to more talk and he got no sort of hearing, the rumbling of bellies, in consequence of the delectable aroma of cooking meats, all but drowning his precise periods. Montrose dispensed with any other reply than a series of graceful bows. He had not failed to notice that none of the city representatives had so much as mentioned the King throughout. It seemed apparent that Glasgow was paying homage to a victorious general whose power might well constrain them, rather than showing loyalty to their monarch and his cause.

Thereafter, leaving the troops to their feasting, a move was made back down the High Street, by the official party, now minus pipers, to the Tolbooth and Town House at the junction of Gallowgate and Trongate, where Montrose and his senior officers were to be entertained by the magistrates. Though not quite all of his senior officers, for he made sure that one or two were always to be on duty outside, to ensure of reasonably good behaviour on the part of the men, and to see that sentries and pickets were on the alert all round the city.

Up in the Town Hall, before ever he was sat down, Sir Robert Douglas and others were bringing individuals to present to the Captain-General. The first was none other than his old colleague and lieutenant, John Lyon, 2nd Earl of Kingborne, in ostrich-feathered hat and much beribboned.

'My lord Marquis, your servant,' Kingborne said, bowing over the hand he took – but keeping his eyes down.

'Ha – John! This is a pleasure. And a surprise. We have not seen each other in many months. You are growing fat, man, I swear. I advise more ... activity! *Military* activity, perhaps!'

The other coughed. 'I came to offer you my congratulations, James. And to assure you of my aid and support.'

'Ah. Aid and support, John? I could have done with them this twelvemonth past – I vow I could! And wrote to you to that effect. More than once.'

'Yes. But it was ... difficult, see you. Very difficult. Situated as I was ...'

'No doubt. A man's duty is not always easy, my friend.'

'A man's duty is not always so clear! As it is to you ...'

'You are one of the King's earls, are you not? Sworn to aid and defend His Grace.' He raised his glance. 'And another behind you, if I mistake not.'

'My lord Marquis – may I present the Earl of ...'

Douglas was brushed aside. 'I need no presentation to my lord

126

of Montrose by such as yourself, sirrah,' a thin and haughty middle-aged exquisite declared, oddly dressed in sky-blue velvet and inlaid half-armour. 'We are well acquaint.'

'Yes, indeed we are,' James Graham agreed affably. 'My lord Earl of Roxburgh and I – we used both to be on the King's side! When he was His Grace's Keeper of the Privy Seal, no less.'

'I . . . my lord, I protest!' the elegant spluttered. '*Used* to be! I am the King's most loyal servant.'

'Ha – but I fear that you cannot be that, i' faith! For such position has long been filled by my esteemed goodsire, my lord of Southesk, he never fails to assure me! Would you claim to be more loyal than Southesk, my Lord Roxburgh ?'

That brought the other up short. He could scarcely insist that he was; yet Southesk's equivocal behaviour was known to all, his association with Argyll. Roxburgh compressed his lips tightly and said nothing.

'When last we forgathered, I think, it was in the Parliament Hall at Edinburgh, was it not, my lord ? I, brought from ward in the castle there, to be tried. With certain friends of mine – and of the King. You, as I mind it, had nothing to say.'

'I . . . the King. He was present. His Grace did not interfere. As one of the King's ministers, then, should I have done so ?'

'Ah. There is a question indeed. A matter for calculation. As to advantage, perhaps ?'

'As to loyalties, I say . . .'

'It may be so. And you have a sure judgment in these matters, it seems. I take it, that you now esteem the King's cause to be in the ascendancy ? Er, profitable, once more ?'

'My lord Marquis – I did not come here to be insulted!'

'I am sure that you did not. Nor do I insult you. I but remark on your judgment. Comment on your careful thought. As when I sent you a commission of lieutenancy. From Carlisle, just thirteen months ago. Seeking your aid and support when I entered Scotland, on His Grace's behalf. You judged the cause less hopeful then, I imagine – for you replied nothing. Nor have you since. Until today. You greatly encourage me, I swear! Why *did* you come, sir, may I ask ?'

'To, ah, offer my services. In the rule of this kingdom. You will require much aid and assistance. I have considerable experience in statecraft . . .'

'That you have, my lord. I shall not forget it. Now, with your permission – we hold up the good Provost . . .'

There were others queuing up to pay their respects to victory, Montrose recognising the two Johnston Earls of Annandale and Hartfell, and the Lord Linton, son of the Earl of Traquair, the Lord Erskine, and others. But, let them wait. They had kept *him*, and his master, waiting for sufficiently long. Coolly courteous, he bowed to all, and let Provost Bell lead him to his seat at the head of the great table.

It was while watching with some wry amusement the scramble thereafter, undignified but revealing, for precedency in seating, on the part of lords, knights, bailies, churchmen, university doctors and prominent citizens, that Montrose gained his clearest indication of all that the tide had turned indeed. Well down the room, a figure very familiar to him was quietly slipping into a modest place at the board, richly but restrainedly dressed. It was James, Lord Carnegie, Magdalen's brother and Southesk's heir. None could now doubt which was the cause most likely to win.

Provost Bell, presiding, seated himself on the Captain-General's left, with Colkitto on *his* left, then the Deacon-Convener. Montrose had on his right the Dean of Guild and then the Earl of Airlie. He was almost thankful that Clanranald, Glengarry, Duart and most of the other Highland chiefs had gone home so quickly; they would never have accepted this sort of placing.

'Are you fine there, lord?' the Provost asked, solicitously. 'Plentys o' room? Och, it's a right clutter, this. There's a wheen mair lords an' great folk arrived than we looked for. They must ha' smelt the guid beef roasting, eh?' He tee-heed.

'They must have smelled *something*,' James Graham agreed. 'But, yes – I am very comfortable, I thank you, Mr. Provost. Although it is many a day since I sat down at such a table.'

'Aye, well – a guid bellyfu' will set you up, man. Ayrshire beef – the best. But a bit salmon first. And hens and siclike trash after. But the beef's the thing. The claret's to your hand. And yon flagon's Bordeaux. Gie me the whisky, mysel' – there's mair body to it . . .'

Glasgow might have its own brand of ecclesiastics, and be something lacking in enthusiasm for its monarch, but there was no faulting its victuals. Quantity, quality and variety vied with each other, as course succeeded course. The heat in the great chamber grew stifling, and the noise grew with it, as the plentitude of wines and spirits began to have their effect. Montrose perceived presently that, if this occasion was to be turned to any good account, other than merely social, it would require to be done soon, while men were still in a state to apprehend it. He informed the Provost that he wished to address the gathering on matters of some importance – even though all were not yet finished eating. That worthy apprised all of the fact by merely banging on the table loud and long with his silver tankard.

James Graham rose – and from somewhere down the table Black Pate's voice rang out strongly.

'When His Grace the King's representative stands, all stand!'

There was a hasty if scarcely well-concerted effort to be up-standing, by all – save those already quite incapable of it.

Montrose gave them a moment or two. Then he raised his tankard. 'I give you the health, prosperity, long life and puissant reign of our beloved, mighty and lawful sovereign, King Charles – and damnation to his enemies!'

None refused to drink that toast – and the failure to actually acclaim it by some quite large percentage of the company was largely overwhelmed by the enthusiasm of those who did.

While they were still on their feet, Colkitto shouted, 'And another to the man who makes the King's reigning possible, whatever – Seumas Graham, *An Greumach Mor*, the Marquis!'

Few indeed allowed themselves to seem backward in drinking that toast, with so much cold steel and hot hands present. The shouting went on and on.

Montrose, noting that not a few were striving to be heard, no doubt to present other toasts, recognised that this process could well end any intelligent reception of what he had to say. He raised his hand for silence – and when that failed in effect, jerked his head towards his personal trumpeter, who sat with the ser-geant-of-the-guard and other attendants at a side-table. The subsequent bugle blast, in that confined space, all but lifted the roofing, not to mention the tops of men's heads.

In the abrupt silence that followed, James Graham bowed all around, smiling. 'I thank you. Pray resume your seats.' He paused, and went on pleasantly. 'Mr. Provost, Mr. Dean of Guild, Mr. Deacon-Convener, my lords and gentlemen. On be-half of my officers and of our good fellows who feast outside, I thank all who have provided for and contributed to our enter-tainment here. Few of us, in His Graces's forces at least, have been indulged so notably hitherto, most of us never, I am sure. Our appreciation is most obvious – in some more obvious than in others, for we have not all the same capacity . . .' And he glanced along at Colkitto, whose face was like the rising sun.

There was a shout of laughter – which was not the reaction Colkitto's presence had been creating in Glasgow earlier in the day.

'And now, my friends, I speak to you in a different voice. The voice of the King's Lieutenant for Scotland, and Captain-General of His Grace's forces.' His voice *was* different, too, and his bearing with it. Only those very far through failed to recognise it. Men sat up straighter.

'I declare to you, by the King's royal commission, that I have all the power of this ancient throne vested in me, here in Scotland, until His Grace comes here in person to reign over you. Which joyful event will, I believe, be very shortly . . .'

There was a stir and murmur at that, not all of it sounding overjoyed at the prospect, men glancing at each other questioningly.

'Before His Grace arrives, much falls to be done, in order to prepare this war-torn kingdom for him, with much of misrule, oppression and rebellion to be wiped out and set to rights. To that end I hereby decree, proclaim and call a parliament of the Estates of this realm to meet, in the King's name. Forty days of notice is required for the due calling of a parliament. Accordingly it will meet six weeks from now, on the 20th of October. And in this city of Glasgow . . .'

Again the stir and exclamation, pleased and otherwise. The Provost leaned across, behind Montrose's back, to the Dean of Guild, agitatedly.

'It is my hope that King Charles himself may be here to preside in person over this important sitting. But if not, he will appoint a High Commissioner, as proper. I need not declare to you how momentous will be this occasion, how important for all in Scotland the decisions taken thereat.' He paused, pointedly, that what lay behind his words should sink in.

Few there failed to realise the implications. It would be a day of reckoning, indeed.

'And so, Mr. Provost, you will prepare your city. As the loyal and worthy setting for this great event. I will give you and your Council all necessary powers to requisition, enforce and act accordingly. You understand, gentlemen?'

Provost Bell darted his red head around like a weasel in a wall, uncertain whether to rejoice or wail. His colleagues looked equally unsure of themselves – but definitely more depressed than elated.

That was nothing to their expressions a moment or two later, however, as Montrose went on, 'Farther to this, I shall require forthwith for the immediate weal and governance of the kingdom, until parliament shall make proper and due provision, a loan of £50,000 Scots. From this city. This loan, which must be paid to me by tomorrow's evening, will no doubt be repaid by that parliament hereafter.'

There was no doubt about the wailing now. Like a chorus of the damned the Glasgow representatives raised their voices in agonised protest, loud and continuous.

'Do not tell me that a wealthy city such as this could find it difficult to raise such paltry sum for their lord the King?'

'It's no' possible, lord – Goad, it's no'!' the Provost croaked. 'Fifty thousand! We . . . we couldna get you money the likes o' that.'

'You got Argyll more, five years past! And the next year sent him a further £10,000, I was told.'

'Nine thousand, lord – only £9,000!' Bell quavered. 'And the first was the toon's siller. The whole plate and treasure . . .'

'Save perhaps these silver tankards and dishes we sup from, sir?'

'*Twenty* thousand we might find, my lord Marquis . . .' Commissary Fleming put in.

'I am not here to bargain and chaffer like any huckster!' they were told sternly. 'Fifty thousand I require. By tomorrow night. Or I requisition what is necessary. And that will be no *loan*!'

A halberdier of the Town Guard came, to hurry apologetically to the Provost's side, pluck at his robe, and whisper.

Bell started up. 'Hech, hech – lord there's a riot! In the streets. Booths afire. Your Hielantmen. Robbery! Looting . . .!'

Montrose looked down. 'I am not finished, Mr. Provost. I will not be interrupted. If what you declare is true, it is against my strictest orders. Any such disobedience is punishable with the utmost severity. In the matter of conduct in the streets – or of failure to obey my other commands. Such as producing this money for loan.' He looked up. 'Colonel Graham, Younger of Inchbrakie – you will go investigate. If you find looting, take the leaders and hang them. Where all may see. And put the officers who should have stopped it in close ward. I will deal with such later. I will not have looting or riot – or disobedience – by any soever.'

'Yes, my lord Marquis.' Black Pate strode from the room.

There was a throbbing silence as men contemplated this abrupt display of harsh realism, in all the talking, and the sheer authority which could command it. The lesson was not lost on those present, nor the threat implied to other than rioters.

James Graham remained on his feet. 'I further have to announce that all men assembled in arms, save those under my authority or otherwise in the King's service, must disperse forthwith or be treated as rebels and traitors; and all who command them to be guilty of high treason. All lords, lairds, chiefs of clans and of names, all landed men, must apply to me, in default of parliament, for licence to muster any tail of armed men, in excess of a dozen, sufficient to guard their persons and homes. All comforting, sheltering and abetting former rebel leaders will also be deemed to be in treason to the Crown. But such rebels, who give themselves up and acknowledge their error, and yield due allegiance to the King, will be treated with the utmost clemency. My word upon it. These decrees will be promulgated throughout the land.'

None raised voice in comment.

'Now, as regards requisitioning for my army. I shall require . . .'

Montrose was interrupted again, this time by the sound of upraised voices, and the door being flung open. Two men pushed past the protesting Town Guards – the Master of Napier and Nat Gordon. James Graham's brows had risen – but it was the sight of the faces which now appeared behind his two lieutenants which caught his breath. And caught the breaths of more than he.

It was as though a party of spectres was filing into Glasgow's Town Hall, pale, gaunt, shrunken, stooping, shuffling, sunken-eyed. Absolute silence fell on the crowded chamber.

It was Montrose himself who broke it. 'Dear God – Archie!' he cried, in a strangled voice; and thrusting aside his chair, hurried forward to greet the newcomers. 'And George! I . . . I . . .' Helplessly he shook his head, unable to continue.

'Jamie!' the Lord Napier of Merchiston, his brother-in-law and one-time guardian, whispered. 'God be praised for this day! To set eyes on you again. Oh, Jamie, Jamie . . .'

Montrose clasped the other to him – and almost choked at the slight and brittle insubstantiality of what he held, the mere skeleton of a man. Young Archie had been supporting his father; clearly he was too weak to stand upright, had become an old, white-headed broken totterer. James Graham took over the duty.

132

Holding the other, he turned to Sir George Stirling of Keir, holding out his hand, silent. For Stirling, although a youngish man, was only in slightly better shape than his uncle, Napier, hunched, parchment-skinned, luminous-eyed, the reddened galling of manacles on his wrists the only colour to his person.

'Victory, James!' Keir got out, stammering. 'At last, victory.'

'Victory, George – at a price!' Montrose dashed a tear from his eye. 'God forgive me – this was my doing. Because you are linked with me, it is, that they did this to you.'

'What matters it, James? Now. We have the victory you fought for, won – although *we* only rotted in prison . . .'

His words were lost, indeed he was all but knocked over, as old Airlie rushed past them to reach and embrace his son. The Lord Ogilvy had just hobbled in, no longer the fresh-faced enthusiast of the English campaigns but a haggard scarecrow looking aged enough to be his own father.

Montrose, shocked, appalled, reached out to him also. 'James – you too!' he groaned. 'The brave one, the stalwart of the Angus glens!' He glanced behind still, biting his lip, as more walking ghosts shuffled in, some with as illustrious names as any in the land. Anxiously he scanned them. Then, feeling Napier reeling within his arm, he half carried him to his own chair.

'Cherish these!' he cried. 'The most honoured men in all Scotland. These paid Argyll in different coin to yours! Make way for them, I say . . .!'

There was no lack of aid, now, sympathy and welcome, for the pathetic band. All were eager to help and comfort. Montrose went from one to another greeting, commiserating, exclaiming – even though always his eyes searched behind all, to the still open door.

'Thirty-two in all, my lord Marquis,' Nat Gordon came up to report. 'Including the ladies. These we brought to Keir, on our way here. Where they might have attention. They . . . they were in ill case. These, the men, insisted on coming on, to pay respects to your lordship. We had not the heart to refuse them. My Lord Napier and Sir George we lifted out of Linlithgow town's jail, in the by-going. The rest were in the Tolbooth of Edinburgh. Held in stinking vaults. No light, no room to stand upright, filth covering the floor. Some were too sick and weak even to ride . . .'

'Aye, man. It is beyond belief. But – my son?' Montrose could

133

stand it no longer. 'My *son*! Jamie ? What of him ? Where is he ?'

'He is well, my lord. But they have him secure in Edinburgh Castle. The town itself yielded to us – but not the castle. They moved him there over a month back. We offered them any they might name, as hostage, in exchange for the Lord James. But they would not. Nor would he, indeed. We spoke with him, he standing on the gatehouse parapet, shouting. He said to tell his father not to waste exchange of a good man for one too young to fight. He said it would ill become his father's son to deprive the King of a single fighter.'

'He said that ? Jamie truly said that, Nat ?'

'Aye.' The Gordon grinned. 'He said more. He said that a man in the castle was teaching him to build boats.'

A faint flicker of a smile crossed Montrose's face. 'Aye – that is Jamie! But – what of the plague ? Does it not rage sorely ? Is he in danger ?'

'The castle is high above the mists and stews of the city. The plague has not touched it. Indeed, Edinburgh is not so sore hit as is Stirling town.'

'You say so ? Ah, well – so his mother will not see Jamie yet awhile.' He sighed. 'Edinburgh yielded, then ? You had no trouble ?'

'None. We sent messengers ahead, as you instructed us, demanding that the city submitted, in the King's name. They sent out a deputation of magistrates and the like, to plead with us to spare the town – as though we were a great army. A mere squadron of horse! They said that they were ever loyal to the King – only that their city had been used by wicked and unscrupulous men, who had now fled and left them defenceless. They offered us money, what we would – but besought us to have mercy. For the hand of God was sore upon them, with this plague. We said that we had come only for the prisoners and hostages – and that your lordship would decide Edinburgh's fate in due course! And suggested that you had little cause to love the place . . .!'

'Yes – this is the pattern, then. I am told that Dundee is likewise clamouring to be admitted to the King's peace. No doubt Aberdeen the same. But – they could turn against us again tomorrow, should our fortunes seem to change. Poor devils – I scarce blame them. They are at the mercy of whosoever wields the heaviest stick! We must gain from them what we can *while* we can.' He paused. 'But, Nat, there is one man I have looked for here. Doctor Wishart, the divine. I have not seen him . . .'

'I am here, my lord,' a voice spoke, from behind them.

Montrose turned, and stared – and realised that his eyes had slid over this man, more than once, unrecognising. The lesson had not fully sunk in. George Wishart, one of the ministers of St. Andrews, and a notably learned man, had been ousted for being a King's man, and had fled to Newcastle. There Montrose had met him, when with Leslie's army, and they had discovered that they saw eye to eye on many matters. No doubt because of this friendship he had been taken into custody at the later surrender of Newcastle by the royalists, and confined to Edinburgh's Tolbooth, He was only three years older than Montrose – but now looked thirty.

'George! George Wishart . . .! Oh, my friend – forgive me! That I did not know you. Save us – you, you . . .!' He swallowed, shaking his head.

'That is no matter, my lord. What matters is yourself. I have never seen you look better – for which God be thanked. It is worth all the weary days and nights in that place. To see you well, triumphant, the noblest face in this land . . .!' The voice, which seemed to have deepened, broke.

James Graham gripped his arm. 'What am I to say to you? When you have suffered so much. My friend. And not to know you . . .'

'Say, my lord, that I may stay with you, now. Be your secretary, perhaps, your chaplain. If you will have me. I ask no greater favour, privilege. Take me with you hereafter. I shall serve you, with all my heart.'

Much moved, Montrose nodded, finding words difficult. 'Aye – it shall be so. To be sure, George. To my joy. I will no doubt require a secretary, now. But . . . what did they do to you? Those marks. On your face. Did they – did they misuse you so . . .?'

'Rats,' the other informed, briefly. 'There were more than prisoners in that Tolbooth!'

The banquet broke up quickly thereafter, Montrose having lost all taste for junketing, as for speech-making and social civilities. He wanted to be alone with Archie Napier, George Sterling, James Ogilvy and George Wishart – and was not in a mood for disguising his preferences. Glasgow's representatives were despatched to collect their £50,000 Scots, and sundry other requirements, and the King's Lieutenant took over their Town

House and Tolbooth for the use of his forces, his first act thereafter to order the cells to be opened below it, and their inmates
freed, fed and pardoned, whatever the reason for their incarceration.

CHAPTER TEN

The great castle of Bothwell, although ruinous, made a magnificent backcloth for the event, towering above the level haughlands of the Clyde. There was space on those flats, dry at this time of the year, for all the complicated manoeuvres and displays that Montrose had planned. At the same time, the site held tactical possibilities, in the unlikely event of trouble. And there was sufficient accommodation in the courtyard and outbuildings of the castle, still roofed, to provide for what might be called his Court – and those lofty personages attending who found such conditions too spartan could roost in the little town nearby, if so they elected.

It was the 3rd of September, and the royalist army had been at Bothwell for over a week. Montrose had cut short this stay at Glasgow, remaining there for only two days in fact. It had been discovered that plague had reached the city; moreover, it was increasingly difficult to control many of the soldiery, who, with insufficient to do and too much liquor to drink, found the temptations towards plunder beyond them. Bothwell was only eight miles south-east of Glasgow, and convenient for a variety of reasons.

To all outwards appearances today's programme was a triumph, a successful flourish by an all-conquering general, the fitting climax to a brilliant campaign. The conqueror reviewed his troops and displayed his might and authority for all to see – and to note. A normal, indeed almost obligatory gesture of total victory. None realised – except perhaps Black Pate Graham, from whom his chief had few secrets – that it was, in fact, something of a last desperate throw, the resort of a worried and distracted man.

This review was perhaps unique in that it was organised and laid on not mainly for public edification and impression but for the sake of the army itself. Or what was left of it. For, of the near 6,000 with which he had fought Kilsyth, Montrose had now less than half. Worse than that, not only was Aboyne threatening to leave any day for the North with his Gordon horse, but

Colkitto himself was insisting on a campaign in Argyll, to pay back old MacDonald scores against the Campbells. In vain James Graham had pointed out that this was no valid activity for the King's army, that it was the way to lose Scotland again. Colkitto, urged on by his clansmen, remained obdurate.

This review, then, was an effort to hold together an army, to re-arouse a spirit of military pride, glory and unity – and to display to the rest of Scotland a show of armed might and confident power while yet he had it to display.

Montrose had planned it all almost as carefully as he would a battle. In a way it *was* a battle, a struggle for the adherence of a highly important part of his strength. A great march past, cavalry manoeuvres, Highland charges, a mock battle and the like, were to be followed by less military events and games, archery contests, races, wrestling, piping and dancing, football. All Clydesdale, Cunningham, Kyle and Carrick was invited to attend – though not plague-struck Glasgow – and it was hoped that not a little recruiting would be a by-product of the day.

Anxious to make under 3,000 men seem more than in fact they were, he had split up his forces into a great many lesser units, and improvised a host of flags and banners. There had been much reclothing, mainly at Glasgow's expense. Extra pipers had actually been hired.

Punctually at noon, the King's Lieutenant and his Court emerged from the castle. And it was a Court now, for half the nobility and gentry of Southern Scotland flooded to join him. For the past six days they had been coming in, in ever-growing numbers. As an indication of public opinion they were welcome – but otherwise more of an embarrassment and problem.

The issuing of the official party was the awaited signal. Cannon boomed out from four different batteries – there was no lack of artillery now that it was not needed, with half a dozen Lowland fortresses to draw upon. The sound of the bagpipes swelled and throbbed on the warm September air. The vice-regal procession moved down towards the saluting base just above the spreading haughland.

It was then, just as the first of the remaining clan regiments was marching in, that there was an unscheduled interlude. A small mounted party came trotting across the Clyde meadows from a south-easterly direction, all colour, nodding plumes, jingling spurs and gallantry. Many such had ridden in this last week, but this group seemed to exude a peculiarly pronounced air of confidence and self-assurance, careless authority in every line of them. Montrose had not seen the like. Here were no humble suppliants for his favours, at any rate.

At the head of the strolling, chattering, magpie throng, James Graham halted, and waited for the new arrivals. He was a little concerned that delay might upset the carefully timed arrangements – but showed no sign of this. He did send Black Pate to slow up the first marchers.

A hush fell on all that far-from-hushed company as the identity of the newcomers' leader was recognised – although it took Montrose himself a few moments to place the extravagantly clad florid individual as William Douglas, Marquis thereof. Willie Douglas had put on a deal of weight, since James Graham had left him, at Padua, to go search fruitlessly for his missing sister Katherine amongst the stews of Europe. Then Willie had been Earl of Angus, and they had been doing the Grand Tour in company. Always something of a playboy, the Marquis, succeeding to the title, had since then managed skilfully to avoid entanglement in matters political, religious or national, an odd condition of the head of the mighty house of Douglas, living largely abroad and ignoring all appeals from either side. That he should have appeared, unsummoned, at Bothwell this day was something of a triumph for Montrose – and all there perceived it. He was the *owner* of the castle, of course. However non-military and superficial, William Douglas was the richest man in Scotland, and could, if he so wished, muster more man-power, and horsed man-power at that, than any save Huntly himself, from the wide Douglas lands of Douglasdale, Clydesdale and Dumfriesshire.

'Jamie! Jamie Graham – well met!' this plumply mature dandy exclaimed, flourishing his wide-brimmed, ostrich-plumed bearer in an elaborate but half-mocking bow from the saddle. 'Dammit, man – you are lean as a fox! And as brown, I swear! How d'ye do it, I say?' They were almost of an age, these two, though the Douglas looked ten years the senior despite his pink, chubby cheeks.

'By going to and fro in the land – on the King's business, Willie,' Montrose answered, moving forward to shake the other's hand. 'I recommend it, my friend! You should try it! But – it is good to see you, after all these years. Old Bloody Heart!' This was always the reigning Douglas's nick-name, from the blood-red symbol they bore on their coat-of-arms, representing the great Bruce's heart taken on crusade by their ancestor, the Good Sir James Douglas, on his dying master's command.

'You ever were a restless devil, James. Full of conscience! Thank God, an ill that never afflicted me! So – now you are as good as king in Scotland, eh ?'

'No. Sir – I am not! I am but the King's servant. As are you, and all here. I but wait to hand over all to His Grace – and thankfully retire to mind my own affairs again. Which, unlike yours Willie, I fear are in sorry state!'

'Mm. Aye. To be sure. A costly matter, conscience!' The Douglas smoothed a hand over his double chins. He did not have to be reminded that amongst his hereditary privileges was that of leading the van of the royal army of Scotland in battle, as well as the first vote in Parliament or Council and carrying the crown at coronations – none of them activities Willie Douglas would have chosen. Moreover, he had married as second wife Huntly's sister, and his brother-in-law's views were not unknown to him. He cleared his throat, and looked round. 'You'll be acquaint with my lord of Home ?'

'We know each other, yes,' Montrose tried to force some cordiality into his voice. This James, 10th lord and 3rd Earl of Home was something of a trimmer, ostensibly a King's man but as liable to support the other side. He had signed the Cumbernauld Bond in 1641, but had done nothing to support that signature so far. But he was kin to Douglas, and moreover could produce a large fighting tail of Border moss-troopers and Mersemen. The King's Captain-General was in no position to offend such as James Home. 'My lord of Home is very welcome,' he said.

'Aye. Here, too, is Sir John Dalziel, brother to the Earl of Carnwath – whose fame you will know!'

'Ah, yes – to be sure.' Carnwath had fought for Charles in England, after his fashion, but had refused to accept Montrose's commission from the King and serve under him. He was still in England, an extraordinary character who kept a hard-riding mistress with him on campaign, wearing man's dress, using the name of Captain Francis Dalziel, and leading a troop of horse in fiery style – an unusual arrangement by any standards. The Covenant had outlawed him. His brother might be a useful adherent, for they had large lands in the Upper Ward of Lanarkshire.

Douglas introduced others of his gay entourage, but Montrose intervened to point out that his fighting-men would be getting impatient, unused to being held up, however illustrious the cause. A move was made to the saluting base. Like a pride of posturing peacocks, this particular cross-section of the Lowland nobility and gentry followed on.

As the pipes resumed, and the clansmen came marching into the great arena from one side, the Gordon horsed squadrons rode in from the other. James Graham stood out in front of the rest, under the Royal Standard which stirred only faintly in the warm breeze, aware that his heart had lifted again. Although sanguine of temperament, he had been much concerned over his inability to hold together his victorious army, now that the fighting was over, however little he dared allow his anxiety to show. The sudden adherence of all these nobles was encouraging, but not really important – for they would all be gone as quickly as they had come, at the first hint of reverse. But William Douglas was in a different category. Having taken all this time to make up his mind, being as devoid of ambition as of political interest, with no need to add to his riches or position, it was conceivable that he might stay the course and be able to provide that source of armed strength and influence which the King's cause so greatly needed. Clydesdale and Douglasdale was one of the greatest horse-rearing areas of the land. Montrose was calculating just how many squadrons of cavalry Douglas might be able to raise, when his dreams were rudely broken into. Despite the fact that his Gordon horse were at that moment trotting in gallant ordered ranks across their front, the Viscount Aboyne came spurring to Montrose's side.

'My Lord James,' he cried, careless of who heard him. 'I do protest! The Lord Crawford has taken command of my men. There he rides at their head. Gordons! It is insufferable! I will not have it. You must remove him . . .'

'*Must*, James? That is scarcely the word, I think?' the other said quietly. 'And might I ask you to lower your voice?'

'But . . . but I will not be treated so. I, Aboyne. And heir to Gordon. By this, this arrogant fool! Even if he is senior earl of Scotland! I ask you to remove him from my squadrons, and forthwith. Or . . . or I withdraw them from this play-acting folly!'

Montrose took his patience in both hands. 'James – the Earl of Crawford is one of His Grace's Major-Generals. He should not have superseded you, taken over your command. But I cannot call him off like some underling. Not before all these. I will speak with him hereafter . . .'

'I fear that I must ask you to do so, my lord Marquis,' the younger man said stiffly. 'I have been insulted. In front of my own clansmen. They are not His Grace's troops, I would remind you. But *mine*. Or my father's. Crawford has no right to ride at their head . . .'

'No right, I agree. But some small excuse, perhaps. He is Major-General of Horse. Yours, and a few Ogilvys, are the only cavalry in the King's Scottish army. At present Crawford has no command. And he has been rotting in Edinburgh Tolbooth. Can you not allow him a little flourish, James ?'

'In front of all these . . . ?'

'All here know well the true position. That you are heir of Gordon and Colonel of Aboyne's Horse. Go back, James, and ride at Crawford's side.'

'I will not !' the other declared stubbornly, flushing. 'I will not go back. To eat dirt before that . . . that interloper! Nor will I allow my Gordons to be commanded by any Lindsay, Major-General or none! That will be his next move, for a wager! I shall withdraw my men, as I wished to do before, and return to Strathbogie.'

Montrose raised his head a little higher. 'You will do what you must, James. But so long as you bear the King's commission under my hand, you will obey my commands. Go back to your place, Colonel. And after this ceremonial ride is over, require Major-General the Lord Crawford to report to me.'

Dark-browed, Aboyne rode off, leaving his leader a deal more perturbed than he seemed.

There were no more hitches, and the review proceeded satisfactorily enough, the skilful dispositions, groupings and rearrangement of formations giving the impression of much greater man-power than was actually involved. To avoid the true numbers becoming evident, the final march past in the formal part of the proceedings, was restricted to colour-parties only, bearing banners. Practically the entire remaining man-power was indeed on parade as alleged colour-parties, and a goodly show they made. If any of the spectators realised that it was all bluff, play-acting as Aboyne had called it, they did not publicise their discovery.

This over, and his officers assembling before the games, races, mock-battles and contests commenced, Montrose had devised a little ceremony. At a sign from him, a middle-aged gentleman of great dignity stepped forward from the over-dressed throng, Sir

Robert Spottiswoode, the King's Secretary of State for Scotland. He had arrived at Bothwell two days earlier, from England, bearing letters and appointments from King Charles. He now read out a letter sent from Hereford on the 25th of June, before the Battles of Alford and Kilsyth, expressing Charles's joy and gratitude for the great victory at Auldearn, and all other suc-successes, declaring that he would come to Scotland at the earliest moment possible, and saying that, thanks to his beloved Marquis of Montrose, his sacred cause was now assured of success. All loyal men in England had taken renewed heart from the Scottish triumphs, and so a great surge forward there was imminent. His Grace, therefore, could not come north imme-diately; but he had commanded the Lord Digby and Sir Marmaduke Langdale to ride to Scotland with a major cavalry force, for the Marquis of Montrose's support.

The fact that this cavalry support had not yet materialised, by the end of August, and that the war had gone from bad to worse in England, was not commented upon.

When the polite applause subsided, James Graham thanked Sir Robert, and called upon Sir Archibald Primrose, Clerk to the Privy Council, to read a royal proclamation which Sir Robert had also brought with him. Primrose cannot have enjoyed the occasion, for he was of the opposition party, but he put a good lawyer's face upon it. The proclamation appointed the King's well-beloved James, Marquis of Montrose, to be Lieutenant-Governor and Viceroy of the realm of Scotland, in addition to being Captain-General of its forces, with all the King's powers during his royal absence, the right to call parliament, preside at Privy Councils, create knights, appoint judges and sheriffs, and otherwise rule and govern the King's Scottish subjects. All men soever were ordered and commanded to give the said Marquis of Montrose fullest aid, duty and support. On pain of high treason. Etcetra.

There was rather louder applause for this, led noticeably by Montrose's own officers, for which James Graham bowed acknowledgment.

'I have to announce, my lords and gentlemen, that by this authority I shall tomorrow hold a Council of State, to deal with sundry urgent matters of government and to prepare for the Parliament called for October. This will not be a Privy Council, since that Council is at present in no state to meet.' He did not add that a goodly proportion of its members were indeed fled the country. 'To this meeting most here will be called to attend, and I shall greatly value your advice and guidance.' He paused. 'And now, by the same authority, rather than as commander of the King's forces, I ask Major-General Alastair MacDonald of Dunaverty, Younger of Colonsay, to stand forward.'

Wondering, obviously, but assuming a typically swaggering air to cover his uncertainty, the giant Highlander pushed his way through the throng. He was very fine today, in a strange mixture of Highland and cavalier garb, hung about with Celtic jewellery, ceremonial dirks and the like. Men drew back from his passage heedfully, for this man's name was more feared in Scotland than any other save that of Argyll himself.

'My friends,' Montrose went on, 'before you, you see one to whom the King's cause owes more than to any other in the land. Most of you know him as Colkitto. Without him and his Ulstermen and Highlanders and Islesmen, we could by no means be here today. We have won victories, yes – but without this man we might well have won none. Auldearn, of which you have just heard the King's praise, was almost wholly *his* victory. To unnumbered others we owe much – but to this man most. So I ask you to kneel, Alastair.'

'Kneel?' that stalwart exclaimed, '*Me* kneel? God's eyes – Colkitto kneels to no man. Not even you, Seumas Graham! Not even the King's Grace!'

'Then kneel before your God, man – for this is done in His name. You'll not grudge your Maker a knee?'

Doubtfully the other sank – but only on one knee, stiffly.

James Graham drew his sword, and tapped the gigantic Islesman on each massive shoulder. 'I dub thee knight, Alastair MacDonald,' he said. 'In the sight of God and of all men. Walk humbly before that God, serve the King as you have well done, assist the poor and needy, set thine hand against tyranny and evil, and remain a good and true knight until thy life's end. Arise, Sir Alastair MacDonald.' He paused, and glanced around. 'This in the King's authority. For myself, I name you Captain-General of the Clans, in the King's army.'

Speechless, his face scarlet, Colkitto got up, looked about him shaking his head like a dog, and then stumbled back to his place, forgetting entirely even to bow, much less to swagger. The buzz of exclamation and comment arose.

Montrose had thought to knight Aboyne also; policy dictated no less. But there was no sign of the Gordon; and if he was indeed hiding himself somewhere, sulking, to call out for him would but publish his absence.

He raised his hand. 'It is enough, gentlemen. Now for the contests of strength, the games. There will be victuals, refreshments, for all. Now – a word with you, if you please, my lord Earl of Crawford . . .'

*   *   *

Next morning, as Montrose was dressing himself with unusual care for the Council of State – for today he was acting the King's part, and concerned to do so worthily – his chaplain and secretary came to inform him that the Lord Aboyne was seeking interview.

'So early, George ? He would see me *now* ?'

'Yes, my lord.' Wishart was looking a different man already from the scarecrow which had entered Glasgow's Town Hall. 'He says that it is urgent. And . . . he is dressed for the road, I think!'

'Eh . . . ? You say so.' James Graham frowned. 'Then I must see him.' He sighed.

Aboyne came in, booted and spurred. 'I have come to take my leave, my lord Marquis,' he blurted out, even as he crossed the threshold. 'I ride north forthwith.'

Montrose eyed him levelly. 'I could say, James, that you come to *seek* leave of absence,' he observed. 'But never heed. I am sorry that you feel that you must go. Is there anything that I may do to change your mind ?'

'No. Nothing.'

'That is unfortunate. But – I hope that you will return. And soon.'

'I think not.'

'James – it is not all this foolish matter of Crawford ? I spoke with him last night. I do not think that he will so offend again. Indeed, I may be able to send him on an errand to His Grace, in England – for I love him little more than do you.'

'It is not only Crawford. There will be others like him. And you have made Ogilvy a Colonel of Horse likewise, equal with me. He has a mere eighty troopers – or his father does . . .'

'Ogilvy, James, is a good officer, as you well know. You were companions-in-arms for long, my two good lieutenants, when in England. Do you grudge him this, after a year in a prison cell ? I need experienced officers still, to lead the new squadrons I intend

145

to raise here in the Lowlands. The King's cause is not won yet, I'd remind you.'

'Who is there to fight you now?' the younger man demanded. 'You have all these, these time-servers coming to laud you, to seek positions, commands. No doubt some of *them* you will make colonels, major-generals! Who have done nothing, hazarded nothing . . .'

'You wish to be a major-general, James?'

'I . . . I care not. I am Gordon. And you owe much to Gordon.'

'I do. I have always declared it. You are an excellent commander of light horse, James – one of the best. But are you a general officer? Capable of commanding a general army in the field? In strategy and tactics? You may well be – even though you are very young for it. We do not know. You have never tried, had occasion to do so . . .'

'I am as capable of it as the Earl of Crawford, God knows!'

'No doubt. But *I* did not make Crawford general. I never would have done so. That was the King's doing. I do not see a general's position as a kind of honour. When the lives of thousands, the decision of battles, are in his hands. Knighthood – now that is something different . . .'

'Gordon needs no knighthoods! No, my lord – we ride forthwith. My father – he commands it. I have given the orders to my men. They await me.'

'Your men? So – it is not only yourself, James? You remove your Gordon horse from my army? My main cavalry!'

'Yes. We are to return to Strathbogie.'

'You realise what this means? For the royal cause? Five hundred trained and experienced horse. Leaving me with a mere 100 or so others . . .'

'The fighting is by with. And you will get more. Now that you have the Lowlands. This Douglas, and the rest. Time that they played *their* part. My father demands that we return. I have disobeyed him for long enough. And my brother Lewis is taking my place, at Strathbogie. Making himself master, in my father's absence. *I* am heir to Gordon now, and must take my place. I am sorry . . .'

'I will not beg of you, James. But . . . this is a sore blow. My information is that David Leslie is at Carlisle. Not so very far away. He is the best soldier the enemy have. Better by far than old Sandy, Lord Leven, his kinsman. And he has an army of 10,000, half of them cavalry. *Half* – 5,000 horse! He plans to get between the King and myself. And His Grace delays. All is seeming triumph here – but *is* not! I am weak, man – weak. And your going will make me direly weaker.'

'If it comes to fighting again, I can return, my lord. Time enough for that when Leslie crosses the border.'

Montrose bowed to the inevitable. He held out his hand. 'So be it. God go with you, then, James. I am sorry that we part thus. After so long a companionship. So many dangers shared. I thank you, from my heart, for all that you have done, you and yours. The King, all Scotland, myself – we are all greatly in your debt. More than words can ever say. I hope that you find affairs none so ill at Strathbogie.'

The other gripped his hand, muttered something incoherent, and hurried from the room.

Grave-faced, James Graham continued with his dressing.

Later, on his way to the Council, Montrose saw a tall, dark, sardonic-looking figure idling near the Great Hall doorway. 'Nat!' he exclaimed. 'You, still here ? You have not gone, with the others ?'

'I have not, my lord,' Colonel Nathaniel Gordon said. 'My place is at *your* side. Huntly may whistle for me, as he will!'

The other stepped over to grip the Gordon's arm, silently, before he moved on into the crowded hall.

If some of his officers found their General somewhat constrained, aloof, stern, at the great Council of State that followed, they could account for it by the exceptional nature of the occasion.

In a brief introductory he outlined the programme. The forthcoming parliament would establish and settle much. But meantime the country was in a lawless and leaderless state. Temporary measures had to be taken, and quickly. The previous rulers had largely abdicated their responsibilities, and fled the country. Half the sheriffdoms of the land were vacant. The Court of Session itself had not sat for months. Taxes and duties went ungathered – and many of them were iniquitous and harsh anyway. Broken soldiery terrorised the land. The plague raged unchecked in cities, and refugees roamed the countryside destitute. Certain nobles had not yet disbanded their private forces, and were using them to ravage their neighbours' property. Moreover certain castles and fortresses still held out against the King's authority, Edinburgh the most prominent. He did not stress that his own son was held therein, but all knew it. Famine would take hold if this present harvest was not ingathered quickly. So much to be done . . .

Nothing was said about raising men for the army. Instinctively Montrose felt that this was a matter for private negotiation – and Napier agreed. When James Alexander sought to raise the subject, on his own initiative, he was courteously but firmly headed off on another tack. It was far too delicate and vital a matter to be tossed around in public discussion.

The afternoon session was devoted to the drawing up of a manifesto or declaration of policy and faith, declaring continued support for the terms of the original National Covenant – though by no means the Solemn League and Covenant – freedom of religious observance and from the domination and tyranny of either prelates or Kirk, the maintenance of government by King and Parliament. They were most of the way through this, without overmuch acrimony – for men were growing sleepy in the sunshine – when Pate Graham came whispering at his chief's ear.

'A messenger. Urgent. From the South.' And when the other looked enquiringly at him. 'Ill news, I fear.'

'Bring him to me. But . . . bid him be discreet. And speak low!'

A dusty, weary-looking man in jack and leather was led in, distinctly abashed by the stare of all the great company. 'My lord Marquis – a message from my Lord Digby,' the man muttered, in a North Country English voice. 'He, and Sir Marmaduke Langdale . . . ambushed! By a force of Ironsides. Psalm-singing devils of the man Cromwell. Routed. With their whole force. Crossing Yorkshire. A great slaughter. On their way to you, in Scotland. All gone, destroyed . . .'

'A-a-ah!' James Graham sought to school his features before that closely watching assembly, but his fingers drummed a tattoo on the table.

'My lord and Sir Marmaduke made good their escape. They head across Lancashire. For Carlisle. They hope to raise another force, see you, in Cumberland. To bring to your side. I was to tell you this, my lord. But . . .' The messenger left the rest unsaid.

'Thank you.' Chokingly Montrose got it out. 'I . . . ah, understand. It is the fortunes of war. And you, friend ? You will be tired. Hungry. Colonel Graham will see to your refreshment. And reward.' He paused. 'The King ? What of the King ? Have you news of His Grace ?'

'The King is still on the Welsh marches, my lord.'

'Aye.' That was a sigh. 'My thanks.' Turning back to the

battery of eyes, Montrose drew a long breath. 'Forgive me, gentlemen. A despatch from my Lord Digby, one of His Grace's generals. Who nears the borders. He raises cavalry in Cumberland. As I did once. Intends to bring them north to Scotland in due course. It is my hope, however, that we shall not require them. But we are grateful for His Grace's thought for us. Now – let us proceed. This matter of ensuring the Kirk's support . . .'

James Graham when he decently could, brought the proceedings to a close.

That evening there was much noise and stir in the Irish and Islesmen's camp, to the west of the haugh. Montrose, seeking to convince the Marquis of Douglas to muster a cavalry force and start its training as soon as possible – while not alarming him with the situation as regards the King and Digby – ignored the to-do, for Colkitto's people were often noisy. But when a cannon-shot crashed out from quite close at hand, to be followed by another, shaking the castle walls, he excused himself from the high-born company and went with Pate and young Napier to investigate.

They found the Gaelic host in high spirits, with much drink taken, dancing, singing, squabbling, the cannon-fire seemingly just *joie-de-vivre*, using up the unaccustomed plenty of gunpowder.

'A saint's day, it must be,' Montrose observed. 'Our Irish friends have saints innumerable. They celebrate.'

'Late in the day for it,' Pate demurred. 'But they celebrate *something*.' He called to a young major of gallow-glasses. 'O'Gormon – wherefore the jollity?'

'*Dia* – do you not know? We march . . .' He hiccupped. 'We march tomorrow, by the Mass! Against the Campbells. At last! Mother o' God – we'll teach them who's m-master in Scotland now . . .!'

Pate and Napier glanced at their chief, and then at each other, quickly.

'Where is Colkitto?' Montrose asked, expressionlessly.

They found the Major-General sitting on an upturned powder-barrel, drinking from a tankard.

'Ha – Seumas! My lord Seumas himself!' the big man cried. 'A drink? A drink for the Captain-General! Have you left all your fine gentlemen, to visit us poor bare-shanked barbarians, heh? Come – sit you. A barrel for Seumas Graham. And a drink, whatever . . .'

'Thank you, no, Sir Alastair,' Montrose declared formally. 'I am not drinking, meantime. I am seeking information. I hear word that there is an expedition against the Campbells, planned. To Argyll?'

'And no lie. We march at tomorrow's dawn. With Your Honour's permission, of course! I was just after coming to inform you.'

James Graham smoothed his tiny beard. 'You know that I need your men *here*. That I can by no means spare them. I have told you. Moreover you know that I am against punitory raiding, Campbells or other.'

'Tut, man – you will not need us for a week or so. My lads grow rusty here, idle in these fat Lowlands. And we have scores to pay in Argyll – by God we have!'

'Nevertheless, Alastair – I ask you not to go.'

'But, save us – what's the difference? You are not fighting, nor like to be. We could be back in four days, whatever – three. We serve you nothing here. Send me word when Leslie crosses the Border, and I will be back with you before he is.'

'That is scarce the point. The point is that it will leave me with a bare 1,000 men. Weak, for all to see. Our enemies will not fail to note. And our nervous friends, likewise. Many will hold back. That you may be sure. Roxburgh, Home, Dalziel and the others. Possibly even Douglas. They will contribute nothing to weakness. Only to obvious strength.'

'You are strong enough, never fear, man. Whether the Marquis of Montrose has 1,000 men more or less matters nothing. Your name will serve you sufficiently well. And the Campbells may well be mustering against you. As they have done before, see you. It is not in that devil Argyll not to do so . . .'

'I will not seek to command you, Alastair. But I *ask* you. Do not go.'

'I must, man. I have given them my word. My gallow-glasses. My MacDonalds. I cannot go back on it now, mercy to God! We march at dawn. But – we will be back, never fear.'

James Graham turned away, to walk slowly back whence he had come.

'You fool, Colkitto!' Black Pate said quietly. 'You great, stiff-necked, Hielant fool! You are failing the finest man in this land, God forgive you!'

Next morning early, as they watched the Gaelic host march off, pipes playing, gallant, devil-may-care, Pate repeated his allegation.

'There goes a fool, a great Hielant stot!' he declared. 'Look at him – the knighted ox!'

'There goes the finest infantry leader in all Christendom,' Montrose corrected, a catch in his voice. 'Aye, and the finest fighting-men, too. All gone. Shall we ever see them back? Or their like, again?'

'Not *all* gone, my lord,' a quiet voice said, from behind.

They turned, to find Colonel Magnus O'Cahan standing there.

'Magnus! You ... you are not going?'

'I am not, my lord James. There are some of us sane. And loyal. Though, God knows, Alastair is that, whatever else. Only headstrong. I, and 500 from Ulster, who think as I do, remain. At your service.'

Montrose looked away quickly. 'Thank you, my friend,' he got out. 'My very good friend ...'

CHAPTER ELEVEN

With the Marquis of Douglas agreeing to raise a cavalry force in his wide Dumfriesshire properties – and the Lord Ogilvy sent with him to guide and advise, and to ensure that he kept his less than enthusiasitcally given word – Montrose marched eastwards from Bothwell on the 4th of September, with about 1,200 men, his assemblage of the illustrious and the high-born dispersing, to meet again at the parliament on the 20th of October. He left Bothwell more to prevent any further defection of his forces than for any particular need to move, with the parliament to be held in Glasgow; but he felt instinctively that he would be more able to hold his remaining numbers together on the march, in at least a posture of campaigning, then idling in camp. Moreover, the only three nobles who had promised any substantial numbers of the now so necessary reinforcements were the Earls of Home, Roxburgh and Traquair. And these all had their lands in the East and Middle Marches of the border. James Graham was of the opinion that he would never see these reinforcements unless he actually went there for them. The situation being as it was, therefore, he was as well making a military progress east and south, while Ogilvy and Douglas went south and west. They would rendezvous centrally as soon as possible, and march in strength towards Glasgow, in plenty of time for the parliament – unless an emergency dictated earlier action.

So then 1,200 marched across country, out of Lanarkshire, by West Lothian, skirting the southern flanks of the Pentland Hills, to pick up some extra horsemen from the Dalziel lands around Carnwath and the Fleming lands of Biggar. In two days unhurried marching they were at Cranstoun eight miles south-east of Edinburgh, carefully avoiding that still plague-stricken city, however much Montrose tended to cast his glance towards its distant fortress towering high on its rock, wherein young Jamie was held. A siege of that all but impregnable citadel was utterly out of the question, in the circumstances; it would fall like a ripe plum in due course. Nevertheless, now that he could command what artillery he wanted, the temptation was there.

On Saturday the 6th September, Montrose ordered a great open-air service of prayer and praise for the morrow, at this Cranstoun on the ridge above Dalkeith. He always made a point of marking the Lord's Day especially, if at all practicable; but since most of his army had been Catholic, in the past, he had not gone in for any mammoth church parades. Now, with the Catholic element so direly reduced, and the advisability of displaying to the Presbyterian Lowlands that he was no Papist monster, as was so often alleged, he took the opportunity. The local parish minister was invited to take the service – but for prudence's sake, George Wishart was to preach.

But it was not to be. The Lord Erskine, heir to the Earl of Mar, rode into camp in the early evening, in a great state of excitement. He had left Bothwell earlier, with Home and Roxburgh, for the Merse. They had barely arrived at Home Castle, when the dread news reached them. General David Leslie was on the East March, indeed was crossing Tweed at Berwick that very day. And with 5,000 seasoned cavalry, the pick of Scotland's regular army in England, however many foot he might have.

To say that Montrose was appalled was not strictly accurate. He had all along been all too well aware of this possibility; indeed, despite all the seeming triumph, the thing had haunted him for many a night. Hence his distress over the defection of Aboyne and Colkitto. But he had understood Leslie to be tied up in the West, at Carlisle, where he might have been expected to be preoccupied with Digby's and Langdale's efforts to raise an army amongst the Cumberland loyalists, and where Callander was said to have moved south to join him with his carefully keeping-out-of-the-way force. This switch to the east, therefore, and actual crossing into Scotland at this stage, was a surprise. As was the figure of 5,000 cavalry – a devastating prospect, when Montrose had a bare 100 Ogilvys and perhaps fifty others. The Tweed at Berwick was not forty miles away.

But this was by no means all Erskine's news. At Berwick-on-Tweed Leslie had been joined by a group of the Covenant leaders who had been hiding in Northern England since Kilsyth – including Argyll himself, the Earl of Lanark and the Lord Lindsay. This no doubt was what had brought Leslie across country so unexpectedly – orders from Argyll.

Given this daunting information. Montrose did not waste valuable time on fruitless lamentation or discussion. He ordered immediate striking of camp and readiness to move. He sent Black Pate off southwards, at his old task in charge of scouts. And he despatched urgent couriers to ride day and night northwards to Strathbogie and north-westwards to Colkitto in Argyll; also south-west to Douglas and Ogilvy, and southwards to Traquair in the Ettrick Forest. Then he gave orders to march.

Erskine's information was that Leslie was making northwards along the coast road, by Coldingham and the Lammermuir passes of Pease and Cockburnspath, no doubt hoping to reach the waist of Scotland between Forth and Clyde, and so cut off the royalists from their northern and Highland bases. He could do it, too, in the present circumstances, with all that cavalry. Montrose decided to deny him the opportunity. He would march southwards, as Leslie marched north, but well to the west, inland. Once more he would strive to make the land fight for him. He must remain in the hills, where cavalry were least effective, where ambush offered opportunity, where he and his would be at home. They would go south by Gala Water, for the Ettrick Forest, refuge of so many a desperate band from Wallace and Bruce onwards.

By Soutra and Fala Muir they crossed the hills to the long, hidden valley of the Gala Water, that September night, fairly certain that Leslie's scouts would not have observed them, nor would even look for them here.

Next day, half-way to the Tweed and the Forest, Montrose sent fast messengers ahead, into the Merse, south-eastwards, to the Earls of Home and Roxburgh, with instructions to meet him, in the King's name, with all available strength, at Kelso, at the junction of Tweed and Teviot, by midday following.

Black Pate, now behind them with his scouts, sent word that Leslie and his army, with Argyll and the others, were at Dunbar and still proceeding northwards. They had eluded them, this time, gained a breathing-space, at least.

But at Kelso, down Tweed, the next day there was no sign of the Lords Home or Roxburgh, with their levies. Montrose waited an entire dangerous day for them – and dared risk nothing longer. Kelso was too far from the hills, on the edge of the wide open Merse, cavalry country. He turned back for the Forest of Ettrick and the lonely heights.

They went by Teviot. Jedburgh they passed by, for if Roxburgh – who was Kerr of Cessford – had failed them, his kinsman, the earl of Lothian, Kerr of Ferniehirst here, was actually a general of horse in Leslie's army. But at Jedburgh, at least they learned interesting tidings. Home and Roxburgh were now with Leslie, allegedly as prisoners – but since neither of their strong castles of Home and Cessford had been besieged, or even assailed, it seemed obvious that they had elected to give themselves up rather than risk any further association with Montrose. Apparently the tide has turned once more, in Scotland.

There was still Douglas and Ogilvy, and the rendezvous in the Forest. And on the way to it, they might see what John Stewart, Earl of Traquair, could do to help, former Lord High Commissioner from the King, and Treasurer of Scotland. After all, he had sent his son to Bothwell with assurances of loyal support, in men and money; and Linton, a cheerful youngster, was still with them.

They reached the handsome white and venerable house of Traquair, on the Tweed near Innerleithen, on the evening of the 11th. It was a peaceful spot, a rich oasis in the great Forest of Ettrick. Too peaceful by far, for though the Earl was at home, and had received Montrose's message days before, there was no sign of any mustering of men.

If Traquair did not actually slam his door in the face of the King's Captain-General, he did everything but. Cold to the point of rudeness, he declared that he had no men to spare – and indeed ordered his son to withdraw from the royalist force forthwith. He said that he had no reason to believe that the King was coming north, and he had heard that Digby had been utterly defeated on the way. In consequence it was folly to oppose the Committee of the Estates at this juncture, and he for one would have none of it. He urged the Marquis of Montrose to retire with all speed possible to his Highland fastnesses, and the redisperse his force.

James Graham recognised that he ought to have learned his lesson by now: never to put any trust in the Scots nobility – or nine-tenths of it. He was sorry to lose young Lord Linton. He had to restrain some of his men from violently showing Traquair what they thought of him.

They moved down Tweed again, to camp near Elibank. They did not see the messenger whom Traquair despatched northwards in haste.

That evening, at least some of James Graham's trust in his fellow-aristocrats was restored. For into the Elibank camp came marching the Marquis of Douglas and the Lord Ogilvy, with some 400 mounted Douglas levies from Dumfriesshire, a sight

to quicken the hearts of all present – even though these were
wholly untrained, raw dalesmen from Annandale and Nithsdale.
They were cavalry, of a sort, and welcome indeed. And as welcome, indeed, was the fact that some men kept their word. And
this was not all. More Douglas and Johnston levies would be
coming, when they had been horsed and equipped in two or three
days. They were to make for the original rendezvous in the heart
of the Forest, at St. Mary's Loch, up Yarrow, on the only
practical road over the hills from Moffat and the head of far-
away Annandale – how Douglas and Ogilvy had just come.
Montrose decided to continue on to this area now, to wait for
them. There was levelish ground, around the loch, and there
they could lie safe while he licked his new cavalry into shape.

Next day, then, they made their way in that direction, following Tweed down to its junction with Ettrick, at Sunderland,
just south of Galashiels and then turning up Ettrick for some
three miles, to where Yarrow joined it below the ancient burgh
of Selkirk. Here, on the riverside meadows of Philiphaugh, they
camped again. One day's more marching up Yarrow would
bring them to the St. Mary's Loch rendezvous. There was no
hurry, however.

As ever, Montrose chose his night's position with care. It was
a fairly strong tactical site, flanked by the river on east and south,
with the Yarrow's confluence protecting their rear and steep
hillsides to the west. Assault could come only from the Tweed
area to the north-east, or down Ettrick from the south-south-
west – which latter seemed unlikely, from the Forest fastnesses.
Montrose felt reasonably secure here – but he did send Charteris
of Amisfield, who had come with Douglas and who claimed to
know the district well and was eager to act the soldier, with a
picket to watch the junction of Ettrick and Tweed and give
warning should there be any approach from the north.

They could sleep secure – or most of them. Montrose himself
had a lengthy despatch and memorandum to send to the King,
which would take him most of the night. With Douglas, Airlie
and others he forded the Ettrick – which was running fairly low
after all the good weather – and rode uphill to the little burgh of
Selkirk. He got no welcome from the townsfolk.

It was very late before James Graham extinguished the lamp
in his lodging in the West Port, his companions asleep hours
before. He had ended his letter to Charles urgently requesting a
personal appearance in Scotland, alone if he need be, at the

earliest possible moment, campaigning season or none.

He was at breakfast not very many hours later, when one of Pate Graham's scout officers, Blackadder by name, burst in on the company unceremoniously, with the dire news.

'We are attacked, my lord!' he exclaimed. 'On two fronts. Both sides of the river. Cavalry attack. In this damned mist . . . !'

Montrose's chair fell with a crash as he jumped to his feet, reaching for his sword. 'Attacks, man? Who attacks? What cavalry? How many?'

'Many. Colonel Graham says regular cavalry. Dragoons . . .'

'Dear God – Leslie!' James Graham was already flinging through the doorway. 'Why was he not seen? Reported? Ere this . . . ?' But he did not wait for an answer.

Neither did he wait for his horse to be saddled, but galloped off bare-back down the hill to the Ettrick haughlands. A white mist rolled thickly over all the lower ground, as so often of a night and early morning blankets the border valleys. He could see neither his own forces nor the enemy under the billowing shroud – but he could hear musketry, shooting.

In the seething jumble of his thoughts the musketry registered – and set him thinking clearly, himself again. That mist was far too thick for musket-fire. Therefore it could only be shooting blind. But it was being kept up. Therefore it was a device. To keep a flank occupied. The only point in that would be from across the river – *this* side. Pinning down forces there. To prevent a crossing. Presumably while the main action developed on the other side. Reasonable tactics in a surprise attack, in mist. The chances were, then, that there would be no assault across the river while the mist remained. Time – time he desperately needed.

Keeping well to the left, upstream, of the shooting, he splashed across Ettrick, his companions not far behind. He cursed its autumnal shallowness now. If it had been running high, as so often, no attack across it would have been possible – and he could not have crossed to Selkirk last night. No point in recriminations and regrets now against himself or others. Somebody had blundered. He had relied too much on others – and so failed in his duty. Now he needed time . . .

He needed more than time, however. When he reached the camp, a scene of dire confusion, it was to find Nathaniel Gordon temporarily in command, the Ogilvy cavalry waiting uncertainly for orders. Colonel O'Cahan was forward somewhere, Gordon reported, beating off an attack from the north. And Colonel

Graham was out in the mist, with his scouts, seeking information. This hellish mist . . . !

'We must make it fight for us, now!' Montrose snapped. 'O'Cahan has all his Ulstermen forward? Then, the rest of the foot? Where?'

'Lining the river-side. Under Lords Erskine and Fleming. To prevent a crossing in flank, my lord.'

'There will be no crossing while the mist lasts. That is a feint, meantime. The cavalry? The Ogilvys are here. What of the Douglas horse? And the rest?'

Gordon coughed. The Marquis of Douglas and the Earl of Crawford had just come up, with Airlie and the others. 'I fear they have . . . dispersed, my lord,' he said. 'At the first charge of Leslie's dragoons. I could not hold them. God knows where they are! This accursed mist . . .'

'Aye. My Lords Crawford and Douglas – search for and find, if you may, these missing squadrons. They will be confused, at a loss. Their first action – and leaderless. Gather them, and hold them ready in reserve. Nat – where is Lord Ogilvy?'

'He has gone seeking to rally the Douglas horse.'

'Yes. My Lord Crawford – when you find him, send my Lord Ogilvy back to me. At once. Nat – marshal the remaining cavalry into two squadrons. The hundred Ogilvys, and a mixed lot of fifty. Now – my trumpeters . . .'

Pate Graham came running up, panting. 'Thank God you are here, James!' For almost the first time, he forgot to address his friend and chief honorifically in public. 'Here's a brawl! There's been treachery – our position betrayed. Traquair, for a wager! No sign of Charteris or his picket. Leslie's entire cavalry army is here, I reckon. I've been forward with O'Cahan. There's a hero! He is holding four regiments of horse, at least, with his 500 Ulster foot. At a burn-channel. But with heavy losses. My scouts say there are two regiments of dragoons across the river – 1,500 at least . . .'

'Any encircling move to the left? On the high ground?'

'Not that I know of. That way the Douglas horse fled. At the first charge.'

'They are untrained, raw. Their first engagement.' He turned. 'Where is Airlie?'

'Here, James,' the old Earl said, quietly, from behind.

May I take your Ogilvys, my friend? To O'Cahan's aid? Myself?'

'To be sure. I come with you.'

'Nat – command here at the centre, meantime. I cannot order a battle, blind. I go forward with the Ogilvy squadron. To discover the position, and aid O'Cahan. Send the Lord Ogilvy after me. Hold all others in reserve until you receive my orders, foot and horse. The camp here a strong-point.' He mounted a saddled horse. 'All trumpeters sound the Advance!' he called. He raised drawn sword to the Ogilvy ranks. 'Come!'

Mist or none there was no doubt as to which direction to take, at least. Down-river, due northwards, the noise of battle was evident enough, though muffled. The trumpets ringing out eerily, they advanced at as fast a trot as was practicable, in the obscurity. Soon their mounts were shying and tripping over dead bodies, some dead and dying horses also. These seemed to be mainly Douglases. A charge had got thus far – although O'Cahan was still forward of it.

They came upon the Irish line suddenly, almost rode it down indeed, where O'Cahan was skilfully using a tree-lined burn-channel as extended trench. Men and horses, moaning, screaming many of them, lay thick here, in the swirling eddies, a scene out of hell. They found O'Cahan himself, in the centre, his shirt-sleeve ripped off to act as bandage and to keep the blood from a sabre cut out of his eyes. He was calm and cool as ever, however.

'Ha, my lord – here's warm work! We were taken by surprise, this once.'

'Aye, Magnus – I blame myself. But – that can wait. You have a good line here, old friend. You I could trust, at least! Pate says you have lost heavily? In saving us all.'

The other shrugged. 'We have casualties, yes. Half of our 500 perhaps. But – I have the other half, yet.!'

'Dear God – so many lost! Already? My brave Irish! And your head, man?'

'A nothing. Think you this mist is lifting, my lord? Or thinning?'

'A little, yes. I know not whether to be glad or sorry. To see – and to be seen! Our scant numbers.' He nodded forward. 'They come in waves? They can scarce charge in this . . . ?'

'They come at a trot. A regiment at a time. We have had Middleton's first. Dalhousie's. Eglinton's. Leven's own. No foot. Pate Graham says that Kirkcudbright's and Fraser's are across the river . . .'

'The entire Covenant cavalry army! God knows how they got

here. David Leslie is something new in their generals! Not many would have dared an attack in this. With cavalry. This burn-channel – it makes a fair barrier. How far does it extend? Upwards?'

'As far as I have men to hold it! Farther. For we are thin on the ground, thin.'

'I have the Ogilvys, here. One hundred. Are they better dismounted, and aiding you? Or horsed? To counter the next attack?'

'So long as the mist remains thick, dismounted I'd say.'

'I agree. I will keep them close, not scattered. In case . . .'

Montrose gave orders for his troopers to dismount, but to remain centrally grouped around himself and O'Cahan. The Irish to spread out farther. Horses to be taken a little way back.

Even as this manoeuvre was being carried out, they were all but taken by surprise. For Leslie too had recognised that foot were the more effective in these circumstances, and had sent forward a dismounted attack – and kept it as quiet as might be. Only the hollow clumping of heavy thigh-boots and the occasional jingle of spurs, with the muffled curse of a stumbling cavalryman out of his element, gave them a little warning. Then the mass of grey figures loomed out of the billowing vapours, to fling themselves on the defended line of the burn.

Montrose was almost glad to lose himself in hard hand-to-hand fighting. But he well knew that this was not his role, however tempting as an alternative to hard and responsible thinking. Deliberately he disentangled himself, and drew back. As well that he did. For, on a soft area of wet ground where the burn had been apt to overflow, he distinctly felt the earth trembling slightly beneath his feet. That could only be horses' hooves. He could not tell from which side it came; but it was highly unlikely that the Douglas yeomen could have been rounded up and brought back into battle so quickly. The chances were that Leslie was putting in a mounted attack on the heels of the dismounted one – a sound tactic.

James Graham yelled for his Ogilvys to break off, to remount. Airlie and his son Sir David took up the cry. Somehow they got back to their horses, and up, however raggedly. Montrose by no means waited for the last of them. Leading his people forward in no sort of formation, he drove his mount through the press of struggling men in the burn-channel, pushing through the scrub trees and stumbling through the shallow water, slashing at dismounted dragoons. Across, waiting agitatedly for the others, hearing the oncoming cavalry now, he found himself joined by the Lord Ogilvy.

'Thank Heaven you are here, James!' he gasped. 'Help me get them into an arrowhead. A wedge-formation. Quickly – we have only moments.'

Desperately they herded their troopers into some sort of tight wedge-shaped grouping, with Airlie, his two sons, and Montrose himself, at the tip. Then, not waiting for any refinement, he shouted for his trumpeter whose duty it was always to be at his master's heels, to sound the stirring cavalry Charge. Breathless but recognisable the well-known and dread strains blared out. Ignoring the fact that he could not see where he was going, James Graham dug in his spurs, yelling 'A Graham! A Graham!'

The shout was taken up at his back, interspersed with 'An Ogilvy! An Ogilvy!' and knee-to-knee they plunged onwards blindly, straight into a canter.

It was seconds only before they saw the trotting line of advancing dragoons – or at least that part of it immediately in front of them; how far it stretched on either hand, none could tell. It was a daunting sight, at a mere thirty yards or so – but safe to say not nearly so daunting as the charging compact mass that bore down upon the enemy, yelling. The dragoons' line was only four deep, and inevitably only three or four files were at the actual point of impact. Small wonder then that they tended to rein back, aside, anywhere, to be out of the path of that hurtling, menacing band. The wedge slammed through almost without a blow struck, cutting the enemy line in seconds.

Montrose was thankful that it was the veteran Ogilvy horse which were involved, with Airlie and his sons in command. For such a breakthrough could be of little advantage, indeed could be a positive death-trap, if not skilfully exploited and followed up, if the enemy ranks closed again and massed, cutting off the attackers from their own base. Now, he shouted to the Lord Ogilvy to take the left flank, himself taking the right. The wedge split into two behind him, and without appreciable loss of momentum began to roll up the two lines of dragoons – which now had to draw up, turn about in the mist, and try to counter this assault of unknown dimension at their rear.

It was a chaotic business on both sides. But at least Montrose's people knew what they were seeking to do and held the initiative.

Probably they inflicted no large number of casualties; but they broke up that assault completely and sent the enemy fleeing blindly in all directions. Montrose had his trumpeter sound the Recall, and led his section trotting back to the burn-channel. The quite distinct upward trend of the ground from east to west at least allowed them to recognise which way to go. They came up against many of the dismounted first wave retiring, and were able to punish these severely. Ogilvy was back with O'Cahan before them.

'Merry work, my lord,' the Irishman acclaimed.' That will set Leslie thinking.'

'Aye – he will learn that mist can be a two-sided blade. But . . . it lifts, I think ?'

'To be sure. Where will the advantage lie, then ?'

'Not with us, I think. They must then see how pitifully few we are. Our dire lack of cavalry. Save that it allowed them to creep up on us, the mist was to *our* advantage.'

'Yes. And in this position we cannot retire, I think ? Can we ?'

'I would give much to know. I would break off and retire, yes – if I might. To fight on better terms another day. But I much fear we may be trapped, Magnus. David Leslie is an able general – and bold. Bolder than any we have had to face, as yet – or he would not be here this morning, attacking in the mist. He knows our position. He has sent regiments along the *east* side of Ettrick. They wait there now. Think you he will have neglected to stop the gap behind us ? Up Yarrow ? *I* would not, in his place – with all the regiments of horse he has. And if Yarrow is blocked, we are held. I have sent Blackadder to discover it. But I am not hopeful.'

'We must cut our way through then,' Ogilvy said.

'*We* might. But the foot could not.'

'They could disperse. Up into the hills.'

'It may come to that. But not yet . . .'

They watched the mist lighten, the morning brighten, with ever larger clear patches. No new attack developed. Leslie had learned his lesson and was waiting for clear vision.

A rider from the Marquis of Douglas came to announce that he and Crawford had collected over 100 of the Douglas horse, and more were coming in. His men had not been craven, merely leaderless and confused. Montrose sent the messenger back with orders to use all men to guard the river-bank meantime.

Gradually visibility improved, with an ominous quiet over

the battlefield. Even the rattle of musketry from across Ettrick died away. The quiet was only relative, of course, since it included the cries and moans of wounded men and the whinnying and screaming of hamstrung and broken-legged horses.

Captain Blackadder cantered up to report that the narrows of the vale of Yarrow behind them were blocked by cavalry. They must have found their way across the hills during the early morning. That way there was no escape.

Montrose nodded grimly.

'What happened to Charteris of Amisfield – tell me that!' the Lord Ogilvy demanded. 'He was sent forward to guard the northern approach. All this descends upon us, and he sends us no word.'

'He may have been overwhelmed. Cut off. I blame myself for sending a man insufficiently experienced. But – I had no reason to believe that Leslie was within fifty miles of us!' Montrose spread his hands. 'That does not absolve me from blame. I have failed in this. Taken too much for granted.'

'Do not assail yourself, James,' old Airlie exclaimed. 'There has been treachery, that is certain. I say Traquair is at the back of it. *He* knew where we were heading for, our state, our numbers – the King's Lord Treasurer! I swear he sent word hot-foot to Leslie. A rider sent forthwith and fast could have reached Leslie, in Lothian, by dawn yesterday. And his cavalry, riding south all yesterday and part of last night, could have reached Tweed in time for this.'

'That is true . . .'

All the time he had been peering ahead of him, northwards. Now, at last, they were beginning to see the enemy. Actually they saw those across the Ettrick first, less than the two regiments reported, probably only one, mounted, waiting. They were unlikely to wait much longer.

The main mass of Leslie's force however was massed half a mile to the north, on the haughland west of the river, a cavalry host under a forest of banners, a gallant and colourful sight such as James Graham, for one, had always most dreaded to see. Amidst all his campaigning he had dreamed of this, and awakened sweating in the night – to see a huge and overwhelming host of well-trained and veteran horse, hopelessly outnumbering his own, and with no avenue of escape open to him. Even counting the Douglas contingent as effective, Leslie outnumbered him in cavalry twenty to one. The nightmare had come true. Lacking his experienced Gordons, to say nothing of Colkitto's warriors, he was as a man naked in the face of his foes.

He dared not show the least hint of his despair, of course. Nor did he let himself dwell on the hopelessness of the situation. He was faced with a grievous choice – to fight the best battle possible, and go down bravely and with honour; or to seek to save as much as he could from the wreckage, at all costs, for the King's cause.

He had no doubts in his mind as to his own preference. He had fought a good enough fight hitherto, and he would choose to end it in the same fashion. His own life was not so full of joy and felicity that he must cling to it, award it over-high a value – so long as his honour survived. But nor was he in any doubt but that this was a selfish attitude, well enough for a private soldier. He was not that. He was a general, and must take a general's view. He was the King's representative, and responsible meantime for the entire future of the royal cause in Scotland. There could be no question as to his over-riding duty, however repugnant to himself. He was not the first commander faced with the same grim choice.

Fortunately he did not have to spell it out to his companions. Magnus O'Cahan did it for him.

'My lord Marquis – neither tactics nor strategy will serve to win this day for us – even yours. The thing is plain to see. But you can still save much that is of value to the King's Grace. The foot can by no means escape this trap – but much of the horse can. You must cut your way out, my lord. As you cut through those, just now. It is the only way, now. All Leslie's cavalry are here. When they attack, on three fronts, you are lost.'

'And leave you, and your Ulstermen? And the rest of my brave infantry? To your fate, Magnus?'

'We are in God's hands,' the other said simply. 'And we have no choice. Nor have you. You must save what you can, my lord.'

There was a murmur of agreement from the other officers clustered around.

Montrose moistened dry lips. 'It may come to that,' he acceded, low-voiced. 'But not yet. Leslie has us cornered, yes – but he has yet to spring the trap. He may yet make a wrong move.'

Bugles blowing to the northwards were the signal for the enemy assault. The attack across the river, being nearest at hand, developed first; but the entire main body began to move forward at the trot. Perhaps a thrust would come from the rear likewise; but the mist had not yet lifted from the narrow mouth of the Yarrow valley, and the commander there might hold back, preferring to act only as stop-gap.

Looking to the right, then front, then right again, Montrose made his decision. 'Try to hold your position, Magnus, for a little,' he jerked, pointing forward. 'Enormous odds. But I will be back, I promise you.' Turning to the waiting Ogilvys, he pointed right-handed, eastwards. 'To the river!' he shouted.

The Covenant regiment there was in process of fording Ettrick, on a fairly wide front, a difficult proceeding when opposed. But with perhaps 1,000 of them, against an opposition of no more than 300, they could hardly fail to succeed.

Montrose neither went to reinforce the defenders nor led directly against the enemy. Instead he spurred down to the river, a fair way below the fording regiment, and plunged straight across, the Ogilvys after him, splashing water high.

Unopposed, and less careful of their horses' footing than the heavier dragoons, they made the crossing a deal more quickly than their foes – who indeed were now faltering doubtfully, some even beginning to turn back. Clambering up the far bank, Montrose swung right-handed, upstream. And now his 100 were behind the enemy. They bore down upon those struggling to get back to dry land, swords slashing.

Caught in a direly exposed and unsteady position in the river, the dragoons' commander was in a quandary, entrenched opposition in front, cavalry behind. That there was only a comparatively small number of the latter was obvious – but so also was the Royal Standard of Scotland which Montrose's trumpeter bore aloft behind his master, worth another squadron in itself, so renowned was the Captain-General's reputation. The dragoons chose to press forward.

Or some of them did. Others decided that survival was more important than victory, and turned off up and down the river, seeking escape. Far from desiring to discourage this, Montrose drew his horse-pistol and pointed at the central splashing group.

'The main body!' he cried. 'Shoot at the main body. Leave these others.'

It was short range, and even pistols were fairly effective. The musketeers on the far bank redoubled their efforts. The dragoons fell like ninepins, amidst considerable panic and confusion. When their colonel splashed heavily into the Ettrick, chaos took over.

But already the sounds of clash were evident from the north, where Leslie's main force had come up against O'Cahan's thin line defending the vital burn-channel. Clearly this could not last long.

Reining his mount round, James Graham waved to his Ogilvys to break off and follow him. He spurred into a full gallop, still down the east bank.

Leslie could not fail to see it, nor the small numbers involved. Still, it might effect some slight easement of the pressure on O'Cahan.

They rode on down Ettrick, the Lion Rampant fluttering above them bravely, well past the level of the enemy ranks. Inevitably Leslie had to detach one of his regiments, to turn back to deal with them. Whenever Montrose saw this, he swung down to ford the river again, at once – before they in turn were faced with an opposed crossing. It was not the best stretch for fording; but nowhere was it so deep, at this season, that horses could not cross. They splashed and floundered over, just in time.

Now they were faced with an entire regiment advancing upon them. But once again this was in extended formation, not in column. Shouting to form wedge behind him again, Montrose wasted not a moment to give the enemy time to reform, but lashed his horse into the charge, there and then.

The spearhead had only just formed at his back, and less tightly than desirable, when Montrose crashed into a section of the enemy line, smiting, Airlie at one knee, Ogilvy at the other, the trumpeter with the banner immediately behind. The shock was fierce and he was all but unseated, but sheer pressure from the others kept him up. He was vaguely aware of a sword grazing his shoulder and clanging against his breastplate, also of a man screaming, open-mouthed but unheard, before him and falling away, with another behind him reining desperately aside. Then they were through, pushed on by the thundering mass at their backs.

This time he did not, dared not, signal for any swing right and left behind the broken line. The dragoons were far too many for anything of the sort. Instead he pressed right on, slantwise, across the haughland, making for the high ground.

Leslie could not ignore this, of course, at his immediate rear. Bugles blowing, he turned most of his remaining force to face the north again.

There was no question of any attack on this major formation

which had turned to face them. And the regiment behind would be re-forming, since it had been only broken, not shattered Montrose swung away, climbing.

The land steepened quickly, and no enemy barred the way. There was a real temptation just to ride on, and away, over the hills – as Magnus had advised. Save at least this Ogilvy horse intact. None could stop them now. It was never seriously considered as a programme, however. Part-way up the hill-side, they reined up.

'Well, my friends,' James Graham panted, 'you see it all. We are trapped. Or our foot is, and Douglas. Here is a battle we can by no means win. Your advice, gentlemen ?'

'What *is* there to say, James ?' Airlie demanded. 'We go down fighting. What else ?'

'Or *some* of us do,' his heir amended. 'My Lord James, and yourself, sir, should go. Now leave the field. While you may. Save at least the high command. Ride off, over this hill. And fight, to win, another day.'

'So say I,' his brother, Sir David, agreed.

'That is all your advice, my friends ? To fall, or to flee ?'

'What else can we do, James ? We are no more than a gadfly against this host. We can dart and sting and harass it. But we cannot beat it. Or even greatly harm it.' That was Airlie.

'A gad-fly may yet sting a man into anger which can breed folly! And folly as we know, can lose battles. I intend to sting further. Before I flee! Or fall.' Montrose raised his hand, to point southwards. 'The enemy force sent to stop the mouth of Yarrow have not moved. Have not shown themselves. That could mean that they are the weakest link in this chain that binds us. If we could break that . . . ?'

The mist had all gone now, and a golden, mellow September sun illumined the Borderland. It glinted on steel, there where the wooded hillsides guarded the entrance to Yarrow's valley; but it was impossible to say how many men might be there.

'It may be strongly held . . .'

'It may. But, if you were Leslie, would you send a strong force there ? Merely to block our retreat ? Not to attack us. With the position itself strong.'

'No-o-o.'

'Nor would I. It is a chance, a mere chance. But lacking any other chances I am inclined to take it.'

'How so ?'

167

'A charge down to the river again. They will try to stop us – but will not, I think. Across, at speed. Then upstream, as before we came down. But farther. Up to the junction of Ettrick and Yarrow rivers. Cross Ettrick again, higher. Into those woods between the two rivers. Then ford Yarrow *behind* that force. They would not see us. Not until we were upon them.'

'Phe-e-ew!'

'That would take time, James.'

'Less time than if we ran away! Or fell! It will not take so long – as I intend to ride! Two miles in all – less. Six minutes?'

'My lord – the regiment we broke up, at the first fording, has re-formed. Beyond the river. It is drawn up there . . .'

'I see it, David. But we have smashed through them once, and can do so again. They will be the more ready to break. And the fact that they have formed up there, across the river again, shows that they have little belly for fight. My lord Viscount Kirk-cudbright's dragoons!'

'We could go more quickly behind. Up this hill. And down upon Yarrow from above,' Lord Ogilvy suggested. 'And save a clash on the way.'

'To be sure. But part of our duty is to aid O'Cahan. This may help him a little. The other would not. Would seem as though we fled. Come, then – enough of talk. The wedge again – and forward!'

Straight into the charge they plunged downhill. Leslie's main force was stretched in a long line to their right, just out of musket-range of O'Cahan; and the regiment which they had already cut through was re-formed and now tightly grouped between them and the river. The sudden headlong advance probably took Leslie by surprise, for there was no visible reaction for a little – and time was of the essence, with only half a mile for the galloping horses to cover to the Ettrick. They were, in fact, half-way there before the long line of the main body began to move forward. The single regiment stayed where it was.

Montrose, concerned at the difficulty in keeping his tight formation at this speed on broken ground, abruptly perceived their dire danger. Leslie's massive line was not hastening forward – as it required to do if it was to try to intercept their rush to the river. It moved only at a trot. This could mean only one thing – musket-fire. Because he had never had dragoons to command, he had forgotten; these were heavy cavalry, equipped not with horse-pistols but with short-barrelled muskets, carbines. These had four times the range of pistols, as well as much greater accuracy. If they rode within range of these, massed close as his people were, it would be massacre, a target none could miss. Cursing his lack of previous perception, Montrose raised his sword high, to gesture with it half-left, to swing away northwards. And at the same time he yelled to disperse, break up the formation, open out.

It was not so easy. Speed, impetus, the downhill slope, even lack of understanding amongst the men, ensured that. The mass was still far too tight-knit, even though veering well to the left, when the first shots cracked out.

Now, at least, there was no need to explain, to persuade. Only fools would fail to see the danger. Lashing their beasts, horsemen sought to draw away from their fellows, as men and horses began to fall.

Now along the entire, long, enemy front there was firing. The range was in most cases extreme. But lead was flying thickly – and finding marks all too frequently. The Ogilvy horse was running the gauntlet.

The ordeal did not last for long, with the targets pulling away even more to the left, and the distance to the river closing fast. But it was grim indeed for a few moments, and losses heavy.

And now there was the second menace. For the isolated regiment, Middleton's Montrose now recognised, had seen its opportunity, the foe no longer a hard-hitting wedge but a scatter of individuals. It strung out to intercept carbines firing here also.

That any sizeable proportion of the royalist cavalry got through the barrier was due to impetus, the advantage of the fast-moving over the static. Montrose, suffering no more than a graze on the thigh from a musket-ball, slashed his way through, with his standard-bearer and old Airlie still close at his back. But neither of the Ogilvy sons were there now. Down to the river they plunged, and across. Barely three minutes had passed since the order to advance.

Across the water, they drew up and looked back, Airlie's features as set as those of James Graham. Men were splashing over, wide scattered – but it was clear that they would be fortunate to muster much more than half of their original strength.

They could not wait for stragglers, for Middleton's regiment, its confidence restored, was coming after them, and shooting as it came. Sir David Ogilvy turned up at the last moment, slightly wounded; but there was no sign of his elder brother.

'I am sorry,' Montrose jerked, to the father. 'He may be well enough. Dismounted only. Did you see him fall ?'

Airlie shook his grey head, and rode on.

Less than sixty of them now, they galloped upstream. They could see Kirkcudbright's regiment – or what remained of it – assembled in front of them, back a little from the river-side, out of range of Nat Gordon's muskets. Without surprise, or any other advantage now, any straightforward attack on them would be madness, with the odds still possibly five-to-one. They would never get through. Montrose's plan had to be scrapped. Anyway, it was doubtful whether he now had enough men to mount a surprise assault on the rear of the Yarrow stop-gap.

He pointed across the river, to their own camp area. Much of Middleton's regiment was in hot pursuit not far behind.

They were barely over Ettrick, water dripping off the horses, when Montrose was shouting.

'Nat – a runner to O'Cahan. To retire. If he can. To a shorter line. Yonder shallow ravine. We are too extended. My Lord Douglas – how many have you gathered ?'

'Near 200, Jamie. We have held these others off . . .'

'Aye. Pate – how many in that Yarrow gap. Have you a notion ?'

'A complete regiment, my lord. Fraser's, I think.'

'One regiment ? Then we must try to fight our way through it. Our only hope. The woodlands. We will hold this river-line till O'Cahan can get back. Then a leap-frogging retiral. Up Yarrow. My Lord Crawford – take two troops of Douglas horse. Up-river. To that bend, there. Wait there, where these enemy may see you. You will pose a threat. Of an upper crossing. The Ogilvys will take your place here, meantime. If Middleton is with his regiment over there, we are like to have another attack. He is no shrinking lily ! He will spur on Kirkcudbright's reluctant warriors . . .'

With or without Colonel John Middleton – who had once served under Montrose – when his dragoons did join up with the waiting ranks across the river, there was a prompt and positive reaction. The combined force was swiftly split up into troops of about seventy strong, some ten of these, to be sent off, up and down stream, to line the banks about 100 yards apart. At a bugle's blast they all began the fording process simultaneously.

Montrose bit his lip. He could not hope to cope with this successfully, with his small numbers. Some must get over almost unopposed. He spread his available men as best he could – but all realised that it was hopeless.

They made the enemy pay dearly for that crossing. But before they were outflanked Montrose issued orders to retire to higher ground, calling back Crawford.

As they moved back, Pate Graham raced up to announce that O'Cahan, with barely 100 men remaining of his 500, had fallen back, as ordered, but could not hold the second line with so few. He proposed to stand, form a square, a hedgehog, and go down to the last man.

James Graham groaned aloud. 'My stout Magnus! Not that – not that! Back to him, Pate. Tell him . . .'

He was interrupted by a horseman clattering up, wounded, hatless, one of Blackadder's scout officers. 'My lord,' he gasped, 'Fraser's regiment advances. To attack your rear. Out of Yarrow. See there . . .' And in the act of turning in his saddle to point, he swayed and crashed to the ground.

Montrose raised his head in a strange gesture that was almost relief, and stared around him. It would all be over in ten minutes now. Complete and utter defeat.

A clamour of voices were urging, demanding, a dash for it immediately – Douglas's, Fleming's, Erskine's, young Archie Napier's, Nat Gordon's – though not Airlie's, whose heir was somewhere on that stricken field. Montrose could do no more, they declared. He was the King's Viceroy. The royal cause must go on. Fight another day. Flee, now . . .

Slowly, gravely, James Graham nodded his head. 'As you will,' he said. 'I accept the full responsibility for this decision. Pate – my salute to Colonel O'Cahan. Tell him that he is *not* to fight on. My command. His men to disperse. Into the hills and woods. As best they can. Some will escape. And, Pate – tell Magnus of my love for him. The truest and bravest! Tell him that when next we meet, God willing, he will be Sir Magnus! Off with you. Then follow me southwards. Up Yarrow. Rendezvous, the Loch of St. Mary. God-speed, Pate . . .!'

As his friend hurried off, Crawford rode up. 'The river-line breaks, Montrose. We cannot hold them longer . . .'

'I know it, my lord. It is enough. My command to all. Horse to me here, quickly. All foot to disperse. Save themselves as best they can. Run. Not to yield – run! Our enemies' slogan is "Jesus and No Quarter!" Remind all. To my sorrow and shame. But my grateful thanks . . .' He turned. 'And now, gentlemen – another wedge! For the last time. All remaining horse. Fraser's regiment has not tasted our steel yet. Form up. We shall give these others a moment to come up.' He reached out to grip Airlie's forearm. 'I am sorry, old friend . . .'

'I leave . . . my son . . . in God's hands,' the other muttered. 'Again!'

In the event, that final dash was less taxing than most feared. The cavalry wedge, about eighty strong, got away before the regiment from the river reached the camp area, and before Leslie's main body had got past O'Cahan. And spurring uphill, they found Fraser's regiment in troop formation, spread over the widest front – ideal to catch stragglers of a defeated army, but hopeless to counter a determined arrowhead charge. In fact, actual contact was with only one troop, and this made a gesture rather than any real attempt to halt them. Then they were past, and driving on hard. Yarrow's wooded hill-sides swallowed them up.

It was all too easy, swift, anti-climax. If pursuit there was, none was evident. It still lacked an hour till noon.

James Graham would have wept if he could, as he rode. But he was beyond tears.

CHAPTER TWELVE

St. Mary's Loch was far too close to Philiphaugh to be a safe
rendezvous at which to linger long. Picking up a few stragglers
there, including Pate Graham, the fugitives pressed on, due
northwards now, deciding that to hang about in the Ettrick
Forest area waiting for possible Douglas recruits would be unrealistic in the circumstances. They went by Mountbenger and
the heights of Minchmoor, and so down to the Quair Water.
They hammered on Traquair's door in the by-going, but gained
no response. That particular bird appeared to have flown.

The Lord Fleming pointed out that his house at Biggar was
within riding distance. They could eat and rest there; none would
seek them in the Upper Ward of Lanarkshire, that night. So, in
the dusk, they climbed out of Tweeddale and westwards over
lower green hills, weary, hungry, jaded. But by no means in
despair. Fiercely James Graham had put anything such from
him. He had suffered his first major defeat, and sacrificed some
of his good friends; but he still had much – or the cause had. He
had chosen to keep alight the King's cause, and he would do
so.

That determination was reinforced when a single horseman,
pursuing them¸ was allowed to catch up, in the Skirling area. To
their surprise, it was an infantryman, one of O'Cahan's Irish
officers, MacDermott by name. Flinging aside the Highland
plaid he wore, he revealed himself to be still more colourfully
clad. Wrapped around him were the silken folds of the Ulster
Brigade's standard. He handed it to Montrose, with a flourish.

'You will find another company to serve under it, sir – but you
will never find a better!' he panted.

'That I well know, friend,' Montrose agreed, touched. 'I
thank you. But – how come you here, thus ?'

'There was a great slaughter at the end, lord. We left it too
late. I feigned dead. Amongst the dead. This flag was nearby.
Under Captain O'Donnell. I dragged it beneath myself. And so
lay. Until they left us. And I found me a riderless horse. Och,
there were many of them . . .'

'A great slaughter, you say? And you left it too late? Do you mean that your people did not disperse? That O'Cahan was taken?'

'Aye, sir. *He* was taken. But the rest slain. Cut down there and then.'

'You mean that they took them prisoner? And then slew them, defenceless?'

'I do so. Every one, yes, by God! Barring Colonel O'Cahan himself. And Major Lachlan. And my own self, whom they thought dead. God's curse on them! They cut them down, standing there. Their priests, it was – the black crows! The ministers...'

'Jesus and No Quarter!' Fleming snarled.

'You tell me that Leslie killed all prisoners save the officers?' Montrose's voice quivered. 'At the demand of the ministers?'

'Not all officers, sir. Only the highest were spared. Spared to be hanged they said!'

'Dear God! Magnus...!'

'I told him, Jamie,' Pate Graham put in. 'I said you commanded him to disperse. To run for it. I said the Covenant zealots were merciless. He still had time, opportunity...'

'He aimed to keep the enemy busy, lord,' MacDermott explained. 'Until *yourself* had got clear away. That was the size of him!'

James Graham bowed his head.

Into the hush, the Earl of Airlie spoke uncertainly. 'My son...? The Lord Ogilvy? Did you see aught of him?'

'Aye, lord. He is prisoner. I saw him. Wounded. Colonel Gordon, also. And the lame one, Rollo. And the other Ogilvy, the young captain...'

'Inverquharity.' Airlie sighed, with a mixture of relief and apprehension. 'Thank God he is alive, at the least. So far!'

None commented on the Earl's last words.

'Did you see the Marquis of Argyll, Captain? Was he there?' Montrose asked.

'I know him not, lord. But many great folk rode up. When the fighting was over. With the ministers – flocks of the ministers.'

With much to think upon, they rode on to Biggar.

After only a few hours for rest and refreshment they were off again next morning, before dawn, still heading northwards, Montrose determined to get back into the Highlands where he could summon renewed support, get Colkitto back, and Aboyne.

He must regroup, and re-attack. He was in a hurry now. Hangings had to be prevented, at all costs. This would best be done by posing a threat. And that required men, many men. The Athollmen who had so gallantly aided him in the past, and were quickly mustered, would have won in their harvest by now. Atholl had been the first to give him large-scale support. He would go to Atholl.

The crossings of Forth would almost certainly be held against him. It must be the secret, devious causeways of the Flanders Moss again, then. Avoiding Stirling, they would make for the Campsie Fells.

They were not challenged, that hard-riding company, as they raced up the centre of Lowland Scotland. The word of the Philiphaugh disaster had not yet reached the country at large, and until it did the Marquis of Montrose was still master of the kingdom – even though Leslie would never have neglected to send swift orders ahead to guard the Forth, the ferries east of Stirling, and the bridges there and to the west.

They passed close to Kilsyth that evening, the site of triumph only a few brief weeks before – a wryly humbling experience. Threading the lonely Carron valley of the Campsies thereafter, they camped therein again, only eight miles from the edge of the great Flanders Moss. They dared not seek to cross that watery waste, in darkness, without MacGregor guides.

At daybreak, amongst the mists, they did so, unimpeded, leading their horses over the under-water causeways and twisting deer-tracks, arousing clouds of protesting wildfowl. Wet and muddy, but relieved, they climbed out beyond, into the Menteith uplands. They were safe now. These were the foothills of the Highland Line. Therein no Lowlander would lay hands on James Graham and his friends.

They spent two days at the hospitable MacGregor house of Glengyle, near Loch Katrine – despite the fact that the mistress of the house was a Campbell – resting themselves and their beasts, and treating wounds. Montrose's own superficial thigh-wound had stiffened up, so that he could barely walk, with even riding painful. Donald MacGregor of Glengyle had left the army after Kilsyth, like so many another, to attend to his harvest. Now it was gathered in, and he was a free man again. He would come with them, and seventy of his clansmen. It was an encouraging start.

The two days were by no means wasted, for Montrose used

them to send out messengers far and near, summoning men to Atholl at the earliest possible moment. He wrote in the King's name, and peremptorily.

On the second evening at Glengyle another refugee from Philiphaugh turned up, son of MacGregor of Comar, who had been with Nat Gordon at the Ettrick. That he had got so far and so quickly, on foot, was a tribute to his stamina as it was to his ability. He had escaped the final massacre by throwing himself into the river, and lying for hours under an overhanging bank. He had not seen the terrible things that were done, therefore – but he had heard them. And had later seen the heaps of slain. The ministers had behaved like madmen, he said, screaming about the Sword of the Lord and of Gideon, and slaying the Ishmaelites, and treading down the Winepress of God. They were drunk with blood. And not only on the battlefield of Philiphaugh. All over the Lowlands all who could be linked with the name of Montrose were being rounded up and slaughtered, camp-followers, villagers who had given food and shelter to the royalist army, the folk of districts where they had camped. There were hangings, shootings, drownings. As far north as Linlithgow Bridge, scores were flung over the bridge-parapet into the Avon – and those who tried to swim ashore driven back by musket-butts to drown, men, women and children. Everywhere terror reigned, with the zealots, not the military, in command. Argyll was master of Scotland again.

Montrose did not sleep that night.

Next morning they rode on northwards, though Breadalbane, to Atholl.

Not to involve too grievously the young Earl of Atholl, who had already suffered much from Argyll's reprisals, Montrose did not make his headquarters at Blair-in-Atholl but in the quiet side-glen of Fincastle, off Tummel, whose Stewart laird was sympathetic. From here he wrote a stiff and formal letter to Argyll. He told him that he was unbelievedly shocked at what was being done to their fellow-subjects of King Charles, the more so as apparently it was done in the name of religion, the final blasphemy. He warned the Campbell, and his colleagues, that all such slaughters and savageries must stop immediately, or the consequences would be visited drastically upon his Campbell lands of Lorne and Argyll, which were now within his, Montrose's, grasp. His Major-General Sir Alastair MacDonald was there now, and could be instructed to take the most vehement reprisals. Also he, Montrose, held a number of Covenant hostages and prisoners and could collect many more. If any hurt came to the prisoners, taken after Philiphaugh, these would be the first to suffer – but only the first.

James Graham did not know how much of this threat he could bring himself to carry out. But the writing of the letter did him good – and might have some effect.

Soon the hanging valley of Glen Fincastle was an armed camp, with contingents coming in from all over Atholl, and from the Graham lands of Strathearn and Mentieth and the Drummond and Hay territories of Almond and Gowrie. There was still no sign of Colkitto from the West, or of the Gordons from the North. But Airlie had gone off, with Douglas, to recruit in Angus – where the latter had large lands, being in fact also Earl of Angus. Individuals arrived, singly and in groups, finding their way to these remote fastnesses by devious routes – and all telling grim tales of the reign of terror prevailing in the South. Amongst them came the old Lord Napier, actually carried in a litter by stalwart MacGregor clansmen, a frail, sick man, but determined – and with probably the shrewdest political brain in Scotland, now that Sir Thomas Hope was laid low. By the end of September, Montrose had 600 men assembled, with twice as many promised.

Soon after, he had a letter from the King. It expressed Charles's condolences in the set-back, his continued confidence in his Captain-General, and his promise of armed assistance. He also expressed renewed optimism over the successful outcome of his affairs in England. All would yet be well.

Montrose did not find cause for major rejoicing over this royal epistle although he made the most of it. Next day, news was brought from Edinburgh. Magnus O'Cahan had been hanged, without trial, on the Castle-hill there, as an Irish interloper and brigand, without rights. And the parliament called for the 20th of October was changed to be a meeting of the Committee of Estates, to sit in judgment on the other prisoners and malignants, on charges of treason against the realm, Sir Archibald Johnston of Warriston prosecuting for the Crown.

James Graham shut himself up in a room of the house of Fincastle, a man desolate. He mourned Magnus O'Cahan as he would his own brother. And the bitterness swelled within him.

It was not in the man, however, to mope inactive. To do what he intended, to save those others who faced a similar fate, he

177

required an army, not of 600 but of 6,000. And above all, cavalry. With still nothing from Aboyne and the Gordons, he decided on a lightning dash across the Mounth, in person, to Strathbogie. Pride could find no place in this; the lives of fine men were at stake.

So he and Pate Graham hurried across the Grampians, by Moulin and Strathardle and Glen Shee, to the Dee. And still northwards, over the Mounth passes, in wild free-riding, to come down to the low ground again just south of Strathbogie.

James Graham had a strange encounter with Aboyne, that young man torn between guilt and defiance, sympathy and uncertainty. While not conceding that his Gordons would have made all the difference at Philiphaugh, he pressed for details of the battle and indicated where mistakes had been made. He was loud in his condemnation of Colkitto, and stigmatised the Douglas horse as south-country sheep. He bewailed the capture of his old colleague Ogilvy, but pointed out that he had ever been rash. Nat Gordon, he declared, deserved all that came to him, little better than a bandit. It was all a grievous business – but the fortunes of war.

Montrose listened to all this, drawing on his reserves of forbearance – for he needed what only this young man could supply. What of the future, he asked? What of Gordon power? Had Aboyne received his messages?

The other admitted that he had – but that it was difficult, difficult. After some beating about the bush he informed that he had in fact some 1,500 men mustered, ready – but his father's hand was heavy. Huntly was, indeed, uncomfortably close at hand, having left his refuge in far-away Strathnaver and come south to the castle of Gight, no less. He was insisting that no move could be made without his authority. And so close as Gight, none could deny that he was still Cock o' the North, master of all the Gordons.

Montrose made up his mind there and then. He must see Huntly in person.

Not to allow that strangely wary and atypical magnate to slip away and avoid him, James Graham did not inform Aboyne of his project until ready to set out – for the sly and hostile Lord Lewis was at Strathbogie and might well warn his father. Then they rode as hard as they might for Gight. But it was not to be, not possible in Gordon country apparently, to approach the Gordon chief unawares. Huntly was gone by the time they reached Gight, having left word with his major-domo that he was gone for some days, destination unspecified.

Disappointed but determined, Montrose set to work again on Aboyne. He had gone counter to his father's unreasonable commands before – why not now ? When so much hung upon it – the King's entire cause in Scotland ? His father claimed to be the King's friend, was his hereditary Lieutenant of the North. If a blow was not struck now against the King's enemies, the campaign would possibly collapse. To say nothing of the lives of many illustrious captives.

Aboyne capitulated. He would give orders to march the next day. Almost he seemed in a hurry, now, the decision taken.

Unfortunately, next day, the Lord Lewis insisted on accompanying them. Montrose could scarcely forbid it, especially as many Gordons looked on the younger brother as their leader, in Huntly's absence, rather than Aboyne who had been so long in England. He was only just nineteen but had been out of control and acting the brigand-leader since he was thirteen. They marched southwards at the head of no fewer than 1,800 Gordons.

It did not take long for Montrose's misgivings to be justified. The second day out, in the Dee valley, the Lord Lewis announced that a messenger had arrived from his father. Middleton, now promoted Major-General for his part at Philiphaugh, with 1,000 horse, had come north to Aberdeenshire, specifically to threaten Gordon – or so said Huntly – and was now at Turriff, enrolling local levies from Forbes, Fraser and other enemies of Gordon. The host was to return at once. Huntly however, according to his younger son, sent the Marquis of Montrose his good wishes, and assured him of his continuing support of the King's cause.

Montrose, trusting neither Lewis nor his sire, was prepared to believe that it was all a trick – but could scarcely say so. Aboyne wanted him to turn back with them, to deal with Middleton. But even if the threat at Turriff was genuine, this was the last thing that James Graham was prepared to do at this juncture. His eyes were firmly fixed on the main danger, in the South, and on the saving of the lives of his captured lieutenants. He insisted that they march on. Huntly could raise 5,000 Gordons if so he wished. He did not need this 1,800. And if he required sons to officer his force, he had four others. And Lord Lewis might like to return to lead them ?

Lewis would return, assuredly – but he would take the Gordons with him. It came to another unseemly clash, the two brothers at loggerheads – and ended with Lewis marching back northwards again, with all who would follow him, slightly more than half the total.

And next day, in Glen Shee, with another and more peremptory command coming from Huntly, Aboyne also turned back, with the remainder of the force.

Montrose humiliated, frustrated, returned to the Dee, and sent urgent messages to Huntly, pointing out that he was Viceroy and Captain-General. He had complete royal authority, in Scotland, to dispose the King's forces as he thought best. Middleton could never seriously threaten Gordon with a force of 1,000 dragoons, two regiments. Let him, Montrose, have the Gordon strength to spearhead a swift assault on Glasgow, before the Committee of Estates' meeting and trials, and to deal with Leslie; then he promised that he would hurry back to the North to dispose of Middleton – if Huntly had not already done so.

While he impatiently waited for a reply, he busied himself with recruiting in Mar and Deeside, raising Farquharsons, Irvines and some northern Douglases. No reply came from Huntly, and when inexorable time allowed him to wait no longer, sore at heart he left Braemar for Atholl, with a bare 300 men, only half of them horsed.

At Fincastle he found Airlie and Douglas already returned, with some 600 recruits. There were also other miscellaneous adherents arrived – but no sign of Colkitto. They now had a force of some 1,600, about one third cavalry – but totally untrained cavalry. And Montrose had no time to train it. It was the 22nd of October, and the ominous meetings of the Committee would have started. He had to do what he could with what he had. He ordered a march on Glasgow.

They were at Loch Earn the day following when a relay of messengers caught up with them. One was from the Reverend Zachary Boyd in Glasgow, announcing that the Committee, concerned at Montrose's near presence, had postponed its meetings, as such, but had started forthwith on hasty trials. Sir William Rollo, Montrose's lame friend who had doggedly taken part in most of the campaigns, had been tried, condemned and executed at the Mercat Cross the same day. Sir Philip Nisbet, who had fought with Montrose in England, had followed him to the scaffold. Then young Ogilvy of Inverquharity, although still only in his teens – and despite many pleas for clemency. There was a long list to follow. This messenger also announced that Leslie was in Glasgow for the moment, to receive the thanks of the Committee, and a gift of 50,000 merks – Middleton also, 30,000 – out of the confiscated estate of the Marquis of Douglas; but that Leslie's army was in the main still in Central Scotland, with rumours of royalist assault from England.

The second courier was, in fact, from the King, He announced that Digby and Langdale were once again on their way north, with 1,500 trained horse. They should reach the border by the end of the month, and Charles requested his Captain-General to move south to meet them there.

The third message was from Aboyne, who declared that he had now convinced his father that Middleton was no major threat meantime, and that 1,000 Gordons might be spared. He hoped therefore to join Montrose in a few days time.

James Graham, it is to be feared, did not nowadays accord his illustrious sovereign's pronouncements the respect that would be seemly in a viceroy. He would believe in Digby's 1,500 when he saw them, and not before. Aboyne's 1,000 likewise. He certainly would not go rushing south to the border. But the execution of Rollo, young Inverquharity and Nisbet appalled him, and the threat of more of it forced his hand. He could not wait for further reinforcements. He had to continue his march on Glasgow forthwith.

Keeping within the skirts of the Highlands, he hastened west by south, burning now, deliberately, as he went. For all the Lennox foothill area formed Glasgow's skyline to the north, and the sight of smoke-clouds drawing ever nearer – even if they were only caused by burning stubbles and heather – could have a salutory effect. If terror was to stalk Scotland, he must try to induce some of it. The MacGregors, to whom this sort of thing was second nature, co-operated enthusiastically.

Montrose's own Graham lands of Fintry, Endrick and Mugdock had been harried and ravaged unmercifully times without number, and were little better than a desert. He halted therefore at Buchanan, at the foot of Loch Lomond, a mere dozen miles north of the city – where he could make a quick retreat into the mountains if necessary – and summoned Glasgow to surrender to the King's forces, on pain of sack. And to deliver up to himself all members of the Committee of Estates therein, and all other rebels and murderers.

He prayed God that the threat would be enough.

To some extent it was. The trials were hastily abandoned, and the inquisitors fled – unfortunately taking their prisoners with them. Provost Bell sent Sir Robert Douglas again, to Montrose, assuring him of the city's goodwill and loyalty, complete lack of sympathy with the Committee of Estates, but lack of power to halt their escape. He sent urgent pleas that no armed descent upon the town should be countenanced. Any reasonable demands for money, provision and gear would be met . . .

Douglas, privately, informed that Leslie, allegedly sickened with atrocities, had hurried off to Stirling where a large part of his force was presently stationed.

Satisfied meantime, James Graham sent in his requisitions, and sat down to wait, at Buchanan – with a weather-eye to the eastwards, for Leslie. With a mere 1,600 men he was very vulnerable; but he would not be caught unawares again, and had a way of retreat kept open.

On the last day of October the news reached him that Digby had been defeated once again, at Skipton in Yorkshire. He and Langdale were allegedly fleeing north to join him – but only as hunted refugees, history repeating itself. There was no sign, nor word, of Aboyne. Nor yet of Colkitto – whom rumour declared to have crossed over to Ulster on affairs of his own.

Restive, well recognising that his present position was dangerous as well as unlikely to be profitable, yet anxious not to seem to withdraw the threat which could keep his captive friends alive, Montrose, early in November, decided that he must do better than this. He left a token force of MacGregors and other local clans at Buchanan, under Glengyle, to maintain the illusion of pressure against Glasgow. He moved his main force back into the mountains of Menteith and Balquhidder, from which they could make frequent forays and keep the South-West in a stir, flourishing the Royal Standard, but safe from Leslie. Then, with a small party of close associates, he set out again, fast and secretly, for the North. He was going to have it out, one way or another, with Huntly.

Not unexpectedly, he had great difficulty in running that elusive Cock o' the North to earth, when he did not want to be found. They criss-crossed Aberdeenshire and Banffshire in the early winter weather, with the first snow already on the hill-tops and hard frosts at night. At last they cornered him at Bog o' Gight Castle, at the mouth of Spey, in a snowstorm. Huntly's horse had slipped on the ice and thrown its master, damaging an ankle.

It was years since Montrose had actually seen George Gordon, 2nd Marquis of Huntly, now in his late fifties but looking older – and was surprised at the change in his appearance. He had always been fairly good-looking, in a well-built, red-haired, foxy-faced way; now he was puffy, flabby, his features coarsened, his beard straggling and flecked with white. The sharp foxy look was almost gone; in its place a frowning concentration which could not disguise a general vagueness, alternating with sudden darting, blinking glances and a constant lip-licking. James Graham wondered if there might not be just the beginnings of madness there. The Gordon was dressed in clothes which had once been rich, highly decorative, but were now tarnished, stained, soiled, as was the broad diagonal ribbon of the Garter which he wore on all occasions, frayed as it was. Even before a roaring log fire in his hall, he had a plaid wrapped round his shoulders like a shawl.

'Well, my lord – I have sought you long,' Montrose greeted. 'I regretted to hear of your fall – but rejoice that it has enabled me to come up with you. You know my friends, I think – the Marquis of Douglas, the Lords Reay, Erskine, Fleming, the Master of Napier, Sir John Dalziel and Colonel Graham of Inchbrakie? Some have already visited you on my behalf!'

'Aye,' the other said, pursing his lips. 'No doubt. You are welcome to my house. In this ill weather. I can offer you shelter, refreshment. If nothing more.'

'We hope for more than that, my lord – from the most powerful man in the North of Scotland. Since we come in the King's name and authority. But we shall be glad of your hospitality, sir.'

'The King's authority, you say? Charles Stewart is far away, man. And free with his authority, his commissions! *I* am his Lieutenant of the North, see you.'

'That I acknowledge,' Montrose agreed diplomatically. 'It is to the King's Lieutenant of the North that I appeal, as his Captain-General, for troops, cavalry, to fight the King's battle.'

'The King's battle? Or *yours*, Graham?' the other jerked, with one of his darting glances.

'*Mine*, my lord? How could it be mine?' Astonished, Montrose gazed at the man. 'What have I ever gained, by fighting for the King's cause? It has all been loss to me – save that I did my duty.'

'Many a man will forfeit much for power, James Graham. The power that you seek. To rule a kingdom. If you win this battle – for which you need my Gordons – who will rule Scotland? Not King Charles, I swear – for he will never live in this land. He's

183

ower fond of London. Like his father. James Graham will rule in Scotland. And why should good Gordons die for that, tell me ?'

Montrose frowned, looking over at his friends, as honestly distressed as he was taken aback. 'My lord – you do me wrong, I assure you. I have no desire to rule Scotland. I do not see myself as ruler. I have become a soldier, reluctantly, because the King's Grace needed such, grievously. But as to ruling afterwards, this is for the King and Parliament to decide. When the fighting is over. I shall not be a candidate for government – for I wish to live my own life hereafter. As I have not done for nine years. Believe me, that is the truth of it.'

Huntly peered, blinking, and tugged at his beard.

'You, sir,' Montrose went on, 'could save the King's cause.' He paused, glancing round. 'My lord Marquis of Douglas, here, can do much – has already done much. Supplying men and horses and moneys. But – he has not the cavalry which Gordon has. The large numbers trained to arms. His Borderers, of Eskdale and Annandale and Nithsdale, are excellent material – but they are hard to muster, unused to serving together, to obeying a single voice. They are not of one clan, but many, unlike Gordon. With no chief whose word is their law.' James Graham was picking his words with care. He was concerned not to offend Douglas – yet anxious to play him off against his fellow-marquis. There were in fact only four marquesses in Scotland, now that Hamilton was made duke, and three of them were in this draughty hall, Argyll the fourth. If he could make Huntly jealous of Douglas, without setting them at each others' throats, make him desire to outdo the other, show his superior power and inffuence . . .

'My lord of Douglas has taken long to hear Charles Stewart calling!' the Gordon jerked. 'He has some way to make up, I swear!'

'I know it, my lord,' Douglas acceded, mildly enough. 'But better perhaps to come to His Grace's aid late than to desert him in his need ?'

'I have never deserted the King. Always I have been his friend. I fought for him when James Graham fought *against* him! What happened at Turriff ? Ask *him*! Who has won most of his battles for him, since ? My Gordon horse. And when they are no longer there ? As at this Philiphaugh. Defeat! Do not speak to me of my duty to the King!'

'For all of which His Grace will show his royal gratitude, I am sure,' Montrose put in smoothly. 'As his viceroy, I myself might offer some small and inadequate recognition, even now. A commission as Major-General, perhaps ? The sheriffship of Moray ? Certain lands of the rebel Lord Forbes, contiguous to Gordon territory – at the King's victory ? Even, it might be, the recommendation to His Grace for the bestowal of a dukedom...!'

Huntly moistened his lips. 'A . . . a dukedom!' He almost rose from his chair, but thought better of it. 'Duke – of Gordon!'

'Perhaps. You understand, my lord, that I cannot commit His Grace in any way. But I can strongly recommend.'

The other swivelled those strange eyes sideways, in the direction of Douglas. 'And this – would he be Duke of Douglas ?'

'I have no such ambition or desire,' that nobleman said quickly. 'I am not of the stuff of dukes!'

Huntly drummed his fingers on his chair-arm. 'How many men would you want, Graham ? I could by no means spare many, mind you.'

Montrose sought to keep his voice steady. 'A minimum of, say, 2,000, my lord. At first. Although, the more you provide, the more quickly will this sorry business be over, and . . . results achieved!'

'Aye – maybe so. But, see you – I will allow you my men under one condition only. That they do not leave the North. I will not have them taken south. They must remain where they may guard my Gordon lands from any attack. That is understood ?'

'But – I cannot field an army under these conditions, sir. If it is Middleton who disturbs you, we will deal with him, yes. But then I must return to the South. The King's cause will not be won here in the North.'

'Middleton has moved to Inverness. He is raiding into my lands of upper Spey and Badenoch. And he chaffers with that snake Seaforth! The Mackenzie will turn his coat once again, and bring the northern clans down upon us. If Inverness is held against us, all the North is lost to the King.'

'Seaforth sent me assurances of his fullest support.' But that was before Philiphaugh. Montrose looked at the Gordon thoughtfully. Was this a private feud of his own, against Seaforth ?

The Lord Reay, who was chief of the Mackays, the most northerly clan of all, spoke up. 'If Seaforth takes to arms against you, James, then you will never get the northern MacDonalds to rejoin your banner – Clanranald, Glengarry, Sleat and the rest.

And leave their lands open to the threat of the Mackenzies. In this, Inverness is key to all the North and West.'

'True, Donald.' Was this what had been holding up Colkitto? 'But – Leslie and Argyll are in the South. And the prisoners – such as are still alive. I have to balance it all out . . .'

'My Gordons do not move south of Tay,' Huntly insisted, finally.

'Very well, sir. I will ride south forthwith. Make some gesture there, to keep the hostages from being murdered, if I may. Then bring my main force north again as quickly as possible. Meanwhile you muster your Gordons. Then we will make a joint attack on Middleton. Thereafter deal with Leslie and Argyll.' He did not say that once he had the Gordon host fighting under his command again, he believed that it might go where *he* wanted.

And so, before they so much as tasted of Huntly's proffered refreshment, the thing was settled – after a fashion.

Making it work, with the Cock o' the North for partner, was, all recognised, another matter.

*   *   *

The next months were amongst the most galling and frustrating of James Graham's military career – as well as the saddest. For return to Fincastle revealed that Lord Napier, his brother-in-law, friend and one-time guardian, had just died there while his son, the Master, was away with Montrose. And two days later, news came that Nat Gordon had been hanged, at St. Andrews. And the next day, even Sir Robert Spottiswoode, the King's Secretary of State and former Lord President of the Court of Session – who had sent a dying message to Montrose urging him, in the mercy of Christ, not to indulge in reprisals. There was one bright gleam, however, as other judicial murders were reported; the Lord Ogilvy, condemned to death, feigned sickness, and when his sister obtained leave to visit him for the last time, contrived to escape in women's clothes she brought him. His arrival at Fincastle was a joyous occasion, for once.

But it was Huntly who made that first half of 1646 a misery for James Graham. His interpretation of their agreement and relationship was extraordinary. He produced his Gordon host, yes – but not only did he keep it entirely under his own command, preferring always to use the Lord Lewis rather than Aboyne as lieutenant, but made little or no attempt to co-operate

186

militarily with Montrose or his part of the army. Indeed frequently he acted in exactly contrary fashion, deliberately, blatantly – and Lewis insolently. He declared openly that, since *he* was the King's Lieutenant of the North, and this campaign was taking place in the North, his position was superior to that of Montrose. Moreover, since he had more men under arms – for his force, though ever fluctuating in numbers, often amounted to as many as 3,000 men – *his* decisions on tactics and strategy should prevail.

In theory they were besieging Middleton in Inverness; in practice Huntly was pursuing vendettas of his own all over the North, sometimes two or three at a time, and Middleton was left to Montrose. Aboyne elected usually to stay with Montrose, despite his father, but was unable to detach more than one squadron of horse. As a result, the royalist force was normally greatly inferior in cavalry to that which it was allegedly besieging, however many in theory it might claim in the background. And they were again without artillery, so that they could not hope to take a walled town by storm, when it was alerted and well-defended. Frequently Montrose had to retire precipitately before Middleton's cavalry thrusts from the town. Yet if the Gordon cavalry had been there in force they could have rolled up the enemy time and again. It was a maddening situation. Its only virtue was that it made the cautious Seaforth think again, and retire once more to his northern fastnesses. In consequence, Montrose could still hope for MacDonald participation thereafter. Colkitto was now known to be in Ulster, negotiating with the MacDonnell Earl of Antrim for a joint expedition to Scotland in the late spring – a piece of independent initiative his Captain-General found singularly inept.

It was a hard winter, and campaigning unpleasant anyway. Argyll and Leslie appeared to have accepted the fact that it was not practical, militarily, and operations in the South were in abeyance. Indeed Leslie returned to Leven's army in England temporarily – no doubt glad to get away from the religious zealots who now ruled in Scotland's southern half. Montrose, however, kept up his activities, for he was concerned that the population at large should recognise that Philiphaugh was only a temporary set-back, and that he was still very much a force to be reckoned with. He intended to be in a good position to take the initiative, on a national scale, when the new campaigning season started.

In pursuance of this intention, and in view of the ineffectiveness of the present follies around Inverness and Strathspey, he sent two sections of his force southwards again, under Lord Ogilvy and the new Lord Napier, to keep the Lowlands preoccupied and to reinforce Donald MacGregor of Glengyle's efforts in the Lennox. He would have gone himself, in disgust – but he feared that without his influence in the North, Huntly might run completely mad. Moreover the man was no longer young, and might weary of his brigandage; in which case Montrose wished to be on hand to ensure that the vital cavalry came into Aboyne's command rather than Lewis Gordon's. So he sat it out, at least largely immobilising Middleton – who was the only Covenant leader who appeared to be prepared to fight in winter conditions – seeking meanwhile to stomach Huntly's arrogance and Lewis's sheer impertinence. It made a grim interlude.

But with the lengthening days, and the melting snows, the position began to improve. Both Ogilvy and Napier reported successes. Antrim and Colkitto actually landed on the Hebridean seaboard, concerned mainly with harrying Argyll and Lorne apparently, but who must be coaxed into more productive warfare – Antrim, curiously enough, announcing himself to be the King's General of the Isles and Highlands. Clanranald sent word that, despite Antrim, he would be at Montrose's disposal, with 2,000 MacDonalds, whenever the first hay was in. And the weathercock Seaforth sent a new set of assurances as to his loyalty to the Throne and his good wishes for Montrose. He was ever the first to reflect a change of wind.

At this stage, for some undisclosed reason, Huntly changed direction altogether and led his force southwards to assault, take and sack Aberdeen – all in the name of King Charles. Horrified, Montrose hurried thither in an attempt to undo as much of the harm as he might. But the Gordon, as ever, got word of his coming, and disappeared into deepest Aberdeenshire, leaving only the Lord Lewis to face the Captain-General – which he did with his usual swaggering audacity, announcing that he took his orders from his father, the Lieutenant of the North and from no other, etcetera. And he had thousands of Gordon horse to back his youthful contumely.

Wearily, at long last, James Graham recognised that he had come to the end of the road as far as the Gordons were concerned. There was a limit even to *his* patience. Moreover the harm now being done to the King's cause all over the North was so great that unless he disassociated himself from Huntly, clearly enough for all to see, he must lose all support and credence. Reluctantly he issued a proclamation declaring that, as the King's Viceroy and Captain-General, he could no longer accept the Marquis of Huntly as a true servant of His Grace and colleague of his own, all men to take note. By the same token he ordered Huntly to disband his forces and return to his own territories.

It was in this extraordinary situation, at the end of May 1646, in Strathspey, that the final blow fell. A messenger arrived with a letter from Charles Stewart – but not from Oxford or any other royalist stronghold. It came, by the hand of Colonel Robin Kerr, from the Earl of Leven's Scottish army headquarters in England. And it announced that the King had decided to do as his good and faithful friend the Marquis of Montrose had long advised, abandon his failing cause in England and throw himself upon the loyal affections of his Scottish subjects. To that end he had secretly left Oxford, in the guise of a servant, and committed himself to the care and keeping of the Earl of Leven, the Earl of Lothian, General David Leslie and others commanding the Scottish army, assured of their leal goodwill. As a result of discussions with them he had agreed to certain terms. He would sign the Covenant and order the royalist forces in England to lay down their arms. Accordingly, he commanded his trusted friend the Marquis of Montrose likewise to disarm and disband the royal forces in Scotland, and enter into discussions with the Covenant leadership there, forthwith.

This official letter was privately amplified by Colonel Kerr. His Grace's treatment by the Leslies and Lothian, on Argyll's instructions, was harsh and unbending, and hardly indicative of clemency in Scotland. The King privately advised Montrose to make the best terms he could over the disbandment of his forces, and then to flee to France – where he would send him further instructions in due course.

Utterly bewildered and appalled, James Graham saw all that he had fought and striven for dissolving, crumbling, thrown away. Like a man mortally wounded his head sank on his chest. This, then was what he had given his all for, and what so many fine men had died for. This was the end of it all – abject folly triumphant.

PART TWO

CHAPTER THIRTEEN

James Graham steadied himself against the thrumming cordage as the vessel rolled and pitched, and stared back at the receding land. Already the features and details of the coastline, dramatic as it was, were fading, levelling out, and the great mass of the inland mountains seemed to grow, to come closer to the shore, to dominate all, in their blue, shadow-slashed infinity – those mountains which for so long had been both his sure ally and his continuing challenge, his refuge and yet his constant problem. Would he ever look on them again, he wondered?

He could no longer distinguish the mouths of the two Esks, North and South, or even the towers and spires of the town of Montrose between the rivers and the rising backcloth of the land. He could not pinpoint exactly where lay Old Montrose and Kinnaird, at the head of the great landlocked bay, where last night he had secretly said goodbye to his wife and children, in as unsatisfactory a parting as might be imagined. Magdalen, he well recognised, he might never see again in this life, the mere husk of a woman, mentally and physically, already next to death in all but name. Surely he need not feel responsibility for all of that? But the children – that was different. What sort of a father had he proved to them, sacrificed on the altar of his crumbled faith, an altar to a false god, a noble image with feet of clay? At least he had got Jamie safely out of Edinburgh Castle – though not out of Covenant tutelage and back to his mother – part of the terms he had won from Middleton over the disbandment of the army. He would have liked to have brought the boy away with him; but even if it had been allowed, it would not have been fair to Magdalen. Nor to Jamie himself, probably, for God alone knew into what sort of exile he was sailing. The lad was better left behind, for Southesk had promised to keep an eye on him – and Southesk at least knew the art of self-preservation. Perhaps he had reason to be thankful for David Carnegie's trimming propensities now, for his family's sake.

A little way to the side, in the shelter of the sloop's deckhouse, a small group of men watched him – all that remained of the galaxy that had attended on the Viceroy and Captain-General of Scotland, and none his closest friends. Respecting Montrose's mood and his need for a measure of privacy, these kept their distance – even the brashest of them, Sir John Hurry, of all men. That extraordinary soldier of misfortune was indeed with them. After his defeats, in such bad odour was he with Argyll and the Estates leadership that, a mercenary at heart anyway, he had decided to sell his sword to the other side. It had proved a bad time to make the change; but there was no going back, in the Scotland that now was. But he had soldiered in the Continental wars before – with more success than at home – and could do so again. That he was on this ship, getting safe out of a country too hot to hold him, was the measure of his former enemy's generosity of spirit, and the respect of one soldier for another.

George Wishart, secretary and chaplain, had organised this escape into exile. He knew, as did Montrose himself, that the moment that the strange conferences with Middleton were over and the army actually disbanded, whatever the terms might say, James Graham himself would be arrested, his protection gone – Archibald Campbell would see to that. Aberdeen harbour had been well watched, as had Montrose itself; but Wishart had discovered a small Norwegian vessel at Stonehaven, unloading, and had paid its master well, too well for their slender resources, to forgo a cargo and slip off in the darkness down the coast, to stand out to sea during that day, and then to move in at evening and pick up, off the mouth of the South Esk, a fishing-coble that had rowed out of Montrose Basin, with a minister of the Kirk aboard, the Reverend James Wood, and his servant. That servant had been James Graham, who was now on his way to Bergen.

Montrose, however bitter and grievous his thoughts as he watched the shoreline of his native land recede, was not at heart despairing or hopeless, of course – for that was not in the nature of the man. His private affairs were in ruin, and his faith in his monarch's judgment and word gone; but the cause to which he had sacrificed all could yet be saved, *must* yet be saved. He now identified himself almost wholly with that cause – since his personal life had been so sacrificed as to be all but non-existent. But Charles Stewart and his throne might yet be saved; it was unthinkable to believe otherwise, whatever the folly of the King. He, James Graham, could and would save it, given a modicum of co-operation, understanding, trust. Before ever he came to terms with Middleton, as commanded, he had in fact received a secret letter from Charles, smuggled out from his semi-captivity with Leven's army, in which he had urged Montrose to bear with him, not to desert him, good cause as he had to do so. He appointed him special ambassador to the Courts of Europe, to solicit money, aid, men and arms, from his fellow-monarchs of Christendom, to build up an army which would return to sweep their enemies from England and Scotland both, of which army Montrose was to be supreme commander. Meantime to make his way, if he could, to the Court of Queen Henrietta Maria, who would welcome him, and who had managed to have most of the royal treasure conveyed into her keeping at St. Germain, in France. Shaking his head not a little over this typical Charlesian outpouring, Montrose had nevertheless managed to send the Earl of Crawford secretly out of the country, for France, to prepare the way, to promise the Queen the restoration of her husband to freedom and at least the Scottish throne, given the men and money and authority. Since Charles's hands were tied meantime, his wife was to be his deputy, acting for him and the young Prince of Wales. With her help, James Graham intended to wipe out this present shame and folly, God willing. So this was not really goodbye to Scotland, he prayed. He would be back.

When he could no longer see even the loom of the land, he turned, sought to speak cheerfully to his friends and went below.

With strong but consistent south-west winds the sloop made a fairly fast passage across the North Sea, to arrive at Bergen in six days, on the 10th of September. Under the shadow of different and more jagged mountains, snow-streaked, harsh, they anchored. But though the surly ship-master, Jens Gunnarsen, wanted to be rid of his passengers and off north to his home port of Trondhjem, Montrose refused to disembark until he was apprised of conditions here. His first main objective was to reach King Christian IV of Denmark, who was King Charles's uncle, brother of his late mother Anne of Denmark. From him he might expect aid for his nephew's cause. But the northern kingdom, Norway, was in only doubtful allegiance and security at this time, the Peace of Broemsebro being only two years old. Montrose's foreign travels could well be cut short before they had rightly begun. So he sent Sir John Hurry, who had campaigned here, with George Wishart, ashore to prospect the situation.

They came back in good cheer, Hurry positively gleeful.

Bergen, it seemed, was sound for King Christian, and the Bergenhus, its castle, whose cannon commanded the harbour and had yawned menacingly at them, was in fact under the command of a former lieutenant of Hurry's own in the Thirty Years War, a Scot named Thomas Gray, now Lieutenant-colonel of the Trondhjem Infantry Regiment. He would be honoured to welcome the Marquis of Montrose.

Just how welcome he was Montrose learned with real astonishment. He had barely set his foot on dry land before a salvo of cannon-fire saluted him, the gates of the castle were flung open and the entire garrison marched forth with flags and banners, a band playing. At their head, on a white horse, resplendent in feathered hat and half-armour, rode Colonel Gray.

Reining up before them, he leapt down, flourished off his hat, and actually sank on one knee, almost as though to royalty.

'My lord Marquis of Montrose – hail!' he cried dramatically. 'I welcome the greatest soldier in Christendom to my master's domains. In the name of His Majesty of Denmark, Norway, Schleswig, Holstein and Oldenburg – hail!'

Distinctly embarrassed, Montrose raised him up. 'You do me overmuch honour, sir,' he protested. 'For a defeated general! But I thank you for your warm welcome and kind words. I am . . . somewhat unused to the like, I confess!'

'No man can do you too much honour, my lord. The world rings with your deeds. My house is yours, and all at my command. Mount this horse, if you will, and come taste of honest meats. You will be deeved with shipboard fare . . .'

It was a strange experience to be fêted. During his all too brief months of rule in Scotland, men had bowed to him as victor, governor, fearing his enmity or desiring favours. But disinterested acclaim and admiration was something different. And it was not only Colonel Gray and his officers, but all the notables of Bergen who thronged to pay their respects. It had never occurred to James Graham that he had been building up a reputation outside Scotland. In Norway, at least, he found himself to be a hero.

Pleasing as it was to savour such esteem and boundless hospitality, Montrose did not long delay at Bergen. Christiania, where he hoped to find King Christian, was his immediate objective. But he quickly discovered that Norway was not a land to ride over readily, even for toughened travellers. Savage mountains of rock and ice, rising steep and trackless from the deep dark fiords which probed vast distances inland, barred the way. Christiania was less than 200 miles away, as the crow flew – but as man must travel more than twice that. The quickest way would have been to go by ship. But their previous vessel had left for Trondhjem, to the north, just as soon as it got rid of its passengers, and no other sea-going craft was immediately available. Moreover, Montrose was practically penniless. Skipper Gunnarsen had required almost all their scant funds to compensate for abandoning his return cargo at Stonehaven. And hero or none, the last thing James Graham would consider was to start borrowing money from his new friends. They would travel by land, as best they could.

In fact, they did sail for almost 100 miles, but in a small fishing-craft, between the mosaic of the clustered offshore islands and then up the long, long gut of Sogne Fiord, between scowling fierce mountains, a spectacular and latterly grim waterway which probed deep into the desolate heart of Norway. At its head, at Laerdalsoyri, they disembarked, cramped and cold, and managed to hire there a guide and a dozen shaggy ponies, not unlike their own Highland garrons, to take them on over the high mountain tracks, eastwards.

The days that followed taxed some of the little party to the utmost, George Wishart, not yet fully recovered from his long incarceration in Edinburgh's Tolbooth, in especial. But not Montrose himself. The physical effort, the constant struggle against a harsh and challenging land, were as meat and drink to him, after the frustrations, disappointments and enforced inactivities of the past. He indeed drugged himself with sheer exertion, embracing the weariness which overwhelmed all regrets, repinings, self-questioning. Despite his comparatively slight and slender build, he was superbly fit, his body the tried servant of his will. Moreover the scenery was magnificent, defiant, a dare in itself, and he was a man to whom such meant much, a poet. If he had had little opportunity, or heart, for poetry these last years, perhaps he might do better hereafter.

Climbing over the lofty, ice-bound watershed above Laerdal and so down into the Valdres valley and along the fifty mile long lake of Randsfiord it took them a week to reach Christiania at the head of the Oslo Fiord – there to find that King Christian had gone to Copenhagen, in his other kindgom of Denmark, for the winter – which seemed to set in earlier here than in Scotland. Christian's Norwegian ministers treated the travellers well, making much of Montrose, before despatching them onwards, down the eastern coast of the Oslo Fiord, on the Gothenburg road. They crossed the Swedish border near Kornsjo – which would not have been possible two years before, when Christian made the Peace of Broemsebro with Queen Christina, Gustavus Adolphus's daughter. Even so, although the Scandinavian nations were now nominally at harmony, it was considered unwise for travellers from Christiania to proceed right to Gothenburg, the great new city Gustavus had founded; so they made the crossing to Denmark from Marstrand, a small port a little to the north, over the stormy Kattegat, to Copenhagen.

Here they were disconcerted to learn that the King had departed for Hamburg, for a conference concerned with trying to bring order out of the end of the Thirty Years War which had for so long so decimated Northern Europe. No speedy return was anticipated. So it was onwards again, southwards. At least this time their almost non-existent funds did not have to stretch to the cost, for despatches and papers of State were being sent to the King by the hands of junior ministers, and Montrose and his party were welcome to travel in the royal sloop.

So, in fair comfort, they crossed the south-west corner of the Baltic – although suffering the usual jangle of seas where the cold current from the Gulf of Bothnia met the constricted waters of the Kattegat off the island of Mon. Disembarking at Lubeck, they crossed the level, cattle-dotted lands of Holstein to Altona, and so into the free Hanse city of Hamburg in the Holy Roman Empire, one of the richest towns in the world. The Danish envoys installed the travellers in a canal-side inn, and declared that they would announce Montrose's presence to His Majesty at the Rathaus.

James Graham knew Hamburg of old, having visited it on his Grand Tour of Europe. That was only twelve years before; but it might have been in another life, so different a man had he become from the idealistic, impulsive youth of those days. Somehow the place seemed smaller, less impressive and exciting, despite all its obvious riches, more drab for all the palaces of its merchant-princes, its magnificent churches all overtopped by St. Catherine's with its 400-foot spire, the tall bulging warehouses that overhung the narrow twisting streets, the houses of pleasure with their painted and half naked whores, the picturesque medley of traders, seamen and Jews which thronged every thoroughfare, market-place and canal-side. All seemed somehow lessened, tarnished, from a mere dozen years before. Or was that merely age talking? At thirty-four, no less. James Graham suspected that it might be.

In anticipation of a summons to the Danish King's presence, he was concerned to be as fittingly attired as was possible. Always neat, almost simple in his dress, eschewing the florid extravagance of most of the cavaliers, he nevertheless liked to dress well, indeed with a sort of sober richness that came natural to him. But his present garb was travel-stained where it was not battleworn, and he had not the means to purchase better. His friends offered him the best of their own – but such were apt to be as hard-worn as his, besides tending to be the wrong size and shape. He could only spruce all up as best he might.

He was so engaged when his room door was thrown open, and one of the Danish envoys, Jorgensen, stood there. 'Excellence,' he declared, 'His Majesty the King will speak with you.'

'Ha – I thank you, sir. A moment, and I will come with you.'

'But no! He is here. King Christian himself is here.' And Jorgensen stood aside, bowing low.

A tall and heavy elderly man with a black eye-patch, who stooped, clad in dark, nondescript clothes, came into the room, peering about him, with but one eye from under grey bushy eyebrows. Astonished, Montrose and his companions made hurried genuflexions.

'Your Majesty – this, this is a scarcely believable honour!' James Graham, still in his shirt-sleeves, got out. 'To – to come here . . .!' For once that assured and eloquent man stammered.

'Honour, my lord? Of God's truth, the honour is mine!' Christian barked, in a hoarse voice, his English excellent though thickly accented. He came forward, hand outstretched. '*You* honour this Hamburg, and every man in it, by your presence here. Permit that I shake the hand of the greatest soldier in Europe!'

Quite overcome, Montrose grasped the proffered hand, and bowing deeply, sought to bring it to his lips. But the other would have none of it, insisting on a hearty handshake.

'Stand up, man. Christian of Denmark has more need to bow to the great Marquis of Montrose. As a soldier, I am not worthy to hold your stirrup!'

'Your Majesty – I pray you not to cozen me! You – one of the most experienced campaigners in all Christendom. You, who even mastered Gustavus Adolphus . . .!'

'Only once – and that by his ill-luck,' the King gave back, in his jerky, harsh voice. '*You*, now, would have fought Gustavus into the earth! With you as my general, *I* would have been Lion of the North, not Adolphus. God's Death – and you young enough to be my grandson!'

'Scarce that, Sire. I am thirty-four – and feel older! But – for Your Majesty to come to me, to this lowly tavern! It is too much . . .'

'Tush – where Montrose is must be the most illustrious place in this, or any city, I say! Not that I will not have you out of here, this kennel, forthwith. That Montrose should be stalled thus, in a city of palaces! We shall see to it.'

'You are too good, Sire. But – may I present my friends? Sir John Hurry, Major-General, whom you may know. The Reverend Dr. George Wishart, my secretary, chaplain and guide. Drummond of Balloch, John Spottiswoode, nephew to Sir Robert, King Charles's late Secretary of State. All good servants of your royal nephew.' Which was being generous to Hurry, at least.

Nodding impatiently, Christian sat himself down, unbidden, on one of the rough benches. 'My royal nephew is a fool!' he said bluntly. 'Only a fool could have lost his throne with you as general! My good-son James, his father, was little better than a mountebank, God knows – but he would not have thrown away two kingdoms for a quibble of religion. Charles is an ass. Not worth your support, my lord.'

James Graham bit his lip. 'I cannot believe that Your Majesty is fair to His Grace,' he said. 'King Charles has made mistakes amany. His judgment, I fear, is often at fault. And he has been unfortunate in his choice of advisers. But he is a noble man . . .'

'A noble blockhead, sir! A saintly numbskull! If he must be a saint, he should have abdicated his throne. Kings cannot afford to be saints. I vow his sister Elizabeth, my niece, would have made a better monarch! She is more of a man than Charles will ever be. To allow himself to be bought and sold like, like a slave!'

'Bought and sold, Sire? What jest is this . . . ?'

'No jest, sirrah! I'd have you know I do not jest about the fate of kings! Have you not heard, man? Charles has been sold by the Scots, by your Argyll and Leven and Lothian. To Cromwell and the English. For £200,000. Sold and delivered.'

'No!' Montrose stared, forgetting that one did not contradict reigning monarchs. 'I'll not believe it! Here is some error, some mistaken story . . .'

'No mistake. I have it, in writing, from my ambassador in London. Charles was handed over at Newcastle. He is taken by the English parliamentmen to Hampton Court. A prisoner . . .'

'They gave him up? For money? £200,000 you said? From the English? For the King of Scots?'

'They did – and joyfully. They declared that it was for the proper payment of Leven's army. The first payment of £100,000 is already made – and divided up. Not to the army, by God! £30,000 for the Duke of Hamilton. £30,000 for the Marquis of Argyll. £15,000 to be divided up amongst those named by Argyll. And, see you, the Scots army will not leave English soil until they get the other £100,000!'

'No-o-o! Merciful God – no!' James Graham groaned. 'This is beyond all conception. Even for Argyll . . .!'

'It is the truth. I believed Hamburg to be the city of merchants. Your Scots lords, it seems, can teach them their business! But – enough of that. I came to speak of more savoury matters. Of things military. At Oldurn now – that is how you say it? Ah, Auldearn – yes. You scarcely used your cavalry there, I heard? They stood by, while your foot did all. And at Alward – Alford, yes – your horse, they say, all but lost you the battle. How could this be? Foot against cavalry hosts? I do not understand.'

When, presently, Jorgensen ventured to remind his master that emissaries at the Rathaus were still awaiting him, the old monarch reluctantly got to his feet.

'We will talk more of this, my lord,' he declared. 'My sorrow that I must go now and talk and chaffer over lands and boundaries and appointments, with hucksters, not soldiers. Meanwhile, Jorgensen will find you a house more suitable to your requirements.'

'You are kind, Sire – but I think that I had best remain here, if Your Majesty pleases.'

'In this hovel? Why, man?'

'Because, Sire, I fear that my resources are not such as to pay for better. Scarce even this.'

'Resources? Money? God's death – are *you*, Montrose, to concern yourself with gold pieces?'

'I must – since I have none! All the little we could bring away has been spent in our journeying. Until Queen Henrietta sends me some from St. Germain, we must harbour our groats!'

'Nonsense, man! The greatest soldier in Europe live like a pauper? Not while Christian of Denmark draws breath. See to it, Jorgensen. A good house – one of these merchant's palaces – for the Marquis of Montrose. And an allowance suitable for his dignity.'

'Sire – I thank you, from my heart. But – I cannot accept your charity. Even from Your Majesty. A small loan, perhaps, until the Queen sends me money? I have expended my all on King Charles's service, and I am to draw on the royal revenues she has, while I build up an army to go to his aid. Draw modestly . . .'

'Charity, sir? Who talks of charity? You will receive the payment of a General-Marshal of the Danish Army – which position I request the honour to bestow upon you. You will not say me nay, my lord?'

His breath all but taken away by this announcement, Montrose could only stammer, and shake his head. Without waiting for thanks or even acceptance, the tall old crane of a monarch turned and stalked from the room – before even his audience had so much as time to bow.

*　　　*　　　*

Less than willingly Montrose settled down for the winter in Hamburg. His intention had been to press on to France, to St. Germain, where the Queen held her exiled Court – although, as a French princess she was more at home there than ever she had been in England. But Henrietta Maria did not answer his letters, did not send him any money, and did not issue the official authority which he required – and which King Charles wrote that he had instructed her to do – appointing Montrose ambassador-extraordinary to the monarchs of Europe, to raise funds and man-power for the liberation attempt. Without this, his required credentials, James Graham had nothing to show as authority save a mere paragraph in a private letter from Charles, unsealed, unauthenticated. Requiring more, he perforce must wait, while sending more urgent messages to St. Germain.

They were all very comfortable, however, in the palatial merchant's house in the Alsterstrasse which Jorgensen had rented for them; and Montrose would have been more than human if he had not found some satisfaction in the high esteem in which he was held in Hamburg, and with the compliments and honours showered upon him, the constant stream of distinguished visitors who came from far and near to be presented to the most consistently victorious general in Christendom. After the treatment he had received at home, for long, it was a heady experience. His salary as a Danish general, duly and meticulously paid by King Christian, monthly, was a great help – although not sufficient to support his friends and entourage, penniless as himself, in any great style, and certainly not enough to tour Europe in the character of King Charles's ambassador.

Christian was consistently friendly, and they spent much time in each other's company. But despite all the generosity, Montrose could not pin the King down to promising any substantial number of soldiers for the liberation attempt. Christian conceded that he would supply a number of officers, and would encourage Scots mercenaries in his employ to volunteer for service back in Scotland, at his expense. Also he would provide funds to an unspecified amount, and shipping perhaps. Further than that he would not go – and Montrose was in no position to press him unduly. The fact was, Christian of Oldenburg scarcely judged his nephew Charles Stewart worth the trouble – a difficult situation for the suppliants to get round.

So, in a winter of snow and ice much more severe than they were used to in Scotland, they passed the time pleasantly enough, even though Montrose fretted to be up and doing. At least it was a change, to have leisure and to live in comfort, and in civilised conditions.

The high spot of the winter was the Yuletide festival, carried out on a scale the visitors had never experienced, three solid weeks of celebration, feasting and winter carnival in which the religious aspect of Christmas was very largely swallowed up in only thinly disguised pagan revelry. Hamburg was a cosmopolitan free city, with multi-religious background, but with German and Scandinavian Lutheran sympathies dominant. For all that, licence and gaiety at this season was worthy of the Old Church at its most unreformed and worldly, and enough to set Presbyterian Scotland by the ears. The two divines, Wishart and Wood, were distinctly upset.

It was in the midst of this festive interlude that Montrose one day received a command to attend at King Christian's official quarters in a wing of the Rathaus, where he was passing the winter as the guest of the city-state, and conducting protracted negotiations regarding the Baltic lands. James Graham had been there many times – although it was more usual for the King to come to him, privately, as it were incognito. But this was in the nature of a peremptory royal summons. Conditioned ever to receive bad news – and having felt for some time that this pleasant interlude could not last – he dressed with care, and walked through the icebound streets to the Rathaus.

Known to all in Hamburg now, he was conducted without delay to the royal apartments, through successive floridly gorgeous reception-rooms. A major-domo with a gold-tipped staff of office tapped three times on great double-doors, and after the requisite pause, threw them open and announced:

'His Excellency the General-Marshal Montrose craves audience of His Serene and Gracious Majesty, King of Denmark and Norway, Duke of Holstein and Schleswig, Count of Oldenburg and Lord of Bornholm.'

James Graham perceived firstly that the King was dressed very differently from his normal careless and undistinguished garb, very fine in a quiet way, being in full royal fig. The second perception was that there were three other persons in the great chamber with its four roaring log fires, and all women.

'Come, my lord,' Christian greeted him warmly. 'It is my privilege to present you to a renowned and beautiful lady, who has expressed a hearty desire to meet you. Indeed I believe that she is come to Hamburg for that principal purpose – for she does not often honour her old uncle with her presence! You are well acquainted with her two sons, I understand. Her daughters, here, dazzle my old eyes. But not more than their mother, my niece.' That was quite a courtier's speech for the old warrior. 'Her Majesty Elizabeth of Bohemia.'

Montrose swallowed, as well he might. Christian was by no means exaggerating about the beauty and renown. The woman who held out her hand to James Graham was in fact the most lovely of feature that man had ever set eyes upon, accepted as the most beautiful in Europe, as well as the most talented. Elizabeth Stewart, Queen of Bohemia and Princess-Royal of Great Britain, was an extraordinary daughter for Shaughlin' Jamie, the Wisest Fool in Christendom, James VI and I – though not quite so extraordinary to be the grand-daughter of Mary Queen of Scots. Almost as strange that she should be the sister of King Charles, nobly handsome as he was – for they were clearly poles apart in their natures. This was the celebrated Winter Queen, the Queen of Hearts to all Europe, to whom fate had been so unkind, yet who was acknowledged to be the most lively royal lady in generations.

'Majesty!' the Graham exclaimed, having a little difficulty with his breathing – and for once could think of nothing more to say.

'My lord of Montrose – Jamie, as my son Rupert calls you. I have longed to see you, speak with you. Up, my lord – do not bow to me. One day, it is my hope, you will allow me also to name you Jamie!' Her voice was light but strong, musical and with a lilt, a joy in itself. Tall, she had a magnificent figure, though scarcely slender, for she had had no less than thirteen children, but her carriage was as lively as the rest of her, though proud. She was dressed all in black and silver, but gave no impression of darkness, only of lightsome vigour, vehement loveliness allied to laughter, the epitome of spirited womanhood, ageless, her hair thick and still fair – although she was exactly fifty. Reaching out, she took both his hands.

'Madam . . . you are good. Kind. Gracious. It is my great joy to see you. I have heard so much of Your Majesty. From Prince Rupert. And Prince Maurice. And others. All of it in your praise . . .'

'*La* – enough! I would not have believed the Marquis Jamie a flatterer! A courtier! My sons will not always speak well of me, I swear! When I chide them – as they need chiding, now and again! As indeed do these two.' Elizabeth turned. 'My daughters, Louise and Sophia. Come, my dears, and pay your respects to the Hero of Scotland!'

The two young women, watching, reacted differently. One curtsied deep, the other bobbed an almost boyish nod, and grinned. They were indeed very different in almost every way. Sophia was fair, plumpish, conventionally pretty, with large blue eyes of seeming innocence, her yellow hair in ringlets, dressed with a sort of artful simplicity, not extravagantly – for her widowed mother, dispossessed and exiled, was not wealthy – but in the latest style and fashion. Whereas her sister was dark, taller, more slender with finely sculptured features, a wide mouth and strong chin, with a strange sort of watchful self-sufficiency about her – wholly womanly but with this boyish streak, and recognisably Prince Rupert's sister.

'Highnesses,' Montrose said, bowing. 'It has not been my good fortune to see at one time so much beauty as graces this room. I am privileged as I am overwhelmed.'

The Princess Sophia giggled, but the Princess Louise eyed him, frankly assessing, saying nothing.

'My daughters are not usually lacking in words!' the Queen observed, drily. 'Your presence, and reputation, must be too much for them, my Lord Jamie.'

'Not so, Mamma,' Sophia protested. 'But none told us the Marquis was so handsome as well as, as . . .' She flushed, prettily. 'Forgive me, my lord.'

'It seems that these minxes take after me in something, at least,' Elizabeth added, with a trill of laughter. 'For I have a sad weakness for good-looking men! So be it they *are* men!'

'Oh, Mamma . . .!'

King Christian chuckled raspingly. 'A captain of men and women both, on my soul!' he said. 'Captain-General, indeed!'

James Graham coughed, not a little embarrassed. 'Not so,' he objected, again forgetting that one did not contradict reigning monarchs. 'You mistake, Sire. I am no lady's man. Or, or . . . Your pardon, Majesty, Highnesses! Say that I lack success with your sex, I think. I am a plain man, in truth. Simple. And no great soldier, either – and that is a fact. I have been fortunate. In war, in some measure. In things military. Though, not altogether.' It was not often that Montrose made such a botch of any pronouncement.

'Then all the world is wrong about the Great Marquis!' Elizabeth cried. 'Or can it be that his judgment lacks something? As to war and women both? I think it must.'

'I would like to draw Your Lordship,' Princess Louise had not spoken until now. Her quite deep and slightly husky voice surprised the man, as much as her strange abrupt statement.

'Draw . . . ?' he echoed.

'Ha – that is the supreme accolade, sir! When Louise would draw a man,' her mother informed. 'She has a certain skill with crayon and brush. Now you *know* that you are a success!'

'Except that Louie is concerned to draw the ugly as much as the handsome!' her sister put in demurely. 'Indeed, her favourite sitter is a pet monkey.'

'Pert, miss!' the Queen said, though not sharply.

'It is character that I am concerned with, not beauty,' Louise declared, but with a shrug, as though the matter was of no importance. She seemed to have a casual way with her, highly unusual in a young woman of no more than twenty.

Montrose eyed her keenly, nevertheless. 'You are a painter, Highness?'

'I am not – although I would wish to be,' she answered, frankly.

'She has done some very fair work,' her mother told him. 'And will do better when she has lived longer, more fully. Gerard van Honthorst, who honours us at the Hague, gives her lessons and has hopes for her. When you come to the Hague – as come you must – you will see something of it.'

'Daubs of paint on canvas,' Sophia decried, in mock criticism. 'In the main, monkeys and ugly old men . . .'

'At least *I* paint canvas – you only your face!' her sister gave back, smilingly, without rancour.

'Ah – I think that the awe of the mighty Marquis of Montrose begins to wear off,' the Queen commented. 'Perhaps we should banish these two to another chamber, Uncle, and so be able to talk in adult fashion.'

'No, Madam – if you please,' Montrose pleaded. 'I would hear more. This of character – it is all, is it not ? All important. What distinguishes men from clods, and masters from men. Character is the essence of a man. Or a woman. But of the *full* man. For it is not something born, I think, but achieved. The painter – the Princess Louise – looks for character to draw. On canvas. I also have ever been concerned with character, in my small way. Not in paint, but in words. And in the assessment of men . . .'

'Ah, yes – you are a poet, of course,' Elizabeth nodded. 'Rupert said so – I had forgot. Forgive me.'

'God's Eyes – a poet!' King Christian looked shocked.

'Scarce that, Your Majesties. A mere versifier, a rhymster, now and again. A makar, as we say in Scotland. I scribble, lacking only talent, not will nor feeling . . .'

'As I draw and paint,' Louise added.

'Much better, I should think!' Sophia averred. 'Now I come to think of it, my lord has the looks of a poet.'

'God forbid!' Christian jerked. 'I would not wish to enrol a poet as General-Marshal of Denmark!'

'You need have no fear, Sire,' Montrose smiled. 'My weakness I keep well in hand. But – Your Majesty may decry poetry but not, surely, the search for character in men, which poetry, *my* poetry, seeks to express ? And the Princess's brush. For is not kingcraft, successful kingcraft, dependent upon the true judgment of character ? If a monarch cannot distinguish character in others, cannot choose the right men to serve him, how can his kingdom stand ?'

'You are right in that, at least,' the King agreed. 'Would God my nephew Charles had learned it.'

207

'Amen!' Elizabeth said, simply.

At the sudden pause, the change in atmosphere in that great room was very noticeable. It was as though a shadow had fallen over them, a noble but somewhat pathetic shadow of nephew, brother, uncle and sovereign, now captive in cruel and mocking hands, bought and sold like merchandise, failed, betrayed, rejected, yet still a King. Montrose, who had not made his references lightly, spoke carefully.

'King Charles and his kingdom can yet be saved – in especial his Scots kingdom. Of England, I do not know. But the Scots I do know. They will not do without their King, the successor of the Kenneths and Malcolms and Alexanders, of the Bruce and the Stewarts, the line that has endured for a thousand years. The monarch, *Ard Righ*, the High King of the Celtic peoples, is something that is part of the Scots, something which completes their polity, which they will not, cannot, do without, and remain themselves. It is otherwise in England, I think, where the monarch was ever the master, rather than the father. Wicked self-seeking men, in Scotland today, have pushed their King aside meantime – one man, in particular, who sees himself as master of the land. But the people are not with him and his supporters – despite the Kirk which he uses and which would use him . . .'

'Yes – the Kirk?' Elizabeth interposed. 'What of Scotland's Church? If it is against him . . . ?'

'The Kirk has gained all that it sought from the King. Freedom of worship, the revenues of the dioceses, even the suppression of the bishops. Only the fanatic few, the zealots who rave and rant, are against the King. And the nobles hate Argyll. Scotland would fall to any competent general – had he the cavalry I always lacked. To that end I am here, in Europe – to gather together the core of that invasion army, its arms and munitions of war. And the moneys to gain it that cavalry. With it, I will put King Charles on his Scottish throne again, if not his English.'

Elizabeth of Bohemia shook her beautiful head. 'Would I could aid you in your noble project, for my brother, my lord,' she said. 'God knows I would if I might. But I am poor, with barely sufficient to maintain my own house and family. I live an exile's life. But . . . I will do what I can to influence others. I have my friends . . .'

That was the reason for Montrose's rather lengthy statement.

He knew well that the Queen herself could not supply him with what he needed. But she was beloved of many, and might sway powerful men. Not least King Christian himself. She might well bring him to the stage of committing men, money and supplies for the venture.

'How will you win Charles out of the man Cromwell's hands, my friend?' the King asked, then. 'The English Parliament will be loth to let go a prize they have paid so highly for!'

'Once I sit in strength in Edinburgh, Sire, I believe they will quickly yield up King Charles – if they have not already done so. I would tell them that I was coming for him! I conceive it to be the last thing that Cromwell and his friends would wish would be another Scottish invasion, this time openly *against* them. There are over-many royalists in England, still. They would trade the King, for peace. Of this I am sure.'

'And then? With Charles back on the Scots throne? What then?'

'Then, Sire, it would be *my* advice to let England be. Meantime. It will not run away! In due course it will, I think, return to its allegiance. To its lawful monarch! Although – do I not know. I think, perhaps, it might be better for His Majesty to be content with being King of Scots, as were his forefathers. The English throne has brought little but sorrow and trouble . . .'

'And wealth! Forget not the wealth, man. Do not tell me that Charles Stewart will be content with ruling Scotland only, when he has ruled England also. He will not be in Scotland a month before he is seeking to get back to London. This is what I fear, why I, and others, hesitate. To see our men and aid squandered in a long campaign with England with Charles in foolish, unsure command. He and his friends have shown that they have no notion of soldiering, dabblers all. Madam's Rupert was the best of them – and him Charles threw out after Bristol siege. To *you*, sir I would trust my men. To my nephew Charles, never!'

Montrose bit his lip. 'Lend *me* the men then, Majesty – and you have my word that, whenever Scotland is won, you will have them back. At once.'

'*You* say so. But what my royal nephew say? He would over-rule you I swear. How think you, Elizabeth?'

'I would trust the Lord Jamie, Uncle. He has failed none, as yet – only been failed by others. Especially my foolish brother, God forgive him. I agree that it were wise to consider the Scots throne only, meantime. In this pass. Tie your aid to the sole command of my lord, here. That clear from the outset. Charles cannot demur. He has no choice.'

'Mm. I cannot provide sufficient of men and arms for the task. I will do what I can. Ships I can find . . .'

'But there are others,' Elizabeth declared. 'The Emperor. The Archduke Leopold. The Prince of Orange. The Electors – Hanover, Brandenburg. The King of France, indeed . . .'

'If I, and other Protestants, take this up, the Catholics will not touch it.'

'All Christian monarchs must deplore the unseating of a fellow-king, by his own subjects,' Montrose put in. 'Religion should not enter into this. Here is a cause to unite Protestant and Catholic both. Although, I admit it, Scotland would take more kindly to Protestant aid.'

'I have friends in both camps,' the Queen said. 'I shall appeal to all – but the Protestants first. I shall be your scribe and adjutant, my Lord Jamie. And enrol my sons Rupert and Maurice first of all!'

The Princess Sophia clapped her hands. 'We will all recruit for the Marquis. I swear I can persuade not a few young officers to go campaigning . . .!'

'Hush, girl – this is serious talk,' her mother told her. 'Not some knightly adventure. Though if any man can make war knightly, it will be this one, I think! But we must plan it with great care. *Our* campaign . . .'

Montrose cleared his throat. 'Madam, you are kind, kindness itself. I shall greatly esteem your royal and gracious help. But I must remind Your Majesty that I, we, require first the Queen's authority. The other Queen – Henrietta. King Charles has sent me to her. She is his deputy, while he is a prisoner. Any request for men and arms to invade his kingdom must go out with her authority . . .'

'That woman! That, that . . .!' Elizabeth swallowed, her fine eyes flashing. 'You must excuse me, my lord. I forget myself. But· Henrietta Maria is . . . difficult. No wife for a man in Charles's situation. She is courageous, yes. She has spirit. But she is shallow as she is obstinate. Oh, you will say that all women are that! But Henrietta is like a weathercock. And selfish. She has little care for aught but her own comfort, I think.'

'Mamma would think more kindly of Aunt Henrietta if she were a man!' the innocently pert Sophia observed.

Elizabeth laughed frankly. 'Perhaps there is some truth in

that. Though it ill becomes my daughter to say it! But I do fear that if you depend on Henrietta, my lord, you are like to suffer much, in delay, procrastination, perhaps betrayal. And you have been betrayed overmuch already. I have known her for over twenty years, and never loved her. She is so *French* – and half a Medici, at that!'

Both daughters laughed at that, and Louise made one of her few contributions. 'Rupert at least agrees with Mamma. He once called her Aunt Hetty – and she boxed his ears!'

'But she also likes good-looking men!' her sister pointed out. 'My lord may be more fortunate than you, Mamma!'

'Our tastes in men scarce coincide!' the Queen commented, drily.

Montrose inclined his head. 'Her Majesty admires my lord Duke of Hamilton,' he said, and left it at that.

'You have not heard from her yet?' King Christian enquired.

'No, Sire. I still await a reply to my letters.'

'And you have no authority, true authority, without her? To raise forces in Charles's name?'

'No written authority. Only a private letter, in the King's own hand, but the page unsigned, unsealed. Instructing me to obtain authority, as ambassador extraordinary, from the Queen.'

'A fool in this, as in all!' Christian grunted. 'The woman is not to be trusted – like the rest of her house. She surrounds herself with time-servers and toadys. Rupert and Maurice soon had enough of her Court, and fled it.'

'All I need from the Queen, Sire, is a paper. Sealed. And some money, if I may . . .'

'Then, when you have got your paper, come back to the Hague, my Lord Jamie, and we will plan our campaign,' Elizabeth told him. 'But do not mention my name to Henrietta Maria, if you are wise!'

'It may not be necessary to go to St. Germain, Madam. If the Queen will but send me the letters of accreditation. As I have requested . . .'

They moved through to an antechamber, to eat, a fairly plain meal considering the illustriousness of the little company, for Christian had no patience with things fancy, in food as in other spheres. Montrose greatly enjoyed the company of the ladies, smiling and laughing and blossoming out more than he had done for long years. He found the Queen a truly kindred spirit, and was wholly captivated by her beauty, her verve, her warm outgoing manner – and by her wits, for he perceived her ability and acute mind, recognising what Christian had meant when he had said that Elizabeth Stewart was more of a man than Charles would ever be. Obviously she had inherited much of her extraordinary father's shrewdness, if apparently little else of his. As for the daughters, the man found the lively and so deceptively demure Sophia a constant challenge – though his eyes tended to stray more often to her quieter sister. Though quiet was hardly the word to apply to Louise; watchful, latent, smouldering, perhaps. She gave the impression of intense vitality, something of her mother's spirits, held as it were on leash, her finely moulded features, high arched brows and slightly hooded dark eyes eloquent of hidden fires. Apparently there were other daughters in this lively family.

It was with a real reluctance that James Graham eventually forced himself to make his adieus, seeking royal permission to retire, determined not to linger over-long in company so lofty, to outstay what was suitable in a first encounter – however much the ladies united in urging him to remain. He promised to visit them at the Queen's place of exile at the Hague, as soon as he might.

When Queen Elizabeth gave him one hand to kiss, she held his other with her own, squeezing it frankly. 'Be not too long in coming, Lord Jamie,' she told him. 'I am old enough to grudge the passage of time!' She was exactly fifty, and looked fifteen years younger.

The princesses bade farewell in typical fashion, Sophia breathless, prominent bosom heaving flatteringly, glance dipping but provocative, fluttering diffident but calculated compliments; Louise brief, almost casual, but her glowing eyes looking deep into the Graham's for a moment before she turned away.

That look stayed longer with the man than her sister's dimpling, as he made his way through the snow-decked streets of Hamburg to his own lodging. But it was their mother's image and presence and voice which presently pushed them both to the back of his mind. Something told him that he had been looking for Elizabeth Stewart all his days.

CHAPTER FOURTEEN

The early months of 1647 were of mixed satisfaction for James Graham. He had seldom been more comfortably quartered. He was still being most flatteringly treated, a constant stream of distinguished visitors coming to greet him and express appreciation and admiration. Invitations came from various Courts, to attend. He had leisure, as seldom before, and a remarkable lack of immediate responsibilities. Moreover, he had a warm feeling somewhere at the back of his mind, which he did not examine too closely but of which he was seldom unaware – and which was the inspiration of more poetry than he had written since his Grand Tour days, even if this tended to be torn up and burned before any other eyes could rest on it. A peculiar sense of well-being permeated the man – even though guilt for it was as consistent. For the thought of his wife and family, and all his friends, back in Scotland, seldom was far from him. That he could do nothing about them was at once both the hurt and the relief of it.

Frustration of a more immediate sort was as constant, however. For the waited-for reply from Queen Henrietta did not come, no royal summons to Paris. He fretted, being the man he was, his work, his duty, held up. His affairs had been awry, now, for so long that he almost forgot what it was like to be otherwise. But in the past action had been the anodyne for his problems and troubles – even with Magdalen and the children, with his estates and tenantry, with his involvement in national affairs, vigorous action had been the saving of his peace of mind. Now, action was denied him; but relaxation did not follow, with all that he stood for trembling on the brink, and he safe, comfortable, but unable to affect the issue. The image of that woman who was not his wife and was not, could not be, for him, while it warmed him like a steady fire, scarcely soothed the frustration.

Elizabeth of Bohemia wrote him a friendly, cheerful and encouraging letter – and uncertain how to answer her, he sent her a careful verse – after tearing up five.

He waited.

213

Then, in a bitter cold February, he had a letter from King Charles, much delayed in transit. It was warm, almost fulsome, assuring his well-beloved cousin and friend of his continuing reliance, affection and trust, commending him to the Queen, hoping for great things – but giving Montrose nothing that he needed. Charles continued to rûn true to form. No proper credentials, no constructive commands or instructions, no recognition of the Graham's helplessness in foreign lands, lacking funds or authority, however resounding his fame. There were even royal commendations, to him, of sundry utterly useless courtiers and captains, now on the Continent, proven incompetents and worse, who would co-operate with the King's Captain-General.

James Graham all but wept.

Then, at last, at the end of February, the long-awaited letter from Queen Henrietta arrived at Hamburg. But it contained no credentials, no authority of any sort, not even a promise thereof, or of funds. Merely platitudes, ineffectual felicitations, and assurances of welcome at her Court at the Louvre should he choose to call there in his sojournings on the Continent of Europe. She promised to write him further despatches hereafter, and signed herself his very good and affectionate cousin and friend.

Sorrowfully, Montrose decided that he had waited sufficiently long. Anyway, King Christian was not well, and was going back to Copenhagen, where he might be in his own palace. James Graham had wrung as much, in promises, out of the old warrior as he was likely to get. He wrote briefly to Henrietta that he was on his way to Paris, with the intention of collecting his credentials, as King Charles had instructed, closed up the house in Hamburg, took a rather troubled leave of King Christian, who had suddenly begun to age noticeably, thanked the Free City's council for its hospitality, and set off westwards, by sea, at the beginning of March.

It was convenient to sail to the Hague, and then to travel overland, by Brabant and Flanders. Elizabeth, in her second letter, had said that Rupert was proposing to be with her that month.

With contrary westerly winds, and fogs off the Friesian islands, it was late in the afternoon, three days later, when their vessel put in at Schevenigen, the port of the Hague, and mid-evening before Montrose could present himself at the couple of large and rambling houses, the Hof te Wassenaer and the

214

Naaldwijk Hof, which William II, Prince of Orange, had generously made available to his aunt-by-marriage – he was wed to King Charles's daughter Mary – on the Kneuterdijk, at the western end of the tree-lined Lange Voorhout and near the city's central Vijver pond. The two adjacent houses scarcely made up a palace, but they served to house quite the gayest and most lively royal establishment in Europe, a mecca for talent, wit and beauty, where laughter, music, good talking and artistic expression flourished, despite the comparative poverty of the exiled Queen.

Impoverished or not, lights were everywhere as James Graham was conducted up a short avenue and into a courtyard surrounded on three sides by a many gabled and dormered red-brick house with notably steep roofs and ornamented chimneys. He heard the music before ever a servant informed him that an orchestral concert was in full swing. But a very gallant young man quickly materialised, to usher him into an ante-room, explaining the situation and announcing that Her Majesty sent assurances to the Lord Marquis that she would not long keep him waiting. Protesting that he had no intention of disturbing the evening's performance, and declaring that he would seek audience the next day, he was for prompt retiral. But any such thing was prevented by the arrival of an imperious young woman, not beautiful but dark with fine eyes, to whom the gallant bowed low, and introduced as the Princess Elizabeth. She looked Montrose up and down, assessingly, evidently decided that she approved of what she saw, and smiled faintly – and her smile transformed features just a little heavy.

'Mamma was right, and Sophia was wrong,' she observed, cryptically, and held out her hand to be kissed.

'I rejoice to meet one more of a family splendid as it is renowned, Highness,' he said. 'But – do I congratulate myself, or otherwise, on this judgment of right and wrong?'

'That is for yourself to decide, my lord. My mother said that she wished that you were ten years older, my sister that you were ten years younger!'

'Ha!' Giving himself time to ponder that intriguing disclosure, the man cleared his throat. 'And . . . what did the Princess Louise say, Highness?'

'Louie keeps her own counsel, sir. But she told Sophie not to be a fool!'

'So – I must make the best I can out of that?' He considered this, at twenty-eight, the eldest daughter of this spirited family, known as Eliza to distinguish her from her mother. 'You also would prefer me ten years older, Highness?'

'Twenty, sir. Then you might be less dangerous to us women-folk!'

He sighed, ruefully. 'The danger, I swear, is all the other way. I am a poor soldier, lacking defences against beautiful women.' He bowed. 'I confess to having had little practice in such . . . campaigning. Circumstances have been less than propitious, I fear.'

'Are your Scotswomen so backward, then? Or blind? You cozen us, I think. You agree, Comte Henri? The Marquis is a cozener, a dangerous man?'

The younger man spread his hands. 'All the world knows of his victories, Highness. And a man who wins victories in one sphere, usually knows how to do so in others.'

'Exactly. Was Her Majesty wise in inviting this, this victor to the Hague, I wonder.'

'The said victor retires, stricken, forthwith,' James Graham assured her. 'I will return again tomorrow, if I may? Girded for battle . . .!'

'Indeed, my lord, and you will do no such thing! My royal mamma would not forgive me if I let the Marquis of Montrose go now — nothing more sure. If your lordship wearies of me, shall I send out Sophie . . .?'

'God forbid, Highness! But — I did not come to intrude. Upon a concert. An entertainment. I will come back . . .'

'Concerts we have, like poverty, always with us — but Montrose is a rare bird! Come, sir — I was to take you to my mother's boudoir. No buts, my lord — a royal command! This way. Henri — I have come to the conclusion that you may safely leave me with my Lord of Montrose . . .!'

So the visitor was conducted, by rather shabby corridors and passages, to a small private apartment, opening on to a bed-chamber, where a wood-fire burned brightly and an elderly serving-woman sat knitting beside it, a homely and domestic scene. The woman was hobbling out, after bobbing a sort of curtsy, when the Princess restrained her.

'Wait, Martha. My lord — this is Martha. Martha Duncan, from Scotland. Who was Mamma's nurse, once. And my own likewise. Martha — here is the great Marquis of Montrose. Of whom we have so often spoken.'

'Mistress Duncan – your servant.' Montrose bowed as low as he had done to Eliza. 'Whoever nursed these ladies deserves the praise of all!'

'Och, mercy – himsel', is it?' the woman exclaimed, in the strong, slightly harsh voice of central Scotland. 'James Graham! God be thankit I have lived to see the face o' King Charles's truest friend! Gin there had been but yin mair like yoursel', sir, the pair gentlemen wouldna be where he is the day.' And coming forward again, she took Montrose's hand and kissed it, then almost flung it away, in a strange gesture, part fervid, part defiant.

Moved, the man shook his head. 'King Charles has been ill-served, yes. But I fear you all have been misled as to my poor efforts. What have I achieved, after all? That has lasted? I have been but ploughing the sands. And so many have paid for that ploughing, so much more dearly than have I.' He changed his sigh to a smile. 'But, I thank you. I see that Her Majesty of Bohemia has been under an excellent Scots influence, this while!'

'Och, I'm frae Falkland, in the Kingdom o' Fife, just. When Her Majesty's mither, the Queen Anne came, nae mair'n a lassie frae Denmark, I was a bit maid in the palace there, dochter to Pate Duncan, the falconer. That was fifty year ago and mair, mind . . .'

A great flurry of activity interrupted her. The door was flung open and two large dogs bounded in, a greyhound and a beagle, all tail-wagging joy. And behind them came Elizabeth of Bohemia, hurrying, breathless. Obviously she had run up the stairs. Yet somehow she remained queenly, assured, mistress of herself and all else. And vivid – so vivid that her daughter and the old Scotswoman might not have been there. Her presence was an extraordinary one, magnetic, positive, compulsive – yet less imperious than that of his eldest daughter. She was like a bright light which makes all lesser luminaries seem dimmer than they really are, by comparison. Yet her brilliance had a gaiety and warmth which countered any hurt and grudging which it might have aroused amongst her own sex.

'My Lord Jamie – forgive me! The good musicians would have been hurt had I left them in mid-flood! Here is delight, to see you in my house. I rejoice that you have come.' She stopped short of an actual embrace of her visitor, but only just, gripping his arm, his shoulder, smiling into his eyes. 'Am I pardoned?'

Quite overwhelmed, James Graham wagged his head. 'Majesty – what can I say ? You shame me, I declare! Mine is all the privilege. That you should receive me in your house, at all. I have interrupted your music, spoiled your concert . . .'

'It is an interruption we relish, my friend. Oh, the music was well enough. But your coming changes all. The word of it went round that salon like a flash, I swear – the great Marquis of Montrose is here! None listened any more.' She laughed. 'Save only I, who most desired to come away. I must make a show of heeding. The Queen must ever set example! Ah, me!'

Her daughter looked heavenwards. 'Mamma – how *can* you!'

'I can, must and do, girl. And gain scant help from my unruly offspring. How has she been entertaining you, my lord ? With the sharp edge of her tongue, this one, I vow! And Martha, here ? Did I hear her declaring my sorry fifty years ? Shame on you, Martha! When my Lord Jamie might have conceived me less. Such treachery!'

'Och wheesht, Mam – it was *my* age, no' yours, I was at. The day *you* look your right age, there'll no' be a weel-favoured man left walking this good earth!'

'Mercy – I do not think I like the sound of that!' the Queen exclaimed, grimacing. 'As you can see, sir, I am accorded scant respect in my own house. My daughters have a conspiracy to keep me down. And this old witch shamefully abets them. But – at least it gives me just cause to banish them now, from my royal presence. So that I may have you to myself, my lord! Begone – both of you! You are dismissed.' With a lofty flourish, Elizabeth waved them out.

'I do not know how to thank Your Majesty for your gracious reception and favour,' Montrose said, when they were alone. 'And for your kind letters, advice and offer of aid. It is for your royal brother's sake, I well know. But it is none the less an enormous satisfaction, encouragement to me. The more so in that others prove less helpful.'

'Ah – you mean Henrietta Maria, I expect ? Has she not sent you your authority yet ? Or moneys ?'

'Neither, Madam. As yet. Only a vague letter. But she has now sent invitation, of a sort, to attend her Court – should I choose to travel in France! So that I may now go to the Louvre. Am on my way there, now, I took the opportunity to call upon Your Majesty, en route. To seek your further guidance. And in hope of seeing Prince Rupert . . .'

'Alas, Rupert is not come. Nor likely to come, for some time, I fear. He is seeking to build up a fleet of ships. For his uncle's aid. And, no doubt, to transport *your* army in due course. But there is trouble – there is always trouble. He is in South Zeeland, I think. A mutiny, no less. He lacks money also, to be sure. To pay the men, as well as to hire the vessels.'

'Aye, money is ever the stumbling-block. And yet, what is money, mere gold, compared with the lives of men ? Shame it is that blood is cheap, but gold, silver, are dear indeed.'

'True – how very true. My sorrow that *I* cannot give you the money that you require. Any more than I can give it to Rupert. I live here in comfort yes – but only on the bounty of others, now that nothing comes to me from England. I am still the Princess-Royal of England – aye, even the First Daughter of Scotland! I have lands, properties, moneys owed me from both kingdoms. But not a groat have I seen from either, for years. Bohemia avails me nothing. And such Palatinate revenues as survive are insufficient even for my son Charles-Louis, the Elector. Were it not for my kinsman, William of Orange, here. And Uncle Christian . . .'

'Majesty – you must not distress yourself so. Myself also,' James Graham cried. 'I did not come to you, seeking money – God forbid! I pray you say no more on that score. I am sorry that I shall not see Prince Rupert. But it was for other help, guidance, introductions, that I sought Your Majesty's good offices . . .'

'Ah, me – and myself foolishly hoping that it might be something of my poor self that brought you. But never heed – at least accept my guidance in this, that we cease, when we are alone, this nonsense of majesty and lordship, and be ourselves. My name is Elizabeth – and I shall call you Jamie. As does Rupert. As, indeed, I intended, from the start! It was my father's name, and so my mother called him – although that may not commend itself to you ? For not all men found my strange sire to their taste! But at least he knew how to manage men – which my brother does not.' She pointed to a chair. 'Come – sit with me by the fire, here. And tell me how Elizabeth Stewart may serve Jamie Graham.'

A little bemused, overwhelmed still, by all this, he waited for the Queen to sit, and then took his chair, at a discreet distance. That would not do.

'Draw close,' she commanded. 'For this Holland and its

creeping mist is plaguey cold of a winter, as it is hot and dusty of a summer. Dear God – how often I long and long for my own pleasant land.' She sighed, who was not a woman for sighing. 'I have been an exile for over thirty years. Almost all your lifetime, Jamie.'

'You would go back? If you might? To England? To Scotland?'

'Scotland I left at the age of six. Forty-four years ago. You see, I insist upon my full fifty years! If *I* do not, my daughters will! And you are but thirty-five. I have made it my business to find that out! So you are quite safe from Elizabeth Stewart, the woman, and may sit close to the fire with her, secure, James Graham. Not back there, as though the flames might scorch you!' She laughed, a shade ruefully. 'Forgive an elderly woman's havers, Jamie. And remember that I am Mary Stewart's grand-daughter. Also god-daughter of Elizabeth Tudor! A fatal heritage for any female, you will agree?'

He bit his lip, but did draw his chair closer. 'It's not the fire that might scorch me, I think,' he said carefully. 'In some matters, many I fear, I am but a weakly man, Madam . . .'

'Elizabeth.'

'Elizabeth.' He nodded. 'I believe that you underestimate your . . . potency. Which has nothing to do with age or years. Or rank, indeed.'

'I underestimate nothing, my friend. Myself – nor you! Nor sad facts. Facts I have been living with, all my days. I am not likely to blink them now.' She sat back a little. 'Your wife, Jamie? Your children? Tell me of them.'

He drew a long breath. 'I do not know. How they do. Now. I left the children well, Magdalen less so. I hope, I believe, that they will not suffer further. On my account. Magdalen's father, the Earl of Southesk, is a careful man. He seldom finds himself at odds with the winning side! He remains friendly with those who rule Scotland today. And she, Magdalen, has long lived with him. In his house. Under his protection. With the younger children. They should be safe, I think.'

Elizabeth considered that. 'Your wife prefers her father's course to yours?'

'She has had reason to, I have brought her little but sorrow and hurt. Our first son died. On campaign with me. Although but fourteen years. Our second is a prisoner, a hostage. Mag-dalen has suffered for my actions, always.'

'It is a wife's lot and duty, is it not ? And yours has the greatest soldier in Europe to husband.'

'I cannot think that she would esteem that – even if it were true. Besides, she is unwell. Much troubled. Has been, for long . . .'

'In her mind ? Or her body ?'

'In both, I think. And, God forgive me, I have been no help to her, in this, either.'

'You have had much else to consider.'

'So I tell myself. But is it sufficient excuse ? For a husband ?'

She eyed him shrewdly. 'So James Graham blames himself ? You have spent more than your treasure, and the risk of your life, in my brother's cause, it seems.'

'A man must be prepared to give all for what he believes in. But . . . it is grievous when the price must be paid by others, who had no choice in the matter.'

'Your wife did not choose ? To support you in this your fight ?'

'No-o-o. She believed always that I made the wrong choice. Perhaps I did. But, having made it, set my hand to it, taken the lead indeed, I must needs see it through. Cost what it may. Or . . . so *I* saw it.'

'Yes – that is how Montrose would see it. So – you lack support in your own house, as well as in my brother's ? More than Charles Stewart is not worthy of James Graham, I think.'

'No – you misjudge, Madam. Elizabeth. You misjudge it. I have thought much on this. Magdalen was married to me as a child, a mere child. Myself I was not seventeen. She had no choice – nor indeed did I. But we were happy enough. For three years. But in her father's house. I blame much on that. It was part of the marriage contract that my guardians drew up – and David Carnegie himself was one of them – that for at least three years after the wedding, until I was of age, his daughter should continue to live in *his* house. So she never escaped from his influence. And he is a dominant man, and thinks other than do I. And I grew to rebel against it. Then, when my good-brother Colquhoun ran off with my younger sister Katherine, to the Continent, I took matters into my own hands and went after her, at the age of twenty. To try to save her, bring her back from shame. It meant putting forward my projected tour of Europe. But I did not take Magdalen with me. I had a wife and two bairns – and I left them behind, in her father's house. For three years. I did not find Katherine, and I lost Magdalen, in those years. She became her father's daughter, rather than my wife, and has remained so. For when I came home at last, it was almost at once to become concerned in Scotland's troubles. I have been no husband to Magdalen Carnegie. And her's not the blame.'

For a while there was silence in that chamber, apart from the snuffling of the two dogs, men's dogs but seemingly the Queen's own, and the whuff and crackle of the wood fire.

Gently Elizabeth spoke, at length. 'Tell me of your children, Jamie. Three survive, I think . . . ?'

He spoke to her of Jamie, and his defiant gesture, imprisoned in Edinburgh Castle; of David who died young; of little Robert and young Jean. Nor did he hide his painful pride in Johnnie, who had played the man before his time, and died in his father's arms. So they talked by the flickering fire, and the man found a comfort in the talking such as he had not known in long years – even though comfort was not usually one of the emotions inspired by this woman. Elizabeth, the Queen of Hearts. She proved herself an excellent listener, understanding, responsive, sympathetic – but never merely that, stimulating, leading on. And she, presently, in return, told him much of her own affairs; of her beloved Frederick's death, by plague, fifteen years previously; of the trials of an exiled widow with no fewer than ten children still to rear; of the problems of maintaining royal state without a kingdom or its revenues; of her pride in her valiant son Rupert, her satisfaction over the more solid Maurice and her disillusion with the eldest, the Elector Palatine Charles-Louis; and so on. She even, ruefully, related something of the semi-scandalous affair of the Sieur de Vaux, Colonel Jacques de l'Epinay, who had come to the Hague a year before and paid court in shameless and flagrant fashion both to herself and to her daughter Louie – and had had his hat knocked off by her nineteen year old son Philip in consequence, this resulting first in a duel between the two, which was interrupted, and then in a more deadly encounter ending in the death of de Vaux and the flight of Prince Philip. The Queen did not seem unduly upset over the gallant Colonel's demise, and her head-shaking over the spirits of her sons gave the impression of being formal rather than distressed. Montrose's grave observation that he was duly warned as to the dangers of association with the Bohemian royal family, brought forth a quick hand to his arm, a chuckle, and the reminder that none of her sons happened to be at the Hague in the meantime.

So it was late when James Graham finally forced himself to depart, still without anything to the point said on the subject of his visit, advice over his approaches to Henrietta Maria and introductions to various crowned heads of Europe. That must await their next interview. The Queen herself saw him down back-stairs and passages to a side-door – a delightfully personal, almost conspiratorial proceeding, that sent the man off through the misty, night-bound streets in a warm glow of sheer pleasure such as had not been his lot to experience heretofore. He was to come back the next day, and with all his little party, to take up residence in the Wassenaer Hoff, before he moved on towards Paris – that was another royal command.

*　　*　　*

Montrose spent a full week at the Hague, entirely pleasantly, indeed enjoyably. Moreover, his ever-active conscience did not greatly trouble him over the delay, for at his next audience with Elizabeth he discovered that, although peace had theoretically descended at last upon war-torn Europe, much of it was still an armed camp and travel across it still impossible without permits and letters of passage. Flanders had to be crossed to reach France, and the Governor of the Spanish Netherlands, the Archduke Leopold, brother of the Emperor Ferdinand III, still scarcely welcomed travellers from Protestant Holland. But he was well-disposed to the Queen of Bohemia it seemed, and she would send to him for a safe-conduct for the Marquis of Montrose. Meantime he had no option, she pointed out, but to put up with her company and that of her daughters.

This was no hardship. Four daughters, though no sons, were presently at the Hague with their mother – Eliza, Louise, Sophia and Henrietta, the last a gentle and pretty girl of twenty-one. They all showed considerable interest in their visitor, each in a different fashion, and the man underwent the highly unusual experience of passing his days amidst a whirl of attractive, high-spirited and demanding womanhood. He did not again have opportunity for any lengthy and purely private association with the Queen; but there was a rapport and sympathy between them, amongst all the flurry and activity of that lively and somewhat overcrowded little Court which did not have to be emphasised by confidential encounters. A glance, a tossed word, an understanding or cryptic allusion, as well as an open and undisguised mutual admiration, served eloquently to link them in a form of delightful intimacy such as James Graham, at least, had never envisaged as linking a man and a woman. It was a strange and totally unlooked for development – but he was scarcely given time to brood on its implications or problems.

Through it all he was aware, too, of other eyes that were apt to dwell on him, in thoughtful, assessing fashion, Sophia flirted with him outrageously, Eliza fenced with him in a kind of intellectual in-fighting, and Henrietta plainly hero-worshipped. But Louise considered him, he was aware, with deeper, more searching scrutiny, from those lustrous eyes. There was no rude staring; but Montrose was a little uncomfortably sensible of being carefully weighed in some sort of balance. Whether this was all in the interests of art and feature delineation, he tended to doubt. Nevertheless, without deliberately debating the matter with himself, he came to accept that the Princess Louise was his favourite amongst the royal daughters.

A most agreeable surprise for James Graham was the fortuitous arrival at the Hague, that week, of the young Lord Napier, direct from Scotland. Archie was, in fact, on his way to Paris, seeking Montrose, and unable to bear Scotland without him any longer; but the only vessel he had been able to find passage in had been bound for Haarlem and Schevenigen. Uncle and nephew made a joyful reunion. They had parted, in sad farewell at Rattray, on the northern rim of Strathmore, the previous July, when Montrose had disbanded what remained of his army, on the King's command and according to the terms he had had to agree with Middleton.

Napier had much and varied news from home. He had not seen Magdalen and the children, but the Lord Carnegie had told him that his sister might as well be dead, for all her interest in living. She was still with her father at Kinnaird. The children were well, and the Lord James still a hostage but not being maltreated.

With this Montrose had to be satisfied.

For the rest of his news, the younger man confirmed the sale of the King for £200,000 – but said that only half had been paid by the English Parliament. Argyll was master in Scotland but, strangely, the Estates were proving more difficult towards him than heretofore. The selling of the King had shocked the Scottish people, of all ranks, and the men responsible were highly unpopular. Hamilton and Argyll had fallen out, whether over their respective shares in the money, or otherwise, was not clear;

but the Duke was now seeking to form a monarchical party – presumably in the interests of King Hamilton instead of King Campbell. The Kirk was split, and the fanatic zealots had lost ground – although the moderates had suffered a blow in the death of Alexander Henderson . . .

Montrose grieved to hear this last. He and Henderson had scarcely agreed these last years; but he had always esteemed the minister honest, and recognised his notable qualities. Scotland in her present sorry state could ill spare Henderson.

As for the rest, the 'pardon' and reversal of all forfeitures, which James Graham had managed to gain for his supporters, by his treaty with Middleton and the disbandment of his army, though grumbled at by the Estates had been respected in the main, and there seemed to have been no major reprisals. Nevertheless, life was made sufficiently difficult for all who had been King's men, with pinpricks innumerable, threats and continued ostracism. But greetings and assurances of renewed support came from all Montrose's former lieutenants and friends – Airlie and his sons, Madderty, Douglas, Atholl, Kinnoull, Wigton, even the Laird of Grant – and, of course, all the Grahams, Inchbrakie in particular, who was like a shackled lion, denied action and his master's presence. They all asked, when would he come back to free Scotland from its purgatory ?

Montrose was touched, moved – but frustrated, in his turn. God knew, he was as anxious as they for his return. But he was under the King's command to raise an army, munitions and money, for that purpose, yet was still denied all the necessary authority to do so. He was, in fact, little farther on than when he had left Scotland, save in the good offices and sponsorship of the Queen of Bohemia, and in certain promises of Christian of Denmark. At this rate he could hold out no hope of any speedy return, grieve him as it did to say so.

Then let him go back to Scotland alone, on his own, his nephew urged, with all the enthusiasm of his twenty-three years. Forget the foreign aid and rely on Scotland itself, Many would rise again, rejoicing at their leader's return, and they would sweep Argyll and Hamilton, with all the sour prophets of doom and hell-fire, from the face of a fair land. As they had done before. Montrose could be master of Scotland again in six months, would he but return and raise his standard.

Patiently his uncle demurred. Was something not being forgotten ? King Charles, and his commands. He, Montrose, had no right, or desire, to be master of Scotland. His only authority to raise any standard was the King's. He was Charles's Captain-General, yes – but it was on the King's command that he had disbanded his army and left Scotland. He could not just return on his *own* authority – not as Captain-General.

While Napier deflatedly considered this, Montrose went on to ask about the Gordons. What of Huntly? Of Aboyne? Aye, and what of Colkitto? And the Clan Donald? Despite the older man's realism as to the priorities of the situation, there was no hiding the eagerness behind the enquiries.

The Gordons were just the Gordons, his nephew asserted. Huntly was lying low, safe behind his ramparts of man-power and vast territories. Aboyne was no one knew where, and the Lord Lewis, a curse on him, to all intents leader of the clan and approved of by Argyll. As for Colkitto, it was said that he had gone back to Ulster in the meantime. Clan Donald was back to internecine feuding, and baiting Seaforth and the Mackenzies. All was folly and a beating of the air. But if Montrose returned . . .

James Graham digested his nephew's news with mixed feelings, glad as he was to see the young man. It made him, at least, the more urgent to get to Henrietta Maria in France, whatever the present delights of the Hague. Indeed when, two days later, the awaited safe-conduct arrived from the Archduke Leopold, plus a pressing invitation to call at the vice-regal seat of Ghent in the by-going, it was Archie Napier who would have held back and dallied amongst the feminine attractions of the Wassenaer Hof.

The young women would have held their visitors back, but the Queen rebuked them. 'Let them go, stupids!' she said. 'No man worth the name thinks the more of women who seek to detain him when he has business on his mind. And the Lord Jamie has much on his – whatever the Lord Archie may have! Let him go while still he loves us – and he will come back the sooner!'

'Her Majesty is as wise as she is beautiful,' Montrose acknowledged. 'Would that we might linger. But with work to do, pressing work – for men's lives are in this – we would make ill company biding in this felicity against our consciences.' And if that sounded too sententious, he added, smiling, 'We are Scots Presbyterians, recollect – uncomfortable folk, wary of all the world's pleasures!'

'You will scarce feel at home where you are going, then!'

226

Elizabeth declared. 'We shall not quarrel with that, never fear – and welcome you back thereafter to our soberer company!'

So they left the Hague on the 10th of March for Ghent, on horseback now, over the canal-seamed levels of the Flanders plain.

*   *   *

The Archduke Leopold, son of the late Emperor Ferdinand II and brother of the present Ferdinand, was Governor of the Spanish Netherlands. He greeted them effusively, loud in his praise of Montrose's achievements, vehement in his vocal support, hinting at translating it into arms and men in due course. This was encouraging, but at the same time somewhat embarrassing. For, of course, this was Catholic support; and if it was over-enthusiastic, or made too much of, Protestant princes might refuse to co-operate. Moreover, any Catholic preponderance in the proposed invasion force would be highly unpopular in Scotland, where Montrose's Catholic supporters had already been too prominent. Money, now – that was different. Catholic money smelled the same as any other. But Leopold, a sallow and rather sinister-looking Hapsburg in his late thirties, with a slight squint in one eye which chillingly reminded James Graham of Argyll, however much he smiled, had nothing to say about money. So his visitor found himself in the strange position of seeking to play down enthusiasm for his cause, meantime. Perhaps he would come back to the Archduke.

On the second day at the great fortress-city of Ghent, another English-speaking visitor arrived – and seeking Montrose, not Leopold. This was a Mr. John Ashburnham, one of Queen Henrietta Maria's Gentlemen-in-Waiting. He had been sent to intercept the Marquis on his way to Paris.

When they could be alone, in the long vaulted gallery of the twelfth-century castle on the Scheldt, the stylishly languid Mr. Ashburnham, slightly older than Montrose and apparently somewhat weary of living, after expressing the Queen's great regard for his lordship and his own humble satisfaction at greeting so eminent a soldier, went on to declare that it therefore gave him no little pleasure to be the means of shortening his lordship's inevitably tedious journey through these benighted lands, and save him much time and trouble. All on Her Majesty's gracious behalf, of course. Even a sympathetic yawn was achieved here.

'You mean, sir, that you have brought me my letters of

227

credence and appointment? As His Majesty's ambassador-extraordinary? You have them with you?' Montrose was indeed prepared to look more kindly on this saturnine and sighful elegant, with his scented gloves, powder and ringlets if he carried the long-sought authority.

'Hm. Not precisely that, my lord. But, shall we say, new and improved instructions? Her Majesty desires you, instead of further delay here on the Continent, to return to Scotland forthwith, there to gather an army and lead it south into England against the man Cromwell, this Fairfax, and the other rebels. In conjunction with a thrust from Ireland, to be led by my lord of Ormonde.'

James Graham stared, bereft of any speech.

'Her Majesty believes that this will be much more profitable to the King's cause than your making of a tour of Europe. Here is a letter, from the Queen, making plain her instructions. So there will be no need for your lordship to continue on this journey to the Louvre.'

Montrose drew a long breath. 'Do I hear aright? Or am I losing my senses?' he demanded. 'You are telling me that Queen Henrietta proposes that I turn back? Do not see her. But instead return to Scotland. Just as I am. Alone! Without men, or money. Or, indeed, credit. And there, in Argyll's Covenant-dominated land, raise an army and invade England! That is what you are saying, sir? And conceiving as possible?'

'You have done it before, my lord, have you not? And can do it again.'

Long seconds passed as the other strove to master his emotions and speak with a controlled voice. 'No, sir,' he said, at length. 'I have not done so before. When last I entered Scotland, to raise it for the King, I was a rich man. With a clan to raise; friends, also rich, and hopeful. The King's cause, in England, was still sound, battles still being won. Now, I am a man utterly impoverished – as are my friends. At the King's command I disbanded my army, submitted myself to his enemies, disappointed all who were loyal to His Grace in Scotland. And now you would have me go back, empty-handed, discredited, alone, and start all over again. One man . . .'

'Scarce discredited, my lord. As a soldier, you still have credit. Your name alone will be sufficient, I vow, to rally thousands to you . . .'

'God save us – do you know anything of soldiering, of armies, warfare, man? Anything at all, to speak of?' It was not often that James Graham was provoked into such discourteous speech.

Offended, Ashburnham turned away, to move to one of the small windows. 'I have served His Majesty in the field, my lord, I assure you,' he threw back over his padded shoulder. 'And not without success. But – I am here to express the Queen's desires and instructions, not my own.'

'Queen Henrietta can know nothing of war. Therefore she takes the advice of others, in this. If not yours, sir – whose?'

'That is not my place to say. I am here conveying the royal commands.'

'Commands? I take my commands, sir, from my master – and yours – King Charles.'

'Her Majesty acts for the King. Since he is imprisoned and cannot act for himself. Read Her Majesty's letter if you doubt my competence, my lord.'

Montrose did break the seals and scanned the neat clerk's pen-work with Henrietta's floriate signature at the foot. Ashburnham had not gone beyond his remit. The Queen had indeed requested her well-beloved cousin and friend to return to Scotland forth-with, there to raise an army and invade England.

Helplessly he shook his head. 'Whoever advised Her Grace to this course was a fool!' he declared. 'I cannot accept it.'

'But . . . my lord! It is the Queen's expressed wish that you should. Clear and beyond question. You cannot reject Her Majesty's written authority.'

'I am the *King*'s Captain-General and ambassador-designate. With the King's personal instructions to visit the Courts of Europe on his behalf. To gain men and materials and shipping from them, to lead a properly equipped and officered invasion of Scotland,' he said. '*That* command I cannot reject, on the whim of his wife, advised by incompetents.'

'You refuse to obey Her Majesty, my lord?'

'No. But I will not carry out foolish proposals without first seeing her, and advising her otherwise. As the King's principal officer and adviser on Scottish affairs. I shall continue on my journey to Paris, sir.'

'Hm.' John Ashburnham turned, and spoke in a rather different tone of voice. 'That will not be necessary, I am sure, my lord Marquis. I have, er, other matters to put to you, which may make you see this policy in a different light.'

'Ah. I wondered why one of the Queen's Gentlemen should

have brought this letter to me, rather than a mere courier. There is more than meets the eye, here?'

'There is policy, my lord – to meet the new situation. The King's captivity and harsh treatment by Fairfax and Cromwell. In the circumstances, we must think anew. How best to serve His Majesty's interests. My Lord Jermyn is convinced that the time has come to make a new and statesmanlike move. In conformity with His Majesty's own wishes.'

'So – it is Jermyn! Harry Jermyn is a lord now! He was ever close to the Queen's ear. So much so that King Charles sentenced him to eternal banishment! So this is where Her Majesty gleans her advice!'

'Lord Jermyn is amongst the ablest of the Queen's advisers, sir.' That was stiffly said.

'And knows little more of warfare and soldiering than does the lady herself!'

'This is policy, statecraft, rather than soldiering, my lord. The Scots, the Covenant Scots, have fallen out with their English allies, with Cromwell and Fairfax and the Independents. They have been paid only half the price they bargained for the King – £200,000. The rest is withheld – not going to be paid, it is clear. Moreover, the Independents have rejected Presbyterianism – Cromwell will have none of it. That was to be the cornerstone of Argyll's Commonwealth of the two kingdoms – Presbyterian worship and government for both. So there is ill-will. We must turn it to the King's advantage. Do you not agree?'

'I await Lord Jermyn's superior understanding of statecraft, sir, to enlighten me as to how this unsavoury squabble between traitors and hucksters may serve the King?'

'Why, it is simple, I'd have thought. The true enemy is Parliament, Cromwell and the Independents, the rebels who hold the King prisoner. The Scots business is a mere nothing, by comparison. So – make friends with the Scots, and use them against the English rebels.'

'Make friends with the Scots?' Montrose searched the man's face. 'The Scots people are the King's friends *now*. His loyal subjects. Can it be . . . can you possibly mean to make friends with the Covenant leadership? Argyll? And the zealot ministers? Not that – you cannot mean that!'

'But yes. Why not? To make use of them against the King's enemies.'

'Dear God! Do you know what you say? *Use* Archibald

Campbell! You and your like ? Mercy of heaven – have you, and Jermyn, taken leave of your wits ?'

'I think you forget yourself, my lord!' Ashburnham said, haughtily. 'I am not accustomed to be spoken to so. Especially when on the Queen's business. This is not some camp of mercenary soldiers, in the Scottish wilds!'

'Then I beg your pardon, sir, if my disbelief offends you. I would offend no man, without cause. But – still I cannot conceive you to be in earnest in this.'

'And why not ? The Marquis of Argyll is an able and astute nobleman – if prejudiced. He will perceive advantage to himself and his Presbyterians in uniting with the King's forces against the English Parliament, which witholds his money. And, once the King is safely back on his throne, he can deal with the Presbyterian fanatics. As he has done before. And if Argyll and his faction will not co-operate, then be sure that the Duke of Hamilton and his *will*. Already he has set up a King's party in Scotland . . .'

'Hamilton, now!' James Graham had difficulty in breathing. Abruptly he turned and paced the length of the gallery and back before committing himself to speech.

'Mr. Ashburnham,' he said, tightly, 'Hamilton is only second to Argyll as the King's enemy and betrayer. He is a fool, where the Campbell is clever – but a dangerous fool. None, of any integrity, or plain sense, would trust him a yard!'

'You must not allow your personal humours and dislikes to sway you in matters of State, my lord Marquis,' the other reproved, raising his brows. 'We cannot all delight in those we work with.'

Somehow Montrose kept his Graham temper. 'Sir – would you work with one who had just *sold* your King, and his ? For money. And pocketed £30,000 therefor ? Dividing the forty pieces of silver with Argyll! And now weeps because another £30,000 is not forthcoming ? You would work with such ?'

'I would *use* such. On the King's service and behalf. Use them to fight the King's greater enemies. They will fight as well as the next, will they not ? Especially when led by a general so able as the Marquis of Montrose.'

'Which they will not be, I assure you, sir!' That was forceful, grim. 'I would no more consider working with these forsworn traitors than would they agree to be led by me. We are anathema to each other.'

'And if your monarch's interests demand it? And your Queen's commands?'

'See you, sir – how can I make you understand? Argyll is a shrewd man, utterly unscrupulous. Compared with him, you and Jermyn – aye, and my own self – are babes at breast! He has played a long, difficult and hazardous game to win to where he is now – ruler of Scotland. He has betrayed, tortured, slaughtered, as few men have ever done, to reach that goal. Think you he will allow *any* to use him now? Will not see through any manoeuvre that you, or I, might envisage? He would no more allow an invasion of England, on the King's behalf, than he would yield the style of *MacCailean Mor* to one of his clansmen. Argyll must be *defeated* before any such move may be attempted. Defeated in the field, and then before the Estates. And defeated soundly. Driven from Scotland.'

'Hamilton, then? The Duke.'

'Fails in all he touches. Save only in imposing on the King. And the Queen! Fails and betrays. Death to any cause. I would not work with him under any circumstances. That is final.'

'You are a harsh judge, my lord.'

'On the contrary. Others claim that I am too trusting. But these two are beyond all association.'

'There are others in the Covenant ranks. Even you, sir, will not call Lauderdale, Lothian. Lanark ...'

'They have sold their monarch once. They would do so again.'

'*You* would be there to ensure that they did not.'

'No, sir. I will not be there. Save with an army at my back. Now – enough. You know my mind. I shall not change it.'

'The Queen's Majesty will be much displeased.'

'Better that than betrayed, her husband's cause further violated. But – I will speak with Her Majesty on this. I ride on to the Louvre, Mr. Ashburnham ...'

CHAPTER FIFTEEN

There was need for haste now, Montrose recognised – for Ashburnham would not linger in getting back to Paris with his news and steps might well be taken to injure, or at least retard, his interests there. But an invited guest of a ruling prince could not just pack up and depart unceremoniously, and James Graham had to take his leave of the Archduke Leopold in due and proper fashion. This could not be done before noon next day – and meanwhile Ashburnham had a major start on the 200-mile road to Paris.

So, once they did win clear of Ghent, Montrose, Napier and Wishart – for Hurry had departed to sell his sword to the highest bidder, and the other exiles gone their own ways – settled down to sheer and sustained hard riding. It was almost like old days, exhilarating indeed, after too much hanging about and soft living, to stretch themselves, to test horse-flesh and their own endurance to the full. Over the flat, poplar-dotted plains and straight hedgeless roads of Flanders, Hainault and Picardy they raced, on and on through a fertile country-side still shamefully devastated by the long years of war, with ruin, neglect and havoc everywhere. Compared with Scotland, however, it was easy riding, the endless canals, ditches, and rivers with often damaged bridges the greatest obstacles. Darkness did not halt them, and they rode on through the night, only the weariness of their horses the limiting factor. By late afternoon of the second day they were riding down the forested reaches of the wide valley of the Oise.

At St. Denis, only four miles from Paris, Montrose sent Archie Napier on ahead, to the Louvre – but he himself slowed his pace only a little. A stratagem was necessary, he believed. If Ashburnham was still ahead, and hurried to inform his mistress that her commands and desires were being contested, Henrietta Maria, a proud and headstrong woman, might possibly refuse to receive her visitor – or her advisers might so sway her. Apart from his personal feelings in the matter, it would do his embassage no good if it was whispered round the Continent that the Marquis of Montrose had either been refused audience of his

Queen, or kept kicking his heels for any lengthy time before she would deign to see him. He must ensure, if at all possible, that this did not happen.

The magnificent royal palace of the Louvre, on the north bank of Seine, had not been occupied by the French royal family since the death of Louis XIII in 1643. His widow, Anne of Austria, mother of the child Louis XIV, had generously handed it over to her exiled sister-in-law with a monthly pension of no less than 30,000 livres, and here the so-called Court of England was set up in surroundings of almost unbelievable splendour, in vast premises and amongst a treasure-house of art, sculpture, tapestries and the like. Nevertheless, despite the pension, the innumerable occupants of this huge establishment were, by this 1647, not a little threadbare, if not tarnished. Henrietta conceived it her duty to maintain a large Court. Support for King Charles's cause amongst his fellow-monarchs of Christendom, she pointed out, would nowise be advanced by the presence of any seedy and second-rate household for his Queen and representative. She was the wife of the reigning monarch of one of the major States of Europe – not the widow of the ex-King of a small country, like her sister-in-law of Bohemia; and it was only suitable and consonant with her husband's dignity that she should maintain a worthy style and entourage. Moreover, she was a Daughter of France, sister of the late King Louis, and in France its princesses were expected to live in a fashion commensurate with the household of His Most Christian Majesty. Hence the princely pension. Unfortunately, Henrietta had always been extravagant however, and though she had in the past engaged in much money-raising for King Charles's cause – the object of her return to France – more and more her Court establishment ate up not only her revenues but also the hoard of jewellery she had brought her from England at an early stage of the Civil War – including the Crown Jewels. The value of that royal treasure had been enormous – King James had remarked at his daughter Elizabeth's wedding to the Elector Palatine in 1612 that he and his wife, Anne of Denmark, between them wore jewellery to the value of over £900,000. But all this was long since gone, and Henrietta was hard put to it to keep her establishment in the style she conceived necessary, much less to find funds for adventures in England and Scotland.

Nevertheless, superficially at least, impoverishment was by no means obvious – compared, for instance with Queen Elizabeth's little establishment at the Hague. In numbers of adherents, for one thing; scores, almost hundreds, of high-born but at present mainly impecunious courtiers decorated the Louvre's already over-decorative halls and salons, English and French, with their families and servants. Gaiety, colour and amusement by no means suffered, and were indeed even more in evidence than when the Court had flourished, at peace, in England. Henrietta Maria was a woman of spirit, although of a very different order from Elizabeth, and was not to be unduly depressed by circumstances. Her Court glittered, and if the glitter was apt to be more tinsel than solid specie, it corruscated but the more brittly brilliant.

Montrose knew enough of this to be prepared, and cautious. The last thing he desired was to antagonise this Queen. Elizabeth's entourage at the Hague was nothing to by go; its friendly, hospitable informality was unlikely to be paralleled by any other in Europe. Courts-in-exile were often the fiercest sticklers for form of any; and Henrietta's, on past performance, was more than likely to be of that order. In theory, he should not approach the royal presence without being summoned. She had, of course, invited him to visit her; but her later request for him to return to Scotland at once might be claimed to have countermanded that invitation. Nevertheless, he was Viceroy of Scotland, in name at least, and ambassador-designate, and as such surely had the *right* to approach the King's consort as one of her advisers. While sending Napier ahead to inform the Master of the Queen's Household of his arrival, therefore, he followed closely enough in the other's wake not to be halted by any hastily decided ban.

He had taken dress into consideration, likewise, and halted for a brief time at an inn on the outskirts of Paris, to change, not into Court dress deliberately, but into clothing sufficiently neat not to stand out offensively in evening company.

Nevertheless, when he entered the ornate portico of the magnificent quarter-mile-long façade of the Louvre Palace, ablaze with lights, and strode authoritatively past the uncertain guards into the first of the great reception-rooms, discarding his travelling-cloak, in the peacock brilliance of the seething, chattering throng his sober black-and-silver garb stood out like a daw's. He moved quietly but purposefully through the staring, painted, posturing groupings.

His purpose, of course, required that he should not now be

kept waiting for any lengthy period, at the royal displeasure, before all – although such of these people as spared him more than a disapproving glance probably assumed him to be a secretary or messenger somehow strayed into the wrong part of the palace, or possibly one of the musicians for the dancing which was in progress in the huge main gallery.

Where the thickest throng was, there he anticipated he would find the Queen. He was fortunate to arrive just as a cotillon was approaching its final measures, in the 300-foot-long pilastered and arcaded gallery under the coved, gilt and painted ceilings and the flashing crystal chandeliers, its blaze and colour reflected to infinity in vast ornate mirrors. Henrietta herself was treading it, at the far top end of the apartment, partnered by a florid, thick-set and fair-headed youngish man with a somewhat petulant mouth, who would have looked better dressed other than in yellow satin – an old acquaintance though scarcely a friend of Montrose's, the Lord Digby, heir to the Earl of Bristol and the former junior commander of royalist forces who had twice failed to come to Scotland. The high throne-like chair raised on the dais-platform at the head of the gallery was obviously where the Queen would make for at the end of the dance. James Graham worked his way thitherwards unobtrusively, as the final flourishes of the orchestra led up to a climax. It all could not have been much more convenient.

But, standing beside the throne, waiting with some evident impatience, was a very large and bulky gentleman, red faced, powdered-haired, dressed in maroon velvet with orange bows and garters and gold lace. Montrose knew this man also – Harry, first Lord Jermyn of St. Edmundsbury, Chamberlain and Master of the Household to Henrietta – and declared by many to be the Queen's lover, likewise. Their eyes met.

'Christ God – Montrose!' Jermyn gasped. 'Here! Already!'

'Greetings, my lord. Accept my belated congratulations on your, hm, elevation. Not unearned, I warrant!' That was smoothly said.

'But . . . damme, sir – my lord . . .' The other's rather prominent blue eyes goggled unhappily, He was superficially an amiable man, and lazy, an unlikely intriguer and meddler in State affairs; but since the Queen had so largely influenced the King, and Jermyn had long found himself in a position to influence the Queen, he had gradually achieved a power which seemed to sit but unsuitably on his massive but rather ungainly person. Now, although he was obviously much upset by the Graham's appearance upon the scene, he found it difficult to be authoritatively angry in the face of this proud interloper. He was the son only of a simple country knight, and was not at his best with such as Montrose.

'Yes, my lord?' the other encouraged, smiling gently – and thereby causing the greater unease.

'Did you not . . .? I sent Napier . . . I told him to tell your lordship that, that . . .'

'That Her Majesty would be happy to greet her principal adviser on Scottish affairs? I have, as you see, hastened to present myself to Her Majesty, as is right and proper, immediately on my arrival in Paris, straight from the saddle. I could do no less.'

'No, my lord Marquis.' Jermyn had partly recovered himself. 'That was not my intention. I sent the Lord Napier back to you, to inform you that it was not possible for Her Majesty to grant you audience. Not at present. Not yet. Until she has considered well. Considered your, your contumely.' The big man puffed. 'Your refusal to obey Her Majesty's specific commands. Reported to me only a short time ago. Scarcely believable, sir – but proved as accurate by your presence here. When you should be on your way to Scotland. I must request you to leave, my lord. To leave the palace at once. Until Her Majesty has had time to consider your situation.'

'You jest, sir! How can Her Majesty consider my, and the Scottish situation, when she is uninformed upon it? Is decision to be taken on Scotland, with Scotland's Lieutenant outside the door?'

'You are no longer Scotland's Lieutenant, my lord. And when the Queen requires your advice, she will send for it. You may not thrust it upon her. She has her advisers on Scottish affairs, never fear.' Those lack-lustre eyes which could look so sleepy darted their glance now towards the dance-floor. The music had ceased and the dancers were bowing. Henrietta Maria was making for the dais, on Digby's arm. 'Now – go, sir. And quickly. Her Majesty approaches.'

'I shall do no such thing. You cannot be serious, sir?'

'God's death, I am! Would you provoke a scene, in front of the Queen's Majesty, man?'

'My lord – I am here on the King's behalf, not the Queen's. In that cause I have made more than dance-floor scenes! I wish nothing such – but am prepared for it, and worse, if thereby His Majesty may be served. I bide.'

Jermyn bit fleshy lips, calculated how close was Henrietta and recognised that there was no time for further argument. He could scarcely summon minions to eject the Marquis of Montrose. All he could do was to step forward to warn the Queen, and put himself between her and the unwanted visitor.

Montrose anticipated just such move. He accordingly stepped out at the same time as the other, smiling, and side by side they paced together to meet the Queen and Digby, Jermyn's red, round face a study.

Henrietta Maria was a tiny and still vivacious creature of thirty-eight years, not beautiful although she had been pretty as a young woman, having too large a nose, heavy eyelids and features becoming a little gaunt; but she was undeniably attractive, despite much ill-health, and all the sorrows of her marriage and motherhood. She was now painfully thin compared with the last time Montrose had seen her, at Oxford four years earlier, having been grievously ill on her flight to France, with the birth of the Princess Henrietta-Anne and childbed-fever en route. But she could summon vigour and energy when she would, and her darkly imperious eyes could sparkle strangely under those misleadingly heavy lids. The dance's exertions had brought colour to cheeks already painted. Her visitor realised that she was *more* formidable, rather than less so, than on their previous encounters.

As she caught sight of him, she hesitated in her step – but only for an instant. She was a great lady, daughter of the renowned Henry of Navarre himself, and both by breeding and her training able to cope with the unexpected in better fashion than did such as Jermyn. She inclined her head very slightly, and spoke – but to Digby at her side, not to James Graham.

'My lord of Montrose, I see, has honoured our Court with his unexpected presence,' she said, her accent still pronounced but her words sufficiently clear, as clear as the intimation to all that he had come lacking her royal summons.

'Majesty – I come straight from the saddle to your presence,' Montrose said quickly, before Jermyn could speak. 'Forgive this attire. But, after so long, it was incumbent upon me to come and pay my respects and duty, at the first possible moment. As representing your royal husband's ancient kingdom of Scotland.'

'Madam – I tried . . .' Jermyn protested, but got no further.

The Graham had stepped the extra two paces forward, and dropping on one knee reached for and took the Queen's beringed hand, to raise it to his lips. Almost she seemed as though she would resist him, but did not actually do so – although she took the hand back quickly, all but snatched it indeed.

'We had anticipated that you would be on your way to Scotland, my lord,' she said shortly.

He rose, as quickly. 'The sooner that the King your husband's cause takes me back to Scotland, the happier I shall be, Your Majesty. But meantime you would not deny me a brief glimpse of the sun ? In my master's service it has been mainly cloud and storm which has been my lot. The opportunity to bask, even for a brief moment, in the presence of his renowned and fair consort was not to be missed. None will blame me for this, I think ?'

It was fulsome, courtier's stuff – but it had its effect. Unexpected from Montrose, it gave the Queen pause. And she was woman enough, and Frenchwoman, to be affected by the sheer beauty of this man and his winsome personality – wholly manly as these were. Allied to his dazzling reputation as a soldier and leader of men, plus the aura of tragedy which went with him, they added up to a total not readily cast aside by any woman.

Henrietta nodded, and moving over to her throne, sat down.

Montrose had been accepted at Court, after a fashion.

He was under no illusions, however, that he was welcome. He was not exactly shunned, thereafter, and was indeed the target for all eyes; but most people kept their distance, and such as greeted him did so briefly, formally, warily. The Queen was stiffly gracious, Digby civil but restrained, Jermyn pointedly ignored him now. The only Scot apparently present, at least in this great gallery, was none other than the Earl of Crawford, Major-General, whom Montrose himself had sent here from Scotland, as forerunner and envoy eight months before, at the King's suggestion – and who, judging by results, seemed to have been as unsuccessful diplomatically as he usually was militarily. He at least greeted his Captain-General affably, but with the sort of patronising effusiveness of the old hand for the new boy – which the other found very little to his taste. The Graham and the Lindsay, heads of two of the oldest lines in Scotland, had never found each other congenial company.

Montrose, having established his position and right, formed a base for future assault, recognised that this was no time to press his case. A strategic retiral was indicated, meantime, and a return at a more suitable moment for discussion of affairs. But Court procedure did not permit that he just up and left. Those with whom the Queen had spoken, or in any way close to her person, might not leave before her, save by her pleasure.

He sought to move close to the throne therefore – but Henrietta was now surrounded by a tight throng of her courtiers, male and female, chattering, laughing, posturing. Undoubtedly the Queen saw that he tried to win close enough to speak – but she gave no sign. He perforce had to wait.

James Graham was not an unduly impatient man – or, at least, he kept his tendency to impatience under close rein; and though proud, he was not prideful. But it taxed his self-control to the full to stand there humbly awaiting for a pause in the inanities and simperings and giggling, in order to take his leave. He told himself that this was a different world from his own, and since he had elected to enter it for the time being, he must adjust himself to it. But he found it hard.

The Court of Great Britain – or England, as it ignorantly called itself – in Paris, certainly was a different world from anything James Graham had known. When he had visited Court at Whitehall and at Oxford, he had been sufficiently disenchanted; but there, at least, the King's personally noble presence had had some restraining effect. Here, there seemed to be none. He recognised, of course, that this was un-Reformed France, not Presbyterian Scotland or even Cavalier England, where different standards applied; and that exiles, in the uncertainty of their future, often tended to a feverish gaiety and search for pleasure. But even making allowances, what he saw about him in this Louvre Palace shocked and dismayed him. License was the prevailing theme here, obviously, extreme depravity in dress, talk, manner and behaviour. Men were painted, powdered and prinked out much as were the women, perfumed, hair-styled, high-heeled, beribboned. Women's bosoms had been prominent enough at Whitehall, with peeping, rouged nipples the smart thing, but here breasts thrust or hung openly out of gowns which scarcely existed above the waist – and men handled and fondled them as they would. Skirts, though as voluminous as the men's breeches, were frequently split, dividing frankly; while others were almost wholly diaphanous, worn without shift or petticoats, revealing gartered silken stockings and bare flesh. Kissing, embracing and intimate caresses went on shamelessly in every alcove and bay amongst the erotic statuary, men with women, men with men, women with women. Wine flowed, drunken casualties of both sexes were dragged into corners, but the music and dancing went on, growing ever the wilder. Henrietta Maria, daughter of the depraved Medicis as well as of the gallant Navarre, had always been known as a fast and sensual woman who had shocked Charles's England – though oddly religious also, with her Jesuit confessor, Father Walter Montagu, ever nearby. It was a strange commentary on her doting husband's complex and at least superficially saintly character, that she had never seemed to shock him.

At length, James Graham could stand neither the scene nor the waiting any longer. It occurred to him, who was not rank-conscious, that in fact he was almost certainly the highest-ranking individual in that palace, next to the Queen herself; he had seen no one loftier than an earl – Crawford. Courteously but authoritatively, he stepped in, to move people firmly aside, right and left, ignoring the gasps and stifled protests, until he found himself once more at Lord Jermyn's bulky side and looking down on the Queen in her chair. Jermyn was speaking, and undoubtedly would go on doing so.

'Majesty,' Montrose said, not loudly but very clearly. 'The Lord Jermyn will forgive me, as I hope you will also, if I make so bold as to intervene. For only a moment. I will not claim seniority, in this – only his indulgence. To seek Your Majesty's permission to retire.'

Henrietta looked from one to the other of them, and said nothing. Jermyn cleared his throat, frowning, but doubtfully. That word seniority, from a marquis to a baron, was not lost on him.

'I have been in the saddle two days and a night, from Ghent, Majesty, coming here. And only came thus immediately, to present himself before you, my liege lord's lady, as in duty bound, and then to seek my couch. I am scarcely in a state to associate with the company I find around me. If I may retire – and seek Your Majesty's presence hereafter – I shall esteem myself fortunate.'

The Queen considered that curious assertion for a moment, and then shrugged her thin, bare shoulders. 'Very well, my lord. You may go. I bid you a good-night. I shall bring myself to overlook your desertion. Like your . . . *recalcitrance*!'

Their eyes met, dark brown and blue-grey, and each realised that the other was no mean opponent – but an opponent, certainly. Smiling faintly, slowly, James Graham bowed twice, once low, a second time two paces back, and briefly – and their eyes held. Then he turned and strode off through the rainbow throng.

In the outer vestibule, itself a palatial salon, he found Archie Napier asleep on a gilded bench and George Wishart pacing the marble floor anxiously.

'Come, my friends,' he said, 'Let us out of this shameful bordello and breathe some clean air! The cheapest inn in Paris will savour sweeter than this Louvre!'

'You were rejected . . . ?'

'No-o-o. Not rejected. But not accepted, either. Challenged, it may be. Aye, challenged. And sickened! That this should be the scene and centre of our liege lord's hopes! God save the King indeed!'

*　　　*　　　*

Montrose was right about the challenge. He had won the first round, by speed and strategy, with Henrietta and her friends; but that it was only the first round was soon made apparent. It was one thing to be accepted at Court; another to gain the Queen's private ear, or to attend on her as a counsellor. It quickly became obvious that Henrietta intended to play with him as a cat with a mouse; and was therefore equally obvious that she had little intention of giving him what he wanted, letters of accreditation for his ambassadorial tour. He applied, and reapplied, for a private audience – and was sent formally gracious acknowledgments and assurances that this would be arranged so soon as it was possible; but it was never arranged. Montrose discovered, if he had not realised it before, that nothing was more difficult than to obtain a personal interview with a queen who does not so desire. And his own nature and character militated against him in this – for he would not crawl and toady to her close associates, to try to arrange it; nor would he hang about in the corridors or gardens of the Louvre, indefinitely, like some wistful and consistently rejected suitor.

He did see, even spoke with, Henrietta Maria on not a few occasions, of course – but never when she was not surrounded by a protective circle of her courtiers. He even, in these circumstances, attempted some initiation of discussion as to his purpose in Paris – but made no progress at all in what was quite obviously a private and State matter unsuitable for public airing. Without being curt or rude, the Queen, on her own ground, was able easily to counter all his efforts.

If grievously and infuriatingly held up in his purpose, however, the man was not left neglected or forlorn elsewhere. His fame and renown seemed to be as greatly acclaimed in France as in other lands; and once it became known that he was in Paris, callers, invitations, honours, descended upon him in a flood. Only at the Louvre, it seemed, was he to be held at arm's length. Princes and great nobles sought him out and gave receptions in honour of the First Soldier of Christendom. Ambassadors of other States and Powers brought him glowing invitations to visit their countries and rulers. Deputations of the municipality, the Sorbonne, the Scots College, the officer-corps, learned societies and the like waited upon him, urging attendance at banquets and gatherings, asking him to address their members. He acceded to many, partly on policy, to make friends for the King's cause; partly because he had little else to do – and moreover was far from antisocial and normally enjoyed the company of his fellow-men, and partly in the hope that word of it all might in some way affect Henrietta in her enclosed, hothouse world at the Louvre.

If the last was in fact achieved, in any degree, no sign of it reached James Graham that spring of 1647.

He was much heartened and warmed, however, to receive a letter at the end of April from that other and so different queen, Elizabeth. She wrote in the most natural and affectionate terms, wondering how he fared, warning him now to escape the Paris ague, and playfully urging him to be on his guard against Frenchwomen, indeed all designing females – save only those at the Hague, whose designs were wholly either artistic or altruistic. Which led her to tell him that Louie's portrait of him was nearly finished and requiring only the sitter's return to give it the final touches – for which return the artist was as impatient as was her mother. She would forbear to comment on the work of art, since she was perhaps prejudiced in having her own picture of Jamie Graham which she conceived to be rather different from her daughter's perhaps. But it might be that she should warn him, in the by-going, that she had a notion that Louie might just possibly have fallen in love with her sitter – a dire matter for an artist, however unexceptionable in less rarefied and mature mortals.

She went on to inform him that she had had a letter from the

243

Emperor Ferdinand, in answer to her own, to the effect that he would eagerly welcome the Marquis of Montrose to his Imperial Court at Prague, and would pay as sympathetic attention to the Marquis's representations as was in his power. Also the warlike and valiant Elector Frederic William of Brandenburg had sent her word that he was prepared to consider allotting men and money for her brother's cause if the Marquis of Montrose would give him detailed information and surety as to its satisfactory employment – and that was *Protestant* aid. She added that her long-standing benefactor and 'landlord' Frederick Henry, Prince of Orange, had fallen seriously ill at the nearby Binnenhoff Palace, where his fifteen and a half year old daughter-in-law, Charles's and Henrietta's elder daughter Mary, was declared to be with child. The girl's brother, the young Charles, Prince of Wales, had arrived – allegedly not so much to comfort his sister during her trial as to try to get some money out of her father-in-law before he died, for the illness was said to be grave. Elizabeth confided that she found her seventeen year old nephew excellent company and a laughing cynic – but she would not trust him an inch! It was hardly his fault, of course, but there was too much of his grandmother's Medici blood in him for her taste. She ended by declaring that she was afraid that she was getting stout, and would certainly turn into a fat old woman very soon now – but was attempting to rumble away the noxious flesh with hard daily horse-riding – no hardship – tennis and archery – of little use – and sawing firewood for faggots – the best of all since it warmed one twice. She looked forward to instructing Jamie Graham in the saw just as soon as he could find his way back to the Hague.

James Graham cherished that letter more than he would admit, even to himself, reading and re-reading it. It helped to make up for so much. The bit about the Princess Louise caused him just a little unease; but, with all the rest, should probably not be taken too seriously, he assured himself. Almost at once he sat down to write a lengthy reply, pouring out his troubles, difficulties and frustrations to one whom he knew could perceive, understand and sympathise – perhaps the only one.

Though that might be unfair to George Wishart, Montrose was not the only writer busy in the modest Trois Plumes *auberge* where they had taken up residence. Wishart was nowadays almost consistently so employed, compiling something which he had begun some time before in a small way and was now tackling seriously – a book on the life and activities of his friend, hero and employer. When he first heard of this, James Graham was far from enthusiastic; but with Wishart pointing out that his enemies would most certainly seek to misrepresent him in every way, his motives, aims and behaviour, to the detriment of his cause as well as his personal honour and reputation, he began to see that there might be some point in it. Accordingly he submitted to much questioning, searching of memory and some embarrassment; and gradually the stack of paper had grown. Now, the first part, ending with his hero's departure from Scotland, was almost completed, and Montrose quite intrigued.

In May, as Montrose was becoming almost desperate about his affairs, there was a development which although at first it seemed just one more empty honour, might well hold the seeds of better things. A clerical messenger, a Vicar-General no less, called upon him at his inn, one morning, to request that the Marquis of Montrose, of his goodness, might honour the Archbishop-Coadjutor of Paris with his company at private dinner the following day. Surprised – for he had heard much of Monseigneur l'Abbé Jean François Paul de Gondi de Retz – James Graham accepted without hesitation. All knew that de Retz, whatever his reputation, held the key to the door of the corridors of power, in France.

So next evening, Montrose presented himself at the huge Archiepiscopal Palace, and was conducted to a small but richly furnished Moroccan-leather panelled chamber in a side-wing, where he found a tall, good-looking, flashing-eyed youngish man of approximately his own age, dressed in the height of fashion and with no hint of the ecclesiastic about him, indeed a dress sword at his side. The Vicar-General, however, introduced him as the Illustrious and Exalted Archbishop-Coadjutor of Paris.

'Greetings to today's reincarnation of the true Roman hero – born into a sadly degenerate world!' this extraordinary character cried, in highly exaggerated fashion, as though taking part in a theatrical masque. 'I am enchanted to meet the victor of a hundred battles, fought against the enemies of Christ!'

Montrose cleared his throat. 'Half a dozen, Excellency,' he amended flatly. 'And my opponents would debate with much vigour, aye and scriptural texts, as to which of us was Christ's enemy! I, the excommunicate, or they the Elect! But . . . I thank you for your courtesy.'

'It is my privilege, Marquis. But – you are young! So much younger than I had realised.'

The other almost said that the same thought had occurred to himself – but perhaps it was less than tactful to comment on an archbishop's youth whatever was the case with a soldier. Especially when one realised that the archbishopric had been obtained by other than normal promotion within the episcopate.

But de Retz went on, in flowery flood. 'Younger – but no less gallant, Monsieur – than I had anticipated. More so, I vow to God! Alas – I had feared the day of the hero dead!'

'The same God knows that I am no hero, Excellency,' James Graham contested, almost roughly for him – the effect of the other's dramatics on his Scots restraint. 'Merely a general, a reluctant general, who was fortunate in his fighting-men. And an unsuccessful one – or I would scarce be here, begging through Europe!' He bowed slightly, and he hoped, less ironically than he felt. 'For success, I had better look to you, Your Eminence.'

'Ha – say it not, Marquis! Eminence is only for cardinals – and I am not that. Not yet!' De Retz laughed gaily. 'Give me another year or two. Perhaps a grey hair, to go with a red hat! It looks the better. It looks the better, yes – especially to the ladies. And it is important to please the ladies, is it not ? Especially in France! And, perhaps, in the Netherlands also ?'

Montrose looked at this strange Archbishop quickly, at that, and recognised that there was shrewdness in those brilliant dark eyes, as well as dramatics and laughter and quick-silver changes of expression. There would be, of course, must be. For this slightly swarthy man-about-town of a cleric was not the second most powerful figure in France by accident. Of fairly humble and Italian stock – like Mazarin himself – he had risen by his own efforts, even though some criticised his methods, like all else about him. But it had not been the usual and easy way, by toadying to the Throne and Court intrigue. Unlikely as it might seem, de Retz was actually a reformer, a liberal, almost a radical, a leader of the liberal-reform party – which was to be called the Fronde, but not quiet yet – and which had campaigned against the undue assumption of power by the Throne, as represented by the late Cardinal Richelieu, to the hurt of Church, nobility and to some extent, people. He had been prepared to make himself unpopular with the highest power in the land, and won in that struggle. He had the great advantage, of course, of having as uncle the Archbishop of Paris; and with the old man's descent towards senility, had got himself appointed, first secretary, then Archbishop-Coadjutor, and gradually taken the archiepiscopal power wholly into his own capable hands – as David Beaton had done, in Scotland, a century before. This despite the fact that he had never wished to enter the Church, indeed had sought a military career more suitable in the son of a general of galleys. Not that he had let episcopal office, or political reforming fervour either, interfere unduly with his private life, as his many amours, affairs of honour settled by the sword, and uninhibited conversation testified. But all that only enhanced his popularity with the people of Paris, and so had the effect of strengthening his position in the Estates – whatever it did with his fellow-clerics. Cardinal Mazarin and he were known to hate each other. But it had come to this that it was only through co-operation with de Retz that Mazarin ruled France, in the name of the infant King Louis XIV.

'Success, Marquis, is relative, qualified and impermanent. Heroism is not,' the Archbishop-Coadjutor went on – and there seemed no doubt that he was speaking seriously. 'In a century – or half as much, perhaps – none will know *my* name. But yours will live for all time. No – not because you won battles. Others have done that, by the score – Wallenstein, Arnim, Tilly, Wrangel. But because you won by gallantry, against overwhelming odds, never counting the cost, leading all in person, sustaining all, doing the impossible. And, I heard, giving God the credit! For that the name of Montrose will never die.'

James Graham looked down, suddenly much moved. He had not thought that it was possible, with this seeming mountebank. But there was obviously much more to Jean François de Retz than appeared at first or second sight.

'I fear that you have mis-heard, Archbishop. Been wrongly informed.' he said. 'Or misinterpreted. Others, you see, think a deal less highly!'

'That I take leave to doubt, Monsieur. Others recognise your greatness – but may hate it. Men like yourself are often a menace to lesser men. And women! Never forget it. But, come – a glass of wine, before we eat. My shame, to have kept you standing thus . . .'

De Retz was not all praise and flattery. He proved to be keenly interested in strategy and military affairs, and knowledgeable too, asking pointed questions, and making accurate deductions from the answers. Also he was particularly concerned with the character, motives and activities of the Marquis of Argyll, whom he declared, he had been at a loss to understand. But, in due course, during an excellent repast, he came to the point of the invitation to this private dinner.

'I have been requested to approach you, Marquis, on your further intentions and employment,' he remarked, apropos of nothing. 'So eminent and talented a commander should not be having to kick his heels, dancing attendance on the whims of royal ladies, however charming! Here, or at the Hague.'

A hot retort almost sprang to James Graham's lips, especially at that last word. But he bit it back. He recognised that this man was probably as well informed as anyone in Europe; nor was he one for a penniless exile to offend.

'My further intentions have never been in doubt, Archbishop,' he said, instead, as calmly as he might. 'If attendance at Courts, Queen Henrietta's or others, is a necessary preliminary, then I must needs accept it. Meantime.'

'You mean, my friend, that you still think to try to build up an army, here on the Continent of Europe ? To go to the aid of King Charles ?'

'I do. Or, if not a full army, at least the equipment, munitions and officer-corps for a Scots army. And the money to pay for it. These were my master the King's commands.'

'No doubt. But – do you see them ever likely to be fulfilled, Marquis ?'

James Graham turned to look at him. 'If I did not, I would not be here.'

'But you are finding little success in your quest, I think ? And, I fear, will continue so to find. King Charles's cause is, shall we say, scarcely the most hopeful. Unfortunately. Not all would wish to risk supporting it.'

'It is my business, then, to convince them otherwise. I know better than most the possibilities of success, Excellency. Not in England, perhaps, at first. But in Scotland. Given some support, I can win back Scotland for King Charles – this I am sure. His ancient kingdom.'

'Perhaps. But, I think, not all to whom you appeal are interested in Scotland. England is the prize. Am I not right ?'

'That is the short-sighted view, if I may say so, Archbishop. Scotland is the first priority. Where the Stewart line belongs.'

'I think that *you* are not greatly concerned with the English throne, my friend? Others are. It is a score of times richer, is it not?'

'Richer? Richer in what, sir? Money? Gold? Numbers? Are these what matter? Or should it be the *kind* of throne, the quality and worth of it, the most ancient throne in Europe? In Scotland Charles is *Ard Righ*, High King. That is, in fact, King of Kings. Is there another in Christendom? Once there was, in Ireland, another land of our ancient Celtic race. But not now for long. Only in Scotland. England's throne is a later, less worthy, thing – a conqueror's. Scotland's a father's.'

The other was keenly interested, obviously. 'So you claim small Scotland's crown superior? To all others?'

'I do. Because it represents something superior. The King of Scots is just that – not the King of Scotland. It is important. He can never be a tyrant, as can, almost *must*, be other kings. For he is not only a king of kings; he must reign through, with and on behalf of his lesser kings. It is the patriarchal system, the father of the family, the chief of the clan – our Celtic heritage. It has been Charles Stewart's great loss and failing that he did not understand it. His father did, however little he loved Scotland. And all his forefathers. He, Charles, must learn it again.'

'Fascinating, Marquis. I knew nothing of this. Tell me – who are these lesser kings? In Scotland. Where does one find them?'

'You need not look far, Archbishop. One sits at your side! The lesser kings are the earls of Scotland. Not perhaps the new earls, of whom Charles has made over-many, after the English pattern. A mistake. Proof that he does not understand. As, indeed, he made me marquis. And Hamilton duke. Alien, all but meaningless titles, in Scotland. The ancient Earls of Scotland, and certain great chiefs such as the Lords of the Isle, descended from the former mormaors – these are the lesser kings to *Ard Righ Albann*. Whose duty was, and is, to guide, advise, support and rule with the High King of Scots, for the good of the whole people and community of the realm. Not for the power of the throne. Do you understand?'

'I think that I do, yes. And a noble concept. I do not wish to dispirit you, Marquis. Nor to cause you offence. But it is my belief, from what I know and hear, that you will not be successful in your project. Even amongst those from whom you would most look for help. They do not seek adventures, change. And such as might move have their eyes set on England. Moreover you are unfortunately beset by the jealousy of smaller men.

249

Forgive my plain speaking. But it would be wise to look facts in the face. As a commander ever must.'

The Graham waited.

'Matters may improve – who knows? Much will depend on Charles himself. How he comports himself with this Cromwell and the English Parliament. But – an invasion of England is out of the question. And of Scotland, I fear, few see the advantage. Meantime, the greatest soldier in Europe is . . . *désœuvré*. Unemployed! Save as an unsuccessful importuner. Almost a beggar – shame as this is. Do I speak too plain, Marquis?'

'I prefer plain speech, sir. But – I am prepared to go on begging. That I may fight the better hereafter.'

'Spoken like Montrose! But why be a beggar? Why be humiliated when you should be raised to the heights you deserve?' De Retz paused. 'I have been authorised to sound you as to certain suggestions, my friend. I am but an intermediary, in this. But the offers are authoritative – that I assure you.'

'Offers, Archbishop? Suggestions? For my cause?'

'For your person, Marquis. Meantime. In the service of France. High service.'

'But . . . I am grateful. But how should that help my master?'

'It is *you* whom we would honour, Marquis, rather than your monarch. But I think it would do his cause no harm to be represented by one highly placed in the service of France.'

'You are kind. But . . .'

'Wait, Monsieur. Hear what is proposed. Firstly, that you should be made Lieutenant-General of the Army of France – a command, my friend, not just an honour. Command over all the Mareschals-of-the-field. Secondly, that you should be, not only commander of the *Garde Ecossais* but general of all the Scots soldiers in France – and, as you know, there are many. Your *private* command. Thirdly, that you be appointed Captain of the Corps of Gentlemen-at-Arms, so placing you ever close to the French throne. And this, my friend, carries a statutory annual payment of 12,000 crowns, with a pension over and above! Lastly, in a year's time – since it could not, by regulation, be done before – you to be appointed Mareschal of France, and Captain of the King's Guard.'

Speechless, Montrose stared at him.

'Is it a fair offer – for one of the lesser kings of the Scots?'

'You . . . you cannot be serious?' his hearer got out. 'Not . . . all this!'

'But, yes. The suggestion comes from, shall we say, the highest source. As indeed it would have to.'

'Mazarin? This is scarcely to be believed. So much. So great a position. For a foreigner. And outsider . . .'

'Scarcely that. The Auld Alliance is not yet forgotten, Marquis. The Scots have always held an especial position here in France. And the privilege would be France's. To possess the greatest soldier in Christendom.'

That word possess brought James Graham up with a jerk. It was not intended in any derogatory way, nothing is more certain – but it was significant. It put all into perspective, brought Montrose abruptly out of his euphoria.

'I thank you,' he said. 'And he who instructed you. From the bottom of my heart. For a most signal honour, undeserved. But – no, sir. My sincere regrets – but it cannot be. I am sorry, but I must refuse. Refuse all.'

The other leaned over to search his guest's face closely. 'You say so? Take longer to think of it, my friend. This is no matter for instant decision. Think well.'

'There is no need, Archbishop. No choice, indeed. I am King Charles's servant, only. I cannot transfer my allegiance to the King of France. Or any other. My service must be to my own High King, and he in need. You must perceive it. I am honoured far beyond my deserts – but I have no choice.'

The Archbishop-Coadjutor let out his breath in a long sigh, almost a whistle. 'So-o-o! I was right. I told the Cardinal – the Marquis of Montrose is incorruptible! I said that I feared that you would not have it. That is why he would have *me* put it to you. Not himself. He, the Minister of the Crown, could not have a refusal, you understand. So – I was right. But I am sorry, nevertheless. I know no other who would have refused so great an offer. That is why it *was* so great. The Cardinal believed none could refuse so much. Why – the Captaincy of the King's Guard alone is a position the highest in the land will pay 150,000 crowns to fill!' He smiled. 'All the more reason for Montrose to refuse it, eh?'

The other shook his head. 'I would not have you think me prudishly pretentious, sir. Puritanical. But when so much hangs in the balance, for King Charles and for Scotland, I cannot involve myself in other matters, however flattered I feel. You understand?'

'I understand – and admire the more. I only wish

that I could aid you in your great and unpromising task.'

'Perhaps you can, Archbishop – if you will?'

'Try me, Monsieur – so be it that it is in my power.'

'I wish to have private speech with the Queen. Yes, my *own* Queen! For though I should be her adviser, she will not see me alone, or even in council. As I think you know well?' As de Retz nodded, he went on. 'It occurs to me that you, or the Cardinal, might arrange it. Of your kindness. *Outside* the Louvre. I need my letters of credence, and time passes. If I am to achieve anything for the King. His wife is badly advised, God knows. If I could but gain private speech with her. Some function to which we were both invited, perhaps? She depends much on the goodwill of France . . .'

The Archbishop-Coadjutor nodded. 'Leave it with me, Monsieur. I will see what may be done. I think the Cardinal will be sympathetic – although disappointed. Though whether such speech will serve you anything to the point, I doubt. But we can try . . .'

CHAPTER SIXTEEN

James Graham was on his travels again, and thankfully, his accreditation, signed and sealed by Henrietta Maria, in his pouch. But it had taken a long time. The Archbishop-Coadjutor de Retz had been as good as his word, and with Cardinal Mazarin's help had engineered an interview between Montrose and his Queen – not indeed in private, but at a great banquet in the Archiepiscopal Palace. Each summer, the Queen Regent, Anne of Austria, removed with her small son and Court to the Palace of Fontainebleau, and Queen Henrietta, with her entourage, to St. Germain-en-Laye, to avoid the heat and smells of Paris. To as it were celebrate this annual departure for the country, the Cardinal had invited the two queens to this farewell entertainment – with Montrose as extra guest-of-honour, but this only divulged at the last moment. He had been ushered in, with trumpets, to a great ovation, only when all the other guests, including the two royal ladies, were already seated, eulogised in a welcoming speech – to his supreme embarrassment – by the swarthy Italianate Mazarin, and then led forward to take his seat beside his Queen. It had all looked natural and uncontrived – and Henrietta could by no means object. Especially with the Queen Regent present and applauding, and Mazarin, her host, in a position to stop her French pension and use of the royal palaces – for he guided Anne in all things. Actually, after an initial stiffness, they had got on fairly well together. Henrietta, true Frenchwoman, was a realist, and no doubt recognised that with such powerful friends any further overt offence to the Graham would be injudicious. Perhaps she allowed herself to savour, just a little, her fellow-guests, undoubted attractiveness to her sex. At any rate, they had conversed amicably enough throughout an interminable repast of no fewer than fifteen courses, interspersed with entertainments; and though it was hardly the occasion for discussion of policies or strategy, the man had managed to say most of what he wanted. She had listened, sounded even gracious, if non-committal towards his needs and requests, and he believed that he had made some impression.

She was not a woman that he could understand, or even like; but he was prepared to accept that she had her qualities, even though her ideas and loyalties were very different from his own. He had at least gained from her an undertaking to let him have the long-awaited and necessary credentials.

Fulfilment had taken a long time, even so. The removal to St. Germain and consequent upheaval and holiday spirit, plus the subsequent round of distracting country pursuits and visits, riding, hunting, hawking, picnics, pageants and the like, all served to delay. Montrose would have been wholly out of patience again, had it not been that a letter from Queen Elizabeth informed that Prince Rupert was intending to visit his aunt and seek her aid, plus official French aid, in his building up of a fleet to help King Charles's cause. A joint assault on Henrietta Maria, with so potent an ally as Rupert, was worth waiting for. But unfortunately Rupert had not come. At length, James Graham had got his papers – though no promise of money for his army, or indeed any firm commitment of active support. He had requested permission to leave Court there and then – and was granted it a deal more promptly than any other requests of his.

So now, at last, he was doing what Charles had sent him to do, after all the wasted months, making a tour of the States and Courts of Europe, a selective tour.

It was a strange progress, by any standards, an absurd mixture of welcome and rejection, of personal success and causal failure. He left George Wishart behind in Paris to finish his book and superintend the printing and publication thereof – which, he had come to recognise, might well prove a useful weapon of propaganda – and with Archie Napier for company made first for Protestant Geneva. But the democratic Swiss, though greatly admiring of Montrose the Victor, would have admired him more were his pockets full of gold. Moreover, they had little interest in saving monarchs, their history being concerned almost wholly with keeping all such at bay. Though notable purveyors of mercenary fighters, rivalling Scotland herself in the commodity, the Swiss demanded cash down for such aid, and certainly were not prepared to subsidise applicants, however illustrious. If the Marquis of Montrose came back with a full purse, they would not fail him. Meanwhile they commended him to Calvin's God.

On through the other cantons of the Swiss Confederation he travelled, experiencing similar receptions, flanking the Bernese

Oberland by the upper Rhone valley, climbing the St. Gotthard Pass and down the Vorder Rhein into the Tyrol. This was Austria, Catholic and in the domains of the Emperor. Montrose had heard that Ferdinand was here, but this proved to be false, and Vienna his goal. But he took the opportunity of approaching the princely and ducal rulers of this part of the Empire in the by-going – and was everywhere received with enormous respect and consistent acclaim, a triumphant succession calculated to turn the head of anyone less used to disappointment than was James Graham. But nowhere could he arouse the least enthusiasm for King Charles's cause. Sympathy with his plight, yes; outrage at upstarts and traitorous subjects, who could thus treat a crowned monarch; acknowledgment that here was a highly dangerous precedent and warning for other rulers. But possible involvement, commitment, no.

It was the same at Munich and Ratisbon, in Bavaria, whither he went on his way to Vienna. The elderly Duke Maximilian of Wittelsbach, with whom Elizabeth of Bohemia had been in touch – although he, as leader of the Catholic League had been mainly responsible for driving her and her husband out of Bohemia in 1619 – greeted Montrose like a long-lost brother, and conferred on him the Order of St. Hubert, to add to the others he had collected, but remained dumb as regards aid and offered not one penny to the campaign-chest.

Jean François de Retz had been right.

At Vienna also he drew a blank – although he was given a civic welcome. The Emperor Ferdinand seemed to rattle about his vast domains like a weaver's shuttle, and had now gone to his winter palace at Prague. Since the Emperor's help and influence with all the lesser rulers could be enormous, possibly decisive, and Montrose was getting desperate, he set out forthwith to travel the further 150 miles northwards. He was already 650 miles from Paris, and the harsh winter of Central Europe upon him.

On the fourth day after leaving Vienna, with a messenger gone on before, and the beautiful and famous walled city of Prague, in its vast amphitheatre ahead, James Graham was brought the extraordinary news that the Emperor himself had come out to meet and receive him. And in due course, at the end of the magnificent sixteen-arched and towered bridge over the Moldau, with the tiered city rising behind, Ferdinand and much of his Court stamped about in the snow beside huge bonfires lit to warm them, waiting to greet the Hero of Scotland, an honour to put all others in the shade.

Ferdinand was much more Germanic in appearance than his brother Leopold, a big, bull-necked, solidly built man of forty, inclining to fatness, beside whom Montrose looked slight and slender. He threw his arms around his guest, embracing him before all, and then took him on his own sled over the bridge with its serried statues and through the narrow crowded streets lined with cheering citizens, to climb to the vast palace-castle of Hrads on its ridge, almost a city in itself, where all 440 of its rooms appeared to be ablaze with light. Debating with himself the reason for this so flattering reception, Montrose sought to keep his hopes from rising too high. No doubt there would be a price to pay. And, of course this was again *Catholic* support, next to the Pope the most Catholic of all, the Holy Roman Empire. He acknowledged to himself, however, that he was reaching the stage where he would clutch at *any* support, so long as it was in more than words.

He was not kept long in doubt as to the Emperor's reasons for all this enthusiasm. The very next day, at a great banquet which followed a review of troops, at which Montrose had stood by Ferdinand's side to take the salute, the Emperor, now just a little drunk, after toasting his honoured guest and brother-in-arms as the most successful general since their own much-lamented Wallenstein, announced his immediate appointment to the Order of the Golden Fleece, the most sought-after decoration in the world. He also declared that he intended to make the Marquis of Montrose an honorary citizen by creating him a Count of the Holy Roman Empire. And this – Ferdinand turned, staggering just a little, and jerking a stiff bob – would in turn make him eligible to receive the highest honour that it was in the Emperor's power to bestow. He would receive the baton of a Marshal of the Empire. The Emperor repeated that, beaming – a Marshal of the Empire. And then added, very slightly slurring his consonants, that he would then have the greatest strategist in Christendom in his ranks – and where would those French condottieri, Turenne and Condé, be then ? Chasing their tails back to Paris ! Long live the Empire's new Marshal !

As the roar of applause burst out, and continued, and Ferdinand sat down beaming, James Graham stared set-faced before him. So that was it ! Those last two sentences, added no doubt only because wine had loosened the imperial tongue, revealed all. And not only this present 'honour'. As in a flash he saw what had really been behind Mazarin's equally flattering offers in Paris – and which, in his own simplicity of mind, had never occurred to him. These great powers, the Empire and France, were not really concerned to honour him, the man, at all. They were at each other's throats, in this unending state of war, and each had seen in the unemployed soldier James Graham, with his reputation for strategy and successful tactics, a means of stealing a march on the other. He was but a pawn in this power-game, this struggle for the hegemony of Europe – for the Thirty Years War had developed into that, between the Empire and France, rather than the religious struggle between Catholicism and Protestantism with which it had started. He was not being given ovations for what he had done for King Charles, but bargained for as a useful weapon. And, by the same token, the last thing either side would wish would be to see him disappear back to Scotland with an army. What an innocent he had been!

Nevertheless, it was necessary that the honoured Marquis of Montrose should get to his feet, there and then, and express his thanks, his sense of deep and humble gratitude, for these signal, indeed unheard-of marks of favour being shown to him – for this was not an offer, like Mazarin's, but a bestowal, an edict not a suggestion, and public refusal was unthinkable. In fairish German – for he had always been good at languages – he expressed his appreciation, although without saying anything about actual military service. And all the time he was sick at heart.

He retired to bed, long afterwards, in the magnificent quarters allotted to him in the Castle of Hrads that night, Golden Fleece, Count and Marshal of the Empire notwithstanding, a saddened and a wiser man. Would he ever, indeed, return with an army to save Scotland from Argyll and for his King?

*   *   *

When the weather eased somewhat, one influence more than any other detained James Graham in Prague. This was the Emperor Ferdinand himself, the man's character, and the stirrings of hope it offered Montrose. For he proved to be a fairly simple man, and friendly, almost childlike in some things, something of a hero-worshipper. He had been a soldier himself before he succeeded his father in 1637, indeed had nominally won a great victory over the Swedes at Nordlingen in 1634, having succeeded the murdered Wallenstein as imperial generalissimo – although

Count Matthias of Gallas was the true victor. Since he ascended the throne he had not lead troops in person. But his admiration of Montrose, as a general, was at least informed and sincere, knowing in fact no bounds. A friendly tussle developed between these two, on one side to manoeuvre the new Marshal into actual command in the field, and so to challenge the French; on the other, to avoid anything of the sort, and at the same time gain concessions which would aid the Scots' cause. It was inevitably a prolonged process – but since Montrose clearly had the stronger character and the nimbler brain, he grew steadily the more hopeful. Nor did he see that he could be more usefully employed elsewhere, in the prevailing circumstances.

So he accompanied the Emperor that spring of 1648, when the snows would let them, in the eastern part of the imperial domains, visiting armies, garrisons and strategically placed rulers – all with hunting, sport and varied junketing as ostensible primary purpose. The war situation had been quiescent for some time, although this last year or two the Empire had done but poorly militarily – in part the reason for Montrose's enthusiastic welcome undoubtedly. But as spring wore on, signs of renewing hostilities were not lacking. By May Turenne and the Swedish General Wrangel were advancing from southern France into Bavaria, and presently achieved a major victory over the imperial forces under Count Melander of Holzappel, at Zusmarhausen. The Elector Maximilian of Bavaria came in flight to Prague. Suddenly it was no longer hypothetical but actual war – and Montrose found himself liable to be caught up in it, willy-nilly.

It went against the grain to seem to desert the Emperor just as danger threatened, and moreover he needed a skilful strategist as never before. But to become actively involved in this massive struggle, which meant nothing to him, would not only have been contrary to his principles but fatal for King Charles's cause – as well as anathema to all Protestants. Moreover, the fighting would in fact be mainly against the French, which was out of the question for Montrose. The Emperor, with Maximilian, marched south to Linz on the Danube, there to threaten the invaders' flank in Bavaria. And there, at last, James Graham went to him and finally told him that, with his gracious permission, he must leave. He could on no account allow himself to appear to be in arms against his master's wife, a French princess, with the royal Court of Great Britain on French soil. He was sorry, but the time had come to part.

In the end, Ferdinand took it in good part, Montrose having established a considerable ascendancy over him. Probably he had seen it coming. Recognising realities, he agreed, made a fine ceremony of presenting the crimson baton of the Empire to his departing Marshal at the castle of Linz, on the 12th of June; and followed it up, at last with what the other had been angling for for so long – the imperial written authority to raise troops under his own command, and to appoint his own colonels and other officers therefor. Clearly neither Austria, Bohemia nor Bavaria was the place to attempt this – but Ferdinand gave him a letter to his brother the Archduke Leopold, in the Netherlands, where there was a large army, with many mercenaries, remote from the present theatre of war and convenient for shipping to Scotland. Leopold would help.

Grateful, and feeling almost absurdly guilty, James Graham took his leave, at last – leaving behind, as his considered advice to his imperial friend that he would be wise to conclude a truce, if not a full peace, with the forces invading Bavaria, just as soon as possible. Before matters got worse. He believed, in fact, that the Emperor could not win.

Feeling like deserters, he and Archie Napier set off actually eastwards from Linz, through Moravia to Cracow on the Polish Marches, to make northwards thereafter, for Danzig. A Swedish army was known to be now threatening the northern German States, and was liable to make travel exceedingly difficult. Montrose would seek to avoid it, and other complications, by skirting eastwards, to make for Denmark. There he would try to keep Christian to his promise regarding shipping. Then by sea to the Spanish Netherlands and the Archduke Leopold.

At last, it almost looked as though he might be getting somewhere. It was his belief that Ferdinand would be forced to make peace, and fairly quickly, to prevent further losses to his Empire. By the time that he himself reached Leopold, the war might well be over – with consequently many soldiers suddenly available for new employment. If only he had the moneys he ought to have, to hire them . . .

CHAPTER SEVENTEEN

The familiar hammer-blows of fate recommenced for James Graham. At Danzig, he learned that Christian of Denmark's illness had proved fatal. The old King had died at Copenhagen on the last day of February. Montrose grieved for the harsh old warrior whom he had come to look upon as a friend; and he was anxious for his cause. The new monarch was Christian's middle-aged son Frederic III, an unknown quantity of no pronounced character, of whom his father had spoken little. He had spoken much, however of his son-in-law Korsitz Ulfeldt, the Lord High Steward, a strong and ambitious man who dominated the Rigsraad, or Parliament. All said that there would be troubles in Denmark. If even Christian had been lukewarm about aid for his nephew Charles, was the new regime likely even to go so far?

Nevertheless they sailed, as planned, from Danzig port, arriving at Copenhagen in high August. They found Frederic amiable, but a weak man compared with his sire – and already moreover shorn of much of his authority, Ulfeldt having played upon the nobles and Rigsraad to unite and to compel the new monarch to accept much reduced powers. Montrose was well received; but it was clear from the first that hopes of substantial aid must be scaled down, and any idea of a sizeable fleet of ships could be abandoned – unless money was forthcoming to hire them commercially. Frederic had difficulties enough of his own, without rushing to his cousin's rescue. Montrose felt compelled to offer, in the circumstances, the termination of the very useful salary which Christian had conferred upon him – which offer was accepted.

James Graham's reaction was controlled. Control was, indeed, becoming almost the dominant factor in this man's life – an unnatural state in which he himself recognised the dangers of rigidity, of atrophy. Moreover, only half of his mind was engaged, concerned. For other letters either awaited him, or caught up with him, at Copenhagen. One of them informed him that Magdalen was dead.

The effect of this news upon him was greater than might have been anticipated. For long his wife had been detached from him, emotionally as well as physically, and indeed more or less withdrawn from the whole business of living. The final break could scarcely come as a great surprise. The letter bringing the tidings was from his father-in-law Southesk, who wrote curtly, giving no details other than using the phrase that she had 'lost all will to live', and had died in the spring. There should have been nothing of shock in this. And yet, James Graham was shocked. Those words bit deeper probably than the writer knew. The reader did not fail to ask himself – if Magdalen had lost the wish to live, whose fault was it ? Only his own, surely. They had been joined together, man and wife, one entity before God. And one of them had chosen to die. The other could not escape the indictment. However ill-matched, however little she had seemed to try to conform herself to him and his way of life, his career, his fate, he had almost certainly failed her. And so, basically, was responsible for her death at the age of thirty-two. That he had also, to some extent, been responsible for their son Johnnie's death, after Inverlochy, was a recognition which he had never sought to blink. Added to this, it was a thought which wakened him of a night, sweating. Also, he had been, in a fashion, responsible for the deaths of so many others, foes, soldiers, friends – this was grievous burden enough, though one any leader or commander in the field had to carry. But this of his wife was different. Even Johnnie had not *blamed* him – however entitled he might have been to do so. But undoubtedly Magdalen had done so. She had said as much.

If, at the back of his mind, there was the recognition of a new freedom, some kind of relief that that chapter was for the time being closed, it was overlaid not only by the feeling of guilt but by sheer sorrow, sadness, for the withered and spoiled life of the comely girl he had married.

News of his master, as well as of his wife, awaited Montrose in Copenhagen. In November, Charles had effected his escape from detention at Hampton Court, unwisely as it now seemed, and fled to the Isle of Wight, en route for France. There, for some reason, he had committed himself to one Colonel Hammond, governor of the royal castle of Carisbrooke. But Hammond was a kinsman of Oliver Cromwell himself, and had detained the King. So now he was a closer prisoner than ever, at Carisbrooke, and in worse case; for while there he had entered into negotiations with Scots emissaries, and the terms he was alleged to have agreed with these, anent the imposition of the Covenant and Presbyterianism to both kingdoms, had infuriated the English Parliamentarians. There was even wild talk of bringing the King to trial for treason against his English realm, as though that were possible.

Montrose groaned for his sovereign lord. Had he no one with any wits or wisdom to advise him?

James Graham had been in Copenhagen only a few days when another Scots visitor arrived in Denmark – William Hay, 3rd Earl of Kinnoull, once Viscount Dupplin, who had joined Montrose after Tippermuir and thought better of it after Fyvie and before Inverlochy. Now, apparently he could stand Covenant-ruled Scotland no longer. Having heard that Montrose was about to invade England with a great army and fleet, from Denmark, he had come to participate.

'Invade England, Will? Are you out of your wits!' The Graham stared at his visitor. 'What nonsense is this?'

'Why, James – is it nonsense, then?' Kinnoull was a stocky, stolid man of early middle years, rather like one of his own Perthshire bulls. He shook his head now, as though to clear it. 'All Scotland resounds with it. And England too, they say. All have heard how great has been your reception by these foreigners. All the crowned heads of Europe showering titles on you, making you marshal, general, offering you men, guns, ships, whatever you seek. Cromwell himself, a curse on the man, has moved his troops, they do say, to East Anglia, to repel your descent upon London. Myself, I'd liefer you came to Scotland, but ...'

'Save us – Cromwell is no such fool, I'll swear! Dear God, I'm in no state to invade the Isle of May! You see there my sole following – Archie Napier! I have no army, no ships. Titles, honours, yes, but nothing that I can grasp. Not yet. Heaven knows, it is not for want of trying. But this Europe has its own troubles ...'

'My God – it is all nothing, then? Wind! Fables! Your success ...?'

'Scarce that, sir!' Napier put in, warmly. 'My lord Marquis has everywhere been received as in a Roman triumph. Hailed, saluted, garlanded. He has the Emperor's authority to recruit, as Marshal ...'

'But no recruits, as yet, Archie! Nothing to show but a marshal's baton – and an empty purse! Not what my lord came to Denmark to find. I am sorry, Will, that you – and so many others, it seems – have been misinformed . . .'

'Sink me – all Scotland has, James. Even the Estates. Argyll himself. I do not believe that he would ever have allowed the Engagers to have their way, had he not believed it was better so than your invasion. He would never have let them go to Carisbrooke – no, nor to the Queen, either – without the threat of your sword constraining him. And it is all . . . nothing!'

'Argyll, you say, believes this? And this of engagers? Who engages? And what?'

Kinnoull stared. 'Do you not know, James? The Engagement. Hamilton, Lauderdale and the rest?'

'I heard Hamilton was seeking to form some new party in Scotland, supposedly favouring the King – but we know Hamilton's favours! Is that what you mean?'

'No, no. It grew out of it, yes. They called themselves the Moderate Covenanters. When the King escaped to this Carisbrooke, they realised that he would never agree with the English Parliament. So they sent emissaries to Charles there – Loudoun, the Chancellor. Lanark, Hamilton's brother. And Lauderdale...'

'Loudoun! But he is a Campbell. In Argyll's pocket!'

'Aye – Argyll ever keeps a road of escape open! As you know well. So, although against these others, he set Loudoun with them. And they came to an agreement with the King. This was at last Yule. It was agreed that Charles should impose the Covenant on England. Impose Presbyterianism as the religion there, for at least three years. And ban all sectaries, the Independents. In return, the Scots would urge on the English Parliament the King's release and restoration to the throne – and if they would not have it, invade England from Scotland, on the King's behalf. That was the Engagement. Covenanted Uniformity, they call it – that is the goal.'

'Sweet March! You are not telling me . . . you do not say that any man could believe in any of this! Back to the old folly. The Solemn League and Covenant again. Impose Presbyterianism on the English, against their wishes! Charles – and the Scots! Ban the Independents – and Cromwell an Independent! God save us – invade against Cromwell's New Model Army!'

'It is true. Those were the agreed terms. Secret, of course. But they leaked out . . .'

'I swear they did! I swear Argyll sent a galloper with them, hot-foot to his friend Cromwell! Loudoun agreed to this madness, you say ? Then it would be only to betray it.'

'Perhaps. It split the Estates, anyway. In a larger parliament than there has been for years. Over fifty lords alone.' Kinnoull coughed, but did not declare that, obviously, he himself had attended and voted. 'In March, it was. They won a great majority. All thinking to aid the King. Then they sent envoys to the Queen and the Prince of Wales, in Paris . . .'

'Ha! So that was it. When was this ?'

'April, it would be.'

Montrose exchanged glances with his nephew. 'April! And we were there, in Paris. We did not leave until June. Were not told of their presence at Court. Kept out!' He took a deep breath. 'This was Hamilton, eh ? Ever the Queen favoured him. But – what came of it ?'

'Why, the invasion. Invasion of England. In July. Hamilton's invasion. The Kirk and Argyll were against it, but the Estates gave him permission . . .'

'If Argyll was against it, he could have stopped it. But did not ? Then he saw a way of getting rid of Hamilton!' James Graham groaned aloud. 'So – they actually did it ? Marched into England. Under Hamilton ? That under-witted clothes-horse! With whom, as general ?'

'Himself as general. Callander second-in-command. Baillie as chief-of-staff. Middleton as master-of-horse. Ten thousand men . . .'

'Middleton ? He, at least, should have known better. How far did they get ?'

'To Preston, only. In Lancashire. The English royalists did not rise, as hoped for . . .'

'Can you wonder at it ? To have Presbyterianism imposed upon them!'

'Langdale, from Cumberland, only. With a small force. Hamilton split his army – why, I know not. Callander and Middleton, with the horse, rode on to the south, to Wigan. Cromwell came up, over the hills from the east, and fell on Hamilton. It was a complete rout. Thousands died. Hamilton surrendered. He is still a prisoner. It was disaster.'

'So-o-o!' Montrose shook his head, helplessly. 'Every move of it could have been foreseen. The sorry folly of it! And the King in worse case than ever, in consequence. What happened to Callander and Middleton ? The rest of the Scots ?'

'They won back to Scotland, in due course. Without battle. Just ahead of the man Cromwell himself.'

'Cromwell? You mean – he invaded Scotland, then?'

'No, no. Not that. He came alone. A private visit. To see Argyll. They got on very well, it is said.'

'I vow they did! They are hand-in-glove, those two – the King's greatest enemies. I doubt not but that it was all planned between them. Argyll got rid of Hamilton, and Cromwell got rid of the Scots threat. And has a further charge against the King. And Queen Henrietta, if she supported Hamilton, has no doubt thrown away on him what moneys she could raise. It is hardly to be believed that there could be so much of foolish incompetence and error.'

'If only they had listened to *you*,' Napier burst out. 'The King's Captain-General and Viceroy! And the only soldier who could have out-fought Cromwell. Yet they turned their backs on you. Why? When the rest of the world unites to do you homage?'

None attempted to answer that rhetorical question.

'So now all wait for you to invade England,' Kinnoull ended. 'It is believed that you have a great mercenary army. All Scotland believes it. And – you have not!'

There was silence in that room of the Rosenborg Castle, as three peers of Scotland contemplated the unhappy state of their native land.

*   *   *

Montrose was going to Gothenburg, across the Kattegat, in Sweden, to seek out, not official aid – which could hardly be looked for with Christina now at active war with the Empire – but the private help of a Scottish merchant-prince there, one John Maclear, immensely rich and said to be prepared to assist King Charles's cause. It might be less than consonant with the dignity of the King's Lieutenant to go cap-in-hand in search of a mere merchant, but James Graham was never one to consider anything of the sort. And he had time to spare, anyway, for the Archduke Leopold himself was now involved in the hostilities, and had left Ghent at the head of his troops – scarcely the best moment to approach him for military aid. The Thirty Years War, which had seemed to be over at last, save for a few local adjustments, apparently and unhappily was warming up again – to the sorrow of more than Montrose.

But on the eve of his setting sail for Gothenburg, news

reached Copenhagen that changed all. The Archduke had been met and soundly defeated by a French army under Marshal the Prince Louis of Condé, at Lens near Liege, on the 20th of August, losing 7,000 men. He had retreated to Tournai. With his brother still unable to avenge the May defeat in Bavaria, and the Swedes now actually besieging Prague, the Empire was making overtures for peace – and apparently prepared to pay the price for it. Mazarin and Christina were sending negotiators to meet the Emperor at Munster. If a final peace was concluded, as seemed likely, it behoved Montrose to be on hand when the Archduke began the inevitable disbandment of his army. It was westwards, therefore, that he must sail, meantime, not eastwards.

With Kinnoull and Napier he was embarking on a Dutch coaster for Groningen, in Holland, when King Frederic sent after them two packages which had just come from thereabouts, addressed to Montrose. One was a letter from George Wishart, enclosing a copy of the first edition of his book, published at the Hague under the imprint of one Samuel Browne and pleasingly bound in calf, the text in Latin, recording the *Annus Mirabilis* of the campaigns of the illustrious Marquis of Montrose. The second was sealed with the royal arms of Bohemia – and this the recipient refrained from opening until he was alone in his tiny cabin and they were tossing their way up the Kattegat. It read:

Jamie Graham,

I have heard that you make for Copenhagen, where my good uncle has died. If he rests in peace now, I swear it will be more than he ever did in life. I send this letter to my cousin Frederic's hand, in hope that it will come to yours in as little time as may be.

This is to greet you, with all my heart. And to wish you well. We have heard here, with much joy, of your triumphs where-ever you go and your deserved honours. Will you be too grand, Marshal of the Empire, when you return to the Netherlands, to keep company with an elderly lady of respectable birth but reduced fortune, and her peculiar daughters ? I pray not.

You have been too long away, Marshal Jamie, and I urge you to return so soon as you may. Not only for my own selfish sake, who find your company to my taste. But for your own good, and for the cause we both do cherish. You may have heard of Leopold's defeat at Lens. It was not expected. I have heard that the Emperor has been making moves towards peace for some time. This defeat will, I am sure, expedite the matter. Indeed peace may be signed ere you receive this. In which case you should be here, in the Netherlands, I do believe. Although it was beat – by bad generalship, it is said – the Archduke's army is in being and as good for your purposes as any you will find in Europe. The Spanishers you will not want, but there are in the army many mercenary corps, men not a few of them Scots, with much experience of war. These will be disbanded, if there is true peace, you may be sure. You might gain whole regiments of veteran soldiers. If so be it that you can hire them. Of this I know not, but hope that you have found the moneys, or some, such as you need – and which alas this impoverished friend cannot find you.

There is more reason than this for your return to the Hague. My nephew Prince Charles is now here, lodging with his sister, Mary, now Princess of Orange. At the age of eighteen he is advanced for his years, but needs better company than he keeps. He is a youth of parts – but not all of the parts such as a king should display – and one day, God willing, he will be King in his father's room. Who am I to speak who, according to my daughters but seldom decently act the queen ? But then, *my* kingdom can be only in the hearts of my friends, Jamie – whereas young Charles will have the rule over many. He does admire you, and speaks of the Great Marquis often. But others about him, I fear, are less admiring – Willoughby, Hopton, Colepeper. That gross fellow-countryman of yours, Earl of Lauderdale, in especial is now ever at his ear. You know him ? A depraved ruffian, but cunning. He came as ambassador of the so-called Engagers, of whom you will certainly have heard, and when their foolhardy cause went down, he bided here. Safer, I doubt not, than back in Scotland at this moment. But he drinks and whores too much with young Charles, gaining over-great an influence. And would persuade him to other courses than yours, I swear. For my brother's sake, as well as for the country's sake, his son requires a better guide and adviser than any he has here. Despite Lauderdale, I reckon that he still conceives James Graham as hero. The more so, I do believe, since he heard the story of your scandal with his mother. It may be that you have not yourself heard of this, my handsome James – but the story being put out from Henrietta's Court is that you left it in haste after making unsuitable advances upon that poor lady's virtue, and boasting indecently of her favours towards you afterwards. Young Charles, who knows his mother – although not quite so well as I do – is highly intrigued. But for myself, I prefer to await the tale from your own lips rather than from such as surround my sister-in-law.

My sons Rupert and Maurice have now built up a fair fleet at Helvoetsluys, but continue to have much trouble in manning it, lacking money also. With Prince Charles they made a sally, by sea across Channel to the mouth of Thames, in August, on Henrietta's instructions, as part of this mismanaged Engagement of Hamilton's. But nothing came of it, and Rupert is angry and sore with waiting. He is determined to sail his ships to Ireland, to join Ormonde, where he conceives there is now more hope for his uncle's cause than in England or Scotland. If you were here it might be that you could convince him otherwise. You will require ships to sail your army to Scotland. Uncle Christian might have given you them, but I think not my cousin Frederic.

Come back to the Hague then, Jamie Graham, to the much comfort and satisfaction of

your affectionate and entirely loving friend,

ELIZABETH.

At the end there was scrawled a postscript, in larger, hasty almost defiant writing:

Louie would send a letter with this, if she but dared. She has written two, to my knowledge. She does not usually lack, daring.

James Graham read and re-read that characteristic epistle, his emotions in a turmoil. He did not know whether to be more disturbed by the postscript or by the canard about himself and Henrietta Maria. The former, probably – since no one who really knew him would believe the latter, surely. Not that these two items bulked overlarge in his mind, or spoiled the rest for him. That letter generated a warmth within him which, deliberately, he did not seek to analyse, which indeed he dared not analyse.

CHAPTER EIGHTEEN

Landing in the Ems estuary for Groningen, in North-East Holland, Montrose and his companions rode due south through an October countryside alive with talk of peace, heady but confused, through Drente and Gelderland and Brabant to Flanders. Some said that the Emperor had already signed the peace treaty at Münster, yielding much that men had died for but bringing hope to the lives of countless more. Just what had been at stake was by now less than clear to most; certainly not any clear-cut religious decision, for Protestants and Catholics had been fighting on both sides. But the power of the Empire and the Pope had suffered a major blow obviously, and that of France an enhancement.

When the travellers arrived at length at Tournai, only a few miles from the French border, it was to discover that the Archduke Leopold had already left for Brussels to meet the States-General. But peace was indeed concluded, and the Spanish-Netherlands' imperial army was kicking its heels in idleness, still at Tournai, disgruntled over its shameful and unnecessary defeat, concerned with future unemployment, discipline relaxed, a trouble to itself and everybody else. Montrose could have recruited thousands there and then – had he the money to pay them. As it was, he interviewed many senior officers, especially Scots ones – of whom there were large numbers – seeking to persuade, promising, all but pleading. He had the fullest authority to enrol them, the Emperor's signed commission to do so; and they wanted to be enrolled. But though some few might be prepared to take a chance on it, not unnaturally most required financial inducement. And the King's Captain-General had now insufficient money even to pay his own daily expenses, and was reduced to spending Kinnoull's. One of the Scots officers here was none other than Sir John Hurry, acting colonel of one of the mercenary regiments. Poor Hurry was not very fortunate in his employment, these days. But he remained the cheerful soldier of fortune, prepared to take the rough with the smooth. Perceiving no better prospects on the present rather gloomy military horizon, he once more attached himself to Montrose's party – and promptly resumed the rank and status of major-general.

Having obtained tentative agreements to join his expeditionary force for Scotland, when the necessary funds were available – unless better alternative employment turned up in the meantime – from a large number of experienced officers, some colonels promising their entire regiments also, James Graham repaired to Brussels in search of the Archduke. His Marshal's baton, commission and letter of recommendation from the Emperor meant less than they had done when they were granted, admittedly, but they must still have value within the imperial domains.

Brussels was the seat of the States-General of the Spanish Netherlands, and the new political situation in Europe consequent on what was now being called the Peace of Westphalia, signed at Münster by the Emperor, meant great changes in the position and influence of this Catholic and Walloon southern section of the Low Countries. Very much on the wrong side in this settlement, it had to swallow much that was unpalatable, and its ruling body, the States-General, was in constant session, the Governor-General, Leopold, no longer the military dictator he had been during a state of war, and in almost as constant attendance. In these circumstances, Montrose was under no illusions as to the difficulties of his task.

Leopold, a harassed man, and never a towering figure personally, received his visitor civilly enough – but did not fail to indicate that he could have done with this new Marshal of the Empire's renowned military services somewhat earlier in the day. He accepted, however, his brother the Emperor's expressed wishes in this matter – even though he all but implied that he could scarcely understand why Ferdinand should have taken so much trouble at this difficult time. The affairs of King Charles, Scotland and England, could hardly be of less importance to the troubled Empire, he inferred. Nevertheless, his brother's word was his command, and all that had been promised the Marquis of Montrose would be fulfilled as far as it was in his – the Archduke's – power to ensure. He could recruit, enlist, appoint his own colonels and officers, marshal and train his force in the imperial domains, and embark it at imperial ports.

All of which was, of course, satisfactory so far as it went. But since Montrose had not funds left to hire himself a body-servant, much less an army, it did not in fact go very far. And when the subject of money was raised, a subvention-in-aid, either loan, credit or outright grant, Leopold Hapsburg referred him to the States-General. Anything such was entirely and solely within the province of that body, which now controlled the exchequer. He himself had no funds at his disposal other than his private purse and what the States-General voted him for expenses, he declared. He could not offer a penny. What he could and would do, however, was to commend an application for financial aid from Montrose to the States-General – and meantime house him in Brussels in a fashion suitable for a Marshal of the Empire. Perhaps, if approached, the Emperor might even grant a small pension...?

With that James Graham had to be satisfied – and seem grateful. He pointed out that the aid required was for King Charles and his kingdom of Great Britain, not in any way for himself; and that, as such, could and would undoubtedly be repaid if and when Charles was restored to his rightful throne. The Archduke advised that he inserted a clause to that effect in a written application to the States-General, and he would undertake to present it, sympathetically. But he warned that it must inevitably take time – for the business before the assembly was lengthy, far-reaching and urgent. Meanwhile, his lordship was to consider himself the guest of the Governor-General.

And so Montrose settled himself down, in a wing of the royal palace in huddled, steep-climbing Brussels, to the familiar and soul-destroying business of waiting, through that winter of 1648/49.

He kept in touch with the residue of the professional army, therefore, with Hurry as his link – and would dearly have liked to move into it in person, to try to save it from demoralisation and indisciplined rampage. But even as a Marshal he had no claim or authority to do anything of the sort, until there was at least some indication that he would be in a position to employ it, or any portion of it. Born to wealth and inherited power, James Graham seemed to himself to have been a beggar for too long.

He was by no means idle that winter, apart from constant lobbying and interviewing soldiers. He wrote long letters. Those he wrote to Elizabeth of Bohemia were indeed in the nature of safety-valves, some release for his pent-up anxieties and impatience. But he also sent messages to her son Rupert and her nephew Prince Charles. Rupert he urged to think again over the projected expedition to Ireland, and instead to help him with the

Scottish project, which he believed to be infinitely more likely to succeed, as well as much more effective for the King's restoration. Especially to hold his fleet available to transport the troops. To young Charles he appealed for help in his plea to the States-General, as indication that the Scottish invasion was indeed royal policy and not just some wild theory of his own. This was important, for Henrietta Maria's influence could be guaranteed to be working against him, and these cautious Flemings had to be convinced that they had at least the chance of getting their money back. He wrote with much tact, for he was in effect asking the son to work against his mother; but it was *for* his father in dire need. Also he urged Charles to approach his sister on his, Montrose's behalf – this on Elizabeth's suggestion. The Princess Mary's husband was now ruling Prince of of Orange, Stadtholder of the Protestant Netherlands, on the winning side, and as such in a position to influence his neighbours. Moreover he was wealthy – and Mary herself had been given a considerable fortune in jewels by her father on her marriage. She was only seventeen, and apparently not concerned with much other than her own domestic affairs; but some of those jewels, sold, could solve the financial problem of this expedition's start.

Rupert replied in friendly fashion, declaring his great admiration for Montrose, and his desire to help, but pointing out that he was hardly his own master, and more or less committed to the Irish venture, with Ormonde, and could not just postpone it indefinitely. The longer he remained in port, with his ships, the more difficulties he had to contend with. If Jamie Graham would give him an approximate date, in the not-distant future, when the Scots expedition would be ready to embark, he would put it to his colleagues that here was a practical proposition. If not, he feared that plans to sail for Ireland, already far advanced, must inevitably go ahead.

Jamie Graham, unable of course to give any possible date, wrote back begging patience, and suggesting a meeting to discuss the whole situation, including overall strategy.

Charles, Prince of Wales, did not reply.

Rupert did continue with the correspondence, to the effect that they were now preparing to embark troops – but that there had been another mutiny amongst the ships' crews, engineered with the aid of English parliamentary gold. He could not leave Helvoetsluys in these circumstances, for a meeting, but would be delighted to see his old friend there on the Dutch coast.

Montrose, expecting any day to be summoned before the States-General to elaborate on his appeal, wrote that he would come just so soon as he might. Meantime, for the King's and old friendship's sake, not to sail away on an Irish expedition which, in truth, even if successful, could not win Charles Stewart his freedom or regain him his throne, as could the Scottish one.

By this time Yule-tide had passed, Montrose's third on the Continent. In a letter of seasonable greetings and good wishes to Elizabeth and her family, he urged her, if she would, to use her influence with her nephew Charles to reply to his overture and proposals, as time was of the essence. With this he enclosed, as Christmas gift, an inscribed copy of the new edition of his book by Wishart – in English now. The first edition was already sold out, and a second printing.

Before the end of January he did, in consequence, receive a reply from Prince Charles, at last – not written but by the lips of a messenger. Unfortunately, the day before he had had a final letter from Rupert, sending his greetings and regrets, but that he was sailing with the morrow's tide. A sudden financial godsend, in the shape of the proceeds of the sale of his cousin the Princess of Orange's jewellery, had enabled him to buy the so necessary provisions and munitions, and at last to pay his mutinous and absentee crews. He had to thank the Prince of Wales for this, he understood. It would be folly to delay longer and risk further trouble. He wished his old comrade-in-arms very well, and hoped that they might indeed meet together before long – preferably somewhere in England, in a joint Irish and Scottish thrust on London. Meantime, God aid them both and King Charles likewise.

It was, in consequence, in a distinctly doubtful not to say incensed frame of mind, that James Graham learned that Sir Edward Nicholas, secretary to the Prince of Wales, waited in an ante-room of the Palais Royale in Brussels, craving an interview.

The very thin, almost emaciated man of late middle years who awaited him in the ante-room, soberly dressed, with deep-set dark eyes and careful speech, seemed an unlikely representative, on the face of it, for the allegedly gay and imprudent Prince of Wales. Montrose had heard of Edward Nicholas, of course – one of the King's former Secretaries of State, no less, appointed by an anxious father, when things were in dissolution around him, to be the guide and secretary to a youthful son and heir lacking parental control. Rumour had it that he was wise, but insufficiently strong of character to exert influence over his high-spirited charge. That he himself had made the journey to Brussels, on Charles's behalf, was at least encouraging.

After mutually courteous greetings, Nicholas did not beat about the bush. 'Your lordship – His Highness has sent me to you in person, rather than commit words to writing,' he declared in a softly lilting Welsh voice. 'That I may explain his situation to you. We conceived it too dangerous to write. His Highness hopes, therefore, that you will forgive the delay in answering your lordship's letter.'

'A delay, sir, which has had dire results! All these weeks I have waited. And now Prince Rupert has sailed, with his fleet, for Ireland. Enabled to do so by the moneys which might have set up a Scottish expedition of infinitely more value. I cannot think that His Highness was well advised in this. Nor in failing to send support for my appeal for credit to the States-General here. The King's cause, I believe, is the sufferer.'

'My lord Marquis – your disappointment and concern are well understood. Personally I agree with you,' the other said earnestly. 'But you must understand the Prince's most difficult position. He has the greatest admiration for you, as a commander, and recognises that you have done more for his royal father than any man living. He conceives you also to be better informed and have a wiser head, than most others who would advise him. Or than Prince Rupert, his cousin, indeed. But his situation is most delicate. And you, my lord, have . . . enemies. In high places.'

'Of that I am well aware, sir. To my sorrow. But need that have prevented a reply to my letter? All this delay? And no message to the States-General?'

'I fear that it needs must. His Highness is heir to the throne, yes – but only eighteen years, and with no true authority of his own. As yet. Whereas his mother, the Queen, has the authority. *She* is His Majesty's personal representative and mouthpiece, in this unhappy situation – by the King's express command. Not his son. Indeed, His Majesty has instructed His Highness to obey his mother in everything. The Queen's authority you have had occasion to know, I think, my lord! Not unnaturally, there-fore, she brings strong influence to bear on Prince Charles. She provides most of the members of his household. To be frank with you, his household at the Hague is little more than a nest of spies! The Queen is informed, in the course of two or three days,

274

of everything His Highness says and does. And he is, of course, kept grievously short of money – for the pension which the French Treasury allows him is paid through Her Majesty, who withholds what she sees fit. I am his secretary, and know, to my cost! The Queen undoubtedly *means* well, my lord – but she still has the power gravely to influence and control His Highness. Save in, h'm, private and personal matters.'

'Ah, yes. I have heard of these. The present young woman – Walters, is it? Mistress Walters has had her child. What says Her Majesty to that?'

'Little or nothing, my lord. Indeed, I think that so long as the Prince does her wishes in matters of State, she cares little how he behaves in private.'

'So – you say that His Highness could not write to me for fear of the Queen's spies knowing of it?'

'Partly that, my lord. We know that his couriers are frequently tampered with. As his other servants. That is why *I* am come here today – in secret. And that is not all, see you. There are the damned Scots also . . .!' Nicholas drew a quick breath, blinking those deep eyes. 'Your pardon, my lord Marquis – a slip of the tongue. No offence meant, I do assure. But – we have at the Hague the Earl of Lauderdale and his party. If you know him . . . ? Then you will understand! *They* have plenty of money, I swear! Where it comes from, who knows?'

'But I understood Lauderdale, whom I much dislike, was something of an exile himself? A refugee, now that the Engagement folly is done with?'

'But it is not done with, my lord. *Hamilton*'s bolt is shot, yes. But the Engagers seem to be very much a power in Scotland still, and Lauderdale their representative here. Indeed, it is whispered that the Marquis of Argyll himself now encourages them, *sub rosa*. If it is so, this could be where their money comes from.'

'If that is true, then it is all for his own evil ends.'

'No doubt. Which is why we have to be so careful, so wary. Secret. And Lauderdale never ceases to speak against your lordship and your enterprises. He holds out to His Highness much hope of support in Scotland – but claims that *you* must be put aside, that you are the stumbling-block of his Scottish support. You will understand, therefore, how His Highness is pulled in many ways. He would have you to meet and confer with Sir Edward Hyde, my lord. If you will. In secret also. On the whole matter of your policy and plans. Hyde is the King's Chancellor.

But not in the Queen's pocket. He has a good head and is to be trusted.'

'I know Ned Hyde. A lawyer, though sourish. Able – but no soldier.'

'No. But a good judge of the practical. He is the King's most senior minister, and the Prince trusts him.'

'Where do I meet him, then? The sooner the better. Can he come here – for I cannot risk to be away from Brussels while the States-General may call upon me.'

'I will take back a message to Hyde from you, my lord. Name a place and date, and I will seek to arrange it . . .'

So it was agreed. Nicholas took back to the Hague with him, that 20th day of January, Montrose's letters to Prince Charles himself and to Sir Edward Hyde, the King's minister.

It was exactly two weeks later, to the hour, that one of the Archduke's men handed a letter to George Wishart, for his master, from Hyde, written from the Hague. He brought it to Montrose as he sat at his desk by a bright log fire, writing – for it was a cold and snowy day of February. James Graham did not open it at once, finishing the paragraph which he was penning, to Elizabeth. Then, breaking the seal, spreading the paper and raising it to gain added light from the fire, he began to read.

Suddenly Wishart, at his own writings, heard a strange choking sound. Glancing up he saw the other to be tugging convulsively at the deep white linen collar at his neck, and swaying noticeably in his chair. The letter had fluttered to the floor. Alarmed, he rose and hurried over.

'My lord – are you unwell? What's to do?' he demanded. 'Of a mercy – what's this?'

Only a strangled gasping came from James Graham, who appeared to be taking some sort of seizure.

Desperately Wishart sought to support his master's and friend's slumping person, to loosen the collar. He shouted for help. The Lord Napier was somewhere about.

Montrose was evidently struggling, fighting some staggering attack upon body or mind, eyes staring but unfocussed, lips trembling but seeking to form words. With one hand he clutched at his friend's arm, with the other he seemed to be pointing downwards, to the floor. Obviously it was the letter that he indicated.

Wishart held him upright, gabbling assurances, comforts, appeals to the Deity.

Archie Napier came in, eyes widening at what he saw. He sprang forward to his uncle's side, with a flood of questions.

'He is ill! Quick – wine!' Wishart panted. 'There – on the board. No – hold him. I will get it . . .'

But when they tried to force wine between Montrose's slack lips, he managed to shake his head, with some kind of decision, mumbling.

'What does he say ? In God's name – what is it ?' Napier cried.

'It sounds like, like the King,' Wishart muttered.

The deep groan from the chair confirmed that. Again there was the palsied pointing towards the floor.

'The letter . . .' Wishart stooped to pick it up.

'What letter ? Who from ? Christ God – what does it say ?'

'Hyde. From Sir Edward Hyde, the Chancellor . . .' The other was swiftly scanning the writing, as he spoke. Then he gagged, gulping for air in his turn. 'They . . . they . . . have slain . . . the King! Dear God – dead! Executed – dead! They have, have cut off King Charles's head! Oh, merciful Jesu . . .!'

Napier snatched the paper from the other's hand, to read. And James Graham, unsupported, collapsed forward over his desk, a tight-coiled spring snapped, broken.

CHAPTER NINETEEN

It was two whole days before Montrose dared emerge from his bedchamber and face the world again, two days in which his friends had tiptoed about their palace suite, continually coming to listen and whisper at the locked door, lost, frightened, as though the death was here, not in far-away London. When he did emerge, however, James Graham was calm, quiet, set-faced, but himself – even though it was a rather different self, steely, eyes hooded, remote. In level tones he apologised for any inconvenience and anxiety he had caused, and declared that he was now fully recovered – but that, of course, His Majesty's death changed all. None there, even the somewhat insensitive Kinnoull, who had hurriedly returned, nor the brash Hurry, thought to discuss or elaborate with him on the King's trial and execution by Cromwell and the Parliamentarians.

And indeed it did change all, for Montrose as for so many others. Any authority Montrose had had stemmed from his monarch. He was no longer, therefore, Viceroy of Scotland, or Captain-General either. He had no further right to appeal to Leopold or the States-General or to seek enlist an army. He was suddenly no more than a private individual, who had staked all – and lost. His desperate grief for Charles Stewart, and his surging hurt and anger at those who had dared to slay the Lord's Anointed, did not blind him to the fact that here was a wholly, radically, new situation, for himself and all his hopes and plans. He might still be a commander of some renown, a Marshal of the Empire; but the *raison d'etre* for it all – indeed for his whole existence, as it seemed – was no longer there. In consequence, he could no longer trespass on the Archduke Leopold's hospitality, nor further impose his claims on the States-General. He sat down at once to write formal statements of withdrawal and expressions of gratitude.

But another aspect of the utterly changed situation did not fail to impress itself ever more clearly upon his recognition. There was no King Charles I to serve, any more; but there was now a King Charles II. Eighteen year old Charles was no longer Prince of Wales but King, in undoubted right and succession – King of Scots, in particular, however much the English Parliamentarians might talk about a Republic or Commonwealth. There was no such possibility for Scotland. Even the most fanatic ministers and Covenanting zealots had never conceived Scotland without a king. Young Charles, whatever else he was, was *Ard Righ*, the High King of Scots. And to be accepted as King of Great Britain also, meantime.

All of which had highly important implications, in its turn. Authority now rested with Charles himself, however immature. At eighteen, and of sound mind, he was beyond the age for regency control. Henrietta Maria was no longer the King's representative in Europe. In theory at least, all the Crown revenues, prerogatives, privileges and powers were his. Honours, appointments, dispensations, charters, were within his gift; treaties, official negotiations, State decisions, were his to make or break. Cromwell, Fairfax, Milton and their friends had, by their wicked sacrilege, exchanged a captive and helpless monarch whom they could dominate and press, whose aim latterly had been to escape to the Continent, for a free monarch who was already there. Apart from the ethics of it all, they had scarcely been well-advised.

It behoved James Graham, therefore, as a loyal subject and moreover one of the Earls of Scotland, to present himself and his allegiance to his new High King forthwith, as well as to be available to advise on Scottish matters. Nothing altered that hereditary privilege and duty. He must repair to the Hague.

*　　*　　*

'Her Majesty requests that you will come this way, Marquis,' the young Count Henri informed. 'If you will follow me – and forgive, h'm, the *desarroi, desordre* ? A reception is in progress in the principal salons. For the ministers of the Elector Palatine, Her Majesty's son, who have come to pay their respects to the new King Charles.'

'Then, sir, let me come again. On another, more suitable occasion.'

'No, Marquis. The Queen commands your attendance. But – this way!'

If Count Henri felt that he must apologise for leading the visitor by the distinctly seedy and humbly domestic back-passages and corridors of the Wassenaer Hof, he did not know, of course, that Montrose had traversed them before, and in good company. The newcomer's heart lifted, indeed, to their shabby intimacy as he followed the younger man.

Climbing the remembered private stairway at the end of one passage, to the better proportioned and decorated but still far from palatial bedroom floor, his escort handed Montrose over to the old Scotswoman, Martha Duncan, who stood waiting there, and discreetly withdrew.

She took him through the dressing room, littered with women's clothing, shaking her grey head and tut-tutting at the untidy sight, and opened the door beyond. But she opened it only a little, to insert her head and peer within. Then she nodded again, opened it wider, and gestured through.

'Aye, well,' she observed, with her own significance, gave him the slightest push in, and shut the door behind him.

Elizabeth stood in the firelight, with no lamps or candles further lighting her boudoir – for it was a grey day of late February sleet. Regally clad – for the reception, of course – the flickering half-light played about her magnificent figure and lovely features. She stood watching him, in a strangely alert, almost wary, questioning stance, as she searched his face. She did not speak.

He bowed low. 'Your Majesty,' he murmured. 'Your . . . very proud . . . servant.'

She drew a long, quite audible breath, and also drew herself up from the slightly tense and peering posture. And she raised her arms, forwards towards him, still unspeaking.

He moved into the room, with a trace of hesitance. 'I intrude, as ever,' he said. 'Interrupt Your Majesty's affairs. I . . .'

He it was who was interrupted. She did not wait for his careful advance, 'Jamie! Jamie!' she cried, and moved swiftly forward, to throw herself directly into his arms.

'Elizabeth!' The name came out almost as a groan, as he enfolded her in his embrace. 'Elizabeth, my dear.' And he buried his lips in her hair.

For long moments they clung thus, saying no more. The man was trembling, and knew it, and the Queen's splendid bosom heaved frankly, strongly against him. She was a big, well-made woman, challenging to any masculine arms and person.

At length she straightened up, and drew a little away – but still held him by both forearms, so that he did not feel compelled to drop his own arms from her sides.

'Jamie – forgive this . . . display!' she breathed, panting just a little her face close to his own. 'A weak woman's foolishness. I should keep myself . . . better in hand. Should I not ?'

Gravely he considered that, and her. 'Should you ?' he asked. As seriously, she nodded. 'Unseemly. That is what it is. Inappropriate. Everyone would say so. Do you not think so ?' But she did not release his arms.

'As a queen ? As a royal lady, to an impoverished Scots lord ?'

'As an old woman! To a man fifteen years younger. There is surely no folly to equal an elderly woman's presumptuous folly! See – I lit no lights lest you should notice the lines on my face!'

'Is this folly, then ? I suppose that it is. For James Graham. But – it is the dearest folly that I have ever known.' He comprehensively scanned the lightly upturned features so near his own. 'Lines ? I see no lines. Only the fairest face that it has ever been my joy to behold. And the kindest, truest, most noble. As for age, there is none so full of years in all this world, I sometimes think, as am I. If this be folly, Elizabeth – let us be fools a little longer!'

'With all my heart!' she said, and her parted lips rose to his.

When at length they moved, it was still hand-in-hand, going slowly over to stare down into the red glow of the fire, silent, too full for words. But presently Elizabeth shook her head, blinking a little.

'Jamie, dear Jamie – bless you! And Elizabeth Stewart, too. God bless us both! This, of all things most wonderful! So very good. See – I am weeping. Weeping for joy. I never thought to do that again. Our folly is . . . blessed. I think that we have paid for it, in advance, you and I! And may pay further, indeed. But we have something, here, now, which no one can ever take from us. Jamie and Elizabeth. Sweet God – Jamie . . . and Elizabeth!'

'Yes,' he said.

'What does the future hold for us, Jamie ? Placed as are you and I ?'

'I am no seer, Elizabeth – save to see that you will ever reign in my heart, here and in eternity.'

'That, then, is perhaps sufficient, my lord! If we have eternity, present uncertainties, problems, obstacles, become the less sore to contemplate. Or should do. As even now, my dear, at this precious moment. Which should be ours, and ours alone. Alas, I have to return to my stupid, honest Germans! Already they will be asking what has become of the Queen ? And Charles Louis, the Elector Palatine, the eldest of my brood – and the least lovable, a pompous ass, indeed! – will be huffing and puffing, at my seeming discourtesy to the ministers he has brought. Aye, and the girls will be doing their best for me – and raising eyebrows to each other over their scandalous mamma! Not that I care, for them – or for Charles Louis. But these German burghers – that is different. I have my duty.' She sighed. 'Charles Louis has arranged – and will pay for, since I cannot – a banquet for them. Seemingly of my giving. Young Charles will be there. He it is they have come to greet – the new British King. If you care to honour it, you will be the most welcome guest. But . . .'

'No – I thank you. Since I cannot be with you this night, I would wish to be by myself. Alone. Where I may hug this joy to me, clutch it to myself, lose myself in it. Is that selfish? To sit through a banquet, with you there, but be unable to talk with you, touch you . . .!' His hand slid from hers, and his arm encircled her, to tighten and draw her close again fiercely, possessively.

'I know, I know . . .'

When she could, breathlessly, she went on. 'I must go, Jamie. But – we have said nothing of, of my brother.'

'No.' He drew a deep breath. 'I dared not. I do not think that I can dare it, even now, Elizabeth. And, and for you . . .!'

'I was less close to Charles than, perhaps, I should have been. I served him not one-tenth so well as did you. But I grieve for him sorely. For all he was – and for all he failed to be. He had great virtues, of a sort. Not as a king. That was the sorrow of it – he was unfitted to be King. If only my brother Henry had lived! But – Charles did not deserve to pay so hideously for his failure.' She stopped, as she perceived the man's face working. 'Oh, forgive me, my dear. I forget myself. Your Lord Napier told me of your, your great hurt. I am sorry . . .'

He shook his head.

She turned, within his arm.' Jamie – we have both had a dire bereavement since last we were together. Myself a brother, you, a wife! You said that you dared not speak of Charles. I, likewise, can scarce dare to speak . . . of her.'

'Then do not,' he said, thickly, almost harshly. 'Magdalen is with God. And better there than she was with me for husband. We were . . . ill-matched. I failed her. But life failed her also. She had no joy in it, for years. Who knows why it should be so? The fault was not her's. But she wished to be gone. It would be as wrong to grudge her the going as it would be to pretend that I did not know a certain . . . relief.'

'Yes. You were ever honest. As, I hope, am I. For I do not pretend that I am sorry. Save for her. For you, I think that I am glad. For myself, more so. Is that cruel? Heartless? I would not have permitted myself this, this happiness, indulgence, had not, had not this happened. Had she still lived.'

He nodded, slowly. 'Nor I. Nor, strangely, Elizabeth, had the *King* lived, I think. You see, I was *his* servant, before all, his instrument, a weapon for his hand. I was not my own man, while he remained constrained in need of my services. I left all for his cause – and must have continued to do so. But . . . I am, God help me, free of that servitude now. After ten years of it. *Both* deaths brought us to this, Elizabeth – for better or worse. Both of them.'

She raised a hand to touch his cheek, wordless.

He turned to her, with something almost like desperation. 'I was lost – a lost man. Suddenly. Do you understand? I came to you. What I have found, in this room, I cannot yet gauge, cannot foresee the end of. But . . . I am not lost, any more.'

'I thank God for that!' she breathed. And then, 'But you come to see young Charles, do you not? Oh, I know that you came to me, as a woman. But – *he* is now your King, is he not? Do you serve him, then, as you served his father?'

'I must serve him, yes – as my liege lord. But . . . it is not quite the same. As you will understand. My full duty I do not yet see. It may be that *you* will show me it.'

'No! Do not put that responsibility upon me, James Graham. I have sufficient, without that! But – I will speak to Charles. Tonight. Arrange that you see him. Privately. And quickly. This I can do. But as to your decision thereafter – that you must take yourself, my dear. For I, I would but work and intrigue to keep you by *my* side! I think that I shall do that, anyway, I warn you!'

He smiled, at last. 'I shall be on my guard! But not tonight. Now I have been overlong at your side, kept you from your guests and duty. Go, my dear – before your delightful daughters come searching for their mother, and find her thus! Which would not do.'

'Would not do . . . ? You think . . . it will not . . . do?' Her voice faltered unqueenlike.

'Net yet, at any rate, I judge. We must be discreet. Very. You are a queen . . .'

'I have never been discreet, all my life! Must I start now – for Jamie Graham ?'

'Yes,' he said. 'And for Elizabeth Stewart, too.'

She searched his eyes, in the firelight, and clung to him.

They embraced again, passionately. Then she broke away, and hurried to the door.

She turned there. 'Tomorrow you will come again. For all to see. Meet all again, my family. Then you will stay here, in this my house. I will not have you staying in an inn. And we shall contrive to be together, frequently.' She was all the Queen again. 'However discreetly . . . !'

'Do you think that wise ?'

'Wise ? Wise! There is more than wisdom and discretion to living!' Then, in a different voice. 'But, Jamie – be kind to Louie, will you ? For a little. I . . . I would not wish her hurt. She cares for you, I know. As I do not think she has done for others. It may pass – you are a hero, and shamefully good-looking – and she is young. You will think of it ?'

'Yes, my dear. I will be kind with Louise. And find it no hardship.'

'But not too kind, sir! I will not see my daughter's affections trifled with!' She held out two hands towards him, and then, as he came forward again, shook her head, turned, and opening the door, hurried out.

CHAPTER TWENTY

The plump and slightly pompous little man in the rich but sober clothing, eyed Montrose warily and scarcely warmly from prominent but shrewd if watery eyes. 'His Majesty is informed, my lord, and will grant you audience presently,' he said. 'Private audience. Save for my humble self, as adviser. As is necessary.' He did not sound humble. But then, why should he? Sir Edward Hyde, although humbly enough born, the son of a country squire, was senior minister of the Crown – whatever the English and Scottish Parliaments might proclaim – Chancellor of the Exchequer, however empty its coffers, and principal adviser to the new King Charles II.

Montrose had never liked the self-important little man, who seemed so much older than his forty years, but he recognised him as able, gifted and moreover honest, attributes not so common at the Courts of monarchs as not to be appreciated when discovered.

The door opened quite suddenly and a young man slipped into this small and obscure chamber of the Naaldwijk Hof, a house adjacent to the Wassenaer Hof and linked thereto for use as overflow by the Bohemian Court. It was no regal entrance – just as this was no regal apartment – merely the unannounced arrival of a tall and angular youth who, by his breathing, had apparently run up the stairs to get here. Coming in, and his glance going straight to Montrose, he halted, began to bow, recollected his station, and raised a hand in a kind of involuntary salute – which itself was cut short as probably unsuitable.

'My lord Marquis,' he said – and smiled ruefully.

James Graham, taken by surprise at such entry, after a first keen gaze, bowed deeply. 'Your Grace!' he said. Then, straightening up, he stepped forward, to take the young man's hand between both of his own, palms vertical, and holding them thus to go down on one knee. 'I take, and hold you for liege lord and High King,' he declared.

Wonderingly Charles Stewart looked down at him, and as the other rose again, shook his dark head. 'My lord – it is rather for

285

me to greet the great Montrose in such lowly fashion, than you me, I swear . . .' he began, and then stopped, biting his lip.

'Lowly, Sire? That is the proudest fashion in which I may greet any man living! *An Greumach Mor* to his *Ard Righ*, in first acceptance. The ancient usage of an Earl of Scotland to his liege, cousin and High King.'

'Ha – I had not heard of this, my lord. I have not been greeted so before. Forgive me. And forgive me also for keeping you waiting. I . . . I was detained. My cousin Sophie . . .'

'Ah, yes.' Gravely James Graham inclined his head. 'The Princess Sophia is most detaining, I agree, Sir. Like all the rest of her family!' And he smiled a little.

The young King grinned at that – and a rather ugly face was quite transformed. Montrose had not been prepared for his appearance, any more than for his abrupt entry. Charles was totally unlike his father, in looks as evidently in all else. He was surprisingly tall, for a Stewart – although his great-grandmother Mary had been tall – and he had little of the traditional Stewart good looks, being sallow, irregularly featured, with too large a mouth. But his eyes were good, large, dark and lustrous – Stewart eyes; but more lively than had been his father's, with something vivid in them, quick-silver. A Medici inheritance, perhaps. It was a strangely contradictory face, young-old, casual-calculating, debonair but wary too.

'Yes. Yes, my aunt and her daughters are not to be denied!' he agreed. 'I wish . . .' He stopped, shrugging eloquently, in true Gallic fashion, his quick glance darting towards Hyde, for the first time. 'But I forget myself, my lord. May I welcome you to the Hague, and my, er, presence, if not my Court! Even in these modest quarters. And say how greatly I am honoured to see you, the greatest soldier in Europe. I, I have longed to meet you, sir – but it has never been possible. But now that I am my own master – or almost . . .' He looked again at Hyde, with that quick-silver smile.

'You are too kind, Sire. I am sure that you have met much greater soldiers than am I, trained soldiers – Condé, Turenne, Wrangel? But, whatever my qualities, successes or failings, I am now at Your Grace's service. As I was . . . at your father's.'

'And you served my father better than did any other, my lord Marquis. He would have me say it, I think.'

Wordless, James Graham shook his head.

Charles looked at him quickly, and changed the subject. Perhaps his aunt had warned him. 'My royal mother, however, has not always fully appreciated your worth, I fear. I am sorry. She has been ill-advised, I think. In this as in other matters. But – that is past, my lord.'

Montrose bowed again, unspeaking.

'I wish to avail myself of your services to the full,' the young man went on. 'I rejoice that they are . . . available. However secret they must be, at this stage.'

'Secret, Sire . . . ?'

'Perhaps secret is not the word? Kept undeclared, un-trumpeted . . . ?' Charles looked for help to Hyde.

'Secret, my lord, is, I would say, fair, accurate. In the cir-cumstances prevailing,' the little man said judicially. 'Secrecy was necessary when we sent Sir Edward Nicholas to you at Brussels. It is still more necessary now.'

'I am afraid that I do not understand, Sir Edward. Conditions have wholly changed, since then. Your master, here, is now King. King of Scots, in fact; King of Great Britain to be. His Grace now commands all. And must be seen to do so. You must explain to me this need for secrecy. Between the King of Scots and one of his earls.'

'But that's it, my lord! It is the confounded Scots that are at the back of it! H'r'm.' The little lawyer had risen on tiptoe, flushing, blinking, puffing. He recovered himself, however. 'I beg Your Majesty's pardon. And yours, my lord Marquis. But – it is all most difficult, most unfortunate. The secrecy is not of *my* choosing, I assure you. Or of His Majesty's.'

'Perhaps if you explained, Ned?' Charles suggested. 'His lordship clearly does not fully comprehend the fix we are in.'

'As Your Majesty wishes. You know, my lord, that the Earl of Lauderdale is here at the Hague. Has been for some time. Repre-senting the Engagers' party in Scotland. He, ah, mislikes yourself. As do his friends, unfortunately. For reasons we need not go into. But now, since his late Majesty's shameful murder, the position is changed somewhat. In this, as in other issues. Lauderdale now represents more than the Engagers. Letters of authority have come from Scotland. Now he represents the whole Estates of that realm. Other representatives are on their way to the Hague, to join him. To explain new proposals to His Majesty. It seems that Scotland is as shocked by his late Majesty's death as, as are we.'

'I rejoice to hear it, sir. I knew it, of course – that it would be so. Scotland's position is wholly different from England's. That is why I said that in *fact* His Grace is already King of Scots and only to *be* King of Great Britain.'

'I noticed that, my lord – and did not quite take your meaning?' Charles said.

'It is because the Scots monarchy is different, Sire. In quality and essence. More patriarchal. The King of Scots cannot be unseated. It seems that the King of England can! If he is a bad king, he may be forced to govern through a regency. As Robert III was. But there *must* be a King of Scots, always. Without interval. At your royal father's last breath, Your Grace became the High King. Your coronation will follow, one day – but you are King now. You need not await any recognition, from the Estates or others. Even from the lesser kings of Scotland, the Earls. Although on *their* acceptance the fullest authority of your reigning depends. That is the Scots monarchial position.'

'I see. This is something I had not known, fully. None ever explained it so.' Charles raised an eyebrow towards his official adviser, even a little annoyed.

'That may be so, my lord. In theory,' the Chancellor declared, frowning. 'But we are, I fear, more concerned with practice. The facts of the situation.'

'And these demand secrecy, sir?'

'So far as your lordship is concerned, unfortunately, they do. This letter from the Scots Chancellor, intimating Lauderdale's new authority and the coming delegation, expressly declares that your lordship must not be included in any discussions or negotiations. As outlaw, and forfeited by the Estates, they say, and excommunicated by their Kirk.'

'Dear God!' Montrose breathed. 'Do you mean to *agree* to this outrageous demand? This insult!'

Charles cleared his throat. 'My lord – it is a condition of the discussions. We, we deplore it. But if anything is to be achieved . . .'

'His Majesty greatly admires and respects your lordship,' Hyde put in quickly, soothingly. 'But he cannot reject the whole of Scotland for one man's position. In especial when, as is here proved, he is anxious to consult and lean on you, privately . . .'

'More than that,' Charles broke in, eagerly. 'To honour you, my lord. I intend to show my great gratitude for all that you have done for my father. And the the realms that are now, in name, mine. And to show my fullest trust in you. So I would confirm you in all your offices and positions. All, my lord.'

'But secretly, Sire ? Not openly.'

'Er . . . yes. I fear, meantime, it must be so.'

'To what end ? So that you may negotiate with Lauderdale
and these others who come ? You, their King ? What can they
offer you, which is not yours already ? The Crown ? It is yours.
In Scotland. Allegiance ? They cannot withhold it. Even Argyll.
What, then ? Power ? Power – that is all they have. The power of
the sword and the pulpit, meantime. And think you, Your Grace,
that they will yield up that power to you ? In any respect ? If they
send to you, here, it is because they would *use* you. A puppet for
their own purposes. For Argyll's. The Campbell will not yield
one inch of his power. He has paid too high a price for it! That
I can assure you. Until he is forced to do so – by a sharper sword
than his own!'

There was silence in that room for a space, as King and Chancellor digested that. Then the latter spoke, blowing out his
cheeks.

'You speak as a soldier, my lord. His Majesty is in no position
to use the sword. Therefore he must use other methods. The
conference-table. Negotiation.'

'What is thus important to be negotiated ?'

Charles answered. 'They offer that I shall be proclaimed King,
formally, from every market cross in Scotland. Also in the
assembled Parliament. They will consider my possible return to
Scotland, and my coronation.'

'As they cannot deny you. And in return . . . ?'

'I am to accept the Covenant.'

'A-a-ah! Which Covenant, Sire ? The Solemn League ?'

'I do not precisely understand the difference, my lord.'

Montrose swung on Hyde. 'You do, Sir Edward – *you* must
know! You cannot conceivably advise His Grace to adhere to the
Solemn League and Covenant. And it can be only that they want.
You – an Englishman!'

'It is only a form of words, sir. A foolish bigoted form of words.
But as a basis for negotiation, we would consider it. To gain a
great advantage. The *National* Covenant is none so grievous. We
might settle for that.'

'But – Sir Edward! You are named a man of sharp wits. Have
you taken leave of them ? Forgive my words, Sire – but this is no
occasion for mere polite exchange. Of course the *National*
Covenant is none so grievous. I had a hand in drawing it up,

289

and know. His Grace your father came to accept it. The terms merely provide for freedom of worship, in Scotland. What I fought for – and would still fight for. It is to be *assumed* that Your Grace would agree to that, anyway. With an Episcopalean father and a Catholic mother, none would expect otherwise. It is the elementary right of every man . . .'

'To be sure, my lord. I agree, most heartily.'

'Then it is not *that* which these come to negotiate. But the damnable Solemn League and Covenant. Argyll's Covenant. The object of which is not religious freedom but religious tyranny, with political power. To impose a narrow Presbyterianism on all, by law. And moreover, to impose it upon your English realm also!' He swung back on Hyde. 'Is that a basis for negotiation ?'

'What would *you* suggest, my lord ?'

'You said, Sire, a little past, that you would confirm me in my offices and positions ? Though in secret. By that do you mean as Captain-General of your Scottish forces, and Viceroy or Governor there ?'

'Yes, my lord – and more than that. I would have you to command all, Commander-in-Chief of *all* my forces whatsoever, by land and sea. And meantime to be my ambassador-at-large, to all the courts and rulers of Europe.'

Montrose bowed, but briefly. 'Your Grace is kind. But the last is significant, is it not ? Ambassador-at-large, meantime! You would have me, therefore, at *other* courts. Not your own! This is the secrecy again ? A kind of banishment, indeed! Meantime.'

Hyde all but choked, and Charles bit his lip.

'Good God – no! Never that, my lord. But, clearly, it would be a sign of my trust and favour. While yet you were not present at these negotiations . . .' The young voice tailed away.

'Precisely, Sire.' Montrose contrived a smile. 'Banishment is too harsh a word, I agree. Forgive me. Shall we say . . . extrusion ? Politic retirement elsewhere ? Think you that you would have any need for a commander-in-chief thereafter ? Or a Viceroy in Scotland. Having yielded your royal authority in advance ?'

The King swallowed, but did not answer.

'But you asked what *I* would advise, Sire. That is simple. Declare now these appointments and offices, publically. Inform Lauderdale and the negotiators that naturally your commander for Scotland must be present at any discussion of the Scottish situation. And throw your whole authority and will behind the raising of an army for me to take back to Scotland just so soon as possible, to place you in *power* there, not as a puppet for Argyll. Aye – and come to Scotland with me, Sire, so that you *need* no Viceroy! Play the King of Scots indeed. That is my advice.'

If that left Charles Stewart and his Chancellor at a loss for words, it also somewhat surprised James Graham himself. He had not entered this room intending to make any such declaration and appeal. It seemed that, somehow, his mind had been made up for him.

The King swallowed audibly. 'You . . . you would do that, my lord? Lead an invasion – and take me with you?' His young – old eyes sparkled.

'It is what must be done if you are to fulfil your destiny, Sire. And to avenge your father's death. For which I also have a duty, I think.'

Hyde coughed loudly. 'Heady talk, my lord – soldier's talk. But scarcely practical, I suggest. His Majesty does not wish to start his reign by invasion and bloodshed. When his subjects are extending the hand of friendship, willing to negotiate. It would be an unstatesmanlike step. And if it failed, could lose him his Crown indeed. For ever. Moreover, to endanger his royal life in such adventure . . .!' The Chancellor shook his head severely. 'I cannot commend such a programme. I suggest, Sire, that this audience has achieved as much as is possible, at this stage.'

'Mm.' Charles looked uncertain, but threw one of his rueful smiles at Montrose.

'I agree with Sir Edward,' that man said, courteously now. 'Enough has been said. And I seek your royal forbearance and pardon if I have spoken over freely, have chosen my words ill. I did not come here, indeed, intending to offer to take up the sword again. I had thought that I had laid it down. But Your Grace's situation, your kindness, and above all, Scotland's need, forced me to say what I did. I trust, and believe, that you – as well as your advisers – will consider it well. I will await the outcome. May I say, Sire, that it has been my great joy to meet you? And to render to you my allegiance. It is yours to command. Have I your royal permission to retire?'

'Why yes, my lord Marquis. You, you have given me much to think upon. I thank you for it. I . . . I find plain speaking, on occasion, to my taste, I think! We shall discuss further, to be sure.'

'I thank you.'

'My lord – this audience, I would remind you, was secret. Was and is,' Hyde put in quickly. 'And must remain so.'

The Graham ignored that, bowed to his liege lord, and left the room.

*   *   *

Back in the Wassenaer Hof on his way to the rooms Elizabeth had insisted on providing for him – and for Napier and Kinnoull as well, so that it might look less personal – Montrose was way-laid by the Princess Sophia, who drew him into the music-room which served more or less as a private parlour for the family.

'Marquis – you have seen Charles? The new King?' she demanded, eagerly. 'How think you of him? Is he not . . . exciting? A prince of princes! You would get along well with him, I vow!'

'I found his Grace friendly and likeable, Highness. As a young man, much to be admired. As a King, it is a little early to say.'

'Oh, he will make a splendid King, I am sure. Not stiff and proud, as kings usually are! His people will love him, when they come to know him, of that I am certain.'

'His Grace has made a good start, it seems – with his cousin!'

She blushed, prettily. 'He is a great improvement on most of the princes. I have met – that is all,' she asserted. 'And he dances divinely. As he skates. He rides well too – like a, a centaur. And plays tennis better than any I have seen. He is so tall and dashing . . .'

'Altogether a most estimable young man, Highness. He is going to have little trouble with his *feminine* subjects, at least! Or . . . is he?'

'You, too! My lord, that is unworthy of you, I swear! Every-one casts up at him that wretched trollope Lucy Walters. A heartless scheming minx who set out to seduce him . . .'

'Our poor wronged Charles! Sophie on her pet subject, again!' The Princess Elizabeth had come into the music-room from a chamber beyond. 'Or should it be that Sophie is *Charles's* pet subject?'

'At least it is not *you*, Eliza, whom Charles dances with, and takes riding and skating! Nor do I blame him . . . !'

'Hush, Sophie – what will my lord of Montrose think of you? He must have a strange enough opinion of this family, as it is, I do declare!'

'My opinion of the Bohemian royal family could scarcely be

292

higher, Highness,' James Graham assured, smiling. 'So much beauty, talent, vigour and kindness, in one household, is hardly to be credited.'

'You perhaps should keep such fine speeches for Louie. Or Mamma, my lord.'

'And you have not met our brother Charles Louis!' Sophie giggled.

'Sophie – restrain yourself!' her elder sister reproved. 'My lord – pay no heed. She has had her head turned by our saturnine cousin's recent attentions . . .'

'I have *not*! And he is not saturnine. He is very good-looking, in one way. You all call him ugly, copying Mamma, just because you are jealous. He is a lot better-looking than that dry old stick Descartes *you* dote on, and write endless screeds to! Pretending it is philosophy! As for Louie and her sighings and moonings...!'

'What of Louie?' Although, as always, slightly husky, the voice came clearly from the other room. 'I can hear very well Sophie.'

'Ha – the Princess Louise is here,' Montrose said. 'I must pay my respects.' Uncertain whether to be glad for the interruption, or otherwise, he moved over to the open doorway, and through.

She was standing at an easel, in an old paint-smudged smock, brushes and palate in hand. She did not turn as he entered the room.

'Princess – you are busy. Forgive me. I would not wish to interrupt. But I could not ignore you when I heard your voice.' It did not fail to occur to him that if she had heard her sister so clearly, she had heard him also, and could have come through had she so desired.

Almost as though she had read his thoughts, Eliza, behind him commented, 'Oh, Louie would *wish* you to interrupt her, I am sure! She merely would have you come to her, not she come to you, my lord!'

'As is but right and proper,' the man acceded mildly.

Louise spoke, still without turning her head from the painting. 'Had you any sisters, my lord? Or brothers, rather – since sisters would be more kindly to a brother, I think. *I* am blessed with mine, you will notice? They are a little trying at times – but much kinder when such as the Marquis of Montrose is not present.'

'That is unfair . . .!' Sophie exclaimed hotly. 'You cannot blame us if you are so, so difficult.'

'Highnesses!' Montrose protested. 'I seem to be the unwitting cause of a rift in the lute, a discord in this music-room! I had better retire, I think – since it seems that you treat each other more kindly when I am not here!'

'No. You have not yet told me how it went with King Charles. Did you agree? He told me that he thinks you the hero of the age. Those were his very words – the hero of the age.' Sophie nodded importantly, with something only she was able to declare.

'If you go before Mamma comes, we all will get the rough side of her tongue,' Eliza said. 'Shall we not, Louie?'

'Probably,' Louise agreed, shrugging slightly. 'But that is no concern of my lord's. He will wish to escape from this nest of idle chattering women, I think. As who would blame him? Or deny him?'

James Graham looked from her stiff, besmocked back to the other two, and shook his head gently. Then he moved over, closer to the easel. 'May I see what you paint, Highness?' he asked. 'I have no talent that way, myself – but I greatly admire those who have.'

'Lord Jamie – you call Mamma Elizabeth, when you think none hear you,' the irrepressible Sophie declared. 'Must you call us all Highness, all the time?'

He drew a hand over his mouth. 'If Your Highnesses prefer otherwise. In private.'

'We do – oh, we do. *You* do, Louie, I swear.'

'My lord of Montrose will do as he thinks best. He always does,' her sister said. But she turned round, at last, and her eyes rose to his.

Meeting her look, the man was strangely moved. The other two young women might not have been present, in those moments. There was a distinct and undeniable rapport and affinity between them, a clear mutual awareness and some sort of bond. It was an alarming and momentarily bewildering recognition for James Graham, bringing with it an immediate sense of both satisfaction and guilt, of pleasure and pain. This should not be, he was well aware. Yet there was delight in it . . .

Neither spoke, and it was Eliza who commented.

'His lordship may prefer to keep his distance. From some of us,' she said drily. 'He must find us something of a . . . confusion.' She had some uncanny knack of mind-reading, that eldest and least beautiful of the sisters.

The man withdrew his gaze, to transfer it to the canvas on the easel – although he was only partially aware of what he saw. It was the painter that preoccupied him, not the painting, mentally, emotionally and physically – that, and an awareness of a sense of betrayal. *His* betrayal of Elizabeth. In thus mentally embracing the daughter when it was the mother whom he loved. What had suddenly happened to him?

Long he peered at the picture, as though examining its every brush-mark. It was the portrait of an old wizened man peering regretfully into an empty tankard. Only the face was completed, the rest only sketched in. But that face was vividly alive, set in lines of experience and constant disappointment, rheumy eyes preoccupied with the obvious emptiness of what he held, and seeking in its dregs for all that the drinker had lost, or failed to find, in a long life. The thing was a clear allegory, but displaying extraordinary depth and understanding, sympathy, especially for a young woman and a princess, insight into character and emotion, and an ability to portray it surely and with vigour. That, of course, was what had allegedly sparked off her interest in himself, at their first meeting in Hamburg, her concern with character wherever it might be found. Not that James Graham consciously perceived all this in those moments, his eye looking inwards rather than outwards. He straightened up.

'A notable work. Great . . . compassion,' he said. 'There is feeling, deeply perceived, Louie. And displayed.' It was the first time he had used her Christian name, let alone the familiar Louie.

'Not deeply enough displayed,' she answered shortly. 'Not one tenth of what I would show, is there.'

'An old drunken sot's maudlin tears?' Sophie cried.

'That old man's tears are my own. And all the world's,' Montrose told her; and he heard the sharp intake of Louie's breath at his side.

'Then you should see her picture of *you*, Lord Jamie!' the younger sister asserted with a quick laugh.

'I heard, yes, that a portrait was being drawn. From memory. I was much flattered – and would be most interested to see it . . .'

'No!' Louise said forcefully. 'He is *not* to see it. I told you all . . .'

'Why not? It is not so bad as *all* that!'

'Because it reveals the artist more truly than the sitter!' Eliza said calmly.

'It is not to be shown, I say . . .'

There was a diversion as Queen Elizabeth swept in, her lovely face flushed from the cold air, hair disordered, eyes sparkling, magnificent in riding-habit and ostrich-feathered wide-brimmed hat.

'Arguing, as always, my nestlings!' she cried. 'And before my lord! On my oath, you are incorrigible! Heigho – I am late. I met my lord Earl of Crawford, new come from Paris and the Louvre. To see the King. A very gallant cavalier, I must say. Vehement. He would have swept even an old lady like myself out of my saddle, had I given him an inch of encouragement.'

'And you did not, Mamma?'

Elizabeth ignored her namesake. 'He is a major-general of your own, my Lord Jamie, he tells me?'

'Hardly of my own, Your Majesty.' Montrose bowed. 'His commission was direct from His late Grace, your brother. Myself, I would have used my lord's undoubted abilities . . . differently.'

'Aha – nicely put! I can just see it. And you two together. Sparks flying, when a fizzing rocket meets a deep-glowing fire! He said that he had gone from Scotland to Henrietta Maria as your ambassador. So I told him that I hoped he soldiered better than he played envoy, or Heaven help the Marquis and the King's cause! I do not think that he liked that.' Her laughter pealed out rich, musical, uninhibited.

Looking from her to her second daughter, James Graham knew a complex feeling, compounded of understanding, relief and sympathy. It was something of her mother in Louie which attracted him to her. But when Elizabeth herself came into the company, her daughters, indeed all others, might almost not be there. Louie had deep, banked-down fires, yes, and much that spoke quietly, directly to something in himself; but her mother was all of her plus so much more, the most alive person, without exception, whom it had ever been his joy and privilege to meet. And she loved him – the miracle of it, she loved him!

'I was admiring Louise's painting, Majesty,' he said, carefully. 'So full of warmth and compassion, seeing below the surface. She sees that old man as *mankind*, I think. Whereas others can see only a drunken sot.' He glanced round, smiling, for Sophia – but she had slipped away, out of the room.

The Queen nodded. 'Kind,' she said. 'Louie has to put up with much raillery, I fear. She will the more cherish your . . . understanding.' And, as Louise turned away abruptly, at that, she shrugged, but cheerfully. 'Ah me – who would be a mother? Now – tell me, how did you fare with my nephew Charles? You are back sooner than I looked for you?'

'I found His Grace an attractive and interesting young man, Your Majesty. We spoke of many matters. And learned to know each other a little, I think.'

'But . . . ? But – you are disappointed in him?'

'Say that I perhaps had not appreciated how young he is. Nor how much he is under Hyde's thumb.'

'Ah! Ned Hyde? That was the trouble? Was he there? All the time?'

'Yes. I could not object to that, with so new a monarch. But his influence was too strong, too much that of the tutor, I fear.'

'He has been in charge of Charles for too long. A complacent little man. But with his uses, also. For he has countered Henrietta Maria's influence with her son, in some measure . . .'

'Has he, Mamma? What of Mistress Walters – Sophie's *bete noire*? And Charles's other ladies, then?'

Sophie came back, as though on the enunciation of her name, carrying something bulky.

'Oh, no!' That was Louise, hotly.

'But yes, Louie!' her sister cried, and turned round her burden, whipping off the cloth that covered it. She held up a painted canvas, the portrait of Montrose, for him to inspect.

'You are cruel! Heartless!' Louise exclaimed. And swinging round, she positively ran from the room.

'That was not kindly done, Sophie,' her mother said. 'But – the Lord Jamie would have to see it, some time.'

James Graham looked at the picture – and did not fail to recognise why its painter had not wished him to see it. Not that it was ill done, or a poor likeness – quite the reverse. It was in fact a very handsome portrait, pleasingly and naturally postured, attractively coloured, and unmistakably Montrose, in his most gallant stance, against a background of smoky war-clouds. Yet there was something wrong with it, something not true. And it did not demand any particular perception to recognise what it was. It was the subject's expression of sheer love and fervour. Not the fervour of battle or loyalty or enthusiasm, but simply and clearly that of a man's love for a woman, for the woman those eyes seemed to feast upon. It was extraordinary that mere paint could be made to express an emotion so frankly, vividly.

'I see,' he said, sighing a little. 'A most . . . telling picture.

Remarkable. Done by a most gifted hand. And mind. And done from memory, to be sure. Or, at least from . . .' he did not finish that.

'Done from *heart* rather than hand, I'd say!' Eliza observed.

'Yes. Well, take it away, Sophie,' the Queen said. 'Louie will not quickly forgive you for this. I think. Off with you.' She turned. 'And you too, Eliza, if you please. I have more important matters I wish to discuss with my lord. Matters of State.'

'Of *State*, Mamma ?' That young woman smiled. 'I will see to it, then, that you are not disturbed!'

'Do that, baggage!',

Montrose spoke. 'And will you be so good as to tell the Princess Louise that I admired her portrait ? And am both flattered . . . and unworthy. Tell her kindly, please.'

Eliza nodded. 'I understand,' she said. She looked back, from the doorway. 'We do not scratch at each other *all* the time,' she added, and went.

Alone, the man and woman eyed each other unspeaking for a long moment, and then came into each other's arms. Her hat fell off.

'Dear Jamie,' she murmured, against his lips. 'You are kind. What a tangle! How can you . . . put up with us all ?'

'I am deeply, humbly, grateful,' he said. 'For all.'

'Are you ? Are you ?' She drew her head back a little, to look at him. 'Can that be true ?'

'The simple truth, Elizabeth. I have had not so much of love in my life that I do not cherish it. When so generously given. By whomsoever.'

'By whomsoever! By mother and daughter! An old woman – and a young one!'

'Years have little to do with true love. Or with a great deal that is important in living. That at least I have learned.'

'Yes. But . . . you are sure ? In your own mind ? Louie has so much more to offer than have I.'

'Yes, I am sure.' He paused, only for a moment. 'To be honest, for a space I wondered. A little. Before you came. But whenever you entered I knew beyond all doubt. And rejoiced to know it.'

'I am glad, then, glad. Selfishly. Had it been otherwise, I do not think that I would have given you up so very readily. Without a fight. And when Elizabeth Stewart fights, I warn you . . .!'

He closed her lips on that threat.

Presently she detached herself. 'Now, to get back to our important matters of state! No, no – do not be greedy, Jamie. Time enough for that. You cannot trifle with kings and queens and look to escape your obligations to their game of kingcraft. What of Charles ? I thought that I had primed him well. And he does admire you – there is no doubt of that. What went wrong ? Can I help ?'

'You could aid me to work on Charles's mind, my dear. To wean him from Hyde's tutorship, at least where Scotland is concerned.' He paused, drawing a breath. 'I offered to take an army back to Scotland to gain *his* throne for him. And asked him to come with me. I had to do it.'

In silence she searched his face, and a prolonged sigh escaped her. Then she nodded. 'Yes. Yes, for you, it had to be that, in the end. I tried to convince myself otherwise. To keep you here. But – I knew in my heart that it could not be. That you would go back to Scotland eventually, to hazard all. James Graham being James Graham. And, leave Elizabeth Stewart.'

'When *Charles* Stewart sits on his Scottish throne, Elizabeth Stewart will be as well in Scotland as in the Hague. And no exile, any more.'

She gazed away beyond him. 'True,' she said, at last. 'Jamie – what is to become of us ? You and me ? Can we ever . . . is it possible . . . ?'

'Anything is possible – if we are determined to have it so, my dear. Greater difficulties than this. It is in God's hands – but if we set *our* hands to it, and our hearts, we shall not fail. Here – or hereafter.'

'Very well.' Elizabeth nodded again. 'I accept that. From James Graham. I do not think that I would accept it from any other. I shall not doubt the future, then. But meantime, thank God, we have the present! Enough of this talk, my dear. Matters of State be damned! We have . . . each other.'

'With all my heart!' he said.

CHAPTER TWENTY-ONE

Once again, therefore, as so often before, it was a matter of waiting, for James Graham. But this waiting was different. Now, indeed, he almost welcomed the delay. For now he had Elizabeth and delight – even though it had to be a very discreet delight.

It was as well that he could feel this way, for in all truth his cause did not make much apparent headway that first half of 1649. Charles and his councillors maintained their attitude of official non-recognition, however ridiculous the consequences in a comparatively small city like the Hague. Everyone knew that the young King personally favoured the Graham, and only kept him at a distance for reasons of state. That they met, on occasion, at the Wassanaer Hof and elsewhere was inevitable and likewise well known. But the fiction was kept up.

The new representatives from Scotland in due course arrived, to reinforce the objectionable Lauderdale – in theory to supersede him, Lanark their leader, now being in name at least the senior. For he was in fact now Duke of Hamilton. His brother, captured after Preston, had recently followed his erstwhile and ill-served master to an English scaffold, the heavy hand of General Cromwell – who now dominated an English Parliament which acknowledged no king and called the Kingdom a Commonwealth – unfaltering with the axe. Montrose had heartily disliked the man, and with reason – but he grieved and was shocked that he should have been slain so. He made a point of letting the former Lanark know of this – Elizabeth inviting one or two of the new Scots Engagers to dinner at the Wassenaer Hof and James Graham appearing thereat as an honoured guest. Nor did, or could, the Queen of Bohemia's other guests make protest; certainly they did not march out. This was typical of the crazy situation which prevailed at the Hague in the year 1649.

William Hamilton was a weaker but rather less arrogant and stupid edition of his brother, and was in fact considerably in awe of Montrose. In public he assiduously, if with evident embarrassment, avoided anything but a monosyllabic exchange with the Graham; but when, with Elizabeth's aid, the latter contrived it so that they might have a brief private conversation, the new Duke was a little more forthcoming. He admitted that the situation in Scotland was bad, that Argyll's rule was hateful, that they needed their King back on the throne, as a civil authority for all decent men to rally round, and to counter the overweening dominance and tyranny of the zealot ministers; but insisted that, with Argyll and the Kirk swaying them, the Estates were wholly set on the King adhering to the Solemn League and Covenant. Nothing else would do. As also, of course, Montrose's own exclusion. He, Hamilton, could not relax on these basic conditions one iota. He was nominally in charge of the negotiations; but he knew Argyll did not trust him. Lauderdale was still the Campbell's man, and in constant secret touch with Scotland. He was sorry, but there was nothing that he could do to ease the situation.

So the charade went on. The negotiations continued seemingly endlessly. Progress was made on a number of minor matters, and some not so minor – for instance a total break with Cromwell and the English Parliamentarians. But on the main issue of contention, that Charles must accept and sign the Solemn League and Covenant, with its essential corollary that Presbyterianism must be imposed on *all* the King's realms, there was no agreement.

So matters stood when, in May, still another deputation arrived from Scotland – and this time, no Engagers. They came direct from the Chancellor – which meant, from Argyll – and proved to be a much tougher and less discursive party. They had the immediate effect of tightening up the Scots position, cancelling much that had been accepted, and generally changing the atmosphere. They were led by the Earl of Cassillis, a sour and hardened West-country Presbyterian, nick-named The Solemn, and one of the actual framers of the Solemn League and Covenant. With him came Master Robert Baillie, one of the Kirk's most vociferous and active zealots, and kinsman of the unfortunate General William Baillie whom Montrose had humiliated so frequently in the field.

The new Commissioners made no attempt to conceal their contempt for Hamilton and his team, even for Lauderdale; and their annoyance – or Argyll's – that negotiations had dragged out thus long and not been satisfactorily concluded. They made it abundantly clear that they considered that they held the whiphand. All would start afresh – and would be dealt with expeditiously from now on. King Charles they treated almost as a cipher. They had not come to bargain, or indeed to negotiate at all. They had come to inform, to state, to demand. Charles had been duly proclaimed as King from the market crosses of Scotland, with trumpet and tuck of drum. In return, if that proclamation was to be followed by a coronation, he must accede to three demands. The Solemn League and Covenant must be subscribed, in total. All Acts of the Scottish Parliament, past, present and future, were to be homologated, and taken as binding on the King. All civil matters and questions must be referred to the said Parliament, hereafter – and all religious to the General Assembly. No matters of State should be decided without their consent. Nothing could be simpler.

They brought other word than that from Scotland. George Gordon, Marquis of Huntly, had been surprised and captured in Aberdeenshire, hurried south to Edinburgh and there executed out of hand – as an enemy of the State. His heir, the Viscount Aboyne, was somewhere in exile and said to be dying. The young Lord Lewis now led the Clan Gordon undisputed – and had come to terms with Argyll. A purge was proceeding in Scotland amongst all who were not wholly for the Solemn League and militant Presbyterianism; even many of the more moderate ministers were being deposed and driven from their parishes. There had been an abortive rising in the North, led by Mackenzie of Pluscarden, the diffident Earl of Seaforth's brother, but this had been put down with vigour by David Leslie, the usual executions following – though Seaforth himself had got out of Scotland in time.

It was all a grim development for Montrose and his cause. But it had its brighter side. The sheer arrogance and lack of all respect on the part of Cassillis and Baillie grievously offended young Charles and set his advisers by the ears. There was now really nothing to negotiate about; it was either complete surrender to the Commissioners, or nothing. Little was to be gained, therefore, by keeping Montrose out of sight any more. After another secret meeting at the Wassenaer Hof, where James Graham pointed out the obvious, and moreover that the news from Scotland had its hopeful side, since clearly Argyll was being forced to hold down the country by arms and terror, the King announced publicly that he was reappointing his illustrious and trusted friend, the Marquis of Montrose, Captain-General and commander-in-chief of all his forces, and that therefore he was entitled to, and must, take part in any further debates and negotiations in which matters military might be involved. Since arms were already in use in Scotland, and none could assert that they would not continue to be so, the Marquis must be present.

That set the cat amongst the pigeons with a vengeance. The Commissioners were faced with the choice of swallowing their condition against Montrose being at the conference-table, or of packing up and going home with nothing decided. They compromised. They declared that they could not accept the excommunicate and malignant James Graham in any degree as a negotiator; but that they would attend one more meeting with the King and his advisers, not to negotiate but to sum up what had been achieved, preparatory to their departure for Scotland.

A confrontation was at last to be effected.

* * *

And so Montrose finally crossed the threshold of the wing of the Binnenhoff Palace lent to His Britannic Majesty. He entered the heavily ornate conference-chamber, in an atmosphere of high tension, immediately behind King Charles, the Commissioners from Scotland, already present and seated, perforce rising to their feet at the monarch's arrival, however galling in that they seemed to be standing for the Captain-General also. Every eye was on James Graham, who came in with grave dignity but no sort of triumph or flourish – even when Charles, taking his throne-like chair at the head of the long table, waved him to the seat immediately on his right, first on that side of the board, hitherto always occupied by Sir Edward Hyde – who now sat one farther down. The message was clear – and something like a growl rose from the ranks of the Scots Commissioners. Though not from all the Scots present, for now the right-hand side of the table was furnished with certain other peers of Scotland, at Montrose's suggestion, the Earls of Crawford, Kinnoull, even Seaforth – who had arrived timeously at the Hague only the day before – and the Lords Napier and Sinclair.

A chair scraped back, and although John Kennedy, 6th Earl of Cassillis did not rise, he drew every eye. He was a stocky, heavy, greying man of middle years, square-faced, with bushy eyebrows and a lowering expression, dressed more like a divine than a great nobleman.

'Your Grace,' he rasped, in a nasal voice 'in the name of this Commission of the Estates, I do protest at the presence of James

Graham, so-called Marquis of Montrose, at this table, and in the company of honest men! He is here against the wishes, advice and consciences of those whose duty and concern it is to guide Your Grace on Scottish matters, an outlaw and renegade, forfeited for crimes unnumbered against the Scottish realm. No negotiation or dealing with him is permissible or possible. I demand that he be dismissed forthwith. In the name of the Commission of the Estates.'

The Reverend Robert Baillie, tall, shock-headed, urgent, hot-eyed, jumped to his feet with all the vigour of a much younger man. 'I further that demand. In the name of the General Assembly of the Kirk of Scotland. I say that I cannot sit at a table with a notorious sinner, excommunicated by the Kirk, a man justly cast out of the Church of God, upon whose head lies more innocent blood than on any other for many years, the most bloody murderer in our nation!' Trembling with his emotion, he pointed at Montrose.

There were gasps around the table at this passionate onslaught, and not all from the King's side, Hamilton especially looking highly uncomfortable. Charles turned to Montrose, dark brows raised – but that man looked straight in front of him, grave expression unchanged. He did not speak.

The young King cleared his throat. 'Master Baillie, I request that you use more temperate language in my royal presence,' he said. 'My lord Marquis is here on my authority, and it is not my desire that he should withdraw. So, I fear . . .' A slight pause, and that flashing smile, '. . . I fear that since you cannot sit at table with him, you will have to remain standing! Or, hm, leave us.'

There were some smothered chuckles at that, and Archie Napier, who had half risen to protest on his uncle's behalf, subsided, grinning.

Baillie, blinking those hot eyes, bit his lip and looked uncertain. Then, pushing back his chair a good yard from the table, he sat down thereon behind the backs of his colleagues. Into the uncomfortable silence, a thick but fruity voice spoke, coarse, spluttering a little, but strong. 'Sire – if the Marquis of Montrose is to be present, then there can be no further negotiation. For this is part of our remit – as was made fell clear before this. If it is your royal wish, then we must accept it, in this house.' The speaker rather underlined that word *this*. He was a burly, almost gross man, younger than the previous spokesmen, but florid, gone to fat, with double chin, thick sensuous lips and small shrewd pig-like eyes, John Maitland, 2nd Earl of Lauderdale, grandson of James VI and I's Chancellor Maitland, and great-grandson of Mary Queen of Scots' agile Secretary Maitland of Lethington. 'But we may at least detail and sum up what has already been discussed and accepted. And so we may not entirely waste our time – and Your Grace's.'

'I am still open to conviction, my lord, therefore to negotiation. If these talks must end without decision, then I call all to witness that it is not my wish or choosing. *I* will still negotiate.'

'How can you say that?' Cassillis – who had looked none too pleased at Lauderdale's apparent taking of the lead – demanded. 'When Your Grace has rejected all three of our main points – that you take the Covenant, homologate all Acts of Parliament, and in future act only with the agreement of the Estates and the General Assembly. Lacking acceptance of these terms, we must return to Scotland, nothing achieved. And Your Grace no nearer your throne!'

'Terms, my lord? Did I hear aright?' That was James Graham. 'Do you, an Earl of Scotland, present *terms* to *Ard Righ*, your liege lord?'

Cassillis's great fist banged down on the table. 'Sire – I'll no' bandy words with this, this felon! But, these are terms, yes. Not mine, but of the Estates of your Scottish realm. Either you accept them – or you do not ascend the throne.'

Charles seemed about to make hot retort, but a cough from Hyde caused him to pause, shrug and produce his rueful grin. 'But, my lord – what would you? I have agreed to sign your Covenant – the National one, not the other, which appears to me to interfere impossibly in the affairs of my other realm of England. I have agreed to consider all the Acts and edicts of the Parliaments which have sat in Scotland since the last accepted by my royal father. You cannot expect me to homologate them un-read? You have not brought them all with you, have you? But I would *wish* to approve them, if I may. And I have said that I will indeed consult with the Estates, as is right and proper, in all major matters of policy and law. The Assembly of the Kirk is another matter. For it is a private body with no civil authority. But I will say that I have no wish or intention to interfere with the governance of the Kirk – any more than it should interfere in the governance of the realm. I cannot see, my lord, wherein we are so far from agreement.'

'Then Your Grace's sight must be much impaired!' Cassillis snapped. 'No doubt through immaturity and ill-advice!' And he glared round the opposite side of the table. 'You canna cozen us with words, see you. The terms are clear – no' to be mistaken. Either you agree to them, without quibble or reserve – or you continue to bide here in exile!'

When the outraged murmur of the King's advisers sank away, Montrose spoke quietly. 'I think there is a third alternative, my Lord Cassillis.'

The Kennedy did not answer him, but he eyed him like a wary bull.

'His Grace may return to Scotland, his kingdom, under other auspices than your unmannerly ones, sir. And *take* what is his own, by right.'

There was silence at that. The two sides were now clearly in naked confrontation, all pretence dropped.

It was Lauderdale who spoke. 'Invasion, my lord of Montrose! Against his Grace's own people? We have had enough of bloodshed.'

'Have you, sir? I have not seen you risking *your* blood. On either side!'

'I am a man of peace, sir.'

'How fortunate you are! Whereas I am a man of blood, it seems? A murderer most vile, according to Master Baillie. Admittedly I have seen blood shed in the cause of His late Majesty. Even a little of my own. And am prepared to shed more, for His Grace here – all of my own, if need be. For I do believe, sir, that right, justice, freedom, truth, are more precious even than blood – mine own, or yours. But, Lord Lauderdale, since you are a proclaimed man of peace, you will not oppose His Grace's landing on the shores of his own ancient kingdom? Or urge others to do so. Thus you will suffer no blood-letting. Will you?'

Frowning, the other did not reply.

There was a general muttering round the table. Robert Baillie began to speak, recollected that he had declared that he could not, and subsided into frustrated silence.

The Reverend Alexander Jaffray spoke instead. 'If Your Highness listens to this evil man, this barbarian who has taken up the sword and will most undoubtedly perish by the sword, you will make your name hated in every corner of the realm,' he cried.

'Master Jaffray – you were at Philiphaugh, I believe,' Montrose said, conversationally. 'Urging on the godly work of slaughter. How many men, aye, and women and children also, did *you* slay, or urge to be slain that day? By the sword, the pike, the bullet, the cudgel, by drowning? Tell His Grace – for they would have been *his* subjects.'

'They were God's enemies, sirrah, whosoever subjects! Idolatrous savages. Catholic Erse and heathenish Highland scum! Do you dare name such in the same breath as God's elect people ...?'

'I do, sir – I do. Christ died for them, as much as for you. Will you, can you, deny that?'

'I am not here to justify the purposes of Almighty God to an excommunicate.'

'Very well. You have your answer, Sire. I say, send these stiff-necked and self-righteous persecutors of your Scottish subjects back to the man who sent them. Archibald Campbell, with the word that you will sign the *National* Covenant, deal well and faithfully with the decisions of Parliament and govern through it, and will allow freedom of worship for all whatsoever, be they Presbyterian, Episcopalean or Roman. And that you will come in person quickly thereafter, for your royal coronation, adequately supported. And that no subject, Argyll or other, will offer the King of Scots terms! Send that message, Sire – and that said, I see no need to detain these gentlemen further.'

Strangely enough it was Edward Hyde who protested. 'Sire – Your Majesty We ... my lord of Montrose goes too fast. We are reasonable men. We must act as statesmen, not swordsmen! Especially when my lord Marquis of Argyll has shown that he would prefer so to act. He has held out a hand ...'

'A hand that grasped £200,000 as price for his master, by God!' That was the Earl of Crawford.

'Sire – do not be distracted by these unhelpful interruptions,' the Chancellor urged. 'We must look at the situation as it is, not as we would wish it to be. Whatever is past, the Marquis of Argyll has extended a hand to Your Majesty. You can, I do conceive, meet two of his conditions. As for the Solemn League and Covenant, it is scarcely possible for you to sign it as it is at present worded, however much you might wish – since it would impose Presbyterian church-government on England. Which is, hm, unacceptable. But not only this, it would in consequence preclude all co-operation between Scots and English royalists, such as is vitally necessary. So I say, as a reasonable man, ask my lord of Argyll and the Estates to amend the wording thereof sufficiently for Your Majesty to sign it. None so difficult, surely. A word here and there – that is all.' Hyde put his plump fingers together, and beamed over them at all concerned, a civilised man triumphant. 'Thus all three conditions will be met, and all resolved. And the fourth matter for consideration will fall into its due and proper sequence . . .'

'Fourth matter, man ? What fourth matter ?'That was Cassillis.

'One which was not entrusted to your Commission – which would have been unsuitable, my lord,' the little man declared primly. 'Since it is a more personal matter. Sent direct from my lord Marquis to His Majesty. Through my humble self. My lord of Argyll, in token of his goodwill and honest and loyal intentions, suggests that his daughter, the Lady Anne Campbell, should be married to His Majesty.'

'Merciful . . . God!' Montrose got out, chokingly.

There was chaos around that table, on both sides, men exclaiming, shouting, thumping the board, jumping to their feet. King Charles sat back, watching, a curious expression on his saturnine features. He made no attempt to halt the uproar – although his Chancellor did, beating on the table with a roll of paper, his shocked voice rising to a squeak, totally without effect.

At length Montrose turned to the young monarch, his poise recovered. 'Sire – you will not control them now. Nor, I think, should wish to. I would advise that you rise and leave. The best way. At this juncture. _Your_ dignity intact, at least. Better tactics for the future, anyway.'

Charles nodded, relievedly, got to his feet, and inclined his head towards the noisy company. Then he turned, and walked unhurriedly to the door. Montrose managed to reach and open it for him, in time. They passed through, and it shut behind them.

'Mary Mother of God!' the King – who was, of course, a good official Protestant – exclaimed. 'That was . . . an experience! Heaven preserve me from many such! Is that what Privy Councils are like in Scotland, my lord ?'

'Do not think too hardly of the Scots, Sire. These were scarcely representative. And at least they did not swallow the Campbell's insult to Your Grace, as Hyde seems to have done.'

Charles looked at him thoughtfully for a moment, and then changed the subject. 'You said, just then, something about better tactics for the future. What did you mean ?'

'I meant, Sire, that after this you cannot sit down again with these Commissioners. Even if they would. Not without seeming to surrender your position. You have given them *something* to take home with them – more I think than they should have. So, I humbly suggest that Your Grace should remove yourself.'

'Remove myself? I? Go away?'

'Yes. Go – before they do. Show that *you* clearly have had sufficient. Not that *they* have left you. Go, meantime, somewhere away from the Hague. And, if you will, seem to link your going with armed preparations. Such will well serve your cause, I am sure.'

'And *your's*, my lord!'

'My cause is your own, Sire. I have no other.'

'Where could I go? To Paris? To my mother? Not that, I think!'

'Your sister and the Prince of Orange are gone to Breda, in Brabant, meantime. Could you not go there? Seem to concern yourself with shipping. Prince Rupert used Breda when he was recruiting ships and men. Busy yourself with that, Sire. Or, if you do not in truth, *seem* to. Nothing will more surely disturb these Commissioners. And Argyll.'

'Ned Hyde will not like it.'

'Hyde has had his chance. And what has it won Your Grace?'

'I . . . I will think on it, my lord. Yes – I believe you have the rights of it . . .'

CHAPTER TWENTY-TWO

James Graham rode through the mellow smiling Rhineland province of Utrecht in the golden late-August sunshine, with only Archie Napier for company, his mind something of a battleground for his all too demanding emotions. At long last the waiting, the uncertainty, the painful frustrations, seemed to be almost over. The action for which his whole nature craved was about to replace the years of delay and disappointment – even though it was not the scale of action he had visualised and there was still much of disappointment, foot-dragging, almost betrayal involved. And he was going to see Elizabeth again, after six weeks of absence. But that was as bitter-sweet as the rest.

The Queen of Bohemia and her family had been lent, for some summers, the small, old and semi-derelict royal castle of Rhenen, on the Nether Rhine, to escape to in the hot months when the dusty plains around the Hague baked, and where she could indulge in the active pursuits which she loved, hunting in the forests, hawking in the low hills, boating excursions on the great river. It was only a roosting-place, primitive, uncomfortable – but Elizabeth greatly enjoyed it, and was grateful to her niece's husband for letting her use it. Montrose had not been there previously.

They rode down to the town by the riverside, jingled through the narrow streets, and on up the circular roadway which climbed round and round the steep rocky bluff behind, past the outer and inner walls and gatehouses. At close range the castle looked a deal less romantic, with here and there decayed outbuildings, sagging roofs, broken masonry and fallen plaster. There were no guards at either gatehouse to challenge callers.

Clattering into the high central courtyard under the soaring towers where pigeons cooed and grass grew between the paving-stones, they found Princess Louise helping an elderly groom at one of the handles of the obviously deep draw-well in the centre. Looking up, at their arrival, she did not fail to look disconcerted and embarrassed, but there was no lack of eagerness in her glance – even though she replaced it by a frown and went on still more vigorously winding her handle. Archie gallantly leapt down and ran to relieve her at her labour, just as the brimming bucket came to the top. A row of already filled buckets stood nearby.

James Graham came to her, smiling, hands outstretched. 'How well you look, Louie. And how lovely!' He leant, to kiss both her flushed cheeks, a proceeding Napier eyed with a touch of envy. 'Rhenen agrees with you, to be sure. Even with all the water to hoist from the depths of the earth. How good to see you again.'

'And you, my lord. My *lords*.' She had excuse for sounding breathless. 'We believed you in Brussels.'

'We have come from there. The more happy to be here.'

'You will find Mamma gathering plums,' Louie said, looking away. 'There is an orchard. On a terrace – over that side. Hugo will show you.'

He was about to suggest that it would be better if she showed him herself, but thought better of it. 'Archie will be glad to aid you with the water, I am sure,' he said easily, and strolled off with the groom.

Through a pend below a corbelled tower, they came out on a sloping terrace grown with old and gnarled fruit-trees, and down the somewhat lessened incline people were working, filling baskets with the fat purple plums. Amongst the leafage Montrose could not identify individuals. Dismissing the guide, he wandered down amongst the trees. The noise of bees was here superseding the cooing of the doves.

He saw the Princess Eliza sitting on a stool, her back against a tree-trunk, eyes apparently closed, and, feeling disinclined for a verbal passage at arms just then, moved discreetly away. Then he heard an inconsequential, crooning singing – and his heart lifted to the voice. He made his way towards the sound.

Elizabeth was up a ladder, head amongst the branches, pulling fruit and putting the plums in a basket hung on an iron hook, humming a melody as she worked. The man bowed to her silken stockings.

'Your elevated Highness,' he observed, judicially, 'has a well-turned ankle!'

She looked down, wide-eyed. 'Jamie!' she cried. 'On my soul – Jamie Graham! Here's joy!' And she came down that ladder in a rush more illustrative of her physical fitness and agility than of her dignity.

But it was the clear and apparent duty of a gentleman to aid her in the business, if not actually to catch her bodily. Montrose did not neglect his responsibilities.

In each other's arms for a moment they clung tightly, before separating, with swift glances around. Dressed in oldest clothing, cheek smudged with green lichen from the tree, fingers stained with the fruit, eyes shining, she looked entirely ravishing nevertheless. He said as much.

'My dear, my dear!' she breathed, in not much more than a whisper, consciously or otherwise seeking not to draw attention to themselves a moment before they must, there amongst the serried, low-branched trees. 'How good, how splendid. And the better for being unexpected. In your letter of a week past you did not say . . . ? Are you finished at Brussels, then ? Or is this but an interlude ?' She shook her head. 'But – never heed. You are here – that is all that matters.'

'Agreed. After the stolid mynheers of the States-General, you can scarcely conceive how glorious a sight you make, Elizabeth, my love – smears and all! Yes, I have finished with Brussels at last, thank God – although less profitably than I had hoped. No more kicking my heels *there*, at least.'

'Good! Then you will be able to stay awhile ? You deserve a diversion, a respite. I shall take you boar-hunting, Jamie – a change from boors! We shall sail the river, fish with spears – a new sport I have discovered – visit the monasteries where they make the wine . . .'

'Do not tempt me!' he broke in on her, pleading. 'Alas, I cannot stay. I am here only, to to . . .' He could not bring himself to use the phrase 'say goodbye'. 'Only two nights, my dear. Then I must be on my way.'

'Jamie – oh, no!' She clutched his arm. 'Not . . . not away ? Going away!' She shook her head, decisively, as though she would not hear it. 'Do not tell me. Not now. Not this happy moment. Let us have this, at least . . .'

'Yes. Assuredly. With all my heart. We are not so rich in moments like these, you and I, to squander them! I . . .' He paused, and touched her elbow. 'But – we are discovered. Here comes Sophie . . .'

That evening, on a high balcony of the castle, with the air still warm, they sat looking out over the gleaming Rhine, and talked, while Eliza played gentle, wistful music on a lute in the room behind them, Louie whittled a block of wood into the shape of a monkey, with chisel and knife, and Henrietta, the youngest of the family, played with a gangling puppy. Sophia had gone walking with Archie Napier.

'So – the States-General finally gave you the moneys? But less than you hoped?' Elizabeth said.

'Yes. After Charles let it be known that he was supporting my plans all seemed set fair, for the money. A loan, of course. But then, when from Breda he of a sudden announced his support for an immediate new expedition to Ireland, the States-General began to doubt again. As I could not blame them. He could not stage both ventures successfully, they said. But I wrote of that, to you, in June.'

'Yes, indeed. It was foolishness. The folly of a young man lacking experience. And badly advised – other than by yourself. *I* felt in part responsible, Jamie – since it was, no doubt, my son Rupert who sent to Charles urging that aid and reinforcement be sent. But – you put that right, did you not? You went to Breda, and changed Charles's mind?'

'It was not so much I who changed it, but Cromwell! Cromwell's successful expedition to Ireland changed all. With Ormonde easily defeated – as I feared he must be – there could be no further Irish adventure. But, although I brought Charles back to Brussels and the States-General, they had lost some of their confidence in my cause. Or, at least, the King's full commitment to it. So, I have got only one-third of what I hoped for.

'I am sorry. In my relief that Rupert and Maurice were safe, I had not realised how much that foolish venture was costing *you*. But I did write to you not to place over much reliance in Charles, urged you to go to Breda earlier, not to let him long out of your sight and influence. He is a strange young man, my nephew, not wholly trustworthy . . .'

'Mamma!' Henrietta protested. 'How unkind.'

'Not unkind, stupid, but looking facts in the face. As one must, when men's whole lives are at stake. I like Charles very well. He is charming, attractive – too attractive. But devious. Perhaps he could not be otherwise with the mother and grandmother he had! Young, he swings too much according to the last advice he receives. Seems to wish to agree with all – yet deep down pursues unspoken ways all his own.'

'But he greatly admires my lord . . .'

'That does not change his nature. Or make his policies the more reliable.' Elizabeth turned back to Montrose. 'And now he has gone to his mother, in France. I cannot think that pleased you, either!'.

'No. Although I could by no means attempt to dissuade him. He will not persuade Queen Henrietta to a Scottish venture, nor to find money for it. He left Brussels for St. Germain before the States-General made its final decision.'

'And now?'

'Before we parted, he gave me all the *authority* I need. Nothing more was said as to me being commander-in-chief of his forces – but that is of no moment. I never sought it. I am Captain-General and Lieutenant-Governor of Scotland, with complete powers to act there as I think fit. In his royal name. I can now move, at last.'

'And the money?' That was Louise. 'Have you sufficient?' For your needs? To hire an Army?'

'No, nothing sufficient,' he admitted. 'Not with shipping to hire. Although I am hopeful, in that respect, of help from a Scots merchant of Gothenburg – a man of great wealth. I cannot take an army. Only an officer-corps – and mainly Scots, at that. But experienced veterans, such as I greatly need. I have this credit from the States-General – although it applies only within the Emperor's territories – and have already made arrangements in Brussels. Hurry will see to the enrolling there. I have sent to the Elector of Brandenburg for the moneys he has promised – through the kindness of your royal mother. Also to the Duke of Courland. I hope to collect more at Hamburg – where also I hope to hire shipping. Then I go to your kinsman the new King of Denmark, at Copenhagen, to try hold him to his father's word. Finally to Gothenburg, and the merchant Maclear.'

'That will take . . . some time?' Elizabeth said.

'Yes. And timing is of the essence, now. I cannot hope to be ready to sail while still this campaigning season lasts. But there may be advantage in that also – if only I can seize it. I know from experience that Argyll and his generals will never contemplate a winter campaign. They esteem it impossible, in a mountainous land like Scotland. So, I shall seek to land in Scotland when and where I am least expected, while it is still winter, God aiding me.'

'A winter crossing, by sea?' the Queen said. 'Is that practicable? Is it not dangerous?'

'Danger? There is danger in all that we do, in this matter. But it is practicable, shipmasters assure me.'

There was silence, then, save for the lute's liquid notes.

'Where will you make for? To land?' Louise asked.

'Where we will not be looked for. Where we may have time and peace to assemble, muster, send out messengers to the clans, without being attacked in the meantime. The Orkney Islands. It is almost the shortest voyage from the Skagerrack, with like to be little Scots shipping to spy us. And Orkney is a little world unto itself; yet close to the Scottish mainland. And the Earl of Morton, Kinnoull's uncle, is master there – and a good King's man. I will send Kinnoull, with a small token force, to Orkney beforehand. At once. From Hamburg, if I may get the ships. So that they have the autumn and most of the winter to prepare, gather and train local men, make ready to receive my main expedition. Even if Argyll learns of their arrival, he will not anticipate any large descent there, I think. And in winter. Then, without delay, we shall cross to Caithness – there is no lack of shipping in Orkney, small boats. And south, down through the Scottish Highlands.'

'And you are sanguine? Of course?' Elizabeth demanded, suddenly urgent. 'You seem, to a mere woman's mind, to be gambling in this. Heavily.'

'I am gambling, yes. War *is* a gamble. Things are not as I would have had them. But I must make the attempt. I have had to delay too long. If a blow is to be struck, it must be soon. While Charles is fresh on his throne. So that the Scots people can perceive a new start. While there is still hope in the land. The longer we wait, the more difficult the task.'

'I understand.' She sighed – and Elizabeth Stewart was not a great sigher. 'So you leave us . . . soon?'

'Two nights from now I have arranged to see Kinnoull and Hurry at the Hague. Then on to Hamburg. I am sorry, so very sorry – but time presses on me, and there is no avoiding my duty.'

Louise got up, and hurried away, wordless. The lute, and the puppy's grunts had it all to themselves.

*   *   *

Leave-taking was a sore business. All would have wished it to be got over as swiftly as possible, in the end. But the decencies had to be observed. Archie Napier was both a help and a nuisance, brisk, unemotional but all too present. To gain a few precious moments of privacy Elizabeth resorted to a device, transparent enough but effective, of suddenly recollecting a message she had for Montrose to deliver at the Hague, and taking him back with her to her own room to collect it, leaving the others in the court-yard.

Out of sight of them all, she turned to him. 'Jamie – this is damnable! I am like a stricken, doting girl – but I can scarcely control myself. This of goodbye – I do not think that I can face it.'

'Nor you alone. But we must, my dear. Must try to make it a memory to cherish, not a misery to be got over.'

'Ah – how noble! So sensible! So like a man!' she exclaimed. 'But – do you realise what this *is*, Jamie ? This is *parting*! It may be the, the end. We may never see each other again.'

'Not the end, Elizabeth – never that. Our love cannot end. Now or ever. It is eternal. And we shall see each other again – of this I have no doubt.'

'But – oh God, you may be killed! You are thrusting yourself into dire danger.'

'Even so, we shall see each other again. Hereafter.'

'I wish that I had your faith. But that is not how I want to see you.' She clutched him. 'It is *you*, in the flesh. My Jamie Graham. Not some, some spirit!'

He held her close, but said nothing.

'Oh, I am weak, weak,' she mumbled into his shoulder. 'I am sorry. But I cannot bear the thought of living without you. Living and living . . . !'

'You will not be without me, ever. That I promise you. What-ever happens, my heart. Dear Elizabeth – we have taken each the other. Two human souls cannot do more. This parting is grievous. But only that. It is not a severance, an ending. I do not fear the future. It is ours.'

'Will you come back to me, Jamie ?'

'Either that – or you will come to me,' he assured her, gravely.

She searched his face, as though to discern all the implications of his words. Then she nodded. 'I will come.'

'Then, then we need care for nothing. For what transpires. You and I. We hold it all. In our hearts. This leave-taking is but a step on our way together.'

'Yes,' she whispered. 'Yes. I will, I will hold to that.'

They clung to each other for a little, and then turned and went back to the others.

In the courtyard, Elizabeth spoke as nearly naturally as she could. 'At the Hague, Jamie, make time to go see Gerard Honthorst. The portrait of you that I commissioned is near

316

finished. He but needs a few brush-strokes for the features, the eyes. Give him that, of your precious time – on my royal command! It is a mite stern, I think – but I will hang it in my cabinet. And at least it will serve to frighten away the Brethren! Your Scots enemies, when they come plaguing me.'

'It shall be done, Madam. But I had rather the artist painted in a smile on me! I have had enough of sternness. As . . . in the other.' And he threw an understanding glance at Louise.

'Tell Honthorst so, then.'

Montrose said goodbye to the young women, Henrietta, Sophia, Eliza. Louise he gripped more tightly.

'The stout and constant heart,' he murmured, in her ear. 'It cannot be defeated. *You* will not be defeated. That I know.'

'And . . . you?'

'Both of us,' he said. And kissed her.

Then he turned to the Queen, straightening up his shoulders. 'I have a journey to make, Highness,' he said. 'Have I Your Majesty's permission to leave?'

Head high, she mustered a smile. 'You have, Jamie Graham. We will receive you to our royal presence . . . another day!' Almost gaily she said it.

'For that day I wait,' he answered, raised her hand to his lips, and bowed low.

Archie Napier flourished his feathered beaver, and held the horses while uncle mounted.

'God save the Queen!' Montrose said, from the saddle, and reining round spurred at once into a trot for the gatehouse arch – and dared not to look back.

PART THREE

CHAPTER TWENTY-THREE

As James Graham had watched Scotland recede from his sight forty-two long months before, so from the heaving bows of another Scandinavian ship he watched it loom again before him, grey and forbidding in the thin rain, on the 20th of March, 1650, a harsh barrier of rocks and cliffs ringed with the white water of great breaking seas, long, low-lying – for this was Orkney, not the mountainous mainland. And if his mood on that other occasion had been grim, sombre as the scene, now, despite the fact that this was what he had waited and longed and prayed for for so long, the return to his native land, his humour was little more cheerful. There was not much lift of the heart for Montrose at this homecoming, weeks later than he had intended.

It was as though almost everything conspired to depress him. Nothing had gone well in the six months since he had taken leave of Elizabeth at Rhenen. Admittedly Kinnoull had successfully managed to sail from Amsterdam for Orkney, via Copenhagen, at the end of August with an advance-party of eighty experienced mercenaries and 100 Danish volunteers, and after a fair voyage had landed without incident. But that was as far as the credit side stretched. At Kirkwall he had found his uncle, Robert Douglas, 8th Earl of Morton, gravely ill – and he had died in November. This was serious, for Morton's influence was paramount, as lord of the islands – and the new earl was only a youth. But this was only the beginning of misfortune; for Kinnoull himself had been suffering from recurring fevers contracted in the Low Countries, and possibly as a result of his transfer to the wet cold of the North, the younger man fell ill at Kirkwall only a few days later, with pleurisy, and followed his uncle to the grave before the end of the year. This grievous news had been brought to Montrose at Gothenburg by Sir James Douglas, Morton's brother, in January. He had other tidings to impart also. Word had not been long in reaching the South as to Kinnoull's landing, and General David Leslie had marched north, with a Covenant army. He had made no attempt at a crossing to Orkney – but the threat was there.

Nevertheless, Douglas was optimistic over the military situation. Leslie's army was not large, and had very much settled into winter quarters. The people of Scotland, by and large, were sickened with the Covenant regime and ready to rise, he assured. He promised 1,000 from Orkney itself, and they could be sure of 2,000 of Seaforth's Mackenzies when they landed on the mainland. Others also had sent promises. Montrose could reckon on 10,000 men from the North to face Leslie. Only arms, munitions, powder and shot, were in desperately short supply.

To aid in this situation Montrose had despatched a squadron of four old vessels from Gothenburg – all that he could hire – filled with guns, and munitions, and 1,200 men, mainly Danes and Netherlanders, with Scots officers. But a frightful gale had caught these vessels in the savage northern seas, and only the one ship had reached Orkney, with 200 men.

People began to say that God's hand was against Montrose.

But this was not the worst of James Graham's anxieties, sorrowful as he was for the lost men. As he braced himself against the thrumming rigging of the Swedish *Herderinnen* and watched the spires of St. Magnus's Cathedral grow out of the rain and scud, his real unease came from a letter in his pocket, a letter from Elizabeth delivered to him a day or two before he sailed from Bergen, on the 16th of March, with his shipload of veteran officers. The letter itself was a joy and a comfort – although it had an ominous postscript to the effect that the Queen was hearing ill rumours from St. Germain. But it had enclosed another letter, this indeed headed from St. Germain, and written on the 19th of September, from his new liege lord and monarch, sent via Rhenen. It was a friendly, even flattering letter. But there was a paragraph therein which, taken in conjunction with Elizabeth's postscript, hit James Graham like a body blow. It ran:

I entreat you to go on vigorously, and with your wonted courage and care, in the preservation of those trusts I have committed to you, and not to be startled with any reports you may hear, as if I were otherwise inclined to the Presbyterians than when I left you. I assure you I am upon the same principles I was, and depend as much as ever upon your undertakings and endeavours for my service, being fully resolved to assist and support you therein to the utter most of my power.

The thought of those words '. . . not to be startled with any reports you may hear . . .' and from that address and source, had remained like a leaden weight with Montrose ever since. Something was wrong, basically wrong, somewhere – he felt it in his bones. 'As if I were otherwise inclined to the Presbyterians than when I left you.' Could he trust young Charles Stewart ? Elizabeth had said that he should not. And if not, what might be the consequences for this venture ?

To counter the sudden fears and doubts which, if they affected him, must still more affect others once they became generally known, Montrose had composed and issued a Declaration before he sailed, a resounding manifesto announcing his intentions to overthrow the evil men who held Scotland in thrall and who had sold their monarch to his death, and were denying men freedom to worship God in their own chosen way. And he committed, advisedly King Charles II to this venture, which was being carried out in his royal name and authority. As a precaution against unnamed doubts, it was the best that he could do. Archie Napier and George Wishart, left behind at Hamburg to muster and send on reinforcements and munitions, would publish it abroad.

Hurry and Sir James Douglas had joined him in the *Herderinnen*'s bows, the latter a small middle-aged man wrapped in a cloak against the weather.

'Not long now, my lord,' Douglas said. 'By God's teeth, I'll not be sorry to set foot on dry land again! In yon storm, I feared we would never win to Pomona.'

'Pomona . . . ?'

'The name for the main island of Orkney. It will gain a new fame as the place where the great Marquis of Montrose returned to deliver his native land!'

'So be it we are kindly received!' Hurry put in. 'How do we know that Leslie has not crossed the Pentland Firth and is waiting for us ?'

'There would have been warnings – beacons, smokes, boats out . . .'

'Nevertheless, we shall not sail blindly in,' Montrose decided. 'Have the shipmaster to lie off the harbour mouth a few cables' length, and send a boat in. Many Swedes and Norwegians trade here. Find out what transpires. There will be little suspicion of a single ship flying the Swedish flag.'

This precaution was carried out, and a group of Swedes rowed ashore. The others had not long to wait, however, before it was seen returning – and rather fuller of folk than when it went.

As he watched from the ship's side, Montrose, suddenly perceiving, straightened up – and the dark mood which had clothed him for a while dropped from him like a cast cloak. 'Pate!' he cried. 'Black Pate!' And he raised an arm, and shouted his delight and greetings.

Colonel Pate Graham of Inchbrakie was the first man up the rope-ladder to the deck, and unashamedly the two friends embraced each other in incoherent joy, while the onlookers grinned and chuckled their amusement – and also their relief. For, if Black Pate could thus sail out openly from Kirkwall, all must be well therein.

'Jamie, Jamie . . .!' was all that Inchbrakie could get out. 'At last, Jamie – at last . . .!'

'Pate – God be praised! Man – how good, how very good! *You*, here. To come to Orkney. This is a joy. A welcome home, indeed!'

'I came two weeks past. When I heard that Kinnoull expected you. To wait for you. You, you heard that he had died . . . ?'

'Yes. A tragedy. A grievous loss. And Morton too. But you, Pate – you look well, your own sturdy black self! Worth a regiment, I swear! And Jean, your wife – she is well also? And your bairns? And, and mine?'

'Aye – all well. Yours with their grandsire, my lord of Southesk. At Kinnaird. James too, released this past year. Confined to Kinnaird, mind. They may not travel abroad or see any but their kin. But they are well . . .'

'Praise God for that!' Montrose recollected his duty. Two young men had climbed up after Pate, and were waiting. 'And these gentlemen . . . ?'

'William Hay, my lord – new Earl of Kinnoull. And James Crichton, my lord Viscount Frendraught. Others await you ashore.'

'My lords, I rejoice to see you. In the King's name, I greet you.' He did not actually say that it was good to find Frendraught on the right side – for he had fought against him previously. 'This is a good augury. I thank you for your courtesy in coming to meet me . . .'

And so the *Herderinnen* drew in to the harbour of Kirkwall, in wind and rain, and James Graham set foot again on Scottish soil. Despite the weather a crowd had gathered, the Provost and magistrates to the fore, and it was in something like a triumph, a canny, undemonstrative Scots triumph, that the Viceroy made his way through the narrowest streets in Europe to the Earl's Palace opposite St. Magnus's Cathedral, the splendid castellated pile started by Mary Queen of Scots' half-brother Robert Stewart, when first Bishop then Earl of Orkney. He had been Elizabeth's great-uncle – however much of a scoundrel.

Here men came flocking to greet the King's representative. But despite the welcome and enthusiasm, it did not take James Graham long to perceive that although Kinnoull's advance-party had been in Orkney for five months, the persons and personages who ought to have been flocking to the Royal Standard were neither present nor represented. Of the great lords, the two who had come out in the boat were in fact the only representatives – and these not of the most powerful. There were a number of Graham lairds, some old companions-in-arms like Ogilvy of Powrie, Hay of Delgatie, Drummond of Balloch and Major David Guthrie; also many local Orkney landowners. But of the men who could provide the necessary major reinforcements, there was no sign.

Montrose said as much to Black Pate when they could be alone together.

'Orkney is a long way north, James,' the other reminded. 'And Argyll's spies are everywhere. Watching especially those known to be your friends. *I* only won away by a stratagem. Airlie, Madderty, Fleming, Erskine and the rest are as good as prisoners in their own houses. They will rise – but only when you are a deal farther south than Kirkwall!'

The other nodded. 'I know well the danger and problems. For these. But I had hoped for others. Reay, chief of the Mackays – I had looked for him here. His lands are just across the Firth. Seaforth is still in Holland, I believe – but his brother, Mackenzie of Pluscarden, has shown that he is a better fighter. I thought to see *him*. And the Rosses? Where are they? Balnagown should be here. The Munroes? They took part in Pluscarden's rising. All these are North Country clans. I told Kinnoull to call them in. Where are they?'

Pate Graham had no answer to that.

Montrose found that he had, as command, a total of some 1,700 men – those whom Kinnoull had brought, the 200 survivors of the ill-fated second expeditionary force, those who had come with himself, plus the men raised locally in Orkney.

A highly unbalanced force, at that, with a great preponderance of mercenary officers, no cavalry, and the Orkneymen almost totally untrained.

Nevertheless it was a nucleus, an armed force, and James Graham was in no state to be over-critical, however far below expectations and requirements it fell. He set about the training and improving of it the very next day, with a will, marshalling it into cadres, at this stage heavily over-officered, which could rapidly be expanded into companies and regiments.

Cavalry was the big problem, as ever, for although Montrose had over £10,000 in cash, largely advanced by the gallant John Maclear in Gothenburg, set aside for the purchase or hiring of horseflesh, Orkney was not the place to do this, the short-legged ponies of the islands being quite unsuitable for military work. A round-up of gentlemen's horses in the area produced only some forty usable animals – his total cavalry meantime. His tactics, for some time ahead therefore, must be to operate where cavalry, enemy cavalry, could not function – however hindering this must be to his eventual campaign.

The third day after their arrival at Kirkwall, a courier landed from a fishing-boat come from the Scottish mainland, a royal courier, one Major Harry May. He had been on Montrose's trail, it seemed, for many weeks, having left the King in Jersey in mid-January. Hearing, at Copenhagen, that the Graham had sailed, he had taken passage in the first ship voyaging to Scotland, and landed at Aberdeen, thereafter making his way overland to John o' Groats. Major May, an Englishman, was caustic in his observations on travel in Scotland in March.

Montrose, who at least had adequate, indeed spacious quarters in the Earl's Palace of Kirkwall, took the royal package, quite a bulky one, to open in a private room. It contained three bundles. The first, unwrapped, proved to be the splendid insignia and ribbon of the Order of the Garter, bestowed by a grateful monarch on his illustrious Viceroy as a mark of confidence and esteem. The recipient was appreciative, but considered the timing odd. Laying it aside, he opened the larger of the remaining packets, which contained a bundle of copies of correspondence, in what he believed to be the neat and spidery handwriting of Edward Hyde. The smaller packet was heavily sealed with the royal arms, and in Charles's own hand, dated the 12th of January, 1650, at Jersey.

As he scanned this, the man's face quickly set and grew grim, and the leaden weight which he had carried about with him since leaving Gothenburg kicked anew and violently. A groan of sheer pain escaped him.

Charles wrote in as friendly and flattering a fashion as ever, declaring how much pleasure it gave him to appoint his most valued and trusted servant to the Most Noble Order of the Garter, the highest honour he could pay him in present circumstances. But then he went on to announce that he had reopened negotiations with Argyll and the Estates, and to such good effects that a treaty was actually in preparation – which might make it possible to gain his Scottish kingdom without distressing bloodshed. And, more important still, could result in a Scots invasion over the border, to link up with the English royalists and so sweep Cromwell and the rebellious Parliamentarians from power, with a consequent restoration to his joint throne of the United Kingdom – which, after all, was his main objective. He, Charles, was most hopeful of this new initiative – as the enclosed documents would show – and was convinced that his Captain-General's venture in the North would greatly strengthen his hand in these new negotiations. He urged Montrose to proceed vigorously and firmly on his undertaking, doubting not that all his loyal and well-affected subjects in Scotland would cordially and effectually join him, to force any who were against an equitable treaty to reconsider. He ended:

> We will not, before or during the treaty, do anything contrary to the power and authority which we have given you by our commission, nor consent to anything that may bring the least degree of diminution to it; and if the said treaty should produce an agreement, we will, with our uttermost care, so provide for the honour and interest of yourself, and of all that shall engage with you, as shall let the whole world see the high esteem we have for you.

All this was most carefully and painstakingly written, as though from a copy. But the letter concluded with an obviously hurried scrawled afterthought, which urged Montrose not to take alarm at any reports or messages from others, and reiterating that he, Charles, would never consent to anything to his friend's prejudice.

Appalled, James Graham stared unseeing out of the window towards St. Magnus's brown-stone towers and spires. The folly of it, the sheer, devious-minded folly! To authorise and despatch an armed invasion – and then to enter into negotiations with those to be assaulted, without warning or consent, behind the invader's back! Especially with such as Argyll. It would, it *must*, be construed by all as sheer weakness, complete lack of confidence in the military attempt, an undermining of all Montrose's aims and authority, whatever Charles wrote about trust and esteem. How many would now risk all by rising to support the invasion, when a treaty was in the offing? And a treaty which, if agreed, could only mean one thing, Charles's signing of the Solemn League and Covenant. Argyll in his strong position – stronger now than ever – would never resile one inch from that basic demand. Which meant that there could be *no* co-operation with the English royalists, who would never draw sword to have Covenant-style Presbyterianism imposed upon them, as the Solemn League demanded. Once this got known, the military venture was as good as doomed. Perhaps it had been doomed from the outset . . . ?

When James Graham at length returned to the others, in the Great Hall, he had schooled himself and his features to calm inscrutability. Rather stiffly for him, however, he questioned Major May as to how much he knew of the new negotiations and proposed treaty, and how much bruited abroad it all was generally?

'Why, my lord, all know of it,' the other answered. 'It is no secret – indeed it was of a purpose published far and wide. His Majesty and his advisers believed it to be a notable step forward, proof that reason and good sense will prevail and that the sword is not the only way to solve the affairs of nations.'

All present were now listening intently, faces tense. Pate Graham began to speak, and then shut his mouth almost with a click.

Montrose went on, level-voiced. 'This notable step has been published abroad? So long ago as January? Then it will of a certainty have reached Scotland. Argyll will have seen to that. It will now be known far and wide.'

'It was spoken of in Aberdeen, yes.'

'It will be the less likely to inspire military fervour I think!'

There was an ominous growl from the listening group of senior officers. Many looked uncomfortable.

James Graham changed the subject. 'Coming north, sir, what did you learn of the enemy? Or perhaps we do not call them that, now? Since the King is in negotiation with them? Say then, the Covenant forces? Do you know how they are said to be disposed?'

'Yes, my lord Marquis – that is well-enough known also. The country is full of the talk of it. General Leslie has returned to Edinburgh, leaving Major-General Strachan in command in the North. Why is not said. Strachan has taken up a position at a place called the Ord of Caithness, some thirty-five miles south of Thurso. A strong place where the hills come down in great cliffs to the sea. I passed near by, in guise of a packman – all travellers must pass there, or climb the mountains. Also he garrisons the strong castles of Dunrobin, Skibo, Skelbo and Dornoch behind him, belonging, they say, to the Earl of Sutherland.'

'Yes, Sutherland was always hot for the Covenant. Have you any notion as to his numbers? Strachan's, not the local Sutherland levies.'

'It is said that he has 3,000 foot, my lord, and 1,500 horse. Dragoons.'

Glances were exchanged all around that noble apartment. Fifteen hundred heavy cavalry. And *they* had forty!

Montrose, well aware of those glances, shrugged. 'He has all of the Northern Highlands to hold, with these. Most of it country of hills, bogs and torrents where dragoons are of little use. Is there any word of the clans? The Northern clans. The Mackenzies in especial. Seaforth's people.'

'I heard that there was some fighting between Mackenzies and MacDonalds in the west, my lord. But I understand that this is nothing unusual amongst these savages.'

'I thank you for your informations, Major,' Montrose said bleakly. 'But when I desire your observations on the qualities of His Grace's Highland subjects, I will ask for it!' He turned away.

Later, as they watched the men training on the sandy links west of the town, Black Pate spoke out, though quietly. 'James – we are betrayed, are we not? Struck in the back. By the young man we have taken up arms to seat on his throne! Can we go on?'

'Can we do other, Pate? We have no choice, as I see it. These negotiations will achieve nothing for the King. He has no least idea of the men with whom he would deal. Even if there *is* a treaty, even if he signs the damnable Solemn League and is brought to Scotland, he will not rule. He will be kept a captive puppet, to do the Campbell's bidding. As much a prisoner as ever was his father. It was not for that I swore allegiance and service.'

329

'But we will be hamstrung, now. Who will join our attempt while the King sits at table with our opponents? Your second Charles is sending us to our deaths!'

Montrose drew a deep breath. 'It may not be so bad as that, Pate. It must sorely hamper us, yes. But it could also hamper Leslie and Strachan. They too will be less than eager for battle, in the circumstances, risking their skins for a cause which may already be won and lost. Leslie in especial – he is a soldier first and foremost; and no soldier likes to campaign with negotiations going on behind him.'

'So – you aim to fight? Despite all?'

'I see no other course. It is that – or returning to the Continent. We shall soon outstay our welcome in Orkney. Moreover, for any peace and good to come to Scotland, Argyll and his minions must be unseated and put down. Whatever Charles Stewart may think. Nothing else will serve. I am still Viceroy and Captain-General of Scotland. Charles himself orders me to press on vigorously – for he believes this will strengthen *his* hand at the conference-table – however much it weakens mine. I am a card to play, no more, no less, But he is still my liege lord and I have accepted his commission. We must go on with the venture.'

'With our hands tied. With not one-tenth of the numbers you looked for. And with none likely to rise in our favour.'

'Even so. But – we have faced like odds before, Pate. This is not like you . . . ?'

'No – God knows it is not for myself, James! It is for you I burn. After all, that you have done, suffered, sacrificed, all you *are* – betrayed again, thrown to the wolves, your counsel rejected. I wonder that you have any regard or loyalty left for the Stewarts!'

'Is my duty, and yours Pate, lessened because our High King makes mistakes? Trusts the wrong advisers? An oath of allegiance is more than a courtesy – at least, *I* deem it so. Especially that of an Earl of Scotland. I am bound by it, man.' He lightened his voice, shook his head. 'Besides, the situation is less ill, I think, than you fear. You know the Highland terrain as well as I do. If we can outfight, out-manoeuvre or outmarch Strachan at this Ord of Caithness, we have the whole of Highland Scotland before us, to cherish us. The Clan Donald Federation – will they not flock to me again? If only in hatred for the Campbells. Even though Colkitto is far away in Ireland. The Farquharsons, the Camerons, the Athollmen, the MacGregors – these care not for conference-tables and treaties, or even for King Charles, I think! But they will follow *me*, I do believe – especially to unseat Argyll, as they have done before. Even Gordon, if we get that far, will have reason to think again . . .'

'That insolent pup, the Lord Lewis, is now Marquis of Huntly, Cock o' the North, with his father and Aboyne dead. He will do nothing for love of you, James.'

'No. But for love of something else, perhaps. If he sees the tide flowing strongly enough. Did you know that he wrote to the new King, declaring himself to be his most loyal and devoted subject, as well as the most powerful, and requesting the Order of the Garter? The sheer, shameless arrogance of it! The Garter!' Montrose mustered a smile. 'I could offer him mine, in exchange for 1,000 Gordon horse!'

Pate Graham muttered something unrepeatable. 'We march, then?' he said.

'Yes. We march. But not just yet. First, I will send a strong advance-party across the Firth, to spy out the land. To settle the best landing-place. To try to rally local support – though I cannot hope for much from the Sinclairs, led by their oaf of an earl! To advance on Strachan – as near as may be without coming to blows. Test the situation. While the main force here completes training and marshalling. It had better be Hurry who goes – rather than yourself, Pate. He is Major-General, after all, and anxious to prove himself a good King's man! Also he is the most experienced soldier – although I know you love him not. Such a venture will suit him very well – for he is bold enough. I will give him a strong brigade – our best-trained 500. And we follow when he sends word.'

Inchbrakie part shrugged, part nodded. 'Perhaps you have the rights of it,' he acceded.

'Can you suggest better?'

'No-o-o . . .'

CHAPTER TWENTY-FOUR

On the 12th of April Montrose and the main Royalist force of about 1,000 sailed across the stormy Pentland Firth in a fleet of fishing-boats, to land without incident near John o' Groats. Hurry had crossed here a week before and recommended it as landing-place. They were unlikely to be opposed, he reported. Caithness was a land unto itself, its Sinclair barons utterly uninterested in national affairs, from which they were so far removed, and concerned only with internecine feuding. Hurry himself had encountered no real difficulties, and had pressed on southwards, as commanded, his first opposition being at the Sinclair castle of Dunbeath, forty miles on, and ten miles north of the Ord, where the laird, Sir John, was a member of the Estates and had made a fortune as a merchant in the South. It was a strong place, and Hurry had by-passed it, proceeding on past Berriedale to the Ord. Here he had discovered that Major May had been wrong with his information. General Strachan was not here, but farther south, rumoured to be at Tain. It was the Earl of Sutherland who held the Ord – but at Hurry's appearance, he had relinquished his strong strategic position and retired southwards without fight. Fearing to put too great a distance between himself and his commander, Hurry had settled in at the Ord, fortifying the cliff-top position still further.

So Montrose marched westwards without delay along the very northern shore of the Scottish mainland, seventeen miles from John o' Groats to Thurso, the Caithness capital, a small grey town at the head of its bay. Here, still without opposition, he unfurled the Royal Standard in the market-place – and with it, the banner the Douglas ladies had made at Kirkwall showing the late King Charles with his head at a rather gruesome distance from his body, and beneath it the legend *Judge and Defend my Cause, Oh Lord*. This was a little embarrassing, but would probably do no harm. At the unfurling, he issued a proclamation, as Viceroy, summoning all loyal and true subjects of the King to come and make their allegiance. The Provost and not a few citizens came and did so – but no Sinclair lairds, the Earl of Caithness biding watchfully in his evil eagle's nest of a hold at Castle Girnigoe, twenty miles away, north of Wick. Montrose let him be.

One hundred or so Mackays from the west arrived next day; but Lord Reay himself was not with them. He sent his greetings, declared that he was gathering his strength, and would join the royal army as soon as he could – although he dared not too greatly denude his lands of fighting-men for fear of raiding Sinclairs and Gunns.

Montrose could not wait for him. He left Sir Harry Graham and 200 men at Thurso, to accept allegiances in his name, keep the Sinclairs preoccupied, and receive and marshal incoming reinforcements. Also to maintain a link with Orkney, where two more shiploads of arms and munitions were expected. Then he marched southwards through the desolate Caithness moors, to join Hurry.

Hurry met them near Dunbeath Castle, having left his advance-party at the Ord. His information was that the Earl of Sutherland had retired south as far as Tain, on the southern side of the Dornoch Firth – why, with his preponderance in numbers, was not clear. But there were rumours that Leslie was hurrying north again, from Edinburgh, with reinforcements, and had reached Brechin in Angus. Probably Strachan, at Tain, on the border of Ross and Sutherland, was waiting for him, and had called the Earl of Sutherland back, delaying encounter until the Covenant could be sure of winning. Hurry urged, therefore, that they marched upon him with all speed.

'Why should Strachan wait – if he has four or five times our numbers? He is no faint-heart.' Montrose shook his head. 'I see another possible reason. He wishes to entice us down into the flat coastal levels around the Dornoch Firth, where his cavalry will be able to operate most effectively. Hereabouts is no cavalry country – so he abandons it. He will know, to be sure, that we have no cavalry. He wants us down on those plains, for a wager!'

'But if we wait, he will be reinforced – with Leslie himself back to take command.'

'Even so, we shall not play his game. If Leslie was only at Brechin when last you heard, it will take him many days to reach the Dornoch Firth, with 150 miles of difficult country to cover, four great firths to win round. So we need not rush into Strachan's trap, I think.'

'You said before that time was of essence. What do we do, then ? Kick our heels at the Ord . . . ?'

'We will give the Mackenzies a day or two more to join us. I have sent Pluscarden urgent couriers. And meanwhile we shall assault this castle of Dunbeath.'

That surprised them all, even Black Pate – for in the past Montrose had always made a point of not wasting time and effort on reducing powerful strongholds, for which he had not the necessary cannon and special techniques, preferring to leave them isolated. He explained.

'I do not mind leaving enemy castles behind me – when I am advancing, when my strategy ahead is clear in my mind. As it is not, here. I do not relish to have the enemy *both* in front and behind me – especially with a sea-coast on my flank. There is this fishertown here at the mouth of the Dunbeath River – Portormin – not large but sufficient for fishing-craft. A fleet of boats could sail up here from Tain. This enemy-held castle overlooking and guarding Portormin might tempt Strachan to send up a sea-borne force behind us. And if they landed here, they could cut our links with Thurso; with Sir Harry, with the Mackays, even with Orkney. That might matter little, soon – but not at this stage. We must have reinforcements. We shall assail Sir John Sinclair, gentlemen, while we wait for the Mackenzies.'

That they did, there on the slanting shelf above the high cliffs. Without artillery, and with small-arms fire more demonstrative than effective against thick stone walling, they could do little more than settle in around the landward side of the castle, beyond its ditch and drawbridge, shout demands for surrender and make other threatening noises, reinforced by the odd sniping shot at windows or glimpsed movement. But that very first evening, a local man, a Sinclair himself, connected to the former line of lairds, who had some grudge against the new Sir John of a different branch, came to the Viceroy, proclaiming himself a good King's man, and declaring that he could stop the water-supply of the castle. There *was* a draw-well in the courtyard, yes – but it was not a true well, tapping no subterranean spring. Its shaft went down to an underground burn – and the informant could show them where that burn *went* underground a mile or so inland, on the hillside. They could cut off the water without difficulty.

Rather foolishly loth to use such methods as he was, Montrose reminded himself that he was dealing with men who used the 'phrase Jesus and No Quarter!' as a slogan and did not fail to act up to those sentiments. He sent a party up the hill, with the renegade Sinclair, to damn and divert the stream.

Dunbeath Castle capitulated on the evening of the second day, without casualties on either side. Sir John Sinclair and his family Montrose treated courteously, saying that he would not turn them out of their home and would only install a garrison in the castle for as short a time as was necessary. That night he held a council-of-war in Sir John's hall, with the noise of great seas smashing themselves into spray on the rocks hundreds of feet below.

'There appear to be three courses open to us, gentlemen,' he summarised. 'We can go down into the level lands around the Dornoch Firth, and fight it out with Strachan who waits for us at Tain. We can bide here until the Mackenzies come – but they are a Highland force, not horsed either. There is, indeed, *no* cavalry to be obtained north of Inverness and the Great Glen, I fear. The Rosses and Munroes may raise a few horsemen – but unfortunately they are on the wrong side of Strachan, south of Tain, and we have no reason to believe that they will rise until we reach them. If then. The third course, as I see it, is to take to the heather, to make a great half-circuit inland to west and south across bog and mountain, and attempt to pass Strachan by altogether, heading south for the Great Glen and the mountain mass of Highland Scotland without coming to blows with the enemy at all. How think you, my friends?'

'I am against bog-hopping and goat-clambering about on hills!' Hurry, the professional soldier said, wrinkling a long nose in disgust at the thought. 'I say take our courage in our hands, and attack Strachan before Leslie can reach him. You, my lord, are notable for making the country fight for you – as I know to my cost! We need not assail the enemy on the ground of *their* choosing, which will suit their cavalry. There is marshland flanking the Dornach Firth estuary. If we could inveigle them into that, bog down their horses . . .'

'If I had Highlanders fighting for me, I would agree with that, Sir John. But I have none. Our army is made up of Orkneymen with no experience of war, and mercenary Netherlanders and Danes. Good troops but not used to fighting as the clansmen fight, light, half-naked, speedy, on only a handful of oatmeal. Would they serve the case in your marshland? For the same reason, I am doubtful of leading them inland over the mountains.'

'Yet we cannot bide here,' the new Earl of Kinnoull declared. 'This will gain us nothing. And Leslie will come up with his reinforcements.'

'It all depends on the Mackenzies, does it not ?' Frendraught asked. 'These are Highlanders, such as we need in this pass. Two or three thousand of them. I say we *must* wait until they come up with us. They come from Kintail, do they not ? Eighty, ninety miles to the west. They must be here soon.'

'If they come!' Pate Graham growled. 'We have waited for Seaforth's Mackenzies before this! His brother may be a better fighter – but little more reliable!'

'That is a risk I am aware of,' Montrose agreed. 'But he did rise last March – and has not dispersed his people. And there are the Mackays – fewer of them, but able fighters.'

'Do we wait here, then, for the Highlanders?' Hurry demanded. 'I say that is folly. We may wait for too long. And have Leslie to face. After your lordship's self, the best general in Scotland. Reinforced.'

There was a murmur of agreement around the table.

Frendraught spoke. 'You, my lord – what do *you* think ? Why do you ask us ? You are accepted as the greatest strategist in Europe. What do our opinions signify ?'

'Much – they signify much,' James Graham reproved him. 'When men are asked to risk their lives, they should be consulted. No commander can consult all his ordinary soldiers. But his senior officers' views *must* weigh with him. But – if I *have* heard them all, here is what I would say. I agree, we should not linger here. I accept that our present troops are not such as could cross the trackless mountains at speed, with any great success – not yet. I recognise that Strachan should be defeated, if it is at all possible, before Leslie arrives. But I fear that we cannot hope to defeat him lacking the arrival of some of our Highland reinforcements, Mackenzies or Mackays. The Mackays would come from the north, behind us. The Mackenzies from the west, by Strathkannaird and Strathoykell, over the spine of North Scotland. Let us therefore put ourselves in a posture to meet the Mackenzies, and where the Mackays can reach us, and at the same time be able to try to manoeuvre Strachan into a battleground where his cavalry do not give him overwhelming advantage. Let us march south from the Ord, by Brora and Golspie, and then turn westwards from the coast, up the strath of the Fleet. We are there still a dozen miles north of Tain, as the crow flies, with the Dornoch Firth between. Safe from Strachan. Then we march up the valley of the Fleet to Lairg – say fifteen miles. There, if our scouts have not already found the Mackenzies for us, we turn south for Strathoykell. Wait for them there. And thereafter, with them, advance down the Oykell upon the Kyle of Sutherland, Dornoch and Tain. Take Strachan in flank, with a choice of battlegrounds. How say you ?'

'How long would that take us ?' Frendraught asked.

'Three days to Lairg, forced marching. From there to the Oykell, only six or seven miles.'

'You have forgotten Dunrobin, my lord,' Hurry said. 'Dunrobin Castle, the Earl of Sutherland's chiefest stronghold, stands in the way. At Golspie, before we reach the Fleet.'

'I have not forgotten Dunrobin. We can summon it to surrender – but it will be too strong for us to take. If it stands out against us, we must leave it behind, intact.'

The others accepted that. In the morning they would start out, making for Lairg and the Oykell – and pray that the Mackenzies were not long delayed.

*   *   *

On the 23rd of April they reached the Oykell, in a wild upland country of long heather ridges, deep wooded valleys and rushing peat-brown torrents, with still no sign of Clan Kenneth, the Mackenzies – or indeed of Clan Hugh, the Mackays. They waited for a day at Rosehall, near Inveroykell, where Glen Cassley came down from the north-west to join Strathoykell, all fretting now. None required to inform James Graham how bad this delay and seeming indecision was for the morale of their troops – although John Hurry did not fail to tell him so. Idling, dawdling, for a new invasion force, was the reverse of good tactics. Yet Montrose had no option, short of a premature battle for which he was hopelessly unfit, unready. Not 200 men had joined him since he had landed on the mainland of Scotland – where he had believed there would be thousands. He had few doubts, of course, as to why. King Charles's negotiations with Argyll had become known; a treaty was to be signed. This was no time to indulge in revolt – especially when it was obvious to all that Argyll held the upper hand. It could mean putting necks in a noose for nothing.

On the 24th one of Montrose's own couriers returned to them at Inveroykell, from the west. He brought news that Thomas

Mackenzie of Pluscarden was on the move, with 2,500 men. He had been dealing with an incursion of Macleods from the Isle of Lewis, in the Loch Broom and Braemore area, a perennial warfare. He intended to obey the vice-regal summons to join the Royal Standard, yes – but he had received a letter from his brother, the Earl of Seaforth in Holland, advising caution, as it was understood that King Charles was likely to command Montrose to lay down his arms and disband. Pluscarden, therefore, was not hastening as he might – despite urgings . . .

James Graham had to exercise all his well-tried restraint to prevent a furious outburst. But hold himself in he did.

'But Pluscarden is coming, you say?' he demanded of the Mackay courier. 'With his thousands. However slowly. He is following you up?'

'He comes, yes. Although whether he will fight, my lord, is another matter.'

'I see.' Montrose was actually trembling, so great was the grip he was exerting upon his temper and emotions. 'I see. Seaforth . . . and his brother! But – even if he will not draw the sword, 2,500 Mackenzie clansmen in battle array joining us may well have a notable effect upon Archibald Strachan! Who knows – it might serve . . . ?' He went pacing the greensward, and then came back. 'Where did you leave them? Coming up Strathkannaird? How far away?'

'He is not coming up Kannaird, lord. He comes by a different route. Which I have never trod, at all. So I came back by the way I knew – as I had gone. Mounted, moving fast. The Mackenzies march by secret mountain tracks, by high passes – but shorter, they say. From Braemore, by the Inverlael hills and the Glens Beg and Mor, to the Carron. Down Strathcarron to salt water. It cuts off twenty miles, they say . . .'

'Strathcarron? That is to the south of us. It joins this strath of Oykell miles to the eastwards, does it not? Ten miles down, at least? At the head of the Kyle of Sutherland, towards Tain!'

'Aye, lord. At Invercharron, below Invershin and Carbisdale. Where the Kyle narrows in. I know Strathcarron – although I have never crossed to it from the west, through the mountains.'

'And Pluscarden saves twenty miles of march, thus? Then, dear God – we must move down there, and quickly! Or he may get in *front* of us, meet Strachan before we do – which would be fatal. If he is reluctant to fight he might come to terms with Strachan. Before I could work on him.' Montrose, urgent now, raised his voice. 'Pate! Pate – quickly! Inform all. We march. At once. With all speed . . .'

Fording the Oykell, which was running high, they marched without delay down the south bank of the river, by wooded hillside, bog and flooded haughland, scouts well ahead under Pate Graham. Nightfall found them some eight miles on, almost opposite Invershin, where the Shin came down from the Lairg. Here word reached them from Pate that he was at Invercharron, where the Carron joined the Oykell from the west, and there was no sign of the Mackenzies. There was a small village here, and the people declared that no large body of men had passed through recently. They did however report the presence of occasional small parties of Covenant horse, obviously scouting – but never more than a troop, less usually, at a time.

Montrose halted for the night opposite Invershin.

Next morning they were on the move again, south by east, down the strath, with the open water of the Kyle of Sutherland appearing before them, looking like a loch but actually an extension of the Dornoch Firth, when another galloper from Pate brought news that there was still no sign of the Mackenzies – and Inchbrakie had a picket out well up the Carron seeking contact. But there were two more positive items. A half-troop of cavalry was reported from the vicinity of Ardchronie two or three miles down the southern shore of the Kyle, from Invercharron; and a fisherman, who had rowed across the Kyle itself from the northern shore, was declaring that the Earl of Sutherland was on the march *northwards*, having ferried a large force over the Firth at the narrows near Edderton, Local talk, the fisherman said, was contradictory about Sutherland's movements after crossing. Some said that he was going to Dunrobin, his great castle near Golspie, which Montrose had summoned to surrender on his way south to the Oykell but had not waited to take; others that he was going to turn west, and march up the Fleet River, as Montrose himself had done, and so get behind the royalist force. All were agreed however that he was on the move northwards with a large force.

Montrose sought to puzzle this out. They were on the edge of Sutherland country – where it would be wise to assume that the Earl thereof was kept well informed of what went on in his domains, better informed than he himself was likely to be. Sutherland would know that Dunrobin was not being besieged – a fishing-boat slipping out of Dunrobin harbour could be at

Tain in a couple of hours. He would need no large force, therefore, to regain his castle. If he was moving north in strength, it must be either to cut the royalist communications with Caithness and Orkney, or to make the suggested encircling move behind them, up Fleet. In either case, it probably meant that Strachan was also moving, or preparing to move, from Tain. Almost certainly it would be a synchronised move, two-pronged. The chances were, then, that Strachan and his Covenant regulars were, or would be, marching towards them, directly up this south side of the Kyle, hoping to trap the royalist force from east and west in the tight valley of the Oykell. The half-troop of cavalry spotted could be his advance scouts.

There were the seeds of disaster in this situation.

But there were one or two considerations to be taken into account. Sutherland, if he was making a circling movement, must be given time to make it – so that Strachan would have to delay his much shorter cavalry advance to conform. Sutherland need not go all the way up to Lairg and down the Shin, of course; he could cut across the low hills which formed the barrier between the straths of Fleet and Oykell – if his people were tough enough. There was a rough route across. But he would still emerge on the wrong side of the Oykell – and it was running high, and the less easy to ford the farther down the strath. How soon would Sutherland be a menace, then ? Pate did not say just *when* the enemy force had crossed the Firth – no doubt the fisherman did not know. But the probability was that it was early that day.

And, presumably, Sutherland was not just coming up the north side of the Kyle – the fisherman would have known *that*. The story was that he was going northwards, not westwards, in the meantime. From his ferry-landing it would be about ten miles up to Loch Fleet, at Skelbo. Then up that strath a short way, and over the hills for a dozen or more very rough miles. Say a thirty-mile circuit in all – more, if he went right up to Lairg. The chances were, then, that Strachan would allow Sutherland at least a whole day, possibly two, before he himself moved.

Had the Covenanters decided on action now, when they had been prepared to wait previously, because they had heard of the Mackenzies' approach ? It could well be. If so, now it was a race. Could Pluscarden and his clansmen come down Strathcarron soon enough to reach the royalist force before they were trapped between Strachen and Sutherland ?

It made a grim situation. If Montrose retired back up the Oykell to safety in the west, while he had time, he missed meeting the Mackenzies whose reinforcements he so vitally needed. And it was not merely a case of missing them; if Pluscarden, on his brother's advice, was so unenthusiastic about fighting as the Mackay courier suggested, he might well make his peace with Strachan when they met – and that would be the end of the Mackenzie aid. Montrose just could not contemplate that. On the other hand, if he moved down to Invercharron and waited there, as intended, and Pluscarden did not materialise, then the royalist foot was at the mercy of Strachan's dragoons, in that more open country.

He decided on a compromise. He would move down to where the strath *began* to widen, at the head of the Kyle, to some point where he had a prospect but still some way short of Invercharron, from whence he could quickly join the Mackenzies when they arrived, but which still left a line of retreat open to him. For a time, at least. Sutherland might block that line fairly soon.

It was a sorry tactical contretemps for the most renowned tactician in Europe.

They marched on eastwards, therefore, to the last major hill on their right, which represented almost the end of the range separating Strathoykell and Strathcarron, a steep and lofty bluff, rocky at summit and with birch-scrub at the foot, named, according to the Mackay, Greag Choineachan. At its south-east base was the small property of Carbisdale, where there was some clearing of the birch-scrub, a little tilled land, and a view down the strath. Here Montrose disposed his troops in a defensive situation, and as far as was possible, out of sight from the lower land. Then, with Hurry and a few other officers, he rode on down to Invercharron. There were no armed men to be seen, anywhere, Mackenzies or Covenanters.

At the Mill of Invercharron, where a ford crossed the Carron River just before it entered the Kyle, they found Pate Graham and his little group, hidden in the scrub. Pate was not happy.

'This is a poor place,' he declared. 'Poor for observing, poor for fighting in. I would be glad to see us out of it, James.'

'I also. But we have little choice. What is the present position, Pate?'

'There is not enough height here to see well, or far, over the firth-shore plain. And it is so covered in this birch-scrub that distant view is impossible. But there is a troop – possibly only half a troop – of dragoons over there. On those braes two miles down, where there are a scattering of croft-houses. They call it Upper Ardchronie. And I would think that they will know we are here, and are keeping watch on us. They do not greatly seek to hide themselves.'

'This is the same group you have watched for a while? Obviously a forward picket. You do not think that they have been reinforced?'

'Not that we have seen. Or heard of. I have sent out scouts. On foot, in disguise. But – with all that thick woodland a mile or so behind, who knows? That is Wester Fearn. A headland juts into the Kyle, there, with a deep bay behind, which we cannot see. All too low-lying for observation. Struie Hill behind you can see clearly enough. But Strachan could move up troops from Tain, by Edderton and the coast, completely hidden from us here by all that woodland at Western Fearn.'

'But your scouts have crept forwards? And have not reported any such movement?'

'No-o-o. They think that there is only this one troop between us and Edderton. The crofter folk here say the same. But – I do not like it.'

'What do you advise then, Pate?'

'I think I would retire. Not up Oykell again, where we could be cut off by Sutherland's force. But up this Carron, Hope to meet the Mackenzies the sooner. If ever we see them! But get away from these firth-side levels. There is danger here.'

'I know it. I would choose the same. But Mackay and others who know these parts, tell me that this Strathcarron quickly narrows into a high steep pass, at a place called Croick. No place for troops who are not mountaineers. We could be trapped in there. With our old Highland host it would have been child's play. But these Netherlanders and Orkneymen . . .! I dare not let them get cooped up in there, Pate.'

'Aye – that is true. James – where in God's name is Pluscarden and his people? They should have been here long since. Think you – think you they will fail us? That they delay, of a purpose?'

'I do not know. Would God I did! All I know is that I must have Highland reinforcements if I am going to fight in this country. All is based on that. I have no choice but to wait for the Mackenzies and the Mackays – if I may!'

So once again they settled to wait. That evening a newcomer was brought to Montrose, a loyalist Munro laird, of Achness, with half a dozen men. His report was not cheering. His own clan, and their neighbours, the Rosses, who had both risen for the King with Pluscarden the previous spring, had found Strachan and his dragoons, on their doorstep, too much for them. With word of King Charles talking peace, they had thought better of joining Montrose – indeed, they had joined Strachan, though not enthusiastically and under threat. Some like himself had objected – and if the lord Marquis made a strong move southwards into their country, they might well think again. But meantime they were on Strachan's side. He had no word about the Mackenzies and Pluscarden; he had understood them still to be far in the West. But as to the Covenant enemy, there was only the one troop of horse north of Tain, with Strachan also waiting. Waiting for Leslie.

Nine-tenths of warfare consisted of waiting, James Graham reminded himself and his colleagues.

They waited, then, strengthening their hill-side position with entrenchments below the Creag Choineachan, with the Culrain Burn in a steepish ravine to guard their flank. But in the early afternoon waiting abruptly ended. The, or a, troop of dragoons suddenly appeared, riding westwards, openly, out of the woodlands of Ardchronie, on over the levels towards them.

It was time now for decision, with the enemy riding straight for their present advanced position at the ford of Invercharron. Something had to be done about it. There were about fifty of them, and Montrose's horse numbered forty, not cavalry as such but mounted officers. Why the dragoons had decided to advance now, after delaying for so long, was anybody's guess – but it could well mean that Strachan's main body was coming up behind, at long last.

Hurry and his aide Major Lisle, a veteran cavalryman, were urgent now. These dragoons must be engaged and destroyed, before they got in amongst the unprotected infantry. Once let these loose on the unblooded Orkneymen, even fifty of them, and it would be massacre. The forty royalist horse were not so greatly outnumbered – and they were all gentlemen, officers and experienced. Pate agreed. A small victory now could have important results – apart from saving the infantry.

James Graham, faced with a united front, bowed to it, despite his own reluctance. Indeed, he had little option. To retire his

1,200 men in the face of fifty dragoons was barely thinkable in its results on morale. Whether the dragoons recognised this, or were in fact completely unaware of their danger, was not to be known. But they were heading straight for the fords across Carron in column of march.

'Very well,' Montrose acceded. 'We shall let them cross the river, so that they can be pinned against it thereafter. Sir John – you will take all our horse, save for a few officers remaining with me. I will lead a detachment of the foot, out of sight, north-abouts, down to the Carron, to hold the fords, so that no dragoons get back, and no reinforcements can reach them. The untried Orkneymen I shall leave here, on the higher ground, meantime. You must deal with the dragoons, thirty-five against fifty, as you think best.'

'Thank the Lord!' Hurry exclaimed. A bold commander of light cavalry, this was an encounter after his own heart. Dividing his thirty-five officers into two groups, one under Lisle the professional, they waited until the advancing dragoons had disappeared into the wooded hollow of the Carron, well over a mile eastwards, and then spurred off to do battle.

Montrose left Sir James Douglas, with Kinnoull, in charge of their own Orkneymen, and with Pate, Frendraught and Sir James's brother John, led the Continental mercenaries, to the number of about 400, down through the open woodland in a circling movement to the north, on the slopes parallel to the shore, at a steady trot, to reach the river below the fords and work up behind the dragoons.

Before they were half-way there they heard the clash of conflict. But as they ran, panting, amongst the birch-woods, Montrose jerked to Pate.

'Do you hear fighting?' he demanded. 'I hear a confusion. Beat of hooves. Shouting. But no clash of steel. Do you?'

'No. They may have broken and run. The dragoons. Hurry has surprised and broken them? Already!'

'Unless it is Hurry who runs!' Frendraught put in.

'No – Hurry would not run, in this. He lacks not for cour-age . . .'

'If the dragoons are fleeing, we should be at the fords. Prevent them escaping . . .'

They ran the faster.

The scrub-birch denied prospects in most directions at this low level. But at one point, near a small headland, a clearing and its thatched blackhouse suddenly revealed to them a group of about a dozen dragoons cantering on an opposite course about 300 yards farther up. These, though they could not help seeing the infantry, and some shook their drawn swords at them, made no attempt to ride them down or even to change course towards them. They rode on. And presently a group of five royalist officers, led by Drummond of Balloch, came dashing in pursuit, riding much faster. All passed out of sight in the trees.

'Save us – what sort of a ploy is that!' Pate panted.

'Poltroons!' Frendraught cried. 'Fleeing from half their number.'

Montrose did not share the Viscount's scorn. There was something wrong here. Those dragoons gave no impression of fleeing. Their cantering looked far more like an exercise. There had been no sign of the confusion of battle, no wounds, no helmets lost.

'I do not like it,' he said, as they ran on.

At the ford area there was no sign of fleeing cavalrymen. Montrose quickly placed his Continental infantry in a position to guard the crossings from either side. Down here, there were no distant views. He called Inchbrakie to him.

'Pate – take a couple of men and hurry up to the higher ground again. We can see nothing here. There is something amiss. These dragoons are neither fighting nor fleeing. I think they have been sent to keep our horse engaged, to bemuse us. A ruse. If so, there must be more enemy near by, to take advantage. I fear an attack in strength. We are as well here, at these fords, as anywhere. Meantime. But – the Orkneymen could be in danger. Hurry and the horse also. Off with you. Be my eyes. Get me information . . .'

It was not Pate who came racing down to them a few minutes thereafter, but the Earl of Kinnoull, gasping for breath.

'They are coming, James!' he exclaimed. 'Hundreds. They are upon us. Whole army! Plain filled with horse. They have us . . .!'

'Thank you, my lord,' Montrose said quietly. 'Regain your breath, pray. Then let us have it in order. Take your time, my friend.'

His calm stilled the incipient panic. Kinnoull managed to make it clear that soon after the fifty dragoons had crossed the fords, he and Douglas, up with the Orkneymen, had had their attention directed to movement away on the slopes to the south, their right front. Soon it was clear that a large infantry force was advancing down the braes that flanked the south side of Strath-carron. At first they were cheered, assuming that it was the Mackenzies at last – but they realised that they came from the wrong direction and had either cavalry support or many mounted officers, which the Mackay said the Mackenzies had not. Then it was seen that out from the same woodland of Ardchronie from which the dragoons had issued were coming large numbers of cavalry, troop upon troop, with banners . . .

'Heading for here ?' Montrose interrupted. 'These fords ?'

'Yes. Straight here. They cannot be far off now . . .'

Raising his voice, James Graham shouted to his officers to prepare all ranks to oppose a crossing of the river in strength from the east. Only a few to stand watch to the rear. Hide so far as possible . . .

They were barely settled into a defensive position when the first ranks of Strachan's horse came up fast through the trees making directly for the fords opposite the Mill of Invercharron. Unfortunately, some over-excited musketeer on their side fired his weapon before the horsemen were fully within range across the water – and then others followed suit. There was no whole-sale decimation of the unsuspecting enemy, therefore. Even so, it was complete surprise. Clearly Strachan had never anticipated that the fords would be manned and held *after* his dragoon advance guard had crossed over. There was much confusion across the Carron, as new troops of horse cantered up to become involved with the first ones pressing back to be out of range.

Montrose passed urgent commands down his line to stop haphazard and wasteful shooting. Fire was to be disciplined, volleyed.

The fordable area was all within a compass of some 300 yards. The enemy appeared to know this, and presently four distinct crossings were attempted, simultaneously, at about seventy-yard intervals, with covering fire from Strachan's heavy dragoons equipped with muskets, to keep the opposition pinned down. But Montrose's Danish, German and Netherland mercenaries knew how to counter this, and zigzagging and bent double, moved into new positions without serious loss. They were able to halt all four crossing attempts.

The enemy withdrew in disorder into the trees again.

James Graham found one of Pate's men crouching at his side. 'Lord,' he said, 'Inchbrakie says to tell you that there is a clan host, it may be 1,000, advancing frae the south. But a mile off. Munroes and Rosses, he jalouses. Stiffened wi' regular musketeers and mounted officers, forbye. And there's cavalry – but, och, you've found them! Maybe six troops, Inchbrakie says. Aye – and General Hurry and his officers are right fully engaged, now, wi' thae dragoons. They've turned to fight, now.'

'Yes. I thank you. Tell me – is there another ford to this river? Higher?'

'Aye, lord – a mile up, nae mair. Naething downstream.'

'A pity!' Montrose turned. 'My lord of Kinnoull – take some five-score men, and this guide. To go guard another ford a mile up. At the run! But climb up into the woodland first, so that the enemy do not see where you go . . .' He stopped. 'Ah – damnation!'

Leaving a couple of troops of horse to face them across Carron, the main body of the Covenant cavalry was wheeling in column to their left, to spur off up the river-side.

'Too late! Strachan must know of the other fords. Do not go, my lord. You cannot outrun horse. We cannot stop them crossing, now.'

'Bravo, my lord Marquis!' Frendraught shouted from a little way off. 'The first joust is ours!'

Montrose muttered that this was no jousting, God help them! But he waved back, smiling encouragement on all. Then he called all but the regimental officers to him.

'Gentlemen – I am concerned for the Orkneymen. And for our horse. *This* is a fair defensive position – but our force is grievously scattered. Hay of Delgatie – I leave you in command here. My lords Kinnoull and Frendraught, and you, Powrie, and John Douglas – come with me.' He did not have to name young Menzies of Pitfodels, who was acting as standard-bearer, and never left the Captain-General's side. 'I shall join Sir James and the Orkneymen, seek to concentrate the horse, with them. And bring all down to the peninsula where this Carron joins the Kyle. It is low and marshy, and we will be protected on three sides by water. They will not overrun us there. Start moving your men, in stages, down-river, Delgatie, when I send you a runner. Is it understood?'

The six men went hurrying up through the open woodland, keeping a wary eye open for dragoons and ready to dive for cover at any moment. They saw no dragoons, but soon came on traces of a running fight. They found a riderless horse standing

347

amongst bushes, and nearby the body of the cavalryman, Major Lisle, dead, shot through the head with a pistol-bullet. Near by a wounded Covenant trooper lay groaning in a pool of blood.

Frendraught caught the horse and brought it to Montrose. He mounted, to get to the Orkneymen the more swiftly, with Menzies of Pitfodels and the Royal Standard riding pillion behind him. He told the others to press on, and if they saw any of Hurry's group to tell them to rejoin the main force on the higher ground immediately. Then he spurred off.

He saw more bodies, and a stray horse or two, but paused for none. Then, half a mile short of the entrenchment area, his heart fell as he perceived a great body of men ahead of him. It was Sir James Douglas and the Orkneymen coming marching down.

'Dear God!' he groaned. 'The fools! The poor purblind fools . . .!'

But he mastered his anger in the interests of morale. Riding up, he called, 'Sir James – well met! But I must request you to turn your men about. The situation is much changed. About turn your men, and back to the prepared positions, if you please.'

'We were marching to your aid, my lord,' the Douglas explained. 'We heard of the assault at the fords.'

'Yes. I thank you. But – four troops of Covenant horse may be upon us at any moment. In column, like this, you could be cut to pieces in minutes. Quickly, now – have your men trot.'

As they hurried back towards the entrenchments, where they could at least have some hope of facing cavalry, Montrose racked his brain for the best way out of this tangle, this tactician's nightmare. He had intended to move the 800 Orkneymen downhill, to the north, to reach the low, marshy peninsula, to be sure – but it would have to be done properly, in an organised series of leap-frogging bounds, in say four companies, three giving covering fire while one ran forward, 200 yards at a time. And if possible with a group of horse to aid. This present straightforward marching in the open invited massacre. They would have to get back to the entrenchments, take up the defensive position they should never have left, and there organise the companies, meantime trying to round up what was left of Hurry's horse . . .

But it was not to be. A group of about a dozen horsed officers, one seriously wounded, did join them, all that was left of Lisle's party, under Major David Guthrie; of Hurry and the others they had seen nothing for some time. Inchbrakie had met them and told them to report back at the entrenchments. Montrose mounted Pitfodels on the wounded man's horse.

A shout from the rear turned all heads. Covenant cavalry was appearing out of the scrub behind them, not a quarter-mile away. And in large numbers. This was not the remnants of the fifty dragoons. These were the first of the troops who had crossed the upper fords.

'Form schiltroms! Two hollow squares,' Montrose shouted to the Orkneymen. 'Front ranks kneeling, others standing. Quickly – two schiltroms.' They had practised this at Kirkwall – pray heaven they had not forgotten how. 'No fire before seventy yards. Front ranks to fire first. Then standing men, as they reload.'

In some fashion the 800 formed into two ragged squares. These were crofters and fishermen, in action for the first time, untrained infantry facing heavy regular cavalry. If they made a poor showing, who could blame them? Certainly not James Graham. He, for his part, now devoted himself to the dozen horsemen.

'Into a wedge behind me. Wedge-formation, gentlemen. Tight. Guthrie – Drummond – the horns of the V. Keep tight, my friends, and we shall drive through anything.' He raised his plumed hat, from under the Lion Rampant standard which Menzies held bravely above him. 'For God and King Charles!'

A cheer arose, faltering at first, but gaining in strength.

The Covenant horse had slowed their approach. There appeared to be two troops, of approximately 100 each. A bugle was blown, no doubt to bring the other two troops up to their aid. Then, still in two formations, they extended into line abreast, obviously preparing to charge. The trees, though scattered, open, hampered them somewhat.

'Sir James – control your fire,' Montrose warned. 'The first charge you should break. The second we will try to disperse. Then, one of your schiltroms to rise. Run 200 yards, while the other covers them. Towards the entrenchments. Then they will cover you. Leap-frogging. You have it? We must get back to the trenches.'

The Douglas raised his hand in acknowledgment at the same moment as the Covenant horse charged.

The Orkneymen's shooting was ragged and premature indeed, and much of it wasted. There was no clear distinction between

349

the volleys. Some horses and riders fell and, as always in a charge tripped up others. But the charge was not halted. These were light dragoons, not heavy, equipped with large horse-pistols which they fired from the saddle, and then drew their sabres. The second troop let the first get half-way to the schiltroms before they followed on in similar style.

Montrose had to wait, or he would run into the Orkneymen's fire. But as this began to die away, he raised his sword high, slashed its point down towards the enemy, and dug in his spurs. Behind him, tight as men and horse could pack themselves, his wedge thundered after him.

He drove over at a tangent, behind the first troop and in front of the second. At this stage, his aim was not actual fighting, sword-play, but to break up the second charge. This rear-ward troop, he knew, were unlikely to fire their pistols meantime, for fear of hitting their comrades in front. Not all of his own people had pistols loaded and ready. Such as had followed their leader's example and fired them into the advancing line.

That first drive of the wedge was a complete success, in that it utterly broke up the second troop's rush. There was no real clash, for as the royalists drove slantwise across the dragoon's front, even though it was twelve to 100, the latter reined aside this way and that, the first rank confusing the rear, so that in only a few seconds the whole was in milling chaos, all forward impetus lost.

Without casualty, Montrose now sought to perform the most difficult of manoeuvres, to swing a racing wedge round upon itself in a restricted space for a charge in the reverse direction, and in tree-dotted terrain. It was less than successful, for most of his dozen were not trained cavalrymen, and though Guthrie and Drummond at the rear did their best to whip the others into formation again swiftly, precious moments were lost.

Montrose waiting, fretting, had a chance to look at the Orkneymen and groaned at what he saw. Utter confusion prevailed there. One schiltrom was already broken and in process of retiring – but the men streaming off in panic, throwing away their arms the better to run from the slashing sabres and trampling hooves. Obviously these would not halt, to form up again. The other formation, Douglas's own, was in better shape, still recognisable as a defensive unit, and most of the dragoons were leaving it alone, milling round after the fleeing men, to leave it to the second troop.

His wedge not quite so tightly marshalled this time, James

Graham drove forward again for the incoherent mass of troopers, the officers of which were now furiously seeking to re-form it. This time pistol-shots cracked out at them, and two of the wedge were hit, before they crashed into the enemy – but owing to the press of horseflesh, neither actually fell to the ground, carried along slumped in their saddles.

At the point of the wedge, sword slashing in figure-of-eight fashion left and right, James Graham bored through the Covenant horse. Men and beasts reared up before him, reined aside, swayed, ducked or went down, steel flashed before his eyes, shots whistled past him, men shouted and cursed, falling, flailing horses screamed high terror. Twice his own mount stumbled, all but throwing him. A buffet from behind, by his own Royal Standard, knocked off his hat as Menzies of Pitfodels reeled in his saddle from a sabre-slash. Then they were through, with only a scattering of troopers fleeing before them.

But now his wedge was in a sorry state. Only seven of them remained, and only four unwounded. Both Guthrie and Drummond, in the dangerous tail positions, were down. Pitfodels was obviously seriously wounded, the Lion Rampant leaning drunkenly.

The second troop of dragoons was dispersed meanwhile, and would take some time to reassemble. Douglas's schiltrom, though battered, was still a unit, the first troop's effectiveness largely dissipated in pursuing the fleeing Orkneymen of the other formation.

James Graham, shaking his long waving hair clear of his face, sought to wipe perspiration from his eyes and found it to be blood, from an unsuspected graze on his forehead.

'A smaller wedge, gentlemen,' he cried. 'We must save Douglas's schiltrom if we can. Pitfodels – can you sit your horse ?'

'Yes-e-es,' that young man got out, through clenched teeth.

Montrose was urging his horse forward once more, towards the schiltrom, when he gained an unexpected reinforcement. It was Kinnoull, Frendraught and John Douglas, on captured horses, dashing up from the east – and even three men were welcome. But not their news. They shouted that two more troops of Covenant cavalry, with Strachan's own banner, were just behind.

By the time they reached the schiltrom, the new enemy was emerging from the trees to the east. In his heart James Graham knew that this was the end. Nothing, no amount of improvising, of heroism, could save them now. The fresh cavalry would rally the earlier troopers, only dispersed, not defeated, the Strachan would know how to control them. It was only a question of time, brief time. Where was Hurry . . . ?

Nevertheless, he shouted his orders with assurance, even with his accustomed courtesy. 'Sir James – here is your brother John. Divide your men in two companies, if you please. John, take one. The leap-frogging move, 200-yard rushes. John's company first – you cover them. Four moves should make the entrenchments. We will try to protect you. My Lord Frendraught – take the Standard. Pitfodels is sore hurt . . .'

'I can . . . make do . . . my lord,' Menzies jerked, white-faced.

'Very well. A tight wedge, gentlemen. One more. Behind me. Out to the flank, here. Till we see how they will attack.'

Strachan was an experienced commander. No doubt told what had happened to the first two troops, he did not repeat their tactics. Instead of a long line-abreast charge, he sent two half-troops forward in column, at the trot, fully 200 yards apart, making but poor targets for a wedge attack. His main body he held back in the centre, and then moved it forward also, but pacing slowly.

Montrose knew well what that meant. Those dragoons in the centre would be heavies, equipped with muskets, not pistols. At that slow pace, when they got within range – and twice the range of the pistols, and more – they would be able to fire from the saddle, then throw away the muskets and charge with the sabre. Musket-fire, so much more accurate and lethal . . .

'The left-hand half-troop first,' he called, to his nine horsemen. 'We will try take them in flank. They'll mask us from musket-fire so. Sir James – those dragoons have muskets. More dangerous. You fire yours at 100 yards. Aim for their horses – larger targets. Then run. Controlled running. To your brother. You have it ?'

Without waiting for an answer, the gallant little party under the red and gold Lion Rampant rode out, half-left, towards the advancing enemy.

The fifty half-troop of Strachan's right was, of course, ready for them. This time there was no surprise. As, presently, Montrose swung his group round in a semicircle to drive straight at the centre of the column, the pistols cracked out. One horse and two riders went down. Then the column sought to open, divide, to let the wedge through. Montrose wrenched his mount's head round hard to the left, and managed to drive into the rear half of the troop, in pounding, slashing fury. He was aware of blood before his eyes, a red-faced man who seemed to yell soundlessly in his face, all teeth and spittle. He felt his horse check, as though to a heavy blow, but plunge on. He heard the rattle of musket-fire from all around, but remotely, only through a great ringing in his head. Then there was nobody in front of him, and he was almost swept out of the saddle by a birch-tree branch.

Turning, swaying, to look behind him, dizzy, he found that he had only four companions now. Menzies of Pitfodels was gone, and Frendraught had the Standard. Kinnoull was there, Ogilvy of Powrie and Sir William Johnston. As he stared, blinking away the blood from his eyes, his horse gently collapsed under him, and died. He managed to throw himself clear, but fell on his knees, sword spinning.

Frendraught and Ogilvy were down beside him in a trice, banner and all, helping him up, bringing back his sword. 'Up on my horse, James!' the Viscount cried.

But Ogilvy brought him a riderless beast, of which there were not a few standing around now, and aided him into the saddle.

The situation elsewhere on that curious battlefield was far from static. Sir James Douglas's truncated schiltrom had now broken before the main Covenant advance, and the men were streaming away westwards with the cavalry in pursuit. Whether they could ever be halted again, was doubtful. His brother's group had indeed formed up farther back, after a fashion. Down upon them bore hunted and hunters both.

There was little effective that Montrose could do – but he had to try. He had brought these Orkneymen here; he could not desert them now. His head was spinning, and coherent thought difficult. Without any very clear idea of what to do, other than to return to action, he led his direly reduced group back into the fray.

But before ever they could affect the issue, John Douglas's formation broke, and now the entire part-wooded slope was covered with fleeing foot chased by savage horsemen. There could be no possible rally. Kinnoull shouted as much at the Graham's back, while Frendraught urged him to save himself, and quickly, for the sake of the cause.

They had rather reckoned without Colonel Archibald Strachan, acting Major-General. As that stern religionist saw the collapse of the Lord's enemies' main force, he drew back a company of heavy dragoons from the general pursuit to turn to look for Montrose. The little party under the Lion Rampant was in the act of pulling round, preparatory to flight, when an unexpected volley of musket-fire from these dragoons crashed out, all directed at them.

The wonder was that any of the five men survived in that sudden hail of lead. Three of the five horses fell, including Montrose's new one, its rider's shoulder grazed by a shot. Kinnoull and Frendraught alone remained in their saddles, the latter slumped over, wounded in the thigh, the Standard dropping to the grass.

As Montrose picked himself up, reeling, Frendraught slid to the ground grimacing with pain.

'Take this beast, James,' he gasped, 'I, I am . . . done. Quick – flee! They come. For God's sake . . .!' And he pitched forward on top of the Lion Rampant.

James Graham, groaning, did not delay. He flung himself up into the vacated saddle, and kicked in his heels, spurring after Kinnoull who was already dashing off. A scatter of musket- and pistol-shots followed them as they plunged away northwards, but this time none found a mark.

Carbisdale was over, not so much a battle as a protracted folly and disaster.

CHAPTER TWENTY-FIVE

It was some time before, pounding along behind Kinnoull, James Graham was really aware of anything other than pain, grief, humiliation and the need to keep upright in his saddle and ahead of pursuit. He did know that they were pursued, though shots had soon ceased behind them. Fortunately they were heavy dragoons that were involved, and their own captured horses were light cavalry mounts, which gave them a slightly better turn of speed. But he knew not where they were, or where they were going.

Gradually however his mind cleared and his will reasserted itself. Gazing about him, he realised that they were heading north-westwards up Strathoykell; that Kinnoull, concerned only with flight, had ridden off directly back whence they had come, in automatic reaction, with the enemy to the south and east and the waters of the Kyle to the north. But up here, at any time, they might run into the Earl of Sutherland's force, marching down.

Forcing himself, with a major effort, to think ahead constructively, coherently, he decided that Sutherland would necessarily be advancing down this southern side of the Oykell, if he was there at all. Somehow, then, they must get across the estuary. He tried to recollect the lie of the land, observed two days before as they had headed south-eastwards. The Oykell, he was fairly sure, had not been fordable, or indeed swimmable, for the last many miles of his course, rushing in a deep channel. But soon after it opened into the tidal Kyle, the latter had narrowed suddenly, for a short distance, with a low headland of sorts reaching out towards the north shore. Just below Invershin, if he remembered rightly. If the tide was not at too strong an ebb, it might be possible to swim horses across there. Not more than half a mile ahead now . . .

He shouted to Kinnoull to pull away right-handed, downhill, towards the waterside.

It was more thickly wooded here, and their progress was slowed. But that would apply also to their pursuers. And the cover was better. Down through the birches and alders they plunged, horses and riders whipped by the branches. At the mud-lined shore, as they reined left-handed along it, Kinnoull groaned, pointing. Two horsemen were there, flailing their mounts, riding in the same direction.

'Only two. And fleeing. Ours,' Montrose jerked, and slowed a little, to let them catch up.

They were two of Hurry's group, both Sinclairs – indeed almost the only Sinclairs they had been able to enroll; Sir Edward, a middle-aged Orkneyman, descendant of the St. Clair Earls of Orkney; and Major Alexander of Brims, a cadet of Caithness. They were obviously much heartened to find themselves in Montrose's company again. They too were trying to find a place to cross the Kyle. They were all that was left of Hurry's party, they panted, all the rest dead, wounded or captured, Hurry with them.

They came to the low marshy point Montrose had remembered, scarcely to be called a headland, but at least narrowing the Kyle to no more than 300 yards, just a little way above Invershin Castle on the northern shore. It was now or never. Dragoons were in sight behind them, but well out of musket-range. James Graham led the way, spurring his reluctant horse through the thick, black, half-tide mud and into the cold water.

There was only some 200 yard of actual swimming. Fortunately the tide was coming in, helping to neutralise the Oykell's current. Even so they were swept downstream quite some distance, strongly as the tired beasts strove, the riders half swimming alongside, urgent, desperate enough scarcely to notice the chill.

They dragged themselves out, over more mud, on to a green cattle-dotted meadow, closer to Invershin Castle, a small Sutherland hold, than was comfortable. Looking back, they saw that the first of the dragoons had reached the opposite shore, but had drawn up there, watching, as yet making no attempt to follow – no doubt hoping that no officer would arrive to order them to take to the water.

Shivering now in wet clothes, the four fugitives rode on north-westwards. The River Shin came in on their right almost immediately, from the Lairg area, and the Sinclairs were for turning up its valley, to get quickly away from this dangerous Strathoykell. But Montrose pointed out that it was a populous valley, and narrow, its people Sutherlands. They could not hope to traverse it without being seen, and the folk would be hostile. Better to ford Shin and continue up the north side of Oykell meantime, and take the next valley on the right, Glen Cassley, some seven or eight miles up. They knew it and its drove-road – it was the way they had come south to Inveroykell some days ago. It was a much wilder route, with little habitation – safer. They must try to cross the mountains north-westwards, to the Mackay country of Reay. If Lord Reay's 1,000 Mackays were indeed marching to join him, they would be as apt to come that way as the long way round by Thurso. If they could meet them . . .

There was still no sign of the Earl of Sutherland's force on the far side of the Oykell. The fact was actually worrying Montrose somewhat now. If Sutherland was not over there, where was he? Delayed, and coming down Shin behind them? Or Cassley in front?

They could see their troop of dragoons now riding parallel with their own progress on the far side of the river, keeping them in view. This was dangerous also. There just might possibly be somewhere that men and horses could cross, short of Inveroykell ford. And they could signal to allies on this side.

He put it to the others. Reluctant as he was, he thought that they should abandon the horses. They were too ken-speckle, would not blend into the background scene. And it was horsemen that the enemy would be on the look-out for. He proposed that they actually turned back a little way, on their beasts, as though they had changed their minds, and were going to flee up the Shin. The dragoons across the valley would see it. Then they would abandon their horses in the thickish wood they had passed half a mile back, and proceed thereafter, north-westwards again, on foot but on the higher ground meantime, as inconspicuously as possible, taking advantage of the cover. James Graham made this a suggestion, not an order. He conceived it proper no longer to command his fellow-fugitives.

None contraverted his proposals, however – little as they relished the thought of having to do their escaping on foot. Or of actually turning back, even for a short distance. But they did it – and had the satisfaction of seeing the dragoons across Oykell pause also, and then turn back.

In the wood of Altass, Montrose abandoned more than his horse. He took off his handsome black chased-steel breast-plate, and his wet coat with the star and ribbon of the Garter – which he had been wearing as visible sign of his authority as Viceroy –

and even his sword-belt and pistol. None of these would solve any problems for them now, where inconspicuousness might. They would undoubtedly require all their strength for the major walking and climbing ahead of them. Unfortunately they could none of them dispense with their heavy thigh-length riding-boots without alternative footwear, unsuitable as these were. Hiding all beneath tree-roots – as unlikely a depository for the insignia of the Garter as probably had yet been conceived – and leaving the horses hitched loosely, they turned westwards once more out of the wood, now making use of hollows, trees, out-cropping rock and all other cover, to hide their progress.

Montrose's shoulder had stiffened up, and his hair-line wound throbbed painfully, Kinnoull also was hurt, his ribs crushed by a fall from his horse, possibly even cracked. Neither of the Sinclairs appeared to be injured, but Sir Edward was the oldest of the party and hardly robust. They had not a morsel of food between them. But at least they were glad of the activity to generate warmth, to dry their clothing.

It was now late afternoon, and for the remainder of that day they made their way up Strathoykell's north bank, high above the river-side road, without incident. They saw much to-ing and fro-ing on the far side of the strath and just before dusk a mounted patrol came cantering down the road on their own side, from the west. But there was no searching of their braesides meantime; presumably it was believed that they had gone up Shin.

Darkness overtook them near the mouth of Glen Cassley; but, weary as they were, they dare not rest yet. They stumbled on a shepherd's cabin in the entrance of the glen, near the ford, where dogs barked vociferously in alarm. The others were for beating a hasty retreat, but Montrose demurred. This would make it clear to the inhabitants that fugitives had passed this way, he reasoned – and in the morning they would be able to tell enquiring dragoons and send them up the glen after them. Better to make use of the opportunity. He gave Major Sinclair some silver and asked him to go forward to the house, to declare that he was a fugitive from battle and had a wounded comrade, and seek to buy food and old clothing, plaids, anything to cover them. But to stress that they were proceeding up Oykell, after fording Cass-ley. Ask about the ford, and how far it was to the west coast, up Oykell. The Mackay had mentioned Elphin, up there. Ask about Elphin. So that, when questioned, the cottagers would be sure to send the hunt in that direction, not up Cassley.

Presently Alexander Sinclair came back. He had managed to procure two plaids and some rags of old clothing. But little food. The shepherd had been friendly enough, but his own meal-kist was sadly low, at the end of the winter, and he had no meat in the house. A couple of bannocks, a handful of oatmeal, and some cold boiled salmon from the river, was all that he could provide.

They shared these morsels, and pressed on up the glen, not crossing the ford.

Some three miles up, they halted from sheer exhaustion, and huddled together in the heather in the lee of a great outcrop. It had begun to rain and they spread the plaids over them. Despite wet, cold and discomfort, they all sank into sleep almost immediately.

They wakened chilled, cramped, hungry and depressed, to the grey misery of dawn, with cold, seeping mist hanging low over all, no vistas, no food. But at least they were still undiscovered, and unlikely to be spotted in the mist. The others prevailed on Montrose, as the most conspicuous, as well as the one most vitally important to avoid capture, to exchange his fine clothing for most of the shepherd's ragged contributions. As had been discovered on an earlier occasion, however, no matter how shabby the clothing, it could not make James Graham look other than distinguished, assured, characterful. His scalp wound was bleeding again, slightly, and he tore up part of his silken shirt to make a bandage.

They moved on.

Although they none of them felt in conversational mood, and the disaster and losses of yesterday were still rather too close for discussion, it was necessary to decide on their immediate aims. There were really only two choices of action. Either they should head north by east to try to reach Sir Harry Graham and his rearguard in the Thurso area; or north-westwards into the friendly Mackay country of Reay. The two Sinclairs preferred the former, as might be expected. Kinnoull the latter. Montrose tended to agree with Kinnoull. His reasoning was that Harry Graham was capable of doing all that could be done up in Caithness, maintaining the links with Orkney; yet he had no large force, and the Sinclairs, as a clan, would not rise before – so would be a deal less likely to do so now. Whereas Lord Reay and the Mackays were committed. And they were a much larger clan, dominating all the very north-west corner of the mainland. Even if, on their way there they missed the promised 1,000 men, in a week or so on Reay they could muster another 1,000 and more. With such Montrose could wage a Highland campaign still, overcome the effects of yesterday's set-back, and be down in Atholl, threatening the Lowlands, in a month.

It was brave talking, on purpose – but not unrealistic. All had not been lost at Carbisdale. Indeed, taken in the context of the entire Scottish cause, it was only a preliminary minor skirmish gone wrong, a false start before the real campaign started, grievous as was the loss of officer-corps personnel and friends, and the sad sacrifice of the Orkneymen. But it was not with these latter that Montrose had hoped to win Scotland for the King. He did not put into words, however, the much more ominous background situation which was, in fact, the real cause of yesterday's defeat – the climate of opinion beginning to prevail in Scotland, caused by Charles's renewed sitting down with the Covenanters, and talk of a treaty which was stifling all enthusiasm for uprising against Argyll meantime, and had almost certainly made the Mackenzies drag their feet and fail him and caused the Munroes and Rosses to attach themselves to Strachen. If the Mackays chose to take the same line . . .!

Unfortunately for their decision, however, none of the fugitives really knew this wild country, save by repute. They had indeed come south down Glen Cassley earlier, but had never left the deep valley-floor. Two-thirds of the way up, they recollected, the side-glen of Muic struck off westwards. They would take that for the Reay country, by Assynt. But meantime they were on the wrong side of the Cassley – and the mist was so thick that they could not see more than fifty yards.

Montrose thought that he remembered crossing from the west to the east side of the glen, on the march down, at a ford fairly soon after Glen Muic came in. They must look out for that ford, therefore, and cross there.

They did not find it so soon as they anticipated. Indeed it was mid-afternoon, and still thick, cloying mist, before they were able to discover a spot where they might get across the rushing torrent – and it was not the place where they had forded before, all recognised.

However, about an hour later, they found a fairly large incoming stream on the left, and felt rather than saw that they were in the mouth of a widish tributary valley. It might be the Muic, or it might not; but at least it led off westwards in the direction they wanted to go. They decided to follow it up.

Soon they were climbing, but there was a track of sorts. They followed it for hour after hour, climbing all the time, and growing more certain that it was not Glen Muic. An early dusk found them, ravenous, weary and uncertain; and when their deteriorating track made a substantial fork, with nothing to indicate which was the major prong, they decided to halt for the night, in the hope that the mist would be gone by morning, and they might see approximately where they were and which was the route.

That was a grim night. This bare expanse of peat-hags was much colder than in the sheltered valley. Their hunger was now a pain, gnawing, and leaving them light-headed. Montrose barely slept at all, the pain in his head throbbing. And as the night progressed, a new anxiety came to him. For Sir Edward Sinclair, who had been noticeably silent all that day and tending to lag behind, was moaning and groaning and sometimes talking wildly, obviously not so much dreaming nightmares as in semi-conscious raving. Never a robust man, he was too old and unused to hard living and campaigning for this sort of thing. That he was going to hold them up on the morrow, to say the least of it, was most apparent.

The mist changed to rain, half sleet indeed at this high altitude, just before dawn. Huddled beneath the plaids, shivering, they waited for the light to grow. Sir Edward was quieter now, but sunk in a heavy lethargy. Montrose forced himself to talk, talk incessantly, cheerfully, about plans for the future, past campaigns, his experiences in Europe. Alexander Sinclair responded well, but Kinnoull, never a talkative young man, was as silent as Sir Edward, hunched, depressed. Hunger ate at their vitals like rats.

When eventually they realised that it would grow no lighter, there were still no distant prospects. The rain had to some extent washed away the mist, but itself formed driving curtains to screen the view. They appeared to be on a lofty peat-pocked plateau, a wilderness of black hags and old heather, with vague hill-sides looming around but no certainty. As far as the forking paths went, there was nothing at all to choose from.

Some discussion arose between Montrose and Alexander Sinclair as to which to take – or even whether possibly to go back down to Cassley – Kinnoull and Sir Edward evincing no interest. Montrose thought the left-hand track ought to be the more hopeful in that it should bring them to lower ground more quickly, more or less due westwards – for he was pretty sure that they were considerably north of Glen Muic and that therefore the vast and daunting mountain massif of the Ben More Assynt group must lie ahead north-westwards, though they could see nothing of it. Sinclair argued that if they bore to the right they would do better, that Ben More was not so near as all that, and that direction should allow them to pass south-westwards of it and its great neighbour Conival, to reach Inchnadamph and the head of Loch Assynt. And even if it did not, the more to the right they swung, the better, for it would bring them ever nearer to the head of Glen Cassley, which, he had heard, swung strongly westwards in its higher reaches. Indeed they ought never to have left Cassley, he declared.

'Then would you prefer that we turn back, down to Cassley glen again, Major?' James Graham asked. 'I am prepared to consider it.'

'No, not that. It might be dangerous to retrace our steps. We may be followed, run into a patrol. No, I say we should take this right-hand track. And if it leads us to upper Glen Cassley, so much the better. From there only a low ridge can separate it from upper Shin – four miles, no more. And we are on the road for Caithness.'

'You are still anxious to get to Caithness, then? You would rather that than go on the longer road to Reay?'

'To be sure – I would. And Sir Edward too, I warrant. Indeed, I doubt if he will survive the long evil tramp across these damnable mountains, my lord. We could get him through to Shin, though. Perhaps put him up in some shepherd's cabin, till he can win safely northwards.'

Montrose nodded. 'You may be right. Yet it is better for the cause that I make for the Mackays, as swiftly as may be,' he declared. He looked at the other two, painful brows wrinkled. They offered no guidance or help. 'See you, Major – I think that we should part company. You and my lord of Kinnoull take Sir Edward and make for the Upper Cassley and upper Shin. The quickest way to food and shelter. And I will press on for Assynt and Reay.'

'But . . . my lord! Alone, you would not survive! We cannot leave you . . .'

'I will do very well . . .'

'*I* do not intend to leave him,' Kinnoull announced thickly. 'I stay with James.' It was the first words he had spoken for long.

Montrose would, in fact, have preferred it otherwise, but could not say so. Kinnoull would more likely be a hindrance than a help, and in his present state not notable company either.

Sir Edward seemed to gain an accession of strength and interest at this prospect of Caithness and the shorter journey. No doubt he felt his own beloved Orkney to be suddenly nearer. They shook hands and parted there, then, taking a plaid and a share of the available money, all in a blatter of sleet that was almost snow, the Sinclairs eager to be off.

Unspeaking, the two peers of Scotland turned westwards.

*   *   *

There are more varieties of hell than one, undoubtedly, and grey, wet cold at a high altitude in peat-hag country can be as terrible a sort as any blazing of eternal fires. All that grievous day James Graham and William Hay forced their stumbling way approximately west by north, into a north-west sleet-laden wind, famished, in pain, all but frozen. The track took them for some miles – how far they could not calculate – and then, bringing them to a rushing peat-stained torrent, did not recommence, so far as they could discover, on the other side. Snow was beginning to lie and presumably covering what slight traces of track there might be, and there was no vantage-point to give them a prospect. They discovered a narrow deer-path heading in roughly the right direction; but it turned and twisted as such do, and after a while petered out. They could only keep facing into the icy wind, staggering and tripping onwards over a broken, savage, endless terrain of tall old heather, quaking peat-sumps, the semi-fossilised roots of huge ancient trees from a warmer era, outcropping rock and innumerable rushing burns. Their pace grew slower and slower. Kinnoull undoubtedly would have halted, laid down and given up, had not Montrose consistently urged him on.

James Graham, for the first time, began to contemplate dying in this empty, ferocious wilderness – he for whom the Highlands had always sounded a clarion-call.

It was mid-afternoon when, at last, there was a break in the weather, the sleet died away and the clouds began to lift – although the wind blew still harder and colder. Gradually colour, distance and dimension returned to the land – but what it revealed was utterly appalling.

They were in the centre of a great basin of the mountains, a sort of amphitheatre two or three miles wide, a place of bogs and moraines and low heather knolls by the hundred, with a small, lost, slate-grey loch over to their right. But it was not the immediate prospect which held their daunted gaze so much as the enormous mountain mass which reared up behind the lochan, seeming almost to overhang them, thousands of feet above, three great, snow-streaked towering peaks, all streaming, glistening rock-face, beetling precipice, white falling water and soaring pinnacles, vast, overpowering. With a groan, Kinnoull sank down in the heather and buried his face in his shivering hands.

Montrose drew a long, quivering breath, but sought to hold his voice steady. 'Look at that, Will,' he said. 'See — we know where we are now. Those giants — they can be none other than Ben More Assynt and Conival. I know not the name of the third. But — I was right.' His voice faltered. 'God help the Sinclairs — they, they must have walked straight into it! Though — perhaps their track swung away in time. It must lead somewhere. But, see you — if we are south of Ben More, then Loch Assynt and its low strath cannot be so far away. To the west. And Neil Macleod of Assynt served with me for a little, after Inverlochy. With one of Seaforth's companies. A King's man.'

Kinnoull did not respond, or even look up.

Montrose turned his gaze towards the south-west, where there was a major gap in the encircling barrier of the mountains, some three miles away.

'Yonder is our route, Will. Through that col. You can see that there are no great hills beyond. That *must* lead into the strath of Assynt, since it lies south-west of Ben More. Three more miles to the col. Then, say another three, and we shall be safe. Six miles, no more ...'

The other raised his head. 'Then you go on, James — if you can. For I cannot.'

'You can, man — you can. And *must*! Together we can do it. We may well find food, a house, before then. Coming to lower ground. It is food that you need. A bite to eat and you will find your strength again. Chew on these heather-stems, as I have done — who knows, there may be good in it. Come.' He put a hand under the other's arm and hoisted him to his feet — although the effort almost toppled himself.

They lurched off in the new direction, arm-in-arm.

That col took an unconscionable time to draw any nearer. The ground, as they approached it, grew ever more waterlogged, with small lochans and peat-pools everywhere – typical West Sutherland landscape. Slithering, ploutering, circling, they dragged themselves on.

Montrose raised a croaking cheer at the first stunted Scots pine, a twisted, poor thing but significant, proof that they were coming down to the tree-level and therefore the possible haunts of men. But soon thereafter they had to wade one more of the countless rushing burns – and crossing this, William Hay slipped on the slimy stones of the bottom and fell his length in the icy water. Montrose managed to grab him before he was swept away and dragged him to the bank.

But now Kinnoull could not stand, much less walk. He had dislocated his hip, it seemed.

James Gordon had no choice. He could by no means carry his friend. They would both die if he was just to lie down beside the man, here. He must go on, try to bring the other help and food – although it was a grievous decision to leave him there. Dragging Kinnoull into the lee of a great outcrop and pulling heather to form a barrier around him, he wrapped the plaid round his soaking, shivering conpanion, promised aid, confided him to God's keeping, and pressed on.

The climb up to the col, although nothing steep nor long, taxed Montrose to the utmost. Darkness descended upon him in that defile, but he stumbled on. There could be no halting now. Weakened with hunger and exhaustion, if he let himself sink down – as his whole being craved – he might well never rise again.

That night had an unreality for him, an utterly unearthly quality beyond all description. Fortunately the floor of the defile contained a fairly well-defined track which carried him onwards, westwards – otherwise, most certainly, he could not long have continued in the darkness. As it was he continually tripped over obstacles – and when he fell it demanded all his will-power each time to rise once more. He lost all impression of time, or even of where he was, relatively. More and more his mind, his consciousness, was far elsewhere, mainly with Elizabeth whose love, warm understanding and support were more real to him than any present conditions. Other presences came to be with him also – Magdalen, young Johnnie, George Gordon, Magnus O'Cahan, Archie Napier – but always Elizabeth was at his elbow. She was his prime strength that night, of the will, where there was no strength of the body left.

More and more frequently he stumbled into trees, as time wore on, and somewhere on his left a rushing river kept him company, he was aware.

Daylight found him still moving forward, however slowly, unsteadily and in fits and starts, in fairly level immediate country with the great hills behind him. Hills remained all round, but they had drawn back and were no longer major mountains although, half-right, in the far distance, a strange jagged saw-tooth ridge soared, blocking all view to the north-west. He believed that he was, indeed, in Assynt, and that would be the great Quinag, of which he had heard – but he was so light-headed that he scarcely felt a lift of the heart in consequence.

Perhaps this was as well. For the reverse also applied, and when, an hour or two later, he saw some way off a low-browed, turf-roofed cabin and made therefor in a sort of dazed eagerness, his disappointment at finding it empty and abandoned was cushioned also. Although he avidly searched every corner and cranny of its peat-smoke-blackened interior for even a grain of meal, he discovered nothing.

Almost automatically now he lurched on.

Sometime that bright windy forenoon it penetrated to his consciousness that he had been aware of some factor for a while, something good, significant. With an effort of concentration he recognised that it was a scent, the scent of peat smoke, on the north-westerly wind. Forcing himself to clamber, partly on all-fours, up a heather-knoll by the track-side, and blinking weak tears from his eyes, he managed to distinguish another cot-house, just like the last one, a short distance half-right – only this one had a blue plume of smoke rising from the centre of its heather thatch. Gabbling aloud, he staggered crazily towards it.

A barking dog heralded his arrival, and an elderly man and woman came to the cavern of a door. But seeing his reeling, tottering state, they hurried forward to aid and support him. Between them they led, half-carried him into the warm, dark interior.

They set him on a bench by the peat fire in mid-floor. The man gave him a quaigh of fiery whisky to drink. Then the woman brought a wooden bowl of venison and oatmeal stew, ladled out of a large black pot which hung from an iron swee above the fire. He gulped it down, scarcely noticing that it burned his mouth, while they patted his shoulders and fussed over him, shaking their heads.

It came to him in his dizzy relief, elation and gratitude, that he was babbling to them in English, and that they were not understanding a word of him. He groped for the Gaelic words – which he knew quite well, but which in his present state it took a major effort to find and bring forth. He told them that he was Montrose, the King's Viceroy; that he had suffered defeat at Carbisdale on the Kyle of Sutherland; that the Earl of Kinnoull was lying injured some miles back beyond the pass – between it and the lochan under Ben More and Conival – and desperately needed help. A pony – had they a garron? To get Kinnoull?

Amidst exclamations of wonder and sympathy, the man declared that, alas, he had no garron. He was a shepherd, and it was a lonely house. The nearest garrons would be down at Chalda, on the shore of the big loch, where Ardvreck had a farm – four miles on. But his son, on the hill seeing to the sheep, would soon be back for his meal. Then he and his son would go find the other lord . . .

Montrose was vaguely agitated that this was insufficient, that he must do better for Kinnoull than that. But his agitation was muted, lacked force. Indeed, he could scarcely remain upright on the bench. What with the warmth of the cabin, the whisky and food in his stomach, on top of utter exhaustion, he could not keep his eyes open. Seeing it, the woman guided him to a pallet of sheepskins in a corner. He was asleep before even he was fully stretched thereon. The couple had to lift his booted legs up after him.

They had considerable difficulty in rousing him, an hour later. 'Lord,' the man was shouting in his ear, shaking him, 'wake you! They are coming. The soldiers. A party of soldiers, whatever. On horses. Coming from the road, from the west. Quickly – you must hide, lord.'

Somehow they got him off those sheepskins. The cabin was built on a slope, and the lower end of the single long chamber served as byre for the cow, no partition separating beast from owners – though it had a different door, and the soil from the byre drained away down the slope beyond. The new season's pasture was not yet sprouting, so the beast was still tethered in its winter stall. At its head was a wooden trough, as manger, and under this Montrose was pushed by his urgent hosts, with an armful of bog-hay piled over him, the cow snuffing and puffing close by.

They were only just in time. The barking of the dog, the thud of hooves and the jingling of bits and bridles was overlaid by the shouts of men. Then an authoritative voice, obviously an officer and within the house, spoke in English. He announced that he came in the name of the Estates of the Realm, and was looking for fugitives, supporters of the excommunicate rebel and man of blood Montrose, who had been defeated in the east. Many fugitives were known to have scattered all over these hills, and were to be hunted down like the ungodly vermin they were. Had any come here, or been seen in the vicinity?

The shepherd declared in the Gaelic that he was sorry but he did not understand the gentleman's English.

The officer apparently had an interpreter, who translated it all, adding a threat or two of his own as to the dire results of lying or hiding aught.

Montrose, beneath his hay, could hear every word.

The shepherd said again that he was sorry, but he could not help. His back was hurting him, from an old fall, and he had not been out this day. But he had seen no strangers on the hill yesterday or the day before.

The officer grunted, and demanded whisky. While it was being brought, he pointed out that anyone caught harbouring any of the traitorous rebels would be hanged from his own rooftree. But that any word of the man Montrose himself would gain the giver a rich reward, if he was captured. There was a price of no less than £25,000 on the malignant's head, promised by the Marquis of Argyll himself. A mighty fortune. So let them keep watch.

Translated, the shepherd assured that he would not fail to watch well.

There was no actual search of the cabin – it was all open to the soldier's gaze. One man did clump into the byre and thrust a bayonet into the heap of hay from which the shepherd had taken the armful to cover the fugitive – but he did not squeeze up past the cow to prod below the manger.

Lying still, Montrose heard the military leave the cabin and ride away.

The couple came for him presently, to assure him that all was clear, that the soldiers had ridden off eastwards, the way he had come. He could come out.

James Graham, although still light-headed, was in command of his senses again. He declared his undying gratitude, that he would never forget the kindness and self-sacrificing Christian charity for a stranger which he had received at the shieling of

Glaschyle. Pressing some money upon them, he would not hear of the woman removing the dirty bandage from his brow and dressing the wound. They had done more than sufficient. He was going, now. He had brought them into dire danger, just to save his own skin. God helping him, he would not let that happen again to innocent strangers. But if they could get food and aid to the Earl of Kinnoull, he would be eternally in their debt still further.

They urged him to stay, and sleep again; but though his every inch cried out to agree, he would not. The military might be back, or another patrol come.

At the cabin door he asked where was Ardvreck? They had mentioned the name in connection with the big loch. Loch Assynt? Macleod of Assynt had served under him once. He was a loyal King's man, and in a position to help him. They told him that the head of Loch Assynt was only two miles to the west, at Inchnadamph, and that the castle of Ardvreck was but two miles farther, on the north shore, easily seen. The soldiers had gone in the other direction, eastwards, so all should be well.

Drinking a coggie of milk, and with a bannock to sustain him on his way, James Graham set out again, with a thankful heart.

It did not take him long to discover, however, that he was still desperately weak and in no state for walking. Soon all was swimming before his eyes, and frequently he had to go down on hands and knees, head hanging, or he would have pitched prostrate. It seemed to take him hours to reach the Inchnadamph vicinity, with the wide spread of the six-mile-long Loch Assynt opening before him.

There were houses here, even a tiny turf-roofed chapel. Even though the dragoons were now presumably far to the east, Montrose decided not to risk calling here, but made a long, difficult and he hoped undetected circuit to the right, at about half a mile's distance, having to ford another quite major river in the process. In his present state it took him almost two hours, before he could proceed again along the track which followed the north shore of the loch.

It seemed, however, that all his sore hiding and skulking had been for nothing; for presently he heard shouting behind him, and turning, saw two men hurrying after him. They were Highlanders, dressed in ragged tartans and plaids. He waited for them, since he was in no condition to do anything else.

They proved to be a rough-looking pair, but were civil

enough, asking who he was and where he had come from, also where he was going – in the Gaelic of course. With his bandaged head and obviously Lowland style, they would have been fools not to guess that he was one of the fugitives from the battle; but he saw no need to inform them of anything else other than that he was a traveller seeking Macleod of Assynt and had unfortunately met with an accident. At mention of Macleod's name, the two men eyed each other, and one announced that they were in fact gillies of Macleod's and that they would take the gentleman to their master.

So they went on together – and perceiving their charge's faltering steps, the pair each took an arm and supported him on his way, for which he was grateful.

They had not far to go. Quite soon, rounding a bend of the loch-shore, they came into view of a low green promontory jutting into the water, at the tip of which rose starkly a tall, narrow tower-house, four storeys and a garret, typical with corbelling, crowstepped gabling and steep roofing, all within a small curtain-walled and loop-holed courtyard. A scattering of cot-houses surrounded the castle, amongst a patchwork of tiny, odd-shaped fields and peat-stacks. It looked a fairly primitive place to be the centre of a lairdship large as a southern county – but, in this mountainous wilderness, reassuring.

Watched with interest from every cabin door, they came to Ardvreck Castle. There, although the iron yett and great oaken door both stood open, Montrose was left at the threshold in care of one gillie while the other went to announce arrival. The visitor understood the reason for this seeming discourtesy in an innately courteous people; once a stranger had crossed a Highland threshold, the laws of hospitality came into force – and such visitor, unwelcome, might prove an embarrassment.

A young man, thick-set and with reddish hair and a straggle of thin beard, came back with the gillie. He was dressed in tartans little better than his servants', with a long calfskin waistcoat. He did not smile any welcome to his unannounced guest.

'So, you have found one of them!' he commented, in Gaelic. 'Where did you pick him up?'

'Assynt,' Montrose said, in English. 'I greet you. It is some time since we foregathered. I make so bold as to crave your hospitality for a little.'

At the speaker's manner and tone of voice, Macleod peered. 'Who are you?' he demanded. He was scarcely to be blamed, perhaps, for failing to recognise his former Captain-General in the gaunt, head-bandaged, peat-stained scarecrow before him.

'James Graham of Montrose – who else? Though . . . scarce at my best, sir!'

'God Almighty!' Assynt gasped. 'Montrose! I . . . I did not know you. Mercy on us – yourself!'

The other nodded. He was leaning against the doorpost now.

'They . . . they have not caught you, then? Och – dear God, and you're wounded, whatever!'

'A little. But more . . . weary.' Montrose closed his eyes, swaying.

'My lord – you are ill.' There was some concern now, in the other's voice. 'Come away in . . .' Belatedly, Macleod made his decision.

'Neil!' The single word halted him and turned him round – and opened James Graham's heavy-lidded eyes. A young woman was there, peering from behind, slight, not uncomely, but sharp-featured. She was looking at the visitor with no kindness.

'It is Montrose himself, Christian – the Marquis of Montrose. Wounded . . .'

'And hunted! With a price on his head,' the young woman added shortly.

'Lady Ardvreck?' The Graham managed even a hint of a bow. 'Your servant, ma'am. A sore sight, to be sure. But . . . still the King's Viceroy!' It was faintly if significantly said. He clung to the doorpost still, for support.

'He must come in,' Macleod said, shaking his red head. 'It is necessary. He must come in, Christian. We cannot . . .' He left the rest unsaid.

Without a word she turned and hurried back into the house. Her husband took Montrose's arm and led him inside, after her.

Aided up the winding turnpike stair to the modest hall of the castle on the first floor, the visitor was set down at a long table, near the peat fire in the moulded stone fireplace. It was all not so very different from the shepherd's cabin, larger but with little of refinement or graciousness, and almost as dark, for the windows were small. But there was one notable difference here – there was little of welcome, and the food and drink given were offered at the hands of the master of the house, not the mistress. Christian Macleod stayed out of sight, her disapproval evident for all that.

But James Graham was in no condition to complain or reproach, hardly to notice. He did say that if his presence was awkward or an embarrassment, he would press on – to which Neil Macleod made no very outraged protest, though he did declare that his lordship must rest before thinking of so doing. Which was a self-evident fact, for twice during the meal James Graham slumped over the table two-thirds asleep, and had to be roused to eat more. Eventually the young man led him up a further and narrower flight of the turnpike stair to a bedchamber on the second floor. The guest collapsed on the bed, and scarcely heard his host say that he would send up hot water and dressings for washing and the wound. Montrose was deep asleep when an old woman arrived with these, and she had to perform her ministrations on a scarcely conscious patient.

*　　　*　　　*

Montrose slept the clock round twice, so that it was the evening of the next day before he wakened sufficiently to be aware of his situation. It was the arrival of another exhausted fugitive, carried in by gillies, to share his room, which roused him – none other than Sinclair of Brims. But the Major was in such a state of fatigue and exposure as to be quite incoherent and wandering in his mind, so that the other could get nothing out of him that night. More food came at the hands of the old woman, but of their host and his wife there was no sign. When Montrose asked to see the laird, he was told that himself was from home. He tried to get some nourishment down his companion's throat, but with scant success, and decided that it was best to leave him to sleep. No lamp was brought for them, and James Graham was glad enough to sink back into slumber himself, once more.

Next morning, Sinclair was tossing and turning in a fever. Montrose grew anxious for him. About noon Neil Macleod made an appearance. He vouchsafed no explanation for his absence, but declared that there were many parties of soldiers quartering all the surrounding valleys, and since some might well come to Ardvreck and search the house, it would be safer for his guests to be down in the vaulted basement cellars. These had dark wall-chambers in which they could hide, if need be. Montrose asked him if he preferred that he, at least, left the castle at once, patrols or none, so that no charge of harbouring the prime fugitive might fall upon him? But Macleod said no, so long as they were safe hidden in the cellarage. So down they went, supporting Sinclair between them.

It was dark, chill and miserable down in the semi-subterranean vault, with only a single narrow slit-window; but there were two mural garderobes in the thickness of the walling, which could be screened with piled peat and would provide hiding-place if need be. Macleod brought down their bedding from aloft, blankets on heaped deerskins, and provided them with ample to eat and drink. It was far from comfortable – but compared with what they had been through, it was not to be complained about.

Macleod seemed less than anxious for converse with his uninvited visitors, but Montrose detained him to speak of the future. They must leave just so soon as Sinclair was fit to travel. He had been heading for the Reay country, and hoping to meet the Lord Reay and a large force of Mackays. But now that the word of the Carbisdale defeat had spread over the countryside, Reay would almost certainly have turned back – and moreover might well be disinclined for further adventuring meantime, until he saw larger backing for the King's cause. As who would blame him? Therefore he, Montrose, now believed that he should make for Caithness, *en route* for Orkney, where he was expecting considerable reinforcements of men and arms at any time. Would Ardvreck aid him to get to Thurso, where Sir Harry Graham and the royalist rearguard was based?

Macleod's expression was hard to distinguish in the gloom; but he sounded anything but enthusiastic.

'It would be difficult, my lord,' he said. 'With all these soldiers scouring the hills. Dangerous. You would likely be captured.'

'Is it not more dangerous to remain here? And bring down trouble upon yourself? Besides, *you* must know secret ways through the mountains, the passes and glens. I swear that you could guide us, my friend, so that we could outwit all these Lowland soldiery – you, in your own Highlands?'

'It is not so easy. For me to get away, see you. It is a bad time. Time for the spring sowing. For the beasts to be got out on to the hill pastures. A busy time, whatever. I am a poor man, my lord Marquis – no great noble. I have to earn my bread . . .'

James Graham sought to keep the contempt out of his voice. 'You shall be richly rewarded for your services, Ardvreck, never fear. And for what I ask of you. You will lose nothing by guiding us to Thurso, providing garrons for us to ride. A week of your time would be well spent so.'

The other, edging towards the door, muttered something

about being unable to leave Ardvreck meantime. Personal matters, his lordship would understand. Perhaps later . . .

'Then send a gillie with us. Two garrons, a gillie and some food. That is all we need. That at least you can do? And for that service, Ardvreck, I will give you a note-of-hand for whatsoever sum you require. Make it sufficiently large, man. Argyll is not the only one in Scotland who can offer rich rewards!'

Macleod had the grace at least to cough, almost to choke, make some sort of protesting disclaimer, and hurry out, slamming the cellar-door after him.

That evening Major Sinclair's fever abated, and he became lucid though very weak. Broken-voiced he informed that there had been disaster, that Sir Edward would be dead by now. They had progressed fairly well for some time after parting from Montrose and Kinnoull. But the snowstorm seemed to sap all the remaining strength out of the older man. They had had to take shelter for the night in a cranny of the rocks, and the next morning Sir Edward had refused to rise. He, Brims, had forcibly dragged him on – but quite soon the other had collapsed, taken some sort of seizure, lost consciousness. He had no option but to leave him there, with the plaid around him, and struggle on. But when the blizzard cleared he had found himself amongst mighty mountains, and he realised that he was far from where he had expected to be, far to the west obviously. Rather than turn back, he had pressed on westwards, making for this Assynt area. For how long he wandered amongst those hellish mountains he knew not. Two days and nights, or three? Then barking dogs had found him, and two men after them, Highlanders, gillies, who had brought him here. They were indeed Macleod's men, and had been searching the hills for fugitives.

'You were fortunate indeed, my friend. They might have been soldiers, dragoons. There are many searching, it seems.'

'Aye, no doubt.' Sinclair did not sound very convinced of his good fortune. 'Can they give us no light in here?' he demanded querulously. 'It is black as a whale's belly!'

'Ardvreck advises against it. He says light would shine out, under the door and through the window-slit. Let it be known that there were occupants of this vault. It could be a wise precaution.'

'Perhaps. My lord – do you trust Ardvreck?'

Montrose took time to answer that. 'I would not wish to say that I did not, Major,' he declared at length, carefully. 'He is our host. We eat his bread. He undoubtedly endangers himself and

374

his house by harbouring us. It would ill become me to say that I mistrusted him.'

'*I* am not so nice, my lord Marquis! I do *not* trust the man. Admittedly, I do not know him. But those gillies of his, who found me, were scarcely friendly. They may have saved me from wandering to my death – but they treated me with scant kindness. I believe that they were more pleased at finding me than saving me! They were searching for fugitives, yes – but my notion is that they were not doing so out of love for our cause.'

'Gillies' behaviour does not matter, Major. It is their master who counts.'

'And their master is married on a daughter of Munro of Lemlair! The Munroes who failed to rise for you – and took the wrong side at Carbisdale.'

'Is she a Munro, then? That I did not know.' Montrose sounded very thoughtful. 'Certainly I do not think that she approves of our being here. She did not want me brought in – and I have not once set eyes on her, since. But . . . Macleod served with me once. I can surely trust one of my own officers . . .'

'Not your's, my lord – Seaforth's, you said. And Seaforth has also failed you, ere this. What happened to his brother, Pluscarden, and the Mackenzies ? Where are they ?'

There was a long silence in that dark vault.

'Perhaps there is something in what you say,' Montrose said at length. 'At least it would be wise to take precautions. If we may. To tell the truth, some such fears have been at the back of my own mind. I put them from me as unworthy. But – you may have the rights of it. Tomorrow, I think, if you are fit to travel, we shall leave this house. Patrols or none.'

'Aye – that would be best. I will travel, yes. On a garron if I may, on foot if I must. I am not done yet!' the younger man declared, determination in his voice. 'It is Caithness for me.' He paused. 'What of my Lord Kinnoull ?'

'I had to leave him – as you left Sir Edward. He put out his hip, falling in a river. But I asked the shepherd who befriended me to go to his aid. With his son. Their dog would find him. They were good folk, most kind – they would not fail to go for him, I am sure. Tomorrow we will ride back that way, see how he fares . . .'

So, next morning, when the old woman brought them their breakfast porridge and milk, Montrose asked to see Ardvreck. She came back presently to say that himself would come when he could, but was unable to do so just then. In a little small while . . .

They waited – but the little while dragged noticeably. Sinclair, though still weak, declared himself fit for the road. Now they were impatient to be gone. At length, courtesy towards their hosts gave way to urgency. They opened the cellar door and entered the short dark passage without.

This also had a massive door – and it was locked.

They stared at each other in the half dark, shaken. It *could* be for their own security, to prevent anyone straying into the basement and discovering them. But to be locked in, unwarned, was ominous.

They knocked on the heavy door, without result. Then they banged and shouted. There was no response. Appalled, they went back to the vault.

Some time later, listening intently, they heard the key turn in the outer door. In a moment they were out in the arched stone lobby. It was the old woman again.

'Himself has been out. But he will see your honours now,' she informed. 'Come, you.'

They followed her up the stairs and into the hall.

Their host was indeed there, with his wife. But also four men, three wearing steel breastplates and helmets. The fourth wore a black, wide-brimmed, Puritan-type hat, with a black cavalry cloak. He bowed, very briefly.

'You are James Graham, sometimes styled Marquis of Montrose?' he said crisply. 'I am Major-General Holbourn, representing the Estates of this Realm. You are my prisoner, sir.'

There was a long silence. Then Montrose bowed. 'At your service, General. You have had to come a long way for this . . . audience. My apologies! Have you breakfasted? I am sure Lady Ardvreck will accommodate you. At *my* charges, of course.'

The other frowned. 'I have not come for dalliance, sir. My instructions are to take you to General Strachan. At once. We ride, sir.'

'Very well. I am at your disposal. But my friend here, Major Sinclair of Brims, is sick. Suffering from exposure. He is in no state to travel . . .'

'He will travel,' Holbourn interrupted shortly.

Inclining his head, Montrose turned to Macleod and his wife. Haggard, clad still in the ragged clothing obtained from the shepherd in Glen Cassley, his bearing and presence nevertheless dominated the scene. 'Ardvreck – you have chosen your bargain,' he said mildly. 'May it sustain you hereafter. We all have to make our choice, and then live with it. Ma'am – I thank you for your hospitality, and regret that you were troubled by my presence. I shall not forget Ardvreck in Assynt!'

With a sort of choking groan, Neil Macleod turned and all but ran from his own hall.

Holbourn signed to his lieutenants. 'Enough,' he said. 'Bring the prisoners out.' And he also made for the door.

'But, sir – you go? So soon?' Christian Macleod asked, urgently.

'We do, Mistress. My orders are to bring the malignant James Graham before General Strachan at Tain, without delay. We will be on our way.'

'But . . . the money, sir? The reward . . . ?' That was almost a wail.

'Do you think that I carry £25,000 Scots about on my person, woman? You will get it, never fear. The meal you shall have from Tain. The money you must await, from my lord Marquis of Argyll. A good day to you.'

James Graham shook his head. 'Campbell gold, ma'am. I fear – I fear that you must labour further ere ever you see it!' There was only sorrow in his voice.

CHAPTER TWENTY-SIX

Outside the castle's little courtyard they tied Montrose's wrists together with rope, and were mounting him on one of the cavalry horses, Sinclair on another, when General Holbourn intervened. 'Not so,' he commanded. 'That broken-down shelt over there. That will serve an excommunicate traitor very well!' He pointed to a miserable ancient grey garron of Macleod's, all bones and sores, standing drooping in the infield – used, no doubt, for carrying in the peats. 'Give Macleod a pound for it – and he will be overpaid!'

'It will delay us, sir . . .'

'We shall see that it does not!'

Throwing some old rags of plaiding over the poor beast's back, with a looped rope for stirrups, the troopers mounted their chief prisoner thereon, and tied his ankles together, under the brute's sagging belly, with more rope. Sinclair they allowed to ride normally on a cavalry charger. Thus, with an escort of a full troop of light dragoons, they left Ardvreck Castle and turned eastwards along Loch Assynt, on the long road to destiny. Not one of the Ardvreck cottagers turned out to watch them go.

Holbourn was accurate when he said that they would not allow the short-legged, aged garron to hold them up. One trooper led it on a rope from in front, and another behind beat it about the croup when it flagged. Spaced well behind the jingling leaders, and as far ahead of the main troop, the sorry creature was hustled along, faster than it had moved for many a year. On its swaying back its rider knew a real sympathy, and indeed protested at the rope's-end floggings from the rear, not a few of which came perilously near to striking himself.

It made a weary journey – but James Graham reminded himself that it was a deal less taxing than had been his journey westwards. Anyway, his mind was scarcely there at all, but far hence, concerned with matters infinitely more important to himself than this pettily spiteful progress. As they passed near the shieling of Glaschyle, however, he did return to the present for a little, to wonder whether William Hay of Kinnoull lay therein. But he did no more than merely glance towards the cabin, for fear of seeming to take too great an interest. The dog barked at them passing, but no figures appeared at the open doorway.

It was nearly fifty miles of savage country to Tain, with only a drove-road pitted with bogs, climbing over high passes and fording innumerable rushing torrents – which, oddly enough, the broad-hooved, short-legged garron crossed a deal better than did the Lowland cavalry mounts. The going became very slow, and Montrose's beast, in consequence, managed well enough. They went by Lochs Awe and Borralin and over the watershed, the very roof of Scotland, to join the upper east-flowing Oykell again, stopping for the night at Rosehall, in the mouth of Glen Cassley, within a mile of the spot where the clothing Montrose was wearing had come from. Wrists and ankles still tied, he was thrown into a cow-byre under strong guard – where the beasts and the hay kept him a deal warmer than he had been in Ardvreck vault. Sinclair was bestowed elsewhere. They seemed determined to keep the two prisoners separate, and to heap the contumely on James Graham the excommunicate.

Next day was wet, thin chill rain with mist low on the hills. So that the scene of the battle – if that it could be called – was mercifully blotted out across the Kyle as they passed Carbisdale. For Holbourn held, for some reason, to this north side of the firth. It made a grim day's riding, and Montrose was beginning to feel light-headed again, partly with the swaying of his saddleless mount's awkward gait. An early dusk found them at the Skibo peninsula, at the ferry-haven opposite Edderton of Tain – but the tide was out and the flat ferry scows needed for transporting cavalry could not ply. They put up for the night at Skibo Castle near by.

There an odd incident took place. Montrose was once again deposited in mean quarters, but to his surprise presently was brought out, his bonds untied, and he was led into the castle proper, indeed upstairs to its hall. There he found Holbourn and his officers seated at table with their hostess, an old, fierce dame, bent and thin, but with a lively eye. It was, of course, a Sutherland house, and Lady Skibo no friend of Montrose's cause. Her son, of the name of Gray, was out with the Earl's force. But she rose, nevertheless, from her seat at the head of the table, as he was led in – which caused some shuffling discomfort amongst her guests, who ought to have risen with her, in common courtesy, but dared not when their commander remained determinedly seated and scowling. The two troopers who had brought the prisoner up thrust him into a chair at the foot of the table, where Holbourn indicated, and stood guard behind him.

'No, sir – not there!' old Lady Skibo exclaimed, in a voice cracked but stern. 'Up here. Have ye no understanding, man?' It was to Holbourn she spoke.

'He will do very well there, Mistress. Too well. Let him be, I say.'

'Let him be, *you* say! You'll no' order me in *my* house, soldier! My lord Marquis – I dinna care overmuch for your policies, but I ken how the King's Captain-General should be treated in a decent house. Come up here, to my side, if you please.'

'Nonsense, woman! The man is an excommunicate felon! He stays where he is – or returns to his cell.' Holbourn glared, as Montrose rose from his seat. 'Sit down!' he roared.

'*You* give orders in Skibo, scum?' the old lady screamed. And reaching forward she picked up the steaming leg of mutton from its ashet and brought it down in splattering fury on the head of the astounded Major-General, covering him with its juices. Two more skelps she got in, left and right, with her odd weapon, before she slapped it down again on its plate.

There was a silence of utter consternation in that hall as, purple with rage and humiliation, Holbourn lurched to his feet, mouth open, wiping his face.

Montrose it was who spoke. 'Lady Skibo – may I congratulate you on your notable courtesy? And judgment. The Major-General, as a soldier, I am sure will commend your aim! And your mutton smells delicious!'

'God damn you, you old bitch! God damn you!' Holbourn spluttered. 'As Christ's my witness, you'll pay for this . . . !'

'Dinna blaspheme in my house, soldier!' their hostess cried. 'This is a God-fearing house, and I'll have no swearing! Sit down and take your meat like a decent body – or leave my table. Come you, Marquis – up here by my side. I kenned your mother . . .'

Holbourn, gasping for words and breath both, stormed from the room. But at the door he turned, and pointed a shaking finger, first at the troopers and then at Montrose.

'Get that man out of here and down to his kennel, fools!' he shouted. And to his officers, 'All of you – leave this house. D'you hear – leave this house.'

So, despite the violent protests of Lady Skibo, James Graham was urgently hustled away below again, to bread and water. But man is nourished not by bread alone. His spirits took a distinct upwards turn, that night.

On the morrow they came across the ferry to Tain, where Holbourn got rid of his objectionable prisoner – not to Strachan as he expected but to General David Leslie himself, who had arrived at last and sent Strachan south personally with the glad news of his own victory.

Montrose was brought before the commander-in-chief in the handsome Tolbooth of the royal burgh of Tain. These two had been not unfriendly once, but after the vile excesses and butchery of Philiphaugh, James Graham retained no respect for the man, however able a soldier. They greeted each other stiffly, before a battery of officers and black-robed ministers, the latter not backward in voicing their hatred for the impious excommunicate renegade who had sold himself to the Devil, and glee at his apprehension.

When he could make himself heard above the divine chorus, Leslie spoke levelly but uneasily, scarcely glancing at his scarecrow of a prisoner.

'James Graham, sometime Earl and Marquis of Montrose, you have been taken in arms against the Estates of the Realm of Scotland. You had previously been outlawed and forfeited by the said Estates, and condemned to death. Also excommunicated by the Kirk of Scotland in Assembly. Therefore it is my duty to conduct you to your deserved end and execution. Not to trial, for you have been tried already and no further debate is necessary. You are to die.'

There was a shout of approval from the clerical committee which the Covenant imposed upon its commanders.

Montrose inclined his head. 'We are all to die, General. Even you. Even these reverend gentlemen. It is all a matter of when, of timing. Personally I have not found my living, of late, of such delight that I cannot bear to leave it. Here, at Tain, is as good a place to die as any, I think.'

'Not so. You go to Edinburgh for your execution, sir.'

'A pity. So long and weary a journey, for nothing, is it not? For us all. Why not exert your undoubted authority, General, as commander-in-chief – on which may I congratulate you? As on the 50,000 merks reward and the gold chain you received for your slaughter at Philiphaugh! Execute me here and save much trouble. After all, a renowned ancestor of your own, betrayed at Tain, would have sought the same felicity, I am sure – instead of being dragged all the way south to Berwick to be hanged, drawn and quartered by English Edward.' He referred to Nigel Bruce, the hero-king's brother, captured here along with the Queen and others, also on the way to Orkney. For the General was a son of of Patrick Leslie, first Lord Lindores, whose mother had been daughter of Robert Stewart, Earl of Orkney, half-brother of Mary Queen of Scots – and therefore descended from the Bruce.

Leslie frowned. 'No, sir. My orders are explicit. You are to be carried to Edinburgh, there to meet your deserved fate.'

'A pity. However – if needs must. I hope, in that case, that you may provide me – at my own charges, I hasten to say – with some rather cleaner wear than this, for the journey. And allow me to shave. Also to ride something more fit for the road than Ard-vreck's broken garron, which has all but died under me. It deserves execution a deal less than I do! One of General Holbourn's . . . economies.'

'No, sir. None of these. Major-General Holbourn was acting strictly to his orders. As I must do. These are the Lord Chancellor's commands, in the name of the Estates. You will travel to Edinburgh in the fullest indignity of your state as an excommunicate traitor. There will be no remission of severity.'

'I am here, General, in the name and on the written authority of His Grace the King of Scots, Charles Stewart. In whose name you also must hold your commission. But mine is by his own hand. How then can I be a traitor to Scotland, excommunicate or otherwise ?'

'Silence!' the other cried, looking unhappy. 'I am not here to answer your questions. We march tomorrow.' He turned to an officer. 'Remove the prisoner . . .'

Leslie made an early start in the morning, with a large company, clerical and lay. Montrose found that he had indeed been allotted a new mount – but it was the seediest nag they had been able to find in Tain, a gaunt and pathetic bag of bones. The same old plaiding still served for saddle, though, since it was raining again, the prisoner was allowed to drape part of the smelly tartan about his shoulders. Wrists and ankles bound as before, he was led fore and aft by troopers. He had merely exchanged gaolers and escort.

They rode by Alness and the Cromarty Firth to Dingwall, and turned up Strathpeffer to Brahan Castle, a thirty-five-mile journey. At Dingwall a sizeable town, a picket spurred ahead to warn the magistrates and people to turn out, and as they entered the crowded streets a herald and trumpeter rode before the entourage chanting 'Here comes James Graham, a traitor to his country.' Over and over again this monotonous proclamation was made – but there was no corresponding raillery or outcry from the watching throng. It was Munro and Ross country, but for all that only silence greeted the procession, save for the occasional God bless you and cry of pity or shame.

Brahan Castle was Seaforth's eastern seat – but the Earl was still prudently on the Continent, and his brother Pluscarden no more in evidence here than he had been at Strathcarron. The Covenanters made very free with the Mackenzie's house and gear; but, as hitherto, Montrose was confined in the poorest quarters. Not that he cared. He had other matters to preoccupy his mind. Moreover, he grew to be on quite good terms with the common soldiers who were his immediate guards, and fared rather better than his captors intended.

Next day, by Beauly they came to Inverness, round the firth. Here again the Provost and magistrates were summoned to watch the parade, and the herald made his repeated proclamation. But here Provost Forbes of Culloden, a laird of some standing in his own right, chose to interpret Leslie's orders in his own way. He had tables of meats and drink laid out at the Mercat Cross, for all to partake, guards and prisoners – and noting Montrose's bound condition, he brought forward refreshments for him with his own hands. Leslie, taken by surprise, could not forbid it without an unedifying scene – and Forbes was an influential man.

'My lord,' the Provost said, bowing to the principal prisoner, 'I am sorry for your circumstances.'

Montrose smiled. 'I thank you, sir, for your kindness. I am no less sorry for being the object of your pity.'

Two of the town's ministers had come up, to stand behind the Provost – and whether because of the other's example, or otherwise, these did not rail upon and castigate the prisoner as others of their kind had done. Leslie sent an officer to announce, belatedly, that there must be no intercourse with the Estates' prisoner. Provost, ministers and captive eyed each other gravely, thoughtfully, for a little, and then turned away.

At Inverness a quite large group of prisoners from Carbisdale had already been assembled – and in fact were gathered here at the Cross to join Leslie's train, and also partaking of the provender. Amongst them James Graham was both glad and sorry

383

to see many friends, some of whom he had feared dead, including Sir John Hurry, Sir James Douglas and Graham of Balgowan. His captors would not allow him to speak with these, of course, but at least they could exchange signals. He noted that Frendraught was not amongst them, and wondered. They were almost all bandaged, one way or another, witness to the fact that, however small the numbers involved, Carbisdale had been no cheaply won victory.

The enlarged cavalcade spent the night at Castle Stewart, near Nairn, a house of the Earl of Moray. Montrose had hoped to be quartered with the other prisoners, but he was still kept segregated – just as he must still ride the sorry nag, in rags, while the others wore their own clothes and rode cavalry chargers. In the towns of Nairn and Forres and Elgin some citizens duly turned out to jeer and mock, notably clergy, as Argyll had sent orders to be done – but very few in relation to the population; and no stones and filth was thrown, as was also the Campbell's instructions. On the contrary, there were many cries of sympathy and goodwill – which the captive acknowledged with the same quiet courtesy as he did the raillery.

They came to Keith, in upland Banffshire, on the Saturday night, the 8th of May, and the ministers with them insisted on a halt for the Sabbbath. In the morning Montrose must attend divine worship in the parish church, after a night spent in an open field. But this was no ordinary service, for he was permitted no change to decent clothing, and led, still bound with ropes, not to a pew amongst the other worshippers, but to a stool-of-repentance set apart and in front of all. And there he was preached at, at length and with vituperative vigour, by Master William Kininmonth, on the texts of 1st Samuel 15, verses 32–35; and 2nd Kings 18 at verse 17, the first concerned with the hewing to pieces of Agag and the fullest slaughter of the Amalekites, with an amplitude of gory details and assurances of eternal damnation. So overcome was the preacher with his religious fervour over the working out of the first text, that he had to pause, tears streaming down his cheeks, preparatory to launching on the second. Into the brief blessed silence, James Graham himself spoke – to the shocked offence of the godly.

'Rail on, Rabshakeh!' he observed, and swivelled round on his stool, to turn his back on the pulpit. The congregation did not know whether to be more distressed by the raising of a non-ministerial voice in church, or by the fact that this excommunicate miscreant knew his Old Testament sufficiently well to cap the text thus appositely.

The endless journey was resumed next day.

They were now moving through the country over which Montrose had campaigned with such success and frequency. His captors sought to make the most of it, organising demonstrations and scenes, the herald who announced the approach of the discredited traitor being so employed almost continuously. Down through the centre of Aberdeenshire they went, avoiding the hill country to the west where Gordons or Farquharsons might just conceivably have attempted a rescue. At Pitcaple Castle, in the valley of the Urie, they spent the night of the 13th of May, and here destiny was almost cheated. For Leslie of Pitcaple had been King's man enough to serve in Hamilton's ill-fated Engagement attempt, and moreover his wife was in fact a far-out kinswoman of Montrose's own. In her husband's absence the lady played a subtle game, not on the face of it objecting to James Graham's treatment and segregation but instead feasting and wining Leslie and his officers in especially lavish fashion. And not only the officers, for she sent down to Montrose's immediate guards a sufficiency of whisky to put them all into a state of temulent beatitude and caring very little what happened to their prisoner. Around midnight, Lady Pitcaple herself came down to the castle vaults – to find her kinsman the only waking inmate. She told him that if he followed her, she could bring him to an underground passage, opening from a contiguous vault, which would bring him out beyond the courtyard's curtain-wall. She could not untie his bonds, but he ought to be able to hobble down to the river-side and get away.

Warmly he thanked her – and refused. 'Whether or not I escaped thus, in my person,' he said, 'I would never escape in my mind or my conscience. And I have reached such stage where my peace of mind is worth more than all else to me. Too many already have suffered and died, on my account. Kin of my own in especial. You are that. There would be no mercy for you. Being a woman would not save you from Argyll's spleen. Moreover, your husband is already in bad odour with the Covenanters, over the Engagement trouble. My escape from his house could put a halter round his neck. I thank you – but no.'

Nothing the lady could say would shake his resolution. Weeping, she left.

For some reason Leslie avoided the city of Aberdeen thereafter, although it had no reason to love Montrose. They marched south by Kintore, Banchory on the Dee, and the Slug Road to Stonehaven, and so into the Mearns. And there, despite consistently rigorous treatment, Leslie showed a trace of humanity by turning eastwards at Brechin, down the River South Esk, and halting for a night at Kinnaird Castle, beside Old Montrose. Perhaps his objective was not all altruistic but partly to display to this Graham district the low estate to which his wickedness had brought James Graham, and the hopelessness of any betterment for him. And perhaps to underline, to the Earl of Southesk, the difficult position he was in through having such a son-in-law. But at least, though still held close captive, the prisoner was able to see his two younger children again, bitter-sweet as was this experience. And in an awkward and cryptic interview with Southesk, attended by guards, he heard something of his wife's last days and death – although he did not learn much thereby, for his father-in-law had never been of a forthcoming nature, or eloquent, especially towards the man whom he held to have encompassed the ruin of his daughter. But young Robert, now aged eleven, and Jean, aged six, were well and sturdy, and seemingly happy enough with their grandfather. Jamie now Earl of Kincardine, was safely out of the country, on his way to the Netherlands – where undoubtedly Elizabeth would look after him. With this Montrose had to be content.

Being led away from Kinnaird the following morning constituted the hardest trial of the entire grim journey.

Riding through the fair land of Angus, they stopped for the next night at the Durham house of Grange of Monifeith, between Arbroath and Dundee. Here again only an old lady was in charge – and of the same calibre as the Ladies Skibo and Pitcaple. Strangely enough she chose the same methods as the latter to display her resentment at the treatment of James Graham, managing to get the guard drunk once more, this time on strong ale and brandy. She came to the prisoner in the night, with women's clothing of her own for him to don – and after whispered argument he agreed to make the escape attempt. He told himself that she was no relative of his, and old enough surely to be free from even Campbell reprisals – at which, when he mentioned it, she snorted vigorously. Also, the laird, her son, was a confirmed Covenanter and member of the Estates. Unfortunately, however, the attempt came to naught, for it was a bright moonlight night, and one of the guard was not only a total abstainer from strong drink but evidently a restless noctambulist. At any rate, he was outside on the prowl, and observing what was seemingly two women emerging furtively from the back quarters, he went to investigate. In his wrist-bound state, and unarmed, Montrose could neither run nor fight and it was all over, amidst much outcry, in a few seconds. Thereafter the guard was changed, and neither befuddled miscreants, officer-in-charge, prisoner nor aged hostess, left in any doubts as to the weight of General Leslie's wrath.

It could be assumed that no similar opportunities for escape would be allowed to occur.

The city of Dundee, despite its sufferings in Montrose's campaigns, received the prisoner kindly, almost warmly, to Leslie's embarrassment, the magistrates insisting on greeting him with wine and refreshments at the Cross, and the streets thronged with quiet, respectful and sympathetic crowds. At sight of his rags, decent clothing was hastily produced, and his captors, not desiring to damn themselves as viciously heartless in the eyes of this consistently Covenanting city, did not refuse permission for the prisoner to change into it. He was still kept bound, however, and though the old grey nag had died under him, another equally decrepit mount had been found.

It was with real gratitude that James Graham left Dundee, dressed in a good black suit of broadcloth and, with head held higher, he faced the hostile Fife across Tay, and the still more hostile Edinburgh's smoke across Forth. A journey, any journey, was what a man made of it. This one had enriched him as much, perhaps, as any he had made.

CHAPTER TWENTY-SEVEN

Leslie had sent messengers ahead, and when the coastal vessel bearing Montrose and the other officer prisoners arrived at Leith on the Saturday afternoon of the 18th of May, 1650, there was no lack of preparations to receive it. A great crowd was present at the dockside, and Provost Sir James Stewart of Coltness and the magistrates of Edinburgh had come down in force to take charge of the captives, with the Town Guard – the same which had escorted James Graham on many another occasion. There was a certain amount of confusion at the harbour, for on the same tide a still larger vessel than Leslie's coaster from Dysart had sailed in, from Holland, bearing no less than King Charles's personal envoy Sir William Fleming, with messages, oddly enough, both for his Captain-General and for the latter's enemies Argyll and the Estates. When Fleming learned that the reception was staged not for himself but for a captive Montrose, he was somewhat put out, especially when he perceived the sort of reception it was, and that he was not to be allowed to present the King's letter to this recipient. His information that it was, amongst other things, King Charles's command to the Captain-General to lay down his arms and disband his forces on agreed and honourable terms, was greeted with considerable hooting and rudery.

Montrose himself, on disembarking, was left in no doubts that from now on nothing would be left to chance. The Provost and Council ceremoniously greeted Leslie and his staff but studiously ignored the prisoners. Not so certain ministers, cheer-leaders and rabble-rousers, commissioned to lead the populace in abuse and contumely, who, at a given signal, raised a great shouting, pointing and jeering at the traitor James Graham, slayer of the innocent, friend of Papists, sold to the Devil, excommunicate and man of blood. The good folk of Leith did not rise to the occasion, however, being always suspicious of orders from Edinburgh anyway, but watched in silence. The eggers-on grew the more hysterical.

The prisoners were not left alone while the Provost collogued with Leslie. The Town Guard roughly marshalled all save Montrose into a column for the two-mile march up to the Capital from the firth-shore – the craft they had sailed in from Fife had had no accommodation for horses and only Leslie's and one or two other mounts had been shipped over. An old heavy cart-horse had been found for Montrose himself, without saddle or bridle, and on this he was placed, tied as before with ropes, with a scullion-boy to lead it. They waited for a considerable time while Leslie, and also the doubtful Fleming, partook of the Provost's refreshment. Then at last the march to Edinburgh began, the herald chanting his monotonous announcement before, the other prisoners shuffling along on foot.

They entered the city by the Water Gate, at the east and bottom end of the Canongate, near Holyroodhouse and the Abbey. Here a new deputation awaited the entourage, consisting now of the city's law officers plus the public hangman. Provost Stewart and the magistrates had apparently played their part, and like Leslie drew aside, while the minions of justice took over.

First of all a lengthy proclamation of the Estates was read out, declaring that since James Graham had already been tried, found guilty of treason, forfeited and excommunicated, there was no need for, nor could there be, further trial. Only the manner of carrying out the sentence of death had had to be decided, and this was now pronounced. The foresworn traitor and renegade, as well as forfeiting all rights, estates, properties, titles and life, had also forfeited the right to die in any seemly fashion appropriate to his former rank and style. He was to be conducted to the Tolbooth of Edinburgh, there to be lodged in the lowest common cell. From thence, in due course, he was to be taken to the town gibbet to be hanged as a common malefactor, not executed on the block like a more worthy rebel. But he was not to escape the axe altogether, for after being hanged his head was to be hewn from off his trunk and placed on a spike above the said Tolbooth; and each of his limbs were likewise to be severed from his body and sent to be displayed in prominent places in the towns of Glasgow, Stirling, Perth and Aberdeen, there to remain for all time coming. What remained of the trunk was to be thrown, unburied, into the felons' pit on the Burgh-muir of Edinburgh. If, however, in God's great mercy, he was to publicly and fully repent of all his wicked misdeeds and shameful treasons and murders and heresies, his excommunication might be withdrawn,

389

and his limbless, headless trunk permitted to be buried in that Greyfriars kirkyard where he had once been first to sign the noble National Covenant which he had so basely and impiously betrayed. In all this process it was hoped, instructed and commanded that the citizens of Edinburgh as representing all whom James Graham had maltreated, shamed and caused to suffer, would display their hatred and revulsion against the said traitor, with every means at their disposal. This was the sentence of the Committee of the Estates of Scotland, given on the 17th day of May, the year of Our Gracious Lord 1650. God save the King!

The reader handed this impressive document to Montrose to scan, that he might verify the writing, signatures, seals and all relevant details, but he shook his head.

'I thank you, sir – no,' he said. ' I have heard it very well, and am sure that you read it accurately. My only concern is that His Grace, my master and yours, whose royal commission I bear, should be thus dishonoured by being invoked in so sorry a matter.'

The hangman, who had his open flat cart with him, drawn by four horses, was now motioned forward. He untied the principal captive's bonds – but only to lead him to the cart, to tie him thereon again, an arm stretched out and bound on either side to the vehicle.

'Why this, friend ?' James Graham asked.

'Orders,' the man muttered, uneasily. 'Sae you'll no' can ward off whit's thrown at you, man.'

'Ah, I see. All is thought of.'

The other snatched off Montrose's old Highland bonnet, which he had worn for so long. 'Orders, tae. You're to be uncovered, see you. And I'm no'.' And he tapped the red bonnet he wore himself.

'You are welcome, indeed.'

So the final short stage of a long journey was commenced, up the Canongate's cobbles, between the tall grey gabled lands and tenements where Scotland's aristocracy had their town-houses amongst the teeming warrens, pig-sties and poultry-sheds of lesser folk. The narrow street was packed, and Montrose braced himself on his cart to face the hail of filth and missiles recommended by authority of State and Church. Yet, strangely, none was forthcoming. At a snail's pace, in complete silence save for the clop-clop of the horses' hooves, the creaking of the cart and the shuffling of feet behind, the procession made its way up the crowded climbing thoroughfare, with scarcely room for it to pass – and whatever men and women thought, not a hand or a voice was raised.

Just the hint of a smile played about James Graham's unwashed, unshaven and wasted, but still supremely handsome, features, as he thought of the day he had ridden up this same street with Johnnie Kilpont, straight from London and King Charles I's rejection, and decided that though he loved Scotland he did not love Edinburgh. He might be seeing Kilpont again soon now – and they could compare impressions! Seeing others too, perhaps, who had gone on ahead – his own eager Johnnie, and poor lost Magdalen, lost no longer, God being good. Aye, and Archie Napier the father, Magnus O'Cahan, Will Rollo, Tom Ogilvy, Nat Gordon. All the best of his friends had gone on already – a blessed thought. Save only Elizabeth – and Black Pate Graham. George Gordon, now – he would rejoice to see George again, George, who had chosen in the end to die for him against his own father, and died a clean death in battle, as consequence . . .

It was by chance that, as his mind dwelt on George, Lord Gordon, whom he had loved, his head-high glance lighted on dark eyes that stared on him from quite close by. Eyes gazed at him, of course, from every window of the teeming lands, rich and poor, nobles and burghers and common folk, and he returned none of the stares. But these eyes were different, seeming to bore into him, filled with venom, hate – the eyes of George Gordon's own sister, the Lady Jean, now married to the young Earl of Haddington. With a group of richly dressed personages she was standing on a stone balcony projecting from one of the windows of the Earl of Moray's townhouse. Because of the projection, and the narrowness of the street, they were only a few feet from the cart, though slightly higher. As Montrose approached, the young Countess suddenly laughed shrilly, a shocking, hysterical sound in the prevalent hush. Then leaning forward, she spat directly in James Graham's face.

He was unable to wipe away the spittle. He did not even turn his face away. Instead he eyed her wonderingly. The Gordons had always been a strange, unpredictable family, George much the best of them – and she had seen her father led to be executed here in Edinburgh, and might well somehow blame himself as partly responsible.

He did not answer her – but someone in the throng below

answered for him, in justice or otherwise. 'You painted whore!' a woman's voice yelled. 'Yoursel' it is should be in the cairt, paying for your adulteries, you!'

There was a low rumble of agreement from the crowd, and then the silence resumed.

James Graham had scarcely heard that last. For, standing next to Jean Gordon on the balcony he had suddenly recognised an exquisite young man to be none other than another Archibald Campbell, Lord Lorne, Argyll's son – and the recognition reminded him that one of his guards had told him a day or two before that his great enemy's heir was being wed that week to the Earl of Moray's daughter. This, then, would be the wedding-party at Moray House, still celebrating. Immediately, as he trundled past, his glance swept the others on the balcony – and there, sure enough, half hidden behind the others, typically, he caught a glimpse of two hooded foxy eyes, one of them squint, under reddish brows, beside the pale cadaverous features of Johnston of Warriston, now Lord Warriston of Session no less. For a timeless moment James Graham and Archibald Campbell eyed each other in eloquent if wordless communion. Then *MacCailean Mor* turned abruptly away, knuckles to mouth, and pushing Warriston aside got back through the window, and flung the shutter to behind him. Montrose continued on his creaking way.

And now his small smile was, although no broader, assured, content, almost triumphant. For, in a way, he had won. Won his last long and personal battle. Only he and the Campbell knew it – but who else did it concern ? That brief exchange proclaimed him the victor, beyond all manner of doubt, an old score settled at last. The rest he could face untroubled – and indeed the sooner the better.

It took a long time to win up the steep mile of Canongate and High Street, past the Canongate Tolbooth, the Netherbow Port and the scores of noblemen's lodgings, where faces peered or peeped from behind glass, curtains or shutters. At the Mercat Cross beside St. Giles, James Graham was paraded round the high gibbet erected for him – and recalled, with even a trace of wry amusement, how the Earl of Rothes had said to him one day, on this very spot, 'Watch you – or you'll no' be at rest till you are lifted up above the rest o' us on three fathoms o' a rope!' He would perhaps have the opportunity to congratulate Rothes on that curious prophecy quite shortly now.

They untied him then and flung him into the filthy, dark, semi-subterranean vault of the city's Tolbooth – from which, by the smells and atmosphere, the usual occupants – thieves, pickpockets and harlots – had only just been removed to make room for him. From the Estates' declaration he had expected to be incarcerated with these felons – and knew not whether to be glad or sorry. He had been denied anyone to talk with, although surrounded by people, for two weeks. He still had a few coins, and instructed the hangman to put hand into his pocket to take them, as was the custom and very wise precaution.

He sank down upon the dirty straw of a corner, and closed his eyes – for he was in fact very tired. It had been a long and trying day – it had taken over two hours to come up from the Water Gate, and the city bells were now ringing for seven o'clock.

He had barely sat down, however, when lamps were brought to light up the sordid scene – and he understood why the cell had been cleared of its former occupants, when a group of black-robed divines and a deputation from the Estates was ushered in. Montrose recognised some of them, including Master James Guthrie, minister of the High Kirk at Stirling, one of the most prominent of the Covenanting party, who appeared to be in charge. These did not greet the prisoner as a person, but set about their business without delay or preamble, Master Guthrie launching into a lengthy prayer which his companions punctu-ated with frequent Amens, evidently to encourage rather than to bring to a halt. Though it was not in fact so much a prayer as a vigorous reminder to Almighty God of the full scale and enor-mity of the sins of the wretched miscreant and ruthless assassin here before Him, a catalogue of accusation in the form of a demand for suitable divine vengeance. When at length this came to a close, one of the clerks of the Estates stepped forward and declared that he was sent and empowered to examine the prisoner on sundry matters, a dull and mumbling lawyer who peered at a paper in the poor light the while. Quickly having enough of this, Montrose interrupted.

'Forgive me, sir – but I fear that I am in no state to give due and proper heed to your remarks. I am somewhat weary with the compliments you and yours have already put upon me this day. I shall be a better listener on another occasion, I promise you. I request that you, and your reverend friends, do me the honour to leave, for this night.'

The clerk puffed, indignant. 'How, how dare you! You, a

condemned prisoner! I come here with the authority of the Estates of Parliament.'

'The Estates of Parliament have no authority, sir, save from the King's Grace. I serve the King, and the King only. I hold his royal commission as his personal representative and Viceroy. Until His Grace supersedes that commission, I decline to accept any lesser authority. I can do no less, without reducing His Grace's position. *Has* King Charles superseded my commission, sir? I understand that letters from him, to myself as also to the Estates, arrived this afternoon.'

The lawyer hesitated, and conferred in a whisper with one of his fellows, while the ministers muttered angrily. Then he cleared his throat. 'The King and the Estates are now come to full agreement,' he declared. 'Your commissions and authority are no longer of any effect.'

'My commission and authority was given me directly by the King. Likewise termination of that authority must also come to me from the King. Have you brought me His Grace's letter, addressed to me?'

'That is unnecessary.'

'It is entirely necessary. Until I have read the signed and sealed writings of King Charles relieving me of my offices and responsibilities, which he put upon me, as King of Scots, I am still Viceroy and Captain-General. You will return and tell the Committee of Estates so, sir. And inform that, as such, I require to appear before them, in the King's royal name. Now, go, if you please. All of you. The day has proved something tedious. I am now going to sleep.'

And, strangely, they went, his authority – whether Charles Stewart had revoked it, or not – sufficiently evident and effective or that, at least.

*   *   *

The morrow was the Lord's Day and James Graham knew well what this was likely to involve. It meant another grim day to live through; for the Kirk would never allow his hanging on a Sunday. He had now reached the stage of wishing it all over, and a day's remission was no cause for satisfaction.

He was not dragged to church, as on the previous Sabbath, but the day's carefully arranged programme was by no means delayed till after the period of public worship. Ministers would no doubt declare his infamy and shame from every city pulpit, but sufficient others were found to repair to the Tolbooth at an early hour, before even the guard had breakfasted, to harangue the prisoner and leave him in no doubt that this was not to be a day of rest for him. Master Guthrie was back again, with the Reverends Robert Traill and Mungo Law and others, set on convincing Montrose that he was the most depraved and abandoned of God's creation, unworthy almost to be so-called – yet the Almighty's mercy, as shown forth by his true Body on earth, the Kirk of Scotland, was such that a contrite and detailed repentance might even yet result in his obtaining the grace of a Christian burial, and his soul's journey towards the terrible judgment-seat might be started at least without the complete and assured eternal damnation involved in dying excommunicate.

James Graham heard them out, thanked them for their concern for his immortal soul, but reminded that he, like them, had been journeying towards judgment all his days, and that he did not see that any last-moment recantations were likely to deceive the all-seeing Father – a Popish doctrine which he was surprised to find his Presbyterian friends clinging to. Moreover he had chosen to make this last stage of his journey uncomplaining and at peace with himself. He was a great sinner undoubtedly, but his sins had not been against the King, the Kirk or the people of Scotland, but against the good God Himself; therefore the matter of repentance was between him and his Maker and Saviour, none other. He therefore wished them all a good day – and sought leave to make his peace with God in private.

Loud were the rejections of this shameful arrogance and indeed blasphemous insult to the Almighty and to Christ's Kirk. *They* were the interpreters of God's laws and commands, not a forsworn, blood-drenched excommunicate. They and only they had the power to grant him Christian burial and lift damnation from his perjured soul. How dare he contemplate his last journey to the gibbet unforgiven by Holy Kirk? If yesterday's progress on the hangman's cart was shame, how much more appalling would be the final unrepentant journey to hell's eternal flames?

Gravely he informed the clerics that, though he was sorry to disappoint them, he had found yesterday's journey quite the most honourable and satisfying he had ever made, with God's loving presence in fact nearer to him than he had been privileged to know previously. But – perhaps they did not worship the same God?

At this ultimate profanity, the divines left him, shocked to the core, and it was the turn of the secular arm. This was represented by members of the Committee of the Estates, led by Warriston and the Provost Sir James Stewart of Coltness again – who was at pains to point out that though the final arrangements for the execution were *his* responsibility, as chief magistrate, the rigorous terms as to the cutting up and disposal of the body were wholly the Committee's.

Montrose sympathised.

Warriston, that hot-eyed fanatic, though seeming older as well as more richly clad, was as tense and perfervid as ever. When the prisoner asked kindly after the Marquis of Argyll, whom he thought had not looked well yesterday, the other swallowed convulsively, his prominent Adam's-apple leaping about as though of independent life, and forthwith launched into a tirade. He declared, amidst a positive spray of saliva which his hearer found distressing, that he, James Graham, was about to suffer the well-merited end of all who betrayed their Creator, their nation, their Church and their fellow-men. That he was a man whose savagery against the State was equalled only by the viciousness of his private life, as was well known. That he had not only signed but helped to word the Covenant – and then had taken up arm against it, and moreover employed heathen Irish barbarians to terrorise Scotland and spill oceans of his own compatriots' blood.

When the speaker had to pause for very panted breath, Montrose shook his head. 'If I was even half of what you call me, my Lord Warriston, I would deserve all that your busy Committee have planned for me. But you, as one of this realm's judges, are surely bound by the common rules of evidence and proof? What evidence do you have that I ever spoke or acted against the National Covenant which I signed? You have none, for I did not do so. As for the so-called Solemn League and Covenant, this I had no part in, nor could have, since it is a shameful denial of the liberties of free men. That I oppose, yes – and will go on opposing so long as there is breath in my body. Which is not like to be long, I thank God! That I led Irish troops, amongst others, I agree and rejoice in, for they were better fighters than any they opposed, and were, moreover, as much subjects of the King for whom they and I fought as were the Scots rebels they so soundly beat. As for their religion, I am no Papist any more than you are, sir – but did General Leslie refuse to fight alongside

General Cromwell's Ironsides because they were not Presbyterians ? Or did you refuse to employ General Middleton because he is an Episcopalian ? That a man's religion is his own is something else that I will gladly die for, yours, mine, or the Irish. As to shedding Scottish blood, this I swear by all that I hold holy – and in my present position, you will agree, I should not so swear lightly – that I grieved sorely for every drop that was shed, and sought with all my power to avoid anything such . . .'

'Liar !' Warriston shouted. 'Liar !'

He shrugged. 'Would *you* lie when you are to die the next day ? And, tell me also – how much good Scots blood was shed after Philiphaugh ? And by whom ? You sir, I heard, demanded the death penalty on many friends of mine.'

'They were traitors, all traitors. And deserved death.'

'Traitors to whom ? Not to their King. So, my lord of Session, Scots blood may be shed, so be it that it is the blood of those who oppose Archibald Campbell and Archibald Johnston! Not others. Is that the Court of Session's justice in 1650 ?'

'It is the Estates of Scotland that condemns you. Not me. Nor the Court of Session.'

'Ah, yes. The Estates. They condemn me ? Sitting as a court ?'

'They did. And most rightly.'

'My lord – you are a judge. And I a magistrate. So that we know something of court procedure. Can you tell me how I could be condemned by any court of justice before which I have not appeared ? To which no evidence of defence has been given, or sought ? Hang me by all means, and the sooner the better for my comfort. But do not cloak your murder under the names of trial or sentence. Or anything other than hatred. Be honest, at least !'

All but frothing at the lips, Warriston rushed out of the cell, and in some confusion the others followed him.

Only then was James Graham allowed his breakfast of oatmeal. His request for water to wash and a razor to shave were, as usual, refused. The officer of the Town Guard, a drunken boorish individual named Weir, leeringly explained that the prisoner might choose to cut his throat with the razor and so cheat the hangman.

All that day Montrose was harassed by relays of ministers, parliamentarians and officials of the law. Never for a moment was he left alone, for when there were no deputations, Major Weir filled the cell with his minions of the Guard and led them in mockery and witticisms. These the prisoner was largely able to ignore, drawing into himself. But it had got around that he disliked tobacco smoke, and most evidently the authorities had seized on this, for the Guard were supplied with unlimited quantities of the weed, with the fumes of which they filled his vault and took delight in puffing in their captive's face. Strangely enough he found this pettiness, of all his trials, the sorest to bear.

It made an endless day. But the evening brought slight relief, for the obnoxious Weir went off duty and was replaced by an older lieutenant of less vicious disposition, who cleared the soldiers out of the cell and actually left Montrose with a lamp, so that he could read the small pocket Bible which had never left his person throughout all his wanderings, and had provided an unfailing source of solace and strength. It did not fail him now.

Later that night the new officer returned, bearing a bundle of clothing, including a quite handsome suit of black and silver, red silken hose and good buckled shoes, with a scarlet cloak laced with gold filigree, also a broad-brimmed black beaver hat with silver cord.

'Ladies gave this in for your lordship,' the lieutenant said. 'They gave no names, but wished you very well, and God-speed.'

'That was kind, indeed.' It would probably be the Napiers, from Merchiston not far away, his niece and his nephew's wife. 'And kind of *you*, my friend, to let me have them. Others would not. I should be sorry if you were to suffer for your actions. Major Weir would not approve, I think.'

'I care not for Weir. He was too drunk to give me any instructions. Besides, I take my orders from the Provost, Sir James Stewart. And he is not a hard man.' He cleared his throat. 'I, I have been through the pockets, my lord. That I had to do, see you. There was a razor. I took it out. Orders. But there is some money. Paper. A quill and ink-horn. I had no orders against such.'

'I am greatly in your debt, sir. These will make so much of difference. Also I thank you for leaving me in peace. And for the lamp. God will reward you one day, if I cannot.'

'I want no reward, lord. I mind well your lordship, in happier days. I am for the King, as are most folk. But what can we do?'

'Your time will come, friend. But – I will pray that you do not suffer for what you have permitted.'

'I heard the Provost saying that you are to be taken before the Estates tomorrow. Your lordship will require to be decently dressed for that. If I am questioned, I will say that I believed it is for that the clothes were fetched. As, belike, it is.'

'The Estates . . . ? This is strange, is it not ? The Estates *sent* me their declaration and sentence. They were finished with me. What more is there to say, or do ? Save hang me.'

'I know not, my lord. But I heard Sir James say something of a letter from the King, just come. It may be – I do not know – that it might be that you are yet to be saved. Reprieved.'

'No, no, my friend. Not that, I assure you. King Campbell rules Scotland still, not King Charles. And the Campbell will not permit any reprieve for *me*, whatever the King's letters may say. That I know well. What the Estates wish of me, other than my speedy end, I do not know. But . . . it means that I will have another grievous day to face. I had hoped for quicker . . . release.'

The lieutenant bit his lip and turned away. At the cell door he paused. 'My lord,' he said hesitantly, 'I'd have you know – many feel for you. Many wish you well. The folk – they are not for this. They know you the King's friend. But . . .' Shrugging, he left the rest unsaid, and Montrose was alone again.

Now, of course, his mind was in a turmoil, much less settled and resigned than heretofore. He believed what he had said about Argyll's implacable resolution to have him dead, and the unlikelihood of any repreive; but he would have been more than human not to have grasped at even this slender straw of hope, however much he told himself not to. And the kindness represented in the bringing of these clothes, and the officer's words, although uplifting his heart, unsettled him. He had steeled himself to accept harshness and savagery; but benevolence, humanity, was another matter, tending to upset. He was scarcely used to it.

The pen and ink was a great comfort, with the lamp. He could write now. Whether letters would be allowed to go out from here, he did not know – but he could try it. He wrote a long letter to Elizabeth, commending his son James to her care, making lighter of his position than the facts warranted, and avoiding any criticism of her nephew Charles. He wrote also, less fully, to his own nephew Archie Napier, again carefully avoiding anything which could be of aid to his enemies, if read – as these letters almost certainly would be. Then, since sleep seemed far away, he tried to compose and discipline his disturbed mind from going over and over the faint possibilities of reprieve, by setting down the poem, or some of it, which he had been turning over in his mind these last days. It was not far from morning before he extinguished the lamp.

The new day brought back Major Weir and renewed harsh conditions. Mocking comment was made on the fine clothes the prisoner now had – but there was no attempt to make him divest himself. No doubt Weir assumed they had been officially ordered and provided for the day's programme. In mid forenoon officers arrived to conduct the captive over to Parliament House, a short distance. The lieutenant had evidently been right, and the Committee of the Estates had had cause to think again.

Wrists still tied with rope, he was put into an ante-room with a guard, and left there for a full hour, wondering. Then he was led into the same Parliament Hall where he had appeared as accused prisoner before this, the last time with King Charles I himself a silent observer. He found himself in the presence of about a dozen men, most of whom he knew well, former colleagues on the Tables and other committees. The Chancellor, the Earl of Loudoun, occupied the chair, so that it was presumably a sitting of the official Committee of the Estates. Of the Chancellor's chief, Argyll, there was no sign – although that strange man might be lurking and peeping from behind any door. Warriston was there, in the capacity of secretary, the Earls of Cassillis and Eglinton, the Lords Balmerino and Balfour of Burleigh, and others. Some way apart sat a group of ministers. By their own Assembly's decision they could not take part in Estates business – but they could watch and scowl. There was not a remotely friendly glance in that chamber.

James Graham bowed briefly, and spoke before any other had time to do so.

'I give you a good morning, my lords and gentlemen,' he said equably, assuredly. 'I am glad to see your faces. At last. And not before time, I think you will agree. You, my Lord Chancellor, have much to make clear to me, the King's Lieutenant, have you not?'

'Silence!' Loudoun banged on his table. 'The prisoner will speak only when spoken to. Only in answer to questions. Remove the man's hat.'

'In this Parliament Hall of our realm, my lord, you cannot prevent me speaking. Apart from His Grace's royal commission which I hold, I am an Earl of Scotland, of somewhat more ancient vintage than any here! I belong to this place, of right, as my fathers have done before me. Had you wished for my silence, you should not have brought me *here*.'

'Watch your insolent tongue, traitor!' Loudoun turned to Warriston. 'Proceed.'

Clearing throat nervously, that uneasy individual began to read from a lengthy paper, with none of the fire and vigour with which he had once read the National Covenant. It was dry, wordy, lawyer's stuff, and it took some time before Montrose perceived what was the gist of it. Presently it became evident however that it was a pronunciamento to the effect that the King had written to his Scots Parliament on the 8th day of May declaring that on the 2nd he had signed a treaty with his loyal Scots commissioners at Breda, by which he agreed to accept the Solemn League and Covenant and all its provisions, and to disband all armed forces mustered against the said Scottish Estates. Further His Majesty had commanded his former Captain-General and Viceroy, James Graham, to lay down his arms. If the said James Graham did so, without further hostile acts against the Estates, then His Majesty recommended him and his men to the mercy of his loyal Estates, and suggested that he and they, if they so wished, should be permitted to leave the country.

With some shuffling of papers, Warriston, pausing, glanced towards Loudoun. There was complete silence in the great chamber.

'However,' he went on, picking his words more carefully now, 'on the 12th day of May there was a further letter from His Majesty, in which he disclaimed all responsibility for the actions of the said James Graham, and declared that the previous letter, of the 8th of May, was not to be delivered and read, or if it had been so, it was to be countermanded. The result therefore of His Majesty's correspondence and wishes is that the prisoner James Graham no longer holds any commission soever of the King's Grace, and that any recommendations to mercy are withdrawn. The authority of the Committee of the Estates, therefore, to pronounce and enforce sentence, is clear and unchallengeable.'

Listening, Montrose groaned in his spirit for Charles Stewart – but also did some quick calculations, and thought that he understood. The Treaty of Breda had been signed on the 2nd of May, and the King had written a letter on the 5th ordering a disbandment of forces and acquainting the Estates that this was done. Then on the 8th he had apparently written another letter to the Estates, which was not here quoted, the one now countermanded. This, no doubt, was the one Sir William Fleming had brought to Leith, with one for himself which he had not been allowed to see. Probably it contained instructions for his, Montrose's safety and good treatment. It had to be nullified therefore, countermanded, if this execution was not to be an obvious and illegal spurning of the King's commands and wishes. Therefore this alleged letter of the 12th of May was either a forgery or had been doctored. The former more likely, for this was only the 20th of May, and this document had been worked upon for at the very least a day before. Given favourable conditions, it would have been just about right for Fleming to reach Leith on the 18th, leaving Breda on the 8th. But for a letter written on the 12th to be here before the 19th was all but impossible.

So he recognised now why he had been brought here this morning. The King's letters brought by Fleming had changed the legalities of the situation as far as the parliamentary forfeiture, trial in absence and condemnation were concerned. Therefore a seeming new condemnation and sentence had to be put through, in a hurry, which did not appear to conflict with the royal wishes – since the Treaty of Breda accepted Charles as the lawful monarch and would bring him to Scotland shortly. That almost certain forgery had been necessary to contrive it would be a small enough matter for Campbell government, and could be blamed on other hands later. It explained the delay in carrying out the death sentence – and undoubtedly implied that such delay would not last much longer.

John Campbell of Loudoun took up the attack. He was a poor speaker, and had nothing new to say. He merely reiterated all the old assertions about betraying Covenant, Kirk and country, soaking the land in blood at the hands of Irish savages, and the imperative need for Scotland to be rid of such a scourge once and for all. God had brought James Graham to a just punishment. Before receiving sentence had the prisoner anything to say ?

Clearly Warriston had passed on Montrose's observations as to the invalidity of a court which condemned a captive unheard and without defence. He knew well that the sentence would be the same, and that this was a formality to give it a more lawful flavour. After all he had answered to his inquisitors in his cell, there was really nothing worth adding. But he had to exercise his right to speak.

He did so restrainedly, declaring that since the Estates had now accepted the King's authority, he looked on this Committee as sitting in the monarch's name and so was content to appear bareheaded as though His Grace was indeed present. He averred that all he had done was done in the name and with the authority of the King. The National Covenant he was still faithful to. As for the Solemn League, he had never had hand in it, for which he thanked his Maker, for it was nothing but a shame and a distress to both kingdoms. As for military matters he admitted that disorders could not entirely be prevented in any army, but that anything such that he learned of amongst his troops he had punished severely, and that instead of indicting him for spilling Scots blood they should rather thank him for preserving many thousands of lives, as had ever been his close concern. Lastly, he had come back to Scotland the last month on their King's direct command, in order to accelerate agreement in instilling an urgency into the situation – whereby this Treaty of Breda had in fact been brought to a speedier conclusion. He sought therefore to be judged by the laws of God, of nature and of nations, and moreover the laws of this land. And if they decided against him, he appealed with more confidence to the righteous Judge of all the world, who one day must be both *their* judge and his own.

They heard him in silence, although the ministers coughed and muttered.

Then, without comment, Loudoun ordered him to his knees to hear sentence in an appropriate posture. When James Graham remained standing, the guards were ordered to bring him to the floor, which they did easily enough by kicking him behind the knees and then holding him down.

Thereafter, Warriston read the same detailed sentence as to hanging, beheading, quartering and displaying, without Christian burial, exactly as it had been pronounced at the Water Gate. The charade over, the Chancellor curtly ordered the prisoner's removal back to his cell, and sentence to be carried out the next day at two o'clock in the afternoon. God save the King!

Before the words were fully out, the Committee-members were rising to leave.

*   *   *

That night, his last in this present state, even though he was not left alone as on the previous evening, James Graham, at peace in his mind again, with all uncertainty past, was able to finish the poem he had started, amidst the bickerings and jeers of his guards, and wrote also a sort of grim little prayer as counterblast to their persistent raillery, his lips curving to a small smile as he penned it.

> Let them bestow on every airt a limb,
>   Then open all my veins that I may swim
> To Thee, my Maker, in that crimson lake;
>   Then place my parboiled head upon a stake,
> Scatter my ashes, strew them in the air –
>   Lord! Since Thou knowest where all these atoms are,
> I'm hopeful Thou'lt recover once my dust,
>   And confident Thou'lt raise me with the just.

He even read this out to his drunken crew, when he could gain silence – and did achieve an abashed hush for a little thereafter. And in it told himself that this was scarcely the note on which to end his earthly compositions. So he set down again these extra lines, which he had made up long before and still saw no reason to refute, as a sort of postscript:

> He either fears his fate too much,
>   Or his deserts are small,
> That dares not put it to the touch,
>   To gain or lose it all.

He blessed the kind thought of his anonymous benefactors who had brought him the pen, ink and paper.

When the last of the guard had staggered through to the guardroom, he arranged his clothes decently for the morrow, extinguished the lamp, and lay down on his straw. Unlike the night before with its questions and errant hopes, he fell asleep almost as soon as he closed his eyes, and slept as peacefully as a child.

To awaken knowingly to one's last morning on earth is by any standards an experience of some profundity, conducive to a sharpening of the perceptions and a discarding of the superficial and the frivolous, even though a sense of relief may be a major reaction. Nevertheless, James Graham took particular care with his toilet on this occasion, in so far as he might. He was still denied the use of a razor, but he obtained cold water to wash his person thoroughly. He dusted his clothing as best he could, sought to sponge off stains, wiped his shoes clean with straw, and combed his hair and beard.

The ministers were back at him from an early hour, and though he requested that his last hours might be private, they would have none of it, determined up to the last moment to effect the saving of his soul. He did ask if he might be permitted to say goodbye to any of his friends who might be available, and would so honour him, but this was refused.

It made an interminable forenoon.

At length the Provost arrived, with the bailies and official execution party, which included Warriston but none of the other principals. Sir James Stewart was uncomfortable, almost apologetic. When the prisoner was ready, they would proceed. There was no hurry. If the godly ministers required longer . . . ?

'No, sir – let us be on our way,' Montrose told him. 'I have been too long a-dying, as it is. If the reverend gentlemen have not been able to recover my soul by now, we must needs just leave it to our Maker! Proceed, Sir James.' And he raised his bound hands to put on his beaver.

Promptly Major Weir snatched it off his head, with a curse, much disarranging his hair in the process. 'You'll no' need that!' he declared.

'True, sir. I thank you for reminding me.' James Graham took his comb from a pocket, with difficulty, and ran it two-handedly through his fine, long, wavy hair, to restore its neatness.

Breathing hard, Warriston protested. 'Man – in your state you would be better taking care for your immortal soul than for your worthless body and appearance, combing the hairs of your head!'

'My lord, my head is still mine own. Tonight, when it shall be yours, treat it as you will.' He finished the combing, and bowed to the Provost.

So at last Montrose finally left Edinburgh's Tolbooth and emerged into the packed High Street. A sudden silence at the sight of him was broken by a resounding roll of drums from massed soldiery drawn up to line both sides of the street.

'Military honours also!' he remarked, to the Provost.

'A precaution, just,' Sir James, a humourless man, corrected. 'That all remember that the guard is sufficient strong. To prevent any attempt at rescue.'

405

'A rescue? Here? Soldiers? Am I still a terror to them, then?'
The prisoner smiled. 'I think, aye I think even my *ghost* will
haunt them! After you, Provost.'

They had only a short distance to walk to the scaffold and
gibbet beside the Mercat Cross, where the hangman awaited
them. James Graham greeted him, as he mounted to the first
platform, almost as an old friend.

'A good day to you. To us both. Our meeting again has been
unduly delayed. Through no will of mine, I assure you. Ah –
who have we here?'

Since now the Kirk had washed its hands of him, at last, and
no friends were permitted to be with the rejected excommunicate, a young boy had been deputed to act as final ministrant,
and to take down on a paper any last-moment confession or
statement – a nice touch. The youngster had in his hands, as well
as paper, pen and ink horn, a leather-bound book and a roll of
parchment. Also a small length of rope. Taking this in at a glance,
Montrose looked to where the Reverends Robert Traill and
Mungo Law stood, at the far side of the gallows-platform, at their
most severe, as though what followed was nothing to do with
them, thank God. He bowed.

'Too young to be contaminated?' he enquired interestedly.

They answered nothing.

He turned back to the boy. 'Your name, young man? Since
you are to help me thus, on my way. And what have you there,
with the Bible?'

'No Bible, sir,' the lad answered clearly. 'It is for, for him.'
And he nodded towards the hangman. 'And my name is Robert
Gordon, sir.'

'Ha – Gordon! Here is a joyful omen. I knew another Gordon
lad, not unlike yourself, once. And loved him well. It may be that
I shall see him very shortly now. I thank you for your attendance,
Robert Gordon.'

'I have to write down what you say, sir.'

'Ah, yes. I know that it is customary to address a speech to the
company on such occasions. Though, to tell truth, I am something weary of words, lad.'

'No, sir – not to the company, sir. It is not allowed. Only to
me – that I may write it down.'

'You say so, Robert? A strange provision. But as well, perhaps. For I have no great deal to say. And you will not be so
rushed, in setting it forth.'

Clearing his throat, the hangman stepped forward. 'First of all sir – there's this. As commanded.' He took the book, the scroll and the rope from the boy, and tied the two items together at either end of the rope. James Graham noted that the man's hands were trembling – and hoped that they would not tremble too greatly for efficiency hereafter. He also perceived that the book was a copy of his own *Life and Memoirs* by George Wishart, and the parchment was the declaration of his sentence of hanging and quartering. By the rope, the hangman hung these around his neck.

'Why, friend, this is a most kindly thought,' he commented. 'My vanity, perhaps? But I am as glad to have one as the other by me, my life and my death conveniently to hand!'

'Speak now,' the other grunted. 'But quietly, see you. No' to the folk. They dinna want a disturbance.'

'Of course. A disturbance would be unseemly.' Montrose looked a little doubtfully at the waiting dark-eyed boy. He seemed an unlikely recipient for a man's last expressed thoughts. It would be Warriston's strange and twisted mind which had thought of that, for a certainty. Warriston was watching now, from just below the front of the scaffold. There was no sign of Argyll, as usual, a modest man who ever preferred the background.

Montrose turned to the Provost and group of bailies who waited on the scaffold behind him, well apart from the two ministers, and spoke conversationally.

'I am sorry if this matter of my end is something scandalous for any good Christian, my friends. Who knows the rights and wrongs of it? For my own sins, I acknowledge it to be just before God. For my public acts, I see it . . . otherwise.' He paused, thinking of the busy scribe. 'I forgive those who have brought it about. I forgive them also, if less heartily than I should, for their oppression of the poor, and their perversion of judgment and justice in this kingdom. If God forgives sins, which I do believe, who am I to do otherwise? Indeed, who am I to say anything, at this juncture? Save that what I have done, in Scotland, was done on the commands of my sovereign, and yours. I acknowledge nothing other than to fear God and honour the King.'

There was some clearing of throats amongst those near enough to hear, at this bringing in of the King – which undoubtedly was the last thing that was wanted. Although Montrose had not lifted up his voice, he spoke clearly and slowly, and the crowd, even though unable to hear, maintained an extraordinary hush, so that a barking dog somewhere in one of the flanking closes, made all the competing sound.

James Graham looked down at Warriston, who certainly could hear him. 'Some would have me to blame the late King – the same men who *sold* the late King. God forbid! He, if as some say he lived a saint, did die a martyr. I pray God that I may make as fair an end as he did. As for His Majesty now living, I die his servant. And say to you that never any people, I believe, might be more happy in a king. I pray that he be so dealt with as not to be betrayed, as his father was.'

Warriston was gesticulating at the hangman – who, however, looked at the Provost. That man gave no sign.

'It is enough,' the prisoner said, turning back to the boy. 'Overmuch perhaps, Robert? I have no more to say, save that I desire your prayers. I leave my soul to God, my service to my prince, my goodwill to my friends, and my name and charity to you all.'

The dog barked and barked, an irrelevant, weary sound.

Montrose turned to the hangman. 'Now, my friend, play your part. My hands are pinioned – but you will find some small further moneys in my pocket.'

The man gestured to him to climb the few steps higher, to the little platform, only large enough for two, where the noose dangled from the thirty-foot-high gibbet.

Bowing right, left and then to the executioner, he climbed the final ladder unhurriedly but firmly. At the top he made way for the man mounting behind him.

'There is little room up here,' he mentioned smilingly, as he perceived the tears streaming down the hangman's cheeks.

It had been a dull cloudy day, with a chill wind off the sea, but as he stood there waiting, while the other put the noose around his neck and adjusted the knot in place, a brilliant golden shaft of sunlight struck down to irradiate the ancient grey street, its cobblestones and soaring tenements. He had never loved this towering city, but in the sudden illumination of light and colour and shadow, he seemed to see it differently, a place of two faces, two characters, ever at war with itself, cold yet seeking warmth, harsh yet wistfully lovely, steeped in blood yet somehow eternally innocent – like the nation for which it was the capital, self-torn to its enduring hurt.

'God have mercy on this afflicted land!' he said aloud,

chokingly – and the man at his back pushed, and launched him from the platform.

A great gulping sigh arose and swept the crowd like a tide that ebbed and flowed, as the rope jerked taut, and James Graham left Edinburgh gladly for a better place.

POSTSCRIPT

Charles II made a bad bargain. When he arrived in Scotland a month after Montrose's execution, even though he signed the Solemn League and Covenant on landing, it was to threats, humiliation, religious brow-beating – six sermons a day – the cynical exploitation by the Covenanting leadership, though the common people greeted him warmly. Cromwell promptly invaded Scotland with 16,000 of his new Model Army, and Charles was hastily packed off to the North as embarrassment, being forced to denounce his father's blood-guiltiness, as sop. Cromwell defeated David Leslie at Dunbar, largely because of clerical intervention, with great slaughter. Charles became a fugitive in his own kingdom, and the victor took up residence in the same Moray House in Edinburgh's Canongate where Argyll had watched Montrose pass on the hangman's cart. The Campbell played a double game, ferrying between Edinburgh and the skulking King in the North; and on New Year's Day, 1651 he actually placed the crown on Charles's head at Scone – but made it abundantly clear that he could take it off again equally well. But Cromwell was more than a match for both of them, outmanoeuvring Argyll and eventually defeating Charles at Worcester. The young King was smuggled back to Holland and nine more years of exile.

After Cromwell's death in 1658 both kingdoms quickly rejected his Protectorate. The Restoration followed, and Charles at last returned to his two thrones. But not to his ancient kingdom of Scotland. Never again would he set foot in that hated land.

In July 1661 the Scots Parliament revoked all sentences on the great Marquis of Montrose. A solemn procession was organised to collect all available portions of his body, to bring them to lie in state in the Abbey of Holyrood, till the parts might come in from farther afield. On the 11th of May next year Edinburgh went *en fete*. The greatest state funeral ever staged carried the remains of James Graham for final burial in St. Giles. The castle cannon thundered, the crowds cheered, fourteen earls carried the splendid coffin, the insignia of the Garter on top – with a clutch of Graham lairds, including Pate Graham of Inchbrakie to see that they did it properly – and twelve other peers bore the pall, including the Lords Madderty and Frendraught who had both survived. And in the same Edinburgh Castle where the cannon belched, Archibald Campbell, Marquis of Argyll, lay prisoner, listening. He was executed for treason a few days later, at the same spot on which James Graham had died, and his head fixed upon the spike which had borne his enemy's. The same court as condemned Argyll did as much for Johnston of Warriston, and he was hanged at the Cross in July the same year.

David Leslie, victor of Philiphaugh, was created Lord Newark by Charles, in August, with a pension for life.

NIGEL TRANTER

THE MACGREGOR TRILOGY

Spanning the first five decades of the 18th century, the MacGregor clan, outlawed and landless, battled against the might of Montrose, the Duke of Cumberland and the English army. Under Rob Roy and later Duncan, MacGregor support for the Stuart cause in the skirmishes of 1715 and 1745 placed the clan in mortal danger. yet, with the aid of beautiful, headstrong women, and with a determination none could defeat, the MacGregors left their mark on one of the most romantic and exciting periods of British history.

CORONET BOOKS

NIGEL TRANTER

UNICORN RAMPANT

The year 1617 was a fateful one for Scotland – and especially for young John Stewart of Methven, bastard son of the Duke of Lennox. King James VI of Scotland and I of England, more often known as 'The Wisest Fool in Christendom', made a rare and disastrous visit to the homeland of which he had been absentee monarch for fourteen years.

Knighted in a rash moment by the eccentric King Jamie, John becomes the reluctant servant of the Court. Much against his will he is commanded to return with the King to London, and is soon caught up in a net of murky political intrigue . . .

CORONET BOOKS

NIGEL TRANTER

THE RIVEN REALM

Two hundred years earlier Robert the Bruce had driven out the English and restored his nation's pride. But now the King of Scotland lay dead amongst the bloody slaughter of Flodden.

Now, as fate decreed, the new king, James V, was a child, just seventeen months old. And that same fate had in store intriguing roles for two young men.

David Lindsay and David Beaton — neither high-born, each the son of a lowland laird — were caught up in the very centre of the storm of hatred, fear, treachery and ambition that followed the young king's coming to the throne. Buffeted by events that would involve England, France, the Empire and even the Vatican, each was to win his own very special place in history . . .

'Vivid and enjoyable'
The Times Literary Supplement

CORONET BOOKS

NIGEL TRANTER

THE STEWART TRILOGY

Through the turbulent, troubled years of 14th and 15th century Scotland this absorbing tale charts the fortunes of the House of Stewart — a house divided between feuding factions, beset by jealousy and hatred. The throne remains theirs only through an astonishing genius for survival and, many say, the luck of the Devil himself.

CORONET BOOKS

NIGEL TRANTER

THE BRUCE TRILOGY

In 1296 Edward Plantaganet, King of England, was determined to hammer the rebellious Scots into submission. Despite internal clashes and his fierce love for his antagonist's god-daughter, Bruce took up the task of uniting his people against the invaders from the South in a deadly fight for national survival. After a desperate struggle which threatened to break Bruce's spirit he rose finally to face the English at the memorable battle of Bannockburn. Far from bringing peace, this was to herald fourteen years of struggle, savagery, heroism and treachery before the English could be brought to sit at a peace-table and to acknowledge Bruce as a Sovereign king. This splendid trilogy charts these years, revealing the flowering of Bruce's character and his determination to continue the fight for an independent Scotland, sustained by a passionate love for his land and people.

'Absorbing . . . a notable achievement'
The Scotsman

CORONET BOOKS

ALSO AVAILABLE FROM CORONET BOOKS

All these books are available at your local bookshop or newsagent, or can be ordered direct from the publisher. Just tick the titles you want and fill in the form below.

Prices and availability subject to change without notice.

Hodder & Stoughton Paperbacks, P.O. Box 11, Falmouth, Cornwall.

Please send cheque or postal order, and allow the following for postage and packing:

U.K. – 55p for one book, plus 22p for the second book, and 14p for each additional book ordered up to a £1.75 maximum.

B.F.P.O. and EIRE – 55p for the first book, plus 22p for the second book, and 14p per copy for the next 7 books, 8p per book there-after.

OTHER OVERSEAS CUSTOMERS – £1.00 for the first book, plus 25p per copy for each additional book.

Name ....

Address ....

....